'Fast, dense, deep, runny, *Neuromancer* mee
The ba Rudy Rucker on

ABOUT THE AUTHOR

Neal Stephenson is author of *The Big U*, *Zodiac*, *Snow Crash*, *The Diamond Age*, winner of a 1996 Hugo Award, and *Cryptonomicon*. He also writes (with J. Frederick George) as 'Stephen Bury' and their books are *Interface* and *Cobweb*. He lives in Seattle, where he is at work on other novels.

THE
DIAMOND AGE

Neal Stephenson

PENGUIN BOOKS

PENGUIN BOOKS

Published by the Penguin Group
Penguin Books Ltd, 80 Strand, London WC2R 0RL, England
Penguin Putnam Inc., 375 Hudson Street, New York, New York 10014, USA
Penguin Books Australia Ltd, 250 Camberwell Road, Camberwell, Victoria 3124, Australia
Penguin Books Canada Ltd, 10 Alcorn Avenue, Toronto, Ontario, Canada M4V 3B2
Penguin Books India (P) Ltd, 11 Community Centre, Panchsheel Park, New Delhi – 110 017, India
Penguin Books (NZ) Ltd, Cnr Rosedale and Airborne Roads, Albany, Auckland, New Zealand
Penguin Books (South Africa) (Pty) Ltd, 24 Sturdee Avenue, Rosebank 2196, South Africa

Penguin Books Ltd, Registered Offices: 80 Strand, London WC2R 0RL, England

www.penguin.com

First published in the USA by Bantam Books 1995
Published in Great Britain in Penguin Books 1996

13

Copyright © Neal Stephenson, 1995
All rights reserved

Printed in England by Clays Ltd, St Ives plc

By nature, men are nearly alike;
by practice, they get to be wide apart.

—*Confucius*

PART
THE FIRST

*Moral reforms and deteriorations are moved by large forces,
and they are mostly caused by reactions from the habits of a
preceding period. Backwards and forwards swings the great
pendulum, and its alternations are not determined by a few
distinguished folk clinging to the end of it.*

—*Sir Charles Petrie,* THE VICTORIANS

*A thete visits a mod parlor; noteworthy features of
modern armaments.*

The bells of St. Mark's were ringing changes up on the
mountain when Bud skated over to the mod parlor to up-
grade his skull gun. Bud had a nice new pair of blades with
a top speed of anywhere from a hundred to a hundred and
fifty kilometers, depending on how fat you were and
whether or not you wore aero. Bud liked wearing skin-tight
leather, to show off his muscles. On a previous visit to the
mod parlor, two years ago, he had paid to have a bunch of
'sites implanted in his muscles—little critters, too small to
see or feel, that twitched Bud's muscle fibers electrically according to a program that was supposed to maximize bulk.
Combined with the testosterone pump embedded in his
forearm, it was like working out in a gym night and day,
except you didn't have to actually do anything and you
never got sweaty. The only drawback was that all the little
twitches made him kind of tense and jerky. He'd gotten used

to it, but it still made him a little hinky on those skates, especially when he was doing a hundred clicks an hour through a crowded street. But few people hassled Bud, even when he knocked them down in the street, and after today *no one* would hassle him *ever again*.

Bud had walked away, improbably unscratched, from his last job—*decoy*—with something like a thousand yuks in his pocket. He'd spent a third of it on new clothes, mostly black leather, another third of it on the blades, and was about to spend the last third at the mod parlor. You could get skull guns a lot cheaper, of course, but that would mean going over the Causeway to Shanghai and getting a back-alley job from some Coaster, and probably a nice bone infection in with the bargain, and he'd probably pick your pocket while he had you theezed. Besides, you could only get into a Shanghai if you were virgin. To cross the Causeway when you were already packing a skull gun, like Bud, you had to bribe the shit out of numerous Shanghai cops. There was no reason to economize here. Bud had a rich and boundless career ahead of him, vaulting up a hierarchy of extremely dangerous drug-related occupations for which decoy served as a paid audition of sorts. A start weapons system was a wise investment.

The damn bells kept ringing through the fog. Bud mumbled a command to his music system, a phased acoustical array splayed across both eardrums like the seeds on a strawberry. The volume went up but couldn't scour away the deep tones of the carillon, which resonated in his long bones. He wondered whether, as long as he was at the mod parlor, he should have the batteries drilled out of his right mastoid and replaced. Supposedly they were ten-year jobs, but he'd had them for six and he listened to music all the time, loud.

Three people were waiting. Bud took a seat and skimmed a mediatron from the coffee table; it looked exactly like a dirty, wrinkled, blank sheet of paper. " 'Annals of Self-Protection,' " he said, loud enough for everyone else in the place to hear him. The logo of his favorite meedfeed co-alesced on the page. Mediaglyphics, mostly the cool animated ones, arranged themselves in a grid. Bud scanned through them until he found the one that denoted a comparison of a bunch of different stuff, and snapped at it with his fingernail. New mediaglyphics appeared, surrounding larger cine panes in which *Annals* staff tested several models of skull guns against live and dead targets. Bud frisbeed the mediatron back onto the table; this was the same review he'd been poring over for the last day, they hadn't updated it, his decision was still valid.

One of the guys ahead of him got a tattoo, which took about ten seconds. The other guy just wanted his skull gun reloaded, which didn't take much longer. The girl wanted a few 'sites replaced in her racting grid, mostly around her eyes, where she was starting to wrinkle up. That took a while, so Bud picked up the mediatron again and went in a ractive, his favorite, called *Shut Up or Die!*

The mod artist wanted to see Bud's yuks before he installed the gun, which in other surroundings might have been construed as an insult but was standard business practice here in the Leased Territories. When he was satisfied that this wasn't a stick-up, he theezed Bud's forehead with a spray gun, scalped back a flap of skin, and pushed a machine, mounted on a delicate robot arm like a dental tool, over Bud's forehead. The arm homed in automatically on the old gun, moving with alarming speed and determination. Bud, who was a little jumpy at the best of times because of his muscle stimulators, flinched a little. But the robot arm was a hundred times faster than he was and plucked out the old gun unerringly. The proprietor was watching all of this on a screen and had nothing to do except narrate: "The hole in your skull's kind of rough, so the machine is reaming it out to a larger bore—okay, now here comes the new gun."

A nasty popping sensation radiated through Bud's skull when the robot arm snapped in the new model. It reminded Bud of the days of his youth, when, from time to time, one of his playmates would shoot him in the head with a BB gun. He instantly developed a low headache.

"It's loaded with a hundred rounds of popcorn," the proprietor said, "so you can test out the yuvree. Soon as you're comfortable with it, I'll load it for real." He stapled the skin of Bud's forehead back together so it'd heal invisibly. You could pay the guy extra to leave a scar there on purpose, so everyone would know you were packing, but Bud had heard that some chicks didn't like it. Bud's relationship with the female sex was governed by a gallimaufry of primal impulses, dim suppositions, deranged theories, over-heard scraps of conversation, half-remembered pieces of bad advice, and fragments of no-doubt exaggerated anecdotes that amounted to rank superstition. In this case, it dictated that he should not request the scar.

Besides, he had a nice collection of Sights—not very tasteful sunglasses with crosshairs budded into the lens on your dominant eye. They did wonders for marksmanship, and they were real obvious too, so that everyone knew you didn't fuck with a man wearing Sights.

"Give it a whirl," the guy said, and spun the chair around—it was a big old antique barber chair upholstered in swirly plastic—so Bud was facing a mannikin in the corner of the room. The mannikin had no face or hair and was speckled with little burn marks, as was the wall behind it.

"Status," Bud said, and felt the gun buzz lightly in response.

"Stand by," he said, and got another answering buzz. He turned his face squarely toward the mannikin.

"Hut," he said. He said it under his breath, through unmoving lips, but the gun heard it; he felt a slight recoil tapping his head back, and a startling POP sounded from the mannikin, accompanied by a flash of light on the wall up above its head. Bud's headache deepened, but he didn't care.

"This thing runs faster ammo, so you'll have to get used to aiming a tad lower," said the guy. So Bud tried it again and this time popped the mannikin right in the neck.

"Great shot! That would have decapped him if you were using Hellfire," the guy said. "Looks to me like you know what you're doing—but there's other options too. And three magazines so you can run multiple ammos."

"I know," Bud said, "I been checking this thing out." Then, to the gun, "Disperse ten, medium pattern." Then he said "hut" again. His head snapped back much harder, and ten POPs went off at once, all over the mannikin's body and the wall behind it. The room was getting smoky now, start-ing to smell like burned plastic.

"You can disperse up to a hundred," the guy said, "but the recoil'd probably break your neck."

"I think I got it down," Bud said, "so load me up. First magazine with electrostun rounds. Second magazine with

Cripplers. Third with Hellfires. And get me some fucking aspirin."

Source Victoria; description of its environs.

Source Victoria's air intakes erupted from the summit of the Royal Ecological Conservatory like a spray of hundred-meter-long calla lilies. Below, the analogy was perfected by an inverted tree of rootlike plumbing that spread fractally through the diamondoid bedrock of New Chusan, terminating in the warm water of the South China Sea as numberless capillaries arranged in a belt around the smartcoral reef, several dozen meters beneath the surface. One big huge pipe gulping up seawater would have done roughly the same thing, just as the lilies could have been replaced by one howling maw, birds and litter whacking into a bloody grid somewhere before they could gum up the works.

But it wouldn't have been ecological. The geotects of Imperial Tectonics would not have known an ecosystem if they'd been living in the middle of one. But they did know that ecosystems were especially tiresome when they got fubared, so they protected the environment with the same implacable, plodding, green-visored mentality that they applied to designing overpasses and culverts. Thus, water seeped into Source Victoria through microtubes, much the same way it seeped into a beach, and air wafted into it silently down the artfully skewed exponential horns of those thrusting calla lilies, each horn a point in parameter space not awfully far from some central ideal. They were strong enough to withstand typhoons but flexible enough to rustle in a breeze. Birds, wandering inside, sensed a gradient in the air, pulling them down into night, and simply chose to fly out. They didn't even get scared enough to shit.

The lilies sprouted from a stadium-sized cut-crystal vase, the Diamond Palace, which was open to the public. Tourists, aerobicizing pensioners, and ranks of uniformed schoolchildren marched through it year in and year out, peering through walls of glass (actually solid diamond, which was cheaper) at various phases of the molecular disassembly line that was Source Victoria. Dirty air and dirty water came in and pooled in tanks. Next to each tank was another tank containing slightly cleaner air or cleaner water. Repeat several dozen times. The tanks at the end were filled with perfectly clean nitrogen gas and perfectly clean water.

The line of tanks was referred to as a cascade, a rather abstract bit of engineer's whimsy lost on the tourists who did not see anything snapshot-worthy there. All the action took place in the walls separating the tanks, which were not really walls but nearly infinite grids of submicroscopic wheels, ever-rotating and many-spoked. Each spoke grabbed a nitrogen or water molecule on the dirty side and released it after spinning around to the clean side. Things that weren't nitrogen or water didn't get grabbed, hence didn't make it through. There were also wheels for grabbing handy trace elements like carbon, sulfur, and phosphorus; these were passed along smaller, parallel cascades until they were also perfectly pure. The immaculate molecules wound up in reservoirs. Some of them got combined with others to make simple but handy molecular widgets. In the end, all of them were funneled into a bundle of molecular conveyor belts known as the Feed, of which Source Victoria, and the other half-dozen Sources of Atlantis/Shanghai, were the fountainheads.

Financial complications of Bud's lifestyle; visit to a banker.

*B*ud surprised himself with how long he went before he had to use the skull gun in anger. Just knowing it was in there gave him such an attitude that no one in his right mind would fuck with him, especially when they saw his Sights and the black leather. He got his way just by giving people the evil eye.

It was time to move up the ladder. He sought work as a lookout. It wasn't easy. The alternative pharmaceuticals industry ran on a start, just-in-time delivery system, keeping inventories low so that there was never much evidence for the cops to seize. The snuff was grown in illicit matter compilers, squirreled away in vacant low-rent housing blocks, and carried by the runners to the actual street dealers. Meanwhile, a cloud of lookouts and decoys circulated probabilistically through the neighborhood, never stopping long enough to be picked up for loitering, monitoring the approach of cops (or cops' surveillance pods) through huds in their sunglasses.

When Bud told his last boss to go fuck himself, he'd been pretty sure he could get a runner job. But it hadn't panned out, and since then a couple more big airships had come in from North America and disgorged thousands of white and black trash into the job market. Now Bud was running out of money and getting tired of eating the free food from the public matter compilers.

The Peacock Bank was a handsome man with a salt-and-pepper goatee, smelling of citrus and wearing an exceedingly snappy double-breasted suit that displayed his narrow waist to good effect. He was to be found in a rather seedy office upstairs of a travel agency in one of the lurid blocks between the Aerodrome and the brothel-lined waterfront.

The banker didn't say much after they shook hands, just crossed his arms pensively and leaned back against the edge of his desk. In this attitude he listened to Bud's freshly composed prevarication, nodding from time to time as though Bud had said something significant. This was a little disconcerting since Bud knew it was all horseshit, but he *had* heard that these dotheads prided themselves on customer service.

At no particular point in the monologue, the banker cut Bud off simply by looking up at him brightly. "You wish to secure a line of credit," he said, as if he were pleasantly surprised, which was not terribly likely.

"I guess you could say that," Bud allowed, wishing he'd known to put it in such fine-sounding terminology.

The banker reached inside his jacket and withdrew a piece of paper, folded in thirds, from his breast pocket. "You may wish to peruse this brochure," he said to Bud, and to the brochure itself he rattled off something in an unfamiliar tongue. As Bud took it from the banker's hand, the blank page generated a nice animated color logo and music. The logo developed into a peacock. Beneath it, a video presentation commenced, hosted by a similar-looking gent—sort of Indian looking but sort of Arab too. " 'The Parsis welcome you to Peacock Bank,' " he said.

"What's a Parsi?" Bud said to the banker, who merely lowered his eyelids one click and jutted his goatee at the piece of paper, which had picked up on his question and already branched into an explanation. Bud ended up regretting having asked, because the answer turned out to be a great deal of general hoo-ha about these Parsis, who evidently wanted to make very sure no one mistook them for dotheads or Pakis or Arabs—not that they had any problem with those very fine ethnic groups, mind you. As hard as he tried not to pay attention, Bud absorbed more than he wanted to know about the Parsis, their oddball religion, their tendency to wander around, even their fucking cuisine, which looked weird but made his mouth water anyway. Then the brochure got back to the business at hand, which was lines of credit.

Bud had seen this all before. The Peacock Bank was running the same racket as all the others: If they accepted you, they'd shoot the credit card right into you, then and there, on the spot. These guys implanted it in the iliac crest of the pelvis, some opted for the mastoid bone in the skull—anywhere a big bone was close to the surface. A bone mount was needed because the card had to talk on the radio, which meant it needed an antenna long enough to hear radio waves. Then you could go around and buy stuff just by asking for it; Peacock Bank and the merchant you were buying from and the card in your pelvis handled all the details.

Banks varied in their philosophy of interest rates, minimum monthly payments, and so on. None of that mattered to Bud. What mattered was what they would do to him if he got into arrears, and so after he had allowed a decent interval to pass pretending to listen very carefully to all this crap about interest rates, he inquired, in an offhanded way, like it was an afterthought, about their collection policy. The banker glanced out the window like he hadn't noticed.

The soundtrack segued into some kind of a cool jazz number and a scene of a multicultural crew of ladies and gentlemen, not looking much like degraded credit abusers at all, sitting around a table assembling chunky pieces of ethnic jewelry by hand. They were having a good time too, sipping tea and exchanging lively banter. Sipping too much tea, to Bud's suspicious eye, so opaque to so many things yet so keen to the tactics of media manipulation. They were making rather a big deal out of the tea.

He noted with approval that they were wearing normal clothes, not uniforms, and that men and women were allowed to mingle. "Peacock Bank supports a global network of clean, safe, and commodious workhouses, so if unforeseen circumstances should befall you during our relationship, or if you should inadvertently anticipate your means, you can rely on being housed close to home while you and the bank resolve any difficulties. Inmates in Peacock Bank workhouses enjoy private beds and in some cases private rooms. Naturally your children can remain with you for the duration of your visit. Working conditions are among the best in the industry, and the high added-value content of our folk jewelry operation means that, no matter the extent of your difficulties, your situation will be happily resolved in practically no time."

"What's the, uh, strategy for making sure people actually, you know, show up when they're supposed to show up?" Bud said. At this point the banker lost interest in the proceedings, straightened up, strolled around his desk, and sat down, staring out the window across the water toward Pudong and Shanghai. "That detail is not covered in the brochure," he said, "as most of our prospective customers do not share your diligent attention to detail insofar as that aspect of the arrangement is concerned."

He exhaled through his nose, like a man eager not to smell something, and adjusted his goatee one time. "The enforcement regime consists of three phases. We have pleasant names for them, of course, but you might think of them, respectively, as: one, a polite reminder; two, well in excess of your pain threshold; three, spectacularly fatal."

Bud thought about showing this Parsi the meaning of fatal right then and there, but as a bank, the guy probably had pretty good security. Besides, it was pretty standard policy, and Bud was actually kind of glad the guy'd given it to him straight. "Okay, well, I'll get back to you," he said. "Mind if I keep the brochure?"

The Parsi waved him and the brochure away. Bud took to the streets again in search of cash on easier terms.

A visit from royalty; the Hackworths take an airship holiday; Princess Charlotte's birthday party; Hackworth encounters a member of the peerage.

Three geodesic seeds skated over the roofs and gardens of Atlantis/Shanghai on a Friday afternoon, like the germs of some moon-size calabash. A pair of mooring masts sprouted and grew from cricket ovals at Source Victoria Park. The smallest of the airships was decorated with the royal ensign; she kept station overhead as the two large ones settled toward their berths. Their envelopes, filled with nothing, were predominantly transparent. Instead of blocking the sunlight, they yellowed and puckered it, projecting vast abstract patterns of brighter and not-as-bright that the children in their best crinolines and natty short-pants suits tried to catch in their arms. A brass band played. A tiny figure in a white dress stood at the rail of the airship *Atlantis*, waving at the children below. They all knew that this must be the birthday girl herself, Princess Charlotte, and they cheered and waved back.

Fiona Hackworth had been wandering through the Royal Ecological Conservatory bracketed by her parents, who hoped that in this way they could keep mud and vegetable debris off her skirts. The strategy had not been completely successful, but with a quick brush, John and Gwendolyn were able to transfer most of the dirt onto their white gloves. From there it went straight into the air. Most gentlemen's and ladies' gloves nowadays were constructed of infinitesimal fabricules that knew how to eject dirt; you could thrust your gloved hand into mud, and it would be white a few seconds later.

The hierarchy of staterooms on Æther matched the status of its passengers perfectly, as these parts of the ship could be decompiled and remade between voyages. For Lord Finkle-McGraw, his three children and their spouses, and Elizabeth (his first and only grandchild so far), the airship lowered a private escalator that carried them up into the suite at the very prow, with its nearly 180-degree forward view.

Aft of the Finkle-McGraws were a dozen or so other Equity Lords, merely earl- or baron-level, mostly ushering grandchildren rather than children into the class B suites. Then it was executives, whose gold watch chains, adangle with tiny email-boxes, phones, torches, snuffboxes, and other fetishes, curved round the dark waistcoats they wore to deemphasize their bellies. Most of their children had reached the age when they were no longer naturally endearing to anyone save their own parents; the size when their energy was more a menace than a wonder; and the level of intelligence when what would have been called innocence in a smaller child was infuriating rudeness. A honeybee cruising for nectar is pretty despite its implicit threat, but the same behavior in a hornet three times larger makes one glance about for some handy swatting material. So on the broad escalators leading to the first-class staterooms, one could see many upper arms being violently grabbed by hissing fathers with their top hats askew and teeth clenched and eyes swiveling for witnesses.

John Percival Hackworth was an engineer. Most engineers were assigned to tiny rooms with fold-down beds, but Hackworth bore the loftier title of Artifex and had been a team leader on this very project, so he rated a second-class stateroom with one double bed and a fold-out for Fiona. The porter brought their overnight bags around just as Æther was clearing her mooring mast—a twenty-meter diamondoid truss that had already dissolved back into the billiard-table surface of the oval by the time the ship had turned itself to the south. Lying as close as it did to Source Victoria, the park was riddled with catachthonic Feed lines, and anything could be grown there on short notice.

The Hackworths' stateroom was to starboard, and so as they accelerated away from New Chusan, they got to watch the sun set on Shanghai, shining redly through the city's eternal cloak of coal-smoke. Gwendolyn read Fiona stories in bed for an hour while John perused the evening edition of the *Times*, then spread out some papers on the room's tiny desk. Later, they both changed into their evening clothes, primping quietly in twilight so as not to wake Fiona. At nine o'clock they stepped into the passageway, locked the door, and followed the sound of the big band to *Æther*'s grand ballroom, where the dancing was just getting underway. The floor of the ballroom was a slab of transpicuous diamond. The lights were low. They seemed to float above the glittering moonlit surface of the Pacific as they did the waltz, minuet, Lindy, and electric slide into the night.

Sunrise found the three airships hovering over the South China Sea, no land visible. The ocean was relatively shallow here, but only Hackworth and a few other engineers knew that. The Hackworths had a passable view from their stateroom window, but John woke up early and staked out a place on the diamond floor of the ballroom, ordered an espresso and a *Times* from a waiter, and passed the time pleasantly while Gwen and Fiona got themselves ready for the day. All around them he could hear children speculating on what was about to happen.

Gwen and Fiona arrived just late enough to make it interesting for John, who took his mechanical pocket watch out at least a dozen times as he waited, and finally ended up clutching it in one hand, nervously popping the lid open and shut. Gwen folded her long legs and spread her skirts out prettily on the transparent floor, drawing vituperative looks from several women who remained standing. But John was relieved to see that most of these women were relatively low-ranking engineers or their wives; none of the higher-ups needed to come to the ballroom.

Fiona collapsed to her hands and knees and practically shoved her face against the diamond, her fundament aloft. Hackworth gripped the creases of his trousers, hitched them up just a bit, and sank to one knee.

The smart coral burst out of the depths with violence that shocked Hackworth, even though he'd been in on the design, seen the trial runs. Viewed through the dark surface of the Pacific, it was like watching an explosion through a pane of shattered glass. It reminded him of pouring a jet of heavy cream into coffee, watching it rebound from the bottom of the cup in a turbulent fractal bloom that solidified just as it dashed against the surface. The speed of this process was a carefully planned sleight-of-hand; the smart coral had actually been growing down on the bottom of the ocean for the last three months, drawing its energy from a supercon that they'd grown across the seafloor for the occasion, extracting the necessary atoms directly from the seawater and the gases dissolved therein. The process happening below looked chaotic, and in a way it was; but each lithocule knew exactly where it was supposed to go and what it was supposed to do. They were tetrahedral building blocks of calcium and carbon, the size of poppyseeds, each equipped with a power source, a brain, and a navigational system. They rose from the bottom of the sea at a signal given by Princess Charlotte; she had awakened to find a small present under her pillow, unwrapped it to find a golden whistle on a chain, stood out on her balcony, and blown the whistle.

The coral was converging on the site of the island from all directions, some of the lithocules traveling several kilometers to reach their assigned positions. They displaced a volume of water equal to the island itself, several cubic kilometers in all. The result was furious turbulence, an upswelling in the surface of the ocean that made some of the children scream, thinking it might rise up and snatch the airship out of the sky; and indeed a few drops pelted the ship's diamond belly, prompting the pilot to give her a little more altitude. The curt maneuver forced hearty laughter from all of the fathers in the ballroom, who were delighted by the illusion of danger and the impotence of Nature.

The foam and mist cleared away at some length to reveal a new island, salmon-colored in the light of dawn. Applause and cheers diminished to a professional murmur. The chattering of the astonished children was too loud and high to hear.

It would be a couple of hours yet. Hackworth snapped his fingers for a waiter and ordered fresh fruit, juice, Belgian waffles, more coffee. They might as well enjoy *Æther*'s famous cuisine while the island sprouted castles, fauns, centaurs, and enchanted forests.

Princess Charlotte was the first human to set foot on the enchanted isle, tripping down the gangway of *Atlantis* with a couple of her little friends in tow, all of them looking like tiny wildflowers in their ribboned sun-bonnets, all carrying little baskets for souvenirs, though before long these were handed over to governesses. The Princess faced *Æther* and *Chinook*, moored a couple of hundred meters away, and spoke to them in a normal tone of voice that was, however, heard clearly by all; a nanophone was hidden somewhere in the lace collar of her pinafore, tied into phased-audio-array systems grown into the top layers of the island itself.

"I would like to express my gratitude to Lord Finkle-McGraw and all the employees of Machine-Phase Systems Limited for this most wonderful birthday present. Now, children of Atlantis/Shanghai, won't you please join me at my birthday party?"

The children of Atlantis/Shanghai all screamed yes and rampaged down the multifarious gangways of *Æther* and *Chinook*, which had all been splayed out for the occasion in hopes of preventing bottlenecks, which might lead to injury or, heaven forbid, rudeness. For the first few moments the children simply burst away from the airships like gas escaping from a bottle. Then they began to converge on sources of wonderment: a centaur, eight feet high if he was an inch, walking across a meadow with his son and daughter cantering around him. Some baby dinosaurs. A cave angling gently into a hillside, bearing promising signs of enchantment. A road winding up another hill toward a ruined castle.

The grownups mostly remained aboard the airships and gave the children a few minutes to flame out, though Lord Finkle-McGraw could be seen making his way toward *Atlantis*, poking curiously at the earth with his walking-stick, just to make sure it was fit to be trod by royal feet.

A man and a woman descended the gangway of *Atlantis*: in a floral dress that explored the labile frontier between modesty and summer comfort, accessorized with a matching parasol, Queen Victoria II of Atlantis. In a natty beige linen suit, her husband, the Prince Consort, whose name, lamentably, was Joe. Joe, or Joseph as he was called in official circumstances, stepped down first, moving in a somewhat pompous one-small-step-for-man gait, then turned to face Her Majesty and offered his hand, which she accepted graciously but perfunctorily, as if to remind everyone that she'd done crew at Oxford and had blown off tension during her studies at Stanford B-School with lap-swimming, roller-blading, and jeet kune do. Lord Finkle-McGraw bowed as the royal espadrilles touched down. She extended her hand, and he kissed it, which was racy but allowed if you were old and stylish, like Alexander Chung-Sik Finkle-McGraw.

"We thank Lord Finkle-McGraw, Imperial Tectonics Limited, and Machine-Phase Systems Limited once again for this lovely occasion. Now let us all enjoy these magnificent surroundings before, like the first Atlantis, they sink forever beneath the waves."

The parents of Atlantis/Shanghai strolled down the gangways, though many had retreated to their staterooms to change clothes upon catching sight of what the Queen and Prince Consort were wearing. The big news, already being uploaded to the *Times* by telescope-wielding fashion columnists onboard *Æther*, was that the parasol was back.

Gwendolyn Hackworth hadn't packed a parasol, but she was untroubled; she'd always had a kind of natural, unconscious alamodality. She and John strolled down onto the island. By the time Hackworth's eyes had adjusted to the sunlight, he was already squatting and rubbing a pinch of soil between his fingertips. Gwen left him to obsess and joined a group of other women, mostly engineers' wives, and even a baronet-level Equity Participant or two.

Hackworth found a concealed path that wound through trees up a hillside to a little grove around a cool, clear pond of fresh water—he tasted it just to be sure. He stood there for a while, looking out over the enchanted island, wondering what Fiona was up to right now. This led to daydreaming: perhaps she had, by some miracle, encountered Princess Charlotte, made friends with her, and was exploring some wonder with her right now. This led him into a long reverie that was interrupted when he realized that someone was quoting poetry to him.

"Where had we been, we two, beloved Friend!
If in the season of unperilous choice,
In lieu of wandering, as we did, through vales
Rich with indigenous produce, open ground

Of Fancy, happy pastures ranged at will,
We had been followed, hourly watched, and noosed,
Each in his several melancholy walk
Stringed like a poor man's heifer at its feed,
Led through the lanes in forlorn servitude."

Hackworth turned to see that an older man was sharing his view. Genetically Asian, with a somewhat twangy North American accent, the man looked at least seventy. His translucent skin was still stretched tight over broad cheekbones, but the eyelids, ears, and the hollows of his cheeks were weathered and wrinkled. Under his pith helmet no fringe of hair showed; the man was completely bald. Hackworth gathered these clues slowly, until at last he realized who stood before him.

"Sounds like Wordsworth," Hackworth said.

The man had been staring out over the meadows below. He cocked his head and looked directly at Hackworth for the first time. "The poem?"

"Judging by content, I'd guess *The Prelude.*"

"Nicely done," the man said.

"John Percival Hackworth at your service." Hackworth stepped toward the other and handed him a card.

"Pleasure," the man said. He did not waste breath introducing himself.

Lord Alexander Chung-Sik Finkle-McGraw was one of several duke-level Equity Lords who had come out of Apthorp. Apthorp was not a formal organization that could be looked up in a phone book; in financial cant, it referred to a strategic alliance of several immense companies, including Machine-Phase Systems Limited and Imperial Tectonics Limited. When no one important was listening, its employees called it John Zaibatsu, much as their forebears of a previous century had referred to the East India Company as John Company.

MPS made consumer goods and ITL made real estate, which was, as ever, where the real money was. Counted by the hectare, it didn't amount to much—just a few strategically placed islands really, counties rather than continents—but it was the most expensive real estate in the world outside of a few blessed places like Tokyo, San Francisco, and Manhattan. The reason was that Imperial Tectonics had geotects, and geotects could make sure that every new piece of land possessed the charms of Frisco, the strategic location of Manhattan, the *feng-shui* of Hong Kong, the dreary but obligatory *Lebensraum* of L.A. It was no longer necessary to send out dirty yokels in coonskin caps to chart the wilderness, kill the abos, and clear-cut the groves; now all you needed was a hot young geotect, a start matter compiler, and a jumbo Source.

Like most other neo-Victorians, Hackworth could recite Finkle-McGraw's biography from memory. The future Duke had been born in Korea and adopted, at the age of six months, by a couple who'd met during grad school in Iowa City and later started an organic farm near the Iowa/South Dakota border.

During his early teens, a passenger jet made an improbable crash-landing at the Sioux City airport, and Finkle-McGraw, along with several other members of his Boy Scout troop who had been hastily mobilized by their scoutmaster, was standing by the runway along with every ambulance, fireman, doctor, and nurse from a radius of several counties. The uncanny efficiency with which the locals responded to the crash was widely publicized and became the subject of a made-for-TV movie. Finkle-McGraw couldn't understand why. They had simply done what was reasonable and humane under the circumstances; why did people from other parts of the country find this so difficult to understand?

This tenuous grasp of American culture might have been owing to the fact that his parents home-schooled him up to the age of fourteen. A typical school day for Finkle-McGraw consisted of walking down to a river to study tadpoles or going to the public library to check out a book on ancient Greece or Rome. The family had little spare money, and vacations consisted of driving to the Rockies for some backpacking, or up to northern Minnesota for canoeing. He probably learned more on his summer vacations than most of his peers did during their school years. Social contact with other children happened mostly through Boy Scouts or church—the Finkle-McGraws belonged to a Methodist church, a Roman Catholic church, and a tiny synagogue that met in a rented room in Sioux City.

His parents enrolled him in a public high school, where he maintained a steady 2.0 average out of a possible 4.

The coursework was so stunningly inane, the other children so dull, that Finkle-McGraw developed a poor attitude. He earned some repute as a wrestler and cross-country runner, but never exploited it for sexual favors, which would have been easy enough in the promiscuous climate of the times. He had some measure of the infuriating trait that causes a young man to be a nonconformist for its own sake and found that the surest way to shock most people, in those days, was to believe that some kinds of behavior were bad and others good, and that it was reasonable to live one's life accordingly.

After graduating from high school, he spent a year running certain parts of his parents' agricultural business and then attended Iowa State University of Science and Technology ("Science with Practice") in Ames. He enrolled as an agricultural engineering major and switched to physics after his first quarter. While remaining a nominal physics major for the next three years, he took classes in whatever he wanted: information science, metallurgy, early music. He never earned a degree, not because of poor performance but because of the political climate; like many universities at the time, ISU insisted that its students study a broad range of subjects, including arts and humanities. Finkle-McGraw chose instead to read books, listen to music, and attend plays in his spare time.

One summer, as he was living in Ames and working as a research assistant in a solid-state physics lab, the city was actually turned into an island for a couple of days by an immense flood. Along with many other Midwesterners, Finkle-McGraw put in a few weeks building levees out of sandbags and plastic sheeting. Once again he was struck by the national media coverage—reporters from the coasts kept showing up and announcing, with some bewilderment, that there had been no looting. The lesson learned during the Sioux City plane crash was reinforced. The Los Angeles riots of the previous year provided a vivid counterexample. Finkle-McGraw began to develop an opinion that was to shape his political views in later years, namely, that while people were not *genetically* different, they were *culturally* as different as they could possibly be, and that some cultures were simply better than others. This was not a subjective value judgment, merely an observation that some cultures thrived and expanded while others failed. It was a view implicitly shared by nearly everyone but, in those days, never voiced.

Finkle-McGraw left the university without a diploma and went back to the farm, which he managed for a few years while his parents were preoccupied with his mother's breast cancer. After her death, he moved to Minneapolis and took a job with a company founded by one of his former professors, making scanning tunneling microscopes, which at that time were newish devices capable of seeing and manipulating individual atoms. The field was an obscure one then, the clients tended to be large research institutions, and practical applications seemed far away. But it was perfect for a man who wanted to study nanotechnology, and McGraw began doing so, working late at night on his own time. Given his diligence, his self-confidence, his intelligence ("adaptable, relentless, but not really brilliant"), and the basic grasp of business he'd picked up on the farm, it was inevitable that he would become one of the few hundred pioneers of nanotechnological revolution; that his own company, which he founded five years after he moved to Minneapolis, would survive long enough to be absorbed into Apthorp; and that he would navigate Apthorp's political and economic currents well enough to develop a decent equity position.

He still owned the family farm in northwestern Iowa, along with a few hundred thousand acres of adjoining land, which he was turning back into a tall-grass prairie, complete with herds of bison and real Indians who had discovered that riding around on horses hunting wild game was a better deal than pissing yourself in gutters in Minneapolis or Seattle. But for the most part he stayed on New Chusan, which was for all practical purposes his ducal estate.

"Public relations?" said Finkle-McGraw.

"Sir?" Modern etiquette was streamlined; no "Your Grace" or other honorifics were necessary in such an informal setting.

"Your department, sir."

Hackworth had given him his social card, which was appropriate under these circumstances but revealed nothing else. "Engineering. Bespoke."

"Oh, really. I'd thought anyone who could recognise Wordsworth must be one of those artsy sorts in P.R."

"Not in this case, sir. I'm an engineer. Just promoted to Bespoke recently. Did some work on this project, as it happens."

"What sort of work?"

"Oh, P.I. stuff mostly," Hackworth said. Supposedly Finkle-McGraw still kept up with things and would recognize the abbreviation for pseudo-intelligence, and perhaps even appreciate that Hackworth had made this assumption.

Finkle-McGraw brightened a bit. "You know, when I was a lad they called it A.I. Artificial intelligence."

Hackworth allowed himself a tight, narrow, and brief smile. "Well, there's something to be said for cheekiness, I suppose."

"In what way was pseudo-intelligence used here?"

"Strictly on MPS's side of the project, sir." Imperial Tectonics had done the island, buildings, and vegetation. Machine-Phase Systems—Hackworth's employer—did anything that moved. "Stereotyped behaviors were fine for the birds, dinosaurs, and so on, but for the centaurs and fauns we wanted more interactivity, something that would provide an illusion of sentience."

"Yes, well done, well done, Mr. Hackworth."

"Thank you, sir."

"Now, I know perfectly well that only the very finest engineers make it to Bespoke. Suppose you tell me how an aficionado of Romantic poets made it into such a position."

Hackworth was taken aback by this and tried to respond without seeming to put on airs. "Surely a man in your position does not see any contradiction—"

"But a man in my position was not responsible for promoting you to Bespoke. A man in an entirely different position was. And I am very much afraid that such men do tend to see a contradiction."

"Yes, I see. Well, sir, I studied English literature in college."

"Ah! So you are not one of those who followed the straight and narrow path to engineering."

"I suppose not, sir."

"And your colleagues at Bespoke?"

"Well, if I understand your question, sir, I would say

that, as compared with other departments, a relatively large proportion of Bespoke engineers have had—well, for lack of a better way of describing it, interesting lives."

"And what makes one man's life more interesting than another's?"

"In general, I should say that we find unpredictable or novel things more interesting."

"That is nearly a tautology." But while Lord Finkle-McGraw was not the sort to express feelings promiscuously, he gave the appearance of being nearly satisfied with the way the conversation was going. He turned back toward the view again and watched the children for a minute or so, twisting the point of his walking-stick into the ground as if he were still skeptical of the island's integrity. Then he swept the stick around in an arc that encompassed half the island. "How many of those children do you suppose are destined to lead interesting lives?"

"Well, at least two, sir—Princess Charlotte, and your granddaughter."

"You're quick, Hackworth, and I suspect capable of being devious if not for your staunch moral character," Finkle-McGraw said, not without a certain archness. "Tell me, were your parents subjects, or did you take the Oath?"

"As soon as I turned twenty-one, sir. Her Majesty—at that time, actually, she was still Her Royal Highness—was touring North America, prior to her enrollment at Stanford, and I took the Oath at Trinity Church in Boston."

"Why? You're a clever fellow, not blind to culture like so many engineers. You could have joined the First Distributed Republic or any of a hundred synthetic phyles on the West Coast. You would have had decent prospects and been free from all this"—Finkle-McGraw jabbed his cane at the two big airships—"behavioural discipline that we impose upon ourselves. Why did you impose it on yourself, Mr. Hackworth?"

"Without straying into matters that are strictly personal in nature," Hackworth said carefully, "I knew two kinds of discipline as a child: none at all, and too much. The former leads to degenerate behaviour. When I speak of degeneracy, I am not being priggish, sir—I am alluding to things well known to me, as they made my own childhood less than idyllic."

Finkle-McGraw, perhaps realizing that he had stepped out of bounds, nodded vigorously. "This is a familiar argument, of course."

"Of course, sir. I would not presume to imply that I was the only young person ill-used by what became of my native culture."

"And I do not see such an implication. But many who feel as you do found their way into phyles wherein a much harsher regime prevails and which view *us* as degenerates."

"My life was not without periods of excessive, unreasoning discipline, usually imposed capriciously by those responsible for laxity in the first place. That combined with my historical studies led me, as many others, to the conclusion that there was little in the previous century worthy of emulation, and that we must look to the nineteenth century instead for stable social models."

"Well done, Hackworth! But you must know that the model to which you allude did not long survive the first Victoria."

"We have outgrown much of the ignorance and resolved many of the internal contradictions that characterised that era."

"Have we, then? How reassuring. And have we resolved them in a way that will ensure that all of those children down there live interesting lives?"

"I must confess that I am too slow to follow you."

"You yourself said that the engineers in the Bespoke department—the very best—had led interesting lives, rather than coming from the straight and narrow. Which implies a correlation, does it not?"

"Clearly."

"This implies, does it not, that in order to raise a generation of children who can reach their full potential, we must find a way to make their lives interesting. And the question I have for you, Mr. Hackworth, is this: Do you think that our schools accomplish that? Or are they like the schools that Wordsworth complained of?"

"My daughter is too young to attend school—but I should fear that the latter situation prevails."

"I assure you that it does, Mr. Hackworth. My three children were raised in those schools, and I know them well. I am determined that Elizabeth shall be raised differently."

Hackworth felt his face flushing. "Sir, may I remind you that we have just met—I do not feel worthy of the confidences you are reposing in me."

"I'm telling you these things not as a friend, Mr. Hackworth, but as a professional."

"Then I must remind you that I am an engineer, not a child psychologist."

"This I have not forgotten, Mr. Hackworth. You are indeed an engineer, and a very fine one, in a company that I still think of as mine—though as an Equity Lord, I no longer have a formal connection. And now that you have brought your part of this project to a successful conclusion, I intend to put you in charge of a new project for which I have reason to believe you are perfectly suited."

Bud embarks on a life of crime; an insult to a tribe
& its consequences.

*B*ud rolled his first victim almost by accident. He'd taken a wrong turn into a cul-de-sac and inadvertently trapped a black man and woman and a couple of little kids who'd blundered in there before him. They had a scared look about them, like a lot of the new arrivals did, and Bud noticed the way the man's gaze lingered on his Sights, wondering whether those crosshairs, invisible to him, were centered on him, his lady, or his kid.

Bud didn't get out of their way. He was packing, they weren't, it was up to them to get out of his way. But instead they just froze up. "You got a problem?" Bud said.

"What do you want?" the man said.

It had been a while since anyone had manifested such sincere concern for Bud's desires, and he kind of liked it. He realized that these people were under the impression that they were being mugged. "Oh, same as anyone else. Money and shit," Bud said, and just like that, the man took some hard ucus out of his pocket and handed them over—and then actually thanked him as he backed away.

Bud enjoyed getting that kind of respect from black people—it reminded him of his noble heritage in the trailer parks of North Florida—and he didn't mind the money either. After that day he began looking for black people with that same scared uncertain look about them. These people bought and sold off the record, and so they carried hard money. He did pretty well for himself for a couple of months. Every so often he would stop by the flat where his bitch Tequila lived, give her some lingerie, and maybe give Harv some chocolate.

Harv was presumed by both Bud and Tequila to be Bud's son. He was five, which meant that he had been conceived in a much earlier cycle of Bud and Tequila's breakup-and-make-up relationship. Now the bitch was pregnant again, which meant that Bud would have to bring even more gifts to her place when he came around. The pressures of fatherhood!

One day Bud targeted a particularly well-dressed family because of their fancy clothes. The man was wearing a business suit and the woman a nice clean dress, and they were carrying a baby all dressed up in a white lacy thing, and they had hired a porter to help them haul their luggage away from the Aerodrome. The porter was a white guy who vaguely reminded Bud of himself, and he was incensed to see him acting as a pack animal for blacks. So as soon as these people got away from the bustle of the Aerodrome and into a more secluded neighborhood, Bud approached them, swaggering in the way he'd practiced in the mirror, occasionally pushing his Sights up on his nose with one index finger.

The guy in the suit was different from most of them. He didn't try to act like he hadn't seen Bud, didn't try to skulk away, didn't cringe or slouch, just stood his ground, feet planted squarely, and very pleasantly said, "Yes, sir, can I be of assistance?" He didn't talk like an American black, had almost a British accent, but crisper. Now that Bud had come closer, he saw that the man had a strip of colored cloth thrown around his neck and over his lapels, dangling down like a scarf. He looked well-housed and well-fed for the most part, except for a little scar high up on one cheekbone.

Bud kept walking until he was a little too close to the guy. He kept his head tilted back until the last minute, like he was kicking back listening to some loud tunes (which he was), and then suddenly snapped his head forward so he was staring the guy right in the face. It was another way to emphasize the fact that he was packing, and it usually did the trick. But this guy did not respond with the little flinch that Bud had come to expect and enjoy. Maybe he was from some booga-booga country where they didn't know about skull guns.

"Sir," the man said, "my family and I are on the way to our hotel. We have had a long journey, and we are tired; my daughter has an ear infection. If you would state your business as expeditiously as possible, I would be obliged."

"You talk like a fucking Vicky," Bud said.

"Sir, I am not what you refer to as a Vicky, or I should have gone directly there. I would be obliged if you could be so kind as to moderate your language in the presence of my wife and child."

It took Bud a while to untangle this sentence, and a while longer to believe that the man really cared about a few dirty words spoken within earshot of his family, and longer yet to believe that he had been so insolent to Bud, a heavily muscled guy who was obviously packing a skull gun.

"I'm gonna fucking say whatever I fucking want to your bitch and your fucking brat," Bud said, very loud. Then he could not keep himself from grinning. Score a few points for Bud!

The man looked impatient rather than scared and heaved a deep sigh. "Is this an armed robbery or something? Are you sure you know what you are getting into?"

Bud answered by whispering "hut" under his breath and firing a Crippler into the man's right bicep. It went off deep in the muscle, like an M-80, blowing a dark hole in the sleeve of the man's jacket and leaving his arm stretched out nice and straight—the trike now pulling without anything to oppose it. The man clenched his teeth, his eyes bulged, and for a few moments he made strangled grunting noises from way down in his chest, making an effort not to cry out. Bud stared at the wound in fascination. It was just like shooting people in a ractive.

Except that the bitch didn't scream and beg for mercy.

She just turned her back, using her body to shield the baby, and looked over her shoulder, calmly, at Bud. Bud noticed she had a little scar on her cheek too.

"Next I take your eye," Bud said, "then I go to work on the bitch."

The man held up his good hand palm out, indicating surrender. He emptied his pocket of hard Universal Currency Units and handed them over. And then Bud made himself scarce, because the monitors—almond-size aerostats with eyes, ears, and radios—had probably picked up the sound of the explosion and begun converging on the area. He saw one hiss by him as he rounded the corner, trailing a short whip antenna that caught the light like a hairline crack in the atmosphere.

Three days later, Bud was hanging around the Aerodrome, looking for easy pickings, when a big ship came in from Singapore. Immersed in a stream of two thousand arrivals was a tight group of some two dozen solidly built, very dark-skinned black men dressed in business suits, with strips of colored cloth draped around their necks and little scars on their cheekbones.

It was later that night that Bud, for the first time in his life, heard the word *Ashanti*. "Another twenty-five Ashanti just came in from L.A.!" said a man in a bar. "The Ashanti had a big meeting in the conference room at the Sheraton!" said a woman on the street. Waiting in a queue for one of the free matter compilers, a bum said, "One of them Ashanti gave me five yuks. They're fine folks."

When Bud ran into a guy he knew, a former comrade in the decoy trade, he said, "Hey, the place is crawling with them Ashanti, ain't it?"

"Yup," said the guy, who had seemed unaccountably shocked to see Bud's face on the street, and who was annoyingly distracted all of a sudden, swiveling his head to look all ways.

"They must be having a convention or something," Bud theorized. "I rolled one of 'em the other night."

"Yeah, I know," his friend said.

"Huh? How'd you know that?"

"They ain't having a convention, Bud. All of those Ashanti—except the first one—came to town hunting for you."

Paralysis struck Bud's vocal cords, and he felt light-headed, unable to concentrate.

"I gotta go," his friend said, and removed himself from Bud's vicinity.

For the next few hours Bud felt as though everyone on the street was looking at him. Bud was certainly looking at them, looking for those suits, those colored strips of cloth. But he caught sight of a man in shorts and a T-shirt—a black man with very high cheeks, one of which was marked with a tiny scar, and almost Asian-looking eyes in a very high state of alertness. So he couldn't rely on the Ashanti wearing stereotyped clothing.

Very soon after that, Bud swapped clothes with an indigent down on the beach, giving up all his black leather and coming away with a T-shirt and shorts of his own. The T-shirt was much too small; it bound him under the armpits and pressed against his muscles so that he felt the eternal twitching even more than usual. He wished he could turn the stimulators off now, relax his muscles even for one night, but that would require a trip to the mod parlor, and he had to figure that the Ashanti had the mod parlors all staked out.

He could have gone to any of several brothels, but he didn't know what kind of connections these Ashanti might have—or even what the hell an Ashanti *was*, exactly—and he wasn't sure he could get a boner under these circumstances anyway.

As he wandered the streets of the Leased Territories, primed to level his Sights at any black person who blundered into his path, he reflected on the unfairness of his fate. How was he to know that guy belonged to a tribe?

Actually, he should have known, just from the fact that he wore nice clothes and didn't look like all the other people. The very apartness of those people should have been a dead giveaway. And his lack of fear should have told him something. Like he couldn't believe anyone would be stupid enough to mug him.

Well, Bud had been that stupid, and Bud didn't have a phyle of his own, so Bud was screwed. Bud would have to go get himself one real quick, now.

He'd already tried to join the Boers a few years back. The Boers were to Bud's kind of white trash what these Ashanti were to most of the blacks. Stocky blonds in suits or the most conservative sorts of dresses, usually with half a dozen kids in tow, and my god did *they* ever stick together. Bud had paid a few visits to the local laager, studied some of their training ractives on his home mediatron, put in some extra hours at the gym trying to meet their physical standards, even gone to a couple of horrific bible-study sessions. But in the end, Bud and the Boers weren't much of a match. The amount of church you had to attend was staggering—it was like *living* in church. And he'd studied their history, but there were only so many Boer/Zulu skirmishes he could stand to read about or keep straight in his head. So that was out; he wasn't getting into any laager tonight.

The Vickys wouldn't take him in a million years, of course. Almost all the other tribes were racially oriented, like those Parsis or whatever. The Jews wouldn't take him unless he cut a piece of his dick off and learned to read a whole nother language, which was a bit of a tall order since he hadn't gotten round to learning how to read English yet. There were a bunch of cœnobitical phyles—religious tribes —that took people of all races, but most of them weren't very powerful and didn't have turf in the Leased Territories. The Mormons had turf and were very powerful, but he wasn't sure if they'd take him as quickly and readily as he needed to be taken. Then there were the tribes that people just made up out of thin air—the synthetic phyles—but most of them were based on some shared skill or weird idea or ritual that he wouldn't be able to pick up in half an hour.

Finally, sometime around midnight, he wandered past a man in a funny gray jacket and cap with a red star on it, trying to give away little red books, and it hit him: Sendero. Most Senderistas were either Incan or Korean, but they'd take anyone. They had a nice clave here in the Leased Territories, a clave with good security, and every one of them, down to the last man or woman, was batshit. They'd be more than a match for a few dozen Ashantis. And you could join anytime just by walking in the gates. They would take anyone, no questions asked.

He'd heard it was not such a good thing to be a Communist, but under the circumstances he figured he could hold his nose and quote from the little red book as necessary. As soon as those Ashantis left town, he'd bolt.

Once he made up his mind, he couldn't wait to get

there. He had to restrain himself from breaking into a jog, which would be sure to draw the attention of any Ashantis on the street. He couldn't bear the idea of being so close to safety and then blowing it.

He rounded a corner and saw the wall of the Sendero Clave four stories high and two blocks long, one solid giant mediatron with a tiny gate in the middle. Mao was on one end, waving to an unseen multitude, backed up by his horsetoothed wife and his beetle-browed sidekick Lin Biao, and Chairman Gonzalo was on the other, teaching some small children, and in the middle was a slogan in ten-meter-high letters: STRIVE TO UPHOLD THE PRINCIPLES OF MAO-GONZALO-THOUGHT!

The gate was guarded, as always, by a couple of twelve-year-old kids in red neckerchiefs and armbands, ancient bolt-action rifles with real bayonets leaning against their collarbones. A blond white girl and a pudgy Asian boy. Bud and his son Harv had whiled away many an idle hour trying to get these kids to laugh: making silly faces, mooning them, telling jokes. Nothing ever worked. But he'd seen the ritual: They'd bar his path with crossed rifles and not let him in until he swore his undying allegiance to Mao-Gonzalo-thought, and then—

A horse, or something built around the same general plan, was coming down the street at a hand-gallop. Its hooves did not make the pocking noise of iron horseshoes. Bud realized it was a chevaline—a four-legged robot thingy.

The man on the chev was an African in very colorful clothing. Bud recognized the patterns on that cloth and knew without bothering to check for the scar that the guy was Ashanti. As soon as he caught Bud's eye, he kicked it up another gear, to a tantivy. He was going to cut Bud off before he could reach Sendero. And he was too far away, yet, to be reached by the skull gun, whose infinitesimal bullets had a disappointingly short range.

He heard a soft noise behind him and swiveled his head around, and something whacked him on the forehead and stuck there. A couple more Ashantis had snuck up on him barefoot.

"Sir," one of them said, "I would not recommend operation of your weapon, unless you want the round to detonate in your own forehead. Hey?" and he smiled broadly,

enormous perfectly white teeth, and touched his own forehead. Bud reached up and felt something hard glued to the
skin of his brow, right over the skull gun.

The chev dropped to a trot and cut toward him. Suddenly Ashantis were everywhere. He wondered how long
they'd been tracking him. They all had beautiful smiles.
They all carried small devices in their hands, which they
aimed at the pavement, trigger fingers laid alongside the
barrels until the guy on the chev told them otherwise. Then,
suddenly, they all seemed to be aimed in his direction.

The projectiles stuck to his skin and clothing and burst
sideways, flinging out yards and yards of weightless filmy
stuff that stuck to itself and shrank. One struck him in the
back of the head, and a swath of the stuff whipped around
his face and encased it. It was about as thick as a soap bubble, and so he could see through it pretty well—it had peeled
one of his eyelids back so he couldn't help but see—and
everything now had that gorgeous rainbow tinge characteristic of soap bubbles. The entire shrink-wrapping process
consumed maybe half a second, and then Bud, mummified
in plastic, toppled over face-forward. One of the Ashantis
was good enough to catch him. They laid him down on the
street and rolled him over on his back. Someone poked the
blade of a pocketknife through the film over Bud's mouth so
that he could breathe again.

Several Ashantis set about the chore of bonding handles to the shrink-wrap, two up near the shoulders and two
down by the ankles, as the man on the chev dismounted and
knelt over him.

This equestrian had several prominent scars on his
cheeks. "Sir," the man said, smiling, "I accuse you of violating certain provisions of the Common Economic Protocol,
which I will detail at a more convenient time, and I hereby
place you under personal arrest. Please be aware that anyone who has been so arrested is subject to deadly force in the
event he tries to resist—which—ha! ha!—does not seem
likely at present—but it is a part of the procedure that I am
to say this. As this territory belongs to a nation-state that
recognizes the Common Economic Protocol, you are entitled
to a hearing of any such charges within the judicial frame-
work of the nation-state in question, which in this case happens to be the Chinese Coastal Republic. This nation-state

may or may not grant you additional rights; we will find out in a very few moments, when we present the situation to one of the relevant authorities. Ah, I believe I see one now."

A constable from the Shanghai Police, legs strapped into a pedomotive, was coming down the street with the tremendous loping strides afforded by such devices, escorted by a couple of power-skating Ashantis. The Ashantis had big smiles, but the constable looked stereotypically inscrutable.

The chief of the Ashantis bowed to the constable and graciously spun out another lengthy quotation from the fine print of the Common Economic Protocol. The constable kept making a gesture that was somewhere between a nod and a perfunctory bow. Then the constable turned to Bud and said, very fast: "Are you a member of any signatory tribe, phyle, registered diaspora, franchise-organized quasi-national entity, sovereign polity, or any other form of dynamic security collective claiming status under the CEP?"

"Are you shitting me?" Bud said. The shrink-wrap squished his mouth together so he sounded like a duck.

Four Ashantis took the four handles and hoisted Bud off the ground. They began to follow the loping constable in the direction of the Causeway that led over the sea to Shanghai. "How 'bout it," Bud quacked through the hole in the shrink-wrap, "he said I might have other rights. Do I have any other rights?"

The constable looked back over his shoulder, turning his head carefully so he wouldn't lose his balance on that pedomotive. "Don't be jerk," he said in pretty decent English, "this is China."

Hackworth's morning ruminations; breakfast and departure for work.

Thinking about tomorrow's crime, John Percival Hackworth slept poorly, rising three times on the pretext of having to use the loo. Each time he looked in on Fiona, who was sprawled out in her white lace nightgown, arms above her head, doing a backflip into the arms of Morpheus. Her face was barely visible in the dark room, like the moon seen through folds of white silk.

At five A.M., a shrill pentatonic reveille erupted from the North Koreans' brutish mediatrons. Their clave, which went by the name Sendero, was not far above sea level: a mile below the Hackworths' building in altitude, and twenty degrees warmer on the average day. But whenever the women's chorus chimed in with their armor-piercing refrain about the all-seeing beneficence of the Serene Leader, it felt as if they were right next door.

Gwendolyn didn't even stir. She would sleep soundly for another hour, or until Tiffany Sue, her lady's maid, came bustling into the room and began to lay out her clothes: stretchy lingerie for the morning workout, a business frock, hat, gloves, and veil for later.

Hackworth drew a silk dressing gown from the wardrobe and poured it over his shoulders. Binding the sash around his waist, the cold tassels splashing over his fingers in the dark, he glanced through the doorway to Gwendolyn's closet and out the other side into her boudoir. Against that room's far windows was the desk she used for social correspondence, really just a table with a top of genuine marble, strewn with bits of stationery, her own and others', dimly identifiable even at this distance as business cards, visiting cards, note cards, invitations from various people still going through triage. Most of the boudoir floor was covered with a tatty carpet, worn through in places all the way down to its underlying matrix of jute, but hand-woven and sculpted by genuine Chinese slave labor during the Mao Dynasty. Its only real function was to protect the floor from Gwendolyn's exercise equipment, which gleamed in the dim light scattering off the clouds from Shanghai: a step unit done up in Beaux-Arts ironmongery, a rowing machine cleverly fashioned of writhing sea-serpents and hard-bodied nereids, a rack of free weights supported by four callipygious caryatids—not chunky Greeks but modern women, one of each major racial group, each tricep, gluteus, latissimus, sartorius, and rectus abdominus casting its own highlight. Classical architecture indeed. The caryatids were supposed to be role models, and despite subtle racial differences, each body fit the current ideal: twenty-two-inch waist, no more than 17% body fat. That kind of body couldn't be faked with undergarments, never mind what the ads in the women's magazines claimed; the long tight bodices of the current mode, and modern fabrics thinner than soap bubbles, made everything obvious. Most women who didn't have superhuman willpower couldn't manage it without the help of a lady's maid who would run them through two or even three vigorous workouts a day. So after Fiona had stopped breast-feeding and the time had loomed when Gwen would have to knacker her maternity clothes, they had hired Tiffany Sue—just another one of the child-related expenses Hackworth had never imagined until the bills had started to come in. Gwen accused him, half-seriously, of having eyes for Tiffany Sue. The accusation was almost a standard formality of modern marriage, as lady's maids were all young, pretty, and flawlessly buffed. But Tiffany Sue was a typical thete, loud and classless and heavily made up, and Hackworth couldn't abide her. If he had eyes for anyone, it was those caryatids holding up the weight rack; at least they had impeccable taste going for them.

Mrs. Hull had not heard him and was still bumping sleepily around in her quarters. Hackworth put a crumpet into the toaster oven and went out on their flat's tiny balcony with a cup of tea, catching a bit of the auroral breeze off the Yangtze Estuary.

The Hackworths' building was one of several lining a block-long garden where a few early risers were already out walking their spaniels or touching their toes. Far down the slopes of New Chusan, the Leased Territories were coming awake: the Senderos streaming out of their barracks and lining up in the streets to chant and sing through their morning calisthenics. All the other thetes, coarcted into the tacky little claves belonging to their synthetic phyles, turning up their own mediatrons to drown out the Senderos, setting off firecrackers or guns—he could never tell them apart—and a few internal-combustion hobbyists starting up their primitive full-lane vehicles, the louder the better. Commuters lining up at the tube stations, waiting to cross the Causeway into Greater Shanghai, seen only as a storm front of neon-stained, coal-scented smog that encompassed the horizon.

This neighborhood was derisively called Earshot. But Hackworth didn't mind the noise so much. It would have been a sign of better breeding, or higher pretentions, to be terribly sensitive about it, to complain of it all the time, and to yearn for a townhouse or even a small estate farther inland.

Finally the bells of St. Mark's chimed six o'clock. Mrs. Hull burst into the kitchen on the first stroke and expressed shame that Hackworth had beaten her to the kitchen and shock that he had defiled it. The matter compiler in the corner of the kitchen came on automatically and began to create a pedomotive for Hackworth to take to work.

Before the last bell had died away, the rhythmic whack-whack-whack of a big vacuum pump could be heard. The engineers of the Royal Vacuum Utility were already at work expanding the eutactic environment. The pumps sounded big, probably Intrepids, and Hackworth reckoned that they must be preparing to raise a new structure, possibly a wing of the University.

He sat down at the kitchen table. Mrs. Hull was already marmalading his crumpet. As she laid out plates and silver, Hackworth picked up a large sheet of blank paper. "The usual," he said, and then the paper was no longer blank; now it was the front page of the *Times.*

Hackworth got all the news that was appropriate to his station in life, plus a few optional services: the latest from his favorite cartoonists and columnists around the world; clippings on various peculiar crackpot subjects forwarded to him by his father, ever anxious that he had not, even after all this time, sufficiently edified his son; and stories relating to the Uitlanders—a subphyle of New Atlantis, consisting of persons of British ancestry who had fled South Africa several decades previously. Hackworth's mother was an Uitlander, so he subscribed to the service.

A gentleman of higher rank and more far-reaching responsibilities would probably get different information written in a different way, and the top stratum of New Chusan actually got the *Times* on paper, printed out by a big antique press that did a run of a hundred or so, every morning at about three A.M.

That the highest levels of the society received news

written with ink on paper said much about the steps New
Atlantis had taken to distinguish itself from other phyles.

Now nanotechnology had made nearly anything possible, and so the cultural role in deciding what *should* be
done with it had become far more important than imagining
what *could* be done with it. One of the insights of the Victorian Revival was that it was not necessarily a good thing for
everyone to read a completely different newspaper in the
morning; so the higher one rose in the society, the more
similar one's *Times* became to one's peers'.

Hackworth almost managed to dress without waking
Gwendolyn, but she began to stir while he was stringing his
watch chain around various tiny buttons and pockets in his
waistcoat. In addition to the watch, various other charms
dangled from it, such as a snuffbox that helped perk him up
now and then, and a golden pen that made a little chime
whenever he received mail.

"Have a good day at work, dear," she mumbled. Then,
blinking once or twice, frowning, and focusing on the chintz
canopy over the bed: "You finish it today, do you?"

"Yes," Hackworth said. "I'll be home late. Quite late."

"I understand."

"No," he blurted. Then he pulled himself up short.
This was it, he realized.

"Darling?"

"It's not that—the project should finish itself. But after
work, I believe I'll get a surprise for Fiona. Something special."

"Being home for dinner would be more special than
anything you could get her."

"No, darling. This is different. I promise."

He kissed her and went to the stand by the front door.
Mrs. Hull was awaiting him, holding his hat in one hand
and his briefcase in the other. She had already removed the
pedomotive from the M.C. and set it by the door for him; it
was smart enough to know that it was indoors, and so its
long legs were fully collapsed, giving him almost no mechanical advantage. Hackworth stepped onto the tread
plates and felt the straps reach out and hug his legs.

He told himself that he could still back out. But a flash
of red caught his eye, and he looked in and saw Fiona creeping down the hallway in her nightie, her flaming hair flying

all directions, getting ready to surprise Gwendolyn, and the look in her eyes told him that she had heard everything. He blew her a kiss and walked out the door, resolute.

Bud is prosecuted; noteworthy features of the Confucian judicial system; he receives an invitation to take a long walk on a short pier.

*B*ud had spent the last several days living in the open, in a prison on the low, smelly delta of the Chang Jiang (as most of his thousands of fellow inmates called it) or, as Bud called it, the Yangtze. The walls of the prison were lines of bamboo stakes, spaced at intervals of a few meters, with strips of orange plastic fluttering gaily from their tops. Yet another device had been mounted on Bud's bones, and it knew where those boundaries were. From place to place one could see a corpse just on the other side of the line, body striped with the lurid marks of cookie-cutters. Bud had mistaken these for suicides until he'd seen a lynching in progress: a prisoner who was thought to have stolen some other fellow's shoes was picked up bodily by the mob, passed from hand to hand overhead like a crowd-surfing rock singer, all the time flailing frantically trying to grab something. When he reached the line of bamboo poles, he was given one last shove and ejected, his body virtually exploding as he flew through the invisible plane of the perimeter.

But the ever-present threat of lynching was a minor irritation compared to the mosquitoes. So when Bud heard the voice in his ears telling him to report to the northeast corner of the compound, he didn't waste any time—partly because he wanted to get away from that place and partly because, if he didn't, they could pop him by remote control. They could have just told him to walk directly to the courtroom and take a seat and he would have done it, but for ceremonial purposes they sent a cop to escort him.

The courtroom was a high-ceilinged room in one of the

old buildings along the Bund, not lavishly furnished. At one end was a raised platform, and on that was an old folding table with a red cloth tossed over it. The red cloth had gold threads woven through it to make a design: a unicorn or a dragon or some shit like that. Bud had trouble discriminating among mythical beasts.

The judge came in and was introduced as Judge Fang by the larger of his two gofers: a bulky, rounded-headed Chinese guy who smelled tantalizingly of menthol cigarettes. The constable who had escorted Bud to the courtroom pointed to the floor, and Bud, knowing his cue, dropped to his knees and touched his forehead to the floor.

The Judge's other gofer was a tiny little Amerasian woman wearing glasses. Hardly anyone used glasses anymore to correct their vision, and so it was a likely bet that this was actually some kind of phantascope, which let you see things that weren't there, such as ractives. Although, when people used them for purposes other than entertainment, they used a fancier word: phenomenoscope.

You could get a phantascopic system planted directly on your retinas, just as Bud's sound system lived on his eardrums. You could even get telæsthetics patched into your spinal column at various key vertebrae. But this was said to have its drawbacks: some concerns about long-term nerve damage, plus it was rumored that hackers for big media companies had figured out a way to get through the defenses that were built into such systems, and run junk advertisements in your peripheral vision (or even spang in the fucking middle) all the time—even when your eyes were closed. Bud knew a guy like that who'd somehow gotten infected with a meme that ran advertisements for roach motels, in Hindi, superimposed on the bottom right-hand corner of his visual field, twenty-four hours a day, until the guy whacked himself.

Judge Fang was surprisingly young, probably not out of his thirties yet. He sat at the red cloth-covered table and started to talk in Chinese. His two gofers stood behind him. A Sikh was here; he stood up and said a few words back to the Judge in Chinese. Bud couldn't figure out why there was a Sikh here, but he'd become accustomed to Sikhs turning up where they were least sought.

Judge Fang said in a New York City accent, "The representative from Protocol has suggested that we conduct these proceedings in English. Any objections?"

Also present was the guy he had mugged, who was holding the one arm rather stiffly but seemed otherwise healthy. His wife was with him too.

"I'm Judge Fang," the Judge continued, looking straight at Bud. "You can address me as Your Honor. Now, Bud, Mr. Kwamina here has accused you of certain activities that are illegal in the Coastal Republic. You are also accused of actionable offenses under the Common Economic Protocol, to which we are a subscriber. These offenses are closely related to the crimes I already mentioned, but slightly different. Are you getting all this?"

"Not exactly, Your Honor," Bud said.

"We think you mugged this guy and blew a hole in his arm," Judge Fang said, "which is frowned upon. *Capiche?*"

"Yes, sir."

Judge Fang nodded at the Sikh, who took the cue.

"The CEP code," said the Sikh, "governs all kinds of economic interactions between people and organizations. Theft is one such interaction. Maiming is another, insofar as it affects the victim's ability to fend for himself economically. As Protocol does not aspire to sovereign status, we work in cooperation with the indigenous justice system of CEP signatories in order to pursue such cases."

"You familiar with the Confucian system of justice, Bud?" said Judge Fang. Bud's head was beginning to get dizzy from snapping back and forth like a spectator at a tennis match. "I'm guessing no. Okay, even though the Chinese Coastal Republic is no longer strictly or even vaguely Confucian, we still run our judicial system that way—we've had it for a few thousand years, and we think it's not half bad. The general idea is that as judge, I actually perform several roles at once: detective, judge, jury, and if need be, executioner."

Bud snickered at this crack, then noticed that Judge Fang did not appear to be in an especially jocose mood. His New Yorkish ways had initially fooled Bud into thinking that Judge Fang was something of a Regular Guy.

"So in the first-mentioned role," Judge Fang continued, "I would like for you, Mr. Kwamina, to tell me whether you recognize the suspect."

"He is the man," said Mr. Kwamina, aiming one index finger at Bud's forehead, "who threatened me, shot me, and stole my money."

"And Mrs. Kum?" Judge Fang said. Then, as an aside to Bud, he added, "In their culture, the woman does not adopt her husband's family name."

Mrs. Kum just nodded at Bud and said, "He is the guilty party."

"Miss Pao, do you have anything to add?"

The tiny woman in the spectacles looked at Bud and said, in Texan-accented English, "From this man's forehead I removed a voice-activated nanoprojectile launcher, colloquially known as a skull gun, loaded with three types of ammunition, including so-called Crippler rounds of the type used against Mr. Kwamina. Nanopresence examination of the serial numbers on those rounds, and comparison of the same with fragments removed from Mr. Kwamina's wound, indicated that the round used on Mr. Kwamina was fired from the gun embedded in the suspect's forehead."

"Dang," Bud said.

"Okay," Judge Fang said, and reached up with one hand to rub his temples for just a moment. Then he turned to Bud. "You're guilty."

"Hey! Don't I get to put up a defense?" Bud said. "I object!"

"Don't be an asshole," Judge Fang said.

The Sikh said, "As the offender has no significant assets, and as the value of his labor would not be sufficient to compensate the victim for his injury, Protocol terminates its interest in this case."

"Got it," Judge Fang said. "Okay, Bud, my man, do you have any dependents?"

"I got a girlfriend," Bud said. "She's got a son named Harv who is my boy, unless we counted wrong. And I heard she's pregnant."

"You think she is, or you know she is?"

"She was last time I checked—a couple months ago."

"What's her name?"

"Tequila."

A muffled snort came from one of the Protocol trainees —the young woman—who put one hand over her mouth. The Sikh appeared to be biting his lip.

"Tequila?" Judge Fang said, incredulous. It was becoming clear that Judge Fang tried a lot of these cases and relished the odd scrap of entertainment value.

"There are nineteen women named Tequila in the Leased Territories," said Miss Pao, reading something out of her phenomenoscope, "one of whom delivered a baby girl named Nellodee three days ago. She also has a five-year-old boy named Harvard."

"Oh, wow," Bud said.

"Congratulations, Bud, you're a pa," Judge Fang said. "I gather from your reaction that this comes as something of a surprise. It seems evident that your relationship with this Tequila is tenuous, and so I do not find that there are any mitigating circumstances I should take into account in sentencing. That being the case, I would like you to go out that door over there"—Judge Fang pointed to a door in the corner of the courtroom—"and all the way down the steps. Leave through the exit door and cross the street, and you will find a pier sticking out into the river. Walk to the end of that pier until you are standing on the red part and await further instructions."

Bud moved tentatively at first, but Judge Fang gestured impatiently, so finally he went out the door and down the stairway and out onto the Bund, the street that ran along the waterfront of the Huang Pu River, and that was lined with big old European-style buildings. A pedestrian tunnel took him under the road to the actual waterfront, which was crowded with Chinese people strolling around, and legless wretches dragging themselves hither and thither. Some middle-aged Chinese people had set up a sound system playing archaic music and were ballroom-dancing. The music and dance style would have been offensively quaint to Bud at any other point in his life, but now for some reason the sight of these somewhat fleshy, settled-looking people, twirling around gently in one another's arms, made him feel sad.

Eventually he found the right pier. As he strolled out onto it, he had to shoulder his way past some slopes carrying a long bundle wrapped in cloth, who were trying to get onto the pier ahead of him. The view was nice here; the old buildings of the Bund behind him, the vertiginous neon wall of the Pudong Economic Zone exploding from the opposite

bank and serving as backdrop for heavy river traffic—
mostly chains of low-lying barges.

The pier did not turn red until the very end, where it
began to slope down steeply toward the river. It had been
coated with some kind of grippy stuff so his feet wouldn't
fly out from under him. He turned around and looked back
up at the domed court building, searching for a window
where he might make out the face of Judge Fang or one of
his gofers. The family of Chinese was following him down
the pier, carrying their long bundle, which was draped with
garlands of flowers and, as Bud now realized, was probably
the corpse of a family member. He had heard about these
piers; they were called funeral piers.

Several dozen of the microscopic explosives known as
cookie-cutters detonated in his bloodstream.

*Nell learns to work the matter compiler; youthful
indiscretions; all is made better.*

Nell had grown too long for her old crib mattress, and so
Harv, her big brother, said he would help get a new one. He
was big enough, he offhandedly mentioned, to do that sort
of thing. Nell followed him into the kitchen, which housed
several important boxy entities with prominent doors. Some
were warm, some cool, some had windows, some made
noises. Nell had frequently seen Harv, or Tequila, or one of
Tequila's boyfriends, removing food from them, in one stage
or another of doneness.

One of the boxes was called the M.C. It was built into
the wall over the counter. Nell dragged a chair and climbed
up to watch as Harv worked at it. The front of the M.C. was
a mediatron, which meant anything that had pictures moving around on it, or sound coming out of it, or both. As Harv
poked it with his fingers and spoke to it, little moving pictures danced around. It reminded her of the ractives she

played on the big mediatron in the living room, when it wasn't being used by someone bigger.

"What are those?" Nell said.

"Mediaglyphics," Harv said coolly. "Someday you'll learn how to read."

Nell could already read some of them.

"Red or blue?" Harv asked magnanimously.

"Red."

Harv gave it an especially dramatic poke, and then a new mediaglyphic came up, a white circle with a narrow green wedge at the top. The wedge got wider and wider. The M.C. played a little tune that meant you were supposed to wait. Harv went to the fridge and got himself a juice box and one for Nell too. He looked at the M.C. disdainfully. "This takes so long, it's ridiculous," he said.

"Why?"

" 'Cause we got a cheap Feed, just a few grams per second. Pathetic."

"Why do we got a cheap Feed?"

"Because it's a cheap house."

"Why is it a cheap house?"

"Because that's all we can afford because of the economics," Harv said. "Mom's gotta compete with all kinds of Chinese and stuff that don't have any self-respect and so they'll work for nothing. So Mom's gotta work for nothing." He looked at the M.C. again and shook his head. "Pathetic. At the Flea Circus they got a Feed that's, like, this big around." He touched his fingertips together in front of him and made a big circle with his arms. "But this one's probly like the size of your pinkie."

He stepped away from the M.C. as if he could no longer stand to share a room with it, sucked powerfully on his juice box, and wandered into the living room to get in a ractive. Nell just watched the green wedge get bigger and bigger until it filled half the circle, and then it began to look like a green circle with a white wedge in it, getting narrower and narrower, and finally the music came to a bouncy conclusion just as the white wedge vanished.

"It's done!" she said.

Harv paused his ractive, swaggered into the kitchen, and poked a mediaglyphic that was an animated picture of a door swinging open. The M.C. took to hissing loudly. Harv watched her scared face and ruffled her hair; she could not fend him off because she had her hands over her ears. "Got to release the vacuum," he explained.

The sound ended, and the door popped open. Inside the M.C., folded up neatly, was Nell's new red mattress.

"Give it to me! Give it to me!" Nell shouted, furious to see Harv's hands on it. Harv amused himself for a second playing keep-away, then gave it to her. She ran to the room that she shared with Harv and slammed the door as hard as she could. Dinosaur, Duck, Peter, and Purple were waiting for her. "I got us a new bed," she told them. She grabbed her old crib mattress and heaved it into the corner, then unfolded the new one precisely on the floor. It was disappointingly thin, more blanket than mattress. But when she had it all laid out on the floor, it made a whooshing noise—not loud—the sound of her brother's breathing late at night. It thickened as it inhaled, and when it was done, it looked like a real mattress. She gathered Dinosaur and Duck and Peter and Purple up into her arms and then, just to make sure, jumped up and down on it several hundred times.

"You like it?" Harv said. He had opened the door.

"No! Get out!" Nell screamed.

"Nell, it's my room too," Harv said. "I gotta deke your old one."

Later, Harv went out with his buddies, and Nell was alone in the house for a while. She had decided that her kids needed mattresses too, and so she dragged the chair to the counter and climbed up on top, right in front of the M.C., and tried to read the mediaglyphics. A lot of them she didn't recognize. But she remembered that Tequila just used words when she couldn't read something, so she tried talking to it instead.

"Please secure the permission of an adult," the M.C. said, over and over again.

Now she knew why Harv always poked at things rather than talking to them. She poked at the M.C. for a long time until finally she came to the same mediaglyphics that Harv had used to choose her mattress. One showed a man and woman sleeping in a very large bed. A man and woman in a somewhat smaller bed. A man by himself. A child by herself. A baby.

Nell poked at the baby. The white circle and red

wedge appeared, the music played, the M.C. hissed and opened.

She spread it out on the floor and formally presented it to Dinosaur, who was too little to know how to jump up and down on it; so Nell showed him for a while. Then she went back to the M.C. and got mattresses for Duck, Peter, and Purple. Now, much of the room was covered with mattresses, and she thought how fun it would be to have the whole room just be one big mattress, so she made a couple of the very largest size. Then she made a new mattress for Tequila and another new one for her boyfriend Rog.

When Harv came back, his reaction swerved between terror and awe. "Mom's gonna have Rog beat the shit out of us," he said. "We gotta deke all this stuff now."

Easy come, easy go. Nell explained the situation to her kids and then helped Harv stuff all of the mattresses, except her own, into the deke hopper. Harv had to use all his strength to shove the door closed. "Now we just better hope this stuff all dekes before Mom gets home," he said. "It's gonna take a while."

Later they went to bed and both lay awake for a while, dreading the sound of the front door opening. But neither Mom nor Rog came home that night. Mom finally showed up in the morning, changed into her maid outfit, and ran for the bus to the Vicky Clave, but she just left all her garbage on the floor instead of throwing it in the hopper. When Harv checked the hopper later, it was empty.

"We dodged a bullet," he said. "You gotta be careful how you use the matter compiler, Nell."

"What's a matter compiler?"

"We call it the M.C. for short."

"Why?"

"Because M.C. stands for matter compiler, or so they say."

"Why?"

"It just does. In letters, I guess."

"What are letters?"

"Kinda like mediaglyphics except they're all black, and they're tiny, they don't move, they're old and boring and really hard to read. But you can use 'em to make short words for long words."

*Hackworth arrives at work; a visit to the Design
Works; Mr. Cotton's vocation.*

Rain beaded on the specular toes of Hackworth's boots as
he strode under the vaulting wrought-iron gate. The little
beads reflected the silvery gray light of the sky as they rolled
off onto the pedomotive's tread plates, and dripped to the
gray-brown cobblestones with each stride. Hackworth excused himself through a milling group of uncertain Hindus.
Their hard shoes were treacherous on the cobblestones, their
chins were in the air so that their high white collars would
not saw their heads off. They had arisen many hours ago in
their tiny high-rise warrens, their human coin lockers on the
island south of New Chusan, which was Hindustani. They
had crossed into Shanghai in the wee hours on autoskates
and velocipedes, probably paid off some policemen, made
their way to the Causeway joining New Chusan to the city.
Machine-Phase Systems Limited knew that they were coming, because they came every day. The company could have
set up an employment office closer to the Causeway, or even
in Shanghai itself. But the company liked to have job-seekers
come all the way to the main campus to fill out their applications. The difficulty of getting here prevented people from
coming on a velleity, and the eternal presence of these people—like starlings peering down hungrily at a picnic—reminded everyone who was lucky enough to have a job that
others were waiting to take their place.

The Design Works emulated a university campus, in
more ways than its architects had really intended. If a campus was a green quadrilateral described by hulking, heder-
ated Gothics, then this was a campus. But if a campus was
also a factory of sorts, most of whose population sat in rows
and columns in large stuffy rooms and did essentially the
same things all day, then the Design Works was a campus
for that reason too.

Hackworth detoured through Merkle Hall. It was
Gothic and very large, like most of the Design Works. Its
vaulted ceiling was decorated with a hard fresco consisting
of paint on plaster. Since this entire building, except for the

fresco, had been grown straight from the Feed, it would have been easier to build a mediatron into the ceiling and set it to display a soft fresco, which could have been changed from time to time. But neo-Victorians almost never used mediatrons. Hard art demanded commitment from the artist. It could only be done once, and if you screwed it up, you had to live with the consequences.

The centerpiece of the fresco was a flock of cybernetic cherubs, each shouldering a spherical atom, converging on some central work-in-progress, a construct of some several hundred atoms, radially symmetric, perhaps intended to look like a bearing or motor. Brooding over the whole thing, quite large but obviously not to scale, was a white-coated Engineer with a monocular nanophenomenoscope strapped to his head. No one really used them because you couldn't get depth perception, but it looked better on the fresco because you could see the Engineer's other eye, steel-blue, dilated, scanning infinity like the steel oculus of Arecibo. With one hand the Engineer stroked his waxed mustache. The other was thrust into a nanomanipulator, and it was made obvious, through glorious overuse of radiant tromp l'oeil, that the atom-humping cherubs were all dancing to his tune, naiads to the Engineer's Neptune.

The corners of the fresco were occupied with miscellaneous busywork; in the upper left, Feynman and Drexler and Merkle, Chen and Singh and Finkle-McGraw reposed on a numinous buckyball, some of them reading books and some pointing toward the work-in-progress in a manner that implied constructive criticism. In the upper right was Queen Victoria II, who managed to look serene despite the gaudiness of her perch, a throne of solid diamond. The bottom fringe of the work was crowded with small figures, mostly children with the occasional long-suffering mom, ordered chronologically. On the left were the spirits of generations past who had shown up too early to enjoy the benefits of nanotechnology and (not explicitly shown, but somewhat ghoulishly implied) croaked from obsolete causes such as cancer, scurvy, boiler explosions, derailments, drive-by shootings, pogroms, blitzkriegs, mine shaft collapses, ethnic cleansing, meltdowns, running with scissors, eating Drano, heating a cold house with charcoal briquets, and being gored by oxen. Surprisingly, none of them seemed sullen; they

were all watching the activities of the Engineer and his che-
rubic workforce, their cuddly, uplifted faces illuminated by
the light streaming from the center, liberated (as Hackworth
the engineer literal-mindedly supposed) by the binding energy of the atoms as they plummeted into their assigned
potential wells.

The children in the center had their backs to Hackworth and were mostly seen in silhouette, looking directly
up and raising their arms toward the light. The kids in bottom right balanced the angelic host on the bottom left; these
were the spirits of unborn children yet to benefit from the
Engineer's work, though they certainly looked eager to get
born as soon as possible. Their backdrop was a luminescent,
undulous curtain, much like the aurora, which was actually
a continuation of the flowing skirts of Victoria II seated on
her throne above.

"Pardon me, Mr. Cotton," Hackworth said, almost
sotto voce. He had worked here once, for several years, and
knew the etiquette. A hundred designers were sitting in the
hall, neatly arranged in rows. All had their heads wrapped
up in phenomenoscopes. The only persons who were aware
of Hackworth's presence in the hall were Supervising Engineer Dürig, his lieutenants Chu, DeGrado, and Beyerley,
and a few water-boys and couriers standing erect at their
stations around the perimeter. It was bad form to startle the
engineers, so you approached them loudly and spoke to
them softly.

"Good morning, Mr. Hackworth," Cotton said.

"Good morning, Demetrius. Take your time."

"I'll be with you in a moment, sir."

Cotton was a southpaw. His left hand was in a black
glove. Laced through it was a network of invisibly tiny rigid
structures, motors, position sensors, and tactile stimulators.
The sensors kept track of his hand's position, how much
each joint of each knuckle was bent, and so on. The rest of
the gear made him feel as though he were touching real
objects.

The glove's movements were limited to a roughly
hemispherical domain with a radius of about one cubit; as
long as his elbow stayed on or near its comfy elastomeric
rest, his hand was free. The glove was attached to a web of
infinitesimal wires that emerged from filatories placed here

and there around the workstation. The filatories acted like motorized reels, taking up slack and occasionally pulling the glove one way or another to simulate external forces. In fact they were not motors but little wire factories that generated wire when it was needed and, when slack needed to be taken up or a wire needed a tug, sucked it back in and digested it. Each wire was surrounded by a loose accordion sleeve a couple of millimeters in diameter, which was there for safety, lest visitors stick their hands in and slice off fingers on the invisible wires.

Cotton was working with some kind of elaborate structure consisting, probably, of several hundred thousand atoms. Hackworth could see this because each workstation had a mediatron providing a two-dimensional view of what the user was seeing. This made it easy for the supervisors to roam up and down the aisles and see at a glance what each employee was up to.

The structures these people worked with seemed painfully bulky to Hackworth, even though he'd done it himself for a few years. The people here in Merkle Hall were all working on mass-market consumer products, which by and large were not very demanding. They worked in symbiosis with big software that handled repetitive aspects of the job. It was a fast way to design products, which was essential when going after the fickle and impressionable consumer market. But systems designed that way always ended up being enormous. An automated design system could always make something work by throwing more atoms at it.

Every engineer in this hall, designing those nanotechnological toasters and hair dryers, wished he could have Hackworth's job in Bespoke, where concinnity was an end in itself, where no atom was wasted and every subsystem was designed specifically for the task at hand. Such work demanded intuition and creativity, qualities neither abundant nor encouraged here in Merkle Hall. But from time to time, over golf or karaoke or cigars, Dürig or one of the other supervisors would mention some youngster who showed promise.

Because Lord Alexander Chung-Sik Finkle-McGraw was paying for Hackworth's current project, the *Young Lady's Illustrated Primer*, price was no object. The Duke would brook no malingering or corner-cutting, so everything was as start as Bespoke could make it, every atom could be justified.

Even so, there was nothing especially interesting about the power supply being created for the Primer, which consisted of batteries of the same kind used to run everything from toys to airships. So Hackworth had farmed that part of the job out to Cotton, just to see whether he had potential.

Cotton's gloved hand fluttered and probed like a stuck horsefly in the center of the black web. On the mediatronic screen attached to his workstation, Hackworth saw that Cotton was gripping a medium-size (by Merkle Hall standards) subassembly, presumably belonging to some much larger nanotechnological system.

The standard color scheme used in these phenomenoscopes depicted carbon atoms in green, sulfur in yellow, oxygen in red, and hydrogen in blue. Cotton's assembly, as seen from a distance, was generally turquoise because it consisted mostly of carbon and hydrogen, and because Hackworth's point of view was so far away that the thousands of individual atoms all blended together. It was a gridwork of long, straight, but rather bumpy rods laid across each other at right angles. Hackworth recognized it as a rod logic system—a mechanical computer.

Cotton was trying to snap it together with some larger part. From this Hackworth inferred that the auto-assembly process (which Cotton would have tried first) hadn't worked quite right, and so now Cotton was trying to maneuver the part into place by hand. This wouldn't fix what was wrong with it, but the telæsthetic feedback coming into his hand through those wires would give him insight as to which bumps were lining up with which holes and which weren't. It was an intuitive approach to the job, a practice furiously proscribed by the lecturers at the Royal Nanotechnological Institute but popular among Hackworth's naughty, clever colleagues.

"Okay," Cotton finally said, "I see the problem." His hand relaxed. On the mediatron, the subassembly drifted away from the main group under its own momentum, then slowed, stopped, and began to fall back toward it, drawn in by weak van der Waals forces. Cotton's right hand was resting on a small chordboard; he whacked a key that froze the simulation, then, as Hackworth noted approvingly, groped the keys for a few seconds, typing in some documentation. Meanwhile he was withdrawing his left hand from the glove and using it to pull the rig off his head; its straps and pads left neat indentations in the nap of his hair.

"Is this the smart makeup?" Hackworth said, nodding at the screen.

"The next step beyond," Cotton said. "Remote-control."

"Controlled how? Yuvree?" Hackworth said, meaning Universal Voice Recognition Interface.

"A specialised variant thereof, yes sir," Cotton said. Then, lowering his voice, "Word has it they considered makeup with nanoreceptors for galvanic skin response, pulse, respiration, and so on, so that it would respond to the wearer's emotional state. This superficial, need I say it, cosmetic issue concealed an undertow that pulled them out into deep and turbulent philosophical waters—"

"What? Philosophy of makeup?"

"Think about it, Mr. Hackworth—is the function of makeup to respond to one's emotions—or precisely *not* to do so?"

"These waters are already over my head," Hackworth admitted.

"You'll be wanting to know about the power supply for Runcible," Cotton said, using the code name for the Illustrated Primer. Cotton had no idea what Runcible was, just that it needed a relatively long-lived power supply.

"Yes."

"The modifications you requested are complete. I ran the tests you specified plus a few others that occurred to me—all of them are documented here." Cotton grabbed the heavy brasslike pull of his desk drawer and paused for a fraction of a second while the embedded fingerprint-recognition logic did its work. The drawer unlocked itself, and Cotton pulled it open to reveal a timeless assortment of office drawer miscellany, including several sheets of paper —some blank, some printed, some scrawled on, and one sheet that was blank except for the word RUNCIBLE printed at the top in Cotton's neat draughtsman's hand. Cotton pulled this one out and spoke to it: "Demetrius James Cotton transferring all privileges to Mr. Hackworth."

"John Percival Hackworth in receipt," Hackworth said, taking the page from Cotton. "Thank you, Mr. Cotton."

"You're welcome, sir."

"Cover sheet," Hackworth said to the piece of paper, and then it had pictures and writing on it, and the pictures moved—a schematic of a machine-phase system cycling.

"If I'm not being too forward by enquiring," Cotton said, "will you be compiling Runcible soon?"

"Today most likely," Hackworth said.

"Please feel free to inform me of any glitches," Cotton said, just for the sake of form.

"Thank you, Demetrius," Hackworth said. "Letter fold," he said to the piece of paper, and it creased itself neatly into thirds. Hackworth put it in the breast pocket of his jacket and walked out of Merkle Hall.

*Particulars of Nell & Harv's domestic situation;
Harv brings back a wonder.*

Whenever Nell's clothes got too small for her, Harv would pitch them into the deke bin and then have the M.C. make new ones. Sometimes, if Tequila was going to take Nell someplace where they would see other moms with other daughters, she'd use the M.C. to make Nell a special dress with lace and ribbons, so that the other moms would see how special Nell was and how much Tequila loved her. The kids would sit in front of the mediatron and watch a passive, and the moms would sit nearby and talk sometimes or watch the mediatron sometimes. Nell listened to them, especially when Tequila was talking, but she didn't really understand all the words.

She knew, because Tequila repeated it often, that when Tequila got pregnant with Nell, she had been using something called the Freedom Machine—a mite that lived in your womb and caught eggs and ate them. Victorians didn't believe in them, but you could buy them from Chinese and

Hindustanis, who, of course, had no scruples. You never knew when they'd all gotten too worn-out to work anymore, which is how Tequila had ended up with Nell. One of the women said you could buy a special kind of Freedom Machine that would go in there and eat a fetus. Nell didn't know what a fetus was, but all of the women apparently did, and thought that the idea was the kind of thing that only the Chinese or Hindustanis would ever think up. Tequila said she knew all about that sort of Freedom Machine but didn't want to use one, because she was afraid it might be gross.

Sometimes Tequila would bring back pieces of real cloth from her work, because she said that the rich Victorians she worked for would never miss them. She never let Nell play with them, and so Nell did not understand the difference between real cloth and the kind that came from the M.C.

Harv found a piece of it once. The Leased Territories, where they lived, had their own beach, and Harv and his friends liked to go prospecting there, early in the morning, for things that had drifted across from Shanghai, or that the Vickys in New Atlantis Clave had flushed down their water-closets. What they were really looking for was pieces of stretchy, slippery Nanobar. Sometimes the Nanobar was in the shape of condoms, sometimes it came in larger chunks that were used to wrap things up and preserve them from the depredations of mites. In any case, it could be gathered up and sold to certain persons who knew how to clean it and weld one piece of Nanobar to another and make it into protective suits and other shapes.

Harv had quietly stuffed the piece of cloth into his shoe and then limped home, not saying a word to anyone. That night Nell, lying on her red mattress, was troubled by vague dreams about strange lights and finally woke up to see a blue monster in her room: It was Harv underneath his blanket with a torch, doing something. She climbed out very slowly so as not to disturb Dinosaur, Duck, Peter, and Purple, and stuck her head beneath the blanket, and found Harv, holding the little flashlight in his teeth, working at something with a pair of toothpicks.

"Harv," she said, "are you working on a mite?"

"No, dummy." Harv's voice was hushed, and he had

to mumble around the little button-shaped torch he was holding in his teeth. "Mites are lots smaller. See, look!"

She crawled forward a little more, drawn as much by warmth and security as by curiosity, and saw a limp mottled brown thing a few centimeters on a side, fuzzy around the edges, resting on Harv's crossed ankles.

"What is it?"

"It's magic. Watch this," Harv said. And worrying at it with his toothpick, he teased something loose.

"It's got string coming out of it!" Nell said.

"Sssh!" Harv gripped the end of the thread beneath his thumbnail and pulled. It looked quite short, but it lengthened as he pulled, and the fuzzy edge of the piece of fabric waffled too fast to see, and then the thread had come loose entirely. He held it up for inspection, then let it drift down onto a heap of others just like it.

"How many does it have?" Nell said.

"Nell," Harv said, turning to face her so that his light shone into her face, his voice coming out of the light epiphanically, "you got it wrong. It's not that the thing has threads *in* it—it *is* threads. Threads going under and over each other. If you pulled out all of the threads, nothing would be left."

"Did mites make it?" Nell asked.

"The way it's made—so digital—each thread going over and under other threads, and those ones going over and under all the other threads—" Harv stopped for a moment, his mind overloaded by the inhuman audacity of the thing, the promiscuous reference frames. "It had to be mites, Nell, nothing else could do it."

Security measures adopted by Atlantis/Shanghai.

Atlantis/Shanghai occupied the loftiest ninety percent of New Chusan's land area—an inner plateau about a mile above sea level, where the air was cooler and cleaner. Parts of it were marked off with a lovely wrought-iron fence, but the real border was defended by something called the dog pod grid—a swarm of quasi-independent aerostats.

Aerostat meant anything that hung in the air. This was an easy trick to pull off nowadays. Nanotech materials were stronger. Computers were infinitesimal. Power supplies were much more potent. It was almost difficult *not* to build things that were lighter than air. Really simple things like packaging materials—the constituents of litter, basically— tended to float around as if they weighed nothing, and air- craft pilots, cruising along ten kilometers above sea level, had become accustomed to the sight of empty, discarded grocery bags zooming past their windshields (and getting sucked into their engines). As seen from low earth orbit, the upper atmosphere now looked dandruffy. Protocol insisted that everything be made heavier than need be, so that it would fall, and capable of being degraded by ultraviolet light. But some people violated Protocol.

Given that it was so easy to make things that would float in air, it was not much of a stretch to add an air turbine. This was nothing more than a small propeller, or series of them, mounted in a tubular foramen wrought through the body of the aerostat, drawing in air at one end and forcing it out the other to generate thrust. A device built with several thrusters pointed along different axes could remain in one position, or indeed navigate through space.

Each aerostat in the dog pod grid was a mirror-sur- faced, aerodynamic teardrop just wide enough, at its widest part, to have contained a Ping-Pong ball. These pods were programmed to hang in space in a hexagonal grid pattern, about ten centimeters apart near the ground (close enough to stop a dog but not a cat, hence "dog pods") and spaced wider as they got higher. In this fashion a hemispherical dome was limned around the sacrosanct airspace of the New Atlantis Clave. When wind gusted, the pods all swung into it like weather vanes, and the grid deformed for a bit as the pods were shoved around; but all of them eventually worked their way back into place, swimming upstream like minnows, propelling the air turbines. The 'bines made a thin hissing noise, like a razor blade cutting air, that, when multi- plied by the number of pods within earshot, engendered a not altogether cheerful ambience.

Enough wrestling with the wind, and a pod's battery

would run down. Then it would swim over and nuzzle its neighbor. The two would mate in midair, like dragonflies, and the weaker would take power from the stronger. The system included larger aerostats called nurse drones that would cruise around dumping large amounts of power into randomly selected pods all over the grid, which would then distribute it to their neighbors. If a pod thought it was having mechanical trouble, it would send out a message, and a fresh pod would fly out from the Royal Security installation beneath Source Victoria and relieve it so that it could fly home to be decompiled.

As numerous eight-year-old boys had discovered, you could not climb the dog pod grid because the pods didn't have enough thrust to support your weight; your foot would just mash the first pod into the ground. It would try to work its way loose, but if it were stuck in mud or its turbines fouled, another pod would have to come out and replace it. For the same reason you could pluck any pod from its place and carry it away. When Hackworth had performed this stunt as a youth, he had discovered that the farther it got from its appointed place the hotter it became, all the while politely informing him, in clipped military diction, that he had best release it or fall victim to vaguely adumbrated consequences. But nowadays you could just steal one or two whenever you felt like it, and a new one would come out and replace it; once they figured out they were no longer part of the grid, the pods would self-scramble and become instant souvenirs.

This user-friendly approach did not imply that grid-tampering went ignored, or that such activities were approved of. You could walk through the grid whenever you chose by shoving a few pods out of the way—*unless* Royal Security had told the pods to electrocute you or blast you into chum. If so, they would politely warn you before doing it. Even when they were in a more passive mode, though, the aerostats were watching and listening, so that nothing got through the dog pod grid without becoming an instant media celebrity with hundreds of uniformed fans down in Royal Joint Forces Command.

Unless it was microscopic. Microscopic invaders were more of the threat nowadays. Just to name one example, there was Red Death, a.k.a. the Seven Minute Special, a tiny aerodynamic capsule that burst open after impact and released a thousand or so corpuscle-size bodies, known colloquially as cookie-cutters, into the victim's bloodstream. It took about seven minutes for all of the blood in a typical person's body to recirculate, so after this interval the cookie-cutters would be randomly distributed throughout the victim's organs and limbs.

A cookie-cutter was shaped like an aspirin tablet except that the top and bottom were domed more to withstand ambient pressure; for like most other nanotechnological devices a cookie-cutter was filled with vacuum. Inside were two centrifuges, rotating on the same axis but in opposite directions, preventing the unit from acting like a gyroscope. The device could be triggered in various ways; the most primitive were simple seven-minute time bombs.

Detonation dissolved the bonds holding the centrifuges together so that each of a thousand or so ballisticules suddenly flew outward. The enclosing shell shattered easily, and each ballisticule kicked up a shock wave, doing surprisingly little damage at first, tracing narrow linear disturbances and occasionally taking a chip out of a bone. But soon they slowed to near the speed of sound, where shock wave piled on top of shock wave to produce a sonic boom. Then all the damage happened at once. Depending on the initial speed of the centrifuge, this could happen at varying distances from the detonation point; most everything inside the radius was undamaged but everything near it was pulped; hence, "cookie-cutter." The victim then made a loud noise like the crack of a whip, as a few fragments exited his or her flesh and dropped through the sound barrier in air. Startled witnesses would turn just in time to see the victim flushing bright pink. Bloodred crescents would suddenly appear all over the body; these marked the geometric intersection of detonation surfaces with skin and were a boon to forensic types, who could thereby identify the type of cookie-cutter by comparing the marks against a handy pocket reference card. The victim was just a big leaky sack of undifferentiated gore at this point and, of course, never survived.

Such inventions had spawned concern that people from Phyle A might surreptitiously introduce a few million lethal devices into the bodies of members of Phyle B, providing the technically sweetest possible twist on the trite, ancient dream of being able instantly to turn a whole society into gravy. A few inroads of that kind had been made, a few mass closed-casket funerals had been held, but not many. It was hard to control these devices. If a person ate or drank one, it might end up in their body, but it might just go into the food chain and get recycled into the body of someone you liked. But the big problem was the host's immune system, which caused enough of a histological fuss to tip off the intended victims.

What worked in the body could work elsewhere, which is why phyles had their own immune systems now. The impregnable-shield paradigm didn't work at the nano level; one needed to hack the mean free path. A well-defended clave was surrounded by an aerial buffer zone infested with immunocules—microscopic aerostats designed to seek and destroy invaders. In the case of Atlantis/Shanghai this zone was never shallower than twenty kilometers. The innermost ring was a greenbelt lying on both sides of the dog pod grid, and the outer ring was called the Leased Territories.

It was always foggy in the Leased Territories, because all of the immunocules in the air served as nuclei for the condensation of water vapor. If you stared carefully into the fog and focused on a point inches in front of your nose, you could see it sparkling, like so many microscopic searchlights, as the immunocules swept space with lidar beams. Lidar was like radar except that it used the smaller wavelengths that happened to be visible to the human eye. The sparkling of tiny lights was the evidence of microscopic dreadnoughts hunting each other implacably through the fog, like U-boats and destroyers in the black water of the North Atlantic.

Nell sees something peculiar; Harv explains all.

One morning Nell looked out the window and saw the world had turned the color of pencil lead. Cars, velocipedes, quadrupeds, even power-skaters left towering black vortices in their wakes.

Harv came back from being out all night. Nell screamed when she saw him because he was a charcoal wraith with two monstrous growths on his face. He peeled back a filter mask to reveal grayish-pink skin underneath. He showed her his white teeth and then took up coughing. He went about this methodically, conjuring tangles of spun phlegm from his deepest alveoli and projecting them into the toilet. Now and then he would stop just to breathe, and a faint whistling noise would come from his throat.

Harv did not explain himself but went about working with his things. He unscrewed the bulges on his mask and took out black things that kicked up little black dust storms when he tossed them onto the floor. He replaced them with a couple of white things that he took from a Nanobar wrapper, though by the time he was finished, the white things were covered with his black fingerprints, the ridges and whorls perfectly resolved. He held the Nanobar wrapper up to the light for a moment.

"Early protocol," he rasped, and pitched it toward the wastebasket.

Then he held the mask up to Nell's face, guided the straps around her head, and tightened them down. Her long hair got caught in the buckles and pinched, but her objections were muffled by the mask. It took a little effort to breathe now. The mask pressed against her face when she inhaled and whooshed when she exhaled.

"Keep it on," Harv said. "It'll protect you from toner."

"What's toner?" she mumbled. The words did not make it out through the mask, but Harv guessed them from the look in her eyes.

"Mites," he said, "or so they say down at the Flea Circus anyway." He picked up one of the black things taken from the mask and flicked it with a fingertip. A cineritious cloud swirled out of it, like a drop of ink in a glass of water, and hung swirling in the air, neither rising nor falling. Sparkles of light flashed in the midst of it like fairy dust. "See, there's mites around, all the time. They use the sparkles to talk to each other," Harv explained. "They're in the air, in food and water, everywhere. And there's rules that these mites are supposed to follow, and those rules are called protocols. And there's a protocol from way back that says they're supposed to be good for your lungs. They're supposed to break down into safe pieces if you breathe one inside of you." Harv paused at this point, theatrically, to summon forth one more ebon loogie, which Nell guessed must be swimming with safe mite bits. "But there are people who break those rules sometimes. Who don't follow the protocols. And I guess if there's too many mites in the air all breaking down inside your lungs, millions—well maybe those safe pieces aren't so safe if there's millions. But anyways, the guys at the Flea Circus say that sometimes the mites go to war with each other. Like maybe someone in Shanghai makes a mite that doesn't follow the protocol, and gets his matter compiler to making a whole lot of them, and sends them all across the water to New Atlantis Clave to snoop on the Vickys, or even maybe to do them harm. Then some Vicky—one of their Protocol Enforcement guys— makes a mite to go out and find that mite and kill it, and they get into a war. That's what's happening today, Nell. Mites fighting other mites. This dust—we call it toner—is actually the dead bodies of all those mites."

"When will the war be over?" Nell asked, but Harv could not hear her, having entered into another coughing jag.

Eventually Harv got up and tied a strip of white Nanobar around his face. The spot over his mouth immediately began turning gray. He ejected used cartridges from his mite gun and inserted new ones. It was shaped like a gun, but it sucked air in instead of shooting things out. You loaded it with drum-shaped cartridges filled with accordion-pleated paper. When you turned it on, it made a little whooshing noise as it sucked air—and hopefully mites—through the paper. The mites got stuck in there. "Gotta go," he said, goosing the trigger on the gun a couple of times. "Never know what I might find." Then he headed for the exit, leaving black toner footprints on the floor, which were scoured away by the swirling air currents in his wake, as if he had never passed that way.

Hackworth compiles the Young Lady's Illustrated Primer; *particulars of the underlying technology.*

Bespoke was a Victorian house on a hill, a block long and replete with wings, turrets, atria, and breezy verandas. Hackworth was not senior enough to merit a turret or a balcony, but he did have a view into a garden where gardenia and boxwood grew. Sitting at his desk, he could not see the garden, but he could smell it, especially when the wind blew in from the sea.

Runcible was sitting on his desk in the form of a stack of papers, most of them signed JOHN PERCIVAL HACK-WORTH. He unfolded Cotton's document. It was still running the little industrial cartoon. Cotton had clearly enjoyed himself. No one ever got fired for going with enhanced photorealism, but Hackworth's own signature look was lifted from nineteenth-century patent applications: black on white, shades of gray implied with nearly microscopic cross-hatching, old-fashioned letterpress font a little rough around the edges. It drove clients wild—they always wanted to blow up the diagrams on their drawing-room mediatrons. Cotton got it. He'd done his diagram in the same style, and so his nanotechnological battery chugged away on the page looking much like the gear train of an Edwardian dread-nought.

Hackworth put Cotton's document atop the Runcible stack and guillotined it against the desktop a couple of times, superstitiously trying to make it look neat. He carried it to the corner of his office, over by the window, where a new piece of furniture had recently been rolled in by the porter: a cherrywood cabinet on brass casters. It came up to his waist. On top was a polished brass mechanism—an automatic document reader with detachable tray. A small door in the back betrayed a Feed port, one-centimeter, typical of household appliances but startlingly wimpy in a heavy industrial works, especially considering that this cabinet contained one of the most powerful computers on earth—five cc's of Bespoke rod logic. It used about a hundred thousand watts of power, which came in over the superconducting part of the Feed. The power had to be dissipated, or else the computer would incinerate itself and most of the building too. Getting rid of that energy had been much more of an engineering job than the rod logic. The latest Feed protocol had a solution built in: a device could now pull ice off the Feed, one microscopic chunk at a time, and output warm water.

Hackworth put the stack of documents into the feed tray on top and told the machine to compile Runcible. There was a card-shuffling buzz as the reader grabbed the edge of each page momentarily and extracted its contents. The flexible Feed line, which ran from the wall into the back of the cabinet, jerked and stiffened orgasmically as the computer's works sucked in a tremendous jolt of hypersonic ice and shot back warm water. A fresh sheet of paper appeared in the cabinet's output tray.

The top of the document read, "RUNCIBLE VERSION 1.0—COMPILED SPECIFICATION."

The only other thing on the document was a picture of the final product, nicely rendered in Hackworth's signature pseudo-engraved style. It looked exactly like a book.

On his way down the vast helical stair in the largest and most central of Bespoke's atria, Hackworth pondered his upcoming crime. It was entirely too late to go back now. It flustered him that he had unconsciously made up his mind months ago without marking the occasion.

Though Bespoke was a design rather than a production house, it had its own matter compilers, including a couple of fairly big ones, a hundred cubic meters. Hackworth had reserved a more modest desktop model, one-tenth of a cubic meter. Use of these compilers had to be logged, so he identified himself and the project first. Then the machine accepted the edge of the document. Hackworth told the matter compiler to begin immediately, and then looked through a transparent wall of solid diamond into the eutactic environment.

The universe was a disorderly mess, the only interesting bits being the organized anomalies. Hackworth had once taken his family out rowing on the pond in the park, and the ends of the yellow oars spun off compact vortices, and Fiona, who had taught herself the physics of liquids through numerous experimental beverage spills and in the bathtub, demanded an explanation for these holes in water. She leaned over the gunwale, Gwendolyn holding the sash of her dress, and felt those vortices with her hands, wanting to understand them. The rest of the pond, simply water in no particular order, was uninteresting.

We ignore the blackness of outer space and pay attention to the stars, especially if they seem to order themselves into constellations. "Common as the air" meant something worthless, but Hackworth knew that every breath of air that Fiona drew, lying in her little bed at night, just a silver glow in the moonlight, was used by her body to make skin and hair and bones. The air became Fiona, and deserving—no, demanding—of love. Ordering matter was the sole endeavor of Life, whether it was a jumble of self-replicating molecules in the primordial ocean, or a steam-powered English mill turning weeds into clothing, or Fiona lying in her bed turning air into Fiona.

A leaf of paper was about a hundred thousand nanometers thick; a third of a million atoms could fit into this span. Smart paper consisted of a network of infinitesimal computers sandwiched between mediatrons. A mediatron was a thing that could change its color from place to place; two of them accounted for about two-thirds of the paper's thickness, leaving an internal gap wide enough to contain structures a hundred thousand atoms wide.

Light and air could easily penetrate to this point, so the works were contained within vacuoles—airless buckminsterfullerene shells overlaid with a reflective aluminum layer so that they would not implode en masse whenever the page was exposed to sunlight. The interiors of the buckyballs, then, constituted something close to a eutactic environment. Here resided the rod logic that made the paper smart. Each of these spherical computers was linked to its four neighbors, north-east-south-west, by a bundle of flexible pushrods running down a flexible, evacuated buckytube, so that the page as a whole constituted a parallel computer made up of about a billion separate processors. The individual processors weren't especially smart or fast and were so susceptible to the elements that typically only a small fraction of them were working, but even with those limitations the smart paper still constituted, among other things, a powerful graphical computer.

And still, Hackworth reflected, it had nothing on Runcible, whose pages were thicker and more densely packed with computational machinery, each sheet folded four times into a sixteen-page signature, thirty-two signatures brought together in a spine that, in addition to keeping the book from falling apart, functioned as an enormous switching system and database.

It was made to be robust, but it still had to be born in the eutactic womb, a solid diamond vacuum chamber housing a start matter compiler. The diamond was doped with something that let only red light pass through; standard engineering practice eschewed any molecular bonds that were tenuous enough to be broken by those lazy red photons, underachievers of the visible spectrum. Thus the growth of your prototype was visible through the window—a good last-ditch safety measure. If your code was buggy and your project grew too large, threatening to shatter the walls of the chamber, you could always shut it down via the ludicrously low-tech expedient of shutting off the Feed line.

Hackworth wasn't worried, but he watched the initial phases of growth anyway, just because it was always interesting. In the beginning was an empty chamber, a diamond hemisphere, glowing with dim red light. In the center of the floor slab, one could see a naked cross-section of an eight-centimeter Feed, a central vacuum pipe surrounded by a collection of smaller lines, each a bundle of microscopic conveyor belts carrying nanomechanical building blocks—individual atoms, or scores of them linked together in handy modules.

The matter compiler was a machine that sat at the terminus of a Feed and, following a program, plucked molecules from the conveyors one at a time and assembled them into more complicated structures.

Hackworth was the programmer. Runcible was the program. It was made up of a number of subprograms, each of which had resided on a separate piece of paper until a few minutes ago, when the immensely powerful computer in Hackworth's office had compiled them into a single finished program written in a language that the matter compiler could understand.

A transparent haze coalesced across the terminus of the Feed, mold on an overripe strawberry. The haze thickened and began adopting a shape, some parts a little higher than others. It spread across the floor away from the Feed line until it had filled out its footprint: one quadrant of a circle with a radius of a dozen centimeters. Hackworth continued to watch until he was sure he could see the top edge of the book growing out of it.

In the corner of this lab stood an evolved version of a copy machine that could take just about any kind of recorded information and transmogrify it into something else. It could even destroy a piece of information and then attest to the fact that it had been destroyed, which was useful in the relatively paranoid environment of Bespoke. Hackworth gave it the document containing the compiled Runcible code and destroyed it. Provably.

When it was finished, Hackworth released the vacuum and lifted the red diamond dome. The finished book stood upright atop the system that had extruded it, which was turned into a junk heap as soon as it was touched by the air. Hackworth picked up the book in his right hand and the extruder in his left, and tossed the latter into a junk bin.

He locked the book in a desk drawer, picked up his top hat, gloves, and walking-stick, stepped into his walker, and set off for the Causeway. Toward Shanghai.

Nell & Harv's general living situation;
the Leased Territories; Tequila.

China was right across the water, and you could see it if you went down to the beach. The city there, the one with skyscrapers, was called Pudong, and beyond that was Shanghai. Harv went there with his friends sometimes. He said it was bigger than you could imagine, old and dirty and full of strange people and sights.

They lived in the L.T., which according to Harv was short for Leased Territories in letters. Nell already knew the mediaglyphics for it. Harv had also taught her the sign for

Enchantment, which was the name of the Territory where they lived; it was a princess sprinkling golden specks from a stick onto some gray houses, which turned yellow and bright when the specks touched them. Nell thought that the specks were mites, but Harv insisted that mites were too small to be seen, that the stick was a magic wand and the specks were fairy dust. In any case, Harv made her remember that mediaglyph so that if she ever got lost, she could find her way home.

"But it's better if you just call me," Harv said, "and I'll come and find you."

"Why?"

"Because there's bad people out there, and you shouldn't walk through the L.T. alone, ever."

"What bad people?"

Harv looked troubled, heaved multiple sighs, fidgeted. "You know that ractive I was in the other day, where there were pirates, and they tied up the kids and were going to make them walk the plank?"

"Yeah."

"There are pirates in the L.T. too."

"Where?"

"Don't bother looking. You can't see 'em. They don't look like pirates, with the big hats and swords and all. They just look like normal people. But they're pirates on the inside, and they like to grab kids and tie 'em up."

"And make them walk the plank?"

"Something like that."

"Call the police!"

"I don't think the police would help. Maybe they would."

Police were Chinese. They came across the Causeway from Shanghai. Nell saw them up close once, when they came into the house to arrest Mom's boyfriend Rog. Rog wasn't home, just Nell and Harv were, and so Harv let them in and let them sit in the living room and fetched tea for them. Harv spoke some words of Shanghainese to them, and they grinned and ruffled his hair. He told Nell to stay in their bedroom and not come out, but Nell came out anyway and peeked. There were three policemen, two in uniforms and one in a suit, and they sat smoking cigarettes and watching something on the mediatron until Rog came back. Then they had an argument with him and took him out, shouting the whole way. After that, Rog didn't come around anymore, and Tequila started going out with Mark.

Unlike Rog, Mark had a job. He worked in the New Atlantis Clave cleaning windows of the Vickys' homes. He would come home late in the afternoon all tired and dirty and take a long shower in their bathroom. Sometimes he would have Nell come into the bathroom with him and help scrub his back, because he couldn't quite reach one spot in the middle. Sometimes he would look at Nell's hair and tell her that she needed a bath, and then she would take off her clothes and climb into the shower with him and he would help wash her.

One day she asked Harv whether Mark ever gave him a shower. Harv got upset and asked her a lot of questions. Later, Harv told Tequila about it, but Tequila had an argument with him and sent him to his room with one side of his face red and puffy. Then Tequila talked to Mark. They argued in the living room, the thumps booming through the wall as Harv and Nell huddled together in Harv's bed.

Harv and Nell both pretended to go to sleep that night, but Nell heard Harv getting up and sneaking out of the house. She didn't see him for the rest of the night. In the morning, Mark got up and went to work, and then Tequila got up and put a lot of makeup all over her face and went to work.

Nell was alone the whole day, wondering if Mark was going to make her take a shower that evening. She knew from the way Harv had reacted that the showers were a bad thing, and in a way it felt good to know this because it explained why it felt wrong. She did not know how to stop Mark from making her take the shower this evening. She told Dinosaur, Duck, Peter, and Purple about it.

These four creatures were the only animals that had survived a great massacre perpetrated during the previous year by Mac, one of Mom's boyfriends, who in a fit of rage had gathered up all of the dolls and stuffed animals in Nell's room and stuffed them into the knacking hatch.

When Harv had opened it up a few hours later, he had found all of the toys vanished except for these four. He had explained that the deke bin would only work on things that had come from the M.C. originally, and that anything that

had been made "by hand" (a troublesome concept to explain) was rejected. Dinosaur, Duck, Peter, and Purple were
old ragged things that had been made "by hand."

When Nell told them her story, Dinosaur was brave
and said that she should fight Mark. Duck had some ideas,
but they were silly ideas, because Duck was just a little kid.
Peter thought she should run away. Purple thought she
should use magic and sprinkle Mark with fairy dust; some
of it would be like the mites that (according to Harv) the
Vickys used to protect themselves from bad people.

In the kitchen was some food that Tequila had brought
home last night, including chopsticks with little mediatrons
built into their handles so that mediaglyphics ran up and
down them while you ate. Nell knew that there must be
mites in there, to make those mediaglyphics, and so she took
one of the chopsticks as her magic wand.

She also had a silvery plastic balloon that Harv had
made her in the M.C. All the air had gone out of it. She
reckoned it would make a nice shield like she had once seen
on the arm of a knight in one of Harv's ractives. She sat in
the corner of the room on her mattress with Dinosaur and
Purple in front of her, and Duck and Peter behind her, and
waited, clutching her magic wand and her shield.

But Mark didn't come home. Tequila came home and
wondered where Mark was, but didn't seem to mind that he
wasn't there. Finally Harv came back, late that night, after
Nell had gone to bed, and hid something under his mattress.
The next day Nell looked: It was a pair of heavy sticks, each
about a foot long, joined in the middle by a short chain, and
the whole thing was smeared with reddish-brown stuff that
had gone sticky and crusty.

The next time Nell saw Harv, he told her that Mark
was never coming back, that he was one of the pirates he'd
warned her about, and that if anyone else ever tried to do
such things to her, she should run away and scream and tell
Harv and his friends right away. Nell was astonished; she
had not understood just how tricky pirates were until this
moment.

Hackworth crosses the Causeway into
Shanghai; ruminations.

The Causeway joining New Chusan and the Pudong Economic Zone was Atlantis/Shanghai's whole reason for existence, being in fact a titanic Feed restrained by mountainous thrust bearings at each end. From the standpoint of mass & cash flow, the physical territory of New Chusan itself, a lung of smart coral respiring in the ocean, was nothing more or less than the fountainhead of China's consumer economy, its only function to spew megatons of nanostuff into the Middle Kingdom's ever-ramifying Feed network, reaching millions of new peasants every month.

For most of its length the Causeway skimmed the high tide level, but the middle kilometer arched to let ships through; not that anyone really needed ships anymore, but a few recalcitrant swabbies and some creative tour operators were still plying the Yangtze estuary in junks, which looked precious underneath the catenary arch of the big Feed, strumming the ancient-meets-modern chord for adherents of the *National Geographic* worldview. As Hackworth reached the apogee, he could see similar Causeways to port and starboard, linking the outskirts of Shanghai with other artificial islands. Nippon Nano looked Fujiesque, a belt of office buildings around the waterline, houses above that, the higher the better, then a belt of golf courses, the whole top third reserved for gardens, bamboo groves, and other forms of micromanaged Nature. In the other direction was a little bit of Hindustan. The geotecture of their island owed less to the Mogul period than to the Soviet, no effort being made to shroud its industrial heart in fractal artifice. It squatted out there some ten kilometers from New Chusan, sabotaging many expensive views and serving as the butt of snotty wog jokes. Hackworth never joined in these jokes because he was better informed than most and knew that the Hindustanis stood an excellent chance of stomping all over the Victorians and the Nipponese in the competition for China. They were just as smart, there were more of them, and they understood the peasant thing.

From the high point of the arch, Hackworth could look across the flat territory of outer Pudong and into the high-rise district of metropolis. He was struck, as ever, by the sheer clunkiness of old cities, the acreage sacrificed, over the centuries, to various stabs at the problem of Moving Stuff Around. Highways, bridges, railways, and their attendant smoky, glinting yards, power lines, pipelines, port facilities ranging from sampan-and-junk to stevedore-and-cargo-net to containership, airports. Hackworth had enjoyed San Francisco and was hardly immune to its charm, but Atlantis/Shanghai had imbued him with the sense that all the old cities of the world were doomed, except possibly as theme parks, and that the future was in the new cities, built from the bedrock up one atom at a time, their Feed lines as integral as capillaries were to flesh. The old neighborhoods of Shanghai, Feedless or with overhead Feeds kludged in on bamboo stilts, seemed frighteningly inert, like an opium addict squatting in the middle of a frenetic downtown street, blowing a reed of sweet smoke out between his teeth, staring into some ancient dream that all the bustling pedestrians had banished to unfrequented parts of their minds. Hackworth was heading for one of those neighborhoods right now, as fast as he could walk.

If you counterfeited directly from a Feed, it would be noticed sooner or later, because all matter compilers fed information back to the Source. You needed your very own private Source, disconnected from the Feed network, and this was a difficult thing to make. But a motivated counterfeiter could, with some ingenuity and patience, put together a Source capable of providing an assortment of simple building blocks in the range of ten to a hundred daltons. There were a lot of people like that in Shanghai, some more patient and ingenious than others.

Hackworth in the hong of Dr. X.

The scalpel's edge was exactly one atom wide; it delaminated the skin of Hackworth's palm like an airfoil gliding through smoke. He peeled off a strip the size of a nailhead and proffered it to Dr. X, who snatched it with ivory chopsticks, dredged it through an exquisite cloisonné bowl filled with chemical dessicant, and arranged it on a small windowpane of solid diamond.

Dr. X's real name was a sequence of shushing noises, disembodied metallic buzzes, unearthly quasi-Germanic vowels, and half-swallowed R's, invariably mangled by Westerners. Possibly for political reasons, he preferred not to pick a fake Western name like many Asians, instead suggesting, in a vaguely patronizing way, that they should just be satisfied with calling him Dr. X—that letter being the first in the Pinyin spelling of his name.

Dr. X placed the diamond slide into a stainless-steel cylinder. At one end was a Teflon-gasketed flange riddled with bolt-holes. Dr. X handed it to one of his assistants, who carried it with both hands, as if it were a golden egg on a silken pillow, and mated it with another flange on a network of massive stainless-steel plumbing that covered most of two tabletops. The assistant's assistant got the job of inserting all the shiny bolts and torque-wrenching them down. Then the assistant flicked a switch, and an old-fashioned vacuum pump whacked into life, making conversation impossible for a minute or two. During this time Hackworth looked around Dr. X's laboratory, trying to peg the century and in some cases even the dynasty of each item. A row of mason jars stood on a high shelf, filled with what looked like giblets floating in urine. Hackworth supposed that they were the gall bladders of now-extinct species, no doubt accruing value by the moment, better than any mutual fund. A locked gun cabinet and a primæval Macintosh desktop-publishing system, green with age, attested to the owner's previous forays into officially discouraged realms of behavior. A window had been cut into one wall, betraying an airshaft no larger than a grave, from the bottom of which grew a gnarled maple. Other than that, the room was packed with so many small, numerous, brown, wrinkled, and organic-looking objects that Hackworth's eyes lost the ability to distinguish one from the next. There were also some samples of calligraphy dangling here and there, probably snatches of poetry. Hackworth had made efforts to learn a few Chinese characters and to acquaint himself with some basics of their intellectual system, but in general, he liked his transcendence out in plain sight where he could keep an eye on it—say, in a nice stained-glass window—not woven through the fabric of life like gold threads through a brocade.

Everyone in the room could tell by its sound when the mechanical pump was finished with its leg of the relay. The vapor pressure of its own oil had been reached. The assistant closed a valve that isolated it from the rest of the system, and then they switched over to the nanopumps, which made no noise at all. They were turbines, just like the ones in jet engines but very small and lots of them. Casting a critical eye over Dr. X's vacuum plumbing, Hackworth could see that they also had a scavenger, which was a cylinder about the size of a child's head, wrinkled up on the inside into a preposterous surface area coated with nanodevices good at latching onto stray molecules. Between the nanopumps and the scavenger, the vacuum rapidly dropped to what you might expect to see halfway between the Milky Way and Andromeda galaxies. Then Dr. X himself quivered up out of his chair and began shuffling around the room, powering up a gallimaufry of contraband technology.

This equipment came from diverse technological epochs and had been smuggled into this, the Outer Kingdom, from a variety of sources, but all of it contributed to the same purpose: It surveyed the microscopic world through X-ray diffraction, electron microscopy, and direct nanoscale probing, and synthesized all of the resulting information into a single three-dimensional view.

If Hackworth had been doing this at work, he would already be finished, but Dr. X's system was a sort of Polish democracy requiring full consent of all participants, elicited one subsystem at a time. Dr. X and his assistants would gather around whichever subsystem was believed to be farthest out of line and shout at each other in a mixture of Shanghainese, Mandarin, and technical English for a while. Therapies administered included but were not limited to: turning things off, then on again; picking them up a couple of inches and then dropping them; turning off nonessential appliances in this and other rooms; removing lids and wiggling circuit boards; extracting small contaminants, such as insects and their egg cases, with nonconducting chopsticks; cable-wiggling; incense-burning; putting folded-up pieces of paper beneath table legs; drinking tea and sulking; invoking unseen powers; sending runners to other rooms, buildings, or precincts with exquisitely calligraphed notes and waiting for them to come back carrying spare parts in dusty, yellowed cardboard boxes; and a similarly diverse suite of troubleshooting techniques in the realm of software. Much of this performance seemed to be genuine, the rest merely for Hackworth's consumption, presumably laying the groundwork for a renegotiation of the deal.

Eventually they were looking at the severed portion of John Percival Hackworth on a meter-wide sheet of mediatronic paper that one of the assistants had, with great ceremony, unfurled across a low, black lacquer table. They sought something that was bulky by nanotech standards, so the magnification was not very high—even so, the surface of Hackworth's skin looked like a table heaped with crumpled newspapers. If Dr. X shared Hackworth's queasiness, he didn't show it. He appeared to be sitting with hands folded in the lap of his embroidered silk robe, but Hackworth leaned forward a bit and saw his yellowed, inch-long fingernails overhanging the black Swiss cross of an old Nintendo pad. The fingers moved, the image on the mediatron zoomed forward. Something smooth and inorganic unfolded at the top of their field of view: some kind of remotely controlled manipulator. Under Dr. X's direction it began to sift through the heap of desiccated skin.

They found a lot of mites, of course, both natural and artificial. The natural ones looked like little crabs and had been quietly inhabiting the outer layers of other creatures' bodies for hundreds of millions of years. The artificial ones had all been developed in the past few decades. Most of them consisted of a spherical or ellipsoidal hull with various attachments. The hull was a vacuole, a wee bit of the eutactic environment to coddle the mite's machine-phase innards. The hull's diamondoid structure was protected from the light by a thin layer of aluminum that made mites look like miniature spaceships—only with the air on the outside and the vacuum inside.

Attached to the hulls were various bits of gear: manipulators, sensors, locomotion systems, and antennas. The antennas were not at all like the ones on an insect—they were usually flat patches studded with what looked like close-cropped fuzz—phased-array systems for sweeping beams of visible light through the air. Most of the mites were also clearly marked with the manufacturer's name and a part number; this was demanded by Protocol. A few of them were unmarked. These were illicit and had been invented either by people like Dr. X; by outlaw phyles who spurned Protocol; or by the covert labs that most people assumed were run by all the zaibatsus.

During half an hour's rooting around through Hackworth's skin, roaming around an area perhaps a millimeter on a side, they observed a few dozen artificial mites, not an unusual number nowadays. Almost all of them were busted. Mites didn't last very long because they were small but complicated, which left little space for redundant systems. As soon as one got hit with a cosmic ray, it died. They also had little space for energy storage, so many of them simply ran out of juice after a while. Their manufacturers compensated for this by making a lot of them.

Nearly all of the mites were connected in some way with the Victorian immune system, and of these, most were immunocules whose job was to drift around the dirty littoral of New Chusan using lidar to home in on any other mites that might disobey Protocol. Finding one, they killed the invader by grabbing onto it and not letting go. The Victorian system used Darwinian techniques to create killers adapted to their prey, which was elegant and effective but led to the creation of killers that were simply too bizarre to have been thought up by humans, just as humans designing a world never would have thought up the naked mole rat. Dr. X took time out to zoom in on an especially freakish killer locked in a death-grip around an unlabeled mite. This did not necessarily mean that Hackworth's flesh had been invaded, rather that the dead mites had become part of the dust on a table somewhere and been ground into his skin when he touched it.

To illustrate the kind of mite he was presently looking for, Hackworth had brought along a cocklebur that he had teased from Fiona's hair after they had gone for a walk in the park. He had shown it to Dr. X, who had understood immediately, and eventually he found it. It looked completely different from all the other mites, because, as a cocklebur, its sole job was to stick to whatever touched it first. It had been generated a few hours previously by the matter compiler at Bespoke, which, following Hackworth's instructions, had placed a few million of them on the outer surface of the Illustrated Primer. Many of them had been embedded in Hackworth's flesh when he had first picked the book up.

Many remained on the book, back at the office, but Hackworth had anticipated that. He made it explicit now, just so Dr. X and his staff wouldn't get any ideas: "The cocklebur has an internal timer," he said, "that will cause it to disintegrate twelve hours after it was compiled. We have six hours left in which to extract the information. It's encrypted, of course."

Dr. X smiled for the first time all day.

Dr. X was the ideal man for this job because of his very disreputability. He was a reverse engineer. He collected artificial mites like some batty Victorian lepidopterist. He took them apart one atom at a time to see how they worked, and when he found some clever innovation, he squirreled it away in his database. Since most of these innovations were the result of natural selection, Dr. X was usually the first human being to know about them.

Hackworth was a forger, Dr. X was a honer. The distinction was at least as old as the digital computer. Forgers created a new technology and then forged on to the next project, having explored only the outlines of its potential. Honers got less respect because they appeared to sit still technologically, playing around with systems that were no longer start, hacking them for all they were worth, getting them to do things the forgers had never envisioned.

Dr. X selected a pair of detachable manipulator arms from his unusually large arsenal. Some of these had been copied from New Atlantan, Nipponese, or Hindustani designs and looked familiar to Hackworth; others, however, were bizarre naturalistic devices that seemed to have been torn loose from New Atlantan immunocules—evolved structures, rather than designed. The Doctor employed two of these arms to grip the cocklebur. It was an aluminum-covered megabuckyball in a sunburst of barbed spines, several of which were decorated with fragments of shish-kebabed skin.

Under Hackworth's direction he rotated the cocklebur until a small spine-free patch came into view. A circular depression, marked with a regular pattern of holes and knobs, was set into the surface of the ball, like a docking port on the side of a spacecraft. Inscribed around the circumference of this fitting was his maker's mark: IOANNI HACVIR-TUS FECIT.

Dr. X did not need an explanation. It was a standard port. He probably had half a dozen manipulator arms designed to mate with it. He selected one and maneuvered its tip into place, then spoke a command in Shanghainese.

Then he pulled the rig off his head and watched his assistant pour him another cup of tea. "How long?" he said.

"About a terabyte," Hackworth said. This was a measure of storage capacity, not of time, but he knew that Dr. X was the sort who could figure it out.

The ball contained a machine-phase tape drive system, eight reels of tape rigged in parallel, each with its own read/write machinery. The tapes themselves were polymer chains with different side groups representing the logical ones and zeroes. It was a standard component, and so Dr. X already knew that when it was told to dump, it would spew out about a billion bytes a second. Hackworth had just told him that the total stored on the tapes was a trillion bytes, so they had a thousand seconds to wait. Dr. X took advantage of the time to leave the room, supported by assistants, and tend to some of the other parallel threads of his enterprise, which was known informally as the Flea Circus.

*Hackworth departs from Dr. X's laboratory; further
ruminations; poem from Finkle-McGraw;
encounter with ruffians.*

Dr. X's assistant swung the door open and nodded insolently. Hackworth swung his top hat into place and stepped
out of the Flea Circus, blinking at the reek of China: smoky
like the dregs of a hundred million pots of lapsang
souchong, mingled with the sweet earthy smell of pork fat
and the brimstony tang of plucked chickens and hot garlic.
He felt his way across the cobbles with the tip of his walking-stick until his eyes began to adjust. He was now poorer
by several thousand ucus. A sizable investment, but the best
a father could make.

Dr. X's neighborhood was in the Ming Dynasty heart
of Shanghai, a warren of tiny brick structures sheathed in
gray stucco, topped with tiled roofs, frequently surrounded
by stucco walls. Iron poles projected from the second-story
windows for drying clothes, so that in the narrow streets the
buildings appeared to be fencing with each other. This
neighborhood was near the foundation of the ancient city
wall, built to keep out acquisitive Nipponese ronin, which
had been torn down and made into a ring road.

It was part of the Outer Kingdom, which meant that
foreign devils were allowed, as long as they were escorted
by Chinese. Beyond it, deeper into the old neighborhood,
was supposedly a scrap of the Middle Kingdom proper—the
Celestial Kingdom, or C.K., as they liked to call it—where no
foreigners at all were allowed.

An assistant took Hackworth as far as the border,
where he stepped into the Chinese Coastal Republic, an entirely different country that comprised, among many other
things, virtually all of Shanghai. As if to emphasize this,
young men loitered on corners in Western clothes, listening
to loud music, hooting at women, and generally ignoring
their filial duties.

He could have taken an auto-rickshaw, which was the
only vehicle other than a bicycle or skateboard narrow
enough to negotiate the old streets. But you never could tell

what kind of surveillance might be present in a Shanghai
taxi. The departure of a New Atlantis gentleman from the
Flea Circus late at night could only stimulate the imagina-
tions of the gendarmes, who had intimidated the criminal
element to such a degree that they were now feeling restless
and looking for ways to diversify. Sages, seers, and theoreti-
cal physicists could only speculate at what, if any, relationship might exist between the Shanghai Police Department's
astonishing scope of activities and actual law enforcement.

Deplorable, but Hackworth was thankful for it as he
sampled the French Settlement's ramified backstreets. A
handful of figures skulked across an intersection several
blocks away, bloody light from a mediatron glancing off
their patchwork Nanobar outfits, the kind of thing only
street criminals would need to wear. Hackworth comforted
himself by reasoning that this must be a gang from one of
the Leased Territories who had just come over the Causeway. They wouldn't possibly be so rash as to assault a gentleman in the street, not in Shanghai. Hackworth detoured
around the intersection anyway. Having never done anything illegal in his life, he was startled to understand, all of a
sudden, that a ruthless constabulary was a crucial resource
to more imaginative sorts of criminals, such as himself.

Countless times that afternoon, Hackworth had been
overcome by shame, and as many times he had fought it off
with rationalization: What was so bad about what he was
doing? He was not selling any of the new technologies that
Lord Finkle-McGraw had paid Bespoke to develop. He was
not profiting directly. He was just trying to secure a better
place in the world for his descendants, which was every
father's responsibility.

Old Shanghai was close to the Huang Pu; the mandarins had once sat in their garden pavilions enjoying the river
view. Within a few minutes Hackworth had crossed a bridge
into Pudong and was navigating narrow ravines between
illuminated skyscrapers, heading for the coast a few miles
farther to the east.

Hackworth had been catapulted out of the rank-and-
file and into Bespoke's elite ranks by his invention of the
mediatronic chopstick. He'd been working in San Francisco
at the time. The company was thinking hard about things
Chinese, trying to one-up the Nipponese, who had already

figured out a way to generate passable rice (five different varieties, yet!) direct from Feed, bypassing the whole paddy/coolie rat race, enabling two billion peasants to hang up their conical hats and get into some serious leisure time—and don't think for one moment that the Nipponese didn't already have some suggestions for what they might do with it. Some genius at headquarters, stewing over Nippon's prohibitive lead in nanotechnological rice production, decided the only thing for it was to leapfrog them by mass-producing entire meals, from wonton all the way to digital interactive fortune cookies. Hackworth got the seemingly trivial job of programming the matter compiler to extrude chopsticks.

Now, doing this in plastic was idiotically simple—polymers and nanotechnology went together like toothpaste and tubes. But Hackworth, who'd eaten his share of Chinese as a student, had never taken well to the plastic chopsticks, which were slick and treacherous in the blunt hands of a *gwailo*. Bamboo was better—and not that much harder to program, if you just had a bit of imagination. Once he'd made that conceptual leap, it wasn't long before he came up with the idea of selling advertising space on the damn things, chopstick handles and Chinese columnar script being a perfect match. Before long he was presenting it to his superiors: eminently user-friendly bamboid chopsters with colorful advertising messages continuously scrolling up their handles in real time, like news headlines in Times Square. For that, Hackworth was kicked upstairs to Bespoke and across the Pacific to Atlantis/Shanghai.

He saw these chopsticks everywhere now. To the Equity Lords, the idea had been worth billions; to Hackworth, another week's paycheck. That was the difference between the classes, right there.

He wasn't doing that badly, compared to most other people in the world, but it still rankled him. He wanted more for Fiona. He wanted Fiona to grow up with some equity of her own. And not just a few pennies invested in common stocks, but a serious position in a major company.

Starting your own company and making it successful was the only way. Hackworth had thought about it from time to time, but he hadn't done it. He wasn't sure why not; he had plenty of good ideas. Then he'd noticed that Bespoke was full of people with good ideas who never got around to starting their own companies. And he'd met a few big lords, spent considerable time with Lord Finkle-McGraw developing Runcible, and seen that they weren't really smarter than he. The difference lay in personality, not in native intelligence.

It was too late for Hackworth to change his personality, but it wasn't too late for Fiona.

Before Finkle-McGraw had come to him with the idea for Runcible, Hackworth had spent a lot of time pondering this issue, mostly while carrying Fiona through the park on his shoulders. He knew that he must seem distant to his daughter, though he loved her so—but only because, when he was with her, he couldn't stop thinking about her future. How could he inculcate her with the nobleman's emotional stance—the pluck to take risks with her life, to found a company, perhaps found several of them even after the first efforts had failed? He had read the biographies of several notable peers and found few common threads between them.

Just when he was about to give up and attribute it all to random chance, Lord Finkle-McGraw had invited him over to his club and, out of nowhere, begun talking about precisely the same issue.

Finkle-McGraw couldn't prevent his granddaughter Elizabeth's parents from sending her to the very schools for which he had lost all respect; he had no right to interfere. It was his role as a grandparent to indulge and give gifts. But why not give her a gift that would supply the ingredient missing in those schools?

It sounds ingenious, Hackworth had said, startled by Finkle-McGraw's offhanded naughtiness. But what is that ingredient?

I don't exactly know, Finkle-McGraw had said, but as a starting-point, I would like you to go home and ponder the meaning of the word *subversive*.

Hackworth didn't have to ponder it for long, perhaps because he'd been toying with these ideas so long himself. The seed of this idea had been germinating in his mind for some months now but had not bloomed, for the same reason that none of Hackworth's ideas had ever developed into companies. He lacked an ingredient somewhere, and as he now realized, that ingredient was subversiveness. Lord Alexander Chung-Sik Finkle-McGraw, the embodiment of the Victorian establishment, was a subversive. He was unhappy because his children were not subversives and was horrified at the thought of Elizabeth being raised in the stodgy tradition of her parents. So now he was trying to subvert his own granddaughter.

A few days later, the gold pen on Hackworth's watch chain chimed. Hackworth pulled out a blank sheet of paper and summoned his mail. The following appeared on the page:

THE RAVEN
A CHRISTMAS TALE, TOLD BY A SCHOOL-BOY TO HIS LITTLE BROTHERS AND SISTERS

by
Samuel Taylor Coleridge (1798)

Underneath an old oak tree
There was of swine a huge company
That grunted as they crunched the mast:
For that was ripe, and fell full fast.
Then they trotted away, for the wind grew high:
One acorn they left, and no more might you spy.
Next came a Raven, that liked not such folly:
He belonged, they did say, to the witch Melancholy!
Blacker was he than blackest jet,
Flew low in the rain, and his feathers not wet.
He picked up the acorn and buried it straight
By the side of a river both deep and great.
  Where then did the Raven go?
  He went high and low,
Over hill, over dale, did the black Raven go.
  Many Autumns, many Springs
  Travelled he with wandering wings:
  Many summers, many Winters—
  I can't tell half his adventures.
At length he came back, and with him a She
And the acorn was grown to a tall oak tree.
They built them a nest in the topmost bough,
And young ones they had, and were happy enow.

But soon came a Woodman in leathern guise,
His brow, like a pent-house, hung over his eyes.
He'd an axe in his hand, not a word he spoke,
But with many a hem! and a sturdy stroke,
At length he brought down the poor Raven's own oak.
His young ones were killed; for they could not depart,
And their mother did die of a broken heart.

The boughs from the trunk the Woodman did sever;
And they floated it down on the course of the river.
They sawed it in planks, and its bark they did strip,
And with this tree and others they made a good ship.
The ship, it was launched; but in sight of the land
Such a storm there did rise as no ship would withstand.
It bulged on a rock, and the waves rush'd in fast;
Round and round flew the Raven, and cawed to the blast.
He heard the last shriek of the perishing souls—
See! see! o'er the topmast the mad water rolls!
   Right glad was the Raven, and off he went fleet,
And Death riding home on a cloud he did meet,
And he thank'd him again and again for this treat:
   They had taken his all, and REVENGE IT WAS SWEET!

Mr. Hackworth:

I hope the above poem illuminates the ideas I only touched on during our meeting of Tuesday last, and that it may contribute to your parœmiological studies.

Coleridge wrote it in reaction to the tone of contemporary children's literature, which was didactic, much like the stuff they feed to our children in the "best" schools. As you can see, his concept of a children's poem is refreshingly nihilistic. Perhaps this sort of material might help to inculcate the sought-after qualities.

I look forward to further conversations on the subject.

Finkle-McGraw

   This was only the starting-point of development that had lasted for two years and culminated today. Christmas was just over a month away. Four-year-old Elizabeth Finkle-McGraw would receive the *Young Lady's Illustrated Primer* from her grandfather.

Fiona Hackworth would be getting a copy of the Illustrated Primer too, for this had been John Percival Hackworth's crime: He had programmed the matter compiler to place the cockleburs on the outside of Elizabeth's book. He had paid Dr. X to extract a terabyte of data from one of the cockleburs. That data was, in fact, an encrypted copy of the matter compiler program that had generated the *Young Lady's Illustrated Primer*. He had paid Dr. X for the use of one of his matter compilers, which was connected to private Sources owned by Dr. X and not connected to any Feed. He had generated a second, secret copy of the Primer.

The cockleburs had already self-destructed, leaving no evidence of his crime. Dr. X probably had a copy of the program on his computers, but it was encrypted, and Dr. X was smart enough simply to erase the thing and free up the storage, knowing that the encryption schemes apt to be used by someone like Hackworth could not be cracked without divine intervention.

Before long the streets widened, and the hush of tires on pavement blended with the buller of waves against the gradual shores of Pudong. Across the bay, the white lights of the New Atlantis Clave rose up above the particolored mosaic of the Leased Territories. It seemed a long way off, so on impulse Hackworth rented a velocipede from an old man who had set up a stall in the lee of the Causeway's thrust bearing. He rode out onto the Causeway and, invigorated by the cool moist air on his face and hands, decided to pedal for a while. When he reached the arch, he allowed the bike's internal batteries to carry him up the slope. At the summit he turned it off and began to coast down the other side, enjoying the speed.

His top hat flew off. It was a good one, with a smart band that was supposed to make these mishaps a thing of the past, but as an engineer, Hackworth had never taken the manufacturer's promise seriously. Hackworth was going too fast to make a safe U-turn, and so he put on the brakes.

When he finally got himself turned around, he was unable to see his hat. He did see another cyclist coming toward him. It was a young man, covered in a slick Nanobar outfit. Except for his head, which was smartly adorned with Hackworth's top hat.

Hackworth was prepared to ignore this jape; it was probably the only way the boy could safely get the hat down the hill, as prudence dictated keeping both hands on the handlebars.

But the boy did not seem to be applying his brakes, and as he accelerated toward Hackworth, he actually sat up, taking both hands off the handlebars, and gripped the brim of the hat with both hands. Hackworth thought the boy was preparing to throw it back as he went by, but instead he pulled it down onto his head and grinned insolently as he shot past.

"Say! Stop right there! You have my hat!" Hackworth shouted, but the boy did not stop. Hackworth stood astride his bicycle and watched unbelievingly as the boy began to fade into the distance. Then he turned on the bicycle's power assist and began chasing him.

His natural impulse had been to summon the police. But since they were on the Causeway, this would mean the Shanghai Police again. In any case, they could not possibly have responded fast enough to catch this boy, who was well on his way to the end of the Causeway, where he could fork off into any of the Leased Territories.

Hackworth nearly caught him. Without the power assist it would have been no contest, as Hackworth exercised daily in his club while this boy had the pudgy, pasty look typical of thetes. But the boy had a considerable head start. By the time they reached the first ramp leading down into the Leased Territories, Hackworth was only ten or twenty meters away, just close enough that he could not resist following the boy down the ramp. An overhead sign read: ENCHANTMENT.

They both picked up more speed on the ramp, and once again the boy reached up to grip the brim of the top hat. This time the bike's front wheel turned the wrong way. The boy erupted from the seat. The bicycle skittered into the irrelevant distance and clattered into something. The boy bounced once, rolled, and skidded for a couple of meters. The hat, its crown partially collapsed, rolled on its brim, toppled, and wobbled to a stop. Hackworth hit the brakes hard and overshot the boy for some distance. As before, it took him longer than he would have liked to get turned around.

And then he knew for the first time that the boy was not alone but part of a gang, probably the same group he'd seen in Shanghai; that they'd followed him onto the Causeway and taken advantage of his fallen top hat to lure him into the Leased Territories; and that the rest of the gang, four or five boys on bicycles, was coming toward him down the ramp, coming fast; and in the fog of light from all of the Leased Territories' mediatronic billboards glittered the chromium chains of their nunchuks.

Miranda; how she became a ractor; her early career.

From the age of five, Miranda wanted to be in a ractive. In her early teens, after Mother had taken her away from Father and Father's money, she'd worked as a maid-of-all-work, chopping onions and polishing people's sterling-silver salvers, cake combs, fish trowels, and grape shears. As soon as she got good enough with hair and makeup to pass for an eighteen-year-old, she worked as a governess for five years, which paid a little better. With her looks she probably could have gotten a job as a lady's maid or parlormaid and become an Upper Servant, but she preferred the governess job. Whatever bad things her parents had done to her along the way, they had at least put her through some nice schools, where she'd learned to read Greek, conjugate Latin verbs, speak a couple of Romance languages, draw, paint, integrate a few simple functions, and play the piano. Working as a governess, she could put it all to use. Besides, she preferred even bratty children to adults.

When the parents finally dragged their worn-out asses home to give their children Quality Time, Miranda would run to her subterranean quarters and get into the cheapest, trashiest ractive she could find. She wasn't going to make the mistake of spending all her money being in fancy ractives. She wanted to be a payee, not a payer, and you could practice your racting just as well in a dead shoot-'em-up as a live Shakespeare.

As soon as she had saved up her ucus, she made the long-dreamed-of trip to the mod parlor, strode in with her jawline riding high as the hull of a clipper ship above a black turtleneck, looking very like a ractor, and asked for the Jodie. *That* turned a few heads in the waiting room. From there on it was all *very good, madam,* and *please make yourself comfortable here* and *would you like tea, madam.* It was the first time since she and her mother had left home that anyone had offered her tea, instead of ordering her to make some, and she knew perfectly well it would be the last time for several years, even if she got lucky.

The tat machine worked on her for sixteen hours; they dripped Valium into her arm so she wouldn't whine. Most tats nowadays went on like a slap on the back. *"You sure you want the skull?" "Yeah, I'm sure." "Positive?" "Positive." "Okay—"* and SPLAT there was the skull, dripping blood and lymph, blasted through your epidermis with a wave of pressure that nearly knocked you out of the chair. But a dermal grid was a whole different thing, and a Jodie was top of the line, it had a hundred times as many 'sites as the lo-res grid sported by many a porn starlet, something like ten thousand of them in the face alone. The grossest part was when the machine reached down her throat to plant a trail of nanophones from her vocal cords all the way up to her gums. She closed her eyes for that one.

She was glad she'd done it on the day before Christmas because she couldn't have handled the kids afterward. Her face swelled up just like they said it would, especially around the lips and eyes where the 'site density was greatest. They gave her creams and drugs, and she used them. The day after that, her mistress double-taked when Miranda came upstairs to fix the children breakfast. But she didn't say anything, probably assuming she'd gotten slapped around by a drunken boyfriend at a Christmas party. Which was hardly Miranda's style, but it was a comfortable assumption for a New Atlantan woman to make.

When her face had gotten back to looking exactly the same as it had before her trip to the tat parlor, she packed everything she owned into a carpet bag and took the tube into the city.

The theatre district had its good end and its bad end. The good end was exactly what and where it had been for centuries. The bad end was a vertical rather than a horizontal development, being a couple of old office skyscrapers now fallen into disreputable uses. Like many such structures they were remarkably unpleasant to look at, but from the point of view of a ractive company, they were ideal. They had been designed to support a large number of people working side by side in vast grids of semiprivate cubicles.

"Let's have a gander at your grid, sweetheart," said a man identifying himself as Mr. Fred ("not my real name") Epidermis, after he had removed his cigar from his mouth and given Miranda a prolonged, methodical, full-body optical grope.

"My grid ain't no Sweetheart," she said. Sweetheart™ and Hero™ were the same grid as purveyed to millions of women and men respectively. The owners didn't want to be ractors at all, just to look good when they happened to be in a ractive. Some were stupid enough to fall for the hype that one of these grids could serve as the portal to stardom; a lot of those girls probably ended up talking to Fred Epidermis.

"Ooh, now I'm all curious," he said, writhing just enough to make Miranda's lip curl. "Let's put you on stage and see what you got."

The cubicles where his ractors toiled were mere head stages. He had a few body stages, though, probably so he could bid on fully ractive porn. He pointed her toward one of these. She walked in, slammed the door, turned toward the wall-size mediatron, and got her first look at her new Jodie.

Fred Epidermis had put the stage into Constellation Mode. Miranda was looking at a black wall speckled with twenty or thirty thousand individual pricks of white light. Taken together, they formed a sort of three-dimensional constellation of Miranda, moving as she moved. Each point of light marked one of the 'sites that had been poked into her skin by the tat machine during those sixteen hours. Not shown were the filaments that tied them all together into a network—a new bodily system overlaid and interlaced with the nervous, lymph, and vascular systems.

"Holy shit! Got a fucking Hepburn or something

here!" Fred Epidermis was exclaiming, watching her on a second monitor outside the stage.

"It's a Jodie," she said, but she stumbled over the words as the field of stars moved, tracking the displacements of her jaw and lips. Outside, Fred Epidermis was wielding the editing controls, zooming in on her face, which was dense as a galactic core. By comparison, her arms and legs were wispy nebulas and the back of her head nearly invisible, with a grand total of maybe a hundred 'sites placed around her scalp like the vertices of a geodesic dome. The eyes were empty holes, except (she imagined) when she closed her eyes. Just to check it out, she winked into the mediatron. The 'sites on her eyelids were dense as grass blades on a putting green, but accordioned together except when the lid expanded over the eye. Fred Epidermis recognized the move and zoomed in so violently on her winking eye that she nearly threw herself back on her ass. She could hear him chortling. "You'll get used to it, honey," he said. "Just hold still so I check the 'sites on your lips."

He panned to her lips, rotated them this way and that, as she puckered and pursed. She was glad they'd drugged her out of her mind while they were doing the lips; thousands of nanosites in there.

"Looks like we got ourselves an *artiste* here," Fred Epidermis said. "Lemme try you in one of our most challenging roles."

Suddenly a blond, blue-eyed woman was standing in the mediatron, perfectly aping Miranda's posture, wearing big hair, a white sweater with a big letter F in the middle, and a preposterously short skirt. She was carrying big colored puffy things. Miranda recognized her, from old passives she'd seen on the mediatron, as an American teenager from the previous century. "This is Spirit. A little old-fashioned to you and me, but popular with tube feeders," said Fred Epidermis. " 'Course your grid's way overkill for this, but hey, we're about giving the customer what they want— moving those bids, you know."

But Miranda wasn't really listening; for the first time ever, she was watching another person move exactly as she moved, as the stage mapped Miranda's grid onto this imaginary body. Miranda pressed her lips together as if she'd just put on lipstick, and Spirit did the same. She winked, and

Spirit winked. She touched her nose, and Spirit got a face full of pom-pom.

"Let's run you through a scene," said Fred Epidermis.

Spirit vanished and was replaced by an electronic form with blanks for names, numbers, dates, and other data. He flashed through it before Miranda could really read it; they didn't need a contract for a dry run.

Then she saw Spirit again, this time from two different camera angles. The mediatron had split up into several panes. One was a camera angle on Spirit's face, which still did whatever Miranda's face did. One was a two-shot showing Spirit and an older man, standing in a room full of big machines. Another pane showed a closeup of the old man, who as Spirit realized was being played by Fred Epidermis. The old man said, "Okay, keep in mind we usually play this through a head stage, so you don't control Spirit's arms and legs, just her face—"

"How do I walk around?" Miranda said. Spirit's lips moved with hers, and from the mediatron came Spirit's voice—squeaky and breathy at the same time. The stage was programmed to take the feeds from the nanophones in her throat and disp them into a different envelope.

"You don't. Computer decides where you go, when. Our dirty little secret: This isn't really that ractive, it's just a plot tree—but it's good enough for our clientele because all the leaves of the tree—the ends of the branches, you understand—are exactly the same, namely what the payer wants—you follow? Well, you'll see," said the old man on the screen, reading Miranda's confusion in Spirit's face. What looked like guarded skepticism on Miranda came across as bubble-brained innocence on Spirit.

"Cue! Follow the fucking cues! This isn't improv workshop!" shouted the old man.

Miranda checked the other panes on the display. One she reckoned was a map of the room, showing her location and the old man's, with arrows occasionally pulsing in the direction of movement. The other was a prompter, with a line waiting for her, flashing red.

"Oh, hello, Mr. Willie!" she said, "I know school's out, and you must be very tired after a long day of teaching shop to all of those nasty boys, but I was wondering if I could ask you for a big, big favor."

"Certainly, go ahead, whatever," said Fred Epidermis through the face and body of Mr. Willie, not even pretending to emote.

"Well, it's just that I have this appliance that's very important to me, and it seems to have broken. I was wondering if you knew how to fix—one of these," Miranda said. On the mediatron, Spirit said the same thing. But Spirit's hand was moving. She was holding something up next to her face. An elongated glossy white plastic thing. A vibrator.

"Well," said Mr. Willie, "it's a scientific fact that all electrical devices work on the same principles, so in theory I should be able to help you. But I must confess, I've never seen an appliance quite like that one. Would you mind explaining what it is and what it does?"

"I'd be more than happy to—" said Miranda, but then the display froze and Fred Epidermis cut her off by shouting through the door. "Enough already," he said. "I just had to make sure you could read."

He opened the stage door and said, "You're hired. Cubicle 238. My commission is eighty percent. The dormitory's upstairs—pick your own bunk, and clean it out. You can't afford to live anywhere else."

Harv brings Nell a present; she experiments with the Primer.

When Harv came back home, he was walking with all of his weight on one foot. When the light struck the smudges on his face in the right way, Nell could see streaks of red mixed in with the dirt and the toner. He was breathing fast, and he swallowed heavily and often, as though throwing up were much on his mind. But he was not empty-handed. His arms were crossed tightly across his belly. He was carrying things in his jacket.

"I made out, Nell," he said, seeing his sister's face and

knowing that she was too scared to talk first. "Didn't get much, but got some. Got some stuff for the Flea Circus."

Nell wasn't sure what the Flea Circus was, but she had learned that it was good to have stuff to take there, that Harv usually came back from the Flea Circus with an access code for a new ractive.

Harv shouldered the light switch on and kneeled in the middle of the room before relaxing his arms, lest some small thing fall out and be lost in a corner. Nell sat in front of him and watched.

He took out a piece of jewelry swinging ponderously at the end of a gold chain. It was circular, smooth gold on one side and white on the other. The white side was protected under a flattened glass dome. It had numbers written around the edge, and a couple of slender metal things like daggers, one longer than the other, joined at their hilts in the center. It made a noise like mice trying to eat their way through a wall in the middle of the night.

Before she could ask about it, Harv had taken out other things. He had a few cartridges from his mite trap. Tomorrow Harv would take the cartridge down to the Flea Circus and find out if he'd caught anything, and whether it was worth money.

There were other things like buttons. But Harv saved the biggest thing for last, and he withdrew it with ceremony.

"I had to fight for this, Nell," he said. "I fought hard because I was afraid the others would break it up for parts. I'm giving it to you."

It appeared to be a flat decorated box. Nell could tell immediately that it was fine. She had not seen many fine things in her life, but they had a look of their own, dark and rich like chocolate, with glints of gold.

"Both hands," Harv admonished her, "it's heavy."

Nell reached out with both hands and took it. Harv was right, it was heavier than it looked. She had to lay it down in her lap or she'd drop it. It was not a box at all. It was a solid thing. The top was printed with golden letters. The left edge was rounded and smooth, made of something that felt warm and soft but strong. The other edges were indented slightly, and they were cream-colored.

Harv could not put up with the wait. "Open it," he said.

"How?"

Harv leaned toward her, caught the upper-right corner under his finger, and flipped it. The whole lid of the thing bent upward around a hinge on the left side, pulling a flutter of cream-colored leaves after it.

Underneath the cover was a piece of paper with a picture on it and some more letters.

On the first page of the book was a picture of a little girl sitting on a bench. Above the bench was a thing like a ladder, except it was horizontal, supported at each end by posts. Thick vines twisted up the posts and gripped the ladder, where they burst into huge flowers. The girl had her back to Nell; she was looking down a grassy slope sprinkled with little flowers toward a blue pond. On the other side of the pond rose mountains like the ones they supposedly had in the middle of New Chusan, where the fanciest Vickys of all had their æstival houses. The girl had a book open on her lap.

The facing page had a little picture in the upper left, consisting of more vines and flowers wrapped around a giant egg-shaped letter. But the rest of that page was nothing but tiny black letters without decoration. Nell turned it and found two more pages of letters, though a couple of them were big ones with pictures drawn around them. She turned another page and found another picture. In this one, the little girl had set aside her book and was talking to a big black bird that had apparently gotten its foot tangled up in the vines overhead. She flipped another page.

The pages she'd already turned were under her left thumb. They were trying to work their way loose, as if they were alive. She had to press down harder and harder to keep them there. Finally they bulged up in the middle and slid out from underneath her thumb and, flop-flop-flop, returned to the beginning of the story.

"Once upon a time," said a woman's voice, "there was a little girl named Elizabeth who liked to sit in the bower in her grandfather's garden and read story-books." The voice was soft, meant just for her, with an expensive Victorian accent.

Nell slammed the book shut and pushed it away. It slid across the floor and came to rest by the sofa.

The next day, Mom's boyfriend Tad came home in a

bad mood. He slammed his six-pack down on the kitchen table, pulled out a beer, and headed for the living room. Nell was trying to get out of the way. She picked up Dinosaur, Duck, Peter Rabbit, and Purple, her magic wand, a paper bag that was actually a car her kids could drive around in, and a piece of cardboard that was a sword for killing pirates. Then she ran for the room where she and Harv slept, but Tad had already come in with his beer and begun rooting through the stuff on the sofa with his other hand, trying to find the control pad for the mediatron. He threw a lot of Harv's and Nell's toys on the floor and then stepped on the book with his bare foot.

"Ouch, god damn it!" Tad shouted. He looked down at the book in disbelief. "What the fuck is this?!" He wound up as if to kick it, then thought better of it, remembering he was barefoot. He picked it up and hefted it, looking straight at Nell and getting a fix on her range and azimuth. "Stupid little cunt, how many times do I have to tell you to keep your fucking shit cleaned up?!" Then he turned away from her slightly, wrapping his arm around his body, and snapped the book straight at her head like a Frisbee.

She stood watching it come toward her because it did not occur to her to get out of the way, but at the last moment the covers flew open. The pages spread apart. They all bent like feathers as they hit her in the face, and it didn't hurt at all.

The book fell to the floor at her feet, open to an illustrated page.

The picture was of a big dark man and a little girl in a cluttered room, the man angrily flinging a book at the little girl's head.

"Once upon a time there was a little girl named Cunt," the book said.

"My name is Nell," Nell said.

A tiny disturbance propagated through the grid of letters on the facing page.

"Your name's mud if you don't fucking clean this shit up," Tad said. "But do it later, I want some fucking privacy for once."

Nell's hands were full, and so she shoved the book down the hallway and into the kids' room with her foot. She dumped all her stuff on her mattress and then ran back and shut the door. She left her magic wand and sword nearby in case she should need them, then set Dinosaur, Duck, Peter, and Purple into bed, all in a neat line, and pulled the blanket up under their chins. "Now you go to bed and you go to bed and you go to bed and you go to bed, and be quiet because you are all being naughty and bothering Tad, and I'll see you in the morning."

"Nell was putting her children to bed and decided to read them some stories," said the book's voice.

Nell looked at the book, which had flopped itself open again, this time to an illustration showing a girl who looked much like Nell, except that she was wearing a beautiful flowing dress and had ribbons in her hair. She was sitting next to a miniature bed with four children tucked beneath its flowered coverlet: a dinosaur, a duck, a bunny, and a baby with purple hair. The girl who looked like Nell had a book on her lap. "For some time Nell had been putting them to bed without reading to them," the book continued, "but now the children were not so tiny anymore, and Nell decided that in order to bring them up properly, they must have bedtime stories."

Nell picked up the book and set it on her lap.

Nell's first experiences with the Primer.

The book spoke in a lovely contralto, with an accent like the very finest Vickys. The voice was like a real person's— though not like anyone Nell had ever met. It rose and fell like slow surf on a warm beach, and when Nell closed her eyes, it swept her out into an ocean of feelings.

Once upon a time there was a little Princess named Nell who was imprisoned in a tall dark castle on an island in the middle of a great sea, with a little boy named Harv, who was her friend and protector. She also had four special friends named Dinosaur, Duck, Peter Rabbit, and Purple.

Princess Nell and Harv could not leave the Dark Castle, but from time to time a raven would come to visit them . . .

"What's a raven?" Nell said.

The illustration was a colorful painting of the island seen from up in the sky. The island rotated downward and out of the picture, becoming a view toward the ocean horizon. In the middle was a black dot. The picture zoomed in on the black dot, and it turned out to be a bird. Big letters appeared beneath. "R A V E N," the book said. "Raven. Now, say it with me."

"Raven."

"Very good! Nell, you are a clever girl, and you have much talent with words. Can you spell *raven*?"

Nell hesitated. She was still blushing from the praise. After a few seconds, the first of the letters began to blink. Nell prodded it.

The letter grew until it had pushed all the other letters and pictures off the edges of the page. The loop on top shrank and became a head, while the lines sticking out the bottom developed into legs and began to scissor. "R is for Run," the book said. The picture kept on changing until it was a picture of Nell. Then something fuzzy and red appeared beneath her feet. "Nell Runs on the Red Rug," the book said, and as it spoke, new words appeared.

"Why is she running?"

"Because an Angry Alligator Appeared," the book said, and panned back quite some distance to show an alligator, waddling along ridiculously, no threat to the fleet Nell. The alligator became frustrated and curled itself into a circle, which became a small letter. "A is for Alligator. The Very Vast alligator Vainly Viewed Nell's Valiant Velocity."

The little story went on to include an Excited Elf who was Nibbling Noisily on some Nuts. Then the picture of the Raven came back, with the letters beneath. "Raven. Can you spell raven, Nell?" A hand materialized on the page and pointed to the first letter.

"R," Nell said.

"Very good! You are a clever girl, Nell, and good with letters," the book said. "What is this letter?" and it pointed to the second one. This one Nell had forgotten. But the book told her a story about an Ape named Albert.

*A young hooligan before the court of Judge Fang; the
magistrate confers with his advisers;
Justice is served.*

"The revolving chain of a nunchuk has a unique radar signature—reminiscent of that of a helicopter blade, but noisier,"
Miss Pao said, gazing up at Judge Fang over the half-lenses
of her phenomenoscopic spectacles. Her eyes went out of
focus, and she winced; she had been lost in some enhanced
three-dimensional image, and the adjustment to dull reality
was disorienting. "A cluster of such patterns was recognized
by one of Shanghai P.D.'s sky-eyes at ten seconds after 2351
hours."

As Miss Pao worked her way through this summary,
images appeared on the big sheet of mediatronic paper that
Judge Fang had unrolled across his brocade tablecloth and
held down with carved jade paperweights. At the moment,
the image was a map of a Leased Territory called Enchantment, with one location, near the Causeway, highlighted. In
the corner was another pane containing a standard picture
of an anticrime sky-eye, which always looked, to Judge
Fang, like an American football as redesigned by fetishists:
glossy and black and studded.

Miss Pao continued, "The sky-eye dispatched a flight
of eight smaller aerostats equipped with cine cameras."

The kinky football was replaced by a picture of a tear-
drop-shaped craft, about the size of an almond, trailing a
whip antenna, with an orifice at its nose protected by an
incongruously beautiful iris. Judge Fang was not really looking; at least three-quarters of the cases that came before him
commenced with a summary almost exactly like this one. It
was a credit to Miss Pao's seriousness and diligence that she
was able to tell each story afresh. It was a challenge to Judge
Fang's professionalism for him to listen to each one in the
same spirit.

"Converging on the scene," Miss Pao said, "they recorded activities."

The large map image on Judge Fang's scroll was replaced by a cine feed. The figures were far away, flocks of

relatively dark pixels nudging their way across a rough gray background like starlings massing before a winter gale. They got bigger and more clearly defined as the aerostat flew closer to the action.

A man was curled on the street with his arms wrapped around his head. The nunchuks had been put away by this point, and hands were busy going through the innumerable pockets that were to be found in a gentleman's suit. At this point the cine went into slow-mo. A watch flashed and oscillated hypnotically at the end of its gold chain. A silver fountain pen glowed like an ascending rocket and vanished into the folds of someone's mite-proof raiment. And then out came something else, harder to resolve: larger, mostly dark, white around the edge. A book, perhaps.

"Heuristic analysis of the cine feeds suggested a probable violent crime in progress," Miss Pao said.

Judge Fang valued Miss Pao's services for many reasons, but her deadpan delivery was especially precious to him.

"So the sky-eye dispatched another flight of aerostats, specialized for tagging."

An image of a tagger stat appeared: smaller and narrower than the cinestats, reminiscent of a hornet with the wings stripped off. The nacelles containing the tiny air turbines, which gave such devices the power to propel themselves through the air, were prominent; it was built for speed.

"The suspected assailants adopted countermeasures," Miss Pao said, again using that deadpan tone. On the cine feed, the criminals were retreating. The cinestat followed them with a nice tracking shot. Judge Fang, who had watched thousands of hours of film of thugs departing from the scenes of their crimes, watched with a discriminating eye. Less sophisticated hoodlums would simply have run away in a panic, but this group was proceeding methodically, two to a bicycle, one person pedaling and steering while the other handled the countermeasures. Two of them were discharging fountains of material into the air from canisters on their bicycles' equipment racks, like fire extinguishers, waving the nozzles in all directions. "Following a pattern that has become familiar to law enforcement," Miss Pao said, "they dispersed adhesive foam that clogged the intakes of the stats' air turbines, rendering them inoperative."

The big mediatron had also taken to emitting tremendous flashes of light that caused Judge Fang to close his eyes and pinch the bridge of his nose. After a few of these, the cine feed went dead. "Another suspect used strobe illumination to pick out the locations of the cinestats, then disabled them with pulses of laser light—evidently using a device, designed for this purpose, that has recently become widespread among the criminal element in the L.T."

The big mediatron cut back to a new camera angle on the original scene of the crime. Across the bottom of the scroll was a bar graph depicting the elapsed time since the start of the incident, and the practiced Judge Fang noted that it had jumped backward by a quarter of a minute or so; the narrative had split, and we were now seeing the other fork of the plot. This feed depicted a solitary gang member who was trying to climb aboard his bicycle even as his comrades were riding away on contrails of sticky foam. But the bike had been mangled somehow and would not function. The youth abandoned it and fled on foot.

Up in the corner, the small diagram of the tagging aerostat zoomed in to a high magnification, revealing some of the device's internal complications, so that it began to look less like a hornet and more like a cutaway view of a starship. Mounted in the nose was a device that spat out tiny darts drawn from an interior magazine. At first these were almost invisibly tiny, but as the view continued to zoom, the hull of the tagging aerostat grew until it resembled the gentle curve of a planet's horizon, and the darts became more clearly visible. They were hexagonal in cross-section, like pencil stubs. When they were shot out of the tag stat's nose, they sprouted cruel barbs at the nose and a simple empennage at the tail.

"The suspect had experienced a ballistic interlude earlier in the evening," Miss Pao said, "regrettably not filmed, and relieved himself of excess velocity by means of an ablative technique."

Miss Pao was outdoing herself. Judge Fang raised an eyebrow at her, briefly hitting the pause button. Chang, Judge Fang's other assistant, rotated his enormous, nearly spherical head in the direction of the defendant, who was looking very small as he stood before the court. Chang, in a characteristic gesture, reached up and rubbed the palm of his hand back over the short stubble that covered his head, as if he could not believe he had such a bad haircut. He opened his sleepy, slitlike eyes just a notch, and said to the defendant, "She say you have road rash."

The defendant, a pale asthmatic boy, had seemed too awed to be scared through most of this. Now the corners of his mouth twitched. Judge Fang noticed with approval that he controlled the impulse to smile.

"Consequently," Miss Pao said, "there were lapses in his Nanobar integument. An unknown number of tag mites passed through these openings and embedded themselves in his clothing and flesh. He discarded all of his clothing and scrubbed himself vigorously at a public shower before returning to his domicile, but three hundred and fifty tag mites remained in his flesh and were later extracted during the course of our examination. As usual, the tag mites were equipped with inertial navigation systems that recorded all of the suspect's subsequent movements."

The big cine feed was replaced by a map of the Leased Territories with the suspect's movements traced out with a red line. This boy did a lot of wandering about, even going into Shanghai on occasion, but he always came back to the same apartment.

"After a pattern was established, the tag mites automatically spored," Miss Pao said.

The image of the barbed dart altered itself, the midsection—which contained a taped record of the dart's movements—breaking free and accelerating into the void.

"Several of the spores found their way to a sky-eye, where their contents were downloaded and their serial numbers checked against police records. It was determined that the suspect spent much of his time in a particular apartment. Surveillance was placed on that apartment. One of the residents clearly matched the suspect seen on the cine feed. The suspect was placed under arrest and additional tag mites found in his body, tending to support our suspicions."

"Oooh," Chang blurted, absently, as if he'd just remembered something important.

"What do we know about the victim?" Judge Fang said.

"The cine stat could track him only as far as the gates of New Atlantis," Miss Pao said. "His face was bloody and swollen, complicating identification. He had also been tagged, naturally—the tagger aerostat cannot make any distinction between victim and perpetrator—but no spores were received; we can assume that all of his tag mites were detected and destroyed by Atlantis/Shanghai's immune system."

At this point Miss Pao stopped talking and swiveled her eyes in the direction of Chang, who was standing quiescently with his hands clasped behind his back, staring down at the floor as if his thick neck had finally given way under the weight of his head. Miss Pao cleared her throat once, twice, three times, and suddenly Chang came awake. "Excuse me, Your Honor," he said, bowing to Judge Fang. He rummaged in a large plastic bag and withdrew a gentleman's top hat in poor condition. "This was found at the scene," he said, finally reverting to his native Shanghainese.

Judge Fang dropped his eyes to the tabletop and then looked up at Chang. Chang stepped forward and placed the hat carefully on the table, giving it a little nudge as if its position were not quite perfect. Judge Fang regarded it for a few moments, then withdrew his hands from the voluminous sleeves of his robe, picked it up, and flipped it over. The words JOHN PERCIVAL HACKWORTH were written in gold script on the hatband.

Judge Fang cast a significant look at Miss Pao, who shook her head. They had not yet contacted the victim. Neither had the victim contacted them, which was interesting; John Percival Hackworth must have something to hide. The neo-Victorians were smart; why did so many of them get mugged in the Leased Territories after an evening of brothel-crawling?

"You have recovered the stolen items?" Judge Fang said.

Chang stepped to the table again and laid out a man's pocket watch. Then he stepped back, hands clasped behind him, bent his neck again, and watched his feet, which could not contain themselves from shuffling back and forth in tiny increments. Miss Pao was glaring at him.

"There was another item? A book, perhaps?" Judge Fang said.

Chang cleared his throat nervously, suppressing the urge to hawk and spit—an activity Judge Fang had barred in his courtroom. He turned sideways and backed up one step, allowing Judge Fang to view one of the spectators: a young girl, perhaps four years old, sitting with her feet up on the chair so that her face was blocked by her knees. Judge Fang heard the sound of a page turning and realized that the girl was reading a book propped up on her thighs. She cocked her head this way and that, talking to the book in a tiny voice.

"I must humbly apologize to the Judge," Chang said in Shanghainese. "My resignation is hereby proffered."

Judge Fang took this with due gravity. "Why?"

"I was unable to wrest the evidence from the young one's grasp," Chang said.

"I have seen you kill adult men with your hands," Judge Fang reminded him. He had been raised speaking Cantonese, but could make himself understood to Chang by speaking a kind of butchered Mandarin.

"Age has not been kind," Chang said. He was thirty-six.

"The hour of noon has passed," said Judge Fang. "Let us go and get some Kentucky Fried Chicken."

"As you wish, Judge Fang," said Chang.

"As you wish, Judge Fang," said Miss Pao.

Judge Fang switched back to English. "Your case is very serious," he said to the boy. "We will go and consult the ancient authorities. You will remain here until we return."

"Yes, sir," said the defendant, abjectly terrified. This was not the abstract fear of a first-time delinquent; he was sweating and shaking. He had been caned before.

The House of the Venerable and Inscrutable Colonel was what they called it when they were speaking Chinese. Venerable because of his goatee, white as the dogwood blossom, a badge of unimpeachable credibility in Confucian eyes. Inscrutable because he had gone to his grave without divulging the Secret of the Eleven Herbs and Spices. It had been the first fast-food franchise established on the Bund, many decades earlier. Judge Fang had what amounted to a private table in the corner. He had once reduced Chang to a state of catalepsis by describing an avenue in Brooklyn that was lined with fried chicken establishments for miles, all of them ripoffs of Kentucky Fried Chicken. Miss Pao, who had grown up in Austin, Texas, was less easily impressed by these legends.

Word of their arrival preceded them; their bucket already rested upon the table. The small plastic cups of gravy, coleslaw, potatoes, and so on had been carefully arranged. As usual, the bucket was placed squarely in front of Chang's seat, for he would be responsible for consumption of most of it. They ate in silence for a few minutes, communicating through eye contact and other subtleties, then spent several minutes exchanging polite formal chatter.

"Something struck a chord in my memory," Judge Fang said, when the time was right to discuss business. "The name Tequila—the mother of the suspect and of the little girl."

"The name has come before our court twice before," Miss Pao said, and refreshed his memory of two previous cases: one, almost five years ago, in which this woman's lover had been executed, and the second, only a few months ago, a case quite similar to this one.

"Ah, yes," Judge Fang said, "I recall the second case. This boy and his friends beat a man severely. But nothing was stolen. He would not give a justification for his actions. I sentenced him to three strokes of the cane and released him."

"There is reason to suspect that the victim in that case had molested the boy's sister," Chang put in, "as he has a previous record of such accomplishments."

Judge Fang fished a drumstick out of the bucket, arranged it on his napkin, folded his hands, and sighed. "Does the boy have any filial relationships whatsoever?"

"None," said Miss Pao.

"Would anyone care to advise me?" Judge Fang frequently asked this question; he considered it his duty to teach his subordinates

Miss Pao spoke, using just the right degree of cautiousness. "The Master says, 'The superior man bends his attention to what is radical. That being established, all practical courses naturally grow up. Filial piety and fraternal submission!—are they not the root of all benevolent actions?' "

"How do you apply the Master's wisdom in this instance?"

"The boy has no father—his only possible filial relationship is with the State. You, Judge Fang, are the only representative of the State he is likely to encounter. It is your duty to punish the boy firmly—say, with six strokes of the cane. This will help to establish his filial piety."

"But the Master also said, 'If the people be led by laws, and uniformity sought to be given them by punishments, they will try to avoid the punishments, but have no sense of shame. Whereas, if they be led by virtue, and uniformity sought to be given them by the rules of propriety, they will have the sense of shame, and moreover will become good.' "

"So you are advocating leniency in this case?" Miss Pao said, somewhat skeptically.

Chang chimed in: " 'Mang Wu asked what filial piety was. The Master said, "Parents are anxious lest their children should be sick." ' But the Master said nothing about caning."

Miss Pao said, "The Master also said, 'Rotten wood cannot be carved.' And, 'There are only the wise of the highest class, and the stupid of the lowest class, who cannot be changed.' "

"So the question before us is: Is the boy rotten wood? His father certainly was. I am not certain about the boy, yet."

"With utmost respect, I would direct your attention to the girl," said Chang, "who should be the true subject of our discussions. The boy may be lost; the girl can be saved."

"Who will save her?" Miss Pao said. "We have the power to punish; we are not given the power to raise children."

"This is the essential dilemma of my position," Judge Fang said. "The Mao Dynasty lacked a real judicial system. When the Coastal Republic arose, a judicial system was built upon the only model the Middle Kingdom had ever known, that being the Confucian. But such a system cannot truly function in a larger society that does not adhere to Confucian precepts. 'From the Son of Heaven down to the mass of the people, all must consider the cultivation of the person the root of everything besides.' Yet how am I to cultivate the persons of the barbarians for whom I have perversely been given responsibility?''

Chang was ready for this opening and exploited it quickly. "The Master stated in his Great Learning that the extension of knowledge was the root of all other virtues."

"I cannot send the boy to school, Chang."

"Think instead of the girl," Chang said, "the girl and her book."

Judge Fang contemplated this for a few moments, though he could see that Miss Pao badly wanted to say something.

" 'The superior man is correctly firm, and not firm merely,' " Judge Fang said. "Since the victim has not contacted the police seeking return of his property, I will allow the girl to keep the book for her own edification—as the Master said, 'In teaching there should be no distinction of classes.' I will sentence the boy to six strokes of the cane. But I will suspend all but one of those strokes, since he has displayed the beginnings of fraternal responsibility by giving the book to his sister. This is correctly firm."

"I have completed a phenomenoscopic survey of the book," Miss Pao said. "It is not an ordinary book."

"I had already surmised that it was a ractive of some sort," Judge Fang said.

"It is considerably more sophisticated than that description implies. I believe that it may embody hot I.P.," Miss Pao said.

"You think that this book incorporates stolen technology?"

"The victim works in the Bespoke division of Machine-Phase Systems. He is an artifex."

"Interesting," Judge Fang said.

"Is it worthy of further investigation?"

Judge Fang thought about it for a moment, carefully wiping his fingertips on a fresh napkin.

"It is," he said.

Hackworth presents the Primer to
Lord Finkle-McGraw.

"Is the binding and so on what you had in mind?" Hackworth said.

"Oh, yes," said Lord Finkle-McGraw. "If I found it in an antiquarian bookshop, covered with dust, I shouldn't give it a second glance."

"Because if you were not happy with any detail," Hackworth said, "I could recompile it." He had come in hoping desperately that Finkle-McGraw would object to something; this might give him an opportunity to filch another copy for Fiona. But so far the Equity Lord had been uncharacteristically complacent.

He kept flipping through the book, waiting for something to happen.

"It is unlikely to do anything interesting just now," Hackworth said. "It won't really activate itself until it bonds."

"Bonds?"

"As we discussed, it sees and hears everything in its vicinity," Hackworth said. "At the moment, it's looking for a small female. As soon as a little girl picks it up and opens the front cover for the first time, it will imprint that child's face and voice into its memory—"

"Bonding with her. Yes, I see."

"And thenceforth it will see all events and persons in relation to that girl, using her as a datum from which to chart a psychological terrain, as it were. Maintenance of that terrain is one of the book's primary processes. Whenever the child uses the book, then, it will perform a sort of dynamic mapping from the database onto her particular terrain."

"You mean the database of folklore."

Hackworth hesitated. "Pardon me, but not precisely, sir. Folklore consists of certain universal ideas that have been mapped onto local cultures. For example, many cultures have a Trickster figure, so the Trickster may be deemed a universal; but he appears in different guises, each appropriate to a particular culture's environment. The Indians of the American Southwest called him Coyote, those of the Pacific Coast called him Raven. Europeans called him Reynard the Fox. African-Americans called him Br'er Rabbit. In twentieth-century literature he appears first as Bugs Bunny and then as the Hacker."

Finkle-McGraw chuckled. "When I was a lad, that word had a double meaning. It could mean a trickster who broke into things—but it could also mean an especially skilled coder."

"The ambiguity is common in post-Neolithic cultures," Hackworth said. "As technology became more important, the Trickster underwent a shift in character and became the god of crafts—of technology, if you will—while retaining the underlying roguish qualities. So we have the Sumerian Enki, the Greek Prometheus and Hermes, Norse Loki, and so on.

"In any case," Hackworth continued, "Trickster/Technologist is just one of the universals. The database is full of them. It's a catalogue of the collective unconscious. In the old days, writers of children's books had to map these universals onto concrete symbols familiar to their audience—like Beatrix Potter mapping the Trickster onto Peter Rabbit. This is a reasonably effective way to do it, especially if the society is homogeneous and static, so that all children share similar experiences.

"What my team and I have done here is to abstract that process and develop systems for mapping the universals onto the unique psychological terrain of one child—even as that terrain changes over time. Hence it is important that you not allow this book to fall into the hands of any other little girl until Elizabeth has the opportunity to open it up."

"Understood," said Lord Alexander Chung-Sik Finkle-McGraw. "I'll wrap it up myself, right now. Compiled some nice wrapping paper this morning." He opened a desk drawer and took out a roll of thick, glossy mediatronic paper bearing animated Christmas scenes: Santa sliding down the chimney, the ballistic reindeer, the three Zoroastrian sovereigns dismounting from their dromedaries in front of the stable. There was a lull while Hackworth and Finkle-McGraw watched the little scenes; one of the hazards of living in a world filled with mediatrons was that conversations were always being interrupted in this way, and that explained why Atlantans tried to keep mediatronic commodities to a minimum. Go into a thete's house, and every object had moving pictures on it, everyone sat around slackjawed, eyes jumping from the bawdy figures cavorting on the mediatronic toilet paper to the big-eyed elves playing tag in the bathroom mirror to . . .

"Oh, yes," Finkle-McGraw said. "Can it be written on? I should like to inscribe it to Elizabeth."

"The paper is a subclass of both input-paper and output-paper, so it possesses all the underlying functionality of the sort of paper you would write on. For the most part these functions are not used—beyond, of course, simply making marks where the nib of the pen has moved across it."

"You can write on it," Finkle-McGraw translated with some asperity, "but it doesn't think about what you're writing."

"Well, my answer to that question must be ambiguous," Hackworth said. "The Illustrated Primer is an extremely general and powerful system capable of more extensive self-reconfiguration than most. Remember that a fundamental part of its job is to respond to its environment. If the owner were to take up a pen and write on a blank page, this input would be thrown into the hopper along with everything else, so to speak."

"Can I inscribe it to Elizabeth or not?" Finkle-McGraw demanded.

"Certainly, sir."

Finkle-McGraw extracted a heavy gold fountain pen from a holder on his desk and wrote in the front of the book for a while.

"That being done, sir, there remains only for you to authorise a standing purchase order for the ractors."

"Ah, yes, thank you for reminding me," said Finkle-McGraw, not very sincerely. "I still would have thought that for all the money that went into this project—"

"That we might have solved the voice-generation problem to boot, yes sir," Hackworth said. "As you know, we took some stabs at it, but none of the results were up to the level of quality you demand. After all of our technology, the pseudo-intelligence algorithms, the vast exception matrices, the portent and content monitors, and everything else, we still can't come close to generating a human voice that sounds as good as what a real, live ractor can give us."

"Can't say I'm surprised, really," said Finkle-McGraw. "I just wish it were a completely self-contained system."

"It might as well be, sir. At any given time there are tens of millions of professional ractors in their stages all over the world, in every time zone, ready to take on this kind of work at an instant's notice. We are planning to authorise payment at a relatively high rate, which should bring in only the best talent. You won't be disappointed with the results."

Nell's second experience with the Primer; the story of Princess Nell in a nutshell.

Once upon a time there was a little Princess named Nell who was imprisoned in a tall dark castle on an island in the middle of a great sea, with a little boy named Harv, who was her friend and protector. She also had four special friends named Dinosaur, Duck, Peter Rabbit, and Purple.

Princess Nell and Harv could not leave the Dark Castle, but from time to time a Raven would come to visit them and tell them of the wonderful things over the sea in the Land Beyond. One day the Raven helped Princess Nell escape from the castle, but alas, poor Harv was too big and had to stay locked up behind the castle's great iron door with twelve locks.

Princess Nell loved Harv like a brother and refused to abandon him, so she and her friends, Dinosaur, Duck, Peter, and Purple, traveled over the sea in a little red boat, having many adventures, until they came to the Land Beyond. This was divided into twelve countries each ruled by a Faery King or a Faery Queen. Each King or Queen had a wonderful Castle, and in each Castle was a Treasury containing gold and jewels, and in each Treasury was a jeweled Key that would open one of the twelve locks on the iron door of the Dark Castle.

Princess Nell and her friends had many adventures as they visited each of the twelve kingdoms and collected the twelve keys.

Some they got by persuasion, some by cleverness, and some they took in battle. By the end of the quest, some of Nell's four friends had died, and some had gone their separate ways. But Nell was not alone, for she had become a great heroine during her adventures.

In a great ship, accompanied by many soldiers, servants, and elders, Nell traveled back over the sea to the island of the Dark Castle. As she approached the iron door, Harv saw her from the top of a tower and gruffly told her to go away, for Princess Nell had changed so much during her Quest that Harv no longer recognized her. "I have come to set you free," Princess Nell said. Harv again told her to go away, saying that he had all the freedom he wanted within the walls of the Dark Castle.

Princess Nell put the twelve keys into the twelve locks and began to open them one by one. When the rusty door of the castle finally creaked open, she saw Harv standing with a bow at the ready, and an arrow drawn, pointed straight at her heart. He let fly the arrow, and it struck her in the chest and would have killed her except that she was wearing a locket Harv had given her many years ago, before she left the castle. The arrow struck and shattered the locket. In the same moment, Harv was cut down by an arrow from one of Princess Nell's soldiers. Nell rushed to her fallen brother to comfort him and wept over his body for three days and three nights. When finally she dried her eyes, she saw that the Dark Castle had become glorious; for the river of tears that had flowed from her eyes had watered the grounds, and beautiful gardens and forests had sprung up overnight, and the Dark Castle itself was no longer dark, but a shining beacon filled with delightful things. Princess Nell lived in that castle and ruled over that island for the rest of her days, and every morning she would go for a walk in the garden where Harv had fallen. She had many adventures and became a great Queen, and in time she met and married a Prince, and had many children, and lived happily ever after.

"What's an adventure?" Nell said.

The word was written across the page. Then both pages filled with moving pictures of glorious things: girls in armor fighting dragons with swords, and girls riding white unicorns through the forest, and girls swinging from vines, swimming in the blue ocean, piloting rocket ships through space. Nell spent a long time looking at all of the pictures, and after awhile all of the girls began to look like older versions of herself.

*Judge Fang visits his district; Miss Pao arranges a
demonstration; the case of the stolen book
takes on unexpected depth.*

As Judge Fang proceeded across the Causeway on his chevaline, accompanied by his assistants, Chang and Miss Pao, he saw the Leased Territories wreathed in a mephitic fog. The emerald highlands of Atlantis/Shanghai floated above the squalor. A host of mirrored aerostats surrounded that lofty territory, protecting it from the larger and more obvious sorts of intruders; from here, miles away, the individual pods were of course not visible, but they could be seen in the aggregate as a subtle gleam in the air, a vast bubble, perfectly transparent, enveloping the sacrosanct territory of the Anglo-Americans, stretching this way and that in the shifting winds but never tearing.

The view was spoiled as they drew closer to the Leased Territories and entered into their eternal fogs. Several times as they rode through the streets of the L.T., Judge Fang made a peculiar gesture: He curled the fingers of his right hand into a cylinder, as though grasping an invisible stalk of bamboo. He cupped his other hand beneath, forming a dark enclosed cavity, and then peeked into it with one eye. When he stared into the pocket of air thus formed, he saw the darkness filled with coruscating light—something like staring into a cavern filled with fireflies, except that these lights came in all colors, and all of the colors were as pure and clear as jewels.

People who lived in the L.T. and who performed this gesture frequently developed a feel for what was going on in the microscopic world. They could tell when something was up. If the gesture was performed during a toner war, the result was spectacular.

Today it was nowhere near toner war levels, but it was fairly intense. Judge Fang suspected that this had something to do with the purpose of this errand, which Miss Pao had declined to explain.

They ended up in a restaurant. Miss Pao insisted on a table out on the terrace, even though it looked like rain. They ended up overlooking the street three stories below. Even at that distance it was difficult to make out faces through the fog.

Miss Pao drew a rectangular package from her bag, wrapped up in Nanobar. She unwrapped it and drew out two objects of roughly the same size and shape: a book and a block of wood. She placed them side by side on the table. Then she ignored them, turning her attention to the menu. She continued to ignore them for several minutes more, as she and Chang and Judge Fang sipped tea, exchanged polite chatter, and began to eat their meals.

"At Your Honor's convenience," Miss Pao said, "I would invite you to examine the two objects I laid on the table."

Judge Fang was startled to notice that, while the block's appearance had not changed, the book had become covered in a layer of thick gray dust, as if it had been growing mildew for several decades.

"Oooh," Chang blurted, sucking a lengthy skein of noodles into his maw and bulging his eyes in the direction of this peculiar exhibit.

Judge Fang rose, walked around the table, and bent down for a closer look. The gray dust was not uniformly distributed; it was much thicker toward the edges of the book cover. He opened the book and was startled to notice that the dust had infiltrated deep between the pages.

"This is dust with a purpose in life," Judge Fang observed.

Miss Pao glanced significantly at the block of wood. Judge Fang picked it up and examined it on all sides; it was clean.

"This stuff is discriminating too!" Judge Fang said.

"It is Confucian toner," Chang said, finally choking down his noodles. "It has a passion for books."

The Judge smiled tolerantly and looked to Miss Pao for

an explanation. "You have examined this new species of mite, I take it?"

"It is more interesting than that," Miss Pao said. "Within the last week, not one but *two* new species of mite have appeared in the Leased Territories—both programmed to seek out anything that looks like a book." She reached into her bag again and handed her master a rolled-up piece of mediatronic paper.

A waitress scurried up and helped move the dishes and teacups aside. Judge Fang unrolled the page and anchored it with various small items of faience. The paper was divided into two panes, each containing a magnified view of a microscopic device. Judge Fang could see that both were made to navigate through the air, but beyond that, they could hardly have been more different. One of them looked like a work of nature; it had several bizarre and elaborate arms and sported four enormous, wildly involuted, scoop-like devices, arranged ninety degrees apart.

"The ears of a bat!" Chang exclaimed, tracing their impossibly complex whorls with the tip of a chopstick. Judge Fang said nothing but reminded himself that this sort of quick insight was just the sort of thing Chang excelled at.

"It appears to use echolocation, like a bat," Miss Pao admitted. "The other one, as you can see, is of a radically different design."

The other mite looked like a spacecraft as envisioned by Jules Verne. It had a streamlined, teardrop shape, a pair of manipulator arms folded neatly against its fuselage, and a deep cylindrical cavity in the nose that Judge Fang took to be its eye. "This one sees light in the ultraviolet range," Miss Pao said. "Despite their differences, each does the same thing: searches for books. When it finds a book, it lands on the cover and crawls to the edge, then creeps between the pages and examines the internal structure of the paper."

"What is it looking for?"

"There is no way to tell, short of disassembling its internal computer system and decompiling its program—which is difficult," Miss Pao said, with characteristic understatement. "When it finds that it has been investigating a normal book made of old-fashioned paper, it deactivates and becomes dust."

"So there are many dirty books in the Leased Territories now," Chang said.

"There aren't that many books to begin with," Judge Fang said. Miss Pao and Chang chuckled, but the Judge showed no sign that he had been making a joke; it was just an observation.

"What conclusions do you draw, Miss Pao?" the Judge said.

"Two different parties are searching the Leased Territories for the same book," Miss Pao said.

She did not have to state that the target of this search was probably the book stolen from the gentleman named Hackworth.

"Can you speculate as to the identity of these parties?"

Miss Pao said, "Of course, neither device carries a maker's mark. The bat-eared one has Dr. X written all over it; most of its features appear to be evolved, not engineered, and the Doctor's Flea Circus is nothing more than an effort to collect evolved mites with useful features. At a first glance, the other device could have come from any of the engineering works associated with major phyles—Nippon, New Atlantis, Hindustan, the First Distributed Republic being prime suspects. But on deeper examination I find a level of elegance—"

"*Elegance?*"

"Pardon me, Your Honor, the concept is not easy to explain—there is an ineffable quality to some technology, described by its creators as concinnitous, or technically sweet, or a nice hack—signs that it was made with great care by one who was not merely motivated but inspired. It is the difference between an engineer and a hacker."

"Or an engineer and an artifex?" Judge Fang said.

A trace of a smile came across Miss Pao's face.

"I fear that I have enmeshed that little girl in a much deeper business than I ever imagined," Judge Fang said. He rolled up the paper and handed it back to Miss Pao. Chang set the Judge's teacup back in front of him and poured more tea. Without thinking about it, the Judge put his thumb and fingertips together and tapped them lightly against the tabletop several times.

This was an ancient gesture in China. The story was that one of the early Emperors liked to dress as a commoner and travel about the Middle Kingdom to see how the peasants were getting along. Frequently, as he and his staff were sitting about the table in some inn, he would pour tea for everyone. They could not kowtow to their lord without giving away his identity, so they would make this gesture, using their hand to imitate the act of kneeling. Now Chinese people used it to thank each other at the dinner table. From time to time, Judge Fang caught himself doing it, and thought about what a peculiar thing it was to be Chinese in a world without an Emperor.

He sat, hands folded into sleeves, and thought about this and other issues for several minutes, watching the vapor rise from his tea and form into a fog as it condensed round the bodies of micro-aerostats.

"Soon we will obtrude upon Mr. Hackworth and Dr. X and learn more by observing their reactions. I will consider the right way to set about this. In the meantime, let us concern ourselves with the girl. Chang, visit her apartment building and see whether there has been any trouble there—suspicious characters hanging about."

"Sir, with all respect, everyone who lives in the girl's building is a suspicious character."

"You know what I mean," said the Judge with some asperity. "The building should have a system for filtering nanosites from the air. If this system is working properly, and if the girl does not take the book out of her building, then she should go unnoticed by these." The Judge drew a streak through the dust on the book's cover and smeared the toner between his fingers. "Speak with the landlord of her building, and let him know that his air-filtering system is due for an inspection, and that this is genuine, not just a solicitation for a bribe."

"Yes, sir," Chang said. He pushed his chair back, rose, bowed, and strode out of the restaurant, pausing only to extract a toothpick from the dispenser by the exit. It would have been acceptable for him to finish his lunch, but Chang had, in the past, evinced concern for the girl's welfare, and apparently wanted to waste no time.

"Miss Pao, plant recording surveillance devices in the girl's flat. At first we will change and review the tapes every day. If the book is not detected soon, we will begin changing them every week."

"Yes, sir," Miss Pao said. She slipped on her phenomenoscopic spectacles. Colored light reflected from the surfaces of her eyes as she lost herself in some kind of interface. Judge Fang refilled his tea, cupped it in the palm of his hand, and went for a stroll round the edge of the terrace. He had much more important things to think about than this girl and her book; but he suspected that from now on he would be thinking about little else.

Description of Old Shanghai; situation of the Theatre Parnasse; Miranda's occupation.

*B*efore the Europeans got their hooks into it, Shanghai had been a walled village on the Huang Pu River, a few miles south of its confluence with the estuary of the Yangtze. Much of the architecture was very sophisticated Ming Dynasty stuff, private gardens for rich families, a shopping street here and there concealing interior slums, a rickety, vertiginous teahouse rising from an island in the center of a pond. More recently the wall had been torn down and a sort of beltway built on its foundations. The old French concession wrapped around the north side, and in that neighborhood, on a corner looking across the ring road into the old city, the Theatre Parnasse had been constructed during the late 1800s. Miranda had been working there for five years, but the experience had been so intense that it often seemed more like five days.

The Parnasse had been built by Europeans back when they were serious and unapologetic about their Europeanness. The facade was classical: a three-quarter-round portico on the streetcorner, supported by Corinthian columns, all done in white limestone. The portico was belted by a white marquee, circa 1990, outlined by tubes of purple and pink neon. It would have been easy enough to tear it off and replace it with something mediatronic, but they enjoyed hauling the bamboo ladders out from the set shop and snapping the black plastic letters into place, advertising whatever they were doing tonight. Sometimes they would lower the big mediatronic screen and show movies, and Westerners would come from all over Greater Shanghai, dressed up in their tuxedos and evening gowns, and sit in the dark watching *Casablanca* or *Dances With Wolves*. And at least twice a month, the Parnasse Company would actually get out on stage and do it: become actors rather than ractors for a night, lights and greasepaint and costumes. The hard part was indoctrinating the audience; unless they were theatre buffs, they always wanted to run up on stage and interact, which upset the whole thing. Live theatre was an ancient and peculiar taste, roughly on par with listening to Gregorian chants, and it didn't pay the bills. They paid the bills with ractives.

The building was tall and narrow, making the most of precious Shanghai real estate, so the proscenium had a nearly square aspect ratio, like an old-fashioned television. Above it was the bust of some forgotten French actress, supported on gilt wings, flanked by angels brandishing trumpets and laurel wreaths. The ceiling was a circular fresco depicting Muses disporting themselves in flimsy robes. A chandelier hung from the center; its incandescent bulbs had been replaced by new things that didn't burn out, and now it cast light evenly onto the rows of tiny, creaking seats closely packed together on the main floor. There were three balconies and three stories of private boxes, two on the left side and two on the right side of each level. The fronts of the boxes and balconies were all painted with tableaux from classical mythology, the predominant color there as elsewhere being a highly French robin's-egg blue. The theatre was crammed with plasterwork, so that the faces of cherubs, overwrought Roman gods, impassioned Trojans, and such were always poking out of columns and soffits and cornices, catching you by surprise. Much of this work was spalled from bullets fired by high-spirited Red Guards during Cultural Revolution times. Other than the bullet holes, the Parnasse was in decent shape, though sometime in the twentieth century great black-iron pipes had been anchored vertically alongside the boxes and horizontally before the balconies so that spotlights could be bolted on. Nowadays the spotlights were coin-size disks—phased-array devices that carried their own batteries—and could be stuck up anywhere and controlled by radio. But the pipes were still there and always required a lot of explaining when tourists came through.

Each of the twelve boxes had its own door, and a curtain rail curving around the front so that the occupants could get some privacy between acts. They'd mothballed the curtains and replaced them with removable soundproof screens, unbolted the seats, and stored them in the basement. Now each box was a private egg-shaped room just the right size to serve as a body stage. These twelve stages generated seventy-five percent of the cash flow of the Theatre Parnasse.

Miranda always checked into her stage half an hour early to run a diagnostic on her tat grid. The 'sites didn't last forever—static electricity or cosmic rays could knock them out, and if you let your instrument go to pot out of sheer laziness, you didn't deserve to call yourself a ractor.

Miranda had decorated the dead walls of her own stage with posters and photos of role models, largely actresses from twentieth-century passives. She had a chair in the corner for roles that involved sitting down. There was also a tiny coffee table where she set down her triple latte, a two-liter bottle of mineral water, and a box of throat lozenges. Then she peeled down to a black leotard and tights, hanging her street clothes on a tree by the door. Another ractor might have gone nude, worn street clothes, or tried to match her costume to the role she'd be playing, if she were lucky enough to know in advance. At the moment, though, Miranda never knew. She had standing bids on Kate in the ractive version of *Taming of the Shrew* (which was a butcherous kludge, but popular among a certain sort of male user); Scarlett O'Hara in the ractive *Gone With the Wind*; a double agent named Ilse in an espionage thriller set on a train passing through Nazi Germany; and Rhea, a neo-Victorian damsel in distress in *Silk Road*, an adventure-comedy-romance ractive set on the wrong side of contemporary Shanghai. She'd created that role. After the good review had come in ("a remarkably Rhea-listic portrayal by newcomer Miranda Redpath!") she had played little else for a couple of months, even though her bid was so steep that most users opted for one of the understudies or contented themselves with watching passively for one-tenth the price.

But the distributor had botched the PR targeting when they tried to take it beyond the Shanghai market, and so now *Silk Road* was in limbo while various heads rolled.

Four leading roles was about as many as she could keep in her head at once. The prompter made it possible to play any role without having seen it before, if you didn't mind making an ass of yourself. But Miranda had a reputation now and couldn't get away with shoddy work. To fill in the blanks when things got slow, she also had standing bids, under another name, for easier work: mostly narration jobs, plus anything having to do with children's media. She didn't have any kids of her own, but she still corresponded with the ones she'd taken care of during her governess days. She loved racting with children, and besides it was good exercise for the voice, saying those silly little rhymes just right.

"Practice Kate from *Shrew*," she said, and the Miranda-shaped constellation was replaced by a dark-haired woman with green, feline eyes, dressed in some costume designer's concept of what a rich woman in the Italian Renaissance would be likely to wear. Miranda had large bunny eyes while Kate had cat eyes, and cat eyes were used differently from bunny eyes, especially when delivering a slashing witticism. Carl Hollywood, the company's founder and dramaturge, who'd been sitting in passively on her *Shrews*, had suggested that she needed more work in this area. Not many payers enjoyed Shakespeare or even knew who he was, but the ones who did tended to be very high on the income scale and worth catering to. Usually this kind of argument had no effect on Miranda, but she'd been finding that some of these (rich sexist snob asshole) gentlemen were remarkably good ractors. And any professional could tell you that it was a rare pleasure to ract with a payer who knew what he was doing.

The Shift comprised the Prime Times for London, the East Coast, and the West Coast. In Greenwich Time, it started around nine P.M., when Londoners were finishing dinner and looking for entertainment, and wound up about seven A.M., when Californians were going to bed. No matter what time zones they actually lived in, all ractors tried to work during those hours. In Shanghai's time zone, The Shift ran from about five A.M. to midafternoon, and Miranda didn't mind doing overtime if some well-heeled Californian wanted to stretch a ractive late into the night. Some of the ractors in her company didn't come in until later in the day, but Miranda still had dreams of living in London and craved attention from that city's sophisticated payers. So she always came to work early.

When she finished her warmups and went on, she found a bid already waiting for her. The casting agent, which was a semiautonomous piece of software, had assembled a company of nine payers, enough to ract all the guest roles in *First Class to Geneva*, which was about intrigue among rich people on a train in Nazi-occupied France, and which was to ractives what *The Mousetrap* was to passive theatre. It was an ensemble piece: nine guest roles to be assumed by payers, three somewhat larger and more glamorous host roles to be assumed by payees like Miranda. One of the characters was, unbeknownst to the others, an Allied spy. Another was a secret colonel in the SS, another was secretly Jewish, another was a Cheka agent. Sometimes there was a German trying to defect to the Allied side. But you never knew which was which when the ractive started up; the computer switched all the roles around at random.

It paid well because of the high payer/payee ratio. Miranda provisionally accepted the bid. One of the other host roles hadn't been filled yet, so while she waited, she bid and won a filler job. The computer morphed her into the face of an adorable young woman whose face and hair looked typical of what was current in London at the moment; she wore the uniform of a British Airways ticket agent. "Good evening, Mr. Oremland," she gushed, reading the prompter. The computer disped it into an even perkier voice and made subtle corrections in her accent.

"Good evening, er, Margaret," said the jowly Brit staring out of a pane on her mediatron. He was wearing half-glasses, had to squint to make out her nametag. His tie was loose on his chest, a gin and tonic in one hairy fist, and he liked the looks of this Margaret. Which was almost guaranteed, since Margaret had been morphed up by a marketing computer in London that knew more about this gentleman's taste in girlflesh than he would like to think.

"Six months without a vacation!? How boring," Mi-

randa/Margaret said. "You must be doing something terribly important," she continued, facetious without being
mean, the two of them sharing a little joke.

"Yes, I suppose even making lots of money does become boring after a while," the man returned, in much the
same tone.

Miranda glanced over at the casting sheet for *First
Class to Geneva*. She'd be pissed if this Mr. Oremland got
overly talkative and forced her to pass on the bigger role.
Though he did seem a reasonably clever sort. "You know,
it's a fine time to visit Atlantan West Africa, and the airship
Gold Coast is scheduled to depart in two weeks—shall I book
a stateroom for you? And a companion perhaps?"

Mr. Oremland seemed iffy. "Call me old-fashioned,"
he said, "but when you say Africa, I think AIDS and parasites."

"Oh, not in West Africa, sir, not in the new colonies.
Would you like a quick tour?"

Mr. Oremland gave Miranda/Margaret one long,
searching, horny look, sighed, checked his watch, and
seemed to remember that she was an imaginary being.
"Thank you just the same," he said, and cut her off.

Just in time too; the playbill for *Geneva* had just filled
up. Miranda only had a few seconds to switch contexts and
get herself into the character of Ilse before she found herself
sitting in a first-class coach of a mid-twentieth-century passenger train, staring into the mirror at a blond, blue-eyed,
high-cheekboned ice queen. Unfolded on her dressing-table
was a letter written in Yiddish.

So tonight she was the secret Jew. She tore the letter
into tiny pieces and fed them out her window, then did the
same with a couple of Stars of David that she rooted out of
her jewelry case. This thing was fully ractive, and there was
nothing to prevent other characters from breaking into her
coach and going through her possessions. Then she finished
putting on her makeup and choosing her outfit, and went to
the dining car for dinner. Most of the other characters were
already in here. The nine amateurs were stiff and stilted as
usual, the two other professionals were circulating among
them, trying to loosen them up, break through that self-
consciousness and get them into their characters.

Geneva ended up dragging on for a good three hours. It

was nearly ruined by one of the payers, who had clearly signed up exclusively for the purpose of maneuvering Ilse into bed. He turned out to be the secret SS colonel too; but he was so hell-bent on fucking Ilse that he spent the whole evening out of character. Finally Miranda lured him into the kitchen in the back of the dining car, shoved a foot-long butcher knife into his chest, and left him in the fridge. She had played this role a couple of hundred times and knew the location of every potentially lethal object on the train.

After a ractive it was considered good form to go to the Green Room, a virtual pub where you could chat out-of-character with the other ractors. Miranda skipped it because she knew that the creep would be waiting for her there.

Next was a lull of an hour or so. Primetime in London was over, and New Yorkers were still eating dinner. Miranda went to the bathroom, ate a little snack, and picked up a few kiddy jobs.

Kids on the West Coast were getting back from school and jumping right into the high-priced educational ractives that their parents made available to them. These things created a plethora of extremely short but fun roles; in quick succession, Miranda's face was morphed into a duck, a bunny, a talking tree, the eternally elusive Carmen Sandiego, and the repulsively cloying Doogie the Dinosaur. Each of them got a couple of lines at most:

"That's right! B stands for balloon! I like to play with balloons, don't you, Matthew?"

"Sound it out, Victoria! You can do it!"

"Soldier ants have larger and stronger jaws than their worker counterparts and play a key role in defending the nest from predators."

"Please don't throw me into that briar patch, Br'er Fox!"

"Hello, Roberta! I've been missing you all day. How was your field trip to Disneyland?"

"Twentieth-century airships were filled with flammable hydrogen, expensive helium, or inefficient hot air, but our modern versions are filled literally with nothing at all. High-strength nanostructures make it possible to pump all the air from an airship's envelope and fill it with a vacuum. Have you ever been on an airship, Thomas?"

Nell's further experiences with the Primer;
the origin of Princess Nell.

"Once upon a time there was a little Princess named Nell who was imprisoned in a tall dark castle on an island—"

"Why?"

"Nell and Harv had been locked up in the Dark Castle by their evil stepmother."

"Why didn't their father let them out of the Dark Castle?"

"Their father, who had protected them from the whims of the wicked stepmother, had gone sailing over the sea and never come back."

"Why did he never come back?"

"Their father was a fisherman. He went out on his boat every day. The sea is a vast and dangerous place, filled with monsters, storms, and other dangers. No one knows what fate befell him. Perhaps it was foolish of him to sail into such danger, but Nell knew better than to fret over things she could not change."

"Why did she have a wicked stepmother?"

"Nell's mother died one night when a monster came out of the sea and entered their cottage to snatch Nell and Harv, who were just babies. She fought with the monster and slew it, but in so doing suffered grievous wounds and died the next day with her adopted children still nestled in her bosom."

"Why did the monster come from the sea?"

"For many years, Nell's father and mother badly wanted children but were not so blessed until one day, when the father caught a mermaid in his net. The mermaid said that if he let her go, she would grant him a wish, so he wished for two children, a boy and a girl.

"The next day, while he was out fishing, he was approached by a mermaid carrying a basket. In the basket were the two little babies, just as he had requested, wrapped up in cloth of gold. The mermaid cautioned him that he and his wife should not allow the babies to cry at night."

"Why were they in gold cloth?"

"They were actually a Princess and a Prince who had been in a shipwreck. The ship sank, but the basket containing the two babies bobbed like a cork on the ocean until the mermaids came and found them. They took care of those two babies until they found a good parent for them.

"He took the babies back to the cottage and presented them to his wife, who swooned for joy. They lived happily together for some time, and whenever one of the babies cried, one of the parents would get up and comfort it. But one night father did not come home, because a storm had pushed his little red fishing boat far out to sea. One of the babies began to cry, and the mother got up to comfort it. But when the other began to cry as well, there was nothing she could do, and shortly the monster came calling.

"When the fisherman returned home the next day, he found his wife's body lying beside that of the monster, and both of the babies unharmed. His grief was very great, and he began the difficult task of raising both the children.

"One day, a stranger came to his door. She said that she had been cast out by the cruel Kings and Queens of the Land Beyond and that she needed a place to sleep and would do any kind of work in exchange. At first she slept on the floor and cooked and cleaned for the fisherman all day long, but as Nell and Harv got bigger, she began to give them more and more chores, until by the time their father disappeared, they toiled from dawn until long after nightfall, while their stepmother never lifted a finger."

"Why didn't the fisherman and his babies live in the castle to protect them from the monster?"

"The castle was a dark forbidding place on the top of a mountain. The fisherman had been told by his father that it had been built many ages ago by trolls, who were still said to live there. And he did not have the twelve keys."

"Did the wicked stepmother have the twelve keys?"

"She kept them buried in a secret place as long as the fisherman was around, but after he sailed away and did not come back, she had Nell and Harv dig them up again, along with a quantity of jewels and gold that she had brought with her from the Land Beyond. She bedecked herself with the gold and jewels, then opened up the iron gates of the Dark Castle and tricked Nell and Harv into going inside. As soon as they were in, she slammed the gates shut behind them and locked the twelve locks. 'When the sun goes down, the trolls will have you for a snack!' she cackled.''

''What's a troll?''

''A scary monster that lives in holes in the ground and comes out after dark.''

Nell started to cry. She slammed the book closed, ran to her bed, gathered her stuffed animals up in her arms, started chewing on her blanket, and cried for a while, considering the question of trolls.

The book made a fluttering sound. Nell saw it opening in the corner of her eye and looked over cautiously, afraid she might see a picture of a troll. But instead, she saw two pictures. One was of Princess Nell, sitting on the grass with four dolls gathered in her arms. Facing it was a picture of Nell surrounded by four creatures: a big dinosaur, a rabbit, a duck, and a woman in a purple dress with purple hair.

The book said, ''Would you like to hear the story of how Princess Nell made some friends in the Dark Castle, where she least expected it, and how they killed all of the trolls and made it a safe place to live?''

''Yes!'' Nell said, and scooted across the floor until she was poised above the book.

*Judge Fang pays a visit to the Celestial Kingdom;
tea served in an ancient setting; a "chance"
encounter with Dr. X.*

Judge Fang was not afflicted with the Westerner's inability to pronounce the name of the man known as Dr. X, unless a combined Cantonese/New York accent counted as a speech impediment. In his discussions with his trusted subordinates he had fallen into the habit of calling him Dr. X anyway.

He had never had cause to pronounce the name at all, until recently. Judge Fang was district magistrate for the Leased Territories, which in turn were part of the Chinese

Coastal Republic. Dr. X almost never left the boundaries of Old Shanghai, which was part of a separate district; more to the point, he stuck to a small but anfractuous subregion whose tendrils were seemingly ramified through every block and building of the ancient city. On the map, this region looked like the root system of a thousand-year-old dwarf tree; its border must have been a hundred kilometers long, even though it was contained within a couple of square kilometers. This region was not part of the Coastal Republic; it styled itself as the Middle Kingdom, a living vestige of Imperial China, prohibitively the oldest and greatest nation of the world.

The tendrils went even farther than that; Judge Fang had known this for a long time. Many of the gang members running around the Leased Territories with Judge Fang's cane marks across their asses had connections on the mainland that could ultimately be traced back to Dr. X. It was rarely useful to dwell upon this fact; if it hadn't been Dr. X, it would have been someone else. Dr. X was unusually clever at taking advantage of the principle of grith, or right of refuge, which in the modern usage simply meant that Coastal Republic officials like Judge Fang could not enter the Celestial Kingdom and arrest someone like Dr. X. So usually when they bothered to trace a criminal's higher connections at all, they simply drew an arrow up the page to a single character, consisting of a box with a vertical slash drawn down through the middle. The character meant Middle, as in Middle Kingdom, though for Judge Fang it had come to mean, simply, trouble.

At the House of the Venerable and Inscrutable Colonel and other Judge Fang hangouts, the name of Dr. X had been pronounced more frequently in recent weeks. Dr. X had tried to bribe everyone on Judge Fang's hierarchy except for the Judge himself. Of course, the overtures had been made by people whose connection with Dr. X was tenuous in the extreme, and had been so subtle that most of those approached had not even realized what was happening until, days or weeks later, they had suddenly sat up in bed exclaiming, "He was trying to *bribe* me! I must tell Judge Fang!"

If not for grith, this might have made for a merry and stimulating couple of decades, as Judge Fang matched his wits against those of the Doctor, a worthy adversary at last and a welcome break from smelly, larcenous barbarian whelps. As it was, Dr. X's machinations were of purely abstract interest. But they were no less interesting for that, and many days, as Miss Pao proceeded through the familiar line of patter about sky-eyes, heuristic mugging detection, and tagger aerostats, Judge Fang found his attention wandering across town to the ancient city, to the hong of Dr. X.

It was said that the Doctor frequently took tea in the morning at an old teahouse there, and so it was that one morning Judge Fang happened to drop in on the place. It had been built, centuries ago, in the center of a pond. Swarms of fire-colored fish hung just beneath the surface of the khaki water, glowing like latent coals, as Judge Fang and his assistants, Miss Pao and Chang, crossed the bridge.

There was a Chinese belief that demons liked to travel only in straight lines. Hence the bridge zigzagged no fewer than nine times as it made its way to the center of the pond. The bridge was a demon filter, in other words, and the teahouse demon-free, which seemed of only limited usefulness if it still hosted people like Dr. X. But for Judge Fang, raised in a city of long straight avenues, full of straight talkers, it was useful to be reminded that from the point of view of some people, including Dr. X, all of that straightness was suggestive of demonism; more natural and human was the ever-turning way, where you could never see round the next corner, and the overall plan could be understood only after lengthy meditation.

The teahouse itself was constructed of unfinished wood, aged to a nice gray. It looked rickety but evidently wasn't. It was narrow and tall, two stories high with a proud winglike roof. One entered through a low narrow door, built by and for the chronically undernourished. The interior had the ambience of a rustic cabin on a lake. Judge Fang had been here before, in mufti, but today he had thrown a robe over his charcoal-gray pinstripe suit—a reasonably subtle brocade, funereal by comparison with what people used to wear in China. He also wore a black cap embroidered with a unicorn, which in most company would probably be lumped in with rainbows and elves but here would be understood for what it was, an ancient symbol of acuity. Dr. X could be relied upon to get the message.

The teahouse staff had had plenty of time to realize he was coming as he negotiated the endless turns in the causeway. A manager of sorts and a couple of waitresses were arrayed before the door, bowing deeply as he approached.

Judge Fang had been raised on Cheerios, burgers, and jumbo burritos bulging with beans and meat. He was just a bit less than two meters in height. His beard was unusually thick, and he had been letting it grow out for a couple of years now, and his hair fell down past the tips of his shoulder blades. These elements, plus the hat and robe, and in combination with the power reposed in him by the state, gave him a certain presence of which he was well aware. He tried not to be overly satisfied with himself, as this would have gone against all Confucian precepts. On the other hand, Confucianism was all about hierarchy, and those who were in high positions were supposed to comport themselves with a certain dignity. Judge Fang could turn it on when he needed to. He used it now to get himself situated at the best table on the first floor, off in the corner with a nice view out the tiny old windows into the neighboring Ming-era garden. He was still in the Coastal Republic, in the middle of the twenty-first century. But he could have been in the Middle Kingdom of yore, and for all intents and purposes, he was.

Chang and Miss Pao separated themselves from their master and requested a table on the second floor, up a narrow and alarming stairway, leaving Judge Fang in peace whilst also making their presence forcibly known to Dr. X, who happened to be up there right now, as he always was at this time in the morning, sipping tea and chatting with his venerable homeboys.

When Dr. X made his way down half an hour later, he was nonetheless delighted and surprised to see the moderately famous and widely respected Judge Fang sitting all by his lonesome staring out at the pond, its schools of fish flickering lambently. When he approached the table to tender his respects, Judge Fang invited him to take a seat, and after several minutes of sensitive negotiations over whether this would or would not be an unforgivable intrusion on the magistrate's privacy, Dr. X finally, gratefully, reluctantly, respectfully took a seat.

There was lengthy discourse between the two men on

which of them was more honored to be in the company of the other, followed by exhaustive discussion of the relative merits of the different teas offered by the proprietors, whether the leaves were best picked in early or late April, whether the brewing water should be violently boiling as the pathetic *gwailos* always did it, or limited to eighty degrees Celsius.

Eventually, Dr. X got around to complimenting Judge Fang on his cap, especially on the embroidery work. This meant that he had noticed the unicorn and understood its message, which was that Judge Fang had seen through all of his efforts at bribery.

Not long afterward, Miss Pao came down and regretfully informed the Judge that his presence was urgently required at a crime scene in the Leased Territories. To spare Judge Fang the embarrassment of having to cut short the conversation, Dr. X was approached, moments later, by one of his staff, who whispered something into his ear. The Doctor apologized for having to take his leave, and the two men then got into a very genteel argument over which one of them was being more inexcusably rude, and then over which would precede the other across the bridge. Judge Fang ended up going first, because his duties were deemed more pressing, and thus ended the first meeting between the Judge and Dr. X. The Judge was quite happy; it had all gone just as planned.

*Hackworth receives an unexpected visit
from Inspector Chang.*

Mrs. Hull had to shake the flour out of her apron to answer the door. Hackworth, working in his study, assumed it was a mere delivery until she appeared in his doorway, harrumphing lightly, holding a salver with a single card centered on it: Lieutenant Chang. His organization was called, in traditional Chinese general-to-specific order, China

Coastal Republic Shanghai New Chusan Leased Territories District Magistrate Office.

"What does he want?"

"To give you your hat back."

"Send him in," Hackworth said, startled.

Mrs. Hull dawdled significantly. Hackworth glanced into a mirror and saw himself reaching for his throat, checking the knot on his necktie. His smoking jacket was hanging loose, and he wrapped it tight and retied the sash. Then he went to the parlor.

Mrs. Hull led Lieutenant Chang into the parlor. He was a burly, ungainly fellow with a short buzz cut. Hackworth's top hat, looking rather ill-used, could be seen indistinctly through a large plastic bag clenched in his hand. "Lieutenant Chang," Mrs. Hull announced, and Chang bowed at Hackworth, smiling a bit more than seemed warranted. Hackworth bowed back. "Lieutenant Chang."

"I will not disturb you for long, I promise," Chang said in clear but unrefined English. "During an investigation—details not relevant here—we got this from a suspect. It is marked your property. Much the worse for wear—please accept it."

"Well done, Lieutenant," said Hackworth, receiving the bag and holding it up to the light. "I did not expect to see it again, even in such a battered condition."

"Well, these boys do not have respect for a good hat, I am afraid," said Lieutenant Chang.

Hackworth paused, not knowing what one was supposed to say at this point. Chang just stood there, seeming more at ease in Hackworth's parlor than Hackworth was. The first exchange had been simple, but now the East/West curtain fell between them like a rusty cleaver.

Was this part of some official procedure? Was it a solicitation for a tip? Or just Mr. Chang being a nice guy?

When in doubt, end the visit sooner rather than later. "Well," said Hackworth, "I don't know and don't care what you arrested him for, but I commend you for having done so."

Lieutenant Chang did not get the hint and realize it was time to leave. On the contrary, he seemed just a bit perplexed now, where before everything had been so simple.

"I cannot help being curious," Chang said, "what gave you the idea that anyone had been arrested?"

Hackworth felt a spear pass through his heart.

"You're a police lieutenant holding what appears to be an evidence bag," he said. "The implication is clear."

Lieutenant Chang looked at the bag, laboriously perplexed. "Evidence? It is just a shopping bag—to protect your hat from the rain. And I am not here in my official capacity."

Another spear, at right angles to the first one.

"Though," Chang continued, "if some criminal activity has taken place of which I was not made aware, perhaps I should recharacterize this visit."

Spear number three; now Hackworth's pounding heart sat at the origin of a bloody coordinate system plotted by Lieutenant Chang, conveniently pinned and exposed for thorough examination. Chang's English was getting better all the time, and Hackworth was beginning to think that he was one of those Shanghainese who had spent much of his life in Vancouver, New York, or London.

"I had assumed that the gentleman's hat had simply been misplaced or perhaps blown off by a gust of wind. Now you say criminals were involved!" Chang looked as though he had never, to this day, suspected the existence of criminals in the Leased Territories. Then shock was transcended by wonder as he segued, none too subtly, into the next phase of the trap.

"It was not important," Hackworth said, trying to derail Chang's relentless train of thought, sensing that he and his family were tied to the tracks. Chang ignored him, as if so exhilarated by the workings of his mind that he could not be distracted.

"Mr. Hackworth, you have given me an idea. I have been trying to solve a difficult case—a mugging that took place a few days ago. The victim was an unidentified Atlantan gentleman."

"Don't you have tag mites for that kind of thing?"

"Oh," Lieutenant Chang said, sounding rather downhearted, "tag mites are not very reliable. The perpetrators took certain precautions to prevent the mites from attaching. Of course, several mites attached themselves to the victim. But before we could track him, he made his way to New Atlantis Clave, where your superb immune system destroyed those mites. So his identity has remained a mystery." Chang reached into his breast pocket and pulled out a folded sheet of paper. "Mr. Hackworth, please tell me whether you recognize any of the figures in this clip."

"I'm actually rather busy—" Hackworth said, but Chang unfolded the paper in front of him and gave it a command in Shanghainese. Initially the page was covered with static Chinese characters. Then a large panel in the middle opened up and began to play back a cine feed.

Watching himself getting mugged was one of the most astonishing things Hackworth had ever seen. He could not stop watching it. The feed went to slow motion, and then out came the book. Tears came to Hackworth's eyes, and he made an effort not to blink lest he dislodge them. Not that it really mattered, since Lieutenant Chang was standing rather close to him and could no doubt see everything.

Chang was shaking his head in wonderment. "So it was you, Mr. Hackworth. I had not made the connection. So many nice things, and such a vicious beating. You have been the victim of a very serious crime!"

Hackworth could not speak and had nothing to say anyway.

"It is striking to me," Chang continued, "that you did not bother to report this serious crime to the magistrate! For some time now we have been reviewing this tape, wondering why the victim—a respectable gentleman—did not step forward to assist us with our inquiries. So much effort wasted," Chang fretted. Then he brightened up. "But it's all water under the bridge, I suppose. We have one or two of the gang in custody, on an unrelated crime, and now I can charge them with your mugging as well. Of course, we will require your testimony."

"Of course."

"The items that were taken from you?"

"You saw it."

"Yes. A watch chain with various items, a fountain pen, and—"

"That's it."

Chang seemed just a bit nonplussed, but more than that he seemed deeply satisfied, suffused by a newly generous spirit. "The book does not even bear mentioning?"

"Not really."

"It looked like an antique of some sort. Quite valuable, no?"

"A fake. That sort of thing is popular with us. A way to build an impressive-seeming library without going broke."

"Ah, that explains it," said Mr. Chang, growing more satisfied by the minute. If Hackworth provided him any more reassurance on the matter of the book, he would no doubt curl up on the sofa and fall asleep. "Still, I should mention the book in my official report—which will be shared with New Atlantis authorities, as the victim in this case belonged to that phyle."

"Don't," said Hackworth, finally turning to look Chang in the eye for the first time. "Don't mention it."

"Ah, I cannot imagine your motive for saying this," Chang said, "but I have little leeway in the matter. We are closely monitored by our supervisors."

"Perhaps you could simply explain my feelings to your supervisor."

Lieutenant Chang received this suggestion with a look of wild surmise. "Mr. Hackworth, you are a very clever fellow—as I already gathered from your demanding and very responsible position—but I am ashamed to tell you that your excellently devious plan may not work. My supervisor is a cruel taskmaster with no regard for human feelings. To be quite frank—and I tell you this in all confidence—he is not entirely without ethical blemishes."

"Ah," Hackworth said, "so if I am following you—"

"Oh, no, Mr. Hackworth, it is I who am following *you.*"

"—the appeal to sympathy won't work, and we will have to sway him using another strategy, perhaps related to this ethical blind spot."

"That is an approach that had not occurred to me."

"Perhaps you should do some thinking, or even some research, as to what level and type of inducement might be required," Hackworth said, suddenly walking toward the exit. Lieutenant Chang followed him.

Hackworth hauled his front door open and allowed Chang to retrieve his own hat and umbrella from the rack. "Then simply get back to me and spell it out as plainly and simply as you can manage. Good night, Lieutenant Chang."

As he rode his bicycle toward the gate on his way back to the Leased Territories, Chang was exultant over the success of tonight's research. Of course, neither he nor Judge Fang was interested in extracting bribes from this Hackworth; but Hackworth's willingness to pay served as proof that the book did, in fact, embody stolen intellectual property.

But then he bridled his emotions, remembering the words of the philosopher Tsang to Yang Fu upon the latter's appointment to chief criminal judge: "The rulers have failed in their duties, and the people consequently have been disorganized for a long time. When you have found out the truth of any accusation, be grieved for and pity them, and do not feel joy at your own ability."

Not that Chang's abilities had even been tested this evening; nothing could be easier than getting the New Atlantans to believe that Chinese police were corrupt.

Miranda takes an interest in an anonymous client.

Miranda scanned her balance sheet at the end of one month and discovered that her leading source of income was no longer *Silk Road* or *Taming of the Shrew*—it was that storybook about Princess Nell. In a way that was surprising, because kid stuff usually didn't pay well, but in another way it wasn't—because she had been spending an incredible amount of time in that ractive lately.

It had started small: a story, just a few minutes long, involving a dark castle, a wicked stepmother, and a gate with twelve locks. It would have been forgettable, except for two things: It paid much better than most kid work, because they were specifically looking for highly rated actresses, and it was rather dark and weird by the standards of contemporary children's literature. Not many people were into that whole Grimm Brothers scene anymore.

She collected a few ucus for her trouble and forgot about it. But the next day, the same contract number came up on her mediatron again. She accepted the job and found herself reading the same story, except that it was longer and more involved, and it kept backtracking and focusing in on tiny little bits of itself, which then expanded into stories in their own right.

Because of the way that the ractive was hooked up, she didn't get direct feedback from her counterpart on the other end. She assumed it was a little girl. But she couldn't hear the girl's voice. Miranda was presented with screens of text to be read, and she read them. But she could tell that this process of probing and focusing was being directed by the girl. She had seen this during her governess days. She knew that on the other end of this connection was a little girl insatiably asking why. So she put a little gush of enthusiasm into her voice at the beginning of each line, as if she were delighted that the question had been asked.

When the session was over, the usual screen came up telling her how much she'd made, the contract number, and so on. Before she signed off on it, she checked the little box labelled MARK HERE IF YOU WOULD LIKE A CONTINU-ING RELATIONSHIP WITH THIS CONTRACT.

The relationship box, they called it, and it only came up with higher-quality ractives, where continuity was important. The disping process worked so well that any ractor, male or female, bass or soprano, would sound the same to the end user. But discriminating customers could of course tell ractors apart anyway because of subtle differences in style, and once they had a relationship with one performer, they liked to keep it. Once Miranda checked the box and signed off, she'd get first crack at any more Princess Nell jobs.

Within a week she was teaching this girl how to read. They'd work on letters for a while and then wander off into more stories about Princess Nell, stop in the middle for a quick practical demonstration of basic math, return to the story, and then get sidetracked with an endless chain of "why this?" and "why that?" Miranda had spent a lot of time with kiddie ractives, both as a child and as a governess, and the superiority of this thing was palpable—like hefting an antique silver fork when you'd been eating with plastic utensils for twenty years, or slithering into a tailor-made evening gown when you were used to jeans.

These and other associations came into Miranda's mind on any of the rare moments when she came into contact with something of Quality, and if she didn't make a conscious effort to stop the process, she would end up remembering just about everything that had happened to her during the first years of her life—the Mercedes taking her to private school, the crystal chandelier that would ring like fairy bells when she climbed up on the huge mahogany dinner table to tickle it, her paneled bedroom with the four-poster bed with the silk-and-goosedown duvet. For reasons still unspecified, Mother had moved them far away from all of that, into what passed for poverty these days. Miranda only remembered that, when she had been physically close to Father, Mother had watched them with more vigilance than seemed warranted.

A month or two into the relationship, Miranda groggily signed off from a long Princess Nell session and was astounded to notice that she'd been going for eight hours without a break. Her throat was raw, and she hadn't been to the loo in hours. She had made a lot of money. And the time in New York was something like six in the morning, which made it seem unlikely that the little girl lived there. She must be in a time zone not many hours different from Miranda's, and she must sit there playing with that ractive storybook all day long instead of going to school like a little rich girl should. It was slim evidence to go on, but Miranda never needed much evidence to confirm her belief that rich parents were just as capable of fucking with their children's minds as anyone.

Further experiences with the Primer; Princess Nell and Harv in the Dark Castle.

Harv was a clever boy who knew about trolls, and so as soon as he knew that they had been locked up inside the Dark Castle by their wicked stepmother, he told Nell that they must go out and

gather all the firewood they could find. Rummaging in the Great
Hall of the castle, he found a suit of armor holding a battle-axe. "I
will chop down some trees with this," he said, "and you must go
out and gather kindling."

"What's kindling?" Nell asked.

An illustration of the castle appeared. In the center was
a tall building with many towers that rose up into the
clouds. Around it was an open space where trees and plants
grew, and around that was the high wall that held them
prisoner.

The illustration zoomed in on an open grassy area and
became very detailed. Harv and Nell were trying to build a
fire. There was a pile of wet logs Harv had chopped up.
Harv also had a rock, which he was striking against the butt
of a knife. Sparks flew out and were swallowed up by the
wet logs.

"You start the fire, Nell," Harv said, and left her alone.

Then the picture stopped moving, and Nell realized,
after a few minutes, that it was fully ractive now.

She picked up the rock and the knife and began to
whack them together (actually she was just moving her
empty hands in space, but in the illustration Princess Nell's
hands did the same thing). Sparks flew, but there was no
fire.

She kept at it for a while, getting more and more frustrated, until tears came to her eyes. But then one of the
sparks went awry and landed in some dry grass. A little curl
of smoke rose up and died out.

She experimented a bit and learned that dry yellow
grass worked better than green grass. Still, the fire never
lasted for more than a few seconds.

A gust of wind came up and blew a few dry leaves in
her direction. She learned that the fire could spread from dry
grass to leaves. The stem of a leaf was basically a small dry
twig, so that gave her the idea to explore a little grove of
trees and look for some twigs. The grove was densely overgrown, but she found what she was looking for beneath an
old dead bush.

"Good!" Harv said, when he came back and found her
approaching with an armload of small dry sticks. "You

found some kindling. You're a smart girl and a good worker."

Soon they had built up a roaring bonfire. Harv chopped down enough trees to make sure that they could keep it going until sunrise, and then he and Nell fell asleep, knowing that trolls would not dare approach the fire. Still, Nell did not sleep very well, for she could hear the mutterings of the trolls off in the darkness and see the red sparks of their eyes. She thought she heard another sound too: muffled voices crying for help.

When the sun came up, Nell explored the Dark Castle, looking for the source of the voices, but found nothing. Harv spent the whole day chopping wood. The day before, he had cut down a third of the trees, and this day he cut down another third.

That night, Nell again heard the voices, but this time they seemed to be shouting, "Look in the trees! Look in the trees!" The next morning, she went into the remaining grove of trees and explored it even as Harv was cutting the last of them down. Again she found nothing.

Neither one of them slept well that night, for they knew that they were burning the last of their wood, and that the next night they would have no protection from the trolls. Nell heard the voices again, and this time they seemed to be shouting, "Look under the ground! Look under the ground!"

Later, after the sun came up, she went exploring again and found a cave whose entrance had been shut up by trolls. When she opened the cave, she found four dolls: a dinosaur, a duck, a rabbit, and a woman with long purple hair. But she did not see anything living that could have made the voices.

Nell and Harv went into the Dark Castle itself that night and shut themselves up in a room high in one tower and pushed heavy furniture against the door, hoping that it would keep the trolls at bay. The room had one tiny window, and Nell stood next to it watching the sun go down, wondering if she would see it rise again. Just as the last glimmer of red light disappeared beneath the horizon, she felt a puff of air at her back and turned around to see an astonishing sight: The stuffed animals had turned into real creatures!

There was a great scary dinosaur, a duck, a clever little bunny rabbit, and a woman in a purple gown with purple hair. They explained to Princess Nell that her wicked stepmother was an evil sorceress in the Land Beyond, and that the four of them had long ago sworn to defeat her evil plans. She had placed an enchantment on them, so that they were dolls in the daytime but returned to their normal selves at night. Then she had imprisoned them in this castle, where the trolls had shut them up inside a cave. They thanked Nell for releasing them.

Then Nell told them her own story. When she mentioned how she and Harv had been plucked from the ocean wrapped in cloth of gold, the woman named Purple said, "This means that you are a true Princess, and so we pledge our undying loyalty to you." And all four of them bent down on one knee and swore an oath to defend Princess Nell to the death.

Dinosaur, who was the fiercest of them all, mounted a campaign to stamp out the trolls, and within a few days they had all been driven away. Thereafter Nell was no longer troubled in her sleep, for she knew that the scary trolls, who had once given her bad dreams, had been replaced by her four night friends.

The torture chamber of Judge Fang; a barbarian is interrogated; dark events in the interior of China; an unignorable summons from Dr. X.

Judge Fang didn't torture people frequently. This was for several reasons. Under the new system of Confucian justice, it was no longer necessary for every criminal to sign a confession before a sentence was carried out; all that was needed was for the magistrate to find him guilty on the strength of the evidence. This alone relieved the Judge of having to torture many of the people who came before his bench, though he was often tempted to force confessions from insolent Western thetes who refused to take responsibility for their own actions. Furthermore, modern surveillance equipment made it possible to gather information without having to rely on (sometimes reticent) human witnesses as the magistrates of yore had done.

But the man with the red dreadlocks was a very reluctant witness indeed, and unfortunately the information locked up in his brain was unique. No airborne cine aerostat or microscopic surveillance mite had recorded the data Judge Fang sought. And so the magistrate had decided to revert to the time-honored methods of his venerable predecessors.

Chang strapped the prisoner (who would only identify himself as a Mr. PhyrePhox) to a heavy X-shaped rack that was normally used for canings. This was purely a humanitarian gesture; it would prevent PhyrePhox from thrashing wildly around the room and injuring himself. Chang also stripped the prisoner from the waist down and situated a bucket under his organs of elimination. In so doing he happened to expose the only actual injury that the prisoner would suffer during this entire procedure: a tiny, neat scab in the base of the spine, where the court physician had thrust in the spinal tap the previous afternoon, and introduced a set of nanosites—nanotechnological parasites—under the supervision of Miss Pao. In the ensuing twelve hours, the 'sites had migrated up and down the prisoner's spinal column, drifting lazily through the cerebrospinal fluid, and situated themselves on whatever afferent nerves they happened to bump up against. These nerves, used by the body to transmit information such as (to name only one example) excruciating pain to the brain, had a distinctive texture and appearance that the 'sites were clever enough to recognize. It is probably superfluous to mention that these 'sites had one other key feature, namely the ability to transmit bogus information along those nerves.

That tiny scab, just above the buttocks, always drew Judge Fang's attention when he presided over one of these affairs, which fortunately was not more than a few times a year. PhyrePhox, being a natural redhead, had deathly pale skin.

"Cool!" the prisoner suddenly exclaimed, swiveling his head around in a spray of dreadlocks, trying as best he could to look down and back over his freckled shoulder. "I got this feeling of, like, stroking some, like, really soft fur or something against my left inner thigh. That is so bitching! Do it again, man! Whoa, wait a minute! Now it's the same feeling, but it's like on the sole of my right foot!"

"The attachment of the nanosites to the nerves is an aleatory process—we never know which nanosite will end up where. The sensations you are experiencing now are a way for us to take inventory, as it were. Of course, nothing is actually happening in your thigh or foot; it all takes place within the spinal column, and you would feel it even if your legs had been amputated."

"That's really weird," PhyrePhox exclaimed, his pale green eyes going wide with amazement. "So you could even, like, torture a basket case." His eye and cheek twitched on one side. "Damn! Feels like someone's tickling my face now. Hey, cut it out!" A grin came over his face. "Oh, no! I'll tell you everything! Just don't tickle me! Please!"

Chang was first stunned and then furious at the prisoner's breach of decorum and made a move toward a rack of canes mounted to the wall. Judge Fang steadied his assistant with a firm hand on the shoulder; Chang swallowed his anger and took a deep breath, then bowed apologetically.

"You know, PhyrePhox," Judge Fang said, "I really appreciate the moments of levity and even childlike wonder that you are injecting into this process. So often when we strap people to the torture rack, they are unpleasantly tense and hardly any fun at all to be around."

"Hey, man, I'm into new experiences. I get lots of experience points for this, huh?"

"Experience points?"

"It's a joke. From swords-and-sorcery ractives. See, the more experience points your character earns, the more power he gets."

Judge Fang straightened one hand and snapped it backward past his head, making a whooshing sound like a low-flying fighter plane. "The reference escaped me," he explained for the benefit of Chang and Miss Pao, who did not recognize the gesture.

"Feels like there's something tickling my right eardrum now," the prisoner said, snapping his head back and forth.

"Good! That means a nanosite happened to attach itself to the nerve running from your eardrum into your brain. We always consider it an omen of good fortune when this happens," Judge Fang said, "as pain impulses delivered into this nerve make a particularly deep impression on the subject. Now, I will ask Miss Pao to suspend this process for a few minutes so that I can have your full attention."

"Cool," said the prisoner.

"Let's review what we have so far. You are thirty-seven years old. Almost twenty years ago, you co-founded a CryptNet node in Oakland, California. It was a very early node—number 178. Now, of course, there are tens of thousands of nodes."

A hint of a smile from the prisoner. "You almost got me there," he said. "No way am I going to tell you how many nodes there are. Of course, no one really knows anyway."

"Very well," Judge Fang said. He nodded to Chang, who made a mark on a sheet of paper. "We will save that inquiry for the latter phase of the investigation, which will commence in a few minutes.

"Like all other CryptNet members," Judge Fang continued, "you started out at the first level and made your way up from there, as the years went by, to your current level of—what?"

PhyrePhox smirked and shook his head knowingly. "I'm sorry, Judge Fang, but we've been through this. I can't deny I started out at level one—I mean, that's, like, obvious—but anything beyond that point is speculation."

"It's only speculation if you don't tell us," Judge Fang said, controlling a momentary spark of annoyance. "I suspect you of being at least a twenty-fifth-level member."

PhyrePhox got a serious look on his face and shook his head, jangling the shiny, colorful fragments of glass and metal worked into his dreadlocks. "That is so bogus. You should know that the highest level is ten. Anything beyond that is, like, a myth. Only conspiracy theorists believe in levels beyond ten. CryptNet is just a simple, innocuous tuple-processing collective, man."

"That is, of course, the party line, which is only believed by complete idiots," Judge Fang said. "In any case, returning to your previous statement, we have established that over the next eight years, Node 178 did a prosperous business—as you said, processing tuples. During this time you worked your way up the hierarchy to the tenth level. Then you claim to have severed your connection with CryptNet and gone into business for yourself, as a mediagrapher. Since then, you have specialized in war zones. Your photo, cine, and sound collages from the battlegrounds of China have won prizes and been accessed by hundreds of thousands of media consumers, though your work is so graphic and disturbing that mainstream acceptance has eluded you."

"That's your opinion, man."

Chang stepped forward, visibly clenching the many stout muscles that enwreathed his big, bony, close-cropped head. "You will address the magistrate as Your Honor!" he hissed.

"Chill out, man," PhyrePhox said. "Jeez, who's torturing whom here?"

Judge Fang exchanged a look with Chang. Chang, out of sight of the prisoner, licked one index finger and made an imaginary mark in the air: Score one for PhyrePhox.

"Many of us who are not part of CryptNet find it hard to understand how that organization can survive its extremely high attrition rate. Over and over again, first-level CryptNet novices work their way up the hierarchy to the tenth and supposedly highest level, then drop out and seek other work or simply fade back into the phyles from which they originated."

PhyrePhox tried to shrug insouciantly but was too effectively restrained to complete the maneuver.

Judge Fang continued, "This pattern has been widely noted and has led to speculation that CryptNet contains many levels beyond the tenth, and that all of the people pretending to be ex-CryptNet members are, in fact, secretly connected to the old network; secretly in communication with all of the other nodes; secretly working their way up to higher and higher levels within CryptNet even while infiltrating the power structures of other phyles and organizations. That CryptNet is a powerful secret society that has spread its tendrils high into every phyle and corporation in the world."

"That is so paranoid."

"Normally we do not concern ourselves with these matters, which may be mere paranoid ravings as you aver. There are those who would claim that the Chinese Coastal Republic, of which I am a servant, is riddled with secret CryptNet members. I myself am skeptical of this. Even if it were true, it would only matter to me if they committed crimes within my jurisdiction."

And it could scarcely make any difference anyway, Judge Fang added to himself, given that the Coastal Republic is completely riddled with corruption and intrigue under the best of circumstances. The darkest and most powerful conspiracy in the world would be chewed up and spat out by the scheming corporate warlords of the Coastal Republic.

Judge Fang realized that everyone was looking at him, waiting for him to continue.

"You were spacing out, Your Honor," PhyrePhox said.

Judge Fang had been spacing out quite a bit lately, usually while pondering this very subject. Corrupt and incompetent government was hardly a new development in China, and the Master himself had devoted many parts of the *Analects* to advising his followers in how they should comport themselves while working in the service of corrupt lords. "A superior man indeed is Chu Po-yu! When good government prevails in his state, he is to be found in office. When bad government prevails, he can roll his principles up and keep them in his breast." One of the great virtues of Confucianism was its suppleness. Western political thought tended to be rather brittle; as soon as the state became corrupt, everything ceased to make sense. Confucianism always retained its equilibrium, like a cork that could float as well in spring water or raw sewage.

Nevertheless, Judge Fang had recently been plagued with doubts as to whether his life made any sense at all in the context of the Coastal Republic, a nation almost completely devoid of virtue.

If the Coastal Republic had believed in the *existence* of virtue, it could at least have aspired to hypocrisy.

He was getting off the track here. The issue was not whether the Coastal Republic was well-governed. The issue was trafficking in babies.

"Three months ago," Judge Fang said, "you arrived in Shanghai via airship and, after a short stay, proceeded into the interior via a hovercraft on the Yangtze. Your stated mission was to gather material for a mediagraphic documentary concerning a new criminal gang"—here Judge Fang referred to his notes—"called the Fists of Righteous Harmony."

"It ain't no small-time triad," PhyrePhox said, smiling exultantly. "It's the seeds of a dynastic rebellion, man."

"I've reviewed the media you transmitted back to the outside world on this subject," Judge Fang said, "and will make my own judgment. The prospects of the Fists are not at issue here."

PhyrePhox was not at all convinced; he raised his head and opened his mouth to explain to Judge Fang how wrong he was, then thought better of it, shook his head regretfully, and acquiesced.

"Two days ago," Judge Fang continued, "you returned to Shanghai in a riverboat badly overloaded with several dozen passengers, most of them peasants fleeing from famine and strife in the interior." He was now reading from a Shanghai Harbormaster document detailing the inspection of the boat in question. "I note that several of the passengers were women carrying female infants under three months of age. The vessel was searched for contraband and admitted into the harbor." Judge Fang did not need to point out that this meant practically nothing; such inspectors were notoriously unobservant, especially when in the presence of distractions such as envelopes full of money, fresh cartons of cigarettes, or conspicuously amorous young passengers. But the more corrupt a society was, the more apt its officials were to brandish pathetic internal documents such as this one as if they were holy writ, and Judge Fang was no exception to this rule when it served a higher purpose. "All of the passengers, including the infants, were processed in the usual way, records taken of retinal patterns, fingerprints, etc. I regret to say that my esteemed colleagues in the Harbormaster's Office did not examine these records with their wonted diligence, for if they had, they might have noticed large discrepancies between the biological characteristics of the young women and their alleged daughters, suggesting that none of them were actually related to each other. But perhaps more pressing matters prevented them from noticing this." Judge Fang let the unspoken accusation hang in the air: that the Shanghai authorities were themselves not out of reach of CryptNet influence. PhyrePhox visibly tried to look ingenuous.

"A day later, during a routine investigation of organized crime activity in the Leased Territories, we placed a surveillance device in an allegedly vacant apartment thought to be used for illegal activities and were startled to hear the sound of many small infants. Constables raided the place immediately and found twenty-four female infants; belonging to the Han racial group, being cared for by eight young peasant women, recently arrived from the country-side. Upon interrogation these women said that they had been recruited for this work by a Han gentleman whose identity has not been established, and who has not been found. The infants were examined. Five of them were on your boat, Mr. PhyrePhox—the biological records match perfectly."

"If there was a baby-smuggling operation associated with that boat," PhyrePhox said, "I had nothing to do with it."

"We have interrogated the boat's owner and captain," Judge Fang said, "and he asserts that this voyage was planned and paid for by you, from beginning to end."

"I had to get back to Shanghai somehow, so I hired the boat. These women wanted to go to Shanghai, so I was cool about letting them come along."

"Mr. PhyrePhox, before we start torturing you, let me explain to you my state of mind," Judge Fang said, coming close to the prisoner so that they could look each other in the eye. "We have examined these babies closely. It appears that they were well cared for—no malnourishment or signs of abuse. Why, then, should I take such an interest in this case?

"The answer has nothing to do, really, with my duties as a district magistrate. It doesn't even relate to Confucian philosophy per se. It is a racial thing, Mr. PhyrePhox. That a European man is smuggling Han babies to the Leased Terri-tories—and thence, I would assume, out to the world be-yond—triggers profound, I might even say primal emotions within me and many other Chinese persons.

"During the Boxer Rebellion, the rumor was spread that the orphanages run by European missionaries were in fact abattoirs where white doctors scooped the eyes out of the heads of Han babies to make medicine for European consumption. That many Han believed these rumors ac-counts for the extreme violence to which the Europeans were subjected during that rebellion. But it also reflects a regrettable predisposition to racial fear and hatred that is latent within the breasts of all human beings of all tribes.

"With your baby-smuggling operation you have stumbled into the same extremely dangerous territory. Perhaps these little girls are destined for comfortable and loving homes in non-Han phyles. That is the best possible outcome for you—you will be punished but you will live. But for all I know, they are being used for organ transplants—in other words, the baseless rumors that incited peasants to storm the orphanages during the Boxer Rebellion may in fact be literally true in your case. Does this help to clarify the purpose of this evening's little get-together?"

At the beginning of this oration, PhyrePhox had been wearing his baseline facial expression—an infuriatingly vacant half-grin, which Judge Fang had decided was not really a smirk, more a posture of detached bemusement. As soon as Judge Fang had mentioned the eyeballs, the prisoner had broken eye contact, lost the smile, and become more and more pensive until, by the end, he was actually nodding in agreement.

He kept on nodding for a minute longer, staring fixedly at the floor. Then he brightened and looked up at the Judge. "Before I give you my answer," he said, "torture me."

Judge Fang, by a conscious effort, remained pokerfaced. So PhyrePhox twisted his head around until Miss Pao was within his peripheral vision. "Go ahead," the prisoner said encouragingly, "give me a jolt."

Judge Fang shrugged and nodded to Miss Pao, who picked up her brush and swept a few quick characters across the mediatronic paper spread out on the writing table before her. As she neared the end of this inscription, she slowed and finally looked up at the Judge, then at PhyrePhox as she drew out the final stroke.

At this point PhyrePhox should have erupted with a scream from deep down in his viscera, convulsed against the restraints, voided himself at both ends, then gone into shock (if he had a weak constitution) or begged for mercy (if strong). Instead he closed his eyes, as if thinking hard about something, tensed every muscle in his body for a few moments, then gradually relaxed, breathing deeply and deliberately. He opened his eyes and looked at Judge Fang. "How's that?" the prisoner said. "Would you like another demonstration?"

"I think I have the general idea," Judge Fang said. "One of your high-level CryptNet tricks, I suppose. Nanosites embedded in your brain, mediating its interchanges with the peripheral nervous system. It would make sense for you to have advanced telæsthetic systems permanently installed. And a system that could trick your nerves into thinking that they were somewhere else could also trick them into thinking that they were not experiencing pain."

"What can be installed can be removed," Miss Pao observed.

"That won't be necessary," Judge Fang said, and nodded to Chang. Chang stepped toward the prisoner, drawing a short sword. "We'll start with fingers and proceed from there."

"You're forgetting something," the prisoner said. "I have already agreed to give you my answer."

"I'm standing here," the Judge said, "I'm not hearing an answer. Is there a reason for this delay?"

"The babies aren't being smuggled anywhere," PhyrePhox said. "They stay right here. The purpose of the operation is to save their lives."

"What is it, precisely, that endangers their lives?"

"Their own parents," PhyrePhox said. "Things are bad in the interior, Your Honor. The water table is gone. The practice of infanticide is at an all-time high."

"Your next goal in life," Judge Fang said, "will be to prove all of this to my satisfaction."

The door opened. One of Judge Fang's constables entered the room and bowed deeply to apologize for the interruption, then stepped forward and handed the magistrate a scroll. The Judge examined the seal; it bore the chop of Dr. X.

He carried it to his office and unrolled it on his desk. It was the real thing, written on rice paper in real ink, not the mediatronic stuff.

It occurred to the Judge, before he even read this document, that he could take it to an art dealer on Nanjing Road and sell it for a year's wages. Dr. X, assuming it was really he who had brushed these characters, was the most impressive living calligrapher whose work Judge Fang had ever seen. His hand betrayed a rigorous Confucian grounding—

many decades more study than Judge Fang could ever aspire to—but upon this foundation the Doctor had developed a distinctive style, highly expressive without being sloppy. It was the hand of an elder who understood the importance of gravity above all else, and who, having first established his dignity, conveyed most of his message through nuances. Beyond that, the structure of the inscription was exactly right, a perfect balance of large characters and small, hung on the page just so, as if inviting analysis by legions of future graduate students.

Judge Fang knew that Dr. X controlled legions of criminals ranging from spankable delinquents up to international crime lords; that half of the Coastal Republic officials in Shanghai were in his pocket; that within the limited boundaries of the Celestial Kingdom, he was a figure of considerable importance, probably a blue-button Mandarin of the third or fourth rank; that his business connections ran to most of the continents and phyles of the wide world and that he had accumulated tremendous wealth. All of these things paled in comparison with the demonstration of power represented by this scroll. *I can pick up a brush at any time,* Dr. X was saying, *and toss off a work of art that can hang on the wall beside the finest calligraphy of the Ming Dynasty.*

By sending the Judge this scroll, Dr. X was laying claim to all of the heritage that Judge Fang most revered. It was like getting a letter from the Master himself. The Doctor was, in effect, pulling rank. And even though Dr. X nominally belonged to a different phyle—the Celestial Kingdom —and, here in the Coastal Republic, was nothing more than a criminal, Judge Fang could not disregard this message from him, written in this way, without abjuring everything he most respected—those principles on which he had rebuilt his own life after his career as a hoodlum in Lower Manhattan had brought him to a dead end. It was like a summons sent down through the ages from his own ancestors.

He spent a few minutes further admiring the calligraphy. Then he rolled the scroll up with great care, locked it in a drawer, and returned to the interrogation room.

"I have received an invitation to dine on Dr. X's boat," he said. "Take the prisoner back to the holding cell. We are finished for today."

A domestic scene; Nell's visit to the playroom;
misbehavior of the other children; the Primer
displays new capabilities; Dinosaur tells a story.

In the morning Mom would put on her maid uniform and go to work, and Tad would wake up sometime later and colonize the sofa in front of the big living-room mediatron. Harv would creep around the edges of the apartment, foraging for breakfast, some of which he'd bring back to Nell. Then Harv would usually leave the apartment and not come back until after Tad had departed, typically in late afternoon, to chill with his homeboys. Mom would come home with a little plastic bag of salad that she'd taken from work and a tiny injector; after picking at the salad, she'd put the injector against her arm for a moment and then spend the rest of the evening watching old passives on the mediatron. Harv would drift in and out with some of his friends. Usually he wasn't there when Nell decided to go to sleep, but he was there when she woke up. Tad might come home at any time of the night, and he'd be angry if Mom wasn't awake.

One Saturday, Mom and Tad were both home at the same time and they were on the couch together with their arms around each other and Tad was playing a silly game with Mom that made Mom squeal and wiggle. Nell kept asking Mom to read her a story from her magic book, and Tad kept shoving her away and threatening to give her a whipping, and finally Mom said, "Get out of my fucking hair, Nell!" and shoved Nell out the door, telling her to go to the playroom for a couple of hours.

Nell got lost in the hallways and started crying; but her book told her a story about Princess Nell getting lost in the endless corridors of the Dark Castle, and how she found her way out by using her wits, and this made Nell feel safe—as though she could never be really lost when she had her book with her. Eventually Nell found the playroom. It was on the first floor of the building. As usual, there were lots of kids there and no parents. There was a special space off to the side of the playroom where babies could sit in strollers and crawl around on the floor. Some mommies were in there, but they told her she was too big to play in that room. Nell went back to the big playroom, which was full of kids who were much bigger than Nell.

She knew these kids; they knew how to push and hit and scratch. She went to one corner of the room and sat with her magic book on her lap, waiting for one kid to get off the swing. When he did, she put her book in the corner and climbed onto the swing and started trying to pump her legs like the big kids did, but she couldn't get the swing to go. Then a big kid came and told her that she was not allowed to use the swing because she was too little. When Nell didn't get off right away, the kid shoved her off. Nell tumbled into the sand, scratching her hands and knees, and ran back toward the corner crying.

But a couple of other kids had found her magic book and started kicking it around, making it slide back and forth across the floor like a hockey puck. Nell ran up and tried to pick the book off the floor, but it slid too fast for her to catch it. The two kids began kicking it back and forth between them and finally tossing it through the air. Nell ran back and forth trying to keep up with the book. Soon there were four kids playing keep-away and six others standing around watching and laughing at Nell. Nell couldn't see things though because her eyes were full of tears, snot was running out of her nose, and her ribcage only quivered when she tried to breathe.

Then one of the kids screamed and dropped the book. Quickly another darted in to grab it, and he screamed too. Then a third. Suddenly all the kids were silent and afraid. Nell rubbed the tears out of her eyes and ran over toward the book again, and this time the kids didn't throw it away from her; she picked it up and cradled it against her chest. The kids who'd been playing keep-away were all in the same pose: arms crossed over chests, hands wedged into armpits, jumping up and down like pogo sticks and screaming for their mothers.

Nell sat in the corner, opened the book, and started to read. She did not know all of the words, but she knew a lot of them, and when she got tired, the book would help her sound out the words or even read the whole story to her, or tell it to her with moving pictures just like a cine.

After the trolls had all been driven away, the castle yard was not a pretty sight to see. It had been unkempt and overgrown to begin with. Harv had had no choice except to chop down all the trees, and during Dinosaur's great battle against the trolls, many of the remaining plants had been torn up.

Dinosaur stood and surveyed it in the moonlight. "This place reminds me of the Extinction, when we had to wander for days just to find something to eat," he said.

DINOSAUR'S TALE

There were four of us traveling through a landscape much like this one, except that instead of stumps, all the trees were burned. The particular part of the world had become dark and cold for a while after the comet struck, so that many of the plants and trees died; and after they died, they dried out, and then it was just a matter of time before lightning caused a great forest fire. The four of us were traveling across this great burned-out country looking for food, and you can guess we were very hungry. Never mind why we were doing it; back then, if things got bad where you were, you just got up and went until things got better.

Besides me there was Utahraptor, who was smaller than me, but very quick, with great curving claws on his feet; with one kick he could cut another dinosaur open like ripe fruit. Then there was Ankylosaurus, who was a slow plant-eater, but dangerous; he was protected all around by a bony shell like a turtle's, and on the end of his tail was a big lump of bone that could dash out the brains of any meat-eating dinosaur that came too close. Finally there was Pteranodon, who could fly. All of us traveled together in a little pack. To be perfectly honest, our band had formerly consisted of a couple of hundred dinosaurs, most of them duck-billed plant-eaters, but Utahraptor and I had been forced to eat most of these—just a few a day, of course, so that they didn't notice at first, as they were not very intelligent.

Finally their number had dwindled to one, a gaunt and gamy fellow named Everett, whom we tried to stretch out for as long as we could. During those last few days, Everett was constantly looking around for his companions. Like all plant-eaters, he had eyes in the side of his head and could see in almost all directions. Everett seemed to think that if he could just swivel his head around in the right direction, a big healthy pack of duck-bills would suddenly rotate into view. At the very end, I think that Everett may have put two and two together; I saw him blink in surprise once, as if the light had finally gone on in his head, and the rest of that day he was very quiet, as if all of his half-dozen or so neurons were busy working out the implications. After that, as we continued across this burned country where Everett had nothing to eat, he became more and more listless and whiny until finally Utahraptor lost his temper, lashed out with one leg, and there was Everett's viscera sitting there on the ground like a sack of groceries. Then there was simply nothing to do except eat him.

I got most of him as usual, though Utahraptor kept darting in around my ankles and snatching up choice bits, and from time to time Pteranodon would swoop in and grab a whorl of intestine. Ankylosaurus stood off to the side and watched. For a long time we'd taken him for an idiot, because he would always just squat there watching us divide up those duck-bills, munching stupidly on the erratic horsetail, never saying much. In retrospect, maybe he was just a taciturn sort. He must have worked out that we would very much like to eat him, if only we could locate some chink in his armor.

If only we had! For many days after Everett had become just another scat on our tracks, Utahraptor and Pteranodon and I trudged across that dead landscape eyeing Ankylosaurus, drooling down our chins as we imagined the unspeakably tender morsels that must lie nestled inside that armored shell. He must have been hungry too, and no doubt his morsels were getting less fat and tender by the day. From time to time we would encounter some sheltered hollow where unfamiliar green plants were poking their shoots through the black and gray debris, and we would encourage Ankylosaurus to stop, take his time, and eat all he wanted. "No, really! We don't mind waiting for you!" He would always fix his tiny little side-mounted eyes on us and look at us balefully as he grazed. "How was your dinner, Anky?" we'd say, and he'd grumble something like, "Tastes like iridium as usual," and then we'd go another couple of days without exchanging a word.

One day we reached the edge of the sea. The salt water lapped up onto a lifeless beach strewn with the bones of extinct sea creatures, from tiny trilobites all the way up to plesiosaurs. Behind us was the desert we'd just crossed. To the south was a range of mountains that would have been impassable even if half of them hadn't been erupting volcanoes. And north of us we could see snow dusting the tops of the hills, and we all knew what that meant: If we went in that direction, we'd soon freeze to death.

So we were stuck there, the four of us, and though we didn't have mediatrons and cine aerostats in those days, we all pretty much knew what was up: We were the last four dinosaurs on earth. Pretty soon we would be three, and then two, and then one, and then none at all, and the only question left to settle was in what order we'd go. You might think this would be awful and depressing, but it wasn't really that bad; being dinosaurs, we didn't spend a lot of time pondering the imponderables, if you know what I mean, and in a way it was kind of fun waiting to see how it would all work out. There was a general assumption on all hands, I think, that Ankylosaurus would be the first to go, but Utah and I would have killed each other in an instant.

So we all kind of faced off on the beach there, Utahraptor and Ankylosaurus and I in a neat triangle with Pteranodon hovering overhead.

After we had been facing off there for some hours, I noticed out of the corner of my eye that the banks to the north and south seemed to be moving, as if they were alive.

Suddenly there was a thundering and rushing sound in the air all around us, and I couldn't help looking up, though I kept one sharp eye on Utahraptor. The world had been such a quiet and dead place for so long that we were startled by any noise or movement, and now it seemed that the air and ground had come alive once more, just as in the old days before the comet.

The noise in the air was caused by a great flock of teensy-tiny Pteranodons, though instead of smooth reptilian skin their wings were covered with oversize scales, and they had toothless, bony beaks instead of proper mouths. These miserable things—these airborne crumbs—were swarming all around Pteranodon, getting in his eyes, pecking at his wings, and it was all he could do to keep airborne.

As I mentioned, I was keeping one eye on Utahraptor as always, and to my surprise he suddenly turned away and ran up onto the north slope, with an eagerness that could be explained only by the availability of food. I followed him, naturally, but pulled up short. Something was wrong. The ground on the north slope was covered with a moving carpet that swarmed around Utahraptor's feet. Focusing my eyes, which frankly were not very good, I saw that this carpet actually consisted of thousands of tiny dinosaurs whose scales had grown very long and slender and numerous—in short, they were furry. I had been seeing these quadrupedal hors d'oeuvres dodging around under logs and rocks

for the last few million years and always taken them for an especially ill-conceived mutation. But suddenly there were thousands
of them, and this at a time when there were only four dinosaurs
left in the whole world. And they seemed to be working together.
They were so tiny that Utahraptor had no way to get them into his
mouth, and whenever he stopped moving for an instant, they
swarmed onto his legs and tail and nipped at his flesh. A plague of
shrews. I was so confounded that I stopped in my tracks.

That was a mistake, for soon I felt a sensation in my legs and
tail like millions of pinpricks. Turning around, I saw that the south
slope was covered with ants, millions of them, and they had apparently decided to eat me. Meanwhile Ankylosaurus was bellowing and swinging his bony ball around without effect, for the
ants were swarming on his body as well.

Well, before long the shrews and the ants and the birds
started to run into each other and have skirmishes of their own,
and so at that point they called a truce. The King of the Birds, the
King of the Shrews, and the Queen of the Ants all got together on
top of a rock to parley. In the meantime they left us dinosaurs
alone, seeing that we were trapped in any case.

The situation struck me as unfair, so I approached the rock
where these despicable micro-monarchs were chattering away, a
mile a minute, and spoke: "Yo! Aren't you going to invite the King
of the Reptiles?"

They looked at me like I was crazy.

"Reptiles are obsolete," said the King of the Shrews.

"Reptiles are just retarded birds," said the King of the Birds,
"and so I am your King, thank you very much."

"There's only zero of you," said the Queen of the Ants. In
ant arithmetic, there are only two numbers: Zero, which means
anything less than a million, and Some. "You can't cooperate, so
even if you were King, the title would be meaningless."

"Besides," said the King of the Shrews, "the purpose of this
summit conference is to decide which of our kingdoms shall eat
which dinosaur, and we do not suppose that the King of the Dinosaurs, even if there were such a thing, would be able to participate
constructively." Mammals always talked this way to show off their
oversize brains—which were basically the same as ours, but bur-
dened with a lot of useless extra business on top—useless, I should
say, but darn tasty.

"But there are three kingdoms and four dinosaurs," I
pointed out. Of course this was not true in ant arithmetic, so the

Queen of the Ants immediately began to make a fuss. In the end I had to go over among the ants and crush them with my tail until I had killed a few million, which is the only way that you can get an ant to take you seriously.

"Surely three dinosaurs would be enough to give all of your subjects a square meal," I said. "May I suggest that the birds peck Pteranodon to the bone, the shrews tear Utahraptor limb from limb, and the ants feast on the corpse of Ankylosaurus?"

The three monarchs appeared to be considering this suggestion when Utahraptor sped up in a huff. "Excuse me, Your Royal Highnesses, but who appointed this fellow king? I am just as qualified to be king as he." In short order, Pteranodon and Ankylosaurus also laid claim to the throne.

The King of the Shrews, the King of the Birds, and the Queen of the Ants told us all to shut up, and then conferred amongst themselves for a few minutes. Finally the King of the Shrews stepped forward. "We have reached a decision," he said. "Three dinosaurs will be eaten, and one, the King of the Reptiles, will be spared; all that remains is for one of you to demonstrate that you are superior to the other three and deserve to wear the crown."

"Very well!" I said, and turned on Utahraptor, who began backing away from me, hissing and swiping the air with his giant claws. If I could dispatch Utahraptor with a frontal assault, Pteranodon would swoop down to steal some of the carrion, and I could ambush her then; having fortified myself by eating the other two, I might be strong enough to overcome Ankylosaurus.

"No, no, no!" screamed the King of the Shrews. "This is just the kind of thing I was talking about when I said you reptiles were obsolete. It's not about who is the biggest and baddest anymore."

"It's about cooperation, organization, regimentation," said the Queen of the Ants.

"It's about brains," said the King of the Shrews.

"It's about beauty, glory, dazzling flights of inspiration!" said the King of the Birds.

This precipitated another stridulent dispute among the two Kings and the Queen. Everyone got very short-tempered, and there probably would have been serious trouble if the tide had not come in and washed a few whale carcasses and dead elasmosaurs onto the beach. As you can imagine, we fell upon these gifts with abandon, and while I was eating my fill, I also managed to swallow innumerable birds, shrews, and ants who were feasting on the same pieces of meat as I.

After everyone had filled their bellies and calmed down somewhat, the Kings and the Queen resumed their discussions. Finally the King of the Shrews, who seemed to be the designated spokesmonarch, stepped forward again. "We cannot come to an agreement as to which of you should be the King of the Reptiles, so each of our nations, Birds, Mammals, and Ants, will put each of you to a trial, and then we will gather again and put it to a vote. If the vote results in a tie, we will eat all four of you and bring the Kingdom of Reptiles to an end."

We drew lots, and I was chosen to go among the ants for the first round of trials. I followed the Queen into the midst of her army, picking my way slowly until the Queen said, "Step lively, lung-breather! Time is food! Don't worry about those ants beneath your feet—you can't possibly kill more than zero!" So from then on, I just walked normally, though my claws became slick with crushed ants.

We traveled south for a day or two and then stopped on a stream bank. "South of here is the territory of the King of the Cockroaches. Your first task is to bring me the head of the King."

Looking across the river, I could see that the entire country-side was swarming with an infinite number of cockroaches, more than I could ever stomp; and even if I could stomp them all, there must be more below the ground, which was doubtless where the King lived.

I waded across the river and traveled through the Kingdom of the Cockroaches for three days until I crossed another river and entered into the Kingdom of the Bees. This place was greener than any I'd seen for a while, with many wildflowers, and bees swarmed everywhere taking nectar back to their nests, which were as big as houses.

This gave me an idea. I toppled several hollow trees filled with honey, dragged them back to the Kingdom of the Cock-roaches, split them open, and made sticky honey trails leading down toward the ocean. The cockroaches followed the trails down to the water's edge, where the waves broke over their heads and drowned them. For three days I kept watch over the beach as the number of cockroaches dwindled, and finally on the third day the King of the Roaches emerged from his throne room to see where everyone had gone. I coaxed him onto a leaf and carried him back north across the river and into the Kingdom of the Ants, much to the amazement of the Queen.

Next I was put into the care of the King of the Birds. He and his chirping, chattering army led me up into the mountains, up above the snowline, and I was sure that I would freeze to death. But as we continued up, it suddenly became warmer, which I did not understand until I realized that we were approaching a live volcano. We finally stopped at the edge of a red-hot lava flow half a mile wide. In the center of the flow, a tall black rock stood out like an island in the middle of a river.

The King of the Birds plucked one golden feather from his tail and gave it to a soldier, who took it in his beak, flew over the lava, and left that feather on the very top of the black rock. By the time that soldier flew back, he was half roasted from the heat radiating from the lava—and don't think my mouth didn't water! "Your job," said the King, "is to bring me that feather."

Now, this was clearly unfair, and I protested that the birds were obviously trying to favor Pteranodon. This kind of argument might have worked with ants or even shrews; but the King of the Birds would hear none of it. For them, virtue consisted in being birdlike, and fairness didn't enter into it.

Well, I stood on the edge of that lava flow until my skin smoked, but I couldn't see how to reach that feather. Finally I decided to give up. I was walking away, cutting my feet on the sharp rock, when suddenly it hit me: The rock I'd been standing on, this whole time, was nothing other than lava that had gotten cold and solidified.

This was high in the mountains, where glaciers and snowfields soared above me like palace walls. I climbed up onto a particularly steep slope and began pounding the snow with my tail until I started an avalanche. Millions of tons of ice and snow thundered down onto the lava flow, throwing up a tremendous blast of steam. For three days and nights I could not see the claws in front of my face for all of the steam, but on the third day it finally cleared away, and I saw a bridge of hardened lava running straight to that black rock. I scampered across (to the extent that a dinosaur can scamper), snatched that golden feather, ran back, and stood in the snow for a while cooling my feet off. Then I marched back to the King of the Birds, who was, of course, astonished.

Next I found myself in the care of the mammals, who were almost all shrews. They led me up into the foothills, to the mouth of a great cave. "Your job," said the King of the Shrews, "is to wait here for Dojo and then defeat him in single combat." Then all the shrews went away and left me there alone.

I waited in front of that cave for three days and three nights, which gave me plenty of time to scope the place out. At first I was rather cocky about this challenge, for it seemed the easiest of the three; while I had no idea who or what Dojo was, I knew that in all the world I had never met my equal when it came to single combat. But on the first day, sitting there on my tail waiting for Dojo, I noticed a sprinkling of small glittering objects on the ground, and examining them carefully I realized that they were, in fact, scales. To be precise, they were dinosaur scales, which I recognized as belonging to Pteranodon, Ankylosaurus, and Utahraptor, and they appeared to have been jarred loose, from their bodies by powerful impacts.

On the second day I prowled around the vicinity and found tremendous gashes in tree trunks, which had undoubtedly been made by Utahraptor as he slashed wildly at Dojo; other trees that had been snapped off entirely by the club at the end of the tail of Ankylosaurus; and long scratches in the earth made by the talons of Pteranodon as she dove again and again at some elusive opponent. At this point, I became concerned. It was clear that all three of my opponents had fought Dojo and lost, so if I lost also (which was inconceivable), I would be even with the others; but the rules of the contest stated that in the event of a tie, all four dinosaurs would be eaten, and the Kingdom of Reptiles would be no more. I spent the night fretting about who or what the terrible Dojo was.

On the third day nothing happened, and I began wondering whether I should go into the cave and look for Dojo. So far the only living thing I had seen around here was a black mouse that occasionally darted out from the rocks at the cave's entrance, foraging for a bit of food. The next time I saw that mouse, I said (speaking softly so as not to scare it), "Say, mouse! Is there anything back inside that cave?"

The black mouse sat up on its haunches, holding a huckleberry between its little hands and nibbling on it. "Nothing special," he said, "just my little dwelling. A fireplace, some tiny pots and pans, a few dried berries, and the rest is full of skeletons."

"Skeletons?" I said. "Of other mice?"

"There are a few mouse skeletons, but mostly they are dinosaurs of one kind or another, primarily meat-eaters."

"Who have become extinct because of the comet," I suggested.

"Oh, pardon me, sir, but I must respectfully inform you that the deaths of these dinosaurs are unrelated to the comet."

"How did they die, then?" I asked.

"I regret to say that I killed them all in self-defense."

"Ah," I said, not quite believing it, "then you must be . . ."

"Dojo the Mouse," he said, "at your service."

"I am terribly sorry to have bothered you, sir," I said, using my best manners, for I could see that this Dojo was an unusually polite sort, "but your fame as a warrior has spread far and wide, and I have come here humbly to seek your advice on how I may become a better warrior myself; for it has not escaped my notice that in the postcomet environment, teeth like carving knives and six tons of muscle may be in some sense outmoded."

What follows is a rather long story, for Dojo had much to teach me and he taught it slowly. Sometime, Nell, I will teach you everything I learned from Dojo; all you need do is ask. But on the third day of my apprenticeship, when I still had not learned anything except humility, good manners, and how to sweep out the cave, I asked Dojo if he would be interested in playing a game of tic-tac-toe. This was a common sport among dinosaurs. We would scratch it out in the mud. (Many paleontologists have been baffled to find tic-tac-toe games littering prehistoric excavations and have chalked it up to the local workers they hire to do their digging and hauling.)

In any case, I explained the rules of the game to Dojo, and he agreed to give it a try. We went down to the nearest mud flat, and there, in plain view of many shrews, I played a game of tic-tac-toe with Dojo and vanquished him, although I will confess it was touch-and-go for a while. It was done; I had defeated Dojo in single combat.

The next morning I excused myself from Dojo's cave and went back down to the beach, where the other three dinosaurs had already gathered, looking much the worse for wear as you can imagine. The King of the Shrews, the King of the Birds, and the Queen of the Ants converged on us with all their armies and crowned me King of the Reptiles, or Tyrannosaurus Rex as we used to say. Then they ate the other three dinosaurs as agreed. Besides me, the only reptiles left were a few snakes, lizards, and turtles, who continue to be my obedient subjects.

I could have lived a luxurious life as King, but by now, Dojo had taught me humility, and so I went back to his cave immediately and spent the next few million years studying his ways. All you need do is ask, Nell, and I will pass his knowledge on to you.

Judge Fang goes for a dinner cruise with a Mandarin; they visit a mysterious ship; a startling discovery; a trap is sprung.

Dr. X's boat was not the traditional sort of wallowing pleasure barge that was fit only for the canals and shallow lakes of the Yangtze's sodden delta; it was a real ocean-going yacht built on Western lines. Judging from the delicacies that began to make their way up to the foredeck shortly after Judge Fang came aboard, the vessel's galley had been retrofitted with all the accoutrements of a professional Chinese kitchen: umbrella-size woks, gas burners like howling turbojets, and extensive storage lockers for innumerable species of fungi as well as bird nests, shark fins, chicken feet, fœtal rats, and odds and ends of many other species both rare and ubiquitous. The courses of the meal were small, numerous, and carefully timed, served up in an array of fine porcelain that could have filled several rooms of the Victoria and Albert Museum, delivered with the precision of surgical air strikes by a team of waiters.

Judge Fang got to eat this way only when someone really important was trying to taint him, and though he had never knowingly allowed his judicial judgment to be swayed, he did enjoy the chow.

They began with tea and some preliminary courses on the foredeck of the yacht, as it made its way down the Huang Pu, with the old European buildings of the Bund on the left, lit up eerily by the wash of colored light radiating from the developments of Pudong, which rose precipitously from the bank on the right. At one point, Dr. X had to excuse himself belowdecks for a few moments. Judge Fang strolled to the very bow of the yacht, nestled himself into the acute angle formed by the converging rails, let the wind tug at his beard, and enjoyed the view. The tallest buildings in Pudong were held up by huge aerostats—vacuum-filled ellipsoids hundreds of stories above street level, much wider than the buildings they supported, and usually covered with lights. Some of these extended out over the river itself. Judge Fang rested his elbows carefully on the rail to maintain his balance, then tilted his head back so that he was staring straight up at the underside of one such, pulsing with oversaturated colored light. The trompe l'oeil was enough to make him dizzy, and so he quickly looked down. Something thumped against the hull of the yacht, and he looked into the water to see a human corpse wrapped up in a white sheet, blundering along a foot or two beneath the surface, dimly luminescent in the light from the building overhead.

In time the yacht made its way out into the estuary of the Yangtze, only a few miles from the East China Sea at this point, miles wide, and much colder and rougher. Judge Fang and Dr. X repaired to a dining cabin belowdecks with panoramic windows that mostly just reflected back the light of the candles and lanterns around the table. Not long after they had taken their seats, the yacht accelerated powerfully, first shooting forward and then leaping up out of the water before resuming its steady, level motion. Judge Fang realized that the yacht was actually a hydrofoil, which had been merely idling along on her hull while they had enjoyed the city view but which had now climbed up out of the water.

The conversation so far had consisted almost entirely of formal courtesies. This had eventually led them into a discussion of Confucian philosophy and traditional culture, clearly a subject of interest to both of them. Judge Fang had complimented the Doctor on his sublime calligraphy, and they talked about that art for a while. Then, obligatorily returning the compliment, Dr. X told the Judge how superbly he was executing his duties as magistrate, particularly given the added difficulty of having to deal with barbarians.

"Your handling of the affair of the girl and the book was, in particular, a credit to your abilities," Dr. X said gravely.

Judge Fang found it interesting that the boy who had actually stolen the book was not mentioned. He supposed that Dr. X was referring not so much to the criminal case as to Judge Fang's subsequent efforts to protect the girl.

"This person is grateful, but all credit should go to the Master," Judge Fang said. "The prosecution of this case was founded entirely upon his principles, as you might have seen, had you been able to do us the honor of joining our discussion of the matter at the House of the Venerable and Inscrutable Colonel."

"Ah, it is indeed a misfortune that I could not attend," the Doctor said, "as it would, no doubt, have helped to improve my own, so imperfect understanding of the Master's principles."

"I meant no such insinuation—rather, that the Doctor might have guided me and my staff to a more nearly adequate resolution of the affair than we were, in fact, able to devise."

"Perhaps it would have been good fortune for both of us for me to have been present in the Colonel's house on that day," Dr. X said, returning neatly to equilibrium. There was silence for a few minutes as a new course was brought out, plum wine poured by the waiter. Then Dr. X continued, "One aspect of the case on which I would have been particularly eager to consult your wisdom would have been the disposition of the book."

So he was still stuck on that book. Though it had been weeks since Dr. X had released any more of those book-hunting mites into the airspace of the Leased Territories, Judge Fang knew that he was still offering a nice bounty to anyone who could tell him the whereabouts of the book in question. Judge Fang was beginning to wonder whether this obsession with the book might be a symptom of a general decline in the Doctor's mental powers.

"Your advice on the subject would have been of inestimable value to me," Judge Fang said, "as this aspect of the case was particularly troublesome for a Confucian judge. If the item of stolen property had been anything other than a book, it would have been confiscated. But a book is different—it is not just a material possession but the pathway to an enlightened mind, and thence to a well-ordered society, as the Master stated many times."

"I see," said Dr. X, slightly taken aback. He seemed genuinely thoughtful as he stroked his beard and stared into the flame of a candle, which had suddenly begun to flicker and gyrate chaotically. It seemed as though the Judge had raised a novel point here, which deserved careful consideration. "Better to leave the book in the hands of one who could benefit from its wisdom, than to let it remain, inert, in a police warehouse."

"That was my no doubt less than perfect conclusion, hastily arrived at," Judge Fang said.

Dr. X continued to ponder the matter for a minute or so. "It does credit to your professional integrity that you are able to focus so clearly upon the case of one small person."

"As you will no doubt appreciate, being a far more accomplished scholar than I, the interests of the society come first. Beside that, the fate of one little girl is nothing. But other things being equal, it is better for society that the girl is educated than that she remain ignorant."

Dr. X raised his eyebrows and nodded significantly at this. The subject did not come up again during the rest of the meal. He assumed that the hydrofoil was swinging around in a lazy circle that would eventually take them back to the mouth of the Huang Pu.

But when the engines were throttled back and the craft settled back onto its hull and began to rock with the waves again, Judge Fang could not see any lights outside the windows. They were nowhere near Pudong, nor any other inhabited land as far as he could tell.

Dr. X gestured out the window at nothing and said, "I have taken the liberty of arranging this visit for you. It touches upon a case that has recently come under your purview and also has to do with a subject that seems of particular interest to you and which we have already discussed this evening."

When Judge Fang followed his host out onto the deck, he was finally able to make out their surroundings. They were on the open ocean, with no land in sight, though the urban glow of Greater Shanghai could clearly be seen to the west. It was a clear night with a nearly full moon that was illuminating the hull of an enormous ship nearby. Even without the moonlight this vessel would have been noticeable for the fact that it blocked out all of the stars in one quadrant of the sky.

Judge Fang knew next to nothing about ships. He had toured an aircraft carrier in his youth, when it docked for a few days at Manhattan. He suspected that this ship was even larger. It was almost entirely dark except for pinpricks of red light here and there, suggesting its size and general shape, and a few horizontal lines of yellow light shining out the windows of its superstructure, many stories above their heads.

Dr. X and Judge Fang were conveyed on board this vessel by a small crew who came out to meet them in a launch. As it drew alongside the Doctor's yacht, the Judge was startled to realize that its crew consisted entirely of young women. Their accents marked them as belonging to an ethnic subgroup, common in the Southeast, that lived almost entirely on the water; but even if they had not spoken, Judge Fang would have inferred this from their nimble handling of the boat.

Within a few minutes, Dr. X and Judge Fang had been conveyed aboard the giant vessel through a hatch set into the hull near the waterline. Judge Fang noted that this was not an old-fashioned steel vessel; it was made of nanotechnological substances, infinitely lighter and stronger. No matter compiler in the world was large enough to compile a ship, so the shipyards in Hong Kong had compiled the pieces one by one, bonded them together, and slid them down the ways into the sea, much as their pre–Diamond Age predecessors had done.

Judge Fang had been expecting that the ship would be some kind of bulk carrier, consisting almost entirely of huge compartments, but the first thing he saw was a long corridor running parallel to the keel, seemingly the length of the entire ship. Young women in white, pink, or occasionally blue dresses and sensible shoes bustled back and forth along this corridor entering into and emerging from its innumerable doors.

There was no formal welcome, no captain or other officers. As soon as the boat girls had assisted them on board, they bowed and took their leave. Dr. X began to amble down the corridor, and Judge Fang followed him. The young women in the white dresses bowed as they approached, then continued on their way, having no time to waste on advanced formalities. Judge Fang had the general sense that they were peasant women, though none of them had the deep tans that were normally a mark of low social status in China. The boat girls had worn blue, so he gathered that this color identified people with nautical or engineering duties. In general, the ones in the pink dresses were younger and slenderer than the ones in the white dresses. The tailoring was different too; the pink dresses closed up the middle of the back, the white ones had two zippers symmetrically placed in the front.

Dr. X chose a door, apparently at random, swung it open, and held it for Judge Fang. Judge Fang bowed slightly and stepped through it into a room about the dimensions of a basketball court, though with a lower ceiling. It was quite warm and humid, and dimly lit. The first thing he saw was more girls in white dresses, bowing to him. Then he realized that the room was otherwise filled with cribs, hundreds of cribs, and that each crib had a perfect little girl baby in it. Young women in pink bustled back and forth with diapers. From place to place, a woman sat beside a crib, the front of her white dress unzipped, breast-feeding a baby.

Judge Fang felt dizzy. He was not willing to acknowledge the reality of what he saw. He had mentally prepared himself for tonight's meeting with Dr. X by reminding himself, over and over, that the Doctor was capable of any trickery, that he could not take anything he saw at face value. But as many first-time fathers had realized in the delivery room, there was something about the sight of an actual baby that focused the mind. In a world of abstractions, nothing was more concrete than a baby.

Judge Fang whirled on his heel and stormed out of the room, brushing rudely past Dr. X. He picked a direction at random and walked, strode, ran down the corridor, past five doors, ten, fifty, then stopped for no particular reason and burst through another door.

It might as well have been the same room.

He felt almost nauseous and had to take stern measures to keep tears from his eyes. He ran out of the room and stormed through the ship for some distance, going up several stairways, past several decks. He stepped into another room, chosen at random, and found the floor covered with cribs, evenly spaced in rows and columns, each one containing a sleeping one-year-old, dressed in fuzzy pink jammies with a hood and a set of mouse ears, each one clutching an identical white security blanket and nestled up with a stuffed animal. Here and there, a young woman in a pink dress sat on the floor on a bamboo mat, reading a book or doing needlework.

One of these women, close to Judge Fang, set her needlework down, rearranged herself into a kneeling position, and bowed to him. Judge Fang gave her a perfunctory bow in return, then padded over to the nearest crib. A little girl with astonishingly thick eyelashes lay there, deeply asleep, breathing regularly, her mouse ears sticking out through the bars of the crib, and as Judge Fang stood and stared at her, he imagined that he could hear the breathing of all the children on this ship at once, combined into a gentle sigh that calmed his heart. All of these children, sleeping so peacefully; everything must be okay. It was going to be fine.

He turned away and saw that the young woman was smiling at him. It was not a flirting smile or a silly girlish smile but a calm and confident smile. Judge Fang supposed that wherever Dr. X was on this ship, he must be smiling in much the same way at this moment.

When Dr. X started the cine, Judge Fang recognized it right away: This was the work of the mediagrapher PhyrePhox, who was still, as far as he knew, languishing in a holding cell in downtown Shanghai. The setting was an outcropping of stones amid a dun, dust-scoured vastitude, somewhere in the interior of China. The camera panned across the surrounding waste, and Judge Fang did not have to be told that these had once been fertile fields, before the water table had been drained out from under them.

A couple of people approached, kicking up a plume of dust as they walked, carrying a small bundle. As they drew closer, Judge Fang could see that they were horrifyingly gaunt, dressed in dirty rags. They came to the center of the rocky outcropping and laid the bundle on the ground, then turned and walked away. Judge Fang turned away from the mediatron and dismissed it with a wave of the hand; he did not have to see it to know that the bundle was a baby, probably female.

"This scene could have happened anytime in the history of China," Dr. X said. They were sitting in a rather spartan wardroom in the vessel's superstructure. "It has always been done with us. The great rebellions of the 1800's were fueled by throngs of angry young men who could not find wives. In the darkest days of the Mao Dynasty's birth control policy, two hundred thousand little ones were exposed in this fashion"—he gestured toward the frozen image on the mediatron—"each year. Recently, with the coming of civil war and the draining of the Celestial Kingdom's aquifers, it has once again become common. The difference is that now the babies are collected. We have been doing it for three years."

"How many?" Judge Fang said.

"A quarter of a million to date," Dr. X said. "Fifty thousand on this ship alone."

Judge Fang had to set his teacup down for a few moments while he grappled with this notion. Fifty thousand lives on this ship alone.

"It won't work," Judge Fang said finally. "You can raise them this way until they are toddlers, perhaps—but what happens when they are older and bigger, and must be educated and given space to run around and play?"

"It is indeed a formidable challenge," Dr. X said gravely, "but I trust you will take to heart the words of the Master: 'Let every man consider virtue as what devolves on himself. He may not yield the performance of it even to his teacher.' I wish you good fortune, Magistrate."

This statement had much the same effect as if Dr. X had hit the Judge over the head with a board: startling, yes, but the full impact was somehow delayed.

"I'm not sure if I follow you, Doctor."

Dr. X crossed his wrists and held them up in the air. "I surrender. You may take me into custody. Torture will not be necessary; I have already prepared a signed confession."

Judge Fang had not hitherto realized that Dr. X had such a well-developed sense of humor. He decided to play along. "As much as I would like to bring you to justice, Doctor, I am afraid that I cannot accept your surrender, as we are out of my jurisdiction."

The Doctor nodded to a waiter, who swung the cabin door open to let in a cool breeze—and a view of the gaudy waterfront of the Leased Territories, suddenly no more than a mile away from them.

"As you can see, I have ordered the ships to come into your jurisdiction, Your Honor," Dr. X said. He gestured invitingly out the door.

Judge Fang stepped out onto an open gangway and looked over the rail to see four other giant ships following in this one's wake.

Dr. X's reedy voice came out through the open door. "You may now take me, and the crew of these ships, to prison for the crime of baby-smuggling. You may also take into custody these ships—and all quarter-million of the little mice on board. I trust you can find qualified caregivers somewhere within your jurisdiction."

Judge Fang gripped the rail with both hands and bowed his head. He was very close to clinical shock. It would be perfectly suicidal to call the Doctor's bluff. The concept of having personal responsibility for so many lives was terrifying enough in and of itself. But to think of what would eventually become of all of these little girls in the hands of the corrupt officialdom of the Coastal Republic . . .

Dr. X continued, "I have no doubt that you will find some way to care for them. As you have demonstrated in the case of the book and the girl, you are too wise a magistrate not to understand the importance of proper upbringing of small children. No doubt you will exhibit the same concern for each one of these quarter of a million infants as you did for one little barbarian girl."

Judge Fang stood up straight, whirled, and strode back through the door. "Shut the door and leave the room," he said to the waiter.

When he and the Doctor were alone together, Judge Fang faced Dr. X, descended to his knees, bent forward, and knocked his forehead against the deck three times.

"Please, Your Honor!" Dr. X exclaimed, "it is I who should be doing honor to you in this way."

"For some time I have been contemplating a change of career," Judge Fang said, rising to an upright kneeling position. He stopped before continuing and thought it through once more. But Dr. X had left him no way out. It would have been uncharacteristic of the Doctor to spring a trap that could be escaped.

As the Master had said, *The mechanic, who wishes to do his work well, must first sharpen his tools. When you are living in any state, take service with the most worthy among its great officers, and make friends of the most virtuous among its scholars.*

"Actually, I am satisfied with my career, but dissatisfied with my tribal affiliation. I have grown disgusted with the Coastal Republic and have concluded that my true home lies in the Celestial Kingdom. I have often wondered whether the Celestial Kingdom is in need of magistrates, even those as poorly qualified as I."

"This is a question I will have to take up with my superiors," Dr. X said. "However, given that the Celestial Kingdom currently has no magistrates whatsoever and therefore no real judicial system, I deem it likely that some role can be found for one with your superb qualifications."

"I see now why you desired the little girl's book so strongly," Judge Fang said. "These young ones must all be educated."

"I do not desire the book itself so much as I desire its designer—the artifex Hackworth," Dr. X said. "As long as the book was somewhere in the Leased Territories, there was some hope that Hackworth could find it—it is the one thing he desires most. If I could have found the book, I could have extinguished that hope, and Hackworth would then have had to approach me, either to get the book back or to compile another copy."

"You desire some service from Hackworth?"

"He is worth a thousand lesser engineers. And because of various hardships over the last few decades, the Celestial Kingdom does not have even that many lesser engineers; they have all been lured away by the promise of riches in the Coastal Republic."

"I will approach Hackworth tomorrow," Judge Fang said. "I will inform him that the man known to the barbarians as Dr. X has found the lost copy of the book."

"Good," Dr. X said, "I shall expect to hear from him."

Hackworth's dilemma; an unanticipated return to
the hong of Dr. X; hitherto unseen ramifications of
Dr. X's premises; a criminal is brought to justice.

Hackworth had some time to run through the logic of the
thing one more time as he waited in the front room of Dr. X's
hong, waiting for the old man to free himself up from what
sounded like a twelve-way cine conference. On his first visit
here he'd been too nervous to see anything, but today he
was settled cozily in the cracked leather armchair in the
corner, demanding tea from the help and thumbing through
Dr. X's books. It was such a relief to have nothing to lose.

Since that deeply alarming visit from Chang, Hackworth had been at his wits' end. He had made an immense
cock-up of the whole thing. Sooner or later his crime would
come out and his family would be disgraced, whether or not
he gave money to Chang. Even if he somehow managed to
get the Primer back, his life was ruined.

When he had received word that Dr. X had won the
race to recover the lost copy of the Primer, the thing had
turned from bad to farcical. He had cut a day at work and
gone for a long hike in the Royal Ecological Conservatory.
By the time he had returned home, sunburned and pleasantly exhausted, he had been in a much better mood. That
Dr. X had the Primer actually improved his situation.

In exchange for the Primer, the Doctor would presumably want something from Hackworth. In this case, it was
not likely to be a mere bribe, as Chang had hinted; all of the
money Hackworth had, or was ever likely to make, could
not be of interest to Dr. X. It was much more likely that the
Doctor would want some sort of a favor—he might ask
Hackworth to design something, to do a little bit of consulting work, as it were. Hackworth wanted so badly to believe
this that he had bolstered the hypothesis with much evidence, real and phantasmal, during the latter part of his
hike. It was well-known that the Celestial Kingdom was
desperately far behind in the nanotechnological arms race;
that Dr. X himself devoted his valuable time to rooting
through the debris of the New Atlantan immune system

proved this. Hackworth's skills could be of measureless value to them.

If this were true, then Hackworth had a way out. He would do some job for the Doctor. In exchange, he would get the Primer back, which was what he wanted more than anything. As part of the deal, Dr. X could no doubt find some way to eliminate Chang from Hackworth's list of things to worry about; Hackworth's crime would never be known to his phyle.

Victorians and Confucians alike had learned new uses for the foyer, anteroom, or whatever it was called, and for the old etiquette of visiting cards. For that matter, all tribes with sophistication in nanotech understood that visitors had to be carefully examined before they could be admitted into one's inner sanctum, and that such examination, carried out by thousands of assiduous reconnaissance mites, took time. So elaborate waiting-room etiquette had flourished, and sophisticated people all over the world understood that when they called upon someone, even a close friend, they could expect to spend some time sipping tea and perusing magazines in a front room infested with unobtrusive surveillance equipment.

One entire wall of Dr. X's front room was a mediatron. Cine feeds, or simple stationary graphics, could be digitally posted on such a wall just as posters and handbills had been in olden times. Over time, if not removed, they tended to overlap each other and build up into an animated collage.

Centered on Dr. X's media wall, partly concealed by newer clips, was a cine clip as ubiquitous in northern China as the face of Mao—Buddha's evil twin—had been in the previous century. Hackworth had never sat and watched it all the way through, but he'd glimpsed it so many times, in Pudong taxicabs and on walls in the Leased Territories, that he knew it by heart. Westerners called it *Zhang at the Shang*.

The setting was the front of a luxury hotel, one of the archipelago of Shangri-Las strung up the Kowloon-Guangzhou superhighway. The horseshoe drive was paved with interlocking blocks, brass door handles gleamed, thickets of tropical flowers sprouted from boat-size planters in the lobby. Men in business suits spoke into cellphones and checked their watches, white-gloved bellhops sprinted into the drive, pulled suitcases from the trunks of red taxicabs, wiped them down with clean moist cloths.

The horseshoe drive was plugged into an eight-lane thoroughfare—not the highway, but a mere frontage road—with a spiked iron fence running down the center to keep pedestrians from crossing in midblock. The pavement, new but already crumbling, was streaked with red dust washed down out of the devastated hills of Guangdong by the latest typhoon.

Traffic suddenly became thin, and the camera panned upstream: Several lanes had been blocked by a swarm of bicycles. Occasionally a red taxi or Mercedes-Benz would squeeze by along the iron fence and burst free, the driver holding down the horn button so furiously that he might detonate the air bag. Hackworth could not hear the sound of the horn, but as the camera zoomed in on the action, it became possible to see one driver take his hand off the horn and turn back to shake his finger at the mob of bicyclists.

When he saw who was pedaling the lead bicycle, he turned away nauseous with fear, and his hand collapsed into his lap like a dead quail.

The leader was a stocky man with white hair, sixtyish but pumping away vigorously on an unexceptional black bicycle, wearing drab worker's clothes. He moved it down the street with deceptive speed and pulled into the horseshoe drive. An embolism of bicycles formed on the street as hundreds tried to crowd in the narrow entrance. And here came another classic moment: The head bellhop skirted his stand-up desk and ran toward the bicyclist, waving him off and hurling abuse in Cantonese—until he got about six feet away and realized he was looking at Zhang Han Hua.

At this point Zhang had no job title, being nominally retired—an ironical conceit that the Chinese premiers of the late twentieth century and early twenty-first had perhaps borrowed from American Mafia bosses. Perhaps they recognized that job titles were beneath the dignity of the most powerful man on earth. People who had gotten this close to Zhang claimed that they never thought about his temporal power—the armies, the nuclear weapons, the secret police. All they could think about was the fact that, during the Great Cultural Revolution, at the age of eighteen, Zhang Han Hua had led his cell of Red Guards into hand-to-hand combat with another cell that they deemed insufficiently fervid, and that, at the conclusion of the battle, Zhang had feasted on the raw flesh of his late adversaries. No one could stand face-to-face with Zhang without imagining the blood streaming down his chin.

The bellhop collapses to his knees and begins literally kowtowing. Zhang looks disgusted, hooks one of his sandaled feet under the bellhop's collarbone, and prods him back upright, then speaks a few words to him in the hillbilly accent of his native Fujien. The bellhop can hardly bow enough on his way back into the hotel; displeasure registers on Zhang's face—all he wants is some fast service. During the next minute or so, progressively higher-ranking hotel officials cringe out the door and abase themselves in front of Zhang, who simply ignores them, looking bored now. No one really knows whether Zhang is a Confucianist or a Maoist at this point in his life, but at this moment it makes no difference: for in the Confucian view of society, as in the Communist, peasants are the highest class and merchants the lowest. This hotel is not for peasants.

Finally a man in a black business suit emerges, preceded and pursued by bodyguards. He looks angrier than Zhang, thinking that he must be the victim of some unforgivable practical joke. This is a merchant among merchants: the fourteenth richest man in the world, the third richest in China. He owns most of the real estate within half an hour's drive of this hotel. He does not break his stride as he steps into the drive and recognizes Zhang; he walks straight up to him and asks him what he wants, why the old man has bothered to come down from Beijing and interfere with his business on his foolish bicycle ride.

Zhang simply steps forward and speaks a few words into the rich man's ear.

The rich man takes a step back, as if Zhang has punched him in the chest. His mouth is open, revealing flawless white teeth, his eyes are not focused. After a few moments, he takes another two steps back, which gives him enough room for his next maneuver: He stoops, puts one knee down, then the other, bends forward at the waist until he is on all fours, then settles himself down full-length on the nicely interlocked paving-stones. He puts his face on the pavement. He kowtows to Zhang Han Hua.

• • •

One by one the Dolbyized voices in the next room signed off until only Dr. X and another gentleman were left, haggling about something desultorily, taking long breaks between volleys of tweeter-busting oratory to stoke pipes, pour tea, or whatever these people did when they were pretending to ignore each other. The discussion petered out rather than building to a violent climax as Hackworth had secretly, mischievously been hoping, and then a young fellow pulled the curtain aside and said, "Dr. X will see you now."

Dr. X was in a lovely, generous mood probably calculated to convey the impression that he'd always known Hackworth would be back. He rustled to his feet, shook Hackworth's hand warmly, and invited him out to dinner "at a place nearby," he said portentously, "of utmost discretion."

It was discreet because one of its cozy private dining rooms was connected directly to one of the back rooms of Dr. X's establishment, so that one could reach it by walking down a sinous inflated Nanobar tube that would have stretched to half a kilometer long if you extricated it from Shanghai, took it to Kansas, and pulled on both ends. Squinting through the translucent walls of the tube as he assisted Dr. X to dinner, Hackworth cloudily glimpsed several dozen people pursuing a range of activities in some half-dozen different buildings, through which Dr. X had apparently procured some kind of right-of-way. Finally it spat them out into a nicely furnished and carpeted dining room, which had been retrofitted with a powered sliding door. The door opened just as they were sitting down, and Hackworth was almost knocked off balance as the tube sneezed nanofiltered wind; a beaming four-foot-tall waitress stood in the doorway, closing her eyes and leaning forward against the anticipated wind-blast. In perfect San Fernando Valley English she said, "Would you like to hear about our specials?"

Dr. X was at pains to reassure Hackworth that he understood and sympathized with his situation; so much so that Hackworth spent much of the time wondering whether Dr. X had already known about it. "Say no more, it is taken care of," Dr. X finally said, cutting Hackworth off in midexplanation, and after that Hackworth was unable to interest

Dr. X in the topic anymore. This was reassuring but unsettling, as he could not avoid the impression that he had just somehow agreed to a deal whose terms had not been negotiated or even thought about. But Dr. X's whole affect seemed to deliver the message that if you were going to sign a Faustian bargain with an ancient and inscrutable Shanghainese organized-crime figure, you could hardly do better than the avuncular Dr. X, who was so generous that he would probably forget about it altogether, or perhaps just stow the favor away in a yellowed box in one of his warrens. By the end of the lengthy meal, Hackworth was so reassured that he had almost forgotten about Lieutenant Chang and the Primer altogether.

Until, that is, the door slid open again to reveal Lieutenant Chang himself.

Hackworth hardly recognized him at first, because he was dressed in a much more traditional outfit than usual: baggy indigo pajamas, sandals, and a black leather skullcap that concealed about seventy-five percent of his knotlike skull. Also, he had begun to grow his whiskers out. Most alarmingly, he had a scabbard affixed to his belt, and the scabbard had a sword in it.

He stepped into the room and bowed perfunctorily to Dr. X, then turned to face Hackworth.

"Lieutenant Chang?" Hackworth said weakly.

"Constable Chang," said the interloper, "of the district tribunal of Shanghai." And then he said the Chinese words that meant Middle Kingdom.

"I thought you were Coastal Republic."

"I have followed my master to a new country," Constable Chang said. "I must regretfully place you under arrest now, John Percival Hackworth."

"On what charge?" Hackworth said, forcing himself to chuckle as if this were all a big practical joke among close friends.

"That on the — day of —, 21—, you did bring stolen intellectual property into the Celestial Kingdom—specifically, into the hong of Dr. X—and did use that property to compile an illegal copy of a certain device known as the *Young Lady's Illustrated Primer*."

There was no point in claiming that this was not true. "But I have come here this evening specifically to regain possession of that same device," Hackworth said, "which is in the hands of my distinguished host here. Certainly you are not intending to arrest the distinguished Dr. X for trafficking in stolen property."

Constable Chang looked expectantly toward Dr. X. The Doctor adjusted his robes and adopted a radiant, grandfatherly smile. "I am sorry to tell you that some reprehensible person has apparently provided you with wrong information," he said. "In fact, I have no idea where the Primer is located."

The dimensions of this trap were so vast that Hackworth's mind was still reeling through it, bouncing haplessly from one wall to another, when he was hauled before the district magistrate twenty minutes later. They had set up a courtroom in a large, ancient garden in the interior of Old Shanghai. It was an open square paved with flat gray stones. At one end was a raised building open to the square on one side, covered with a sweeping tile roof whose corners curved high into the air and whose ridgeline was adorned with a clay frieze portraying a couple of dragons facing off with a large pearl between them. Hackworth realized, dimly, that this was actually the stage of an open-air theatre, which enhanced the impression that he was the sole spectator at an elaborate play written and staged for his benefit. A judge sat before a low, brocade-covered table in the center of the stage, dressed in magnificent robes and an imposing winged hat decorated with a unicorn emblem. Behind him and off to one side stood a small woman wearing what Hackworth assumed were phenomenoscopic spectacles. When Constable Chang had pointed to a spot on the gray flagstones where Hackworth was expected to kneel, he ascended to the stage and took up a position flanking the Judge on the other side. A few other functionaries were arranged on the square, mostly consisting of Dr. X and members of his retinue, arranged in two parallel lines forming a tunnel between Hackworth and the Judge.

Hackworth's initial surge of terror had worn off. He had now entered into morbid fascination with the incredible dreadfulness of his situation and the magnificent performance staged by Dr. X to celebrate it. He knelt silently and waited in a stunned, hyper-relaxed state, like a pithed frog on the dissection table.

Formalities were gone through. The Judge was named Fang and evidently came from New York. The charge was repeated, somewhat more elaborately. The woman stepped forward and introduced evidence: a cine record that was played on a large mediatron covering the back wall of the stage. It was a film of the suspect, John Percival Hackworth, slicing a bit of skin from his hand and giving it to (the innocent) Dr. X, who (not knowing that he was being gulled into committing a theft) extracted a terabyte of hot data from a cocklebur-shaped mite, and so on, and so on.

"The only thing that remains is to prove that this information was, indeed, stolen—though this is strongly implied by the suspect's behavior," Judge Fang said. In support of this assertion, Constable Chang stepped forward and told the story of his visit to Hackworth's flat.

"Mr. Hackworth," said Judge Fang, "would you like to dispute that this property was stolen? If so, we will hold you here while a copy of the information is supplied to Her Majesty's Police; they can confer with your employer to determine whether you did anything dishonest. Would you like us to do that?"

"No, Your Honour," Hackworth said.

"So you are not disputing that the property was stolen, and that you deceived a subject of the Celestial Kingdom into colluding with your criminal behavior?"

"I am guilty as charged, Your Honour," Hackworth said, "and I throw myself on the mercy of the court."

"Very well," Judge Fang said, "the defendant is guilty. The sentence is sixteen strokes of the cane and ten years' imprisonment."

"Goodness gracious!" Hackworth murmured. Inadequate as this was, it was the only thing that came to him.

"Insofar as the strokes of the cane are concerned, since the defendant was motivated by his filial responsibility to his daughter, I will suspend all but one, on one condition."

"Your Honour, I shall endeavour to comply with whatever condition you may choose to impose."

"That you supply Dr. X with the decryption key to the data in question, so that additional copies of the book may be made available to the small children crowding our orphanages."

"This I will gladly do," Hackworth said, "but there are complications."

"I'm waiting," Judge Fang said, not sounding very pleased. Hackworth got the impression that this business about the caning and the Primer was a mere prelude to something bigger, and that the Judge just wanted to get through it.

"In order for me to weigh the seriousness of these complications," Hackworth said, "I will need to know how many copies, approximately, Your Honour intends to make."

"In the range of hundreds of thousands."

Hundreds of thousands! "Please excuse me, but does Your Honour understand that the book is engineered for girls starting around the age of four?"

"Yes."

Hackworth was taken aback. Hundreds of thousands of children of both sexes and all ages would not have been difficult to believe. Hundreds of thousands of four-year-old girls was hard for the mind to grasp. Just one of them was quite a handful. But it was, after all, China.

"The magistrate is waiting," Constable Chang said.

"I must make it clear to Your Honour that the Primer is, in large part, a ractive—that is, it requires the participation of adult ractors. While one or two extra copies might go unnoticed, a large number of them would overwhelm the built-in system provided for paying for such services."

"Then part of your responsibility will be to make alterations in the Primer so that it is suitable for our requirements—we can make do without those parts of the book that depend heavily on outside ractors, and supply our own ractors in some cases," Judge Fang said.

"This should be feasible. I can build in automatic voice-generation capabilities—not as good, but serviceable." At this point, John Percival Hackworth, almost without thinking about it and without appreciating the ramifications of what he was doing, devised a trick and slipped it in under the radar of the Judge and Dr. X and all of the other people in the theatre, who were better at noticing tricks than most other people in the world. "While I'm at it, if it pleases the court, I can also," Hackworth said, most obsequiously, "make changes in the content so that it will be more suitable for the unique cultural requirements of the Han readership. But it will take some time."

"Very well," said Judge Fang, "all but one stroke of the cane are suspended, pending the completion of these alterations. As for the ten years of imprisonment, I am embarrassed to relate that this district, being very small, does not have a prison, and so the suspect will have to be released this evening after the business with the cane is finished. But rest assured, Mr. Hackworth, that your sentence will be served, one way or another."

The revelation that he would be released to his family this very evening hit Hackworth like a deep lungful of opium smoke. The caning went by quickly and efficiently; he did not have time to worry about it, which helped a little. The pain sent him straight into shock. Chang pulled his flaccid body off the rack and bore him over to a hard cot, where he lay semiconscious for a few minutes. They brought him tea—a nice Keemun with distinct lavender notes.

Without further ado he was escorted straight out of the Middle Kingdom and into the streets of the Coastal Republic, which had never been more than a stone's throw away from him during all of these proceedings, but which might as well have been a thousand miles and a thousand years distant. He made his way straight to a public matter compiler, moving in a broad-based gait, with tiny steps, bent over somewhat, and compiled some first-aid supplies—painkillers and some hæmocules that supposedly helped to knit wounds together.

Thoughts about the second part of the sentence, and how he might end up serving it, did not come back to him until he was halfway back across the Causeway, borne swiftly on autoskates, the wind keening through the fabric of his trousers and inflaming the laceration placed neatly across his buttocks, like the track of a router. This time, he was surrounded by a flock of hornet-size aerostats flying in an ellipsoidal formation all around him, hissing gently and invisibly through the night and waiting for an excuse to swarm.

This defensive system, which had seemed formidable to him when he compiled it, now seemed like a pathetic gesture. It might stop a youth gang. But he had insensibly transcended the plane of petty delinquents and moved into a new realm, ruled by powers almost entirely hidden from his ken, and knowable to the likes of John Percival Hackworth only insofar as they perturbed the trajectories of the insignificant persons and powers who happened to be in his vicinity. He could do naught but continue falling through the orbit that had been ordained for him. This knowledge relaxed him more than anything he had learned in many years, and when he returned home, he kissed the sleeping Fiona, treated his wounds with more therapeutic technology from the M.C., covered them with pajamas, and slid beneath the covers. Drawn inward by Gwendolyn's dark radiant warmth, he fell asleep before he had even had time to pray.

More tales from the Primer; the story of Dinosaur and Dojo; Nell learns a thing or two about the art of self-defense; Nell's mother gets, and loses, a worthy suitor; Nell asserts her position against a young bully.

She loved all of her four companions, but her favorite had come to be Dinosaur. At first she'd found him a little scary, but then she'd come to understand that though he could be a terrible warrior, he was on her side and he loved her. She loved to ask him for stories about the old days before the Extinction, and about the time he had spent studying with the mouse Dojo.

There were other students too . . .

said the book, speaking in Dinosaur's voice, as Nell sat by herself in the corner of the playroom.

. . . In those days we had no humans, but we did have monkeys, and one day a little girl monkey came to the entrance of our cave looking quite lonely. Dojo welcomed her inside, which surprised me because I thought Dojo only liked warriors. When the little monkey saw me, she froze in terror, but then Dojo flipped me over his shoulder and bounced me off the walls of the cave a few times to demonstrate that I was fully under control. He made her a bowl of soup and asked her why she was wandering around the forest all by herself. The monkey, whose name was Belle, explained that her mother and her mother's boyfriend had kicked her out of the family tree and told her to go swing on the vines for a couple of hours. But the bigger monkeys hogged all the vines and wouldn't let Belle swing, so Belle wandered off into the forest looking for companionship and got lost, finally stumbling upon the entrance to Dojo's cave.

"You may stay with us for as long as you like," Dojo said. "All we do here is play games, and you are invited to join our games if it pleases you."

"But I am supposed to be home soon," Belle complained. "My mother's boyfriend will give me a whipping otherwise."

"Then I will show you the way from your family tree to my cave and back," Dojo said, "so that you can come here and play with us whenever your mother sends you out."

Dojo and I helped Belle find her way back through the forest to her family tree. On our way back to the cave, I said, "Master, I do not understand."

"What seems to be the trouble?" Dojo said.

"You are a great warrior, and I am studying to become a great warrior myself. Is there a place in your cave for a little girl who just wants to play?"

"I'll be the judge of who does and doesn't make a warrior," Dojo said.

"But we are so busy with our drills and exercises," I said. "Do we have time to play games with the child, as you promised?"

"What is a game but a drill that's dressed up in colorful clothing?" Dojo said. "Besides, given that, even without my instruction, you weigh ten tons and have a cavernous mouth filled with teeth like butcher knives, and that all creatures except me flee in abject terror at the mere sound of your footsteps, I do not think that you should begrudge a lonely little girl some play-time."

At this I felt deeply ashamed, and when we got home, I swept out the cave seven times without even being asked. A couple of days later, when Belle came back to our cave looking lonely and forlorn, we both did our best to make her feel welcome. Dojo began playing some special games with her, which Belle enjoyed so much that she kept coming back, and believe it or not, after a couple of years of this had gone by, Belle was able to flip me over her shoulder just as well as Dojo.

Nell laughed to think of a little girl monkey flipping a great dinosaur over her shoulder. She went back one page and reread the last part more carefully:

A couple of days later, when Belle came back to our cave looking lonely and forlorn, we both did our best to make her feel welcome. Dojo made a special meal in his kitchen out of rice, fish, and vegetables and made sure that she ate every scrap. Then he began playing a special game with her called somersaults.

An illustration materialized on the facing page. Nell recognized the open space in front of the entrance to Dojo's cave. Dojo was sitting up on a high rock giving instructions to Dinosaur and Belle. Dinosaur tried to do a somersault, but his tiny front arms could not support the weight of his massive head, and he fell flat on his face. Then Belle gave it a try and did a perfect somersault.

Nell tried it too. It was confusing at first, because the world kept spinning around her while she did it. She looked at the illustration in the book and saw Belle doing exactly what Nell had done, making all of the same mistakes. Dojo scampered down from his rock and explained how Belle could keep her head and body straight. Nell followed the advice as she gave it another try, and this time it felt better. Before her time was up, she was doing perfect somersaults all over the playground. When she went back to the apartment, Mom wouldn't let her in at first, so she did somersaults up and down the hall for a while. Finally Mom let her in, and when she saw that Nell had gotten sand in her hair and shoes down at the playground, she gave her a spanking and sent her to bed without any food.

But the next morning she went to the M.C. and asked it for the special meal Dojo made for Belle. The M.C. said it couldn't really make fish, but it could make nanosurimi, which was kind of like fish. It could make rice too. Vegetables were a problem. Instead it gave her some green paste she could eat with a spoon. Nell told the M.C. that this was her Belle food and that she was going to have it all the time from now on, and after that the M.C. always knew what she wanted.

Nell didn't call it her magic book anymore, she called it by the name printed plain as day on the title page, which she'd only been able to read recently:

> **YOUNG LADY'S ILLUSTRATED PRIMER**
> **a Propædeutic Enchiridion**
> **in which is told the tale of**
> *Princess Nell*
> **and her various friends, kin, associates, &c.**

The Primer didn't speak to her as often as it used to. She had found that she could often read the words more quickly than the book spoke them, and so she usually ordered it to be silent. She often put it under her pillow and had it read her bedtime stories, though, and sometimes she even woke up in the middle of the night and heard it whispering things to her that she had just been dreaming about.

Tad had long since vanished from their home, though not before giving Mom a broken nose. He'd been replaced by Shemp, who had been replaced by Todd, who had given way to Tony. One day the Shanghai Police had come to arrest Tony, and he had plugged one of them right in the living room with his skull gun, blowing a hole in the guy's stomach so that intestines fell out and trailed down between his legs. The other policemen nailed Tony with a Seven Minute Special and then dragged their wounded comrade out into the hallway, while Tony, bellowing like a cornered, rabid animal, ran into the kitchen and grabbed a knife and began hacking at his chest where he thought the Seven Minute Special had gone into his body. By the time the seven minutes had gone by and the policemen burst back into the apartment, he had dug a hole in his pectoral muscle all the way down to his ribs. He menaced the cops with his bloody knife, and the cop in charge punched in some numbers on a little black box in his hand, and Tony buckled and screamed as a single cookie-cutter detonated inside his thigh. He dropped the knife. The cops rushed in and shrink-wrapped him, then stood around his body, mummified in glistening plastic, and kicked him and stomped him for a minute or two, then finally cut a hole in the plastic so Tony could breathe. They bonded four handles onto the shrink-wrap and then carried him out between them, leaving Nell to clean up the blood in the kitchen and the living room. She wasn't very good at cleaning things up yet and ended up smearing it around. When Mom got home, she screamed and cried for a while and then spanked Nell for making a mess. This made Nell sad, and so she went to her room and picked up the Primer and made up a story of her own, about how the wicked stepmother had made Princess Nell clean up the house and had spanked her for doing it wrong. The Primer made up pictures as she went along. By the time she was finished, she had forgotten about the real things that had happened and remembered only the story she had made up.

After that, Mom swore off men for a while, but after a couple of months she met a guy named Brad who was actually nice. He had a real job as a blacksmith in the New Atlantis Clave, and one day he took Nell to work with him and showed her how he nailed iron shoes onto the hooves of the horses. This was the first time Nell had actually seen a horse, and so she did not pay much attention to Brad and his hammers and nails. Brad's employers had a giant house with vast green fields, and they had four kids, all bigger than Nell, who would come out in fancy clothes and ride those horses.

But Mom broke up with Brad; she didn't like crafts-men, she said, because they were too much like actual Victorians, always spouting all kinds of crap about how one thing was better than another thing, which eventually led, she explained, to the belief that some people were better than others. She took up with a guy named Burt who even-tually moved in with them. Burt explained to Nell and Harv that the house needed discipline and that he intended to provide it, and after that he spanked them all the time, sometimes on the butt and sometimes on the face. He spanked Mom a lot too.

Nell was spending much more time at the playground, where it was easier for her to do all of the exercises that Dojo was teaching to Belle. She also played games with the other kids sometimes. One day she was playing tetherball with a friend of hers and kept beating her every time. Then a boy came up, a boy bigger than either Nell or her friend, and insisted that he be allowed to play. Nell's friend gave up her place, and then Nell played against the boy, whose name was Kevin. Kevin was a big solid boy who was proud of his bulk and his strength, and his philosophy of tetherball was winning through intimidation. He would grab the ball, wind up melodramatically, baring his teeth and getting his face bright red, then smash the ball with a windmill punch, complete with sound effects that always showered the ball with spit. The performance was so impressive that many children just stood and watched it in awe, afraid to get in the way of the tetherball, and after that Kevin would just keep smashing the ball faster and faster on each revolution while vomiting profanity at his opponent. Nell knew that Kevin's mom had lived with a lot of the same guys that Nell's mom had lived with; he frequently sported black eyes that he certainly hadn't gotten on the playground.

Nell had always been afraid of Kevin. But today when he wound up for his big serve, he just looked silly; kind of like Dinosaur did sometimes when sparring with Belle. The ball swung toward her, dewy with spit and not really going all that fast. Kevin was shouting things at her, calling her a cunt and other words, but for some reason Nell didn't hear it and didn't care, she just lunged toward the ball and punched it hard, putting her whole body behind her knuckles in a straight line, just as Dojo taught. She hit the ball so hard, she didn't even feel it; it shot up in a wide arc that took it behind and above Kevin's head, and after that all she had to do was give it a few more slaps as it whizzed by, and she'd won the game.

"Two out of three," Kevin said, and they played again, with the same result. Now all the kids were laughing at Kevin, and he lost his temper, turned bright red, and charged at Nell.

But Nell had watched Kevin use this tactic on other kids, and she knew that it only worked because usually the kids were too scared to move. Dojo had explained to Belle that the best way to fight Dinosaur was simply to get out of his way and let his own strength defeat him, so that's what Nell did with Kevin: stepped aside at the last minute, made one foot into a hook, and tripped him. Kevin smashed tremendously into a swingset, gathered himself up, and charged a second time. Nell dodged him and tripped him again.

"Okay," Kevin said, "you win." He approached Nell holding out his right hand to shake. But Nell had seen this one too, and she knew it was a trick. She reached out with her right hand as if she were going to shake. But as Kevin was groping at this bait, every muscle in his arm tense, Nell turned her palm toward the floor and drew her hand down, then back across the middle of her body. She was watching Kevin as she did this and saw that his eyes were tracking her hand, mesmerized. She continued to move her hand around in a long ellipse, turning her palm upward, thrusting it forward, poking her fingers into Kevin's staring eyes.

He put his hands to his face. She kicked him between the legs as hard as she could, taking her time and striking the target precisely. As he bent over, she grabbed his hair and kneed him in the face, then shoved him down on his butt and left him there, too surprised, for the moment, to start bawling.

Hackworth lunches in distinguished company; a disquisition on hypocrisy; Hackworth's situation develops new complications.

Hackworth arrived at the pub first. He got a pint of porter at the bar, cask-conditioned stuff from the nearby Dovetail community, and strolled around the place for a few minutes while he waited. He had been fidgeting at his desk all morning and enjoyed the opportunity to stretch his legs. The place was done up like an ancient London publican house circa World War II, complete with fake bomb damage to one corner of the structure and taped X's over each windowpane —which only made Hackworth think of Dr. X. Autographed photos of British and American airmen were stuck up on the walls here and there, along with other miscellany recalling the heyday of Anglo-American cooperation:

**SEND
a gun
TO DEFEND
A BRITISH HOME
British civilians, faced with threat of
invasion, desperately need arms for
the defense of their homes.
YOU CAN AID
American Committee for Defense of British Homes**

Bowler hats hung in clusters from poles and wall hooks all over the room, like great bunches of black grapes. A lot of engineers and artifexes seemed to come to this place. They hunched over pints of beer at the bar and delved into steak-and-kidney pies at the little tables, chatting and chuckling. There was nothing prepossessing about the place or its patrons, but Hackworth knew that the odds and ends of nanotechnological lore collected in the heads of these middle-class artisans was what ultimately kept New Atlantis wealthy and secure. He had to ask himself why he hadn't been satisfied with simply being one of them. John Percival Hackworth projected his thoughts into matter and did it better than anyone else in this place. But he had felt the need to go beyond that—he had wanted to reach beyond mere matter and into someone's soul.

Now, whether he wanted to or not, he was going to reach hundreds of thousands of souls.

The men at the tables watched him curiously, then nodded politely and looked away when he caught their eye. Hackworth had noticed a full-lane Rolls-Royce parked in front of the place on his way in. Someone important was here, evidently in a back room. Hackworth and everyone else in the place knew it, and they were all in a heightened state of alertness, wondering what was up.

Major Napier rode up on a standard-issue cavalry chevaline and came in at noon on the dot, pulling off his officer's hat and exchanging a hilarious greeting with the barkeep. Hackworth recognized him because he was a hero, and Napier recognized Hackworth for reasons left provocatively unspecified.

Hackworth translated his pint to the left and exchanged a vigorous handshake with Major Napier in front of the bar. They strolled toward the back of the place, exchanging some hearty, forgettable, balderdash-laden banter. Napier stepped nimbly in front of him and pulled open a small door in the back wall. Three steps led down into a little snuggery with mullioned windows on three sides and a single copper-covered table in the middle. A man was sitting by himself at the table, and as Hackworth descended the steps, he realized that it was Lord Alexander Chung-Sik Finkle-McGraw, who stood up, returned his bow, and greeted him with a warm and hearty handshake, taking such evident measures to put Hackworth at ease that, in some respects, the opposite result was achieved.

More banter, a bit more restrained. A waiter came in; Hackworth ordered a steak sandwich, today's special, and Napier simply nodded to the waiter to indicate his complete agreement, which Hackworth took as a friendly gesture. Finkle-McGraw declined to eat anything.

Hackworth was not really hungry anymore. It was clear that Royal Joint Forces Command had figured out at least some of what had happened, and that Finkle-McGraw knew about it too. They had decided to approach him privately instead of simply lowering the boom on him and drumming him out of the phyle. This should have filled him with boundless relief, but it didn't. Things had seemed so simple after his prosecution in the Celestial Kingdom. Now he suspected they were about to get infinitely more complicated.

"Mr. Hackworth," Finkle-McGraw said after the pleasantries had petered out, speaking in a new tone of voice, a the-meeting-will-come-to-order sort of voice, "please favour me with your opinion of hypocrisy."

"Excuse me. Hypocrisy, Your Grace?"

"Yes. You know."

"It's a vice, I suppose."

"A little one or a big one? Think carefully—much hinges upon the answer."

"I suppose that depends upon the particular circumstances."

"That will never fail to be a safe answer, Mr. Hackworth," the Equity Lord said reproachfully. Major Napier laughed, somewhat artificially, not knowing what to make of this line of inquiry.

"Recent events in my life have renewed my appreciation for the virtues of doing things safely," Hackworth said. Both of the others chuckled knowingly.

"You know, when I was a young man, hypocrisy was deemed the worst of vices," Finkle-McGraw said. "It was all because of moral relativism. You see, in that sort of a climate, you are not allowed to criticise others—after all, if there is no absolute right and wrong, then what grounds is there for criticism?"

Finkle-McGraw paused, knowing that he had the full attention of his audience, and began to withdraw a calabash pipe and various related supplies and implements from his pockets. As he continued, he charged the calabash with a blend of leather-brown tobacco so redolent that it made Hackworth's mouth water. He was tempted to spoon some of it into his mouth.

"Now, this led to a good deal of general frustration, for people are naturally censorious and love nothing better than to criticise others' shortcomings. And so it was that they seized on hypocrisy and elevated it from a ubiquitous peccadillo into the monarch of all vices. For, you see, even if there is no right and wrong, you can find grounds to criticise another person by contrasting what he has espoused with what he has actually done. In this case, you are not making any judgment whatsoever as to the correctness of his views or the morality of his behaviour—you are merely pointing out that he has said one thing and done another. Virtually all political discourse in the days of my youth was devoted to the ferreting out of hypocrisy.

"You wouldn't believe the things they said about the original Victorians. Calling someone a Victorian in those days was almost like calling them a fascist or a Nazi."

Both Hackworth and Major Napier were dumbfounded. "Your Grace!" Napier exclaimed. "I was naturally aware that their moral stance was radically different from ours—but I am astonished to be informed that they actually *condemned* the first Victorians."

"Of course they did," Finkle-McGraw said.

"Because the first Victorians were hypocrites," Hackworth said, getting it.

Finkle-McGraw beamed upon Hackworth like a master upon his favored pupil. "As you can see, Major Napier, my estimate of Mr. Hackworth's mental acuity was not ill-founded."

"While I would never have supposed otherwise, Your Grace," Major Napier said, "it is nonetheless gratifying to have seen a demonstration." Napier raised his glass in Hackworth's direction.

"Because they were hypocrites," Finkle-McGraw said, after igniting his calabash and shooting a few tremendous fountains of smoke into the air, "the Victorians were despised in the late twentieth century. Many of the persons who held such opinions were, of course, guilty of the most nefandous conduct themselves, and yet saw no paradox in holding such views because they were not hypocrites themselves—they took no moral stances and lived by none."

"So they were morally superior to the Victorians—" Major Napier said, still a bit snowed under.

"—even though—in fact, *because*—they had no morals at all."

There was a moment of silent, bewildered head-shaking around the copper table.

"We take a somewhat different view of hypocrisy," Finkle-McGraw continued. "In the late-twentieth-century *Weltanschauung*, a hypocrite was someone who espoused high moral views as part of a planned campaign of deception—he never held these beliefs sincerely and routinely violated them in privacy. Of course, most hypocrites are not like that. Most of the time it's a spirit-is-willing, flesh-is-weak sort of thing."

"That we occasionally violate our own stated moral code," Major Napier said, working it through, "does not imply that we are insincere in espousing that code."

"Of course not," Finkle-McGraw said. "It's perfectly obvious, really. No one ever said that it was easy to hew to a strict code of conduct. Really, the difficulties involved—the missteps we make along the way—are what make it interesting. The internal, and *eternal*, struggle, between our base impulses and the rigorous demands of our own moral system is quintessentially human. It is how we conduct ourselves in that struggle that determines how we may in time be judged by a higher power."

All three men were quiet for a few moments, chewing mouthfuls of beer or smoke, pondering the matter.

"I cannot help but infer," Hackworth finally said, "that the present lesson in comparative ethics—which I thought was nicely articulated and for which I am grateful—must be thought to pertain, in some way, to my situation."

The other men raised their eyebrows in a not very convincing display of mild astonishment. The Equity Lord turned toward Major Napier, who took the floor briskly and cheerfully.

"We do not know all the particulars of your situation—as you know, Atlantan subjects are entitled to polite treatment from all branches of H.M.'s Joint Forces unless they violate the tribal norms, and that means, in part, that we don't go round putting people under high-res surveillance just because we are curious about their, er, *avocations.* In an era when everything can be surveiled, all we have left is politeness. However, we do quite naturally monitor comings and goings through the border. And not long ago, our curiosity was piqued by the arrival of one Lieutenant Chang of the District Magistrate's Office. He was also clutching a plastic bag containing a rather battered top hat. Lieutenant Chang proceeded directly to your flat, spent half an hour there, and departed, minus the hat."

The steak sandwiches arrived at the beginning of this bit of exposition. Hackworth began messing about with condiments, as if he could belittle the importance of this conversation by paying equal attention to having just the right goodies on his sandwich. He fussed with his pickle for a while, then began examining the bottles of obscure sauces arrayed in the center of the table, like a sommelier appraising a wine cellar.

"I had been mugged in the Leased Territories," Hackworth said absently, "and Lieutenant Chang recovered my hat, somewhat later, from a ruffian." He had fixed his gaze, for no special reason, on a tall bottle with a paper label printed in an ancient crabbed typeface. *"McWhorter's Original Condiment"* was written large, and everything else was too small to read. The neck of the bottle was also festooned with black-and-white reproductions of ancient medals awarded by pre-Enlightenment European monarchs at exhibitions in places like Riga. Just a bit of violent shaking and thwacking ejected a few spurts of the ochre slurry from the pore-size orifice at the top of the bottle, which was guarded by a quarter-inch encrustation. Most of it hit his plate, and some impacted on his sandwich.

"Yes," Major Napier said, reaching into his breast pocket and taking out a folded sheet of smart foolscap. He told it to uncrease itself on the table and prodded it with the nib of a silver fountain pen the size of an artillery shell. "Gatehouse records indicate that you do not venture into the L.T. often, Mr. Hackworth, which is certainly understandable and speaks well of your judgment. There have been two forays in recent months. On the first of these, you left in midafternoon and returned late at night bleeding from lacerations that seemed to have been recently incurred, according to the"—Major Napier could not repress a tiny smile—"evocative description logged by the border patrol officer on duty that night. On the second occasion, you again left in the afternoon and returned late, this time with a single deep laceration across the buttocks—not visible, of course, but picked up by surveillance."

Hackworth took a bite of his sandwich, correctly anticipating that the meat would be gristly and that he would have plenty of time to think about his situation while his molars subdued it. He did have plenty of time, as it turned out; but as frequently happened to him in these situations, he could not bring his mind to bear on the subject at hand. All he could think about was the taste of the sauce. If the manifest of ingredients on the bottle had been legible, it would have read something like this:

Water, blackstrap molasses, imported habanero peppers, salt, garlic, ginger, tomato puree, axle grease, real hickory smoke, snuff, butts of clove cigarettes, Guinness Stout fermentation dregs, uranium mill tailings, muffler cores, monosodium glutamate, nitrates, nitrites, nitrotes and nitrutes, nutrites, natrotes, powdered pork nose hairs, dynamite, activated charcoal, match-heads, used pipe cleaners, tar, nicotine, single-malt whiskey, smoked beef lymph nodes, autumn leaves, red fuming nitric acid, bituminous coal, fallout, printer's ink, laundry starch, drain cleaner, blue chrysotile asbestos, carrageenan, BHA, BHT, and natural flavorings.

He could not help smiling at his own complete haplessness, both now and on the night in question. "I will concede that my recent trips to the Leased Territories have not left me disposed to make any more." This comment produced just the right sort of clubby, knowing smiles from his interlocutors. Hackworth continued, "I saw no reason to report the mugging to Atlantan authorities—"

"There *was* no reason," Major Napier said. "Shanghai Police might have been interested, though."

"Ah. Well, I did not report it to them either, simply because of their reputation."

This bit of routine wog-bashing would have elicited naughty laughter from most. Hackworth was struck by the fact that neither Finkle-McGraw nor Napier rose to the bait.

"And yet," Napier said, "Lieutenant Chang belied that reputation, did he not, when he went to the trouble of bringing your hat—now worthless—to you in person, when he was off-duty, rather than simply mailing it or for that matter throwing it away."

"Yes," Hackworth said, "I suppose he did."

"We found it rather singular. While we would not dream of enquiring into the particulars of your conversation with Lieutenant Chang, or of prying into your affairs in any other way, it did occur to some suspicious minds here—ones that have perhaps been exposed to the Oriental milieu for too long—that Lieutenant Chang's intentions might not be entirely honourable, and that he might bear watching. At the same time, for your own protection, we decided to keep a motherly eye on you during any later sojourns beyond the dog pod grid." Napier did some more scrawling on his paper. Hackworth watched his pale blue eyes hopjumping back and forth as various records materialized on its surface.

"You took one more trip to the Leased Territories— actually, across the Causeway, across Pudong, into the old city of Shanghai," Napier said, "where our surveillance machinery either malfunctioned or was destroyed by countermeasures. You returned several hours later with a chunk taken out of your arse." Napier suddenly slapped the paper down on his desk, looked up at Hackworth for the first time in quite a while, blinking his eyes a couple of times as he refocused, and relaxed against the sadistically designed wooden back of his chair. "Hardly the first time that one of H.M. subjects has gone for a nocturnal prowl on the wild side and come back having suffered a beating—but normally the beatings are much less severe, and normally they are bought and paid for by the victim. My assessment of you, Mr. Hackworth, is that you are not interested in that particular vice."

"Your assessment is correct, sir," Hackworth said, a bit hotly. This self-vindication left him in the position of having to provide some better explanation of the puckered cicatrice running across his buttocks. Actually, he didn't have to explain anything—this was an informal luncheon, not a police interrogation—but it would not do much for his already tatterdemalion credibility if he let it pass without comment. As if to emphasize this fact, both of the other men were now silent for some time.

"Do you have any more recent intelligence about the man named Chang?" Hackworth asked.

"It is singular that you should ask. As it happens, the whilom Lieutenant; his colleague, a woman named Pao; and their superior, a magistrate named Fang, all resigned on the same day, about a month ago. They have resurfaced in the Middle Kingdom."

"You must have been struck by the coincidence—that a judge who is in the habit of caning people enters the service of the Middle Kingdom, and shortly thereafter, a New Atlantan engineer returns from a visit to said clave bearing marks of having been caned."

"Now that you mention it, it is quite striking," Major Napier said.

The Equity Lord said, "It might lead one to conclude that the engineer in question owed some debt to a powerful figure within that clave, and that the judicial system was being used as a sort of collection agency."

Napier was ready for his leg of the relay. "Such an engineer, if one existed, might be surprised to know that John Zaibatsu is intensely curious about the Shanghainese gentleman in question—an honest-to-god Mandarin of the Celestial Kingdom, if he is who we think he is—and that we have been trying for some time, with little success, to obtain more information about his activities. So, if the Shanghainese gentleman were to request that our engineer partake in activities that we would normally consider unethical or even treasonous, we might take an uncharacteristically forgiving stance. Provided, that is, that the engineer kept us well-informed."

"I see. Would that be something like being a double agent, then?" Hackworth said.

Napier winced, as if he were being caned himself. "It is a crashingly unsubtle phrase. But I can forgive your using it in this context."

"Would John Zaibatsu then make some kind of formal commitment to this arrangement?"

"It is not done that way," Major Napier said.

"I was afraid of that," Hackworth said.

"Typically such commitments are superfluous, as in most cases the party has very little choice in the matter."

"Yes," Hackworth said, "I see what you mean."

"The commitment is a moral one, a question of honour," Finkle-McGraw said. "That such an engineer falls into trouble is evidence of mere hypocrisy on his part. We are inclined to overlook this sort of routine caducity. If he goes on to behave treasonously, then that of course is a different matter; but if he plays his role well and provides information of value to Her Majesty's Joint Forces, then he has rather deftly parlayed a small error into a grand act of heroism. You may be aware that it is not unusual for heroes to receive knighthoods, among other more tangible rewards."

For a few moments, Hackworth was too startled to speak. He had expected exile and perhaps deserved it. Mere forgiveness was more than he could have hoped for. But Finkle-McGraw was giving him the opportunity for something much greater: a chance to enter the lower ranks of the nobility. An equity stake in the tribal enterprise. There was only one answer he could make, and he blurted it out before he had time to lose his nerve.

"I thank you for your forbearance," he said, "and I accept your commission. Please consider me to be at Her Majesty's service from this moment forward."

"Waiter! Bring some champagne, please," Major Napier called. "I believe we have something to celebrate."

*From the Primer, the arrival of a sinister Baron;
Burt's disciplinary practices; the plot against the
Baron; practical application of ideas gleaned
from the Primer; flight.*

Outside the Dark Castle, Nell's wicked stepmother continued to live as she pleased and to entertain visitors. Every few weeks a ship would sail over the horizon and anchor in the little bay where Nell's father had once kept his fishing boat. An important fellow would be rowed ashore by his servants and would live in the house with Nell's stepmother for a few days, weeks, or months. In the end, she always got into shouting arguments with her visitors, which Nell and Harv could hear even through the thick walls of the Dark Castle, and when the visitor had gotten sick of it, he would row back out to his ship and sail away, leaving the wicked Queen heartbroken and sobbing on the shore. Princess Nell, who had hated her stepmother at first, came to feel sorry for her in a way and to realize that the Queen was locked into a prison of her own making, even darker and colder than the Dark Castle itself.

One day a barentine with red sails appeared in the bay, and a red-headed man with a red beard came to shore. Like the other visitors, he moved in with the Queen and lived with her for a time. Unlike the others, he was curious about the Dark Castle and would ride up to its gates every day or two, rattle the door handles, and walk all around it, staring at its high walls and towers.

In the third week of the man's visit, Nell and Harv were astonished to hear the twelve locks on the gate being opened, one by one. In walked the red-headed man. When he saw Nell and Harv, he was just as astonished as they were. "Who are you?" he demanded in a low, gruff voice.

Princess Nell was about to answer, but Harv stopped her. "You are the visitor here," he said. "Identify yourself."

At this, the man's face turned almost as red as his hair, and he strode forward and struck Harv across the face with his mailed fist. "I am Baron Jack," he said, "and you may consider that my calling card." Then, just for spite, he aimed a kick at Princess Nell; but his foot in its heavy metal armor was too slow, and Princess Nell, remembering the lessons Dinosaur had taught her, dodged it easily. "You must be the two brats the Queen told me about," he said. "You were supposed to be dead by now—eaten up by trolls. Well, tonight you shall be, and tomorrow the castle will be mine!" He seized Harv and began to bind his arms with a stout rope. Princess Nell, forgetting her lessons, tried to stop him, and in a flash he had grabbed her by the hair and tied her up as well. Soon both of them were lying helpless on the ground. "We'll see how well you can fight off the trolls tonight!" Baron Jack said, and giving each of them a slap and a kick just for spite, he strode off through the gate and locked the twelve locks again.

Princess Nell and Harv had a long wait until the sun went down and her Night Friends came to life and untied her and Harv. Princess Nell explained that the evil Queen had a new lover who intended to take the Dark Castle for himself.

"We must fight him," Purple said.

Princess Nell and all the other friends were startled to hear these words, for usually Purple was patient and wise and counseled against fighting. "There are many shades of gray in the world," she explained, "and many times when the hidden way is best; but some things are purely evil and must be fought to the death."

"If he were but a man, I could crush him with one foot," Dinosaur said, "but not during the daytime; and even at night, the Queen is a sorceress, and her friends have mickle powers. We will need a plan."

That night there was hell to pay. Kevin, the boy whom Nell had defeated over tetherball, had learned everything he knew about being a bully from none other than Burt, because Burt had lived with Kevin's mom for a while and might even have been Kevin's dad, so Kevin went to Burt and told him that he'd been beaten up by Harv and Nell acting together. That night, both Harv and Nell got the worst spanking of their lives. It went on so long that finally Mom tried to step in and get Burt to calm down. But Burt slapped Mom across the face and shoved her down on the floor. Finally, Harv and Nell ended up in their room together. Burt was in the living room having a few beers and getting into a Burly Scudd ractive. Mom had run out of the apartment, and they had no idea where she was.

One of Harv's eyes was swollen shut, and one hand was not working. Nell was terribly thirsty, and when she went to pee, it came out red. Also she had burns on her arms from Burt's cigarettes, and the pain just kept getting worse.

They could sense Burt's movements through the wall, and they could hear the Burly Scudd ractive. Harv could tell when Burt had gone to sleep because a single-user ractive eventually went into pause mode if the user stopped racting. When they were sure Burt was sleeping, they stole into the kitchen to get some medicine from the M.C.

Harv got a bandage for his wrist and a cold-pack for his eye, and he asked the M.C. for something to put on their cuts and burns so they wouldn't get infected. The M.C. displayed a whole menu of mediaglyphs for different kinds of remedies. Some of them were premiums, which you had to pay money for, and there were a few freebies. One of the freebies was a cream that came in a tube, like toothpaste. They took it back to their room and took turns spreading it on each other's cuts and burns.

Nell lay quietly in bed until she could tell that Harv had gone to sleep. Then she got out the *Young Lady's Illustrated Primer*.

When Baron Jack came back to the castle the following day, he was angry to find the ropes piled on the ground, and no bones cracked and gnawed by trolls. He stormed into the castle with drawn sword, bellowing that he would kill Harv and Princess Nell himself; but entering into the dining room, he stopped in wonderment as he saw a great feast that had been laid out on the table for him: loaves of brown bread, pots of fresh butter, roasted fowl, a suckling pig, grapes, apples, cheese, broth, and wine. Standing next to the table were Harv and Princess Nell, dressed in servants' uniforms.

"Welcome to your castle, Baron Jack," Princess Nell said. "As you can see, we your new servants have prepared a small snack that we hope will be to your liking." Actually, Duck had prepared all of the food, but as this was the daytime, she had turned back into a little toy along with all the other Night Friends.

Baron Jack's anger subsided as his greedy eyes traveled over the feast. "I will try a few bites," he said, "but if any of the food is not perfect, or if you do not serve me to my liking, I'll have your heads spiked on the gates of the castle like that!" and he snapped his fingers in Harv's face.

Harv looked angry and was about to blurt out something

terrible, but Princess Nell remembered the words of Purple, who said that the hidden way was best, and she said in a sweet voice, "For imperfect service we would deserve nothing better."

Baron Jack began to eat, and such was the excellence of Duck's cooking that once he started, he could barely stop himself. He sent Harv and Nell scurrying back to the kitchen again and again to bring him more food, and though he constantly found fault with them and rose from his chair to give them beatings, he had apparently decided that they were worth more to him alive than dead.

"Sometimes he would burn their skin with cigarettes too," Nell whispered.

The letters changed on the page of the Primer.

"Princess Nell's pee-pee turned red too," Nell said, "because the Baron was a very bad man. And his real name wasn't Baron Jack. His real name was Burt."

As Nell spoke the words, the story changed in the Primer.

"And Harv couldn't use his arm because of the wrist, so he had to carry everything with one hand, and that's because Burt was a bad man and he hurt it really bad," Nell said.

After a long silence, the Primer began to speak again, but the lovely voice of the Vicky woman who told the story sounded thick and hoarse all of a sudden and would stumble in the middle of sentences.

Baron Burt ate all day, until finally the sun went down.

"Bar the doors," said a high squeaking voice, "or the trolls will be after us!"

These words came from a little man in a suit and top hat who had just scurried through the doors and was now eyeing the sunset nervously.

"Who is that pipsqueak interrupting my dinner!?" roared Baron Burt.

"This is our neighbor," Princess Nell said. "He comes to visit us in the evening. Please let him sit by the fire."

Baron Burt looked a bit suspicious, but at this moment Harv set a delicious strawberry cheesecake in front of him, and he forgot about the little man entirely, until a few minutes later, when the high squeaking voice piped up again:

There once was a Baron named Burt
Who was so tough he couldn't be hurt
And could wrestle a bear; but I think
After two or three drinks
Like a child he'd throw up on his shirt.

"Who dares mock the Baron!?" bellowed Baron Burt, and looked down to see the new visitor leaning insouciantly on his walking stick and raising a glass as if to toast his health.

Your Majesty, don't be upset
And please feel free now to get
Into bed; for it's been a long day
And you're in a bad way
And your trousers you're soon going to wet.

"Bring me a cask of ale!" shouted Baron Burt. "And bring another for this upstart, and we'll see who can hold his drink."

Harv rolled two casks of strong ale into the room. Baron Burt raised one to his lips and drained it in single pull. The little man on the floor then did the same.

Two skins of wine were then brought, and once again both Baron Burt and the little man easily finished them.

Finally, two bottles of strong liquor were brought, and the Baron and the little man took turns drinking one swallow at a time until the bottles were empty. The Baron was confounded by the small man's ability to drink; but there he stood, upright and sober, while Baron Burt was becoming very drunk.

Finally the little man pulled a small bottle from his pocket and said,

For a young man, ale is fine
While grown-ups much prefer wine
Liquor's a thing
That's fit for a king
But it's kid stuff compared to moonshine.

The little man uncorked the bottle and took a drink, then handed it to Baron Burt. The Baron took one swallow and fell asleep instantly in his chair.

"Mission accomplished," said the little man, sweeping off

his top hat with a deep bow, revealing a set of long furry ears—for he was none other than Peter in disguise.

Princess Nell ran back to the kitchen to tell Dinosaur, who was sitting by the fire with a long wooden pole, poking it in the coals and turning it round and round to make the point very sharp. "He's asleep!" she whispered.

Miranda, sitting in her stage at the Parnasse, felt an overwhelming sense of relief as her next line appeared on the prompter. She took a deep breath before she delivered it, closed her eyes, settled her mind, tried to put herself there in the Dark Castle. She looked deep into Princess Nell's eyes and sold the line with every scrap of talent and technique she had.

"Good!" said Dinosaur. "Then the time has come for you and Harv to flee from the Dark Castle! You must be as stealthy as you can. I will come out later and join you."

Please get out of there. Please run away. Get out of that chamber of horrors where you've been living, Nell, and get to an orphanage or a police station or something, and I will find you. No matter where you are, I'll find you.

Miranda had it worked out already: she could compile an extra mattress, put Nell on the floor of her bedroom and Harv in the living room of her flat. If only she could figure out who the hell they were.

Princess Nell hadn't responded. She was thinking, which was the wrong thing to do right now. *Get out. Get out.*

"Why are you putting that stick in the fire?"

"It is my duty to see that the evil Baron never troubles you again," Miranda said, reading from the prompter.

"But what are you going to do with that stick?"

Please don't do this. It's not the time to ask why. "You must make haste!" Miranda read, trying once again to sell the line as best she could. But Princess Nell had been playing with the Primer for a couple of years now and had gotten in the habit of asking endless questions.

"Why are you making the stick sharper?"

"This is how Odysseus and I took care of the Cyclops," Dinosaur said. *Shit. It's going all wrong.*

"What's Cyclops?" Nell said.

A new illustration grew on the next page, facing the illustration of Dinosaur by the fire. It was a picture of a one-eyed giant herding some sheep.

Dinosaur told the story of how Odysseus killed the Cyclops with a pointed stick, just as he was about to do to Baron Burt. Nell insisted on hearing what happened after that. One story led to another. Miranda tried to tell the stories as fast as she could, tried to put a tone of boredom and impatience into her voice, which wasn't easy because she was actually on the verge of panic. She had to get Nell out of that apartment before Burt woke up from his drunk.

The eastern sky was beginning to glow . . .

Shit. Get out of there, Nell!

Dinosaur was just in the middle of telling Princess Nell about a witch who turned men into swine when suddenly, poof, he turned back into a stuffed animal. The sun had come up.

Nell was a bit startled by this turn of events, and closed the Primer for a while, and sat in the dark listening to Harv wheeze and Burt snore in the next room. She'd been looking forward to the moment when Dinosaur would kill Baron Burt, just as Odysseus had done to the Cyclops. But now it wasn't going to happen. Baron Burt would wake up, realize he'd been tricked, and hurt them worse. They'd be stuck in the Dark Castle forever.

Nell was tired of being in the Dark Castle. She knew it was time to get out.

She opened the Primer.

"Princess Nell knew what she had to do," Nell said. Then she closed the Primer and left it on her pillow.

Even if she hadn't learned how to read pretty well, she would have had no trouble finding what she wanted just by using the M.C.'s mediaglyphics. It was a thing she'd seen people use in the old passives, a thing she'd seen when Mom's old boyfriend Brad had taken her to visit the horse barn in Dovetail. It was called a screwdriver, and you could have the M.C. make them in all different shapes: long, short, fat, skinny.

She had it make one that was very long and very

skinny. When it was finished, it made the hissing sound that it always made, and she thought she heard Burt stirring on the sofa.

She peeked into the living room. He was still lying there, his eyes closed, but his arms were moving around. His head turned from side to side once, and she could see a glimmer between his half-opened eyelids.

He was about to wake up and hurt her some more.

She held the screwdriver out in front of her like a lance and ran straight toward him.

At the last instant she faltered. The tool went astray and skidded across his forehead, leaving a trail of red stitches. Nell was so horrified that she dropped it and jumped back. Burt was shaking his head violently back and forth.

He opened his eyes and looked right at Nell. Then he put his hand to his forehead and brought it back all bloody. He sat up on the sofa, still uncomprehending. The screwdriver rolled off and bounced on the floor. He picked it up and found the tip bloody, then fixed his eyes on Nell, who had shrunk into the corner of the room.

Nell knew that she had done the wrong thing. Dinosaur had told her to run away, and she had pestered him with questions instead.

"Harv!" she said. But her voice came out all dry and squeaky, like a mouse's. "We must fly!"

"Yeah, you're gonna fly all right," Burt said swinging his feet around to the floor. "Right out the fucking window you're gonna fly."

Harv came out. He was carrying his nunchuks under his injured arm and the Primer in his good hand. The book hung open to an illustration of Princess Nell and Harv running away from the Dark Castle with Baron Burt in pursuit. "Nell, your book talked to me," he said. "It said we should run away." Then he saw Burt rising from the sofa with the bloody screwdriver in his hand.

Harv didn't bother with the nunchuks. He bolted across the room and dropped the Primer, freeing his good hand to fling the front door open. Nell, who had been frozen in a nearby corner for some time, shot toward the door like a bolt finally loosed from a crossbow, snatching up the Primer as she ran past it. They ran into the hallway with Burt only a few paces behind.

The lobby with the elevators was some distance away from them. On impulse, Nell stopped and dropped to a crouch in Burt's path. Harv turned toward her, terrified. "Nell!" he cried.

Burt's pumping legs struck Nell in the side. He spun forward and landed hard on the hallway floor, skidding for a short distance. This brought him to the feet of Harv, who had turned to face him and deployed his nunchuks. Harv went upside Burt's head a few times, but he was panicked and didn't do a very good job of it. Burt groped with one hand and managed to catch the chain that joined the halves of the weapon. Nell had gotten to her feet by this point and ran up Burt's back; she lunged forward and sank her teeth into the fleshy base of Burt's thumb. Something fast and confusing happened, Nell was rolling on the floor, Harv was dragging her back to her feet, she reached back to snatch up the Primer, which she had dropped again. They made it into the emergency stairs and began to skitter down the tunnel of urine, graffiti, and refuse, jumping over the odd slumbering body. Burt entered the stairwell in pursuit, a couple of flights behind them. He tried to make a shortcut by vaulting over the banister as he had seen and done in ractives, but his drunk body didn't do it as well as a media hero, and he tumbled down one flight, cursing and screaming, now rabid with pain and anger. Nell and Harv kept running.

Burt's pratfall gave them enough of a lead to make it to the ground floor. They ran straight across the lobby and into the street. It was the wee hours of the morning, and there was almost no one out here, which was slightly unusual; normally there would have been decoys and lookouts for drug sellers. But tonight there was only one person on the whole block: a bulky Chinese man with a short beard and close-cropped hair, wearing traditional indigo pajamas and a black leather skullcap, standing in the middle of the street with his hands stuck in his sleeves. He gave Nell and Harv an appraising look as they ran past. Nell did not pay him much attention. She just ran as fast as she could.

"Nell!" Harv was saying. "Nell! Look!"

She was afraid to look. She kept running.

"Nell, stop and look!" Harv cried. He sounded exultant.

Finally Nell ran around the corner of a building, stopped, turned, and peeked back cautiously.

She was looking down the empty street past the building where she had lived her whole life. At the end of the street was a big mediatronic advertising display currently running a big Coca-Cola ad, in the ancient and traditional red used by that company.

Silhouetted against it were two men: Burt and the big round-headed Chinese man.

They were dancing together.

No, the Chinese man was dancing. Burt was just staggering around like a drunk.

No, the Chinese man was not dancing, but doing some of the exercises that Dojo had taught Nell about. He moved slowly and beautifully except for some moments when every muscle in his body would join into one explosive movement. Usually these explosions were directed toward Burt.

Burt fell down, then struggled up to his knees.

The Chinese man gathered himself together into a black seed, rose into the air, spun around, and unfolded like a blooming flower. One of his feet struck Burt on the point of his chin and seemed to accelerate all the way through Burt's head. Burt's body fell back to the pavement like a few gallons of water sloshed out of a bucket. The Chinese man became very still, settled his breathing, adjusted his skullcap and the sash on his robe. Then he turned his back to Nell and Harv and walked away down the middle of the street.

Nell opened her Primer. It was showing a picture of Dinosaur, seen in silhouette through a window in the Dark Castle, standing over the corpse of Baron Burt with a smoking stake in his claws.

Nell said, "The little boy and the little girl were running away to the Land Beyond."

Hackworth departs from Shanghai; his speculations
as to the possible motives of Dr. X.

Would-be passengers skidded to a halt on the saliva-slick-
ened floor of the Shanghai Aerodrome as the announcer
brayed the names of great and ancient Chinese cities into his
microphone. They set bags down, shushed children, furrowed brows, cupped hands around ears, and pursed lips in
utter bewilderment. None of this was made any easier by
the extended family of some two dozen just-arrived Boers,
women in bonnets and boys in heavy coarse farmer's pants,
who had convened by one of the gates and begun to sing a
hymn of thanksgiving in thick hoarse voices.

When the announcer called out Hackworth's flight
(San Diego with stops in Seoul, Vladivostok, Magadan,
Anchorage, Juneau, Prince Rupert, Vancouver, Seattle, Port-
land, San Francisco, Santa Barbara, and Los Angeles), he
apparently decided that it was beneath his dignity, above his
abilities, or both to speak Korean, Russian, English, French,
Coast Salish, and Spanish in the same sentence, and so he
just hummed into the microphone for a while as if, far from
being a professional announcer, he were a shy, indifferent
vocalist hidden within in a vast choir.

Hackworth knew perfectly well that hours would pass
before he actually found himself on an airship, and that
having achieved that milestone, he might have to wait hours
more for its actual departure. Nonetheless, he had to say
good-bye to his family at some point, and this seemed no
worse a time than any other. Holding Fiona (so big and solid
now!) in the crook of one arm, and holding hands with
Gwen, he pushed insistently across a riptide of travelers,
beggars, pickpockets, and entrepreneurs trading in everything from bolts of real silk to stolen intellectual property.
Finally they reached a corner where a languid eddy had
separated itself from the flow of people, and where Fiona
could safely be set down.

He turned first to Gwen. She still looked as stunned
and vacant as she had, more or less consistently, since he
told her that he had received a new assignment "whose

nature I am not at liberty to disclose, save to say that it concerns the future, not merely of my department, nor of John Zaibatsu, but of that phyle into which you had the good fortune to have been born and to which I have sworn undying loyalty," and that he was making a trip "of indefinite duration" to North America. It had been increasingly clear of late that Gwen simply didn't get it. At first, Hackworth had been annoyed by this, viewing it as a symptom of hitherto unevidenced intellectual shortcomings. More recently, he had come to understand that it had more to do with emotional stance. Hackworth was embarking on a quest of sorts here, real Boy's Own Paper stuff, highly romantic. Gwen hadn't been raised on the proper diet of specious adventure yarns and simply found the whole concept unfathomable. She did a bit of rote sniffling and tear-wiping, gave him a quick kiss and a hug, and stepped back, having completed her role in the ceremony with nothing close to enough histrionics. Hackworth, feeling somewhat disgruntled, squatted down to face Fiona.

His daughter seemed to have a better intuitive grasp of the situation; she had been up several times a night recently, complaining of bad dreams, and on the way to the Aerodrome she had been perfectly quiet. She stared at her father with large red eyes. Tears came to Hackworth's eyes, and his nose began to run. He blew his nose plangently, held the handkerchief over his face for a moment, and composed himself.

Then he reached into the breast pocket of his overcoat and drew out a flat package, wrapped up in mediatronic paper of spring wildflowers bending in a gentle breeze. Fiona brightened up immediately, and Hackworth could not help chuckling, not for the first time, at the charming susceptibility of small people to frank bribery. "You will forgive me for ruining the surprise," he said, "by telling you that this is a book, my darling. A magic book. I made it for you, because I love you and could not think of a better way to express that love. And whenever you open its pages, no matter how far away I might be, you will find me here."

"Thank you ever so much, Father," she said, taking it with both hands, and he could not help himself from sweeping her up in both arms and giving her a great hug and a kiss. "Good-bye, my best beloved, you will see me in your dreams," he whispered into her tiny, flawless ear, and then he set her free, spun around, and walked away before she could see the tears that had begun to run down his face.

Hackworth was a free man now, wandering through the Aerodrome in an emotional stupor, and only reached his flight by participating in the same flock instinct that all the natives used to reach theirs. Whenever he saw more than one *gwailo* heading purposefully in one direction, he followed them, and then others started following him, and thus did a mob of foreign devils coalesce among a hundred times as many natives, and finally, two hours after their flight was supposed to leave, they mobbed a gate and climbed aboard the airship *Hanjin Takhoma*—which might or might not have been their assigned vessel, but the passengers now had a sufficient numerical majority to hijack it to America, which was the only thing that really counted in China.

He had received a summons from the Celestial Kingdom. Now he was on his way to the territory still known vaguely as America. His eyes were red from crying over Gwen and Fiona, and his blood was swarming with nanosites whose functions were known only to Dr. X; Hackworth had lain back, closed his eyes, rolled up his sleeve, and hummed "Rule, Atlantis" while Dr. X's physicians (at least he hoped they were physicians) shoved a fat needle into his arm. The needle was fed by a tube that ran directly into a special fitting on the matter compiler; Hackworth was plugged directly into the Feed, not the regulation Atlantan kind but Dr. X's black-market kludge. He could only hope that they'd given it the right instructions, as it would be a shame to have a washing machine, a mediatronic chopstick, or a kilo of China White materialize in his arm. Since then, he'd had a few attacks of the shivers, suggesting that his immune system was reacting to something Dr. X had put in there. His body would either get used to it or (preferably) destroy the offending nanosites.

The airship was a dromond, the largest class of non-cargo vessel. It was divided into four classes. Hackworth was second from the bottom, in third. Below that was steerage, which was for migrating thetes, and for sky-girls, prostitutes of the air. Even now, these were bribing their way past the conductors and into the third-class lounge, making eyes at Hackworth and at the white-shirted *sararimen* who tended to travel this way. Those gentlemen had grown up in one crowded Dragon or another, where they knew how to generate a sort of artificial privacy field by determinedly ignoring each other. Hackworth had arrived at the point where he frankly didn't care, and so he stared directly at these men, front-line soldiers of their various microstates, as each one primly folded his navy blue suit jacket and elbow-crawled into a coffinlike microcabin like a GI squirming under a roll of concertina wire, accompanied or not by a camp follower.

Hackworth pointlessly wondered whether he was the only one of this ship's some two thousand passengers who believed that prostitution (or *anything*) was immoral. He did not consider this question in a self-righteous way, more out of rueful curiosity; some of the sky-girls were quite fetching. But as he dragged his body into his microberth, he suffered another attack of the shivers, reminding him that even if his soul had been willing, his flesh was simply too weak.

Another possible explanation for the chills was that Dr. X's nanosites were seeking out and destroying the ones that H.M. Joint Forces had put in there, waging a turf war inside his body, and his immune system was doing overtime trying to pick up the carnage. Hackworth unexpectedly fell asleep before the dromond had even pulled away from her mooring mast, and had dreams about the murderous implements he had seen magnified on Dr. X's mediatron during his first visit. In the abstract they were frightening enough. Having a few million of them in his veins didn't do much for his peace of mind. In the end it wasn't as bad as knowing your blood was full of spirochetes, which people used to live with for decades. Amazing what a person could get used to.

When he settled into bed, he heard a small chime, like faery bells. It was coming from the little pen dangling from his watch chain, and it meant that he had mail. Perhaps a thank-you note from Fiona. He couldn't sleep anyway, and so he took out a sheet of mediatronic paper and spoke the commands that transferred the mail from the pen charm onto the page.

He was disappointed to note that it was printed, not handwritten; some kind of official correspondence, and not, unfortunately, a note from Fiona. When he began to read it, he understood that it wasn't even official. It wasn't even from a human. It was a notification sent back to him automatically by a piece of machinery he had set into motion two years ago. The central message was wreathed in pages of technical gibberish, maps, graphs, and diagrams. The message was:

THE YOUNG LADY'S ILLUSTRATED PRIMER
HAS BEEN FOUND.

It was accompanied by an animated, three-dimensional map of New Chusan with a red line drawn across it, starting in front of a rather seedy-looking high-rise apartment building in the Leased Territory called Enchantment and making its way erratically around the island from there.

Hackworth laughed until his neighbors pounded on the adjoining walls and asked him to shut up.

Nell and Harv at large in the Leased Territories; encounter with an inhospitable security pod; a revelation about the Primer.

The Leased Territories were too valuable to leave much room for Nature, but the geotects of Imperial Tectonics Limited had heard that trees were useful for cleaning and cooling the air, and so they had built in greenbelts along the borders between sectors. In the first hour that they lived free in the streets, Nell glimpsed one of those greenbelts, though it looked black at the time. She broke away from Harv and ran toward it down a street that had developed into a luminescent tunnel of mediatronic billboards. Harv chased her, just barely matching her speed because he had gotten a worse spanking than she had. They were almost the only people on the street, certainly the only ones moving purposefully, and so, as they ran, the messages on the billboards pursued them like starving wolves, making sure they understood that if they used certain ractives or took certain drugs, they could rely on being able to have sex with certain unrealistically perfect young persons. Some of the billboards made an even more elemental pitch, selling the sex directly. The mediatrons on this street were exceptionally large because they were made to be seen clearly from the heaths, bluffs, terraces, and courts of the New Atlantis Clave, miles up the mountain.

Unremitting exposure to this kind of thing produced mediatron burnout among the target audience. Instead of turning them off and giving people a break for once, the proprietors had joined in an arms race of sorts, trying to find the magic image that would make people ignore all the other adverts and fix raptly on theirs. The obvious step of making their mediatrons bigger than the others had been taken about as far as it could go. Quite some time ago the content issue had been settled: tits, tires, and explosions were the only things that seemed to draw the notice of their supremely jaded focus groups, though from time to time they would play the juxtaposition card and throw in something incongruous, like a nature scene or a man in a black turtleneck reading poetry. Once all the mediatrons were a hundred feet high and filled with tits, the only competitive strategy that hadn't already been pushed to the redline was technical tricks: painfully bright flashes, jump-cuts, and simulated 3-D phantoms that made bluff charges toward specific viewers who didn't seem to be paying enough attention.

It was down a mile-long gallery of these stimuli that Nell made her unexpected breakaway, looking from Harv's increasingly distant point of view like an ant scuttling across a television screen with the intensity and saturation turned all the way up, violently changing course from time to time as she was menaced by a virtual pitch-daemon lunging at her from the false parallax of a moving z-buffer, flaring like a comet against a bogus firmament of video black. She knew that they were fake and in most cases didn't even recognize the products they were pitching, but her life had taught her everything about dodging. She couldn't not dodge.

They hadn't figured out a way to make the adverts come at you head-on, and so she maintained a roughly consistent direction down the middle of the street until she vaulted an energy-absorbing barrier at its end and vanished into the forest. Harv followed her a few seconds later, though his arm didn't support vaulting and so he ended up hurtling ignominiously over the top, like a hyped autoskater who hadn't seen the barrier at all, just body-kissed it full tilt. "Nell!" he was already hollering, as he came to rest in a nest of colorful discarded packaging materials. "You can't stay in here! You can't stay in the trees, Nell!"

Nell had already worked her way deep into the woods, or as deep as you could get in a narrow greenbelt made to separate one Leased Territory from another. She fell down a couple of times and banged her head on a tree until, with childish adaptivity, she realized that she was on one of those surfaces that wasn't flat like a floor, street, or sidewalk. The ankles would actually have to show some versatility here. It was like one of those places she had read about in the Illustrated Primer, a magical zone where the fractal dimension of the terrain had been allowed to struggle off the pin, bumps supporting smaller copies of themselves, repeat until microscopic, throw dirt over it, and plant some of those creepy new Douglas firs that grow as fast as bamboo. Nell soon encountered a big Doug that had blown down in a recent typhoon, popping its own rootball out of the ground and thereby excavating a handy depression that invited nestling. Nell jumped in.

For a few minutes she found it strangely hilarious that Harv could not find her. Their flat had only two hiding places, both closets, and so their traditional exploits in the hide-and-go-seek field had provided them with minimal entertainment value and left them wondering what the big deal was anyway about that stupid game. But now, here in the dark woods, Nell was beginning to get it.

"Do you give up?" she finally said, and then Harv found her. He stood at the edge of the rootball pit and demanded that she come out. She refused. Finally he clambered down, though to an eye more critical than Nell's it might have looked as if he were falling. Nell jumped into his lap before he could get up. "We gotta go," he said.

"I want to stay here. It's nice," Nell said.

"You ain't the only one who thinks so," Harv said. "That's why they got pods here."

"Pods?"

"Aerostats. For security."

Nell was delighted to hear it and could not fathom why her brother spoke of security with such dread in his voice.

A soprano turbojet seemed to bear down on them, fading in and out as it tacked through the flora. The creepy afflatus Dopplered down a couple of notes as it came to a stop directly above them. They couldn't see more than the odd glint of colored light, picked up by whatever-it-was from the distant mediatrons. A voice, flawlessly reproduced and just a hair too loud, came out of it: "Visitors are welcome to stroll through this park at any time. We hope you have enjoyed your stay. Please inquire if you need directions, and this unit will assist you."

"It's nice," Nell said.

"Not for long," Harv said. "Let's get out of here before it gets pissed."

"I like it here."

Bluish light exploded out of the aerostat. They both hollered as their irises convulsed. It was hollering right back at them: "Allow me to light your way to the nearest exit!"

"We're running away from home," Nell explained. But Harv was scrambling up out of the hole, yanking Nell behind him with his good hand.

The thing's turbines screeched briefly as it made a bluff charge. In this fashion it herded them briskly toward the nearest street. When they had finally climbed over a barrier and gotten their feet back on concreta firma, it snapped off its light and zoomed off without so much as a fare-thee-well.

"It's okay, Nell, they always do that."

"Why?"

"So this place don't fill up with transients."

"What's that?"

"That's what we are, now," Harv explained.

"Let's go stay with your buds!" Nell said. Harv had never introduced Nell to any of his buds before, she knew them only as children of earlier epochs knew Gilgamesh, Roland, or Superman. She was under the impression that the streets of the Leased Territories were rife with Harv's buds and that they were more or less all-powerful.

Harv's face squirmed for a while, and then he said, "We gotta talk about your magic book."

"The *Young Lady's Illustrated Primer*?"

"Yeah, whatever it's called."

"Why must we talk about it?"

"Huh?" Harv said in the dopey voice he affected whenever Nell talked fancy.

"Why do we gotta talk about it?" Nell said patiently.

"There's something I never told you about that book, but I gotta tell you now," Harv said. "Come on, let's keep moving, or some creep's gonna come hassle us." They headed toward the main street of Lazy Bay Towne, which was the Leased Territory into which the pod had ejected them. The main street curved along the waterfront, separating a beach from a very large number of drinking establishments fronted with lurid, bawdy mediatrons. "I don't want to go that way," Nell said, remembering that last gauntlet of electromagnetic pimps. But Harv grabbed her wrist and hobbled downhill, pulling her behind. "It's safer than being in the back streets. Now let me tell you about that book. My buds and I pinched it and some other stuff from a Vicky we rolled. Doc told us to roll him."

"Doc?"

"This Chinese guy who runs the Flea Circus. He said we should roll him, and make sure we made it good so it'd get picked up on the monitors."

"What does that mean?"

"Never mind. He also said he wanted us to lift something from this Vicky—a certain package about yay big." Harv formed right angles with his thumbs and index fingers and defined the vertices of a rectangle, book-size. "Gave us to understand it was valuable. Well, we didn't find any such package. We did find a shitty old book on him, though. I mean, it looked old and fine, but no one reckoned it could be the thing Doc was looking for, since he's got lots of books. So I took it for you.

"Well, a week or two later, Doc wants to know where is the package, and we told him this story. When he heard about that book, he flipped and told us that the book and the package were one and the same. By that time, you were already playing with that book all night and all day, Nell, and I couldn't bear to take it away from you, so I lied. I told him I threw the book down on the sidewalk when I saw it was junk, and if it wasn't still there, then someone else must have come along and picked it up. Doc was pissed, but he fell for it.

"That's why I never brought my buds to the flat. If anyone finds out you still have that book, Doc'll kill me."

"What should we do?"

Harv got a look on his face like he'd rather not talk about it. "For starters, let's get some free stuff."

They took a sneaky and indirect route to the waterfront, staying as far as possible from the clusters of drunks winding through the constellation of incandescent bordellos like cold dark clumps of rock wending their way through a bright nebula of young stars. They made their way to a public M.C. on a streetcorner and picked out items from the free menu: boxes of water and nutri-broth, envelopes of sushi made from nanosurimi and rice, candy bars, and packages about the size of Harv's hand, festooned with implausible block letter promises ("REFLECTS 99% OF INFRARED!") that folded out into huge crinkly metallized blankets. Nell had been noticing a lot of rough shapes strewn around on the beach like giant chrome-plated larva. Must be fellow transients wrapped up in these selfsame. As soon as they had scored the goodies, they ran down to the beach and picked out their own spot. Nell wanted one closer to the surf, but Harv made some very well-considered observations about the inadvisability of sleeping below high tide. They trudged along the seawall for a good mile or so before finding a relatively abandoned bit of beach and wrapped themselves up in their blankets there. Harv insisted that one of them had to stay awake at all times to act as a sentry. Nell had learned all about this kind of thing from her virtual adventures in the Primer, and so she volunteered to stay up first. Harv went to sleep pretty soon, and Nell opened up her book. At times like this, the paper glowed softly and the letters stood out crisp and black, like tree branches silhouetted against a full moon.

*Miranda's reactions to the evening's events; solace
from an unexpected quarter; from the Primer, the
demise of a hero, flight to the Land Beyond, and the
lands of King Magpie.*

The Theatre Parnasse had a rather nice bar, nothing spectacular, just a sort of living room off the main floor, with the bar itself recessed into one wall. The old furniture and pictures had been looted by the Red Guards and later replaced with post-Mao stuff that was not as fine. The management kept the booze locked up when the ractors were working, not sharing any romantic notions about substance-abusing creative geniuses. Miranda stumbled down from her box, fixed herself a club soda, and settled into a plastic chair. She put her shaking hands together like the covers of a book and then buried her face in them. After a few deep breaths she got tears to come, though they came silently, a temporary letting-off-steam cry, not the catharsis she was hoping for. She hadn't earned the catharsis yet, she knew, because what had happened was just the first act. Just the initial incident, or whatever they called it in the books.

"Rough session?" said a voice. Miranda recognized it, but just barely: It was Carl Hollywood, the dramaturge, in effect her boss. But he didn't sound like a gruff son of a bitch tonight, which was a switch.

Carl was in his forties, six and a half feet tall, massively built and given to wearing long black coats that almost swept the floor. He had long wavy blond hair drawn back from his forehead and affected a sort of King Tut beard. Either he was celibate, or else he believed that the particulars of his sexual orientation and needs were infinitely too complex to be shared with those he worked with. Everyone was scared shitless of him, and he liked it that way; he couldn't do his job if he was buddies with all of the ractors.

She heard his cowboy boots approaching across the bare, stained Chinese rug. He confiscated her club soda. "Don't want to drink this fizzy stuff when you're having a cry. It'll come out your nose. You need something like tomato juice—replace those lost electrolytes. I tell you what," he said, rattling his tremendous keychain, "I'll break the rules and fix you an honest-to-god Bloody Mary. Usually I make 'em with tabasco, which is how we do it where I'm from. But since your mucus membranes are already irritated enough, I'll just make a boring one."

By the time he was finished with this oration, Miranda had gotten her hands away from her face at least. She turned away from him.

"Kind of funny racting in that little box, ain't it," Carl said, "kind of isolating. Theatre didn't used to be that way."

"Isolating? Sort of," Miranda said. "I could use a little more isolation tonight."

"You telling me to leave you alone, or—"

"No!" Miranda said, sounding desperate to herself. She brought her voice to heel before continuing. "No, that's not how I meant it. It's just that you never know what role you're going to play. And some of the roles can cut pretty deep. If someone handed me a script for what I just did and asked me if I were interested in the part, I'd refuse it."

"Was it a porn thing?" Carl Hollywood said. His voice sounded a bit strangled. He was angry all of a sudden. He had stopped in the middle of the room, clenching her Bloody Mary as if he might pop the glass in his fist.

"No. It wasn't like that," Miranda said. "At least, it wasn't porn in the sense you're talking about," Miranda said, "though you never know what turns people on."

"Was the payer looking to get turned on?"

"No. Absolutely not," Miranda said.

Then, after a long time, she said, "It was a kid. A little girl."

Carl gave her a searching look, then remembered his manners and glanced away, pretending to appraise the carving on the front of the bar.

"So the next question is," Miranda said after she'd steadied herself with a few gulps of the drink, "why I should get so upset over a kiddie ractive."

Carl shook his head. "I wasn't going to ask it."

"But you're wondering."

"What I'm wondering about is my problem," Carl said. "Let's concentrate on your problems for now." He frowned, sat down across from her and ran his hand back through his hair absentmindedly. "Is this that big account?"

He had access to her spreadsheets; he knew how she'd been spending her time.

"Yeah."

"I've sat in on a few of those sessions."

"I know you have."

"Seems different from normal kiddie stuff. The education is there, but it's darker. Lots of unreconstructed Grimm Brothers content. Powerful."

"Yeah."

"It's amazing to me that one kid can spend that much time—"

"Me too." Miranda took another swallow, then bit off the end of the celery stick and chewed awhile, stalling. "What it comes down to," she said, "is that I'm raising someone's kid for them."

Carl looked her straight in the eye for the first time in a while. "And some heavy shit just went down," he said.

"Some very heavy shit, yes."

Carl nodded.

"It's so heavy," Miranda said, "that I don't even know if this girl is alive or dead."

Carl glanced up at the fancy old clock on the wall, its face yellowed from a century and a half's accumulation of tar and nicotine. "If she's alive," he said, "then she probably needs you."

"Right," Miranda said. She stood up and headed for the exit. Then, before Carl could react, she spun on the ball of her foot, bent down, and kissed him on the cheek.

"Aw, stop it," he said.

"See you later, Carl. Thanks." She ran up the narrow staircase, heading for her box.

Baron Burt lay dead upon the floor of the Dark Castle. Princess Nell was terrified of the blood that gushed from his wound, but she approached him bravely and plucked the keychain with the twelve keys from his belt. Then she gathered up her Night Friends, tucking them into a little knapsack, and hurriedly packed a picnic lunch while Harv gathered up blankets and ropes and tools for their journey.

They were walking across the courtyard of the Dark Castle, heading for the great gate with its twelve locks, when suddenly the evil Queen appeared before them, as tall as a giant, wreathed in lightning and thunderclouds! Tears gushed from her eyes and turned to blood as they rolled down her cheeks. "You have taken him away from me!" she cried. And Nell understood that this was a terrible thing for her wicked stepmother, because she was weak and helpless without a man. "For this," the Queen continued, "I shall curse you to remain locked up in this Dark Castle forever!" And she reached down with one hand like talons and snatched the keychain from Princess Nell's hand. Then she turned into a great vulture and flew away across the ocean toward the Land Beyond.

"We are lost!" Harv cried. "Now we shall never escape from this place!" But Princess Nell did not lose hope.

Not long after the Queen had vanished over the horizon, another bird came flying toward them. It was the Raven, their friend from the Land Beyond, who frequently came to visit them and to entertain them with stories of far-off countries and famous heroes. "Now is your chance to escape," said the Raven. "The evil Queen is engaged in a great battle of sorcery with the Faery Kings and Queens who rule the Land Beyond. Throw a rope out of yon arrow-slit, and climb down to freedom."

Princess Nell and Harv climbed the stairway into one of the bastions flanking the Dark Castle's main gate. These had narrow windows where in olden times soldiers should shoot arrows down at invaders. Harv tied one end of a rope to a hook in the wall and threw it out one of these slits. Princess Nell threw her Night Friends out, knowing that they would land harmlessly below. Then she climbed out through the slit and down the rope to freedom.

"Follow me, Harv!" she cried. "All is well down here, and it is a much brighter place than you can possibly imagine!"

"I cannot," he said. "I am too big to pass through the slit." And he began to throw out the loaves of bread, pieces of cheese, wineskins, and pickles that they had packed for their lunch.

"Then I will come back up the rope and stay with you," Princess Nell said generously.

"No!" Harv said, and reeled in the rope, trapping Nell on the outside.

"But I will be lost without you!" Princess Nell cried.

"That's your stepmother talking," Harv said. "You are a strong, smart, and brave girl and can do fine without me."

"Harv is right," said the Raven, flying overhead. "Your destiny is in the Land Beyond. Hurry, lest your stepmother return and trap you here."

"Then I will go to the Land Beyond with my Night Friends," said Princess Nell, "and I will find the twelve keys, and I will come back here one day and free you from this Dark Castle."

"I'm not holding my breath," Harv said, "but thanks anyway."

Down on the shore was a little boat that Nell's father had once used to row around the island. Nell climbed in with her Night Friends and began to row.

Nell rowed for many hours until her back and shoulders ached. The sun set in the west, the sky became dark, and it became harder to make out the Raven against the darkling sky. Then, much to her relief, her Night Friends came alive as they always did. There was plenty of room in the boat for Princess Nell, Purple, Peter, and Duck, but Dinosaur was so big that he nearly swamped it; he had to sit in the bow and row while the others sat in the stern trying to balance his weight.

They moved much faster with Dinosaur's strong rowing; but early in the morning a storm blew up, and soon the waves were above their heads, above even Dinosaur's head, and rain was coming down so fast that Purple and Princess Nell had to bail using Dinosaur's shiny helmet as a bucket. Dinosaur threw out all of his armor to lighten the load, but it soon became evident that this was not enough.

"Then I shall do my duty as a warrior," Dinosaur said. "My usefulness to you is finished, Princess Nell; from now, you must listen to the wisdom of your other Night Friends and use what you have learned from me only when nothing else will work." And he dove into the water and disappeared beneath the waves. The boat bobbed up like a cork. An hour later, the storm began to diminish, and as dawn approached, the ocean was smooth as glass, and filling the western horizon was a green country vaster than anything Princess Nell had ever imagined: the Land Beyond.

Princess Nell wept bitterly for lost Dinosaur and wanted to wait on the shore in case he had clung to a piece of flotsam or jetsam and drifted to safety.

"We must not dawdle here," Purple said, "lest we be seen by one of King Magpie's sentries."

"King Magpie?" said Princess Nell.

"One of the twelve Faery Kings and Queens. This shore is part of his domain," Purple said. "He has a flock of starlings who watch his borders."

"Too late!" cried sharp-eyed Peter. "We are discovered!"

At that moment, the sun rose, and the Night Friends turned back into stuffed animals.

A solitary bird was diving toward them out of the morning sky. When it drew closer, Princess Nell saw that it was not one of King Magpie's starlings after all; it was their friend the Raven. He landed on a branch above her head and cried, "Good news! Bad news! Where shall I start?"

"With the good news," Princess Nell said.

"The wicked Queen lost the battle. Her power has been broken by the other twelve."

"What is the bad news?"

"Each of them took one of the twelve keys as spoil and locked it up in his or her royal treasury. You will never be able to collect all twelve."

"But I am sworn to get them," said Princess Nell, "and Dinosaur showed me last night that a warrior must hold to her duty even if it leads her into destruction. Show me the way to the castle of King Magpie; we will get his key first."

She plunged into the forest and, before long, found a dirt road that the Raven said would lead her toward King Magpie's castle. After a break for lunch she started down this road, keeping one sharp eye on the sky.

There followed a funny little chapter in which Nell encountered the footprints of another traveler on the road, who was soon joined by another traveler, and another. This continued until nightfall, when Purple examined the footprints and informed Princess Nell that she had been walking in circles all day.

"But I have followed the road carefully," Nell said.

"The road is one of King Magpie's tricks," Purple said. "It is a circular road. In order to find his castle, we must put on our thinking-caps and use our own brains, for everything in this country is a trick of one kind or another."

"But how can we find his castle if all of the roads are made to deceive us?" Peter Rabbit said.

"Nell, do you have your sewing-needle?" Purple said.

"Yes," said Nell, reaching into her pocket and taking out her mending kit.

"Peter, do you have your magic stone?" Purple continued.

"Yes," Peter said, taking it out of his pocket. It did not look magic, being just a gray lump, but it had the magic property of attracting small bits of metal.

"And Duck, can you spare a cork from one of the lemonade bottles?"

"This one's almost empty," Duck said.

"Very well. I will also need a bowl of water," Purple said, and collected the three items from her three friends.

Nell read on into the Primer, learning about how Purple made a compass by magnetizing the needle, thrusting it through the cork, and floating it in the bowl of water. She read about their three-day journey through the land of King Magpie, and of all the tricks it contained—animals that stole their food, quicksand, sudden rainstorms, appetizing but poisonous berries, snares, and pitfalls set to catch uninvited guests. Nell knew that if she wanted, she could go back and ask questions about these things later and spend many hours reading about this part of the adventure. But the important part seemed to be the discussions with Peter that ended each day's journey.

Peter Rabbit was their guide through all of these perils. His eyes were sharp from eating carrots, and his giant ears could hear trouble coming from miles away. His quivering nose sniffed out danger, and his mind was too sharp for most of King Magpie's tricks. Before long they had reached the outskirts of King Magpie's city, which did not even have a wall around it, so confident was King Magpie that no invader could possibly pass through all of the traps and pitfalls in the forest.

Princess Nell in the city of King Magpie; hyena trouble; the story of Peter; Nell deals with a stranger.

The city of King Magpie was more frightening to Princess Nell than any wilderness, and she would have sooner trusted her life to the wild beasts of the forest than to many of its people. They tried to sleep in a nice glade of trees in the middle of the city, which reminded Princess Nell of the glades on the Enchanted Isle. But before they could even make themselves comfortable, a hissing hyena with red eyes and dripping fangs came and chased them all away.

"Perhaps we can sneak back into the glade after it gets dark, when the hyena will not see us," Nell suggested.

"The hyena will always see us, even in the dark, because it can see the infrared light that comes out of our bodies," Purple said.

Eventually, Nell, Peter, Duck, and Purple found a place to camp in a field where other poor people lived. Duck set up a little camp and lit a fire, and they had some soup before going to bed. But try as she might, Princess Nell could not sleep. She saw that Peter Rabbit could not sleep either; he only sat with his back to the fire looking off into the darkness.

"Why are you looking into the darkness and not into the fire as we do?" Nell asked.

"Because the darkness is where danger comes from," Peter said, "and from the fire comes only illusion. When I was a little bunny running away from home, that is one of the first lessons I learned."

Peter went on to tell his own story, just as Dinosaur had earlier in the Primer. It was a story about how he and his brothers had run away from home and fallen afoul of various cats, vultures, weasels, dogs, and humans who tended to see them, not as intrepid little adventurers but as lunch. Peter was the only one of them who had survived, because he was the cleverest of them all.

"I made up my mind that one day I would avenge my brothers," Peter said.

"Did you?"

"Well, that's a long story in itself."

"Tell it to me!" Princess Nell said.

But before Peter could launch into the next part of his story, they became aware of a stranger who was approaching them. "We should wake up Duck and Purple," Peter said.

"Oh, let them sleep," Princess Nell said. "They can use the rest, and this stranger doesn't look so bad."

"What does a bad stranger look like exactly?" Peter said.

"You know, like a weasel or a vulture," Princess Nell said.

"Hello, young lady," said the stranger, who was dressed in expensive clothes and jewelry. "I couldn't help noticing that you are new to beautiful Magpie City and down on your luck. I can't sit in my comfortable, warm house eating my big, tasty meals without feeling guilty, knowing that you are out here suffering. Won't you come with me and let me take care of you?"

"I won't leave my friends behind," said Princess Nell.

"Of course not—I wasn't suggesting *that*," the stranger said. "Too bad they're asleep. Say, I have an idea! You come with me, your rabbit friend stays awake here to keep an eye on your sleeping friends, and I'll show you my place—y'know, prove to you that I'm not some kind of creepy stranger who's trying to take advantage of you, like you see in all those dumb kids' stories that only little babies read. You're not a little baby, are you?"

"No, I don't think so," Princess Nell said.

"Then come with me, give me a fair hearing, check me out, and if I turn out to be an okay guy, we'll come back and pick up the rest of your little group. Come on, time's a wasting!"

Princess Nell found it very hard to say no to the stranger. "Don't go with him, Nell!" Peter said. But in the end, Nell went with him anyway. In her heart she knew it was wrong, but her head was foolish, and because she was still just a little girl, she did not feel she could say no to a grown-up man.

At this point the story became very ractive. Nell stayed up for a while in the ractive, trying different things. Sometimes the man gave her a drink, and she fell asleep. But if she refused to take the drink, he would grab her and tie her up. Either way, the man always turned out to be a pirate, or else he would sell Princess Nell to some other pirates who would keep her and not let her go. Nell tried every trick she could think of, but it seemed as though the ractive were made in such a way that, once she'd made the decision to go away with the stranger, nothing she could do would prevent her from becoming a slave to the pirates.

After the tenth or twelfth iteration she dropped the book into the sand and hunched over it, crying. She cried silently so Harv wouldn't wake up. She cried for a long time, seeing no reason to stop, because she felt that she was trapped now, just like Princess Nell in the book.

"Hey," said a man's voice, very soft. At first Nell thought it was coming out of the Primer, and she ignored it because she was angry at the Primer.

"What's wrong, little girl?" said the voice. Nell tried to look up toward the source, but all she saw was fat colored light from the mediatrons filtered through tears. She rubbed her eyes, but her hands had sand on them. She got panicky for a moment, because she had realized there was definitely someone there, a grown-up man, and she felt blind and helpless.

Finally she got a look at him. He was squatting about six feet away from her, a safe enough distance, watching her with his forehead all wrinkled up, looking terribly concerned.

"There's no reason to be crying," he said. "It can't be that bad."

"Who are you?" Nell said.

"I'm just a friend who wants to help you. C'mon," he said, cocking his head down the beach. "I need to talk to you for a second, and I don't want to wake up your friend there."

"Talk to me about what?"

"How I can help you out. Now, come on, do you want help or not?"

"Sure," Nell said.

"Okay. C'mon then," the stranger said, rising to his feet. He took a step toward Nell, bent down, and held out one hand.

Nell reached for him with her left and at the last minute flung a handful of sand into his face with her right. "Fuck!" the stranger said. "You little bitch, I'm gonna get you for that."

The nunchuks were, as always, under Harv's head. Nell yanked them out and turned back toward the stranger, spinning her whole body around and snapping her wrist at the last moment just as Dojo had taught her. The end of the nunchuk struck the stranger's left kneecap like a steel cobra, and she heard something crack. The stranger screamed, astonishingly loud, and toppled into the sand. Nell spun the nunchuks around, working them up to a hum, and drew a bead on his temporal bone. But before she could strike, Harv grabbed her wrist. The free end of the weapon spun around

out of control and bonked her on the eyebrow, splitting it
open and giving her a total-body ice-cream headache. She
wanted to throw up.

"Good one, Nell," he said, "but now's the time to get
the hell out of here."

She snatched up the Primer. The two of them ran off
down the beach, jumping over the silver larvae that glittered
noisily in the mediatronic light. "The cops are probably
gonna be after us now," Harv said. "We gotta go somewhere."

"Grab one of those blankets," Nell said. "I have an
idea."

They had left their own silvery blanket behind. A discarded one was overflowing from a wastebasket by the seawall, so Harv snatched it as they ran by and crumpled it into
a wad.

Nell led Harv back to the little patch of forest. They
found their way to the little cavity where they had stopped
earlier. This time, Nell spread the blanket over both of them,
and they tucked it in all around themselves to make a bubble. They waited quietly for a minute, then five, then ten.
From time to time they heard the thin whine of a pod going
by, but they always kept on going, and before they knew it
they were asleep.

*Mysterious souvenir from Dr. X; Hackworth's
arrival in Vancouver; the Atlantan quarter of that
city; he acquires a new mode of conveyance.*

Dr. X had dispatched a messenger to the Shanghai Aerodrome with instructions to seek out Hackworth. The messenger had sidled up next to him while he was addressing a
piss-trough, greeted him cheerfully, and taken a piss himself. Then the two men had exchanged business cards, accepting them with both hands and a slight bow.

Hackworth's card was about as flashy as he was. It

was white, with his name stamped out in rather severe capitals. Like most cards, it was made of smart paper and had lots of memory space left over to store digitized information. This particular copy contained a matter compiler program descended from the one that had created the original *Young Lady's Illustrated Primer*. This revision used automatic voice generation algorithms instead of relying on professional ractors, and it contained all of the hooks that Dr. X's coders would need to translate the text into Chinese.

The Doctor's card was more picturesque. It had a few Hanzi characters scrawled across it and also bore Dr. X's chop. Now that paper was smart, chops were dynamic. The stamp infused the paper with a program that caused it to run a little graphics program forever. Dr. X's chop depicted a poxy-looking gaffer with a conical hat slung on his back, squatting on a rock in a river with a bamboo pole, hauling a fish out of the water—no wait, it wasn't a fish, it was a dragon squirming on the end of the line, and just as you realized it, the gaffer turned and smiled at you insolently. This kitschy tableau then freeze-framed and morphed cleverly into the characters representing Dr. X's name. Then it looped back to the beginning. On the back of the card were a few mediaglyphs indicating that it was, in fact, a chit: that is to say, a totipotent program for a matter compiler, combined with sufficient ucus to run it. The mediaglyphs indicated that it would run only on a matter compiler of eight cubic meters or larger, which was enormous, and which made it obvious he was not to use it until he reached America.

He debarked from the *Hanjin Takhoma* at Vancouver, which besides having the most scenic airship moorage in the world, boasted a sizable Atlantan clave. Dr. X hadn't given him a specific destination—just the chit and a flight number—so there didn't seem any point in staying aboard all the way to the end of the line. From here he could always bullet-train down the coast if necessary.

The city itself was a sprawling bazaar of claves. Consequently it was generously supplied with agoras, owned and managed by Protocol, where citizens and subjects of different phyles could convene on neutral ground and trade, negotiate, fornicate, or whatever. Some of the agoras were simply open plazas in the classical tradition, others looked more like convention centers or office buildings. Many of

Old Vancouver's pricier and more view-endowed precincts had been acquired by the Hong Kong Mutual Benevolent Society or the Nipponese, and the Confucians owned the tallest office building in the downtown area. East of town in the fertile delta of the Fraser River, the Slavs and the Germans were both supposed to have large patches of *Lebensraum* staked out, surrounded by grids of somewhat nastier than usual security pods. Hindustan had a spray of tiny claves all over the metropolitan area.

The Atlantis clave climbed out of the water half a mile west of the university, to which it was joined by a causeway. Imperial Tectonics had made it look like just another island, as if it had been sitting there for a million years. As Hackworth's rented velocipede took him over the causeway, cool salt air flowing through his stubble, he began to relax, finding himself once again on home territory. On an emerald green playing field above the breakwater, young boys in short pants were knotted into a scrum, playing at fieldball.

On the opposite side of the road was the girls' school, which had its own playing field of equal size, except that this one was surrounded by a dense twelve-foot hedge so that the girls could run around in very little or skin-tight clothing without giving rise to etiquette problems. He hadn't slept well in his microberth and wouldn't have minded checking into the guest hostel and taking a nap, but it was only eleven in the morning and he couldn't see wasting the day. So he rode his velocipede to the center of town, stopped in at the first pub he saw, and had lunch. The bartender gave him directions to the Royal Post Office, which was just a few blocks away.

The post office was a big one, sporting a variety of matter compilers, including a ten-cubic-meter model directly adjacent to the loading dock. Hackworth shoved Dr. X's chit into its reader and held his breath. But nothing dramatic happened; the display on the control panel said that this job was going to take a couple of hours.

Hackworth killed most of the time wandering around the clave. The middle of town was smallish and quickly gave way to leafy neighborhoods filled with magnificent Georgian, Victorian, and Romanesque homes, with the occasional rugged Tudor perched on a rise or nestled into a verdant hollow. Beyond the homes was a belt of gentrified farms mingled with golf courses and parks. He sat down on a bench in one flowery public garden and unfolded the sheet of mediatronic paper that was keeping track of the movements of the original copy of the *Young Lady's Illustrated Primer*.

It seemed to have spent some time in a greenbelt and then made its way up the hill in the general direction of the New Atlantis Clave.

Hackworth took out his fountain pen and wrote a short letter addressed to Lord Finkle-McGraw.

Your Grace,

Since accepting the trust you have reposed in me, I have endeavoured to be perfectly frank, serving as an open conduit for all information pertaining to the task at hand. In that spirit, I must inform you that two years ago, in my desperate search for the lost copy of the Primer, I initiated a search of the Leased Territories . . . (&c., &c.)

Please find enclosed a map and other data regarding the recent movements of this book, whose whereabouts were unknown to me until yesterday. I have no way of knowing who possesses it, but given the book's programming, I suspect it to be a young thete girl, probably between the ages of five and seven. The book must have remained indoors for the last two years, or else my systems would have detected it. If these suppositions are correct, and if my invention has not fallen desperately short of intentions, then it is safe to assume that the book has become an important part of the girl's life . . .

He went on to write that the book should not be taken from the girl if this were the case; but thinking about it a bit more carefully, he scribbled out that part of the letter and it vanished from the page. It was not Hackworth's role to tell Finkle-McGraw how to manage affairs. He signed the letter and dispatched it.

Half an hour letter, his pen chimed again and he checked his mail.

Hackworth,

Message received. Better late than never. Can't wait to meet the girl.

Yours &c.
Finkle-McGraw

When Hackworth got back to the post office and looked through the window of the big matter compiler, he saw a large machine taking shape in the dim red light. Its body had already been finished and was now rising slowly as its four legs were compiled underneath. Dr. X had provided Hackworth with a chevaline.

Hackworth noted, not without approval, that this one's engineers had put a high priority on the virtues of simplicity and strength and a low priority on comfort and style. Very Chinese. No effort was made to disguise it as a real animal. Much of the mechanical business in the legs was exposed so that you could see how the joints and pushrods worked, a little like staring at the wheels of an old steam locomotive. The body looked gaunt and skeletal. It was made of star-shaped connectors where five or six cigarette-size rods would come together, the rods and connectors forming into an irregular web that wrapped around into a geodesic space frame. The rods could change their length. Hackworth knew from seeing the same construction elsewhere that the web could change its size and shape to an amazing degree while providing whatever combination of stiffness and flexibility the controlling system needed at the moment. Inside the space frame Hackworth could see aluminum-plated spheres and ellipsoids, no doubt vacuum-filled, containing the mount's machine-phase guts: basically some rod logic and an energy source.

The legs compiled quickly, the complicated feet took a little longer. When it was finished, Hackworth released the vacuum and opened the door. "Fold," he said. The chevaline's legs buckled, and it lay down on the floor of the M.C. Its space frame contracted as much as it could, and its neck shortened. Hackworth bent down, laced his fingers through the space frame, and lifted the chevaline with one hand. He carried it through the lobby of the post office, past bemused customers, and out the door onto the street.

"Mount," he said. The chevaline rose into a crouch. Hackworth threw one leg over its saddle, which was padded with some kind of elastomeric stuff, and immediately felt it shoving him into the air. His feet left the ground and flailed around until they found the stirrups. A lumbar support pressed thoughtfully on his kidneys, and then the chevaline trotted into the street and began heading back toward the causeway.

It wasn't supposed to do that. Hackworth was about to tell it to stop. Then he figured out why he'd gotten the chit at the last minute: Dr. X's engineers had been programming something into this mount's brain, telling it where to take him.

"Name?" Hackworth said.

"Unnamed," the chevaline said.

"Rename Kidnapper," Hackworth said.

"Name Kidnapper," said Kidnapper; and sensing that it was reaching the edge of the business district, it started to canter. Within a few minutes they were blasting across the causeway at a tantivy. Hackworth turned back toward Atlantis and looked for pursuing aerostats; but if Napier was tracking him, he was doing so with some subtlety.

A morning stroll through the Leased Territories;
Dovetail; a congenial Constable.

High up the mountain before them, they could see St. Mark's Cathedral and hear its bells ringing changes, mostly just tuneless sequences of notes, but sometimes a pretty melody would tumble out, like an unexpected gem from the permutations of the *I Ching*. The Diamond Palace of Source Victoria glittered peach and amber as it caught the sunrise, which was still hidden behind the mountain. Nell and Harv had slept surprisingly well under the silver blanket, but they had not by any means slept late. The martial reveille from the Sendero Clave had woken them, and by the time they hit the streets again, Sendero's burly Korean and Incan evangelists were already pouring out of their gate into the common byways of the Leased Territories, humping their folding mediatrons and heavy crates of little red books. "We could go in there, Nell," Harv said, and Nell thought he must be joking. "Always plenty to eat and a warm cot in Sendero."

"They wouldn't let me keep my book," Nell said.

Harv looked at her, mildly startled. "How do you know? Oh, don't tell me, you learned it from the Primer."

"They only have one book in Sendero, and it tells them to burn all the other books."

As they climbed toward the greenbelt, the way got steeper and Harv started wheezing. From time to time he would stop with his hands on his knees and cough in high hoarse bursts like the bark of a seal. But the air was cleaner up here, they could tell by the way it felt going down their throats, and it was colder too, which helped.

A band of forest surrounded the high central plateau of New Chusan. The clave called Dovetail backed right up against this greenbelt and was no less densely wooded, though from a distance it had a finer texture—more and smaller trees, and many flowers.

Dovetail was surrounded by a fence made of iron bars and painted black. Harv took one look at it and said it was a joke if that was all the security they had. Then he got to noticing that the fence was lined with a greensward about a stone's throw in width, smooth enough for championship croquet. He raised his eyebrows significantly at Nell, implying that any unauthorized personnel who tried to walk across it would be impaled on hydraulic stainless-steel spikes or shot through with cookie-cutters or rent by robot dogs.

The gates to Dovetail stood wide open, which deeply alarmed Harv. He got in front of Nell lest she try to run through them. At the boundary line, the pavement changed from the usual hard-but-flexible, smooth-but-high-traction nanostuff to an irregular mosaic of granite blocks.

The only human in evidence was a white-haired Constable whose belly had created a visible divergence between his two rows of brass buttons. He was bent over using a trowel to extract a steaming turd from the emerald grass. Circumstances suggested that it had come from one of two corgis who were even now slamming their preposterous bodies into each other not far away, trying to roll each other over, which runs contrary to the laws of mechanics even in the case of corgis that are lean and trim, which these were not. This struggle, which appeared to be only one skirmish in a conflict of epochal standing, had driven all lesser considerations, such as guarding the gate, from the combatants' sphere of attention, and so it was the Constable who first noticed Nell and Harv. "Away with you!" he hollered cheerfully enough, waving his redolent trowel down the hill. "We've no work for such as you today! And the free matter compilers are all down by the waterfront."

The effect of this news on Harv was contrary to what the Constable had intended, for it implied that sometimes there *was* work for such as him. He stepped forward alertly. Nell took advantage of this to run out from behind him. "Pardon me, sir," she called, "we're not here for work or to get free things, but to find someone who belongs to this phyle."

The Constable straightened his tunic and squared his shoulders at the appearance of this little girl, who looked like a thete but talked like a Vicky. Suspicion gave way to benevolence, and he ambled toward them after shouting a few imprecations at his dogs, who evidently suffered from advanced hearing loss. "Very well," he said. "Who is it that you're looking for?"

"A man by the name of Brad. A blacksmith. He works at a stable in the New Atlantis Clave, taking care of horses."

"I know him well," the Constable said. "I'd be glad to ring him for you. You're a . . . friend of his, then?"

"We should like to think that he remembers us favorably," Nell said. Harv turned around and made a face at her for talking this way, but the Constable was eating it up.

"It's a brisk morning," the Constable said. "Why don't you join me inside the gatehouse, where it's nice and cozy, and I'll get you some tea."

On either side of the main gate, the fence terminated in a small stone tower with narrow diamond-paned windows set deeply into its walls. The Constable entered one of these from his side of the fence and then opened a heavy wooden

door with huge wrought-iron hinges, letting Nell and Harv
in from their side. The tiny octagonal room was cluttered
with fine furniture made of dark wood, a shelf of old books,
and a small cast-iron stove with a red enamel kettle on top,
pocked like an asteroid from ancient impacts, piping out a
tenuous column of steam. The Constable directed them into
a pair of wooden chairs. Trying to scoot them back from the
table, they discovered that each was ten times the weight of
any other chair they'd seen, being made of actual wood, and
thick pieces of it too. They were not especially comfortable,
but Nell liked sitting in hers nevertheless, as something
about its size and weight gave her a feeling of security. The
windows on the Dovetail side of the gatehouse were larger,
and she could see the two corgi dogs outside, peering in
through the lead latticework, flabbergasted that they had,
through some enormous lacuna in procedure, been left on
the outside, wagging their tails somewhat uncertainly, as if,
in a world that allowed such mistakes, nothing could be
counted on.

The Constable found a wooden tray and carried it
about the room, cautiously assembling a collection of cups,
saucers, spoons, tongs, and other tea-related armaments.
When all the necessary tools were properly laid out, he man-
ufactured the beverage, hewing closely to the ancient procedure, and set it before them.

Resting on a counter by the window was an outland-
ishly shaped black object that Nell recognized as a telephone, only because she had seen them on the old passives
that her mother liked to watch—where they seemed to take
on a talismanic significance out of proportion to what they
actually did. The Constable picked up a piece of paper on
which many names and strings and digits had been handwritten. He turned his back to the nearest window, then
leaned backward over the counter so as to bring most of him
closer to its illumination. He tilted the paper into the light
and then adjusted the elevation of his own chin through a
rather sweeping arc, converging on a position that placed
the lenses of his reading spectacles between pupil and page.
Having maneuvered all of these elements into the optimal
geometry, he let out a little sigh, as though the arrangement
suited him, and peered up over his glasses at Nell and Harv
for a moment, as if to suggest that they could learn some

valuable tricks by keeping a sharp eye on him. Nell watched him, fascinated not least because she rarely saw people in spectacles.

The Constable returned his attention to the piece of paper and scanned it with a furrowed brow for a few minutes before suddenly calling out a series of several numbers, which sounded random to his visitors but seemed both deeply significant and perfectly obvious to the Constable.

The black telephone sported a metal disk with finger-size holes bored around its edge. The Constable hooked the phone's handset over his epaulet and then began to insert his finger into various of these holes, using them to torque the disk around against the countervailing force of a spring. A brief but exceedingly cheerful conversation ensued. Then he hung up the telephone and clasped his hands over his belly, as if he had accomplished his assigned tasks so completely that said extremities were now superfluous decorations. "It'll be a minute," he said. "Please take your time, and don't scald yourselves on that tea. Care for some shortbread?"

Nell was not familiar with this delight. "No thank you, sir," she said, but Harv, ever pragmatic, allowed as he might enjoy some. Suddenly the Constable's hands found a new reason for existence and began to busy themselves exploring the darker corners of old wooden cupboards here and there around the little room. "By the way," he said absentmindedly, as he pursued this quest, "if you had in mind actually passing *through* the gate, that is to say, if you wanted to *visit* Dovetail, as you would be abundantly welcome to do, then you should know a few things about our rules."

He stood up and turned toward them, displaying a tin box labeled SHORTBREAD.

"To be specific, the young gentleman's chocky sticks and switchblade will have to come out of his trousers and lodge here, in the loving care of me and my colleagues, and I will have to have a good long look at that monstrous chunk of rod logic, batteries, sensor arrays, and what-have-you that the young lady is carrying in her little knapsack, concealed, unless I am mistaken, in the guise of a book. Hmmm?" And the Constable turned toward them with his eyebrows raised very high on his forehead, shaking the plaid box.

Constable Moore, as he introduced himself, examined Harv's weapons with more care than really seemed warranted, as if they were relics freshly exhumed from a pyramid. He took care to compliment Harv on their presumed effectiveness, and to meditate aloud on the grave foolishness of anyone's messing about with a young fellow like Harv. The weapons went into one of the cupboards, which Constable Moore locked by talking to it. "And now the book, young lady," he said to Nell, pleasantly enough.

She didn't want to let the Primer out of her hands, but she remembered the kids at the playroom who had tried to take it from her and been shocked, or something, for their trouble. So she handed it over. Constable Moore took it very carefully in both hands, and a tiny little moan of appreciation escaped his lips. "I should inform you that sometimes it does rather nasty things to people who, as it supposes, are trying to steal it from me," Nell said, then bit her lip, hoping she hadn't implied that Constable Moore was a thief.

"Young lady, I should be crestfallen if it didn't."

After Constable Moore had turned the book over in his hands a few times, complimenting Nell on the binding, the gold script, the feel of the paper, he set it down gingerly on the table, first rubbing his hand over the wood to ensure no tea or sugar had earlier been spilled there. He wandered away from the table and seemed to stumble at random upon an oak-and-brass copier that sat in one of the obtuse corners of the octagonal room. He happened upon a few pages in its output tray and went through them for a bit, from time to time chuckling ruefully. At one point he looked up at Nell and shook his head wordlessly before finally saying, "Do you have any idea . . ." but then he just chuckled again, shook his head, and went back to the papers.

"Right," he finally said, "right." He fed the papers back into the copier and told it to destroy them. He thrust his fists into his trouser pockets and walked up and down the length of the room twice, then sat down again, looking not at Nell and Harv and not at the book, but somewhere off into the distance. "Right," he said. "I will not confiscate the book during your stay in Dovetail, if you follow certain conditions. First of all, you will not under any circumstances make use of a matter compiler. Secondly, the book is for your use, and your use only. Third, you will not copy or reproduce any of the information contained in the book. Fourth, you will not show the book to anyone here or make anyone aware of its existence. Violation of any of these conditions will lead to your immediate expulsion from Dovetail and the confiscation and probable destruction of the book. Do I make myself clear?"

"Perfectly clear, sir," Nell said. Outside, they heard the *thrudalump thrudalump* of an approaching horse.

A new friend; Nell sees a real horse; a ride through Dovetail; Nell and Harv are separated.

*T*he person on the horse was not Brad, it was a woman Nell and Harv didn't know. She had straight reddish-blond hair, pale skin with thousands of freckles, and carrot-colored eyebrows and eyelashes that were almost invisible except when the sun grazed her face. "I'm a friend of Brad's," she said. "He's at work. Does he know you?"

Nell was about to pipe up, but Harv shushed her with a hand on her arm and gave the woman a somewhat more abridged version than Nell might have provided. He mentioned that Brad had been "a friend of" their mother's for a while, that he had always treated them kindly and had actually taken them to the NAC to see the horses. Not far into the story, the blank expression on the woman's face was replaced by one that was somewhat more guarded, and she stopped listening. "I think Brad told me about you once," she finally said when Harv had wandered into a blind alley. "I know he remembers you. So what is it that you would like to happen now?"

This was a poser. Nell and Harv had settled into a habit of concentrating very strongly on what they would like *not* to happen. They were baffled by options, which to them seemed like dilemmas. Harv left off clutching Nell's arm and took her hand instead. Neither of them said anything.

"Perhaps," Constable Moore finally said, after the

woman had turned to him for a cue, "it would be useful for the two of you to set awhile in some safe, quiet place and gather your thoughts."

"That would do nicely, thank you," Nell said.

"Dovetail contains many public parks and gardens . . ."

"Forget it," the woman said, knowing her cue when she heard it. "I'll take them back to the Millhouse until Brad gets home. Then," she said significantly to the Constable, "we'll figure something out."

The woman stepped out of the gatehouse briskly, not looking back at Nell and Harv. She was tall and wore a pair of loose khaki trousers, much worn at the knees but hardly at all in the seat, and splotched here and there with old unidentifiable stains. Above that she wore a very loose Irish fisherman's sweater, sleeves rolled up and safety-pinned to form a dense woolen torus orbiting each of her freckled forearms, the motif echoed by a whorl of cheap silver bangles on each wrist. She was muttering something in the direction of her horse, an Appaloosa mare who had already swung her neck down and begun to nuzzle at the disappointingly close-cropped grass inside the fence, looking for a blade or two that had not been marked by the assiduous corgis. When she stopped to stroke the mare's neck, Nell and Harv caught up with her and learned that she was simply giving a simplified account of what had just happened in the gatehouse, and what was going to happen now, all delivered rather absentmindedly, just in case the mare might want to know. For a moment Nell thought that the mare might actually be a chevaline dressed up in a fake horse skin, but then it ejected a stream of urine the dimensions of a fencepost, glittering like a light saber in the morning sun and clad in a torn cloak of steam, and Nell smelled it and knew the horse was real. The woman did not mount the horse, which she had apparently ridden bareback, but took its reins as gently as if they were cobwebs and led the horse on. Nell and Harv followed, a few paces behind, and the woman walked across the green for some time, apparently organizing things in her mind, before finally tucking her hair behind her ear on one side and turning toward them. "Did Constable Moore talk to you about rules at all?"

"What rules?" Harv blurted before Nell could get into

it in a level of detail that might have cast a negative light on them. Nell marveled for the hundredth time at her brother's multifarious trickiness, which would have done Peter himself proud.

"We make things," the woman said, as if this provided a nearly perfect and sufficient explanation of the phyle called Dovetail. "Brad makes horseshoes. But Brad's the exception because mostly he provides services relating to horses. Doesn't he, Eggshell?" the woman added for the mare's benefit. "That's why he had to live down in the L.T. for a while, because there was disagreement as to whether grooms, butlers, and other service providers fit in with Dovetail's charter. But we had a vote and decided to let them in. This is boring you, isn't it? My name's Rita, and I make paper."

"You mean, in the M.C.?"

This seemed like an obvious question to Nell, but Rita was surprised to hear it and eventually laughed it off. "I'll show you later. But what I was getting at is that, unlike where you've been living, everything here at Dovetail was made by hand. We have a few matter compilers here. But if we want a chair, say, one of our craftsmen will put it together out of wood, just like in ancient times."

"Why don't you just compile it?" Harv said. "The M.C. can make wood."

"It can make fake wood," Rita said, "but some people don't like fake things."

"Why don't you like fake things?" Nell asked.

Rita smiled at her. "It's not just us. It's them," she said, pointing up the mountain toward the belt of high trees that separated Dovetail from New Atlantis territory.

Light dawned on Harv's face. "The Vickys buy stuff from you!" he said.

Rita looked a little surprised, as if she'd never heard them called Vickys before. "Anyway, what was I getting at? Oh, yeah, the point is that everything here is unique, so you have to be careful with it."

Nell had a rough idea of what unique was, but Harv didn't, and so Rita explained it for a while as they walked through Dovetail. At some length it dawned on both Nell and Harv that Rita was actually trying to tell them, in the most bewilderingly circumspect way imaginable, that she didn't want them to run around and break stuff. This approach to child behavior modification was so at odds with everything they knew that, in spite of Rita's efforts to be pleasant, the conversation was blighted by confusion on the children's part and frustration on hers. From time to time her freckles vanished as her face turned red.

Where Dovetail had streets, they were paved with little blocks of stone laid close together. The vehicles were horses, chevalines, and velocipedes with fat knobby tires. Except for one spot where a number of buildings clustered together around a central green, houses were widely spaced and tended to be very small or very large. All of them seemed to have nice gardens though, and from time to time Nell would dart off the road to smell a flower. At first Rita would watch her nervously, telling her not to pick any of the flowers as they belonged to other people.

At the end of a road was a wooden gate with a laughably primitive latch consisting of a sliding plank, glossy with use. Past the gate, the road became a very rough mosaic of flagstones with grass growing between them. It wound between undulating pastures where horses and the occasional dairy cow grazed and eventually terminated at a great three-story stone building perched on the bank of a river that ran down the mountain from the New Atlantis Clave. A giant wheel grew out of the side of the building and spun slowly as the river pushed on it. A man stood outside before a large chopping-block, using a hatchet with an exceptionally wide blade to split thin wedges of red wood from a log. These were piled into a wicker basket that was hauled up on a rope by a man who stood on the roof, replacing some of the old gray shingles with these new red ones.

Harv was paralyzed with wonder at this exhibition and stopped walking. Nell had seen much the same sort of process at work in the pages of her Primer. She followed Rita over to a long low building where the horses lived.

Most of the people did not live in the Millhouse proper but in a couple of long outbuildings, two stories each, with workshops below and living quarters above. Nell was a little surprised to see that Rita did not actually live with Brad. Her apartment and her shop were each twice the size of Nell's old flat and filled with fine things of heavy wood, metal, cotton, linen, and porcelain that, as Nell was beginning to understand, had all been made by human hands, probably right here in Dovetail.

Rita's shop had great kettles where she would brew thick fibrous stew. She spread the stew thinly over screens to draw out the water and flattened it with a great hand-cranked press to make paper, thick and rough-edged and subtly colored from the thousands of tiny fibers wending through it. When she had a stack of paper made, she would take it next door to a shop with a sharp oily smell, where a bearded man with a smudged apron would run it through another big hand-cranked machine. When it came out of this machine, it had letters on the top, giving the name and address of a lady in New Atlantis.

Since Nell had been decorous so far and not tried to stick her fingers into the machinery and not driven anyone to distraction with her questions, Rita gave her leave to visit some of the other shops, as long as she asked permission at each one. Nell spent most of the day making friends with various shop owners: a glassblower, a jeweler, a cabinet-maker, a weaver, even a toymaker who gave her a tiny wooden doll in a calico dress.

Harv spent awhile bothering the men who were putting shingles on the roof, then wandered about in the fields for most of the day, kicking small rocks from place to place, generally scoping out the boundaries and general condition of the community centered on the Millhouse. Nell checked in on him from time to time. At first he looked tense and skeptical, then he relaxed and enjoyed it, and finally, late in the afternoon, he became surly and perched himself on a boulder above the running stream, tossing pebbles into it, chewing his thumbnail, and thinking.

Brad came home early, riding a bay stallion straight down the mountain from the New Atlantis Clave, angling through the greenbelt and piercing the dog pod grid with scant consequences as the authorities knew him. Harv approached him with a formal mien, harrumphing phlegm out of the way as he prepared to offer up an explanation and a plea. But Brad's eyes merely glanced over Harv, settled on Nell, appraised her for a moment, then looked away shyly. The verdict was that they could stay the night, but all else depended on legal niceties that were beyond his powers.

"Have you done anything the Shanghai Police might

find interesting?" Brad asked Harv gravely. Harv said no, a simple no without the usual technicalities, provisos, and subclauses.

Nell wanted to tell Brad everything. But she had been noticing how, in the Primer, whenever someone asked Peter Rabbit a direct question of any kind, he always lied.

"To look at our green fields and big houses, you might think we're on Atlantis turf here," Brad said, "but we're under Shanghai jurisdiction just like the rest of the Leased Territories. Now usually the Shanghai Police don't come around, because we are peaceable folk and because we have made certain arrangements with them. But if it were known that we were harboring runaway gang members—"

" 'Nuff said," Harv blurted. It was clear that he had already worked all of this out in his head as he sat on the riverbank and was only waiting for the adults to catch up with his logic. Before Nell understood what was going on, he came up to her and gave her a hug and a kiss on the lips. Then he turned away from her and began running across a green field, down toward the ocean. Nell ran after him, but she could not keep up, and finally she fell down in a stand of bluebells and watched Harv dissolve into a curtain of tears. When she could no longer see him, she curled up sobbing, and in time Rita came and gathered her up in her strong arms and carried her slowly back across the field to the Millhouse where the steady wheel rolled.

Orphans of the Han are exposed to the benefits of modern educational technology; Judge Fang reflects on the fundamental precepts of Confucianism.

The orphanage ships had built-in matter compilers, but they could not, of course, be hooked up to Sources. Instead they drew their supplies of matter from cubical containers, rather like tanks of atoms arranged very precisely. These containers could be loaded on board with cranes and hooked up to the matter compilers in the same way that Feed lines would be if they resided on shore. The ships put in to Shanghai frequently, offloaded empty containers, and took new ones on board—their hungry populations were fed almost exclusively on synthetic rice produced by the matter compilers.

There were seven ships now. The first five had been named after the Master's Five Virtues, and after that they had taken to naming them after major Confucian philosophers. Judge Fang flew out to the one named (as best it could be translated into English) *Generosity of Soul*, personally carrying the M.C. program in the sleeve of his garment. This was the very ship he had visited on the eventful night of his boat ride with Dr. X, and ever since then he had somehow felt closer to these fifty thousand little mice than any of the other quarter-million in the other vessels.

The program was written to work in a bulk compiler, extruding dozens of Primers each cycle. When the first batch was finished, Judge Fang plucked out one of the new volumes, inspected its cover, which had the appearance of marbled jade, flipped through the pages admiring the illustrations, and cast a critical eye over the calligraphy.

Then he carried it down a corridor and into a playroom where a few hundred little mice were running around, blowing off steam. He caught the eye of one girl and beckoned her over. She came, reluctantly, chivvied along by an energetic teacher who alternated between smiling to the girl and bowing to Judge Fang.

He squatted so that he could look her in the eye and handed her the book. She was much more interested in the book than in Judge Fang, but she had been taught the proper formalities and bowed and thanked him. Then she opened it up. Her eyes got wide. The book began to talk to her. To Judge Fang the voice sounded a bit dull, the rhythm of the speech not exactly right. But the girl didn't care. The girl was hooked.

Judge Fang stood up to find himself surrounded by a hundred little girls, all facing toward the little jade book, standing on tiptoes, mouths open.

Finally he had been able to do something unambiguously good with his position. In the Coastal Republic it wouldn't have been possible; in the Middle Kingdom, which hewed to the words and spirit of the Master, it was simply part of his duties.

He turned and left the room; none of the girls noticed, which was just as well, as they might have seen a quiver in his lip and a tear in his eye. As he made his way through the corridors toward the upper deck where his airship awaited him, he reviewed for the thousandth time the Great Learning, the kernel of the Master's thought: *The ancients who wished to demonstrate illustrious virtue throughout the kingdom, first ordered well their own states. Wishing to order well their states, they first regulated their families. Wishing to regulate their families, they first cultivated their persons. Wishing to cultivate their persons, they first rectified their hearts. Wishing to rectify their hearts, they first sought to be sincere in their thoughts. Wishing to be sincere in their thoughts, they first extended to the utmost their knowledge. Such extention of knowledge lay in the investigation of things. . . . From the Son of Heaven down to the mass of the people, all must consider the cultivation of the person the root of everything besides.*

Hackworth receives an ambiguous message; a ride through Vancouver; tattooed woman and totem poles; he enters the hidden world of the Drummers.

Kidnapper had a glove compartment of sorts hollowed into the back of its neck. As he was riding across the causeway, Hackworth opened it up because he wanted to see whether it was large enough to contain his bowler without folding, bending, spindling, or mutilating the exquisite hyperboloid of its brim. The answer was that it was just a wee bit too small. But Dr. X had been thoughtful enough to toss in some snacks: a handful of fortune cookies, three of them to be exact. They looked good. Hackworth picked one and snapped it open. The strip of paper bore some kind of gaudily animated geometric pattern, long strands of something tumbling end over end and bouncing against one another. It looked vaguely familiar: These were supposed to be yarrow stalks, which Taoists used for divination. But instead of forming a hexagram of the *I Ching*, they began falling into place, one after another, in such a way as to form letters in the pseudo-Chinese typeface used in the logos of one-star Chinese restaurants. When the last one had bounced into place, the fortune read:

SEEK THE ALCHEMIST.

"Thanks ever so much, Dr. X," Hackworth snapped. He continued to watch the fortune for a while, hoping that it would turn into something a little more informative, but it was dead, just a piece of litter now and forever.

Kidnapper slowed to a canter and cruised purposefully through the university, then turned north and crossed a bridge into the peninsula that contained most of Vancouver proper. The chevaline did a perfectly good job of not stepping on anyone, and Hackworth soon learned to stop worrying and trust its instincts. This left his eyes free to wander through the sights of Vancouver, which had not been advisable when he'd come this way on the velocipede. He had not noticed, before, the sheer maddening profusion of the place, each person seemingly an ethnic group of one, each with his or her own costume, dialect, sect, and pedigree. It was as if, sooner or later, every part of the world became India and thus ceased to function in any sense meaningful to straight-arrow Cartesian rationalists like John Percival Hackworth, his family and friends.

Shortly after passing the Aerodrome they reached Stanley Park, an unruined peninsula several miles around, which had, thank God, been forked over to Protocol and kept much as it had always been, with the same Douglas firs and mossy red cedars that had been growing there forever. Hackworth had been here a few times and had a vague idea of how it was laid out: restaurants here and there, paths along the beach, a zoo and aquarium, public playing fields.

Kidnapper took him for a nice lope along a pebbly beach and then somewhat abruptly bounded up a slope, for that purpose switching into a gait never used by any real horse. Its legs shortened, and it clawed its way surefootedly up the forty-five-degree surface like a mountain lion. An alarmingly quick zigzag through a stand of firs brought them into an open grassy area. Then Kidnapper slowed to a mere walk, as if it were a real horse that had to be cooled down gradually, and took Hackworth into a semicircle of old totem poles.

A young woman was here, standing before one of the poles with her hands clasped behind her back, which would have given her an endearingly prim appearance if she had not been stark naked and covered with constantly shifting mediatronic tattoos. Even her hair, which fell loosely to her waist, had been infiltrated with some kind of nanosite so that each strand's color fluctuated from place to place according to a scheme not just now apparent to Hackworth. She was looking intently at the carving of a totem pole and apparently not for the first time, for her tattoos were done in much the same style.

The woman was looking at a totem pole dominated by a representation of an orca, head down and tail up, dorsal fin projecting horizontally out of the pole and evidently carved from a separate piece of wood. The orca's blowhole had a human face carved around it. The face's mouth and the orca's blowhole were the same thing. This promiscuous denial of boundaries was everywhere on the totem poles and on the woman's tattoo: The staring eyes of a bear were also the faces of some other sort of creature. The woman's navel was also the mouth of a human face, much like the orca's blowhole, and sometimes that face became the mouth of a larger face whose eyes were her nipples and whose goatee was her pubic hair. But as soon as he'd made out one pattern, it would change into something else, because unlike the totem poles the tattoo was dynamic and played with images in time the same way that the totem poles did in space.

"Hello, John," she said. "It's too bad I loved you because you had to leave."

Hackworth tried to find her face, which should have been easy, it being the thing in the front of her head; but his eyes kept snagging on all the other little faces that came and went and flowed into one another, time-sharing her eyes, her mouth, even her nostrils. And he was starting to recognize patterns in her hair too, which was more than he could handle. He was pretty sure he had just caught a glimpse of Fiona in there.

She turned her back on him, her hair spinning out

momentarily like a twirling skirt, and for that instant he could see through it and begin to make sense of the image. He was positive that somewhere in there he'd seen Gwen and Fiona walking along a beach.

He dismounted from Kidnapper and followed her on foot. Kidnapper followed him silently. They walked across the park for half a mile or so, and Hackworth kept his distance because when he got too close to her, the images in her hair bewildered his eyes. She took him to a wild stretch of beach where immense Douglas fir logs lay scattered around. As Hackworth clambered over the logs trying to keep up with the woman, he occasionally caught a handhold that appeared to have been carved by someone long ago.

The logs were palimpsests. Two of them rose from the water's edge, not quite vertical, stuck like darts into the impermanent sand. Hackworth walked between them, the surf crashing around his knees. He saw weathered intimations of faces and wild beasts living in the wood, ravens, eagles, and wolves tangled into organic skeins. The water was bitterly cold on his legs, and he whooped in a couple of breaths, but the woman kept walking; the water was up past her waist now, and her hair was floating around her so that the translucent images once again became readable. Then she vanished beneath a collapsing wave two meters high.

The wave knocked Hackworth on his backside and washed him along for a short distance, flailing his arms and legs. When he got his balance back, he sat there for a few moments, letting smaller waves embrace his waist and chest, waiting for the woman to come up for a breath. But she didn't.

There was something down there. He rolled up onto his feet and tramped straight into the ocean. Just as the waves were coming up into his face, his feet contacted something hard and smooth that gave way beneath him. He was sucked downward as the water plunged into a subterranean void. A hatch slammed shut above his head, and suddenly he was breathing air again. The light was silver. He was sitting in water up to his chest, but it rapidly drained away, drawn off by some kind of a pumping system, and then he found himself looking down a long silvery tunnel. The woman was descending it, a stone's throw ahead of him.

Hackworth had been in a few of these, normally in

more industrial settings. The entrance was dug into the beach, but the rest of it was a floating tunnel, a tube full of air, moored to the bottom. It was a cheap way to make space; the Nipponese used these things as sleeping quarters for foreign guest workers. The walls were made of membranes that drew oxygen from the surrounding seawater and ejected carbon dioxide, so that seen from a fish's point of view, the tunnels steamed like hot pasta on a cold steel plate as they excreted countless microbubbles of polluted CO_2. These things extruded themselves into the water like the roots that grew out of improperly stored potatoes, forking from time to time, carrying their own Feeds forward so that they could be extended on command. They were empty and collapsed to begin with, and when they knew they were finished, they inflated themselves with scavenged oxygen and grew rigid.

Now that the cold water had drained out of Hackworth's ears, he could hear a deep drumming that he'd mistaken at first for the crash of the surf overhead; but this had a steadier beat that invited him forward.

Down the tunnel Hackworth walked, following the woman, and as he went the light grew dimmer and the tunnel narrower. He suspected that the walls of the tunnel had mediatronic properties because he kept seeing things from the corners of his eyes that were no longer there when he snapped his head around. He'd assumed that he would soon reach a chamber, a swelling in the tunnel where this woman's friends would sit pounding on enormous kettledrums, but before reaching any such thing, he came to a place where the tunnel had gone completely dark, and he had to crouch to his knees and feel his way along. When he touched the taut but yielding wall of the tunnel with his knees and his hands, he felt the drumming in his bones and realized that audio was built into the stuff; the drumming could be anywhere, or it could be recorded. Or maybe it was a lot simpler than that, maybe the tubes happened to transmit sound well, and somewhere else in the tunnel system, people were just pounding on the walls.

His head contacted the tunnel. He dropped to his belly and began to crawl along. Swarms of tiny sparkling lights kept lunging past his face, and he realized that they were his hands; light-emitting nanosites had become embedded in his flesh. They must have been put there by Dr. X's physician; but they had not come alight until he entered these tunnels.

If the woman hadn't already come through here, he would have given up at this point, thinking it a dead end, a busted tunnel that had failed to expand. The drumming was now coming into his ears and bones from all sides. He could not see a thing, though from time to time he thought he caught a glimmer of flickering yellow light. The tunnel undulated slightly in the deep currents, rivers of bitterly cold water swirling along the floor of the straits. Whenever he allowed his mind to wander, reminding himself that he was deep below the surface of the ocean here, he had to stop and force himself not to panic. Concentrate on the nice air-filled tunnel, not what surrounds it.

There was definitely light ahead. He found himself in a swelling in the tube, just wide enough to sit up in, and rolled over on his back for a moment to rest. A lamp was burning in here, a bowl filled with some kind of melting hydrocarbon that left no ash or smoke. The mediatronic walls had animated scenes on them, barely visible in the flickering light: animals dancing in the forest.

He followed the tubes for some period of time that was quite long but difficult to estimate. From time to time he would come to a chamber with a lamp and more paintings. As he crawled through the long perfectly black tunnels, he began to experience visual and auditory hallucinations, vague at first, just random noise knocking around in his neural net, but increasingly well-resolved and realistic. The hallucinations had a dreamlike quality in which things he'd actually seen recently, such as Gwen and Fiona, Dr. X, the airship, the boys playing fieldball, were mingled with images so alien he scarcely recognized them. It troubled him that his mind was taking something as dear to him as Fiona and blending her into a farrago of alien sights and ideas.

He could see the nanosites in his skin. But for all he knew, he might have a million more living in his brain now, piggybacking on axons and dendrites, sending data to one another in flashes of light. A second brain intermingled with his own.

There was no reason that information could not be relayed from one such nanosite to another, through his body and outward to the nanosites in his skin, and from there across the darkness to others. What would happen when he came close to other people with similar infestations?

When he finally reached the grand chamber, he could not really tell whether it was reality or another machine-made hallucination. It was shaped like a flattened ice-cream cone, a domed ceiling above a gently sloping conical floor. The ceiling was a vast mediatron, and the floor served as an amphitheatre. Hackworth spilled into the room abruptly as the drumming reached a crescendo. The floor was slick, and he slid down helplessly until he reached the central pit. He rolled onto his back and saw a fiery scene sprawling across the dome above, and in his peripheral vision, covering the floor of the theatre, a thousand living constellations pounding on the floor with their hands.

PART
THE SECOND

Bred and born in the Foreign regions beyond, there is much in the administration of the Celestial Dynasty that is not perfectly comprehensible to the Barbarians, and they are continually putting forced constructions on things of which it is difficult to explain to them the real nature.

—*Qiying*

Hackworth has a singular experience;
the rite of the Drummers.

In a cavernous dark space lit by many small fires, a young woman, probably not much more than a girl, stands on a pedestal naked except for an elaborate paint job, or maybe it is a total-body mediatronic tattoo. A crown of leafy branches is twined around her head, and she has thick voluminous hair spreading to her knees. She is clutching a bouquet of roses to her breast, the thorns indenting her flesh. Many people, perhaps thousands, surround her, drumming madly, sometimes chanting and singing.

Into the space between the girl and the watchers, a couple of dozen men are introduced. Some come running out of their own accord, some look as if they've been pushed, some wander in as if they've been walking down the street (stark naked) and gone in the wrong door. Some are Asian, some European, some African. Some have to be prodded by frenzied celebrants who charge out of the crowd and shove them here and there. Eventually they form a circle around the girl, and then the drumming builds to a deafening crescendo, speeds up until it devolves into a rhythmless hailstorm, and then suddenly, instantly, stops.

Someone wails something in a high, purposeful, ululating voice. Hackworth can't understand what this person is saying. Then there is a single massive drumbeat. More wailing. Another drumbeat. Again. The third drumbeat establishes a ponderous rhythm. This goes on for a while, the beat slowly speeding up. After a certain point the wailer no longer stops between beats, he begins to weave his rap through the bars in a sort of counterpoint. The ring of men standing around the girl begin to dance in a very simple shuffling motion, one way and then the other way around the girl. Hackworth notes that all of them have erections, sheathed in brightly colored mediatronic condoms—rubbers that actually make their own light so that the bobbing boners look like so many cyalume wands dancing through the air.

The drumbeats and the dancing speed up very slowly. The erections tell Hackworth why this is taking so long: He's watching foreplay here. After half an hour or so, the excitement, phallic and otherwise, is unbearable. The beat is now a notch faster than your basic pulse rate, lots of other beats and counterrhythms woven through it, and the chanting of the individual singer has become a wild semi-organized choral phenomenon. At some point, after seemingly nothing has happened for half an hour, everything happens at once: The drumming and chanting explode to a new, impossible level of intensity. The dancers reach down, grip the flaccid reservoir tips of their radioactive condoms, stretch them out. Someone runs out with a knife and cuts off the tips of the condoms in a freakish parody of circumcision, exposing the glans of each man's penis. The girl moves for the first time, tossing her bouquet up in the air like a bride making her move toward the limo; the roses fountain, spinning end over end, and come down individually among the dancers, who snatch them out of the air, scrabble for them on the floor, whatever. The girl faints, or something, falling backward, arms out, and is caught by several of the dancers, who hoist her body up over their heads and parade her around the circle for a while, like a crucified body just crowbarred off the tree. She ends up flat on her back on the ground, and one of the dancers is between her legs, and in a very few thrusts he has finished. A couple of others grab his arms and yank him out of there before he's even had a chance to tell her he'll still love her in the morning, and another one is in there, and he doesn't take very long either—all this foreplay has got these guys in hair-trigger mode. The dancers manage to rotate through in a few minutes. Hackworth can't see the girl, who's completely hidden, but she's not struggling, as far as he can tell, and they don't seem to be holding her down. Toward the end, smoke or steam or something begins to spiral up from the middle of the orgy. The last participant grimaces even more than the average person who's having an orgasm, and yanks himself back from the woman, grabbing his dick and hopping up and down and hollering in what looks like pain. That's the signal for all of the dancers to jump back away from the woman, who is now kind of hard to make out, just a fuzzy motionless package wrapped in steam.

Flames erupt from several locations, all over her body, at once, seams of lava splitting open along her veins and the heart itself erupting from her chest like ball lightning. Her body becomes a burning cross spread out on the floor, the bright apex of an inverted cone of turbulent steam and smoke. Hackworth notices that the drumming and chanting have completely stopped. The crowd observes a long moment of silence while the body burns. Then, when the last of the flames have died out, an honor guard of sorts descends from the crowd: four men in black body paint with white skeletons painted on top of that. He notes that the woman was lying on a square sheet of some kind when she burned. Each of the guys grabs a corner of the sheet. Her remains tumble into the center, powdery ash flies, flecks of red-hot coals spark. The skeleton men carry the remains over to a fifty-five-gallon steel drum and dump it in. There is a burst of steam and lots of sizzling noises as the hot coals contact some kind of liquid that was in the drum. One of the skeleton men picks up a long spoon and gives the mix a stir, then dips a cracked and spalled University of Michigan coffee mug into it and takes a long drink.

The other three skeleton men each drink in their turn. By now, the spectators have formed a long queue. One by one they step forward. The leader of the skeleton men holds the mug for them, gives each one a sip. Then they all wander off, individually or in small, conversing groups. Show's over.

Nell's life at Dovetail; developments in the Primer; a trip to the New Atlantis Clave; she is presented to Miss Matheson; new lodgings with an "old" acquaintance.

Nell lived in the Millhouse for several days. They gave her a little bed under the eaves on the top floor, in a cozy place only she was tiny enough to reach. She had her meals with Rita or Brad or one of the other nice people she knew there. During the days she would wander in the meadow or dangle her feet in the river or explore the woods, sometimes going as far as the dog pod grid. She always took the Primer with her. Lately, it had been filled with the doings of Princess Nell and her friends in the city of King Magpie. It kept getting more like a ractive and less like a story, and by the end of each chapter she was exhausted from all the cleverness she had expended just to get herself and her friends through another day without falling into the clutches of pirates or of King Magpie himself.

In time, she and Peter came up with a very tricky plan to sneak into the castle, create a diversion, and seize the magic books that were the source of King Magpie's power. This plan failed the first time, but the next day, Nell turned the page back and tried it again, this time with a few changes. It failed again, but not before Princess Nell and her friends had gotten a little farther into the castle. The sixth or seventh time, the plan worked perfectly—while King Magpie was locked in a battle of riddles with Peter Rabbit (which Peter won), Purple used a magic spell to smash open the door to his secret library, which was filled with books even more magical than the *Young Lady's Illustrated Primer*. Hidden inside one of those books was a jeweled key. Princess Nell took the key, and Purple made off with several of King Magpie's magic books while she was at it.

They made a breathtaking escape across a river into the next country, where King Magpie could not chase them, and camped in a nice meadow for a few days, resting. During the daytime, when the others were just stuffed animals, Princess Nell would peruse some of the new magic books that Purple had stolen. When she did, its image in the illustration would zoom toward her until it filled the page, and then the Primer itself would become that magical book until she decided to put it away.

Nell's favorite book was a magical Atlas which she could use to explore any land, real or imaginary. During the nighttime, Purple spent most of her time reading a very large, crusty, worn, stained, burnt tome entitled *PANTECHNICON*. This book had a built-in hasp with a padlock. Whenever Purple wasn't using it, she locked it shut. Nell asked to see it a few times, but Purple told her she was too young to know such things as were written in this Book.

During this time, Duck as usual made herself busy around the camp, tidying up and fixing their meals, doing laundry on the rocks by the river, and mending their clothes that had become ragged during their wanderings. Peter became restless. He was quick with words, but he had not learned the trick of reading, and so the books from King Magpie's library were of no use to him save as nest-lining material. He got into the habit of exploring the surrounding forests, particularly the ones to the north. At first he would be gone for a few hours at a time, but once he stayed away all night and did not come back until the following noon. Then he began to go on trips for several days at a time.

Peter vanished into the north woods one day, staggering under a heavy pack, and didn't come back at all.

Nell was in the meadow one day, gathering flowers, when a fine lady—a Vicky—came riding toward her on a horse. When she drew closer, Nell was surprised to see that the horse was Eggshell and the lady was Rita, all dressed up in a long dress like the Vicky ladies wore, with a riding hat on her head, and riding sidesaddle of all things.

"You look pretty," Nell said.

"Thank you, Nell," Rita said. "Would you like to look like this too, for a little while? I have a surprise for you."

One of the ladies who lived in the Millhouse was a milliner, and she had made Nell a dress, sewing it all together by hand. Rita had brought this dress with her, and she helped Nell change into it, right there in the middle of the meadow. Then she braided Nell's hair and even tucked some tiny wildflowers into it. Finally she helped Nell climb up on top of Eggshell with her and began riding back toward the Millhouse.

"You will have to leave your book here today," Rita said.

"Why?"

"I'm taking you through the grid, into New Atlantis Clave," Rita said. "Constable Moore told me that I should not on any account allow you to carry your book through the grid. He said it would only stir things up. I know you're about to ask me why, Nell, but I don't have an answer."

Nell ran upstairs, tripping over her long skirts a couple of times, and left the Primer in her little nook. Then she climbed back on Eggshell with Rita. They rode over a little stone bridge above the waterwheel and through the woods, until Nell could hear the faint afflatus of the security aerostats. Eggshell slowed to a walk and pushed gingerly through the field of shiny hovering teardrops. Nell even reached out and touched one, then snapped her hand back, even though it hadn't done anything except push back. The reflection of her face slithered backward across the surface of this pod as they went by.

They rode across the territory of New Atlantis for some time without seeing anything other than trees, wildflowers, brooks, the occasional squirrel, or deer.

"Why do the Vickys have such a big clave?" Nell asked.

"Don't ever call them Vickys," Rita said.

"Why?"

"It's a word that people who don't like them use to describe them in kind of a bad, unfriendly way," Rita said.

"Like a pejorative term?" Nell said.

Rita laughed, more nervous than amused. "Exactly."

"Why do the Atlantans have such a big clave?"

"Well, each phyle has a different way, and some ways

are better suited to making money than others, so some have a lot of territory and others don't."

"What do you mean, a different way?"

"To make money you have to work hard—to live your life in a certain way. The Atlantans all live that way, it's part of their culture. The Nipponese too. So the Nipponese and the Atlantans have as much money as all the other phyles put together."

"Why aren't you an Atlantan?"

"Because I don't want to live that way. All the people in Dovetail like to make beautiful things. To us, the things that the Atlantans do—dressing up in these kinds of clothes, spending years and years in school—are irrelevant. Those pursuits wouldn't help us make beautiful things, you see. I'd rather just wear my blue jeans and make paper."

"But the M.C. can make paper," Nell said.

"Not the kind that the Atlantans like."

"But you make money from your paper only because the Atlantans make money from working hard," Nell said.

Rita's face turned red and she said nothing for a little while. Then, in a tight voice, she said, "Nell, you should ask your book the meaning of the word *discretion*."

They came across a riding-trail dotted with great mounds of horse manure, and began following it uphill. Soon the trail was hemmed in between dry stone walls, which Rita said that one of her friends in Dovetail had made. Forest gave way to pastures, then lawns like jade glaciers, and great houses on hilltops, surrounded by geometric hedges and ramparts of flowers. The trail became a cobblestone road that adopted new lanes from time to time as they rode into town. The mountain kept rising up above them for some distance, and on its green summit, half veiled behind a thin cloud layer, Nell could see Source Victoria.

From down in the Leased Territories, the New Atlantis Clave had always looked clean and beautiful, and it was certainly those things. But Nell was surprised at how cool the weather was here compared to the L.T. Rita explained that the Atlantans came from northern countries and didn't care for hot weather, so they put their city high up in the air to make it cooler.

Rita turned down a boulevard with a great flowery park running down the middle. It was lined with red stone row-houses with turrets and gargoyles and beveled glass everywhere. Men in top hats and women in long dresses strolled, pushed perambulators, rode horses or chevalines. Shiny dark green robots, like refrigerators tipped over on their sides, hummed down the streets at a toddler's walking pace, squatting over piles of manure and inhaling them. From place to place there was a messenger on a bicycle or an especially fancy personage in a black, full-lane car.

Rita stopped Eggshell in front of a house and paid a little boy to hold the reins. From the saddlebags she took a sheaf of new paper, all wrapped up in special wrapping-paper that she'd also made. She carried it up the steps and rang the bell. The house had a round tower on the front, lined with bow windows with stained-glass inserts above them, and through the windows and the lace curtains Nell could see, on different stories, crystal chandeliers and fine plates and dark brown wooden bookcases lined with thousands and thousands of books.

A parlormaid let Rita in the door. Through the window, Nell could see Rita putting a calling-card on a silver tray held out by the maid—a salver, they called it. The maid carried it back, then emerged a couple of minutes later and directed Rita into the back of the house.

Rita didn't come back for half an hour. Nell wished she had the Primer to keep her company. She talked to the little boy for a bit; his name was Sam, he lived in the Leased Territories, and he put on a suit and took the bus here every morning so that he could hang around on the street holding people's horses and doing other small errands.

Nell wondered whether Tequila worked in any of these houses, and whether they might run into her by accident. Her chest always got a tight feeling when she thought of her mother.

Rita came out of the house. "Sorry," she said, "I got out as fast as I could, but I had to stay and socialize. Protocol, you know."

"Explain protocol," Nell said. This was how she always talked to the Primer.

"At the place we're going, you need to watch your manners. Don't say 'explain this' or 'explain that.' "

"Would it impose on your time unduly to provide me with a concise explanation of the term *protocol*?" Nell said.

Again Rita made that nervous laugh and looked at Nell with an expression that looked like poorly concealed alarm. As they rode down the street, Rita talked about protocol for a little bit, but Nell wasn't really listening because she was trying to figure out why it was that, all of a sudden, she was capable of scaring grown-ups like Rita.

They rode through the most built-up part of town, where the buildings and gardens and statues were all magnificent, and none of the streets were the same: Some were crescents, some were courts, or circles or ovals, or squares surrounding patches of greenery, and even the long streets turned this way and that. They passed from there into a less built-up area with many parks and playing fields and finally pulled up in front of a fancy building with ornate towers, surrounded by a wrought-iron fence and a hedge. Over the door it said MISS MATHESON'S ACADEMY OF THE THREE GRACES.

Miss Matheson received them in a cozy little room. She was between eight hundred and nine hundred years of age, Nell estimated, and drank tea from fancy thimble-size cups with pictures painted on them. Nell tried to sit up straight and be attentive, emulating certain proper young girls she had read about in the Primer, but her eye kept wandering to the contents of the bookshelves, the pictures painted on the tea service and the painting on the wall above Miss Matheson's head, which depicted three ladies prancing about in a grove in diaphanous attire.

"Our rolls are filled, the term has already begun, and you have none of the prerequisites. But you come with compelling recommendations," Miss Matheson said after she had peered lengthily at her small visitor.

"Pardon me, madam, but I do not understand," Nell said.

Miss Matheson smiled, her face blooming into a sunburst of radiating wrinkles. "It is not important. Let us only say that we have made room for you. This institution makes it a practice to accept a small number of students who are not New Atlantan subjects. The propagation of Atlantan memes is central to our mission, as a school and as a society. Unlike some phyles, which propagate through conversion or through indiscriminate exploitation of the natural biological capacity that is shared, for better or worse, by all persons, we appeal to the rational faculties. All children are born with rational faculties, which want only development. Our academy has recently welcomed several young ladies of extra-Atlantan extraction, and it is our expectation that all will go on to take the Oath in due time."

"Pardon me, madam, but which one is Aglaia?" Nell said, looking over Miss Matheson's shoulder at the painting.

"I beg your pardon?" Miss Matheson said, and initiated the procedure of turning her head around to look, which at her age was a civil-engineering challenge of daunting complexity and duration.

"As the name of your school is the Three Graces, I have ventured to assume that yonder painting depicts the same subject," Nell said, "since they look more like Graces than Furies or Fates. I wonder if you would be so kind as to inform me which of the ladies represents Aglaia, or brilliance."

"And the other two are?" Miss Matheson said, speaking out of the side of her mouth as she had almost got herself turned around by this point.

"Euphrosyne, or joy, and Thalia, or bloom," Nell said.

"Would you care to venture an opinion?" Miss Matheson said.

"The one on the right is carrying flowers, so perhaps she is Thalia."

"I would call that a sound assumption."

"The one in the middle looks so happy that she must be Euphrosyne, and the one on the left is lit up with rays of sunlight, so perhaps she is Aglaia."

"Well, as you can see, none of them is wearing a nametag, and so we must satisfy ourselves with conjecture," Miss Matheson said. "But I fail to see any gaps in your reasoning. And no, I don't suppose they are Fates or Furies."

"It's a boarding school, which means many of the pupils live there. But you won't live there," Rita said, "because it isn't proper." They were riding Eggshell home through the woods.

"Why isn't it proper?"

"Because you ran away from home, which raises legal problems."

"Was it illegal for me to run away?"

"In some tribes, children are regarded as an economic asset of their parents. So if one phyle shelters runaways from another phyle, it has a possible economic impact which is covered under the CEP."

Rita looked back at Nell, appraising her coolly. "You have a sponsor of sorts in New Atlantis. I don't know who. I don't know why. But it seems that this person cannot take the risk of being the target of CEP legal action. Hence arrangements have been made for you to stay in Dovetail for now.

"Now, we know that some of your mother's boyfriends treated you badly, and so there is sentiment in Dovetail to take you in. But we can't keep you at the Millstone community, because if we got into a fracas with Protocol, it could sour our relations with our New Atlantis clients. So it's been decided that you will stay with the one person in Dovetail who doesn't have any clients here."

"Who's that?"

"You've met him," Rita said.

Constable Moore's house was dimly lit and so full of old stuff that even Nell had to walk sideways in some places. Long strips of yellowed rice paper, splashed with large Chinese characters and pimpled with red chop marks, hung from a molding that ran around the living room a foot or two beneath the ceiling. Nell followed Rita around a corner into an even smaller, darker, and more crowded room, whose main decoration was a large painting of a furious chap with a Fu Manchu mustache, goatee, and tufts of whiskers sprouting in front of his ears and trailing down below his armpits, wearing elaborate armor and chain mail decorated with lion's faces. Nell stepped away from this fierce picture despite herself, tripped over the drone of a large bagpipe splayed across the floor, and crashed into a large beaten-copper bucket of sorts, which made tremendous smashing noises. Blood welled quietly from a smooth cut on the ball of her thumb, and she realized that the bucket was being used as a repository for a collection of old rusty swords of various descriptions.

"You all right?" Rita said. She was backlit with blue light coming in through a pair of glass doors. Nell put her thumb in her mouth and picked herself up.

The glass doors looked out on Constable Moore's garden, a riot of geraniums, foxtails, wisteria, and corgi droppings. On the other side of a small khaki-colored pool rose a small garden house. Like this one, it was built from blocks of reddish-brown stone and roofed with rough-edged slabs of green-gray slate. Constable Moore himself could be descried behind a screen of somewhat leggy rhododendrons, hard at work with a shovel, continually harassed by the ankle-biting corgis.

He was not wearing a shirt, but he *was* wearing a *skirt*: a red plaid number. Nell hardly noticed this incongruity because the corgis heard Rita turning the latch on the glass doors and rushed toward them yapping, and this drew out the Constable himself, who approached them squinting through the dark glass, and once he was out from behind the rhodies, Nell could see that there was something amiss with the flesh of his body. Overall he was well proportioned, muscular, rather thick around the middle, and evidently in decent health. But his skin came in two colors, which gave him something of a marbled look. It was as though worms had eaten through his torso, carving out a network of internal passageways that had later been backfilled with something that didn't quite match.

Before she could get a better look, he plucked a shirt from the back of a lawn chair and shrugged it on. Then he subjected the corgis to a minute or so of close-order drill, using a patch of moss-covered flagstones as parade ground, and stringently criticizing their performance in tones loud enough to penetrate through the glass doors. The corgis pretended to listen attentively. At the end of the performance, Constable Moore burst in through the glass doors. "I shall be with you momentarily," he said, and disappeared into a back room for a quarter of an hour. When he returned, he was dressed in a tweed suit and a rough-hewn sweater over a very fine-looking white shirt. The last article looked too thin to prevent the others from being intolerably scratchy, but Constable Moore had reached the age when men can subject their bodies to the worst irritations—whiskey, cigars, woolen clothes, bagpipes—without feeling a thing or, at least, without letting on.

"Sorry to have burst in on you," Rita said, "but there was no answer when we rang the bell."

"I don't care," said Constable Moore, not entirely convincingly. "There's a reason why I don't live up there." He pointed upward, vaguely in the direction of the New Atlantis Clave. "Just trying to trace the root system of some infernal vine back to its source. I'm afraid it might be kudzu." The Constable narrowed his eyes as he spoke this word, and Nell, not knowing what kudzu was, supposed that if kudzu were something that could be attacked with a sword, burned, throttled, bludgeoned, or blown up, it would not stand a chance for long in Constable Moore's garden—once, that is, he got round to it.

"Can I interest you in tea? Or"—this was directed to Nell—"some hot chocolate?"

"Sounds lovely, but I can't stay," Rita said.

"Then let me see you to the door," Constable Moore said, standing up. Rita looked a little startled by this abruptness, but in another moment she was gone, riding Eggshell back toward the Millhouse.

"Nice lady," Constable Moore muttered out in the kitchen. "Fine of her to do what she did for you. Really a very decent lady. Perhaps not the sort who deals very well with children. Especially peculiar children."

"Am I to live here now, sir?" Nell said.

"Out in the garden house," he said, coming into the room with a steaming tray and nodding through the glass windows and across the garden. "Vacant for some time. Cramped for an adult, perfect for a child. The decor of this house," he said, glancing around the room, "is not really suitable for a young one."

"Who is the scary man?" Nell said, pointing to the big painting.

"Guan Di. Emperor Guan. Formerly a soldier named Guan Yu. He was never really an emperor, but later on he became the Chinese god of war, and they gave him the title just to be respectful. Terribly respectful, the Chinese—it's their best and worst feature."

"How could a man become a god?" Nell asked.

"By living in an extremely pragmatic society," said Constable Moore after some thought, and provided no further explanation. "Do you have the book, by the way?"

"Yes, sir."

"You didn't take it through the border?"

"No, sir, as per your instructions."

"That's good. The ability to follow orders is a useful thing, especially if you're living with a chap who's used to giving them." Seeing that Nell had gotten a terribly serious look on her face, the Constable huffed and looked exasperated. "It doesn't really matter, mind you! You have friends in high places. It's just that we are trying to be discreet." Constable Moore brought Nell her cup of cocoa. She needed one hand for the saucer and another for the cup, so she took her hand out of her mouth.

"What did you do to your hand?"

"Cut it, sir."

"Let me see that." The Constable took her hand in his and peeled the thumb away from the palm. "Quite a nice little slash. Looks recent."

"I got it from your swords."

"Ah, yes. Swords are that way," the Constable said absently, then screwed up his brow and turned back to Nell. "You did not cry," he said, "and you did not complain."

"Did you take all of those swords away from burglars?" Nell said.

"No—that would have been relatively easy," Constable Moore said. He looked at her for a while, pondering. "Nell, you and I will do just fine together," he said. "Let me get my first-aid kit."

Carl Hollywood's activities at the Parnasse;
conversation over a milk shake; explanation of the
media system; Miranda perceives the
futility of her quest.

Miranda found Carl Hollywood sitting fifth row center in the Parnasse, holding a big sheet of smart foolscap on which he had scrawled blocking diagrams for their next live production. He apparently had it crosslinked to a copy of the script, because as she sidestepped her way down the narrow aisle, she could hear voices rather mechanically reading lines, and as she came closer she could see the little X's and O's representing the actors moving around on the diagram of the stage that Carl had sketched out.

The diagram also included some little arrows along the periphery, all aimed inward. Miranda realized that the arrows must be the little spotlights mounted to the fronts of the balconies, and that Carl Hollywood was programming them.

She rolled her head back and forth, trying to loosen up her neck, and looked up at the ceiling. The angels or Muses or whatever they were, were all parading around up there, accompanied by a few cherubs. Miranda thought of Nell. She always thought of Nell.

The script came to the end of its scene, and Carl paused it. "You had a question?" he asked, a bit absently.

"I've been watching you work from my box."

"Naughty girl. Should be making money for us."

"Where'd you learn to do that stuff?"

"What—directing plays?"

"No. The technical stuff—programming the lights and so on."

Carl turned around to look at her. "This may be at odds with your notion of how people learn things," he said, "but I had to teach myself everything. Hardly anyone does live theatre anymore, so we have to develop our own technology. I invented all of the software I was just using."

"Did you invent the little spotlights?"

"No. I'm not as good at the nanostuff. A friend of mine in London came up with those. We swap stuff all the time— my mediaware for his matterware."

"Well, I want to buy you dinner somewhere," Miranda said, "and I want you to explain to me how it all works."

"That's a rather tall order," Carl said calmly, "but I accept the invitation."

"Okay, do you want a complete grounding in the whole thing, starting with Turing machines, or what?" Carl said pleasantly—humoring her. Miranda decided not to become indignant. They were in a red vinyl booth at a restaurant near the Bund that supposedly simulated an American diner on the eve of the Kennedy assassination. Chinese hipsters— classic Coastal Republic types in their expensive haircuts and sharp suits—were lined up on the rotating stools along the lunch counter, sucking on their root beer floats and flashing wicked grins at any young women who came in.

"I guess so," Miranda said.

Carl Hollywood laughed and shook his head. "I was being facetious. You need to tell me exactly what you want to know. Why are you suddenly taking up an interest in this stuff? Aren't you happy just making a good living from it?"

Miranda sat very still for a moment, hypnotized by the colorful flashing lights on a vintage jukebox.

"This is related to Princess Nell, isn't it?" Carl said.

"Is it that obvious?"

"Yeah. Now, what do you want?"

"I want to know who she is," Miranda said. This was the most guarded way she could put it. She didn't suppose that it would help matters to drag Carl down through the full depth of her emotions.

"You want to backtrace a payer," Carl said.

It sounded terrible when he translated it into that kind of language.

Carl sucked powerfully on his milk shake for a bit, his eyes looking over Miranda's shoulder to the traffic on the Bund. "Princess Nell's a little kid, right?"

"Yes. I would estimate five to seven years old."

His eyes swiveled to lock on hers. "You can tell that?"

"Yes," she said, in tones that warned him not to question it.

"So she's probably not paying the bill anyway. The payer is someone else. You need to backtrace the payer and then, from there, track down Nell." Carl broke eye contact again, shook his head, and tried unsuccessfully to whistle through frozen lips. "Even the first step is impossible."

Miranda was startled. "That seems pretty unequivocal. I expected to hear 'difficult' or 'expensive.' But—"

"Nope. It's impossible. Or maybe"—Carl thought about it for a while—"maybe 'astronomically improbable' is a better way of putting it." Then he looked mildly alarmed as he watched Miranda's expression change. "You can't just trace the connection backward. That's not how media works."

"How does media work, then?"

"Look out the window. Not toward the Bund—check out Yan'an Road."

Miranda swiveled her head around to look out the big window, which was partly painted over with colorful Coke ads and descriptions of blue plate specials. Yan'an Road, like all of the major thoroughfares in Shanghai, was filled, from the shop windows on one side to the shop windows on the other, with people on bicycles and powerskates. In many places the traffic was so dense that greater speed could be attained on foot. A few half-lane vehicles sat motionless, polished boulders in a sluggish brown stream.

It was so familiar that Miranda didn't really see anything. "What am I looking for?"

"Notice how no one's empty-handed? They're all carrying something."

Carl was right. At a minimum, everyone had a small plastic bag with something in it. Many people, such as the bicyclists, carried heavier loads.

"Now just hold that image in your head for a moment, and think about how to set up a global telecommunications network."

Miranda laughed. "I don't have any basis for thinking about something like that."

"Sure you do. Until now, you've been thinking in terms of the telephone system in the old passives. In that system, each transaction had two participants—the two people having the conversation. And they were connected by a wire that ran through a central switchboard. So what are the key features of this system?"

"I don't know—I'm asking you," said Miranda.

"Number one, only two people, or entities, can interact. Number two, it uses a dedicated connection that is made and then broken for the purposes of that one conversation. Number three, it is inherently centralized—it can't work unless there is a central switchboard."

"Okay, I think I'm following you so far."

"Our media system today—the one that you and I make our livings from—is a descendant of the phone system only insofar as we use it for essentially the same purposes, plus many, many more. But the key point to remember is that *it is totally different from the old phone system*. The old phone system—and its technological cousin, the cable TV system—tanked. It crashed and burned decades ago, and we started virtually from scratch."

"Why? It worked, didn't it?"

"First of all, we needed to enable interactions between more than one entity. What do I mean by entity? Well, think about the ractives. Think about *First Class to Geneva*. You're on this train—so are a couple of dozen other people. Some of those people are being racted, so in that case the entities happen to be human beings. But others—like the waiters and porters—are just software robots. Furthermore, the train is full of props: jewelry, money, guns, bottles of wine. Each one of those is also a separate piece of software—a separate entity. In the lingo, we call them objects. The train itself is another object, and so is the countryside through which it travels.

"The countryside is a good example. It happens to be a digital map of France. Where did this map come from? Did the makers of *First Class to Geneva* send out their own team of surveyors to make a new map of France? No, of course they didn't. They used existing data—a digital map of the world that is available to any maker of ractives who needs it, for a price of course. That digital map is a separate object. It resides in the memory of a computer somewhere. Where exactly? I don't know. Neither does the ractive itself. It doesn't matter. The data might be in California, it might be in Paris, it might be down at the corner—or it might be distributed among all of those places and many more. *It doesn't matter.* Because our media system no longer works like the old system—dedicated wires passing through a central switchboard. It works like *that.*" Carl pointed to the traffic on the street again.

"So each person on the street is like an object?"

"Possibly. But a better analogy is that the objects are people like us, sitting in various buildings that front on the street. Suppose that we want to send a message to someone over in Pudong. We write the message down on a piece of paper, and we go to the door and hand it to the first person who goes by and say, 'Take this to Mr. Gu in Pudong.' And he skates down the street for a while and runs into someone on a bicycle who looks like he might be headed for Pudong, and says, 'Take this to Mr. Gu.' A minute later, that person gets stuck in traffic and hands it off to a pedestrian who can negotiate the snarl a little better, and so on and so on, until eventually it reaches Mr. Gu. When Mr. Gu wants to respond, he sends us a message in the same way."

"So there's no way to trace the path taken by a message."

"Right. And the real situation is even more complicated. The media net was designed from the ground up to provide privacy and security, so that people could use it to transfer money. That's one reason the nation-states collapsed—as soon as the media grid was up and running, financial transactions could no longer be monitored by governments, and the tax collection systems got fubared. So if the old IRS, for example, wasn't able to trace these messages, then there's no way that you'll be able to track down Princess Nell."

"Okay, I guess that answers my question," Miranda said.

"Good!" Carl said brightly. He was obviously pleased that he'd been able to help Miranda, and so she didn't tell him how his words had really made her feel. She treated it as an acting challenge: Could she fool Carl Hollywood, who was sharper about acting than just about anyone, into thinking that she was fine?

Apparently she did. He escorted her back to her flat, in a hundred-story high-rise just across the river in Pudong, and she held it together long enough to bid him good-bye, get out of her clothes, and run a bath. Then she climbed into the hot water and dissolved in awful, wretched, blubbery, self-pitying tears.

Eventually she got it under control. She had to keep this in perspective. She could still interact with Nell and still did, every day. And if she paid attention, sooner or later she would find some way to penetrate the curtain. Barring that, she was beginning to understand that Nell, whoever she was, had been marked out in some way, and that in time she would become a very important person. Within a few years, Miranda expected to be reading about her in the newspaper. Feeling better, she got out of the bath and climbed into bed, getting a good night's sleep so she'd be ready for her next day of taking care of Nell.

*General description of life with the Constable; his
avocations and other peculiarities; a disturbing
sight; Nell learns about his past;
a conversation over dinner.*

The garden house had two rooms, one for sleeping and one for playing. The playing room had a set of double doors, made of many small windows, that opened onto Constable Moore's garden. Nell had been told to be careful with the little windows, because they were made of real glass. The glass was bubbly and uneven, like the surface of a pot of water just before it breaks into a boil, and Nell liked to look at things through it because, even though she knew it was not as strong as a common window, it made her feel safer, as though she were hiding behind something.

The garden itself was forever trying to draw the little house into it; many vast-growing vines of ivy, wisteria, and briar rose were deeply engaged in the important project of climbing the walls, using the turtle-shell-colored copper drainpipes, and the rough surfaces of the brick and mortar, as fingerholds. The slate roof of the cottage was phosphorescent with moss. From time to time, Constable Moore would charge into the breach with a pair of trimmers and cut away some of the vines that so prettily framed the view through Nell's glass doors, lest they imprison her.

During Nell's second year living in the cottage, she asked the Constable if she might have a bit of garden space of her own, and after an early phase of profound shock and misgivings, the Constable eventually pulled up a few flagstones, exposing a small plot, and caused one of the Dovetail artisans to manufacture some copper window boxes and attach them to the cottage walls. In the plot, Nell planted some carrots, thinking about her friend Peter who had vanished so long ago, and in the window boxes she planted some geraniums. The Primer taught her how to do it and also reminded her to dig up a carrot sprout every few days and examine it so that she could learn how they grew. Nell learned that if she held the Primer above the carrot and stared at a certain page, it would turn into a magic illustration that would grow larger and larger until she could see the tiny little fibers that grew out of the roots, and the one-celled organisms clinging to the fibers, and the mitochondria inside them. The same trick worked on anything, and she spent many days examining flies' eyes, bread mold, and blood cells that she got out of her own body by pricking her finger. She could also go up on hilltops during cold clear nights and use the Primer to see the rings of Saturn and the moons of Jupiter.

Constable Moore continued to work his daily shift at the gatehouse. When he came home in the evening, he and Nell would often dine together inside his house. At first they got food straight from the M.C., or else the Constable would fry up something simple, like sausage and eggs. During this period, Princess Nell and the other characters in the Primer found themselves eating a lot of sausage and eggs too, until Duck lodged a protest and taught the Princess how to cook healthier food. Nell then got in the habit of cooking a healthy meal with salad and vegetables, several afternoons a week after she got home from school. There was some grumbling from the Constable, but he always cleaned up his plate and sometimes washed the dishes.

The Constable spent a lot of time reading books. Nell was welcome to be in his house when he was doing this, as long as she was quiet. Frequently he would shoo her out, and then he would get in touch with some old friend of his over the big mediatron on the wall of his library. Usually Nell would just go back to her little cottage during these times, but sometimes, especially if the moon was full, she would wander around in the garden. This seemed larger than it really was by virtue of being divided into many small compartments. On late full-moon nights, her favorite place was a grove of tall green bamboo with some pretty rocks strewn around. She would sit with her back against a rock, read her Primer, and occasionally hear sound emanating from the inside of Constable Moore's house as he talked on the mediatron: mostly deep bellowing laughter and explosions of good-natured profanity. For quite some time she assumed that it was not the Constable who was making these sounds, but rather whomever he was talking to; because in her presence the Constable was always very polite and reserved, albeit somewhat eccentric. But one night she heard loud moaning noises coming from his house, and crept down out of the bamboo grove to see what was happening.

From her vantage point through the glass doors, she couldn't see the mediatron, which was facing away from her. Its light illuminated the whole room, painting the normally warm and cozy space with lurid flashing colors, and throwing long jagged shadows. Constable Moore had shoved all the furniture and other obstructions to the walls and rolled up the Chinese carpet to expose the floor, which Nell had always assumed was made of oak, like the floor in her cottage; but the floor was, in fact, a large mediatron itself, glowing rather dimly compared to the one on the wall, and displaying a lot of rather high-resolution material: text documents and detailed graphics with the occasional cine feed. The Constable was down on his hands and knees amidst this, bawling like a child, the tears collecting in the shallow saucers of his half-glasses and spattering onto the mediatron, which illuminated them weirdly from below.

Nell wanted badly to go in and comfort him, but she was too scared. She stood and watched, frozen in indecision, and realized as she did so that the flashes of light coming from the mediatrons reminded her of explosions—or rather pictures of explosions. She backed away and went back into her little house.

Half an hour later, she heard the unearthly noise of Constable Moore's bagpipes emanating from the bamboo grove. In the past he had occasionally picked them up and made a few squealing noises, but this was the first time she'd heard a formal recital. She was not an expert on the pipes, but she thought he sounded not bad. He was playing a slow number, a coronach, and it was so sad that it almost tore Nell's heart asunder; the sight of the Constable weeping helplessly on his hands and knees was not half so sad as the music he was playing now.

In time he moved on to a faster and happier pibroch. Nell emerged from her cottage into the garden. The Constable was just a silhouette slashed into a hundred ribbons by the vertical shafts of the bamboo, but when she moved back and forth, some trick of her eye reassembled the image. He was standing in a pool of moonlight. He had changed clothes: now he was wearing his kilt, and a shirt and beret that seemed to belong to some sort of a uniform. When his lungs were empty, he would draw in a great breath, his chest would heave, and an array of silvery pins and insignia would glimmer in the moonlight.

He had left the doors open. She walked into the house, not bothering to be stealthy because she knew that she could not possibly be heard over the sound of the bagpipe.

The wall and the floor were both giant mediatrons, and both had been covered with a profusion of media windows, hundreds and hundreds of separate panes, like a wall on a busy city street where posters and bills have been pasted up in such abundance that they have completely covered the substrate. Some of the panes were only as big as the palm of Nell's hand, and some of them were the size of wall posters. Most of the ones on the floor were windows into written documents, grids of numbers, schematic diagrams (lots of organizational trees), or wonderful maps, drawn with breathtaking precision and clarity, with rivers, mountains, and villages labeled in Chinese characters. As Nell surveyed this panorama, she flinched once or twice from the impression that something small was creeping along the floor; but there were no bugs in the room, it was just an illusion created by small fluctuations in the maps and in the rows and columns of numbers. These things were ractive, just like the words in the Primer; but unlike the Primer, they were responding not to what Nell did but, she supposed, to events far away.

When she finally raised her gaze from the floor to view the mediatrons lining the walls, she saw that most of the panes there were much larger, and most of them carried cine feeds, and most of these had been frozen. The images were very sharp and clear. Some of them were landscapes: a stretch of rural road, a bridge across a dried-up river, a dusty village with flames bubbling from some of the houses. Some of them were pictures of people: talking-head shots of Chinese men wearing dirty uniforms with dark mountains, clouds of dust, or drab green vehicles as backdrops.

In one of the cine feeds, a man was lying on the ground, his dusty uniform almost the same color as the dirt. Suddenly this image moved; the feed had not been frozen like the others. Someone was walking past the camera: a Chinese man in indigo pajamas, decorated with scarlet ribbons tied round his head and his waist, though these had gone brown with grime. When he had passed out of the frame, Nell focused on the other man, the one who was lying in the dust, and she realized for the first time that he did not have a head.

Constable Moore must have heard Nell's screaming over the sound of his bagpipes, for he was in the room within a few moments, shouting commands to the mediatrons, which all went black and became mere walls and a floor. The only image remaining in the room now was the big painting of Guan Di, the god of war, who glowered down upon them as always. Constable Moore was extremely ill at ease whenever Nell showed any kind of emotion, but he seemed more comfortable with hysteria than he was with, say, an invitation to play house or an attack of the giggles. He picked Nell up, carried her across the room at arm's length, and set her down in a deep leather chair. He left the room for a moment and came back with a large glass of water, then carefully molded her hands around it. "You must breathe deeply and drink water," he was saying, almost sotto voce; he seemed to have been saying it for a long time.

She was a little surprised to find that she did not cry forever, though a few aftershocks came along and had to be managed in the same way. She kept trying to say, "I can't stop crying," stabbing the syllables one at a time.

The tenth or eleventh time she said this, Constable Moore said, "You can't stop crying because you're all fucked up psychologically." He said it in a kind of bored professional tone that might have sounded cruel; but to Nell it was, for some reason, most reassuring.

"What do you mean?" she said finally, when she could speak without her throat going all funny.

"I mean you're a veteran, girl, just like me, and you've got scars"—he suddenly ripped his shirt open, buttons flying and bouncing all over the room, to reveal his particolored torso—"like I do. The difference is, I know I'm a veteran. You persist in thinking you're just a little girl, like those bloody Vickys you go to school with."

From time to time, perhaps once a year, he would turn down the offer of dinner, put that uniform on, climb onto a horse, and ride off in the direction of the New Atlantis Clave. The horse would bring him back in the wee hours of the morning, so drunk he could barely remain in the saddle. Sometimes Nell would help get him into bed, and after he had lapsed into unconsciousness, she could examine his pins and medals and ribbons by candlelight. The ribbons in particular used a fairly elaborate color-coding system. But the Primer had some pages in the back that were called the Encyclopædia, and by consulting these, Nell was able to establish that Constable Moore was, or at least had used to be, a brigadier general in the Second Brigade of the Third Division of the First Protocol Enforcement Expeditionary Force. One ribbon implied that he had spent some time as an exchange officer in a Nipponese division, but his home division was apparently the Third. According to the Encyclopædia, the Third was often known as the Junkyard Dogs or, simply, the Mongrels, because it tended to draw its members from the White Diaspora: Uitlanders, Ulster Loyalists, whites from Hong Kong, and rootless sorts from all of the Anglo-American parts of the world.

One of the pins on the Constable's uniform said that he had graduate-level training in nanotechnological engineering. This was consistent with his belonging to the Second Brigade, which specialized in nanotech warfare. The Encyclopædia said that it had been formed some thirty years ago to tackle some nasty fighting in Eastern Europe where primitive nanotech weapons were being employed.

A couple of years later, the division had been sent off to South China in a panic. Trouble had been brewing there since Zhang Han Hua had gone on his Long Ride and forced the merchants to kowtow. Zhang had personally liberated several lao gai camps, where slave laborers were hard at work making trinkets for export to the West, smashing computer display screens with the massive dragon's-head grip of his cane, beating the overseers into bloody heaps on the ground. Zhang's "investigations" of various thriving businesses, mostly in the south, had thrown millions of people out of work. They had gone into the streets and raised hell and been joined by sympathetic units of the People's Liberation Army. The rebellion was eventually put down by PLA units from the north, but the leaders had vanished into the "concrete countryside" of the Pearl Delta, and so Zhang had been forced to set up a permanent garrison state in the south. The northern troops had kept order crudely but effectively for a few years, until, one night, an entire division of them, some 15,000 men, was wiped out by an infestation of nanosites.

The leaders of the rebellion emerged from their hiding places, proclaimed the Coastal Republic, and called for Protocol Enforcement troops to come in and protect them. Colonel Arthur Hornsby Moore, a veteran of the fighting in Eastern Europe, was brought in to command. He had been born in Hong Kong, left as a small child when the Chinese took it over, spent much of his youth wandering around Asia with his parents, and eventually settled in the British Isles. He was picked for the job because he was fluent in Cantonese and not half bad in mandarin. Looking at the old cine clips in the Encyclopædia, Nell could see a younger Constable Moore, the same man with more hair and fewer doubts.

The Chinese Civil War began in earnest three years later, when the Northerns, who didn't have access to nanotech, started lobbing nukes. Not long afterward, the Muslim nations had finally gotten their act together and overrun much of Xinjiang Province, killing some of the Han Chinese population and driving the rest eastward into the maw of the civil war. Colonel Moore suffered an extremely dire infestation of primitive nanosites and was removed from the action and put on extended convalescent leave. By that time, the truce line between the Celestial Kingdom and the Coastal Republic had been established.

Since then, as Nell knew from her studies at the Academy, Lau Ge had succeeded Zhang as the northern leader—the leader of the Celestial Kingdom. After a decent interval had passed, he had thoroughly purged all remaining traces of Communist ideology, denouncing it as a Western imperialist plot, and proclaimed himself Chamberlain to the Throneless King. The Throneless King was Confucius, and Lau Ge was now the highest-ranking of all the mandarins.

The Encyclopædia did not say much more about Colonel Arthur Hornsby Moore, except that he'd resurfaced as an adviser a few years later during some outbreaks of nanotech terrorism in Germany, and later retired and became a security consultant. In this latter capacity he had helped to promulgate the concept of defense in depth, around which all modern cities, including Atlantis/Shanghai, were built.

Nell cooked the Constable an especially nice dinner one Saturday, and when they were finished with dessert, she began to tell him about Harv and Tequila, and Harv's tales of the incomparable Bud, their dear departed father. Suddenly it was about three hours later, and Nell was still telling the Constable stories about Mom's boyfriends, and the Constable was continuing to listen, reaching up occasionally to fiddle with his white beard but otherwise displaying an extremely grave and thoughtful countenance. Finally she got to the part about Burt, and how Nell had tried to kill him with the screwdriver, and how he had chased them down the stairs and apparently met his demise at the hands of the mysterious round-headed Chinese gentleman. The Constable found this extremely interesting and asked many questions, first about the detailed tactical development of the screwdriver assault and then about the style of dancing used by the Chinese gentleman, and what he was wearing.

"I have been angry at my Primer ever since that night," Nell said.

"Why?" said the Constable, looking surprised, though he was hardly more surprised than Nell herself. Nell had *said* a remarkable number of things this evening without having ever, to her memory, *thought* them first; or at least she didn't *believe* she had ever thought them before.

"I cannot help but feel that it misled me. It made me suppose that killing Burt would be a simple matter, and that it would improve my life; but when I tried to put these ideas into practice . . ." She could not think of what to say next.

". . . the rest of your life happened," the Constable said. "Girl, you must admit that your life with Burt dead has been an improvement on your life with Burt alive."

"Yes."

"So the Primer was correct on that point. Now, as to the fact that killing people is a more complicated business in practice than in theory, I will certainly concede your point. But I think it is not likely to be the only instance in which real life turns out to be more complicated than what you have seen in the book. This is the Lesson of the Screwdriver, and you would do well to remember it. All it amounts to is

that you must be ready to learn from sources other than your
magic book."

"But of what use is the book then?"

"I suspect it is very useful. You want only the knack of
translating its lessons into the real world. For example," the
Constable said, plucking his napkin from his lap and crush-
ing it into the tabletop, "let us take something very concrete,
such as beating the bejesus out of people." He stood up and
tromped out into the garden. Nell ran after him. "I have seen
you doing your martial-arts exercises," he said, switching to
a peremptory outdoor voice, an addressing-the-troops voice.
"Martial arts means beating the bejesus out of people. Now,
let us see you try your luck with me."

Negotiations ensued as Nell endeavored to establish
whether the Constable was serious. This being accomplished, she sat down on the flagstones and began getting
her shoes off. The Constable watched her with raised eyebrows.

"Oh, that's very formidable," he said. "All evildoers
had best be on the lookout for little Nell—unless she happens to be wearing her bloody shoes."

Nell did a couple of stretching exercises, ignoring
more derisive commentary from the Constable. She bowed
to him, and he waved his hand at her dismissively. She got
set into the stance that Dojo had taught her. In response, the
Constable moved his feet about an inch farther apart than
they had been, and pooched his belly out, which was apparently the chosen stance of some mysterious Scottish fighting
technique.

Nothing happened for a long time except for a lot of
dancing around. Nell danced, that is, and the Constable
blundered around desultorily. "What's this?" he said. "All
you know is defense?"

"Mostly, sir," Nell said. "I do not suppose it was the
Primer's intention to teach me how to assault people."

"Oh, what good is that?" the Constable sneered, and
suddenly he reached out and grabbed Nell by the hair—not
hard enough to hurt. He held her for a few moments, and
then let her go. "Thus endeth the first lesson," he said.

"You think that I should cut my hair off?"

The Constable looked terribly disappointed. "Oh, no,"

he said, "never, ever, ever cut your hair off. If I grabbed you by your wrist"—and he did—"would you cut your arm off?"

"No, sir."

"Did the Primer teach you that people would pull your hair?"

"No, sir."

"Did it teach you that your mother's boyfriends would beat you up, and your mother not protect you?"

"No, sir, except insofar as it told me stories about people who did evil."

"People doing evil is a good lesson. What you saw in there a few weeks ago"—and by this Nell knew he was referring to the headless soldier on the mediatron—"is one application of that lesson, but it's too obvious to be of any good. Ah, but your mother not protecting you from boyfriends—that has some subtlety, doesn't it?

"Nell," the Constable continued, indicating through his tone of voice that the lesson was concluding, "the difference between ignorant and educated people is that the latter know more facts. But that has nothing to do with whether they are stupid or intelligent. The difference between stupid and intelligent people—and this is true whether or not they are well-educated—is that intelligent people can handle subtlety. They are not baffled by ambiguous or even contradictory situations—in fact, they expect them and are apt to become suspicious when things seem overly straightforward.

"In your Primer you have a resource that will make you highly educated, but it will never make you intelligent. That comes from life. Your life up to this point has given you all of the experience you need to be intelligent, but you have to think about those experiences. If you don't think about them, you'll be psychologically unwell. If you do think about them, you will become not merely educated but intelligent, and then, a few years down the road, you will probably give me cause to wish I were several decades younger."

The Constable turned and walked back into his house, leaving Nell alone in the garden, pondering the meaning of that last statement. She supposed it was the sort of thing she might understand later, when she had become intelligent.

*Carl Hollywood returns from abroad; he and
Miranda discuss the status and future of
her racting career.*

Carl Hollywood came back from a month-long trip to London, where he'd been visiting old friends, catching some live theatre, and making face-to-face contacts with some of the big ractive developers, hoping to swing some contracts in their direction. When he got back, the whole company threw a party for him in the theatre's little bar. Miranda thought she handled it pretty well.

But the next day he cornered her backstage. "What's up?" he said. "And I don't mean that in the usual offhanded way. I want to know what's going on with you. Why have you switched to the evening shift during my absence? And why were you acting so weird at the party?"

"Well, Nell and I have had an interesting few months."

Carl looked startled, stepped back half a pace, then sighed and rolled his eyes.

"Of course, her altercation with Burt was traumatic, but she seems to have dealt with it well."

"Who's Burt?"

"I have no idea. Someone who was physically abusing her. Apparently she managed to find some kind of new living situation in short order, probably with the assistance of her brother Harv, who has, however, not stayed with her—he's stuck in the same old bad situation, while Nell has moved on to something better."

"She has? That's good news," said Carl, only half sarcastically.

Miranda smiled at him. "See? That's exactly the kind of feedback I need. I don't talk about this stuff to anyone because I'm afraid they'll think I'm mad. Thank you. Keep it up."

"What is Nell's new situation?" Carl Hollywood asked contritely.

"I think she's in school somewhere. She appears to be learning new material that isn't explicitly covered in the Primer, and she's developing more sophisticated forms of social interaction, suggesting that she's spending more time around a higher class of people."

"Excellent."

"She's not as concerned with immediate issues of physical self-defense, so I gather that she's in a safe living situation. However, her new guardian must be an emotionally distant sort, because she frequently seeks solace under the wings of Duck."

Carl looked funny. "Duck?"

"One of four personages who accompanies and advises Princess Nell. Duck embodies domestic, maternal virtues. Actually, Peter and Dinosaur are now gone—both male figures who embodied survival skills."

"Who's the fourth one?"

"Purple. I think she'll become a lot more relevant to Nell's life around puberty."

"Puberty? You said Nell was between five and seven."

"So?"

"You think you'll still be doing this—" Carl's voice wound down to a stop as he worked out the implications.

"—for at least six or eight years. Oh yes, I should certainly think so. It's a very serious commitment, raising a child."

"Oh, god!" Carl Hollywood said, and collapsed into a big, tatty, overstuffed chair they kept backstage for such purposes.

"That's why I've switched to the evening shift. Ever since Nell started going to school, she's started using the Primer exclusively in the evening. Apparently she's in a time zone within one or two hours of this one."

"Good," Carl muttered, "that narrows it down to about half of the world's population."

"What's the problem here?" Miranda said. "It's not like I'm not getting paid for this."

Carl gave her a good, dispassionate, searching look. "Yes. It brings in adequate revenue."

*Three girls go exploring; a conversation between
Lord Finkle-McGraw and Mrs. Hackworth;
afternoon at the estate.*

Three girls moved across the billiard-table lawn of a great manor house, circling and swarming about a common center of gravity like gamboling sparrows. Sometimes they would stop, turn inward to face one another, and engage in animated discussion. Then they would suddenly take off running, seemingly free from the constraints of inertia, like petals struck by a gust of spring wind. They wore long heavy wool coats over their dresses to protect them from the cool damp air of New Chusan's high central plateau. They seemed to be making their way toward an expanse of broken ground some half-mile distant, separated from the great house's formal gardens by a gray stone wall splashed with bits of lime green and lavender where moss and lichen had taken hold. The terrain beyond the wall was a muted hazel color, like a bolt of Harris tweed that has tumbled from the back of a wagon and come undone, though the incipient blooming of the heather had flung a pale violet mist across it, nearly transparent but startlingly vivid in those places where the observer's line of sight grazed the natural slope of the terrain—if the word *natural* could properly be applied to any feature of this island. Otherwise as light and free as birds, the girls were each weighed down by a small burden that seemed incongruous in the present setting, for the efforts of the adults to persuade them to leave their books behind had, as ever, been unavailing.

One of the observers had eyes only for the little girl with long flame-colored hair. Her connexion to that child was suggested by her auburn hair and eyebrows. She was dressed in a hand-sewn frock of woven cotton, whose crispness betrayed its recent provenance in a milliner's atelier in Dovetail. If the gathering had included more veterans of that elongated state of low-intensity warfare known as Society, this observation would have been keenly made by those *soi-disant* sentries who stood upon the battlements, keeping vigil against bounders who would struggle their way up the vast glacis separating wage slaves from Equity Participants. It would have been duly noted and set forth in the oral tradition that Gwendolyn Hackworth, though attractive, hard-waisted, and poised, lacked the confidence to visit Lord Finkle-McGraw's house in anything other than a new dress made for the occasion.

The gray light suffusing the drawing room through its high windows was as gentle as mist. As Mrs. Hackworth stood enveloped in that light, sipping beige tea from a cup of translucent bone china, her face let down its guard and betrayed some evidence of her true state of mind. Her host, Lord Finkle-McGraw, thought that she looked drawn and troubled, though her vivacious comportment during the first hour of their interview had led him to suppose otherwise.

Sensing that his gaze had lingered on her face for longer than was strictly proper, he looked to the three little girls ambling across the garden. One of the girls had raven hair that betrayed her partly Korean heritage; but having established her whereabouts as a sort of reference point, he shifted his attention to the third girl, whose hair was about halfway through a natural and gradual transition from blond to brown. This girl was the tallest of the three, though all were of about the same age; and though she participated freely in all of their lighthearted games, she rarely initiated them and, when left to her own devices, tended toward a grave mien that made her seem years older than her playmates. As the Equity Lord watched the trio's progress, he sensed that even the style of her movement was different from the others'; she was lithe and carefully balanced, while they bounded unpredictably like rubber balls on rough-hewn stone.

The difference was (as he realized, watching them more keenly) that Nell always knew where she was going. Elizabeth and Fiona never did. This was a question not of native intelligence (Miss Matheson's tests and observations proved that much) but of emotional stance. Something in the girl's past had taught her, most forcefully, the importance of thinking things through.

"I ask you for a prediction, Mrs. Hackworth. Which one shall reach the moor first?"

At the sound of his voice, Mrs. Hackworth recomposed her face. "This sounds like a letter to the etiquette columnist of the *Times*. If I try to flatter you by guessing that it will be your granddaughter, am I implicitly accusing her of impulsiveness?"

The Equity Lord smiled tolerantly. "Let us set aside etiquette—a social convention not relevant to this enquiry—and be scientific."

"Ah. If only my John were here."

He is here, Lord Finkle-McGraw thought, *in each one of those books*. But he didn't say it. "Very well, I will expose myself to the risk of humiliation by predicting that Elizabeth reaches the wall first; that Nell finds the secret way through; but that your daughter is the first one to venture through it."

"I'm sure you could never be humiliated in my presence, Your Grace," Mrs. Hackworth said. It was something she had to say, and he did not really hear it.

They turned back to the windows. When the girls had reached to within a stone's throw of the wall, they began to move toward it more purposefully. Elizabeth broke free from the group, ran forward, and was the first to touch the cool stones, followed a few paces later by Fiona. Nell was far behind, not having altered her steady stride.

"Elizabeth is a Duke's granddaughter, accustomed to having her way, and has no natural reticence; she surges to the fore and claims the goal as her birthright," Finkle-McGraw explained. "But she has not really thought about what she is doing."

Elizabeth and Fiona both had their hands on the wall now, as if it were Home in a game of tag. But Nell had stopped and was turning her head from side to side, surveying the length of the wall as it clambered and tumbled over the increasingly rough shape of the land. After some time she held out one hand, pointing at a section of the wall a short distance away, and began to move toward it.

"Nell stands above the fray and thinks," Finkle-McGraw said. "To the other girls, the wall is a decorative feature, no? A pretty thing to run to and explore. But not to Nell. Nell knows what a wall is. It is a knowledge that went into her early, knowledge she doesn't have to think about. Nell is more interested in gates than in walls. Secret hidden gates are particularly interesting."

Fiona and Elizabeth moved uncertainly, trailing their tiny pink hands across the damp stone, unable to see where

Nell was leading them. Nell strode across the grass until she had reached a small declivity. She almost disappeared into it as she clambered down toward the foundation of the wall.

"An opening for drainage," Finkle-McGraw explained. "Please do not be concerned. I happened to ride that way this morning. The current is only ankle-deep, and the diameter of the culvert just right for eight-year-old girls. The passage is several meters long—more promising than threatening, I should hope."

Fiona and Elizabeth moved cautiously, startled by Nell's discovery. All three of the girls disappeared into the cleft. A few moments later, a blaze of fiery red could be descried bouncing rapidly across the moor beyond the wall. Fiona clambered up a small outcropping of rocks that marked the beginning of the moor, and beckoned excitedly to her companions.

"The secret passage is found by Nell, but she is cautious and patient. Elizabeth is taken aback by her early impulsiveness—she feels foolish and perhaps even a bit sullen. Fiona—"

"Fiona sees a magical gateway to an enchanted kingdom, no doubt," Mrs. Hackworth said, "and even now is crestfallen to find that you have not stocked the premises with unicorns and dragons. She would not hesitate for a moment to fly down that tunnel. This world is not where my Fiona wants to live, Your Grace. She wants another world, where magic is everywhere, and stories come to life, and . . ."

Her voice trailed away, and she cleared her throat uncomfortably. Lord Finkle-McGraw glanced at her and saw pain in her face, quickly masked. He understood the rest of her sentence without hearing it: . . . *and my husband is here with us.*

A pair of riders, a man and a woman, trotted up a gravel path that ran along the edge of the gardens, through a pair of wrought-iron gates in the stone wall, which opened for them. The man was Lord Finkle-McGraw's son Colin, the woman was his wife, and they had ridden out onto the moor to keep an eye on their daughter and her two little friends. Seeing that their supervision was no longer required, Lord Finkle-McGraw and Mrs. Hackworth turned away from the window and drew instinctively closer to a fire burning in a stone fireplace the size of a garage.

Mrs. Hackworth sat down in a small rocker, and the Equity Lord chose an old and incongruously battered leather wing chair. A servant poured more tea. Mrs. Hackworth set the saucer and cup in her lap, guarding it with her hands, and collected herself.

"I have been desirous of making certain enquiries regarding my husband's whereabouts and activities, which have been a mystery to me almost since the moment he departed," she said, "and yet I was led to believe, from the very general and guarded statements he made to me, that the nature of those activities is secret, and that, if Your Grace has any knowledge of them—and that you do, is of course merely a convenient supposition on my part—you must treat that knowledge with flawless discretion. It goes without saying, I trust, that I would not use even my feeble powers of persuasion to induce you to violate the trust reposed in you by a higher power."

"Let us take it as a given that both of us will do what is honourable," Finkle-McGraw said with a reassuringly casual smile.

"Thank you. My husband continues to write me letters, every week or so, but they are extremely general, nonspecific, and perfunctory. But in recent months, these letters have become full of strange images and emotions. They are —bizarre. I have begun to fear for my husband's mental stability, and for the prospects of any undertaking that relies upon his good judgment. And while I would not hesitate to tolerate his absence for as long as is necessary for him to carry out his duties, the uncertainty has become most trying for me."

"I am not wholly ignorant of the matter, and I do not think I am violating any trust when I say that you are not the only person who has been surprised by the duration of his absence," Lord Finkle-McGraw said. "Unless I am very much mistaken, those who conceived of his mission never imagined that it would last for so long. It may ease your suffering in some small degree to know that he is not thought to be in danger."

Mrs. Hackworth smiled dutifully, and not for very long.

"Little Fiona seems to handle her father's absence well."

"Oh, but to Fiona, he has never been gone," Mrs. Hackworth said. "It is the book, you see, that ractive book. When John gave it to her, just before he departed, he said that it was magic, and that he would talk to her through it. I know it's nonsense, of course, but she really believes that whenever she opens that book, her father reads her a story and even plays with her in an imaginary world, so that she hasn't really missed him at all. I haven't the heart to tell her that it's nothing more than a computerized media programme."

"I am inclined to believe that, in this case, keeping her in ignorance is a very wise policy," Finkle-McGraw said.

"It has served her well thus far. But as time goes on, she is more and more flighty and less disposed to concentrate on her schoolwork. She lives in a fantasy and is happy there. But when she learns that the fantasy is just that, I fear it will not go well for her."

"She is hardly the first young lady to display signs of a vivid imagination," the Equity Lord said. "Sooner or later they seem to turn out all right."

The three little explorers, and their two adult outriders, returned to the great house shortly. Lord Finkle-McGraw's desolate private moor was as alienated from the tastes of little girls as single malt whiskey, Gothic architecture, muted colors, and Bruckner symphonies. Once they had reached it and found that it was not equipped with pink unicorns, cotton candy vendors, teen idol bands, or fluorescent green water slides, they lost interest and began to gravitate toward the house—which in and of itself was far from Disneyland, but in which a practiced and assertive user like Elizabeth could find a few consolatory nuggets, such as a full-time kitchen staff, trained in (among many other, completely useless skills) the preparation of hot chocolate.

Having come as close to the subject of John Percival Hackworth's disappearance as they dared, and careened past it with no damage except some hot faces and watery eyes, Lord Finkle-McGraw and Mrs. Hackworth had withdrawn, by mutual consent, to cooler subjects. The girls would come inside to drink some hot chocolate, and then it would be time for the guests to repair to the quarters assigned them for the day, where they could freshen up and dress for the main event: dinner.

"I should be pleased to look after the other little girl—Nell—until the dinner hour," Mrs. Hackworth said. "I noticed that the gentleman who brought her round this morning has not returned from the hunt."

The Equity Lord chuckled as he imagined General Moore trying to help a little girl dress for dinner. He was graceful enough to know his limits, and so he was spending the day shooting on the remoter stretches of the estate. "Little Nell has a talent for looking after herself and may not need or wish to accept your most generous offer. But she might enjoy spending the interim with Fiona."

"Forgive me, Your Grace, but I am startled that you would consider leaving a child of her age unattended for most of the afternoon."

"She would not view it in that way, I assure you, for the same reason that little Fiona does not think of her father as ever having left your house."

The expression that passed over Mrs. Hackworth's face as she heard this statement suggested less than perfect comprehension. But before she could explain to her host the error of his ways, they were interrupted by the sound of a shrill and bitter conflict making its way down the hall toward them. The door swung open halfway, and Colin Finkle-McGraw appeared. His face was still ruddy from the wind on the moor, and it bore a forced grin that was not terribly distant from a smirk; though his brow knit up periodically as Elizabeth emitted an especially piercing shriek of anger. In one hand he held a copy of the *Young Lady's Illustrated Primer*. Behind him, Mrs. Finkle-McGraw could be seen holding Elizabeth by the wrist in a grip that recalled the blacksmith's tongs holding a dangerously hot ingot ready for smiting; and the radiant glow of the little girl's face perfected that analogy. She had bent down so that her face was level with Elizabeth's and was hissing something to her in a low and reproaching tone.

"Sorry, Father," the younger Finkle-McGraw said in a voice slathered with not very convincing synthetic good humor. "Nap time, obviously." He nodded to the other. "Mrs. Hackworth." Then his eyes returned to his father's face and followed the Equity Lord's gaze downward to the book.

"She was rude to the servants, Father, and so we have confiscated the book for the rest of the afternoon. It's the only
punishment that seems to sink in—we employ it with some
frequency."

"Then perhaps it is not sinking in as well as you suppose," Lord Finkle-McGraw said, looking sad and sounding
bemused.

Colin Finkle-McGraw chose to interpret this remark as
a witticism targeted primarily at Elizabeth—but then, parents of small children must perforce have an entirely different sense of irony than unimpaired humankind.

"We can't let her spend her life between the covers of
your magical book, Father. It is like a little interactive empire, with Elizabeth the empress, issuing all sorts of perfectly
bloodcurdling decrees to her obedient subjects. It's important to bring her back to reality from time to time, so that she
can get some perspective."

"Perspective. Very well, I shall look forward to seeing
you and Elizabeth, with her new perspective, at dinner."

"Good afternoon, Father. Mrs. Hackworth," the
younger man said, and closed the door, a heavy masterpiece
of the woodcarver's art and a fairly effective decibel ab-
sorbant.

Gwendolyn Hackworth now saw something in Lord
Finkle-McGraw's face that made her want to leave the room.
After speeding through the obligatory pleasantries, she did.
She collected Fiona from the chimney-corner where she was
cherishing the dregs of her hot chocolate. Nell was there too,
reading her copy of the Primer, and Gwendolyn was startled
to see that she had not touched her drink at all.

"What is this?" she exclaimed in what she took to be
an appropriately sugary voice. "A little girl who doesn't like
hot chocolate?"

Nell was deeply absorbed in her book, and for a moment Gwendolyn thought that her words had gone unheard.
But a few beats later it became evident that the child was
merely postponing her response until she reached the end of
a chapter. Then she raised her eyes slowly from the page of
the book. Nell was a reasonably attractive girl in the way
that almost all girls are before immoderate tides of hormones start to make different parts of their faces grow out of
proportion to others; she had light brown eyes, glowing or-

ange in the light of the fire, with a kind of feral slant to them. Gwendolyn found it difficult to break her gaze; she felt like a captured butterfly staring up through a magnifying lens into the calm, keen eye of the naturalist.

"Chocolate is fine," Nell said. "The question is, do I need it."

There was a rather long pause in the conversation as Gwendolyn groped for something to say. Nell did not seem to be awaiting a response; she had delivered her opinion and was done with it.

"Well," Gwendolyn finally said, "if you should decide that there is anything you *do* need, please know that I would be happy to assist you."

"Your offer is most kind. I am in your debt, Mrs. Hackworth," Nell said. She said it perfectly, like a princess in a book.

"Very well. Good afternoon," Gwendolyn said. She took Fiona's hand and led her upstairs. Fiona dawdled in a way that was almost perfectly calculated to annoy, and responded to her mother's questions only with nods and shakes of the head, because, as always, her mind was elsewhere. Once they had reached their temporary quarters in the guest wing, Gwendolyn got Fiona settled into bed for a nap, then sat down at an escritoire to work her way through some pending correspondence. But now Mrs. Hackworth found that her own mind was elsewhere, as she pondered these three very strange girls—the three smartest little girls in Miss Matheson's Academy—each with her very strange relationship with her Primer. Her gaze drifted away from the sheets of mediatronic paper scattered about the escritoire, out the window, and across the moor, where a gentle shower had begun to fall. She devoted the better part of an hour to worrying about girls and Primers.

Then she remembered an assertion that her host had made that afternoon, which she had not fully appreciated at the time: These girls weren't any stranger than any other girls, and to blame their behavior on the Primers was to miss the point entirely.

Greatly reassured, she took out her silver pen and began to write a letter to her missing husband, who had never seemed so far away.

*Miranda receives an unusual ractive message; a
drive through the streets of Shanghai; the Cathay
Hotel; a sophisticated soirée; Carl Hollywood
introduces her to two unusual characters.*

*I*t was a few minutes before midnight, and Miranda was
about to sign off from the evening shift and clear out of her
body stage. This was a Friday night. Nell had apparently
decided not to pull an all-nighter this time.

On school nights, Nell reliably went to bed betwee..
ten-thirty and eleven, but Friday was her night to immerse
herself in the Primer the way she had as a small child, six or
seven years ago, when all of this had started. Right now,
Nell was stuck in a part of the story that must have been
frustrating for her, namely, trying to puzzle out the social
rituals of a rather bizarre cult of faeries that had thrown her
into an underground labyrinth. She'd figure it out eventually—she always did—but not tonight.

Miranda stayed onstage for an extra hour and a half,
playing a role in a samurai ractive fairly popular in Japan, in
which she was a platinum blond missionary's daughter ab-
ducted from Nagasaki by ronin. All she had to do was
squeal a lot and eventually be rescued by a good samurai. It
was a pity she didn't speak Nipponese and (beyond that)
wasn't familiar with the theatrical style of that nation, because supposedly they were doing some radical and interesting things with *karamaku*—"empty screen" or "empty
act." Eight years ago, she would have taken the one-hour
airship ride to Nippon and learned the language. Four years
ago, she at least would have been disgusted with herself for
playing this stupid role. But tonight she spoke her lines on
cue, squealed and wriggled at the right times, and took her
money, along with a hefty tip and the inevitable mash note
from the payer—a middle-management type in Osaka who
wanted to get to know her better. Of course, the same technology that made it impossible for Miranda to find Nell,
made it impossible for this creep to find Miranda.

An urgent job offer flashed over her screen just as she
was putting her stuff together. She checked the *ENQUIRY*

screen; the job didn't pay that much, but it was of very short duration. So she accepted it. She wondered who was sending her urgent job offers; six years ago it had happened frequently, but since she'd gone into her habit of working the evening shift she had, in general, become just another interchangeable Western bimbo with an unpronounceable name.

It looked like some kind of weird bohemian art piece, some ractors'-workshop project from her distant past: a surreal landscape of abstract colored geometric forms with faces occasionally rising out of flat surfaces to speak lines. The faces were texture-mapped, as if wearing elaborately painted makeup, or were sculpted to the texture of orange peels, alligator hide, or durian fruit.

"We miss her," said one of the faces, the voice a little familiar, but disped into a weird ghostly echoing moan.

"Where is she?" said another face, rather familiar in its shape.

"Why has she abandoned us?" said a third face, and even through the texture-mapping and the voice disping, Miranda recognized Carl Hollywood.

"If only she would come to our party!" cried another one, whom Miranda recognized as a member of the Parnasse Company named Christine something-or-other.

The prompter gave her a line: *Sorry, guys, but I'm working late again tonight.*

"Okay, okay," Miranda said, "I'm going to ad lib. Where are you?"

"The cast party, dummy!" said Carl. "There's a cab waiting for you outside—we sprung for a half-laner!"

Miranda pulled out of the ractive, finished tidying up the body stage, and left it open so that some other member of the company could come in a few hours later and work the gold shift. She ran down the helical gauntlet of plaster cherubs, muses, and Trojans, across the lobby where a couple of bleary-eyed apprentice ractors were cleaning up the debris from this evening's live performance, and out the front doors. There in the street, illuminated by the queasy pink-and-purple neon of the marquee, was a half-lane cab with its lights on.

She was dully surprised when the driver headed toward the Bund, not toward the midrise districts in

Pudong, where tribeless, lower-income Westerners typically had their flats. Cast parties usually happened in someone's living room.

Then she reminded herself that the Parnasse was a successful theatre company nowadays, that they had a whole building somewhere full of developers coming up with new ractives, that the current production of *Macbeth* had cost a lot of money. Carl had flown to Tokyo and Shenzhen and San Francisco seeking investors and had not come back empty-handed. The first month of performances was sold out.

But tonight, there had been a lot of empty seats in the house, because most of the opening-night crowd was non-Chinese, and non-Chinese were nervous about going out on the streets because of rumors about the Fists of Righteous Harmony.

Miranda was nervous too, though she wouldn't admit it. The taxi turned a corner, and its headlights swept across a knot of young Chinese men gathered in a doorway, and as one of them lifted a cigarette to his mouth, she caught a glimpse of a scarlet ribbon knotted around his wrist. Her chest clenched up, her heart fluttered, and she had to swallow hard a few times. But the young men could not see into the silvered windows of the cab. They did not converge on her, brandishing weapons and crying "*Sha! Sha!*"

The Cathay Hotel stood in the middle of the Bund, at the intersection with Nanjing Road, the Rodeo Drive of the Far East. As far as Miranda could see—all the way to Nanjing, maybe—it was lined with Western and Nipponese boutiques and department stores, and the airspace above the street was besprent with almond-size aerostats, each with its own cine camera and pattern-recognition ware to watch for suspicious-looking congregations of young men who might be Fist cells.

Like all of the other big Western buildings on the waterfront, the Cathay was outlined in white light, which was probably a good thing because otherwise it wouldn't have looked like much. The exterior was bleak and dingy in the daytime.

She played a little game of chicken with the doorman. She strode toward the entrance, confident that he'd haul the door open for her, but he stood there with his hands clasped behind his back, staring back at her sullenly. Finally he gave way and hauled the door open, though she had to break her stride so as not to smash into it.

George Bernard Shaw had stayed here; Noel Coward had written a play here. The lobby was high and narrow, Beaux Arts marble, glorious ironwork chandeliers, white light from the Bund buildings filtering in through stained-glass arches. An ancient jazz band was playing in the bar, slap bass over trashcan drums. Miranda stood on tiptoe in the entrance, looking for the party, and saw nothing except middle-aged Caucasian airship tourists slow-dancing and the usual lineup of sharp young Chinese men along the bar, hoping she'd come in.

Eventually she found her way up to the eighth floor, where all the fancy restaurants were. The big banquet room had been rented out by some kind of garishly wealthy organization and was full of men wearing intimidatingly sophisticated suits, women wearing even more intimidating dresses, and the odd sprinkling of Victorians wearing far more conservative—but still dapper and expensive—stuff. The music was fairly restrained, just one tuxedoed Chinese man playing jazz on a grand piano, but on a stage at one end of the room, a larger band was setting up its equipment.

She was just cringing away, wondering in what back room the scruffy actors' bash might be found, when she heard someone calling her name from inside.

Carl Hollywood was approaching, striding across the middle of the banquet hall like he owned the place, resplendent in hand-tooled cowboy boots made of many supple and exotic bird and reptile skins, wearing a vast raiment, sort of a cross between a cape and a Western duster, that nearly brushed the floor, and that made him look seven feet tall rather than a mere six and a half. His long blond hair was brushed back away from his forehead, his King Tut beard was sharp and straight as a hoe. He was gorgeous and he knew it, and his blue eyes were piercing right through Miranda, holding her there in front of the open elevator doors, through which she'd almost escaped.

He gave her a big hug and whirled her around. She shrank against him, shielded from the crowd in the banquet hall by his enveloping cloak. "I look like shit," she said.

"Why didn't you tell me it was going to be this kind of a party?"

"Why didn't you know?" Carl said. As a director, one of his talents was to ask the most difficult imaginable questions.

"I would have worn something different. I look like—"

"You look like a young bohemian *artiste*," Carl said, stepping back to examine her typically form-fitting black bodysuit, "who doesn't give a shit about pretentious clothes, who makes everyone else in the room feel overdressed, and who can get away with it because she's got that special something."

"You silver-tongued dog," she said, "you know that's bullshit."

"A few years ago you would have sailed into that room with that lovely chin of yours held up like a battering ram, and everyone would have stepped back to look at you. Why not now?"

"I don't know," Miranda said. "I think with this Nell thing, I've incurred all the disadvantages of parenthood without actually getting to have a child."

Carl relaxed and softened, and Miranda knew she'd spoken the words he was looking for. "C'mere," he said. "I want you to meet someone."

"If you're going to try to fix me up with some wealthy son of a bitch—"

"Wouldn't dream of it."

"I'm not going to become a housewife who acts in her spare time."

"I realize that," Carl said. "Now calm yourself for a minute."

Miranda was forcibly ignoring the fact that they were walking through the middle of the room now. Carl Hollywood was drawing all of the attention, which suited her. She exchanged smiles with a couple of ractors who had appeared in the interactive invitation that had summoned her here; both of them were having what looked like very enjoyable conversations with fine-looking people, probably investors.

"Who are you taking me to meet?"

"A guy named Beck. An old acquaintance of mine."

"But not a friend?"

Carl adopted an uncomfortable grin and shrugged. "We've been friends sometimes. We've also been collaborators. Business partners. This is how life works, Miranda: After a while, you build up a network of people. You pass them bits of data they might be interested in and vice versa. To me, he's one of those guys."

"I can't help wondering why you want me to meet him."

"I believe," Carl said very quietly, but using some actor's trick so that she could hear every word, "that this gentleman can help you find Nell. And that you can help him find something he wants."

And he stepped aside with a swirl of cloak, pulling out a chair for her. They were in the corner of the banquet hall. Sitting on the opposite side of the table, his back to a large marble-silled window, the illuminated Bund and the mediatronic cacophony of Pudong spilling bloody light across the glossy shoulder-pads of his suit, was a young African man in dreadlocks, wearing dark glasses with minuscule circular lenses held in some kind of ostentatiously complex metallic space grid. Sitting next to him, but hardly noticed by Miranda, was a Nipponese businessman wearing a dark formal kimono and smoking what smelled like an old-fashioned, fully carcinogenic cigar.

"Miranda, this is Mr. Beck and Mr. Oda, both privateers. Gentlemen, Ms. Miranda Redpath."

Both men nodded in a pathetic vestige of a bow, but neither made a move to shake hands, which was just as well —nowadays some amazing things could be transferred through skin-to-skin contact. Miranda didn't even nod back to them; she just sat down and let Carl scoot her in. She didn't like people who described themselves as privateers. It was just a pretentious word for a thete—someone who didn't have a tribe.

Either that, or they really did belong to tribes—from the looks of them, probably some weird synthetic phyle she'd never heard of—and, for some reason, were pretending not to.

Carl said, "I have explained to the gentlemen, without getting into any details, that you would like to do the impossible. Can I get you something to drink, Miranda?"

After Carl Hollywood left, there was a rather long silence during which Mr. Beck presumably stared at Miranda, though she could not tell because of the dark glasses. Mr. Oda's primary function appeared to be that of nervous spectator, as if he had wagered half of his net worth on whether Miranda or Mr. Beck would speak first.

A stratagem occurred to Mr. Oda. He pointed in the direction of the bandstand and nodded significantly. "You like this band?"

Miranda looked over at the band, half a dozen men and women in an assortment of races. Mr. Oda's question was difficult to answer because they had not yet made any music. She looked back at Mr. Oda, who pointed significantly at himself.

"Oh. You're the backer?" Miranda said.

Mr. Oda withdrew a small glittering object from his pocket and slid it across the table toward Miranda. It was a cloisonné pin shaped like a dragonfly. She had noticed similar ones adorning several partygoers. She picked it up cautiously. Mr. Oda tapped himself on the lapel and nodded, encouraging her to put it on.

She left it sitting there on the table for the time being.

"I'm not seeing anything," Mr. Beck finally said, apparently for Mr. Oda's benefit. "To a first approximation, she is clean." Miranda realized that Mr. Beck had been checking her out using some kind of display in his phenomenoscopic glasses.

Miranda was still trying to work out some kind of unpleasant response when Mr. Oda leaned forward into his own cloud of cigar smoke. "It is our understanding," he said, "that you wish to make a connection. Your wish is very strong."

Privateers. The word also implied that these gentlemen, at least in their own minds, had some kind of an angle, some way of making money off of their own lack of tribal affiliation.

"I've been told that such things are impossible."

"It's more correct to speak in probabilistic terms," said Mr. Beck. His accent was more Oxford than anything else, with a Jamaican lilt, and a crispness that owed something to India.

"Astronomically improbable, then," Miranda said.

"There you go," said Mr. Beck.

Now, somehow, the ball had found its way into Miranda's court. "If you guys think you've found a way to beat probability, why don't you go into the Vegas ractives and make a fortune?"

Misters Beck and Oda were actually more amused by that crack than she had expected them to be. They were capable of irony. That was one good sign in the almost overwhelming barrage of negative signals she'd been getting from them so far.

The band started up, playing dance music with a good beat. The lights came down, and the party began to glitter as light flashed from the dragonfly pins.

"It wouldn't work," Mr. Beck said, "because Vegas is a game of pure numbers with no human meaning to it. The mind doesn't interface to pure numbers."

"But probability is probability," Miranda said.

"What if you have a dream one night that your sister is in a crash, and you contact her the next day and learn that she broke up with her boyfriend?"

"It could be a coincidence."

"Yes. But not a very probable one. You see, maybe it's possible to beat probability, when the heart as well as the mind is involved."

Miranda supposed that neither Mr. Beck nor Mr. Oda understood the essential cruelty of what they were saying. It was much better not to have any hope at all. "Are you guys involved in some kind of religious thing?" she said.

Misters Beck and Oda looked at each other significantly. Mr. Oda went into some peculiar routine of tooth-sucking and throat-clearing that would probably convey a torrent of information to another Nipponese person but meant nothing to Miranda, other than giving her a general hint that the situation was rather complicated. Mr. Beck produced an antique silver snuffbox, or a replica of one, took out a pinch of nanosite dust, and hoovered it up into one of his great circular nostrils, then nervously scratched the underside of his nose. He slid his glasses way down, exposing his big brown eyes, and stared distractedly over Miranda's shoulder into the thick of the party, watching the band and the dancers' reaction to it. He was wearing a dragonfly pin, which had begun to glow and to flash gorgeous colored lights, like a fleet of police cars and firetrucks gathered round a burning house.

The band segued into a peculiar, tuneless, beatless miasma of noise, spawning lazy convection currents in the crowd.

"How do you guys know Carl?" Miranda said, hoping to break the ice a bit.

Mr. Oda shook his head apologetically. "I have not had the pleasure of making his acquaintance until recently."

"Used to do *thyuh-tuh* with him in London."

"You're a ractor?"

Mr. Beck snorted ironically. A variegated silk hankie flourished in his hand, and he blew his nose quickly and cleanly like a practiced snuff-taker. "I am a technical boy," he said.

"You program ractives?"

"That is a subset of my activities."

"You do lights and sets? Or digital stuff? Or nanotech?"

"Invidious distinctions do not interest me. I am interested in one thing," said Mr. Beck, holding up his index finger, topped with a very large but perfectly manicured claw of a fingernail, "and that is use of tech to convey meaning."

"That covers a lot of areas nowadays."

"Yes, but it shouldn't. That is to say that the distinctions between those areas are bogus."

"What's wrong with just programming ractives?"

"Nothing at all," said Mr. Beck, "just as nothing is wrong with traditional live theatre, or for that matter, sitting round a campfire telling stories, like I used to enjoy on the beach when I was a lad. But as long as there are new ways to be found, it is my job, as a technical boy, to find them. Your art, lady, is racting. Searching for the new tech is mine."

The noise coming from the band had begun to pulse irregularly. As they talked, the pulses gathered themselves into beats and became steadier. Miranda turned around to look at the people on the dance floor. They were all standing around with faraway looks on their faces, concentrating on something. Their dragonfly pins were flashing wildly now, joining in a coherent pulse of pure white on each beat. Miranda realized that the pins were somehow patched into the wearers' nervous systems and that they were talking to each other, creating the music collectively. A guitarist began to weave an improvised melodic line through the gradually coalescing pattern of sound, and the sound condensed around it as all of the dancers heard the tune. They had a feedback loop going. A young woman began to chant out some kind of tuneless rap that sounded improvised. As she went on, she broke into melody. The music was still weird and formless, but it was beginning to approach something you might hear on a professional recording.

Miranda turned back to face Mr. Beck. "You think you've invented a new way to convey meaning with technology—"

"Medium."

"A new medium, and that it can help me get what I want. Because when meaning is involved, the laws of probability can be broken."

"There are two misconceptions in your statement. One: I did not invent the medium. Others did, perhaps for different purposes, and I have stumbled across it, or actually just heard intimations.

"As far as the laws of probability, my lady, these cannot be broken, any more than any other mathematical principle. But laws of physics and mathematics are like a coordinate system that runs in only one dimension. Perhaps there is another dimension perpendicular to it, invisible to those laws of physics, describing the same things with different rules, and those rules are written in our hearts, in a deep place where we cannot go and read them except in our dreams."

Miranda looked to Mr. Oda, hoping he'd wink or something, but he was staring into the dance floor with a terribly serious expression, as though enfolded in deep thoughts himself, nodding slightly. Miranda drew a deep breath and sighed.

When she looked up at Mr. Beck again, he was watching her, noting her curiosity about Mr. Oda. He turned one hand palm up and rubbed the ball of his thumb over his fingertips.

So Beck was the hacker and Oda was the backer. The oldest and most troublesome relationship in the technological world.

"We require a third participant," Mr. Beck said, dovetailing into her thoughts.

"To do what?" Miranda said, evasive and defensive at the same time.

"All technomedia ventures have the same structure," said Mr. Oda, bestirring himself for the first time in a while. By now a nice synergy had developed between band and crowd, and a lot of dancing was going on—some intimidatingly sophisticated stuff, and also some primal moshing. "Three-legged tripod." Oda held up a fist and began to extend fingers as he enumerated the same. Miranda noted that his fingers were gnarly and bent, as if they'd all been broken frequently. Mr. Oda was, perhaps, a veteran practitioner of certain martial arts now disdained by most Nipponese because of their lower-class provenance. "Leg number one: new technological idea. Mr. Beck. Leg number two: adequate financial backing. Mr. Oda. Leg number three: the artist."

Misters Beck and Oda looked significantly at Miranda. She threw back her head and managed a nice solid laugh, hitting that sweet spot down in her diaphragm. It felt good. She shook her head, letting her hair swing back and forth across her shoulders. Then she leaned forward across the table, shouting to be heard above the band. "You guys must be desperate. I'm old hat, guys. There's half a dozen ractors in this room with better prospects than me. Didn't Carl fill you in? I've been holed up in a body stage for six years doing kid stuff. I'm not a star."

"Star means a master of conventional ractives, which are precisely the technology we are trying to move beyond," said Mr. Beck, a bit scornful that she wasn't getting it.

Mr. Oda pointed to the band. "None of these people were professional musicians—some not even amateurs. Musician skills are not relevant for this—these people were new kinds of artists born too early."

"*Almost* too early," Mr. Beck said.

"Oh, my god," Miranda said, starting to get it. For the first time, she believed that what Beck and Oda were talking about—whatever the hell it was—was a real possibility. Which meant that she was ninety percent convinced—though only Beck and Oda understood that.

It was too loud to talk. A mosher backed into Miranda's chair and nearly fell over her. Beck stood up, came round the table, and extended one hand, asking her to dance. Miranda looked into the Dionysian revel filling the floor and understood that the only way to be safe was to join it. She plucked her dragonfly pin from the tabletop and followed Beck into the midst of the dance. As she pinned it on, it began to flash, and she thought she heard a new strain woven into the song.

*From the Primer, Princess Nell enters into
the lands of King Coyote.*

All that hot afternoon Nell toiled up the numberless switchbacks, occasionally reaching into the bag that dangled at her waist, drawing out a handful of Purple's ashes and scattering them behind her like seeds. Whenever she stopped to rest, she could look out across the burnt desert she had just crossed: a tawny plain scabbed with reddish-brown volcanic rock, patches of aromatic greenish-gray shrubs clinging like bread mold to any parts that were sheltered from the eternal wind. She had hoped that when she climbed the face of this mountain, she would rise up above the dust, but it had followed her, coating her lips and her toes. When she drew a breath through her nose, it only stung her parched nostrils, and so she had given up trying to smell anything. But late in the afternoon a cool moist draft spilled down the mountain and over her face. She drew in a breath of it, hoping to catch some of the cold air before it trickled down into the desert. It smelled of evergreens.

As she climbed the switchbacks, she forded those delightful currents of air over and over, so that as she rounded each hairpin turn in the trail, she had an incentive to climb toward the next one. The little shrubs that clutched rocks and cowered in cracks became bigger and more numerous, and flowers began to appear, first tiny little white ones like handfuls of salt strewn over the rocks, then larger blossoms, blue and magenta and brilliant orange, brimming with scented nectar that attracted bees all fuzzy and yellow with stolen pollen. Gnarled oaks and short dense evergreens cast tiny shadows across the path. The skyline grew closer, and the turns in the path became wider as the mountain became less steep. Nell rejoiced when the switchbacks ended and the trail took off straight across an undulating mountaintop meadow thick with purple-flowered heather and marked with occasional stands of tall firs. For a moment she was afraid that this meadow was nothing more than a ledge, and that she had more mountains to ascend; but then the path turned downhill, and treading heavily as new muscles caught her descending weight, she half-ran across a vast boulder, pocked with tiny pools of clear water and occasional lozenges of wet snow, until she reached a point where it fell away from under her and she skidded to a precarious stop, looking down like a peregrine falcon over an immense country of blue lakes and green mountains, shrouded in a whirling storm of silver mist.

Nell turned the page and saw it, just as the book said. This was a two-page illustration—a color painting, she reckoned. Any one part of it looked just as real as a cine feed. But the geometry of the thing was funny, borrowing some suprarealistic tricks from classical Chinese landscape painting; the mountains were too steep, and they marched away forever into the distance, and if Nell stared, she could see tall castles clinging to their impossibly precipitous slopes, colorful banners waving from their flagpoles bearing heraldic devices that were dynamic: The gryphons crouched, the lions roared, and she could see all of these details, even though the castles should have been miles away; whenever she looked at something it got bigger and turned into a different picture, and when her attention wavered—when she blinked and shook her head—it snapped back to the first view again.

She spent a long time doing that, because there were dozens of castles at the very least, and she got the feeling that if she kept looking and counting she might look forever. But it wasn't all castles: there were mountains, cities, rivers, lakes, birds and beasts, caravans, and travelers of all kinds.

She spent a while staring at a group of travelers who had drawn their wagons into a roadside meadow and set up a camp, clapping hands round a bonfire while one of them played a reel on some small bellows-powered bagpipes, barely audible these many miles away. Then she realized that the book hadn't said anything for a long time. "What happened then?" she said.

The *Young Lady's Illustrated Primer* said nothing.

"Nell looked for a safe way down," Nell essayed.

Her vantage point began to move. A patch of snow swung into view. "No, wait!" she said, "Nell stuffed some clean snow into her water bottles."

In the painting, Nell could see her bare pink hands scooping up snow and packing it bit by bit into the neck of her bottle. When it was full, she put the cork back in (Nell didn't have to specify that) and began moving around on the rock, looking for a place that wasn't so steep. Nell didn't have to explain that in detail either; in the ractive, she searched the rock in a fairly rational way and in a few minutes found a stairway chiseled into the rock, winding down the mountain endlessly until it pierced a cloud layer far below. Princess Nell began descending the steps, one at a time.

After a while, Nell tried an experiment: "Princess Nell descended the stairs for many hours."

This triggered a series of dissolves like she'd seen on old passives: Her current view dissolved into a closeup of her feet, trudging down a couple of steps, which dissolved into a view from considerably farther down the mountain, followed by a closeup of Princess Nell unscrewing her water bottle and drinking melted snow; another view from farther down; Nell sitting down for a rest; a soaring eagle; the approaching cloud layer; big trees; descending through the mist; and finally, Nell tramping wearily down the last ten steps, which left her in a clearing in a dark coniferous forest, carpeted with rust-colored pine needles. It was twilight, and the wolves were beginning to howl. Nell made the usual arrangements for the night, lit a fire, and curled up to sleep.

Having reached a good stopping-place, Nell started to close the book. She'd have to continue this later.

She had just entered the land of the oldest and most powerful of all the Faery Kings. The many castles on the

mountains belonged to all of his Dukes and Earls, and she
suspected she would have to visit them all before she had
gotten what she'd come for. It was not a quick adventure for
an early Saturday morning. But just as she was clasping the
book together, new words and an illustration appeared on
the page she'd been reading, and something about the illustration made her open the book back up. It showed a crow
perched on a tree branch above Princess Nell, holding a
necklace in its beak. It was eleven jeweled keys strung on a
golden chain. Princess Nell had been wearing it around her
neck; apparently the next event in the story was that this
bird stole it while she was sleeping. Beneath the picture was
a poem, spoken by the crow from his perch:

> Castles, gardens, gold, and jewels
> Contentment signify, for fools
> Like Princess Nell; but those
> Who cultivate their wit
> Like King Coyote and his crows
> Compile their power bit by bit
> And hide it places no one knows.

Nell closed up the book. This was too upsetting to think
about just now. She had been collecting those keys for most
of her life. The first she'd taken from King Magpie just after
she and Harv had arrived at Dovetail. She had picked up the
other ten one at a time during the years since then. She had
done this by traveling to the lands of the Faery Kings and
Queens who owned those keys and using the tricks she had
learned from her Night Friends. Each key had come to her in
a different way.

One of the hardest keys to get had belonged to an old
Faery Queen who had seen through every trick that Nell
could think up and fought off every assault. Finally, in des-
peration, Princess Nell had thrown herself on the mercy of
that Queen and told her the sad story of Harv locked up in
the Dark Castle. The Queen had fed Nell a nice bowl of
chicken soup and handed over the key with a smile.

Not much later, Duck had encountered a nice young
mallard on the road and flown away with him to start a
family. Purple and Princess Nell then traveled together for

several years, and on many a dark night, sitting around the campfire under a full moon, Purple had taught Nell secret things from her magic books and from the ancient lore she kept in her head.

Recently they had traveled for a thousand miles on camelback across a great desert full of djinns, demons, sultans, and caliphs and finally reached the great onion-domed palace of the local Faery King—himself a djinn of great power—who ruled over all the desert lands. Princess Nell had devised a complicated plan to trick their way into the djinn's treasury. To carry it out, she and Purple had to live in the city around the palace for a couple of years and make many treks into the desert in search of magic lanterns, rings, secret caverns, and the like.

Finally, Princess Nell and Purple had penetrated to the djinn king's treasury and found the eleventh key. But they had been surprised by the djinn himself, who attacked them in the guise of a fire-breathing serpent. Purple had transformed herself into a giant eagle with metallic wings and talons that could not be burned—much to the surprise of Princess Nell, who had never imagined that her companion possessed such power.

The battle between Purple and the djinn raged for a day and a night, both combatants transforming themselves into any number of fantastical creatures and hurling all manner of devastating spells at each other, until finally the mighty castle lay in ruins, the desert was scorched and blasted for many miles around, and Purple and the djinn king both lay dead on the floor of what had been the treasury.

Nell had picked up the eleventh key from the floor, put it on her chain, cremated Purple's body, and scattered her ashes across the desert as she walked, for many days, toward the mountains and the green land, where the eleven keys had now been stolen away from her.

*Nell's experiences at school; a confrontation with
Miss Stricken; the rigors of Supplementary
Curriculum; Miss Matheson's philosophy of
education; three friends go separate ways.*

AGLAIA	*BRILLIANCE*
EUPHROSYNE	*JOY*
THALIA	*BLOOM*

The names of the three graces, and diverse artists' conceptions of the ladies themselves, were chiseled, painted, and sculpted freely about the interior and exterior of Miss Matheson's Academy. Nell could hardly look anywhere without seeing one of them prancing across a field of wildflowers, distributing laurel wreaths to the worthy, jointly thrusting a torch toward heaven, or shedding lambent effulgence upon the receptive pupils.

Nell's favorite part of the curriculum was Thalia, which was scheduled for an hour in the morning and an hour in the afternoon. When Miss Matheson hauled once on the old bellrope dangling down from the belfry, belting a single dolorous clang across the campus, Nell and the other girls in her section would arise, curtsy to their teacher, walk in single file down the corridor to the courtyard—then break into a chaotic run until they reached the Hall of Physical Culture, where they would strip out of their heavy, scratchy complicated uniforms and climb into lighter, looser, scratchy complicated uniforms with more freedom of movement.

The Bloom curriculum was taught by Miss Ramanujan or one of her assistants. Usually they did something vigorous in the morning, like field hockey, and something graceful in the afternoon, like ballroom dance, or peculiar, giggle-inducing exercises in how to walk, stand, and sit like a Lady.

Brilliance was Miss Matheson's department, though she mostly left it to her assistants, occasionally wheeling in and out of various classrooms in an old wood-and-wicker wheelchair. During the Aglaia period, the girls would get together in groups of half a dozen or so to answer questions or solve problems put to them by the teachers: For example, they counted how many species of plants and animals could be found in one square foot of the forest behind the school. They put on a scene from a play in Greek. They used a ractive simulation to model the domestic economy of a Lakota band before and after the introduction of horses. They designed simple machines with a nanopresence rig and tried to compile them in the M.C. and make them work. They wove brocades and made porcelain as Chinese ladies used to do. And there was an ocean of history to be learned: first biblical, Greek, and Roman, and then the history of many other peoples around the world that essentially served as backdrop for History of the English-Speaking Peoples.

The latter subject was, curiously, not part of the Brilliance curriculum; it was left firmly in the hands of Miss Stricken, who was mistress of Joy.

In addition to two one-hour periods each day, Miss Stricken had the attention of the entire assembled student body once in the morning, once at noon, and once in the evening. During these times her basic function was to call the students to order; publicly upbraid those sheep who had prominently strayed since the last such assembly; disgorge any random meditations that had been occupying her mind of late; and finally, in reverential tones, introduce Father Cox, the local vicar, who would lead the students in prayer. Miss Stricken also had the students all to herself for two hours on Sunday morning and could optionally command their attention for up to eight hours on Saturdays if she came round to the opinion that they wanted supplementary guidance.

The first time Nell sat down in one of Miss Stricken's classrooms, she found that her desk had perversely been left directly behind another girl's, so that she was unable to see anything except for the bow in that girl's hair. She got up, tried to skooch the desk, and found that it was fixed to the floor. All the desks, in fact, were arranged in a perfectly regular grid, facing in the same direction—which is to say, toward Miss Stricken or one of her two assistants, Miss Bowlware and Mrs. Disher.

Miss Bowlware taught them History of the English-Speaking Peoples, starting with the Romans at Londinium and careening through the Norman Conquest, Magna Carta,

Wars of the Roses, Renaissance, and Civil War; but she didn't really hit her stride until she got to the Georgian period, at which point she worked herself up into a froth explaining the shortcomings of that syphilitic monarch, which had inspired the right-thinking Americans to break away in disgust. They studied the most ghastly parts of Dickens, which Miss Bowlware carefully explained was *called* Victorian literature because it was *written* during the reign of Victoria I, but was actually *about* pre-Victorian times, and that the mores of the original Victorians—the ones who built the old British Empire—were actually a reaction against the sort of bad behavior engaged in by their parents and grandparents and so convincingly detailed by Dickens, their most popular novelist.

The girls actually got to sit at their desks and play a few ractives showing what it was like to live during this time: generally not very nice, even if you selected the option that turned off all the diseases. At this point, Mrs. Disher stepped in to say, if you thought *that* was scary, look at how poor people lived in the late twentieth century. Indeed, after ractives told them about the life of an inner-city Washington, D.C., child during the 1990s, most students had to agree they'd take a workhouse in pre-Victorian England over *that* any day.

All of the foregoing set the stage for a three-pronged, parallel examination of the British Empire; pre-Vietnam America; and the modern and ongoing history of New Atlantis. In general, Mrs. Disher handled the more modern stuff and anything pertaining to America.

Miss Stricken handled the big payoff at the end of each period and at the end of each unit. She stormed in to explain what conclusion they were being led to and to make sure that all of them got it. She also had a way of lunging predatorily into the classroom and rapping the knuckles of any girl who had been whispering, making faces at the teachers, passing notes, doodling, woolgathering, fidgeting, scratching, nose-picking, sighing, or slumping.

Clearly, she was sitting in her closetlike office next door watching them with cine monitors. Once, Nell was sitting in Joy diligently absorbing a lecture about the Lend-Lease Program. When she heard the squeaky door from Miss Stricken's office swing open behind her, like all the other girls she suppressed the panicky urge to look around. She heard Miss Stricken's heels popping up her aisle, heard the whir of the ruler, and then suddenly felt her knuckles explode.

"Hairdressing is a private not a public activity, Nell," Miss Stricken said. "The other girls know this; now you do too."

Nell's face burned, and she wrapped her good hand around her damaged one like a bandage. She did not understand anything until one of the other girls caught her eye and made a corkscrewing motion with her index finger up near one temple: Apparently Nell had been twisting her hair around her finger, which she often did when she was reading the Primer or thinking hard about any one thing.

The ruler was such a pissant form of discipline, compared to a real beating, that she could not take it seriously at first and actually found it funny the first few times. As the months went by, though, it seemed to get more painful. Either Nell was becoming soft, or—more likely—the full dimensions of the punishment were beginning to sink in. She had been such an outsider at first that nothing mattered. But as she began to excel in the other classes and to gain the respect of teachers and students alike, she found herself with pride to lose. Part of her wanted to rebel, to throw everything away so that it could not be used against her. But she enjoyed the other classes so much that she couldn't bear to think further of the possibility.

One day Miss Stricken decided to concentrate all her attentions on Nell. There was nothing unusual about that—it was standard to randomly single out particular scholars for intensive enforcement. With twenty minutes left in the hour, Miss Stricken had already gotten Nell on the right hand for hair-twisting and on the left for nail-biting, when, to her horror, Nell realized that she was scratching her nose and that Miss Stricken was standing in the aisle glaring at her like a falcon. Both of Nell's hands shot into her lap, beneath the desk.

Miss Stricken walked up to her deliberately, pop pop pop. "Your right hand, Nell," she said, "just about here." And she indicated with the end of the ruler an altitude that would be a convenient place for the assault—rather high above the desk, so that everyone in the room could see it.

Nell hesitated for a moment, then held her hand up.

"A bit higher, Nell," Miss Stricken said.

Nell moved her hand a bit higher.

"Another inch should do it, I think," Miss Stricken said, appraising the hand as if it were carved in marble and recently excavated from a Greek temple.

Nell could not bring herself to raise the hand any higher.

"Raise it one more inch, Nell," Miss Stricken said, "so that the other girls can observe and learn along with you."

Nell raised her hand just a bit.

"That was rather less than an inch, I should think," Miss Stricken said.

Other girls in the class began to titter—their faces were all turned back toward Nell, and she could see their exultation, and somehow Miss Stricken and the ruler became irrelevant compared to the other girls. Nell raised her hand a whole inch, saw the windup out of the corner of her eye, heard the whir. At the last moment, on an impulse, she flipped her hand over, caught the ruler on her palm, grabbed it, and twisted in a way that Dojo had taught her, bending it against the grain of Miss Stricken's fingers so that she was forced to let go. Now Nell had the ruler, and Miss Stricken was disarmed.

Her opponent was a bulging sort of woman, taller than average, rather topheavy on those heels, the sort of teacher whose very fleshiness becomes the object of morbid awe among her gamine pupils, whose personal toilet practices— the penchant for dandruff, the habitually worn-out lipstick, the little wad of congealed saliva at the corner of the mouth —loom larger in her students' minds than the Great Pyramids or the Lewis and Clark Expedition. Like all other women, Miss Stricken benefited from a lack of external genitalia that would make it more difficult for Nell to incapacitate her, but nevertheless, Nell could think of half a dozen ways to leave her a bloody knot on the floor and not waste more than a quarter of a minute in the process. During her time with Constable Moore, noting her benefactor's interest in war and weapons, she had taken up a renewed interest in martial arts, had paged back in the Primer to the Dinosaur's Tale and been pleased but hardly surprised to discover that

Dojo was still holding lessons there, picking up just where he and Belle the Monkey had left off.

Thinking of her friend Dinosaur and her sensei, Dojo the Mouse, she suddenly felt shame far deeper than anything Miss Stricken or her sniggering classmates could inflict. Miss Stricken was a stupid hag, and her classmates were snot-nosed clowns, but Dojo was her friend and her teacher, he had always respected her and given her his full attention, and he had carefully taught her the ways of humility and self-discipline. Now she had perverted his teachings by using her skill to take Miss Stricken's ruler. She could not have been more ashamed.

She handed the ruler back, raised her hand high in the air, and heard but did not feel the impacts of the ruler, some ten in all. "I shall expect you in my office after evening prayers, Nell," Miss Stricken said when she was finished.

"Yes, Miss Stricken," Nell said.

"What are you girls looking at?" blurted Mrs. Disher, who was running the class today. "Turn around and pay attention!" And with that it was all over. Nell sat in her desk for the rest of the hour as if carved from a solid block of gypsum.

Her interview with Miss Stricken at the end of the day was short and businesslike, no violence or even histrionics. Nell was informed that her performance in the Joy phase of the curriculum was so deficient that it placed her in danger of failing and being expelled from the school altogether, and that her only hope was to come in each Saturday for eight hours of supplementary study.

Nell wished more than anything that she could refuse. Saturday was the only day of the week when she did not have to attend school at all. She always spent the day reading the Primer, exploring the fields and forests around Dovetail, or visiting Harv down in the Leased Territories.

She felt that, through her own mistakes, she had ruined her life at Miss Matheson's Academy. Until recently, Miss Stricken's classes had been nothing more than a routine annoyance—an ordeal that she had to sit through in order to experience the fun parts of the curriculum. She could look back on a time only a couple of months ago when she would come home with her mind aglow from all the things she had learned in Brilliance, and when the Joy part was just an indistinct smudge around the edge. But in recent weeks, Miss Stricken had, for some reason, loomed larger and larger in her view of the place. And somehow, Miss Stricken had read Nell's mind and had chosen just the right moment to step up her campaign of harassment. She had timed today's events perfectly. She had brought Nell's most deeply hidden feelings out into the open, like a master butcher exposing the innards with one or two deft strokes of the knife. And now everything was ruined. Now Miss Matheson's Academy had vanished and become Miss Stricken's House of Pain, and there was no way for Nell to escape from that house without giving up, which her friends in the Primer had taught her she must never do.

Nell's name went up on a board at the front of the classroom labeled, in heavy brass letters, *SUPPLEMENTARY CURRICULUM STUDENTS*. Within a few days, her name had been joined by two others: Fiona Hackworth and Elizabeth Finkle-McGraw. Nell's disarming of the fearsome Miss Stricken had already become the stuff of oral legend, and her two friends had been so inspired by the act of defiance that they had gone to elaborate lengths to get themselves in trouble too. Now, the three best students of Miss Matheson's Academy were all doomed to Supplementary Curriculum.

Each Saturday, Nell, Fiona, and Elizabeth would arrive at the school at seven o'clock, enter the room, and sit down in the front row in adjacent desks. This was part of Miss Stricken's fiendish plan. A less subtle tormentor would have placed the girls as far apart as possible to prevent them from talking to each other, but Miss Stricken wanted them right next to each other so that they would be more tempted to visit and pass notes.

There was no teacher in the room at any time. They assumed that they were being monitored, but they never really knew. When they entered, each one of them had a pile of books on her desk—old books bound in chafed leather. Their job was to copy the books out by hand and leave the pages neatly stacked on Miss Stricken's desk before they went home. Usually, the books were transcripts of debates from the House of Lords, from the nineteenth century.

During their seventh Saturday in Supplementary Curriculum, Elizabeth Finkle-McGraw suddenly dropped her pen, slammed her book shut, and threw it against the wall.

Nell and Fiona could not keep themselves from laughing. But Elizabeth did not convey the impression of being in a very lighthearted mood. The old book had scarcely come to rest on the floor before Elizabeth had run over to it and begun kicking at it. With each blow a furious grunt escaped from her gorge. The book absorbed this violence impassively, driving Elizabeth into a higher rage; she dropped to her knees, flung the cover open, and began to rip out pages by the fistful.

Nell and Fiona looked at each other, suddenly serious. The kicking had been funny, but something about the tearing of pages disturbed them both. "Elizabeth! Stop it!" Nell said, but Elizabeth gave no signs of having heard her. Nell ran up to Elizabeth and hugged her from behind. Fiona scurried in a moment later and picked up the book.

"God damn it!" Elizabeth bellowed, "I don't care about any of the goddamn books, and I don't care about the Primer either!"

The door banged open. Miss Stricken stomped in, dislodged Nell with a simple body check, got both arms around Elizabeth's shoulders, and manhandled her out the door.

A few days later, Elizabeth left on a lengthy vacation with her parents, jumping from one New Atlantis clave to another in the family's private airship, working their way across the Pacific and North America and finally to London itself, where they settled in for several months. In the first few days, Nell received one letter from her, and Fiona received two. After that they received no response to their letters and eventually stopped trying. Elizabeth's name was removed from the Supplementary Curriculum plaque.

Nell and Fiona soldiered on. Nell had reached the point where she could transcribe the old books all day long without actually absorbing a single word. During her first weeks in Supplementary Curriculum she had been frightened; in fact, she had been surprised at the level of her own fear and had come to realize that Authority, even when it refrained from violence, could be as disturbing a specter as anything she had seen in her earlier years. After the incident with Elizabeth, she became bored for many months, then furious for quite a while until she realized, in conversations with Duck and Purple, that her anger was eating her up inside. So with a conscious effort, she went back to being bored again.

The reason she'd been furious was that copying out those books was such an unforgivably stupid waste of time. There was no end to what she could have learned reading the Primer for those eight hours. For that matter, the normal curriculum at Miss Matheson's Academy would have been perfectly fine as well. She was tormented by the irrationality of this place.

One day, when she returned from a trip to the washroom, she was startled to notice that Fiona had hardly copied out a single page, though they had been there for hours.

After this, Nell made it a practice to look at Fiona from time to time. She noticed that Fiona never stopped writing, but she was not paying attention to the old books. As she finished each page, she folded it up and placed it in her reticule. From time to time, she would stop and stare dreamily out the window for a few minutes, and then resume; or she might place both hands over her face and rock back and forth silently in her chair for a while before giving herself over to a long burst of ardent writing that might cover several pages in as many minutes.

Miss Stricken cruised into the room late one afternoon, took the stack of completed pages from Nell's desk, flipped through them, and allowed her chin to decline by a few minutes of arc. This nearly imperceptible vestige of a nod was her way of saying that Nell was dismissed for the day. Nell had come to understand that one way for Miss Stricken to emphasize her power over the girls was for her to make her wishes known through the subtlest possible signs, so that her charges were forced to watch her anxiously at all times.

Nell took her leave; but after proceeding a few steps down the corridor, she turned and stole back to the door and peeked through the window into the classroom.

Miss Stricken had gotten the folded-up pages out of Fiona's bag and was perusing them, strolling back and forth across the front of the room like the slow swing of a pendulum, a devastatingly ponderous motion. Fiona sat in her chair, her head bowed and her shoulders drawn together protectively.

After reading the papers for an eternity or two, Miss

Stricken dropped them on her desk and made some kind of brief statement, shaking her head in hopeless disbelief. Then she turned and walked out of the room.

When Nell reached her, Fiona's shoulders were still shaking silently. Nell put her arms around Fiona, who finally began to draw in sobbing breaths. During the next few minutes she gradually moved on to that stage of crying where the body seems to swell up and poach in its own fluids.

Nell suppressed the urge to be impatient. She well knew, as did all of the other girls, that Fiona's father had disappeared several years ago and never come back. He was rumored to be on an honorable and official mission; but as years went by this belief was gradually supplanted by the suspicion that something disgraceful had taken place. It would be easy enough for Nell to make the point that she had been through much worse. But seeing the depth of Fiona's unhappiness, she had to consider the possibility that Fiona was in a worse situation now.

When Fiona's mother came by in a little half-lane car to pick her up, and saw her daughter's red and ruinous face, an expression of black rage came over her own visage and she drove Fiona away without so much as a glance at Nell. Fiona showed up for church the next day as if nothing had happened and said nothing of it to Nell during the next week at school. In fact, Fiona hardly said a word to anyone, as she spent all of her time now daydreaming.

When Nell and Fiona showed up at seven o'clock the next Saturday morning, they were astonished to find Miss Matheson waiting for them at the front of the classroom, sitting in her wood-and-wicker wheelchair, wrapped up in a thermogenic comforter. The stacks of books, paper, and fountain pens were not there, and their names had been removed from the plaque at the front of the room. "It's a lovely spring day," Miss Matheson said. "Let's gather some foxgloves."

They went across the playing fields to the meadow where the wildflowers grew, the two girls walking and Miss Matheson's wheelchair carrying her along on its many-spoked smart wheels.

"Chiselled Spam," Miss Matheson said, sort of mumbling it to herself.

"Pardon me, Miss Matheson?" Nell said.

"I was just watching the smart wheels and remembering an advertisement from my youth," Miss Matheson said. "I used to be a thrasher, you know. I used to ride skateboards through the streets. Now I'm still on wheels, but a different kind. Got a few too many bumps and bruises during my earlier career, I'm afraid."

"It's a wonderful thing to be clever, and you should never think otherwise, and you should never stop being that way. But what you learn, as you get older, is that there are a few billion other people in the world all trying to be clever at the same time, and whatever you do with your life will certainly be lost—swallowed up in the ocean—unless you are doing it along with like-minded people who will remember your contributions and carry them forward. That is why the world is divided into tribes. There are many Lesser phyles and three Great ones. What are the Great ones?"

"New Atlantis," Nell began.

"Nippon," said Fiona.

"Han," they concluded together.

"That is correct," Miss Matheson said. "We traditionally include Han in the list because of its immense size and age—even though it has lately been crippled by intestine discord. And some would include Hindustan, while others would view it as a riotously diverse collection of microtribes sintered together according to some formula we don't get.

"Now, there was a time when we believed that what a human mind could accomplish was determined by genetic factors. Piffle, of course, but it looked convincing for many years, because distinctions between tribes were so evident. Now we understand that it's all cultural. That, after all, is what a culture is—a group of people who share in common certain acquired traits.

"Information technology has freed cultures from the necessity of owning particular bits of land in order to propagate; now we can live anywhere. The Common Economic Protocol specifies how this is to be arranged.

"Some cultures are prosperous; some are not. Some value rational discourse and the scientific method; some do not. Some encourage freedom of expression, and some discourage it. The only thing they have in common is that if they do not propagate, they will be swallowed up by others. All they have built up will be torn down; all they have accomplished will be forgotten; all they have learned and written will be scattered to the wind. In the old days it was easy to remember this because of the constant necessity of border defence. Nowadays, it is all too easily forgotten.

"New Atlantis, like many tribes, propagates itself largely through education. That is the raison d'être of this Academy. Here you develop your bodies through exercise and dance, and your minds by doing projects. And then you go to Miss Stricken's class. What is the point of Miss Stricken's class? Anyone? Please speak up. You can't get in trouble, no matter what you say."

Nell said, after some dithering, "I'm not sure that it has any point." Fiona just watched her saying it and smiled sadly.

Miss Matheson smiled. "You are not far off the mark. Miss Stricken's phase of the curriculum comes perilously close to being without any real substance. Why do we bother with it, then?"

"I can't imagine," Nell said.

"When I was a child, I took a karate class," Miss Matheson said, astonishingly. "Dropped out after a few weeks. Couldn't stand it. I thought that the sensei would teach me how to defend myself when I was out on my skateboard. But the first thing he did was have me sweep the floor. Then he told me that if I wanted to defend myself, I should buy a gun. I came back the next week and he had me sweep the floor again. All I ever did was sweep. Now, what was the point of that?"

"To teach you humility and self-discipline," Nell said. She had learned this from Dojo long ago.

"Precisely. Which are moral qualities. It is upon moral qualities that a society is ultimately founded. All the prosperity and technological sophistication in the world is of no use without that foundation—we learned this in the late twentieth century, when it became unfashionable to teach these things."

"But how can you say it's moral?" said Fiona. "Miss Stricken isn't moral. She's so cruel."

"Miss Stricken is not someone I would invite to dinner at my house. I would not hire her as a governess for my children. Her methods are not my methods. But people like her are indispensable.

"It is the hardest thing in the world to make educated Westerners pull together," Miss Matheson went on. "That is the job of people like Miss Stricken. We must forgive them their imperfections. She is like an avatar—do you children know about avatars? She is the physical embodiment of a principle. That principle is that outside the comfortable and well-defended borders of our phyle is a hard world that will come and hurt us if we are not careful. It is not an easy job to have. We must all feel sorry for Miss Stricken."

They brought sheaves of foxgloves, violet and magenta, back to the school and set them in vases in each classroom, leaving an especially large bouquet in Miss Stricken's office. Then they took tea with Miss Matheson, and then they each went home.

Nell could not bring herself to agree with what Miss Matheson had said; but she found that, after this conversation, everything became easy. She had the neo-Victorians all figured out now. The society had miraculously transmutated into an orderly system, like the simple computers they programmed in the school. Now that Nell knew all of the rules, she could make it do anything she wanted.

"Joy" returned to its former position as a minor annoyance on the fringes of a wonderful schoolday. Miss Stricken got her with the ruler from time to time, but not nearly so often, even when she was, in fact, scratching or slumping.

Fiona Hackworth had a harder time of it, and within a couple of months she was back on the Supplementary Curriculum list. A few months after that, she stopped coming to school entirely. It was announced that she and her mother had moved to Atlantis/Seattle, and her address was posted in the hall for those who wished to write her letters.

But Nell heard rumors about Fiona from the other girls, who had picked up snatches from their parents. After Fiona had been gone for a year or so, word got out that Fiona's mother had obtained a divorce—which, in their tribe, only happened in cases of adultery or abuse. Nell wrote Fiona a long letter saying she was terribly sorry if her father had been abusive, and offering her support in that case. A few days later she got back a curt note in which

Fiona defended her father from all charges. Nell wrote back a letter of apology but didn't hear from Fiona Hackworth again.

It was about two years later that the news feeds filled up with astonishing tales of the young heiress Elizabeth Finkle-McGraw, who had vanished from her family's estate outside of London and was rumored to have been sighted in London, Los Angeles, Hong Kong, Miami, and many other places, in the presence of people suspected of being high-ranking members of CryptNet.

Hackworth awakes from a dream; retreat from the world of the Drummers; chronological discrepancies.

Hackworth woke from a dream of unsustainable pleasure and realized it wasn't a dream; his penis was inside someone else, and he was steaming like a runaway locomotive toward ejaculation. He had no idea what was going on; but couldn't he be forgiven for doing the wrong thing? With a wiggle here and a thrust there, he finally nudged himself over the threshold, the smooth muscles of the tract in question executing their spinal algorithm.

Just a few deep breaths into the refractory period, and he had already disengaged, yelping a little from the electric spark of withdrawal, and levered himself up on one arm to see whom he'd just violated. The firelight was enough to tell him what he already knew: Whoever this woman was, it wasn't Gwen. Hackworth had violated the most important promise he'd ever made, and he didn't even know the other party.

But he knew it wasn't the first time. Far from it. He'd had sex with a lot of people in the past few years—he'd even been *buggered*.

There was, for example, the woman—
Never mind, there was the man who—
Strange to say, he could not think of any specific exam-

ples. But he knew he was guilty. It was precisely like waking up from a dream and having a clear train of thought in your mind, something you were working on just a few seconds ago, but being unable to remember it, consciousness peeled away from cognition. Like a three-year-old who has a talent for vanishing into crowds whenever you turn your back, Hackworth's memories had fled to the same place as words that are on the tip of your tongue, precedents for déjà vu, last night's dreams.

He knew he was in big trouble with Gwen, but that Fiona still loved him—Fiona, taller than Gwen now, so self-conscious about her still linear figure, still devoid of the second derivatives that add spice to life.

Taller than Gwen? How's that?

Better get out of this place before he had sex with someone else he didn't know.

He wasn't in the central chamber anymore, rather in one of the tunnel's aneurysms with some twenty other people, all just as naked as he was. He knew which tunnel led to the exit (why?) and began to crawl down it, rather stiffly as it seemed that he was stiff and laden with cricks and cramps. Must not have been very athletic sex—more in the Tantric mode.

Sometimes they had sex for days.

How did he know that?

The hallucinations were gone, which was fine with him. He crawled through the tunnels for a long time. If he tried to think about where he was going, he got lost and eventually circled back to where he started. Only when his mind began to wander did he make his way on some kind of autopilot to a long chamber filled with silvery light, sloping upward. This was beginning to look familiar, he had seen this when he was still a young man. He followed it upward until he reached the end, where something unusually stony was under his feet. A hatch opened above him, and several tons of cold seawater landed on his head.

He staggered up onto dry land and found himself in Stanley Park again, gray floor aft, green wall fore. The ferns rustled, and out stepped Kidnapper, who looked fuzzy and green. He also looked unusually dapper for a robotic horse, as Hackworth's bowler hat was perched on top of his head.

Hackworth reached up to feel himself and was as-

tounded to feel his face covered with hair. Several months'
growth of beard was there. But even stranger, his chest was
much hairier than it had been before. Some of the chest hair
was gray, the only gray hairs he had ever seen coming out of
his own follicles.

Kidnapper was fuzzy and green because moss had
been growing on him. The bowler looked terrible and had
moss on it too. Hackworth reached out instinctively and put
it on his head. His arm was thicker and hairier than it used
to be, a not altogether unpleasing change, and even the hat
felt a little tight.

*From the Primer, Princess Nell crosses the trail of
the enigmatic Mouse Army; a visit to an invalid.*

The clearing dimly visible through the trees ahead was a welcome sight, for the forests of King Coyote were surpassingly deep
and forever shrouded in cool mists. Fingers of sunlight had begun
to thrust between the clouds, and so Princess Nell decided to rest
in the open space and, with any luck, bask in the sunlight. But
when she reached the clearing, she found that it was not the
flower-strewn greensward she had expected; it was rather a swath
that had been carved through the forest by the passage of some
titanic force, which had flattened trees and churned up the soil as
it progressed. When Princess Nell had recovered from her astonishment and mastered her fear, she resolved to make use of the
tracking skills she had learned during her many adventures, so as
to learn something about the nature of this unknown creature.

As she soon discovered, the skills of an advanced tracker
were not necessary in this case. The merest glance at the trampled
soil revealed not (as she had anticipated) a few enormous footprints, but millions of tiny ones, superimposed upon one another
in such numbers that no scrap of ground was unmarked by the
impressions of tiny claws and footpads. A torrent of cats had
passed this way; even had Princess Nell not recognized the foot-

prints, the balls of loose hair and tiny scats, strewn everywhere, would have told the story.

Cats moving in a herd! It was most unfeline behavior. Nell followed their track for some time, hoping to divine the cause of this prodigy. After a few miles the road widened into an abandoned camp freckled with the remains of innumerable small campfires. Nell combed this area for more clues, not without success: she found many mouse droppings here, and mouse footprints around the fires. The pattern of footprints made it clear that the cats had been concentrated in a few small areas, while the mice had apparently had the run of the place.

The final piece of the puzzle was a tiny scrap of twisted rawhide that Nell found abandoned near one of the little campfires. Turning it around in her fingers, Nell realized that it was much like a horse's bridle—except sized to fit around the head of a cat.

She was standing on the trail of a vast army of mice, who rode on the backs of cats in the way that knights ride on horses.

She had heard tales of the Mouse Army in other parts of the Land Beyond and dismissed them as ancient superstitions.

But once, several years ago, in an inn high in the mountains, where Princess Nell had stayed for the night, she had been awakened early in the morning by the sound of a mouse rooting through her pack. . . .

Princess Nell uttered a light-making spell that Purple had taught her, kindling a ball of luminance that hung in the air in the center of the room. The words of the spell had been concealed in the howl of the mountain winds through the rickety structure of the old inn, and so the mouse was caught entirely by surprise, blinded by the sudden light. Nell was startled to see that the mouse was not gnawing its way into her supply of food, as any mouse should have done, but rather was going through some of her papers. And this was not the usual destructive search for nesting material—this mouse knew how to read and was looking for information.

Princess Nell trapped the mouse spy under her hands. "What are you looking for? Tell me, and I shall let you escape!" she said. Her adventures had taught her to be on the lookout for tricks of all kinds, and it was important that she learn who had dispatched this tiny, but effective, spy.

"I am but a harmless mouse!" the spy squealed. "I do not even desire your food—information only!"

"I will give you a big piece of cheese, all to yourself, if you give me some information," Princess Nell said. She caught the mouse's tail and lifted him up into the air so that they could talk face-to-face. Meanwhile, with her other hand, she loosened the drawstring of her bag and drew out a nice piece of blue-veined Stilton.

"We are seeking our lost Queen," the mouse said.

"I can assure you that none of my papers have any information about a missing mouse monarch," Princess Nell said.

"What is your name?" the mouse said.

"That is none of your business, spy!" Princess Nell said. "I will ask the questions."

"But it is very important that I know your name," the mouse said.

"Why? I am not a mouse. I have not seen any little mice with crowns on their heads."

The mouse spy said nothing. He was staring carefully at Princess Nell with his little beady eyes. "Did you, by any chance, come from an enchanted island?"

"You have been listening to too many fairy tales," Princess Nell said, barely concealing her astonishment. "You have been most uncooperative and so do not deserve any cheese—but I admire your pluck and so will give you some anyway. Enjoy yourself!" She set the mouse down on the floor and took out her knife to cut off a bit of the cheese; but by the time she was finished, the mouse had disappeared. She just caught sight of his pink tail disappearing under the door.

The next morning, she found him dead on the hallway floor. The innkeeper's cat had caught him. . . .

So the Mouse Army did exist! Princess Nell wondered whether they had ever located their lost Queen. She followed their trail for another day or two, as it went in approximately the right direction and was almost as convenient as a road. She passed through a few more campsites. At one of them, she even found a little gravesite, marked with a tiny headstone carved from a chip of soapstone.

The carvings on this tiny monument were much too small to see. But Princess Nell carried with her a magnifying glass that she had pilfered from the treasury of one of the Faery Kings, and so now she removed it from its padded box and its velvet bag and used it to examine the inscription.

At the top of the stone was a little bas-relief of a mouse knight, dressed in armor, with a sword in one hand, bowing before an empty throne. The inscription read,

> Here lies Clover, tail and all
> Her virtues far outweighed her flaws
> She from the saddle took a fall
> And perished 'neath her charger's paws.
> We know not if her final ride
> Hath led her into Heaven or Hell
> Wherever she doth now abide
> She's loyal yet to Princess Nell.

Princess Nell examined the remains of the fires, and the surfaces of the wood that the Mouse Army had cut, and the state of their droppings, and estimated that they had passed by here many weeks previously. One day she would rendezvous with them and find out why they had formed such an attachment to her; but for now, she had more pressing considerations.

She'd have to see about the Mouse Army later. Today was Saturday, and on Saturday morning she always went down to the Leased Territories to visit her brother. She opened up the wardrobe in the corner of her sleeping room and took out her traveling dress. Sensing her intentions, the chaperone flew out of its niche in the back and whined over to the door.

Even at her still-tender age, just a few years past the threshold of womanhood, Nell had already had cause to be grateful for the presence of the droning chaperone pod that followed her everywhere when she ventured from home alone. Maturity had given her any number of features that would draw the attention of the opposite sex, and of women so inclined. Commentators rarely failed to mention her eyes, which were said to have a vaguely exotic appearance. There was nothing particularly unusual about their shape or size, and their color—a tweedy blend of green and light brown flecked with gold—did not make them stand out in a predominantly Anglo-Saxon culture. But Nell's eyes had an appearance of feral alertness that seized the attention of anyone who met her. Neo-Victorian society produced many young women who, though highly educated and well-read, were still blank slates at Nell's age. But Nell's eyes told a different story. When she had been presented to society a few months ago, along with several other External Propagation girls at Miss Matheson's Academy, she had not been the prettiest girl at the dance, and certainly not the best dressed or most socially prominent. She had attracted a crowd of young men anyway. They did not do anything so obvious as mill around her; instead they tried to keep the distance between themselves and Nell below a certain maximum, so that wherever she went in the ballroom, the local density of young men in her area became unusually high.

In particular she had excited the interest of a boy who was the nephew of an Equity Lord in Atlantis/Toronto. He had written her several ardent letters. She had responded saying that she did not wish to continue the relationship, and he had, perhaps with the help of a hidden monitor, encountered her and her chaperone pod one morning as she had been riding to Miss Matheson's Academy. She had reminded him of the recent termination of their relationship by declining to recognize him, but he had persisted anyway, and by the time she had reached the gates of the Academy, the chaperone pod had gathered enough evidence to support a formal sexual harassment accusation should Nell have wished to bring one.

Of course she did not, because this would have created a cloud of opprobrium that would have blighted the young man's career. Instead, she excerpted one five-second piece of the cine record from the chaperone pod: the one in which, approached by the young man, Nell said, "I'm sorry, but I'm afraid you have me at a disadvantage," and the young man, failing to appreciate the ramifications, pressed on as if he had not heard. Nell placed this information into a smart visiting card and arranged to have it dropped by the young man's family home. A formal apology was not long in coming, and she did not hear again from the young man.

Now that she had been introduced to society, her preparations for a visit to the Leased Territories were just as elaborate as for any New Atlantis lady. Outside of New Atlantis, she and her chevaline were surrounded everywhere by a shell of hovering security pods serving as a first line of personal defense. A modern lady's chevaline was designed with a sort of Y-shaped body that made it unnecessary to ride sidesaddle, so Nell was able to wear a fairly normal-looking sort of dress: a bodice that took advantage of her fashionably narrow waist, so carefully honed on the Academy's exercise machines that it might have been turned on a lathe from walnut. Beyond that, her skirts, sleeves, collar, and hat saw to it that none of the young ruffians of the Leased Territories would have the opportunity to invade her body space with their eyes, and lest her distinctive face prove too much of a temptation, she wore a veil too.

The veil was a field of microscopic, umbrellalike aerostats programmed to fly in a sheet formation a few inches in front of Nell's face. The umbrellas were all pointed away from her. Normally they were furled, which made them nearly invisible; they looked like the merest shadow before her face, though viewed sideways they created a subtle wall of shimmer in the air. At a command from Nell they would open to some degree. When fully open, they nearly touched each other. The outside-facing surfaces were reflective, the inner ones matte black, so Nell could see out as if she were looking through a piece of smoked glass. But others saw only the shimmering veil. The umbrellas could be programmed to dangle in different ways—always maintaining the same collective shape, like a fencing mask, or rippling like a sheet of fine silk, depending on the current mode.

The veil offered Nell protection from unwanted scrutiny. Many New Atlantis career women also used the veil as a way of meeting the world on their own terms, ensuring that they were judged on their own merits and not on their appearance. It served a protective function as well, bouncing back the harmful rays of the sun and intercepting many deleterious nanosites that might otherwise slip unhindered into the nose and mouth.

The latter function was of particular concern to Constable Moore on this morning. "It's been nasty of late," he said. "The fighting has been very bad." Nell had already inferred this from certain peculiarities of the Constable's behavior: he had been staying up late at night recently, managing some complicated enterprise spread out across his mediatronic floor, and she suspected that it was something along the lines of a battle or even a war.

As she rode her chevaline across Dovetail, she came to a height-of-land that afforded a fine view across the Leased Territories, Pudong, and Shanghai on a clear day. But the humidity had congealed into drifts of clouds forming a seamless layer about a thousand feet below their level, so that this high territory at the top of New Chusan seemed to be an island, the only land in all the world except for the snowcapped cone of the Nippon Clave a few miles up the coast.

She departed through the main gate and rode down the hill. She kept approaching the cloud layer but never quite reached it; the lower she went, the softer the light became, and after a few minutes she could no longer see the rambling settlements of Dovetail when she turned around, nor the spires of St. Mark's and Source Victoria above it. After another few minutes' descent the fog became so thick that she could not see more than a few meters, and she smelled the elemental reek of the ocean. She passed the former site of the Sendero Clave. The Senderos had been bloodily uprooted when Protocol Enforcement figured out that they were working in concert with the New Taiping Rebels, a fanatical cult opposed to both the Fists and the Coastal Republic. This patch of real estate had since passed into the hands of the Dong, an ethnic minority tribe from southwestern China, driven out of their homeland by the civil war. They had torn down the high wall and thrown up one of their distinctive many-layered pagodas.

Other than that, the L.T. didn't look all that different. The operators of the big wall-size mediatrons that had so terrified Nell on her first night in the Leased Territories had turned the brightness all the way up, trying to compensate for the fog.

Down by the waterfront, not far from the Aerodrome, the compilers of New Chusan had, as a charitable gesture, made some space available to the Vatican. In the early years it had contained nothing more than a two-story mission for thetes who had followed their lifestyle to its logical conclusion and found themselves homeless, addicted, hounded by debtors, or on the run from the law or abusive members of their own families.

More recently those had become secondary functions, and the Vatican had programmed the building's foundation to extrude many more stories. The Vatican had a number of serious ethical concerns about nanotech but had eventually decided that it was okay as long as it didn't mess about with DNA or create direct interfaces with the human brain. Using nanotech to extrude buildings was fine, and that was fortunate, because Vatican/Shanghai needed to add a couple of floors to the Free Phthisis Sanatorium every year. Now it loomed high above any of the other waterfront buildings.

As with any other extruded building, the design was drab in the extreme, each floor exactly alike. The walls were of an unexceptional beige material that had been used to construct many of the buildings in the L.T., which was unfortunate, because it had an almost magnetic attraction for the cineritious corpses of airborne mites. Like all the other buildings so constituted, the Free Phthisis Sanatorium had, over the years, turned black, and not evenly but in vertical rain-streaks. It was a cliché to joke that the outside of the Sanatorium looked much like the inside of its tenants' lungs. The Fists of Righteous Harmony had, however, done their best to pretty it up by slapping red posters over it in the dead of night.

Harv was lying on the top of a three-layer bunkbed on the twentieth floor, sharing a small room and a supply of purified air with a dozen other chronic asthma sufferers. His face was goggled into a phantascope, and his lips were wrapped around a thick tube plugged into a nebulizer socket on the wall. Vaporized drugs, straight from the matter compiler, were flowing down that tube and into his lungs, working to keep his bronchi from spasming shut.

Nell stopped for a moment before breaking him out of his ractive. Some weeks he looked better than others; this week he did not look good. His body was bloated, his face round and heavy, his fingers swollen to puffy cylinders; they had been giving him heavy steroid treatments. But she would have known he'd had a bad week anyway, because usually Harv didn't go in for immersive ractives. He liked the kind you held in your lap on a sheet of smart paper. Nell tried to send Harv a letter every day, simply written in mediaglyphics, and for a while he had tried to respond in kind. Last year he had even given up on this, though she wrote him faithfully anyway.

"Nell!" he said when he had peeled the goggles away from his eyes. "Sorry, I was chasing some rich Vickys."

"You were?"

"Yeah. Or Burly Scudd was, I mean. In the ractive. See, Burly's bitch gets pregnant, and she's got to buy herself a Freedom Machine to get rid of it, so she gets a job as a maid-of-all-work for some snotty Vickys and rips off some of their nice old stuff, figuring that's a faster way to get the money. So the bitch is running away and they're chasing her on their chevs, and then Burly Scudd shows up in his big truck and turns the tables and starts chasing them. If you do it right, you can get the Vickys to fall into a big pit of manure! It's great! You should try it," Harv said, then, exhausted by this effort, grabbed his oxygen tube and pulled on it for a while.

"It sounds entertaining," Nell said.

Harv, temporarily gagged by the oxygen tube, watched her face carefully and was not convinced. "Sorry," he blurted between breaths, "forgot you don't care for my kind of ractive. Don't they have Burly Scudd in that Primer of yours?"

Nell made herself smile at the joke, which Harv had been making every week. She handed him the basket of cookies and fresh fruit that she had brought down from Dovetail and sat with him for an hour, talking about the things he enjoyed talking about, until she could see his attention wandering back toward the goggles. Then she said good-bye until next week and kissed him good-bye.

She turned her veil to its highest level of opacity and made her way toward the door. Harv impulsively grabbed his oxygen tube and sucked on it mightily a few times, then called her name just as she was about to leave.

"Yes?" she said, turning toward him.

"Nell, I want to tell you how fine you look," he said, "just like the finest Vicky lady in all of Atlantis. I can't believe you're my same Nell that I used to bring things to in the old flat—remember those days? I know that you and I have gone different ways, ever since that morning in Dovetail, and I know it's got a lot to do with that Primer. I just want to tell you, sister, that even though I say bad stuff about Vickys sometimes, I'm as proud of you as I could be, and I hope when you read that Primer—so full of stuff I could never understand or even read—you'll think back on your brother Harv, who saw it lying in the gutter years ago and took it into his mind to bring it to his kid sister. Will you remember that, Nell?" With that he plugged the oxygen tube back into his mouth, and his ribs began to heave.

"Of course I will, Harv," Nell said, her eyes filling with tears, and blundered her way back across the room until she could sweep Harv's bloated body up in her strong arms. The veil swirled like a sheet of water thrown into Harv's face, all the little umbrellas drawing themselves out of the way as she brought his face up to hers and planted a kiss on his cheek.

The veil congealed again as he sank back down onto the foam mattress—just like the mattresses he had taught her to get from the M.C., long ago—and she turned and ran out of the room sobbing.

Hackworth is brought up-to-date by the great Napier.

"Have you had the opportunity to speak with your family?" Colonel Napier said, speaking out of a mediatronic tabletop from his office in Atlantis/Shanghai. Hackworth was sitting in a pub in Atlantis/Vancouver.

Napier looked good now that he was deeper into middle age—somewhat more imposing. He'd been working on his bearing. Hackworth had been temporarily impressed when Napier's image had first materialized on the mediatron, then he remembered his own image in the mirror. Once he'd gotten himself cleaned up and trimmed his beard, which he'd decided to keep, he realized that he had a new bearing of his own. Even if he was desperately confused about how he got it.

"Thought I'd find out what the hell happened first. Besides—" He stopped talking for a while. He was having trouble getting his conversational rhythm back.

"Yes?" Napier said in a labored display of patience.

"I just spoke to Fiona this morning."

"After you left the tunnels?"

"No. Before. Before I—woke up, or whatever."

Napier was slightly taken aback and only popped his jaw muscles a couple of times, reached for his tea, looked irrelevantly out the window at whatever view he had out his office window in New Chusan. Hackworth, on the other side of the Pacific, contented himself with staring into the inky depths of a pint of stout.

A dream-image surfaced in Hackworth's mind, like a piece of debris rising to the surface after a shipwreck, inexorably muscling tons of green murk out of its path. He saw a glistening blue projectile shoot into the Doctor's beige-gloved hands, trailing a thick cord, watched it unfold, nay bloom into a baby.

"Why did I think of that?" he said.

Napier seemed puzzled by this remark. "Fiona and Gwendolyn are in Atlantis/Seattle now—half an hour from your present location by tube," he said.

"Of course! They live—we live—in Seattle now. I knew that." He was remembering Fiona hiking around in the caldera of some snow-covered volcano.

"If you are under the impression that you've been in contact with her recently—which is quite out of the question, I'm afraid—then it must have been mediated through the Primer. We were not able to break the encryption on the signals passing out of the Drummers' cave, but traffic analysis suggests that you've spent a lot of time racting in the last ten years."

"*Ten years!?*"

"Yes. But surely you must have suspected that, from evidence."

"It feels like ten years. I sense that ten years of things have happened to me. But the engineer hemisphere has a bit of trouble coming to grips."

"We are at a loss to understand why Dr. X would choose to have you serve out your sentence among the Drummers," Napier said. "It would seem to us that your engineer hemisphere, as you put it, is your most desirable feature as far as he is concerned—you know that the Celestials are still terribly short of engineers."

"I've been working on something," Hackworth said.

Images of a nanotechnological system, something admirably compact and elegant, were flashing over his mind's eye. It seemed to be very nice work, the kind of thing he could produce only when he was concentrating very hard for a long time. As, for example, a prisoner might do.

"What sort of thing exactly?" Napier asked, suddenly sounding rather tense.

"Can't get a grip on it," Hackworth finally said, shaking his head helplessly. The detailed images of atoms and bonds had been replaced, in his mind's eye, by a fat brown seed hanging in space, like something in a Magritte painting. A lush bifurcated curve on one end, like buttocks, converging to a nipplelike point on the other.

"What the hell happened?"

"Before you left Shanghai, Dr. X hooked you up to a matter compiler, no?"

"Yes."

"Did he tell you what he was putting into your system?"

"I guessed it was hæmocules of some description."

"We took blood samples before you left Shanghai."

"You did?"

"We have ways," Colonel Napier said. "We also did a full workup on one of your friends from the cave and found several million nanosites in her brain."

"Several million?"

"Very small ones," Napier said reassuringly. "They are introduced through the blood, of course—the hæmocules circulate through the bloodstream until they find themselves passing through capillaries in the brain, at which point they cut through the blood/brain barrier and fasten themselves to a nearby axon. They can monitor activity in the axon or trigger it. These 'sites all talk to each other with visible light."

"So when I was on my own, my 'sites just talked to themselves," Hackworth said, "but when I came into close proximity with other people who had these things in their brains—"

"It didn't matter which brain a 'site was in. They all talked to one another indiscriminately, forming a network. Get some Drummers together in a dark room, and they become a gestalt society."

"But the interface between these nanosites and the brain itself—"

"Yes, I admit that a few million of these things piggybacking on randomly chosen neurons is only a feeble interface to something as complicated as the human brain," Napier said. "We're not claiming that you shared one brain with these people."

"So what did I share with them exactly?" Hackworth said.

"Food. Air. Companionship. Body fluids. Perhaps emotions or general emotional states. Probably more."

"That's all I did for ten years?"

"You did a lot of things," Napier said, "but you did them in a sort of unconscious, dreamlike state. You were sleepwalking. When we figured that out—after doing the biopsy on your fellow-troglodyte—we realised that in some sense you were no longer acting of your own free will, and we engineered a hunter-killer that would seek out and destroy the nanosites in your brain. We introduced it, in a dormant mode, into this female Drummer's system, then reintroduced her to your colony. When you had sex with her —well, you can work out the rest for yourself."

"You have given me information, Colonel Napier, and I am grateful, but it has only made me more confused. What do you suppose the Celestial Kingdom wanted with me?"

"Did Dr. X ask anything of you?"

"To seek the Alchemist."

Colonel Napier looked startled. "He asked that of you ten years ago?"

"Yes. In as many words."

"That is very singular," Napier said, after a prolonged interlude of mustache-twiddling. "We have only been aware of this shadowy figure for some five years and know virtually nothing about him—other than that he is a wizardly artifex who is conspiring with Dr. X."

"Is there any other information—"

"Nothing that I can reveal," Napier said brusquely, perhaps having revealed too much already. "Do let us know if you find him, though. Er, Hackworth, there is no tactful way to broach this subject. Are you aware that your wife has divorced you?"

"Oh, yes," Hackworth said quietly. "I suppose I did know that." But he hadn't been conscious of it until now.

"She was remarkably understanding about your long absence," Napier said, "but at some point it became evident that, like all the Drummers, you had become sexually promiscuous in the extreme."

"How did she know?"

"We warned her."

"Pardon me?"

"I mentioned earlier that we found things in your blood. These hæmocules were designed specifically to be spread through exchange of bodily fluids."

"How do you know that?"

Napier seemed impatient for the first time. "For god's sake, man, we know what we are doing. These particles had two functions: spread through exchange of bodily fluids, and interact with each other. Once we saw that, we had no ethical choice but to inform your wife."

"Of course. That's only right. As a matter of fact, I thank you for it," Hackworth said. "And it's not hard to understand Gwen's feelings about sharing bodily fluids with thousands of Drummers."

"You shouldn't beat yourself up," Napier said. "We've sent explorers down there."

"Really?"

"Yes. The Drummers don't mind. The explorers relate that the Drummers behave much the way people do in dreams. 'Poorly defined ego boundaries' was the phrase, as I recall. In any event, your behaviour down there wasn't necessarily a moral transgression as such—your mind wasn't your own."

"You said that these particles interact with each other?"

"Each one is a container for some rod logic and some memory," Napier said. "When one particle encounters another either *in vivo* or *in vitro*, they dock and seem to exchange data for a few moments. Most of the time they disengage and drift apart. Sometimes they stay docked for a while, and computation takes place—we can tell because the rod logic throws off heat. Then they disconnect. Sometimes both particles go their separate ways, sometimes one of them goes dead. But one of them always keeps going."

The implications of that last sentence were not lost on Hackworth. "Do the Drummers only have sex with one another, or—"

"That was our first question too," Napier said. "The answer is no. They have a very good deal of sex with many, many other people. They actually run bordellos in Vancouver. They cater especially to the Aerodrome-and-tube-station crowd. A few years ago they came into conflict with the established bordellos because they were hardly charging any money at all for their services. They raised their prices just to be diplomatic. But they don't want the money—what on earth would they do with it?"

From the Primer, a visit to Castle Turing; a final chat with Miss Matheson; speculation as to Nell's destiny; farewell; conversation with a grizzled hoplite; Nell goes forth to seek her fortune.

The new territory into which Princess Nell had crossed was by far the largest and most complex of all the Faery Kingdoms in the Primer. Paging back to the first panoramic illustration, she counted seven major castles perched on the mountaintops, and she knew perfectly well that she would have to visit all of them, and do something difficult in each one, in order to retrieve the eleven keys that had been stolen from her and the one key that remained.

She made herself some tea and sandwiches and carried them in a basket to a meadow, where she liked to sit among the wildflowers and read. Constable Moore's house was a melancholy place without the Constable in it, and it had been several weeks since she had seen him. During the last two years he had been called away on business with increasing frequency, vanishing (as she supposed) into the interior of China for days, then weeks at a time, coming back depressed and exhausted to find solace in whiskey, which he consumed in surprisingly moderate quantities but with fierce concentration, and in midnight bagpipe recitals that woke up everyone in Dovetail and a few sensitive sleepers in the New Atlantis Clave.

During her trip from the campsite of the Mouse Army to the first of the castles, Nell had to use all the wilderness skills she had learned in years of traveling around the Land Beyond: She fought with a mountain lion, avoided a bear, forded streams, lit fires, built shelters. By the time Nell had maneuvered Princess Nell to the ancient moss-covered gates of the first castle, the sun was shining horizontally across the meadow and the air was becoming a bit chilly. Nell wrapped herself up in a thermogenic shawl and set the thermostat for something a little on the cool side of comfortable; she had found that her wits became dull if she got too cozy. The basket had a thermos of hot tea with milk, and the sandwiches would hold out for a while.

The highest of the castle's many towers was surmounted by a great four-sailed windmill that turned steadily, even though only a mild breeze could be noticed at Princess Nell's altitude, hundreds of feet below.

Set into the main gate was a judas gate, and set into the judas was a small hatch. Below the hatch was a great bronze knocker made in the shape of a letter T, though its shape had become indistinct from an encrustation of moss and lichens. Princess Nell operated the knocker only with some effort and, given its decrepit state, did not expect a response; but hardly had the first knock sounded than the hatch opened up, and she was confronted by a helmet: For the gatekeeper on the other side was dressed from head to toe in a rusty and moss-covered suit of battle armor. But the gatekeeper said nothing, simply stared at Princess Nell; or so she assumed, as she could not see his face through the helmet's narrow vision-slits.

"Good afternoon," said Princess Nell. "I beg your pardon, but I am a traveler in these parts, and I wonder if you would be so good as to give me a place to stay for the night."

Without a word, the gatekeeper slammed the hatch closed. Nell could hear the creaking and clanking of his armor as he slowly marched away.

Some minutes later, she heard him coming toward her again, though this time the noise was redoubled. The rusty locks on the judas gate grumbled and shrieked. The gate door swung open, and Princess Nell stepped back from it as rust flakes, fragments of lichens, and divots of moss showered down around her. Two men in armor now stood there, beckoning her forward.

Nell stepped through the gate and into the dark streets of the castle. The gate slammed behind her. An iron vise clamped around each of Princess Nell's upper arms; the men had seized her with their gauntlets. They lifted her into the air and carried her for some minutes through the streets, stairs, and corridors of the castle. These were completely deserted. She did not see so much as a mouse or a rat. No smoke rose from the chimneys, no light came from any window, and in the long hallway leading to the throne room, the torches hung cold and blackened in their sconces. From place to place Princess Nell saw another armored soldier standing at attention, but, as none of them moved, she did not know whether these were empty suits of armor or real men.

Nowhere did she see the usual signs of commerce and human activity: horse manure, orange peels, barking dogs, running sewers. Somewhat to her alarm, she did see an inordinate number of chains. The chains were all of the same, somewhat peculiar design, and she saw them everywhere: piled up in heaps on streetcorners, overflowing from metal baskets, dangling from rooftops, strung between towers.

The clanking and squeaking of the men who bore her along made it difficult for her to hear anything else; but as they proceeded higher and deeper into the castle, she slowly became conscious of a deep grinding, growling noise that pervaded the very ashlars. This noise crescendoed as they hustled down the long final hallway, and became nearly earth-shaking as they finally entered the vaulted throne room at the very heart of the castle.

The room was dark and cold, though some light was admitted by clerestory windows high up in the vaults. The walls were lined with men in armor, standing stock-still. Sitting in the middle of the room, on a throne twice as high as a man, was a giant, dressed in a suit of armor that gleamed like a looking-glass. Standing below him was a man in armor holding a rag and a wire brush, vigorously buffing one of the lord's greaves.

"Welcome to Castle Turing," said the lord in a metallic voice.

By this time, Princess Nell's eyes had adjusted to the dimness, and she could see something else behind the throne: a tremendous Shaft, as thick as the mainmast of a dromond, made of the trunk of a great tree bound and reinforced with brass plates and bands. The Shaft turned steadily, and Princess Nell realized that it must be transmitting the power of the giant windmill far above them. Enormous gears, black and sticky with grease, were attached to the Shaft and transferred its power to other, smaller shafts that ran off horizontally in every direction and disappeared through holes in the walls. The turning and grinding of all these shafts and gears made the omnipresent noise she had noted earlier.

One horizontal shaft ran along each wall of the throne room at about the height of a man's chest. This shaft passed through a gearbox at short, regular intervals. A stubby, square shaft projected from each gearbox at a right angle, sticking straight out of the wall. These gearboxes tended to coincide with the locations of the soldiers.

The soldier who was polishing the lord's armor worked his way around to one of the lord's spiked knee protectors and, in so doing, turned his back on Princess Nell. She was startled to see a large square hole in the middle of his back.

Nell knew, vaguely, that the name Castle Turing was a hint; she'd learned a bit about Turing at Miss Matheson's Academy. He had something to do with computers. She could have turned to the Encyclopædia pages and looked it right up, but she had learned to let the Primer tell the story its own way. Clearly the soldiers were not men in armor, but simply wind-up men, and the same was probably true of the Duke of Turing himself.

After a short and not very interesting conversation, during which Princess Nell tried unsuccessfully to establish whether the Duke was or was not human, he announced, unemotionally, that he was throwing her into the dungeon forever.

This sort of thing no longer surprised or upset Nell because it had happened hundreds of times during her relationship with the Primer. Besides, she had known, from the very first day Harv had given her the book, how the story would come out in the end. It was just that the story was anfractuous; it developed more ramifications the more closely she read it.

One of the soldiers detached himself from his gearbox on the wall, stomped into the corner, and picked up a metal basket filled with one of those peculiar chains Princess Nell had seen everywhere. He carried it to the throne, fished through it until he found the end, and fed the end into a hole on the side of the throne. In the meantime, a second soldier had also detached himself from the wall and taken up a position on the opposite side of the throne. This soldier flipped his visor open to expose some sort of mechanical device in the space where his head ought to have been.

A tremendous chattering noise arose from inside the throne. The second soldier caught the end of the chain as it was emerging from his side and fed it into the opening in his visor. A moment later it popped out of a hatch on his chest. In this fashion, the entire length of the chain, some twenty or thirty feet in all, was slowly and noisily drawn out of the basket, into the noisy mechanism hidden beneath the throne, down the second soldier's throat, out the hatch in his chest, and down to the floor, where it gradually accumulated into a greasy heap. The process went on for much longer than Princess Nell first anticipated, because the chain frequently changed direction; more than once, when the basket was nearly empty, the chain began to spew back into it until it was nearly full again. But on the whole it was more apt to go forward than backward, and eventually the last link lifted free from the basket and disappeared into the throne. A few seconds later, the din from the throne stopped; now Nell could only hear a somewhat lesser chattering from the second soldier. Finally that stopped as well, and the chain fell from his chest. The soldier scooped it up in his arms and deposited it in an empty basket that was sitting handily nearby. Then he strode toward Nell, bent forward at the waist, put his hard cold shoulder rather uncomfortably into the pit of her stomach, and picked her up off the floor like a sack of corn. He carried her for some minutes through the castle, most of that time spent descending endless stone staircases, and finally brought her to a very deep, dark, and cold dungeon, where he deposited her in a small and perfectly dark cell.

Nell said, "Princess Nell used one of the magic spells Purple had taught her to make light."

Princess Nell could see that the room was about two by three paces, with a stone bench on one wall to serve as a bed, and a hole in the floor for a toilet. A tiny barred window in the back wall led to an air shaft. Evidently this was quite deep and narrow, and Nell was close to the very bottom, because no light came through it. The soldier walked out of the cell and pulled the door shut behind him; as he did, she saw that the lock was extraordinarily large, about the size of an iron breadbox mounted to the door, full of clockwork and with a large crank dangling from its center.

The door was equipped with a small peephole. Peering out through it, Nell could see that the soldier did not have a key as such. Instead, he took a short length of chain, about as long as his arm, from a peg near the door and fed it into the giant lock. Then he began to turn the crank. The clockwork clicked, the chain clanked, and eventually the bolt shot out and engaged the jamb, locking Princess Nell into the dungeon. Immediately the chain crashed out of the lock and landed on the floor. The soldier picked it up and hung it back on the wall. Then he clanked away and did not come back until several hours later, when he brought her some bread and water, shoving it through a little hatch in the middle of the door, just above the mechanical lock.

It did not take Princess Nell long to explore the limited confines of her cell. In one corner, buried under dust and debris, she found something hard and cold and pulled it out for a better look: It was a fragment of chain, quite rusty, but clearly recognizable as the same sort of chain that she saw all over Castle Turing.

The chain was flat. Each link had a toggle: a movable bit of metal in the center, capable of rotating about and snapping into place in either of two positions, either parallel or perpendicular to the chain.

During her first night in the cell, Nell discovered two other things. First, the latch on the little door through which her food was delivered was partly accessible from her side, and with a little effort she was able to jam it so that it no longer locked properly. After that, she was able to stick her head out of the hatch and examine her surroundings, including the mechanical lock. Or she could reach out with one arm and feel the lock, spin the crank, and so on.

The second discovery came in the middle of the night, when she was awakened by a metallic clanking sound coming through the tiny window on the air shaft. Reaching out with one hand, she felt the end of a chain dangling there. She pulled on it, and after initial resistance, it came freely. In short order she was able to pull many yards of chain into her cell and pile it up on the floor.

Nell had a pretty good idea what to do with the chain. Starting with the end, she examined the toggles and began to mark their positions down (the Primer always gave her scratch pages when she needed them). She made a horizontal mark for toggles parallel to the chain and a vertical mark for those that were perpendicular, and came up with this:
|||||||||-|||||-||||||||||||-|||||||||||-|||||||||||||||--|||||||||||--|-|||||||||||||
---||||-|||||||||||||||||-||||||||||-|||||-----||||||||||||||||-
||||||||||||||||||||-||||||||||||||||-|||||||||-|||||||||||||-|||||||-

If she counted the vertical marks and replaced them with numbers, this amounted to
8-5-12-12-15- -9- -1-13- - -4-21-11-5- - - - -20-21-18-9-14-7-

and if the numbers stood for letters of the alphabet, horizontal marks divided the letters, and double horizontals were spaces, this was
HELLO I AM- - -DUKE- - - - -TURING

Perhaps the multiple horizontals were codes for commonly used words:
- - -   *the*
- - - -   (not used; possibly *a/an?*)
- - - - -   *of*

If that was right, then the message was HELLO I AM THE DUKE OF TURING, which was interesting, since the giant fellow in the armor had previously identified himself as such, and she deemed it unlikely that he would be sending her a message by this route. This must have come from someone else calling himself the Duke of Turing—perhaps a real, living human being.

A few years ago Nell could have relied on it. But in recent years the Primer had become much subtler than it used to be, full of hidden traps, and she could no longer make comfortable and easy assumptions. It was just as likely that this chain had descended straight from the throne room itself, and that the mechanical Duke was, for some unfathomable reason, trying to dupe her. So while she was happy to respond to this message in kind, she intended to take a guarded approach until she had established whether the sender was human or mechanical.

The next part of the message was GIVE---CHAIN
----TUG------ANSWER. Assuming that four horizontal
marks stood for *a/an* and six stood for *to*, this was GIVE THE
CHAIN A TUG TO ANSWER.

Nell began to flip the toggles on the chain, erasing the
message from this personage calling himself the Duke and
replacing it with I AM PRINCESS NELL WHY DID YOU
IMPRISON ME. Then she gave the chain a tug, and after a
moment it began to withdraw from her cell. A few minutes
later, back came the message:

WELCOME PRINCESS NELL LET US DEVISE A
MORE EFFICIENT MEANS OF COMMUNICATION

followed by instructions on how to use a more compact system of toggles to represent numbers, and how to
convert the numbers into letters and punctuation marks.
Once this was settled, the Duke said

I AM THE REAL DUKE. I CREATED THESE MA-
CHINES, AND THEY IMPRISONED ME IN A HIGH
TOWER FAR ABOVE YOU. THE MACHINE CALLING
HIMSELF THE DUKE IS MERELY THE LARGEST AND
MOST SOPHISTICATED OF MY CREATIONS.

Nell responded, THIS CHAIN WEIGHS HUNDREDS
OF POUNDS. YOU MUST BE STRONG FOR A HUMAN.

The Duke responded YOU ARE A SHARP ONE PRIN-
CESS NELL! THE FULL WEIGHT OF THE CHAIN IS AC-
TUALLY SEVERAL THOUSAND POUNDS, AND I
MANAGE IT BY MEANS OF A WINCH LOCATED IN MY
ROOM AND DERIVING ITS MOTIVE POWER FROM THE
CENTRAL SHAFT.

Night had long since fallen on the meadow. Nell
closed the Primer, packed up her basket, and returned
home.

She stayed up late into the night with the Primer, just
as she had when she was a small child, and as a result was
late for church the next morning. They said a special prayer
for Miss Matheson, who was at home and said to be feeling
poorly. Nell called on her for a few minutes after the service,
then went straight back home and dove into the Primer
again.

She was attacking two problems at once. First, she
needed to figure out how the lock on the door worked. Second, she needed to find out whether the person sending her

the message was human or mechanical. If she could be confident that he was a human, she could ask him for assistance in opening the lock, but until she had settled this issue, she had to keep her activities a secret.

The lock only had a few parts that she could observe: the crank, the bolt, and a pair of brass drums set into the top with digits from 0 to 9 engraved in them, so that by spinning different ways, they could display all the integers from 00 to 99. These drums were in almost constant motion whenever the crank was turning.

Nell had managed to detach several yards of chain from the one that she was using to converse with the Duke, and so she was able to feed different messages into the lock and see what result they had.

The number on the top changed with every link that went into the machine, and it seemed to determine, in a limited way, what the machine would do next; for example, she had learned that the number happened to be 09, and if the next link in the chain was in the vertical position (which the Duke referred to as a one), the drums would spin around and change the number to 23. But if the next link was, instead, a zero (as the Duke referred to links with horizontal toggles), the number drums would change to 03. But that wasn't all: In this case, the machine would, for some reason, reverse the direction in which the chain was moving through the machine, and also flick the toggle from zero to one. That is, the machine could write on the chain as well as read from it.

From idle chitchat with the Duke she learned that the numbers on the drums were referred to as states. At first she did not know which states led to other states, and so she wandered aimlessly from one state to the next, recording the connections on scratch paper. This soon grew to a table listing some thirty-two different states and how the lock would respond to a one or a zero when it was in each of those states. It took a while for Nell to fill out all the blank spaces in the table, because some of the states were hard to get to—they could be reached only by getting the machine to write a certain series of ones and zeros on the chain.

She would have gone crazy with ones and zeros were it not for the frequent interruptions from the Duke, who evidently had nothing better to do than to send her messages. These two parallel courses of inquiry occupied all of Nell's free time for a couple of weeks, and she made slow but steady progress.

"You must learn how to operate the lock on your door," the Duke said. "This will enable you to effect an escape and to come and rescue me. I will instruct you."

All he wanted to talk about was technology, which wouldn't help Nell in figuring out whether he was a human or a machine. "Why don't you pick your own lock," she responded, "and come and rescue me? I am just a poor helpless young thing all alone in the world, and so scared and lonely, and you seem so brave and heroic; your story really is quite romantic, and I cannot wait to see how it all comes out now that our fates have become intertwined."

"The machines placed a special lock on my door, not a Turing machine," responded the Duke.

"Describe yourself," Nell wrote.

"Nothing special, I'm afraid," wrote the Duke. "How about yourself?"

"Slightly taller than average, flashing green eyes, raven hair falling in luxuriant waves to my waist unless I pin it up to emphasize my high cheekbones and full lips. Narrow waist, pert breasts, long legs, alabaster skin that flushes vividly when I am passionate about something, which is frequently."

"Your description is reminiscent of my late wife, God rest her soul."

"Tell me about your wife."

"The subject fills me with such unutterable sadness that I cannot bear to write about it. Now, let's buckle down to work on the Turing machine."

Since the prurient approach had dead-ended, Nell tried a different tack: playing stupid. Sooner or later, the Duke would become a little testy. But he was always terribly patient with her, even after the twentieth repetition of "Could you explain it again with different words? I still don't get it." Of course, for all she knew, he was upstairs punching the walls until his knuckles were bloody and simply pretending to be patient with her. A man who'd been locked up in a tower for years would learn to be extremely patient.

She tried sending him poetry. He sent back glowing

reviews but declined to send her any of his own, saying it wasn't good enough to be committed to metal.

On her twentieth day in the dungeon, Princess Nell finally got the lock open. Rather than making an immediate escape, she locked herself back in and sat down to ponder her next move.

If the Duke was human, she should notify him so that they could plan their escape. If he was a machine, doing so would lead to disaster. She had to figure out the Duke's identity before she made another move.

She sent him another poem.

> For the Greek's love she gave away her heart
> Her father, crown and homeland.
> They stopped to rest on Naxos
> She woke up alone upon the strand
> The sails of her lover's ship descending
> Round the slow curve of the earth. Ariadne
> Fell into a swoon on the churned sand
> And dreamed of home. Minos did not forgive her
> And holding diamonds in the pouches of his eyes
> Had her flung into the Labyrinth.
> She was alone this time. Through a wilderness
> Of blackness wandered Ariadne many days
> Until she tripped on the memory.
> It was still wound all through the place.
> She spun it round her fingers
> Lifted it from the floor
> Knotted it into lace
> Erased it.
> The lace made a gift for him who had imprisoned her.
> Blind with tears, he read it with his fingers
> And opened his arms.

The answer came back much too quickly, and it was the same answer as always: "I do so envy your skill with words. Now, if you do not object, let us turn our attention to the inner workings of the Turing machine."

She had made it as obvious as she dared, and the Duke still hadn't gotten the message. He must be a machine.

Why the deception?

Clearly, the mechanical Duke desired for her to learn

about the Turing machines. That is, if a machine could ever be said to desire something.

There must be something wrong with the Duke's programming. He knew there was something wrong with it, and he needed a human to fix it.

Once Nell had figured these things out, the rest of the Castle Turing story resolved itself quickly and neatly. She slipped out of her cell and stealthily explored the castle. The soldiers rarely noticed her, and when they did, they could not improvise; they had to go back to the Duke to be reprogrammed. Eventually, Princess Nell found her way into a room beneath the windmill that contained a sort of clutch mechanism. By disengaging the clutch, she was able to stop the Shaft. Within a few hours, the springs inside the soldiers' back had all run down, and they had all stopped in their tracks. The whole castle was frozen, as if she had cast an enchantment over it.

Now roaming freely, she opened up the Duke's throne and found a Turing machine beneath it. On either side of the machine was a narrow hole descending straight through the floor and into the earth for as far as her torch light could illuminate it. The chain containing the Duke's program dangled on either side into these holes. Nell tried throwing stones into the holes and never heard them hit bottom; the chain must be unfathomably long.

High up in one of the castle's towers, Princess Nell found a skeleton in a chair, slumped over a table piled high with books. Mice, bugs, and birds had nibbled away all of the flesh, but traces of gray hair and whiskers were still scattered around the table, and around the cervical vertebrae was a golden chain bearing a seal with the T insignia.

She spent some time going through the Duke's books. Most of them were notebooks where he would sketch the inventions he hadn't had time to build yet. He had plans for whole armies of Turing machines made to run in parallel, and for chains with links that could be set in more than two positions, and for machines that would read and write two-dimensional sheets of chain mail instead of one-dimensional chains, and for a three-dimensional Turing grid a mile on a side, through which a mobile Turing machine would climb about, computing as it went.

No matter how complicated his designs became, the

Duke always found a way to simulate their behavior by putting a sufficiently long chain into one of the traditional Turing machines. That is to say that while the parallel and multidimensional machines worked more quickly than the original model, they didn't really do anything different.

One afternoon, Nell was sitting in her favorite meadow, reading about these things in the Primer, when a riderless chevaline emerged from the woods and galloped directly toward her. This was not highly unusual, in and of itself; chevalines were smart enough to be sent out in search of specific persons. People rarely sent them in search of Nell, though.

The chevaline galloped at her full-tilt until it was just a few feet away, and then planted its hooves and stopped instantly—a trick it could easily do when it wasn't carrying a human. It was carrying a note written in Miss Stricken's hand: "Nell, please come immediately. Miss Matheson has requested your presence, and time is short."

Nell didn't hesitate. She gathered her things, stuffed them into the mount's small luggage compartment, and climbed on. "Go!" she said. Then, getting herself well situated and clenching the hand-grips, she added, "Unlimited speed." Within moments the chevaline was threading gaps between trees at something close to a cheetah's sprint velocity, clawing its way up the hill toward the dog pod grid.

From the way the tubes ran, Nell guessed that Miss Matheson was plugged into the Feed in two or three different ways, though everything had been discreetly hidden under many afghans, piled up on top of her body like the airy layers of a French pastry. Only her face and hands were visible, and looking at them Nell remembered for the first time since their introduction just how old Miss Matheson was. The force of her personality had blinded Nell and all the girls to the blunt evidence of her true age.

"Please let us be, Miss Stricken," Miss Matheson said, and Miss Stricken backed out warily, strewing reluctant and reproving glances along her trail.

Nell sat on the edge of the bed and carefully lifted one of Miss Matheson's hands from the coverlet, as if it were the desiccated leaf of some rare tree. "Nell," Miss Matheson said, "do not waste my few remaining moments with pleasantries."

"Oh, Miss Matheson—" Nell began, but the old lady's eyes widened and she gave Nell a certain look, practiced through many decades in the classroom, that still had not lost its power to silence.

"I have requested that you come here because you are my favorite student. No! Do not say a word," Miss Matheson admonished her, as Nell leaned her face closer, eyes filling with tears. "Teachers are not supposed to have favorites, but I am approaching that time when I must confess all my sins, so there it is.

"I know that you have a secret, Nell, though I cannot imagine what it is, and I know that your secret has made you different from any other girl I have ever taught. I wonder what you suppose you will do with your life when you leave this Academy, as you must soon, and go out into the world?"

"Take the Oath, of course, as soon as I reach the age of eligibility. And I suppose that I should like to study the art of programming, and how ractives are made. Someday, of course, after I have become one of Her Majesty's subjects, I should like to find a nice husband and perhaps raise children—"

"Oh, stop it," Miss Matheson said. "You are a young woman—of course you think about whether you shall have children—every young woman does. I haven't much time left, Nell, and we must dispense with what makes you like all the other girls and concentrate on what makes you different."

At this point, the old lady gripped Nell's hand with surprising force and raised her head just a bit off the pillow. The tremendous wrinkles and furrows on her brow deepened, and her hooded eyes took on an intense burning appearance. "Your destiny is marked in some way, Nell. I have known it since the day Lord Finkle-McGraw came to me and asked me to admit you—a ragged little thete girl—into my Academy.

"You can try to act the same—we have tried to make you the same—you can pretend it in the future if you insist, and you can even take the Oath—but it's all a lie. You are different."

These words struck Nell like a sudden cold wind of pure mountain air and stripped away the soporific cloud of sentimentality. Now she stood exposed and utterly vulnerable. But not unpleasantly so.

"Are you suggesting that I leave the bosom of the adopted tribe that has nurtured me?"

"I am suggesting that you are one of those rare people who transcends tribes, and you certainly don't need a bosom anymore," Miss Matheson said. "You will find, in time, that this tribe is as good as any other—better than most, really." Miss Matheson exhaled deeply and seemed to dissolve into her blankets. "Now, I haven't long. So give us a kiss, and then be on your way, girl."

Nell leaned forward and pressed her lips against Miss Matheson's cheek, which looked leathery but was surprisingly soft. Then, unwilling to leave so abruptly, she turned her head and rested it on Miss Matheson's chest for a few moments. Miss Matheson stroked feebly at her hair and tut-tutted.

"Farewell, Miss Matheson," Nell said. "I will never forget you."

"Nor I you," Miss Matheson whispered, "though admittedly that is not saying much."

A very large chevaline stood stolidly in front of Constable Moore's house, somewhere between a Percheron and a small elephant in size and bulk. It was the dirtiest object Nell had ever seen in her life—its encrustations alone must have weighed hundreds of pounds and were redolent with the scent of night soil and stagnant water. A fragment of a mulberry branch, still bearing leaves and even a couple of actual berries, had gotten wedged into a flexing joint between two adjoining armor plates, and long ropes of milfoil trailed from its ankles.

The Constable was sitting in the middle of his bamboo grove, enveloped in a suit of hoplite armor, similarly filthy and scarred, that was twice as big as he was, and that made his bare head look absurdly small. He had ripped the helmet off and dropped it into his fish pond, where it floated around like the eviscerated hull of a scuttled dreadnought. He looked very gaunt and was staring vacantly, without blinking, at some kudzu that was slowly but inexorably conquering the wisteria. As soon as Nell saw the look on his face, she made him some tea and brought it to him. The

Constable reached for the tiny alabaster teacup with armored hands that could have crumbled stones like loaves of stale bread. The thick barrels of the guns built into the arms of his suit were scorched on the inside. He plucked the cup from Nell's hands with the precision of a surgical robot, but did not lift it to his lips, perhaps afraid that he might, in his exhaustion, get the distance a bit wrong and inadvertently crush the porcelain into his jaw, or even decapitate himself. Merely holding the cup, watching the steam rise from its surface, seemed to calm him. His nostrils dilated once, then again. "Darjeeling," he said. "Well chosen. Always thought of India as a more civilised place than China. Have to throw out all of the oolong now, all the keemun, the lung jang, the lapsang souchong. Time to switch over to Ceylon, pekoe, assam." He chuckled.

White trails of dried salt ran back from the corners of the Constable's eyes and disappeared into his hairline. He had been riding fast with his helmet off. Nell wished that she had been able to see the Constable thundering across China on his war chevaline.

"I've retired for the last time," he explained. He nodded in the direction of China. "Been doing a bit of consulting work for a gentleman there. Complicated fellow. Dead now. Had many facets, but now he'll go down in history as just another damn Chinese warlord who didn't make the grade. It is remarkable, love," he said, looking at Nell for the first time, "how much money you can make shovelling back the tide. In the end you need to get out while the getting is good. Not very honourable, I suppose, but then, there is no honour among consultants."

Nell did not imagine that Constable Moore wanted to get into a detailed discussion of recent events, so she changed the subject. "I think I have finally worked out what you were trying to tell me, years ago, about being intelligent," she said.

The Constable brightened all at once. "Pleased to hear it."

"The Vickys have an elaborate code of morals and conduct. It grew out of the moral squalor of an earlier generation, just as the original Victorians were preceded by the Georgians and the Regency. The old guard believe in that code because they came to it the hard way. They raise their children to believe in that code—but their children believe it for entirely different reasons."

"They believe it," the Constable said, "because they have been indoctrinated to believe it."

"Yes. Some of them never challenge it—they grow up to be small-minded people, who can tell you what they believe but not why they believe it. Others become disillusioned by the hypocrisy of the society and rebel—as did Elizabeth Finkle-McGraw."

"Which path do you intend to take, Nell?" said the Constable, sounding very interested. "Conformity or rebellion?"

"Neither one. Both ways are simple-minded—they are only for people who cannot cope with contradiction and ambiguity."

"Ah! Excellent!" the Constable exclaimed. As punctuation, he slapped the ground with his free hand, sending up a shower of sparks and transmitting a powerful shock through the ground to Nell's feet.

"I suspect that Lord Finkle-McGraw, being an intelligent man, sees through all of the hypocrisy in his society, but upholds its principles anyway, because that is what is best in the long run. And I suspect that he has been worrying about how best to inculcate this stance in young people who cannot understand, as he does, its historical antecedents—which might explain why he has taken an interest in me. The Primer may have been Finkle-McGraw's idea to begin with—a first attempt to go about this systematically."

"The Duke plays his cards close," Constable Moore said, "and so I cannot say whether your suppositions are correct. But I will admit it hangs together nicely."

"Thank you."

"What do you intend to do with yourself, now that you have pieced all of this together? A few more years' education and polishing will place you in a position to take the Oath."

"I am, of course, aware that I have favorable prospects in the Atlantan phyle," Nell said, "but I do not think that it would be fitting for me to take the straight and narrow path. I am going to China now to seek my fortune."

"Well," Constable Moore said, "look out for the Fists."

His gaze wandered over his battered and filthy armor and came to rest on the floating helmet. "They are coming now."

The best explorers, like Burton, made every effort to blend in. In this spirit, Nell stopped at a public M.C., doffed her long dress, and compiled a new set of clothes—a navy blue skin-tight coverall emblazoned with SHIT HAPPENS in pulsating orange letters. She swapped her old clothes for a pair of powered skates on the waterfront, and then headed straight for the Causeway. It rose gently into the air for a few miles, and then the Pudong Economic Zone came into view at her feet, and Shanghai beyond that, and she suddenly began to pick up speed and had to cut the skates' power assist. She'd passed over the watershed now. Nell was alone in China.

The Hackworths have a family reunion; Hackworth strikes out on his quest; an unexpected companion.

Atlantis/Seattle was designed small and to the point; the narrow, convoluted straits of Puget Sound, already so full of natural islands, did not leave much room for artificial ones. So they had made it rather long and slender, parallel to the currents and the shipping lanes, and been rather stingy when it came to the parks, meadows, heaths, gentleman farms, and country estates. Much of the Seattle area was still sufficiently rich, civilized, and polite that New Atlantans did not object to living there, and little Victorian mini-claves were scattered about the place, particularly east of the lake, around the misty forest domains of the software khans. Gwen and Fiona had taken a townhouse in one of these areas.

These tiny bits of New Atlantis stood out from the surrounding forest in the same way that a vicar in morning coat and wing collar would have in the cave of the Drummers. The prevailing architecture here, among those who had not adopted neo-Victorian precepts, was distinctly sub-

terranean; as if these people were somehow ashamed of
their own humanity and could not bear to fell even a handful of the immense Douglas firs that marched monotonously
up the tumbling slopes toward the frozen, sodden ridge of
the Cascades. Even when it was half buried, a house wasn't
even a proper house; it was an association of modules, scattered about here and there and connected by breezeways or
tunnels. Stuck together properly and built on a rise, these
modules might have added up to a house of substance, even
grandeur; but to Hackworth, riding through the territory on
his way to visit his family, it was all depressing and confusing. Ten years among the Drummers had not affected his
neo-Victorian aesthetics. He could not tell where one house
left off and the next one began, the houses were all intertan-
gled with one another like neurons in the brain.

His mind's eye again seemed to seize control of his
visual cortex; he could not see the firs anymore, just axons
and dendrites hanging in black three-dimensional space,
packets of rod logic maneuvering among them like space
probes, meeting and copulating among the nerve fibers.

It was a bit too aggressive to be a reverie and too
abstract to be a hallucination. It didn't really clear away until
a gust of cold mist hit him in his face, he opened his eyes,
and realized that Kidnapper had stopped after emerging
from the trees at the crest of a mossy ridgeline. Below him
was a rocky bowl with a few cobblestone streets sketched
out in a grid, a green park lined with red geraniums, a
church with a white steeple, whitewashed four-story Georgian buildings surrounded by black wrought-iron fences.
The security grid was tenuous and feeble; the software
khans were at least as good at that kind of thing as Her
Majesty's specialists, and so a New Atlantis clave in this area
could rely on the neighbors to shoulder much of that burden.

Kidnapper picked its way carefully down the steep
declivity as Hackworth looked out over the tiny clave, mus-
ing at how familiar it seemed. Since leaving the Drummers,
he hadn't gone more than ten minutes without being seized
by a feeling of déjà vu, and now it was especially strong.
Perhaps this was because, to some degree, all New Atlantis
settlements looked alike. But he suspected that he had seen

this place, somehow, in his communications with Fiona over the years.

A bell clanged once or twice, and teenaged girls, dressed in plaid uniform skirts, began to emerge from a domed school. Hackworth knew that it was Fiona's school, and that she was not entirely happy there. After the crush of girls had gone out of the place, he rode Kidnapper into the school yard and sauntered once around the building, gazing in the windows. Without much trouble he saw his daughter, sitting at a table in the library, hunched over a book, evidently as part of some disciplinary action.

He wanted so badly to go in and put his arms around her, because he knew that she had spent many hours suffering like punishments, and that she was a lonely girl. But he was in New Atlantis, and there were proprieties to be observed. First things first.

Gwendolyn's townhouse was only a few blocks away. Hackworth rang the bell, determined to observe all of the formalities now that he was a stranger in the house.

"May I ask what your visit is regarding?" asked the parlourmaid, as Hackworth spun his card onto the salver. Hackworth didn't like this woman, who was named Amelia, because Fiona didn't like her, and Fiona didn't like her because Gwen had given her some disciplinary authority in the household, and Amelia was the sort who relished having it.

He tried not to confuse himself by wondering how he could possibly know all of these things.

"Business," Hackworth said pleasantly. "Family business."

Amelia was halfway up the stairs when her eyes finally focused on Hackworth's card. She nearly dropped the salver and had to clutch at the banister with one hand in order to keep her balance. She froze there for a few moments, trying to resist the temptation to turn around, and finally surrendered to it. The expression on her face was one of perfect loathing mixed with fascination.

"Please carry out your duties," Hackworth said, "and dispense with the vulgar theatrics."

Amelia, looking crestfallen, stormed up the stairs with the tainted card. There followed a good deal of muffled commotion upstairs. After a few minutes, Amelia ventured as far down as the landing and encouraged Hackworth to make himself comfortable in the parlor. He did so, noting that in his absence, Gwendolyn had been able to consummate all of the long-term furniture-buying strategies she had spent so much time plotting during the early years of their marriage. Wives and widows of secret agents in Protocol Enforcement could rely on being well cared for, and Gwen had not allowed his salary to sit around collecting dust.

His ex-wife descended the stairway cautiously, stood outside the beveled-glass parlor doors for a minute peering at him through the gauze curtains, and finally slipped into the room without meeting his gaze and took a seat rather far away from him. "Hello, Mr. Hackworth," she said.

"Mrs. Hackworth. Or is it back to Miss Lloyd?"

"It is."

"Ah, that's hard." When Hackworth heard the name Miss Lloyd, he thought of their courtship.

They sat there for a minute or so, not saying anything, just listening to the ponderous ratcheting of the grandfather clock.

"All right," Hackworth said, "I won't trouble you talking about extenuating circumstances, as I don't ask for your forgiveness, and in all honesty I'm not sure that I deserve it."

"Thank you for that consideration."

"I would like you to know, Miss Lloyd, that I am sympathetic to the step you have taken in securing a divorce and harbour no bitterness on that account."

"That is reassuring to know."

"You should also know that whatever behaviour I engaged in, as inexcusable as it was, was not motivated by rejection of you or of our marriage. It was not, in fact, a reflection upon you at all, but rather a reflection upon myself."

"Thank you for clarifying that point."

"I realize that any hope I might harbour in my breast of rekindling our former relationship, sincere as it might be, is futile, and so I will not trouble you after today."

"I cannot tell you how relieved I am to hear that you understand the situation so completely."

"However, I would like to be of service to you and Fiona in helping to resolve any loose ends."

"You are very kind. I shall give you my lawyer's card."

"And, of course, I look forward to reestablishing some sort of contact with my daughter."

The conversation, which had been running as smoothly as a machine to this point, now veered off track and crashed. Gwendolyn reddened and stiffened.

"You—you *bastard*."

The front door opened. Fiona stepped into the foyer carrying her schoolbooks. Amelia was there immediately, maneuvering around with her back to the foyer doors, blocking Fiona's view, talking to her in low angry tones.

Hackworth heard his daughter's voice. It was a lovely voice, a husky alto, and he would have recognized it anywhere. "Don't lie to me, I recognised his chevaline!" she said, and finally shouldered Amelia out of the way, burst into the parlor, all lanky and awkward and beautiful, an incarnation of joy. She took two steps across the oriental rug and then launched herself full-length across the settee into her father's arms, where she lay for some minutes alternately weeping and laughing.

Gwen had to be escorted from the room by Amelia, who came back immediately and stationed herself nearby, hands clasped behind back like a military sentry, observing Hackworth's every move. Hackworth couldn't imagine what they suspected he might be capable of—incest in the parlor? But there was no point in spoiling the moment by thinking of galling things, and so he shut Amelia out of his mind.

Father and daughter were allowed to converse for a quarter of an hour, really just queuing up subjects for future conversation. By that time, Gwen had recovered her composure enough to reenter the room, and she and Amelia stood shoulder-to-shoulder, quivering in sympathetic resonance, until Gwen interrupted.

"Fiona, your—*father*—and I were in the midst of a very serious discussion when you burst in on us. Please leave us alone for a few minutes."

Fiona did, reluctantly. Gwen resumed her former position, and Amelia backed out of the room. Hackworth noticed that Gwen had fetched some documents, bound up in red tape.

"These are papers setting out the terms of our divorce, including all conditions relating to Fiona," she said. "You are already in violation, I'm afraid. Of course, this can be forgiven, as your lack of a forwarding address as such made it impossible for us to acquaint you with this information. Needless to say, it is imperative for you to familiarise yourself with these documents before darkening my door again."

"Naturally," Hackworth said. "Thank you for retaining them for me."

"If you will be so good as to withdraw from these premises—"

"Of course. Good day," Hackworth said, took the roll of papers from Gwen's trembling hand, and let himself out briskly. He was a bit surprised when he heard Amelia calling to him from the doorway.

"Mr. Hackworth. Miss Lloyd wishes to know whether you have established a new residence, so that your personal effects may be forwarded."

"None as yet," Hackworth said. "I'm in transit."

Amelia brightened. "In transit to where?"

"Oh, I don't really know," Hackworth said. A movement caught his eye and he saw Fiona framed in a second-story window. She was undoing the latches, raising the sash. "I'm on a quest of sorts."

"A quest for what, Mr. Hackworth?"

"Can't say precisely. You know, top secret and all that. Something to do with an alchemist. Who knows, maybe there'll be faeries and hobgoblins too, before it's all over. I'll be happy to fill you in when I return. Until then, please ask Miss Lloyd if she would be so understanding as to retain those personal effects for just a bit longer. It can't possibly take more than another ten years or so."

And with that, Hackworth prodded Kidnapper forward, moving at an extremely deliberate pace.

Fiona was on a velocipede with smart wheels that made short work of the cobblestone road. She caught up with her father just short of the security grid. Mother and Amelia had just materialized a block behind them in a half-lane car, and the sudden sensation of danger inspired Fiona to make an impetuous dive from the saddle of her velocipede onto Kidnapper's hindquarters, like a cowboy in a movie switching horses in midgallop. Her skirts, poorly adapted to cowboy maneuvers, got all fouled up around her legs, and she ended up slung over Kidnapper's back like a sack of beans, one hand clutching the vestigial knob where its tail would have been if it were a horse, and the other arm thrown round her father's waist.

"I love you, Mother!" she shouted, as they rode through the grid and out of the jurisdiction of New Atlantis family law. "Can't say the same for you, Amelia! But I'll be back soon, don't worry about me! Good-bye!" And then the ferns and mist closed behind them, and they were alone in the deep forest.

Carl Hollywood takes the Oath; stroll along the Thames; an encounter with Lord Finkle-McGraw.

Carl took the Oath at Westminster Abbey on a surprisingly balmy day in April and afterward went for a stride down the river, heading not too directly toward a reception that had been arranged in his honor at the Hopkins Theatre near Leicester Square. Even without a pedomotive, he walked as fast as many people jogged. Ever since his first visit to London as a malnourished theatre student, he had preferred walking to any other way of getting around the place. Walking, especially along the Embankment where fellow-pedestrians were relatively few, also gave him freedom to smoke big old authentic cigars or the occasional briar pipe. Just because he was a Victorian didn't mean he had to give up his peculiarities; quite the opposite, in fact. Cruising along past old shrapnel-pocked Cleopatra's Needle in a comet-like corona of his own roiling, viscous smoke, he thought that he might get to like this.

A gentleman in a top hat was standing on the railing, gazing stolidly across the water, and as Carl drew closer, he could see that it was Lord Alexander Chung-Sik Finkle-McGraw, who, a day or two earlier, had stated during a cinephone conversation that he should like to meet him face-to-face in the near future for a chat.

Carl Hollywood, remembering his new tribal affilia-

tion, went so far as to doff his hat and bow. Finkle-McGraw
acknowledged the greeting somewhat distractedly. "Please
accept my sincere congratulations, Mr. Hollywood. Welcome to the phyle."

"Thank you."

"I regret that I have not been able to attend any of your
productions at the Hopkins—my friends who have could
hardly have been more complimentary."

"Your friends are too kind," said Carl Hollywood. He
was still a little unsure of the etiquette. To accept the compliment at face value would have been boastful; to imply that
His Grace's friends were incompetent judges of theatre was
not much of an improvement; he settled for the less dangerous accusation that these friends had a superfluity of goodness.

Finkle-McGraw detached himself from the railing and
began to walk along the river, keeping a brisk pace for a
man of his age.

"I daresay that you shall make a prized addition to our
phyle, which, as brilliantly as it shines in the fields of commerce and science, wants more artists."

Not wanting to join in criticism of the tribe he'd just
sworn a solemn Oath to uphold, Carl pursed his lips and
mulled over some possible responses.

Finkle-McGraw continued, "Do you suppose that we
fail to encourage our own children to pursue the arts, or fail
to attract enough men such as yourself, or perhaps both?"

"With all due respect, Your Grace, I do not necessarily
agree with your premise. New Atlantis has many fine artists."

"Oh, come now. Why do all of them come from outside the tribe, as you did? Really, Mr. Hollywood, would
you have taken the Oath at all if your prominence as a theatrical producer had not made it advantageous for you to do
so?"

"I think I will choose to interpret your question as part
of a Socratic dialogue for my edification," Carl Hollywood
said carefully, "and not as an allegation of insincerity on my
part. As a matter of fact, just before I encountered you, I was
enjoying my cigar, and looking about at London, and thinking about just how well it all suits me."

"It suits you well because you are of a certain age now.

You are a successful and established artist. The ragged bohemian life holds no charm for you anymore. But would you have reached your current position if you had not lived that life when you were younger?"

"Now that you put it that way," Carl said, "I agree that we might try to make some provision, in the future, for young bohemians—"

"It wouldn't work," Finkle-McGraw said. "I've been thinking about this for years. I had the same idea: Set up a sort of young artistic bohemian theme park, sprinkled around in all the major cities, where young New Atlantans who were so inclined could congregate and be subversive when they were in the mood. The whole idea was self-contradictory. Mr. Hollywood, I have devoted much effort, during the last decade or so, to the systematic encouragement of subversiveness."

"You have? Are you not concerned that our young subversives will migrate to other phyles?"

If Carl Hollywood could have kicked himself in the arse, he would have done so as soon as finishing that sentence. He had forgotten about Elizabeth Finkle-McGraw's recent and highly publicized defection to CryptNet. But the Duke took it serenely.

"Some of them will, as the case of my granddaughter demonstrates. But what does it really mean when such a young person moves to another phyle? It means that they have outgrown youthful credulity and no longer wish to belong to a tribe simply because it is the path of least resistance—they have developed principles, they are concerned with their personal integrity. It means, in short, that they are ripe to become members in good standing of New Atlantis—as soon as they develop the wisdom to see that it is, in the end, the best of all possible tribes."

"Your strategy was much too subtle for me to follow. I thank you for explaining it. You encourage subversiveness because you think that it will have an effect opposite to what one might naively suppose."

"Yes. And that's the whole point of being an Equity Lord, you know—to look after the interests of the society as a whole instead of flogging one's own company, or whatever. At any rate, this brings us to the subject of the advertisement I placed in the ractives section of the *Times* and our consequent cinephone conversation."

"Yes," Carl Hollywood said, "you are looking for ractors who performed in a project called the *Young Lady's Illustrated Primer*."

"The Primer was my idea. I commissioned it. I paid the racting fees. Of course, owing to the way the media system is organised, I had no way to determine the identity of the ractors to whom I was sending the fees—hence the need for a public advertisement."

"Your Grace, I should tell you immediately—and would have told you on the cinephone, had you not insisted that we defer all substantive discussion to a face-to-face— that I myself did not ract in the Primer. A friend of mine did. When I saw the advertisement, I undertook to respond on her behalf."

"I understand that ractors are frequently pursued by overly appreciative members of their audience," said Finkle-McGraw, "and so I suppose I understand why you have chosen to act as intermediary in this case. Let me assure you that my motives are perfectly benign."

Carl adopted a wounded look. "Your Grace! I would never have supposed otherwise. I am arrogating this role to myself, not to protect the young lady in question from any supposed malignity on your part, but simply because her current circumstances make establishing contact with her a somewhat troublesome business."

"Then pray tell me what you know about the young woman."

Carl gave the Equity Lord a brief description of Miranda's relationship with the Primer.

Finkle-McGraw was keenly interested in how much time Miranda had spent in the Primer each week. "If your estimates are even approximately accurate, this young woman must have singlehandedly done at least nine-tenths of the racting associated with that copy of the Primer."

"*That* copy? Do you mean to say there were others?"

Finkle-McGraw walked on silently for a few moments, then resumed in a quieter voice. "There were three copies in all. The first one went to my granddaughter—as you will appreciate, I tell you this in confidence. A second went to

Fiona, the daughter of the artifex who created it. The third fell into the hands of Nell, a little thete girl.

"To make a long story short, the three girls have turned out very differently. Elizabeth is rebellious and high-spirited and lost interest in the Primer several years ago. Fiona is bright but depressed, a classic manic-depressive artist. Nell, on the other hand, is a most promising young lady.

"I prepared an analysis of the girls' usage habits, which were largely obscured by the inherent secrecy of the media system, but which can be inferred from the bills we paid to hire the ractors. It became clear that, in the case of Elizabeth, the racting was done by hundreds of different performers. In Fiona's case, the bills were strikingly lower because much of the racting was done by someone who did not charge money for his or her services—probably her father. But that's a different story. In Nell's case, virtually all of the racting was done by the same person."

"It sounds," Carl said, "as if my friend established a relationship with Nell's copy—"

"And by extension, with Nell," said Lord Finkle-McGraw.

Carl said, "May I inquire as to why you wish to contact the ractor?"

"Because she is a central part of what is going on here," said Lord Finkle-McGraw, "which I did not expect. It was not a part of the original plan that the ractor would be important."

"She did it," Carl Hollywood said, "by sacrificing her career and much of her life. It is important for you to understand, Your Grace, that she was not merely Nell's tutor. She became Nell's mother."

These words seemed to strike Lord Finkle-McGraw quite forcefully. His stride faltered, and he ambled along the riverbank for some time, lost in thought.

"You gave me to believe, several minutes ago, that establishing contact with the ractor in question would not be a trivial process," he said finally, in quieter voice. "Is she no longer associated with your troupe?"

"She took a leave of absence several years ago in order to concentrate on Nell and the Primer."

"I see," said the Equity Lord, leaning into the words a little bit and turning it into an exclamation. He was getting excited. "Mr. Hollywood, I hope you will not be offended by my indelicacy in inquiring as to whether this has been a *paid* leave of absence."

"Had it been necessary, I would have underwritten it. Instead there is another backer."

"Another backer," repeated Finkle-McGraw. He was obviously fascinated, and slightly alarmed, by the use of financial jargon in this context.

"The transaction was fairly simple, as I suppose all transactions are *au fond*," said Carl Hollywood. "Miranda wanted to locate Nell. Conventional thinking dictates that this is impossible. There are, however, some unconventional thinkers who would maintain that it can be done through unconscious, nonrational processes. There is a tribe called the Drummers who normally live underwater—"

"I am familiar with them," said Lord Finkle-McGraw.

"Miranda joined the Drummers four years ago," Carl said. "She had entered into a partnership. The two other partners were a gentleman of my acquaintance, also in the theatrical business, and a financial backer."

"What did the backer hope to gain from it?"

"A leased line to the collective unconscious," said Carl Hollywood. "He thought it would be to the entertainment industry what the philosopher's stone was to alchemy."

"And the results?"

"We have all been waiting to hear from Miranda."

"You have heard nothing at all?"

"Only in my dreams," Carl Hollywood said.

Nell's passage through Pudong; she happens upon the offices of Madame Ping; interview with the same.

Shanghai proper could be glimpsed only through vertical apertures between the high buildings of the Pudong Economic Zone as Nell skated westward. Downtown Pudong erupted from the flat paddy-land on the east bank of the Huang Pu. Almost all of the skyscrapers made use of media-tronic building materials. Some bore the streamlined characters of the Japanese writing system, rendered in sophisticated color schemes, but most of them were written in the denser high-resolution characters used by the Chinese, and these tended to be stroked out in fiery red, or in black on a background of that color.

The Anglo-Americans had their Manhattan, the Japanese had Tokyo. Hong Kong was a nice piece of work, but it was essentially Western. When the Overseas Chinese came back to the homeland to build their monument to enterprise, they had done it here, and they had done it bigger and brighter, and unquestionably redder, than any of those other cities. The nanotechnological trick of making sturdy structures that were lighter than air had come along just at the right time, as all of the last paddies were being replaced by immense concrete foundations, and a canopy of new construction had bloomed above the first-generation undergrowth of seventy- and eighty-story buildings. This new architecture was naturally large and ellipsoidal, typically consisting of a huge neon-rimmed ball impaled on a spike, so Pudong was bigger and denser a thousand feet above the ground than it was at street level.

Seen from the apex of the big arch in the Causeway through several miles of bad air, the view was curiously flattened and faded, as if the whole scene had been woven into a fabulously complex brocade that had been allowed to gather dust for several decades and then been hung in front of Nell, about ten feet away. The sun had gone down not long before and the sky was still a dim orange fading up into purple, divided into irregular segments by half a dozen pillars of smoke spurting straight up out of the horizon and toward the dark polluted vault of the heavens, many miles off to the west, somewhere out in the silk and tea districts between Shanghai and Suzhou.

As she power-skated down the western slope of the arch and crossed the coastline of China, the thunderhead of neon reached above her head, spread out to embrace her, developed into three dimensions—and she was still several miles away from it. The coastal neighborhoods consisted of block after block of reinforced-concrete apartment buildings, four to five stories high, looking older than the Great Wall though their real age could not have exceeded a few decades, and decorated on the ends facing the street with large cartoonish billboards, some mediatronic, most just painted on. For the first kilometer or so, most of these were targeted at businessmen just coming in from New Chusan, and in particular from the New Atlantis Clave. Glancing at these billboards as she went by them, Nell concluded that visitors from New Atlantis played an important role in supporting casinos and bordellos, both the old-fashioned variety and the newer scripted-fantasy emporia, where you could be the star in a little play you wrote yourself. Nell slowed down to examine several of these, memorizing the addresses of ones with especially new or well-executed signs.

She had no clear plan in mind yet. All she knew was that she had to keep moving purposefully. Then the young men squatting on the curbs talking into their cellphones would keep eyeing her but leave her alone. The moment she stopped or looked the tiniest bit uncertain, they would descend.

The dense wet air along the Huang Pu was supporting millions of tons of air buoys, and Nell felt every kilogram of their weight pressing upon her ribs and shoulders as she skated up and down the main waterfront thoroughfare, trying to maintain her momentum and her false sense of purposefulness. This was the Coastal Republic, which appeared to have no fixed principles other than that money talked and that it was a good thing to get rich. Every tribe in the world seemed to have its own skyscraper here. Some, like New Atlantis, were not actively recruiting and simply used the size and magnificence of their buildings as a monument to themselves. Others, like the Boers, the Parsis, the Jews, went for the understated approach, and in Pudong anything understated was more or less invisible. Still others—the Mormons, the First Distributed Republic, and the Chinese Coastal Republic itself—used every square inch of their mediatronic walls to proselytize.

The only phyle that didn't seem to appreciate the ecumenical spirit of the place was the Celestial Kingdom itself. Nell stumbled across their territory, half a square block surrounded with a stucco-sheathed masonry wall, circular gates here and there, and an old three-story structure inside, done in high Ming style with eaves that curved way up at the corners and sculpted dragons along the ridgeline of the roof. The place was so tiny compared to the rest of Pudong that it looked as if you might trip over it. The gates were guarded by men in armor, presumably backed up by other, less obvious defensive systems.

Nell was fairly certain that she was being followed, unobtrusively, by at least three young men who had locked on to her during her initial passage in from the coast, and who were waiting to find out whether she really had somewhere to go or was just faking it. She had already made her way from one end of the waterfront to the other, pretending to be a tourist who just wanted to take in a view of the Bund across the river. She was now heading back into the heart of downtown Pudong, where she had better look as if she were doing something.

Passing by the grand entrance to one of the skyscrapers—a Coastal Republic edifice, not barbarian turf—she recognized its mediaglyphic logo from one of the signs she had seen on the way into town.

Nell could at least fill out an application without committing herself. It would allow her to kill an hour in relatively safe and clean surroundings. The important thing, as Dojo had taught her long ago in a different context, was not to stop; without movement she could do nothing.

Alas, Madame Ping's office suite was closed. A few lights were on in the back, but the doors were locked and no receptionist was on duty. Nell did not know whether to be amused or annoyed; whoever heard of a brothel that closed down after dark? But then these were only the administrative offices.

She loitered in the lobby for a few minutes, then caught a down elevator. Just as the doors were closing, someone jumped into the lobby and slammed the button, opening them back up again. A young Chinese man with a small, slender body, large head, neatly dressed, carrying some papers. "Pardon me," he said. "Did you require something?"

"I'm here to apply for a job," Nell said.

The man's eyes traveled up and down her body in a coolly professional fashion, almost completely devoid of prurience, starting and stopping on her face. "As a performer," he said. The intonation was somewhere between a question and a declaration.

"As a scriptwriter," she said.

Unexpectedly, he broke into a grin.

"I have qualifications that I will explain in detail."

"We have writers. We contract for them on the network."

"I'm surprised. How can a contract writer in Minnesota possibly provide your clients with the personalized service they require?"

"You could almost certainly get a job as a performer," said the young man. "You would start tonight. Good pay."

"Just by looking at the billboards on the way in, I could see that your customers aren't paying for bodies. They are paying for ideas. That's your value added, right?"

"Pardon me?" said the young man, grinning again.

"Your value added. The reason you can charge more than a whorehouse, pardon my language, is that you provide a scripted fantasy scenario tailored to the client's requirements. I can do that for you," Nell said. "I know these people, and I can make you a lot of money."

"You know what people?"

"The Vickys. I know them inside and out," Nell said.

"Please come inside," said the young man, gesturing toward the diamondoid door with MADAME PING'S written on it in red letters. "Would you care for tea?"

"There are only two industries. This has always been true," said Madame Ping, enfolding a lovely porcelain teacup in her withered fingers, the two-inch fingernails interleaving neatly like the pinions of a raptor folding its wings after a long hard day of cruising the thermals. "There is the industry of things, and the industry of entertainment. The industry of things comes first. It keeps us alive. But making things is easy now that we have the Feed. This is not a very interesting business anymore.

"After people have the things they need to live, everything else is entertainment. Everything. This is Madame Ping's business."

Madame Ping had an office on the hundred-and-eleventh floor with a nice unobstructed view across the Huang

Pu and into downtown Shanghai. When it wasn't foggy, she could even see the facade of her theatre, which was on a side street a couple of blocks in from the Bund, its mediatronic marquee glowing patchily through the dun limbs of an old sycamore tree. She had a telescope mounted in one of her windows, fixed upon the theatre's entrance, and noting Nell's curiosity, she encouraged her to look through it.

Nell had never looked through a real telescope before. It had a tendency to jiggle and go out of focus, it didn't zoom, and panning was tricky. But for all that, the image quality was a lot better than photographic, and she quickly forgot herself and began sweeping it back and forth across the city. She checked out the little Celestial Kingdom Clave in the heart of the old city, where a couple of Mandarins stood on a zigzag bridge across a pond, contemplating a swarm of golden carp, wispy silver beards trailing down over the colorful silk of their lapels, blue sapphire buttons on their caps flashing as they nodded their heads. She looked into a high-rise building farther inland, apparently a foreign concession of some type, where some Euros were holding a cocktail party, some venturing onto the balcony with glasses of wine and doing some eavesdropping of their own. Finally she leveled the 'scope toward the horizon, out past the vast dangerous triad-ridden suburbs, where millions of Shanghai's poor had been forcibly banished to make way for high-rises. Beyond that was real agricultural land, a fractal network of canals and creeks glimmering like a golden net as they reflected the lambency of the sunset, and beyond that, as always, a few scattered pillars of smoke in the ultimate distance, where the Fists of Righteous Harmony were burning the foreign devils' Feed lines.

"You are a curious girl," Madame Ping said. "That is natural. But you must never let any other person—especially a client—see your curiosity. Never seek information. Sit quietly and let them bring it to you. What they conceal tells you more than what they reveal. Do you understand?"

"Yes, madam," Nell said, turning toward her interlocutor with a little curtsy. Rather than trying to do Chinese etiquette and making a hash of it, she was taking the Victorian route, which worked just as well. For purposes of this interview, Henry (the young man who had offered her tea) had advanced her a few hard ucus, which she had used to compile a reasonably decent full-length dress, hat, gloves, and reticule. She had gone in nervous and realized within a few minutes that the decision to hire her had already been made, somehow, and that this little get-together was actually more along the lines of an orientation session.

"Why is the Victorian market important to us?" Madame Ping asked, and fixed Nell with an incisive glare.

"Because New Atlantis is one of the three first-tier phyles."

"Not correct. The wealth of New Atlantis is great, yes. But its population is just a few percent. The successful New Atlantis man is busy and has just a bit of time for scripted fantasies. He has much money, you understand, but little opportunity to spend it. No, this market is important because everyone else—the men of all other phyles, including many of Nippon—want to be like Victorian gentlemen. Look at the Ashantis—the Jews—the Coastal Republic. Do they wear traditional costume? Sometimes. Usually though, they wear a suit on the Victorian pattern. They carry an umbrella from Old Bond Street. They have a book of Sherlock Holmes stories. They play in Victorian ractives, and when they have to spend their natural urges, they come to me, and I provide them with a scripted fantasy that was originally requested by some gentleman who came sneaking across the Causeway from New Atlantis." Somewhat uncharacteristically, Madame Ping turned two of her claws into walking legs and made them scurry across the tabletop, like a furtive Vicky gent trying to slip into Shanghai without being caught on a monitor. Recognizing her cue, Nell covered her mouth with one gloved hand and tittered.

"This way, Madame Ping does a magic trick—she turns one satisfied client from New Atlantis into a thousand clients from all tribes."

"I must confess that I am surprised," Nell ventured. "Inexperienced as I am in these matters, I had supposed that each tribe would exhibit a different preference."

"We change the script a little," Madame Ping said, "to allow for cultural differences. But the story never changes. There are many people and many tribes, but only so many stories."

*Peculiar practices in the woods; the Reformed
Distributed Republic; an extraordinary conversation
in a log cabin; CryptNet; the Hackworths depart.*

Half a day's slow eastward ride took them well up into the
foothills of the Cascades, where the clouds, flowing in eternally from the Pacific, were forced upward by the swelling
terrain and unburdened themselves of their immense stores
of moisture. The trees were giants, rising branchless to far
above their heads, the trunks aglow with moss. The landscape was a checkerboard of old-growth forest alternating
with patches that had been logged in the previous century;
Hackworth tried to guide Kidnapper toward the latter, because the scarcity of undergrowth and deadfalls made for a
smoother ride. They passed through the remains of an abandoned timber town, half small clapboard buildings and half
moss-covered and rust-streaked mobile homes. Through
their dirty windows, faded signs were dimly visible, sten-
ciled THIS HOUSEHOLD DEPENDS ON TIMBER MONEY.
Ten-foot saplings grew up through cracks in the streets. Narrow hedges of blueberry shrubs and blackberry canes
sprouted from the rain gutters of houses, and gigantic old
cars, resting askew on flat and cracked tires, had become
trellises for morning glories and vine maples. They also
passed through an old mining encampment that had been
abandoned even longer ago. For the most part, the signs of
modern habitation were relatively subtle. The houses up
here tended to be of the same unassuming style favored by
the software khans closer to Seattle, and from place to place
a number of them would cluster around a central square
with playground equipment, cafés, stores, and other ameni-
ties. He and Fiona stopped at two such places to exchange
ucus for coffee, sandwiches, and cinnamon rolls.

The unmarked, decussating paths would have been
confusing to anyone but a native. Hackworth had never
been here before. He had gotten the coordinates from the
second fortune cookie in Kidnapper's glove compartment,
which was much less cryptic than the first had been. He had
no way to tell whether he was really going anywhere. His

faith did not begin to waver until evening approached, the eternal clouds changed from silver to dark gray, and he noticed that the chevaline was taking them higher and toward less densely populated ground.

Then he saw the rocks and knew he had chosen the right path. A wall of brown granite, dark and damp from the condensing fog, materialized before them. They heard it before they saw it; it made no sound, but its presence changed the acoustics of the forest. The fog was closing in, and they could barely see the silhouettes of scrubby, wind-gnarled mountain trees lined up uncomfortably along the top of the cliff.

Amid those trees was the silhouette of a human being.

"Quiet," Hackworth mouthed to his daughter, then reined Kidnapper to a stop.

The person had a short haircut and wore a bulky waist-length jacket with stretch pants; they could tell by the curve of the hips that it was a woman. Around those hips she had fastened an arrangement of neon green straps: a climbing harness. She wore no other outdoor paraphernalia, though, no knapsack or helmet, and behind her on the clifftop they could just make out the silhouette of a horse, prodding the ground with its nose. From time to time she checked her wristwatch.

A tenuous neon strand of rope hung down the bulging face of the cliff from where the woman stood. The last several meters dangled loosely in the mist in front of a small cozy pocket sheltered by the overhang.

Hackworth turned around to get Fiona's attention, then pointed something out: a second person, making his way along the base of the cliff, out of sight of the woman above. Moving carefully and quietly, he eventually reached the shelter of the overhang. He gingerly took the dangling end of the rope and tied it to something, apparently a piece of hardware fixed into the rock. Then he left the way he had come, moving silently and staying close to the cliff.

The woman remained still and silent for several minutes, checking her watch more and more frequently.

Finally she backed several paces away from the edge of the cliff, took her hands out of her jacket pockets, seemed to draw a few deep breaths, then ran forward and launched herself into space. She screamed as she did it, a scream to drive out her own fear.

The rope ran through a pulley fixed near the top of the cliff. She fell for a few meters, the rope tightened, the man's knot held, and the rope, which was somewhat elastic, brought her to a firm but not violent stop just above the wicked pile of rubble and snags at the base of the cliff. Swinging at the end of the rope, she grabbed it with one hand and leaned back, baring her throat to the mist, allowing herself to dangle listlessly for a few minutes, basking in relief.

A third person, previously unseen, emerged from the trees. This one was a middle-aged man, and he was wearing a jacket that had a few vaguely official touches such as an armband and an insignia on the breast pocket. He walked beneath the dangling woman and busied himself for a few moments beneath the overhang, eventually releasing the rope and letting her safely to the ground. The woman detached herself from the rope and then the harness and fell into a businesslike discussion with this man, who poured both of them hot drinks from a thermal flask.

"Have you heard of these people? The Reformed Distributed Republic," Hackworth said to Fiona, still keeping his voice low.

"I am only familiar with the First."

"The First Distributed Republic doesn't hang together very well—in a way, it was never designed to. It was started by a bunch of people who were very nearly anarchists. As you've probably learned in school, it's become awfully factionalized."

"I have some friends in the F.D.R.," Fiona said.

"Your neighbors?"

"Yes."

"Software khans," Hackworth said. "The F.D.R. works for them, because they have something in common—old software money. They're almost like Victorians—a lot of them cross over and take the Oath as they get older. But for the broad middle class, the F.D.R. offers no central religion or ethnic identity."

"So it becomes balkanized."

"Precisely. These people," Hackworth said, pointing to the man and the woman at the base of the cliff, "are

R.D.R., Reformed Distributed Republic. Very similar to F.D.R., with one key difference."

"The ritual we just witnessed?"

"Ritual is a good description," Hackworth said. "Earlier today, that man and that woman were both visited by messengers who gave them a place and time—nothing else. In this case, the woman's job was to jump off that cliff at the given time. The man's job was to tie the end of the rope before she jumped. A very simple job—"

"But if he had failed to do it, she'd be dead," Fiona said.

"Precisely. The names are pulled out of a hat. The participants have only a few hours' warning. Here, the ritual is done with a cliff and a rope, because there happened to be a cliff in the vicinity. In other R.D.R. nodes, the mechanism might be different. For example, person A might go into a room, take a pistol out of a box, load it with live ammunition, put it back in the box, and then leave the room for ten minutes. During that time, person B is supposed to enter the room and replace the live ammunition with a dummy clip having the same weight. Then person A comes back into the room, puts the gun to his head, and pulls the trigger."

"But person A has no way of knowing whether person B has done his job?"

"Exactly."

"What is the role of the third person?"

"A proctor. An official of the R.D.R. who sees to it that the two participants don't try to communicate."

"How frequently must they undergo this ritual?"

"As frequently as their name comes up at random, perhaps once every couple of years," Hackworth said. "It's a way of creating mutual dependency. These people know they can trust each other. In a tribe such as the F.D.R., whose view of the universe contains no absolutes, this ritual creates an artificial absolute."

The woman finished her hot drink, shook hands with the proctor, then began to ascend a polymer ladder, fixed to the rock, that took her back toward her horse. Hackworth spurred Kidnapper into movement, following a path that ran parallel to the base of the cliff, and rode for half a kilometer or so until it was joined by another path angling down from above. A few minutes later, the woman approached, riding her horse, an old-fashioned biological model.

She was a healthy, open-faced, apple-cheeked woman, still invigorated by her leap into the unknown, and she greeted them from some distance away, without any of the reserve of neo-Victorians.

"How do you do," Hackworth said, removing his bowler.

The woman barely glanced at Fiona. She reined her horse to a gentle stop, eyes fixed on Hackworth's face. She was wearing a distracted look. "I know you," she said. "But I don't know your name."

"Hackworth, John Percival, at your service. This is my daughter Fiona."

"I'm sure I've never heard that name," the woman said.

"I'm sure I've never heard yours," Hackworth said cheerfully.

"Maggie," the woman said. "This is driving me crazy. Where have we met?"

"This may sound rather odd," Hackworth said gently, "but if you and I could both remember all of our dreams— which we can't, of course—and if we compared notes long enough, we would probably find that we had shared a few over the years."

"A lot of people have similar dreams," Maggie said.

"Excuse me, but that's not what I mean," Hackworth said. "I refer to a situation in which each of us would retain his or her own personal point of view. I would see you. You would see me. We might then share certain experiences to-gether—each of us seeing it from our own perspective."

"Like a ractive?"

"Yes," Hackworth said, "but you don't have to pay for it. Not with money, anyway."

The local climate lent itself to hot drinks. Maggie did not even take off her jacket before going into her kitchen and putting a kettle on to boil. The place was a log cabin, airier than it looked from the outside, and Maggie apparently shared it with several other people who were not there at the moment. Fiona, walking to and from the bathroom, was fascinated to see evidence of men and women living and sleeping and bathing together.

As they sat around having their tea, Hackworth persuaded Maggie to poke her finger into a thimble-size device. When he took this object from his pocket, Fiona was struck by a powerful sense of déjà vu. She had seen it before, and it was significant. She knew that her father had designed it; it bore all the earmarks of his style.

Then they all sat around making small talk for a few minutes; Fiona had many questions about the workings of the R.D.R., which Maggie, a true believer, was pleased to answer. Hackworth had spread a sheet of blank paper out on the table, and as the minutes went by, words and pictures began to appear on it and to scroll up the page after it had filled itself up. The thimble, he explained, had placed some reconnaissance mites into Maggie's bloodstream, which had been gathering information, flying out through her pores when their tape drives were full, and offloading the data into the paper.

"It seems that you and I have a mutual acquaintance, Maggie," he said after a few minutes. "We are carrying many of the same tuples in our bloodstreams. They can only be spread through certain forms of contact."

"You mean, like, exchange of bodily fluids?" Maggie said blankly.

Fiona thought briefly of old-fashioned transfusions and probably would not have worked out the real meaning of this phrase had her father not flushed and glanced at her momentarily.

"I believe we understand each other, yes," Hackworth said.

Maggie thought about it for a moment and seemed to get irked, or as irked as someone with her generous and contented nature was ever likely to get. She addressed Hackworth but watched Fiona as she tried to construct her next sentence. "Despite what you Atlantans might think of us, I don't sleep . . . I mean, I don't have s . . . I don't have that many partners."

"I am sorry to have given you the mistaken impression that I had formed any untoward preconceptions about your moral standards," Hackworth said. "Please be assured that I do not regard myself as being in any position to judge others in this regard. However, if you could be so forthcoming as to tell me who, or with whom, in the last year or so . . ."

"Just one," Maggie said. "It's been a slow year." Then she set her tea mug down on the table (Fiona had been startled by the unavailability of saucers) and leaned back in her chair, looking at Hackworth alertly. "Funny that I'm telling you this stuff—you, a stranger."

"Please allow me to recommend that you trust your instincts and treat me not as a stranger."

"I had a fling. Months and months ago. That's been it."

"Where?"

"London." A trace of a smile came onto Maggie's face. "You'd think living here, I'd go someplace warm and sunny. But I went to London. I guess there's a little Victorian in all of us.

"It was a guy," Maggie went on. "I had gone to London with a couple of girlfriends of mine. One of them was another R.D.R. citizen and the other, Trish, left the R.D.R. about three years ago and co-founded a local CryptNet node. They've got a little point of presence down in Seattle, near the market."

"Please pardon me for interrupting," Fiona said, "but would you be so kind as to explain the nature of CryptNet? One of my old school friends seems to have joined it."

"A synthetic phyle. Elusive in the extreme," Hackworth said.

"Each node is independent and self-governing," Maggie said. "You could found a node tomorrow if you wanted. Nodes are defined by contracts. You sign a contract in which you agree to provide certain services when called upon to do so."

"What sorts of services?"

"Typically, data is delivered into your system. You process the data and pass it on to other nodes. It seemed like a natural to Trish because she was a coder, like me and my housemates and most other people around here."

"Nodes have computers then?"

"The people themselves have computers, typically embedded systems," Maggie said, unconsciously rubbing the mastoid bone behind her ear.

"Is the node synonymous with the person, then?"

"In many cases," Maggie said, "but sometimes it's several persons with embedded systems that are contained within the same trust boundary."

"May I ask what level your friend Trish's node has attained?" Hackworth said.

Maggie looked uncertain. "Eight or nine, maybe. Anyway, we went to London. While we were there, we decided to take in some shows. I wanted to see the big productions. Those were nice—we saw a nice *Doctor Faustus* at the Olivier."

"Marlowe's?"

"Yes. But Trish had a knack for finding all of these little, scruffy, out-of-the-way theatres that I never would have found in a million years—they weren't marked, and they didn't really advertise, as far as I could tell. We saw some radical stuff—really radical."

"I don't imagine you are using that adjective in a political sense," Hackworth said.

"No, I mean how they were staged. In one of them, we walked into this bombed-out old building in Whitechapel, full of people milling around, and all this weird stuff started happening, and after a while I realized that some of the people were actors and some were audience and that all of us were both, in a way. It was cool—I suppose you can get stuff like that on the net anytime, in a ractive, but it was so much better to be there with real, warm bodies around. I felt happy. Anyway, this guy was going to the bar for a pint, and he offered to get me one. We started talking. One thing led to another. He was really intelligent, really sexy. An African guy who knew a lot about the theatre. This place had back rooms. Some of them had beds."

"After you were finished," Hackworth said, "did you experience any unusual sensations?"

Maggie threw back her head and laughed, thinking that this was a bit of wry humor on Hackworth's part. But he was serious.

"*After* we were finished?" she said.

"Yes. Let us say, several minutes afterward."

Suddenly Maggie became disconcerted. "Yeah, actually," she said. "I got hot. Really hot. We had to leave, 'cause I thought I had a flu or something. We went back to the hotel, and I took my clothes off and stood out on the balcony. My temperature was a hundred and four. But the next morning I felt fine. And I've felt fine ever since."

"Thank you, Maggie," Hackworth said, rising to his feet and pocketing the sheet of paper. Fiona rose too, following her father's cue. "Prior to your London visit, had your social life been an active one?"

Maggie got a little pinker. "Relatively active for a few years, yes."

"What sort of crowd? CryptNet types? People who spent a lot of time near the water?"

Maggie shook her head. "The water? I don't understand."

"Ask yourself why you have been so inactive, Maggie, since your liaison with Mr.—"

"Beck. Mr. Beck."

"With Mr. Beck. Could it be that you found the experience just a bit alarming? Exchange of bodily fluids followed by a violent rise in core temperature?"

Maggie was poker-faced.

"I recommend that you look into the subject of spontaneous combustion," Hackworth said. And without further ceremony, he reclaimed his bowler and umbrella from the entryway and led Fiona back out into the forest.

Hackworth said, "Maggie did not tell you everything about CryptNet. To begin with, it is believed to have numerous unsavoury connexions and is a perennial focus of Protocol Enforcement's investigations. And"—Hackworth laughed ruefully—"it is patently untrue that ten is the highest level."

"What is the goal of this organisation?" Fiona asked.

"It represents itself as a simple, moderately successful data-processing collective. But its actual goals can only be known by those privileged to be included within the trust boundary of the thirty-third level," Hackworth said, his voice slowing down as he tried to remember why he knew all of these things. "It is rumoured that, within that select circle, any member can kill any other simply by thinking of the deed."

Fiona leaned forward and wrapped her arms snugly around her father's body, nestled her head between his shoulder blades, and held tight. She thought that the subject of CryptNet was closed; but a quarter of an hour later, as Kidnapper carried them swiftly through the trees down toward Seattle, her father spoke again, picking up the sentence where he had left it, as if he had merely paused for breath. His voice was slow and distant and almost trancelike, the memories percolating outward from deep storage with little participation from his conscious mind. "CryptNet's true desire is the Seed—a technology that, in their diabolical scheme, will one day supplant the Feed, upon which our society and many others are founded. Protocol, to us, has brought prosperity and peace—to CryptNet, however, it is a contemptible system of oppression. They believe that information has an almost mystical power of free flow and self-replication, as water seeks its own level or sparks fly upward—and lacking any moral code, they confuse inevitability with Right. It is their view that one day, instead of Feeds terminating in matter compilers, we will have Seeds that, sown on the earth, will sprout up into houses, hamburgers, spaceships, and books—that the Seed will develop inevitably from the Feed, and that upon it will be founded a more highly evolved society."

He stopped for a moment, took a deep breath, and seemed to stir awake; when he spoke again, it was in a clearer and stronger voice. "Of course, it can't be allowed—the Feed is not a system of control and oppression, as CryptNet would maintain. It is the only way order can be maintained in modern society—if everyone possessed a Seed, anyone could produce weapons whose destructive power rivalled that of Elizabethan nuclear weapons. This is why Protocol Enforcement takes such a dim view of CryptNet's activities."

The trees parted to reveal a long blue lake below them. Kidnapper found its way to a road, and Hackworth spurred it on to a hand-gallop. Within a few hours, father and daughter were settling into bunkbeds in a second-class cabin of the airship *Falkland Islands*, bound for London.

*From the Primer, Princess Nell's activities as
Duchess of Turing; the Castle of the Water-gates;
other castles; the Cipherers' Market; Nell prepares
for her final journey.*

Princess Nell remained in Castle Turing for several months. During her quest for the twelve keys, she had entered many castles, outwitted their sentries, picked their locks, and rifled their treasuries; but Castle Turing was an altogether different place, a place that ran on rules and programs that were devised by men and that could be rewritten by one who was adept in the language of the ones and zeroes. She need not content herself with sneaking in, seizing a trinket, and fleeing. Castle Turing she made her own. Its demesne became Princess Nell's kingdom.

First she gave the Duke of Turing a decent burial. Then she studied his books until she had mastered them. She acquainted herself with the states by which the soldiers, and the mechanical Duke, could be programmed. She entered a new master program into the Duke and then restarted the turning of the mighty Shaft that powered the castle. Her first efforts were unsuccessful, as her program contained many errors. The original Duke himself had not been above this; he called them bugs, in reference to a large beetle that had become entangled in one of his chains during an early experiment and brought the first Turing machine to a violent halt. But with steadfast patience, Princess Nell resolved these bugs and made the mechanical Duke into her devoted servant. The Duke in turn had the knack of putting simple programs into all of the soldiers, so that an order given him by Nell was rapidly disseminated into the entire force.

For the first time in her life, the Princess had an army and servants. But it was not a conquering sort of army, because the springs in the soldiers' backs unwound rapidly, and they did not have the adaptability of human soldiers. Still, it was an effective force behind the walls of the castle and made her secure from any conceivable aggressor. Following maintenance schedules that had been laid down by the original Duke, Princess Nell set the soldiers to work greasing the gears, repairing cracked shafts and worn bearings, and building new soldiers out of stockpiled parts.

She was heartened by her success. But Castle Turing was

only one of seven ducal seats in this kingdom, and she knew she had much work to do.

The territory around the castle was deeply forested, but grassy ridges rose several miles away, and standing on the castle walls with the original Duke's spyglass, Nell was able to see wild horses grazing there. Purple had taught her the secrets of mastering wild horses, and Duck had taught her how to win their affection, and so Nell mounted an expedition to these grasslands and returned a week later with two beautiful mustangs, Coffee and Cream. She equipped them with fine tack from the Duke's stables, marked with the T crest—for the crest was hers now, and she could with justification call herself the Duchess of Turing. She also brought a plain, unmarked saddle so that she could pass for a commoner if need be—though Princess Nell had become so beautiful over the years and had developed such a fine bearing that few people would mistake her for a commoner now, even if she were dressed in rags and walking barefoot.

Lying in her bunkbed in Madame Ping's dormitory, reading these words from a softly glowing page in the middle of the night, Nell wondered at that. Princesses were not genetically different from commoners.

On the other side of a fairly thin wall she could hear water running in half a dozen sinks as young women performed their crepuscular ablutions. Nell was the only scripter staying in Madame Ping's dormitory; the others were performers and were just coming back from a long vigorous shift, rubbing liniment on their shoulders, sore from wielding paddles against clients' bottoms, or snorting up great nostril-loads of mites programmed to seek out their inflamed buttocks and help to repair damaged capillaries overnight. And of course, many more traditional activities were going on, such as douching, makeup removal, moisturizing, and the like. The girls went through these motions briskly, with the unselfconscious efficiency that the Chinese all seemed to share, discussing the day's events in the dry Shanghainese dialect. Nell had been living among these girls for a month and was just starting to pick up a few words. They all spoke English anyway.

She stayed up late reading the Primer in the dark. The dormitory was a good place for this; Madame Ping's girls were professionals, and after a few minutes of whispering, giggling, and scandalized communal shushing, they always went to sleep.

Nell sensed that she was coming close to the end of the Primer.

This would have been evident even if she hadn't been closing in on Coyote, the twelfth and final Faery King. In the last few weeks, since Nell had entered the domain of King Coyote, the character of the Primer had changed. Formerly, her Night Friends or other characters had acted with minds of their own, even if Nell just went along passively. Reading the Primer had always meant racing with other characters in the book while also having to think her way through various interesting situations.

Recently the former element had been almost absent. Castle Turing had been a fair sample of King Coyote's domain: a place with few human beings, albeit filled with fascinating places and situations.

She made her lonesome way across the domain of King Coyote, visiting one castle after another, and encountering a different conundrum in each one. The second castle (after Castle Turing) was built on the slope of a mountain and had an elaborate irrigation system in which water from a bubbling spring was routed through a system of gates. There were many thousands of these gates, and they were connected to each other in small groups, so that one gate's opening or closing would, in some way, affect that of the others in its group. This castle grew its own food and was suffering a terrible famine because the arrangement of gates had in some way become fubared. A dark, mysterious knight had come to visit the place and apparently sneaked out of his bedroom in the middle of the night and fiddled with connections between some gates in such a way that water no longer flowed to the fields. Then he had disappeared, leaving behind a note stating that he would fix the problem in exchange for a large ransom in gold and jewels.

Princess Nell spent some time studying the problem and eventually noticed that the system of gates was actually a very sophisticated version of one of the Duke of Turing's machines. Once she understood that the behavior of the water-gates was orderly and predictable, it was not long before she was able to program their behavior and locate the bugs that the dark knight had introduced into the system. Soon water was flowing through the irrigation system again, and the famine was relieved.

The people who lived in this castle were grateful, which she had expected. But then they put a crown on her head and made her their ruler, which she had not expected.

On some reflection, though, it only made sense. They would die unless their system functioned properly. Princess Nell was the only person who knew how it worked; she held their fate in her hands. They had little choice but to submit to her rule.

So it went, as Princess Nell proceeded from castle to castle, inadvertently finding herself at the helm of a full-fledged rebellion against King Coyote. Each castle depended on some kind of a programmable system that was a little more complicated than the previous one. After the Castle of the Water-gates, she came to a castle with a magnificent organ, powered by air pressure and controlled by a bewildering grid of push-rods, which could play music stored on a roll of paper tape with holes punched through it. A mysterious dark knight had programmed the organ to play a sad, depressing tune, plunging the place into a profound depression so that no one worked or even got out of bed. With some playing around, Princess Nell established that the behavior of the organ could be simulated by an extremely sophisticated arrangement of water-gates, which meant, in turn, that it could just as well be reduced to an unfathomably long and complicated Turing machine program.

When she had the organ working properly and the residents cheered up, she moved on to a castle that functioned according to rules written in a great book, in a peculiar language. Some pages of the book had been ripped out by the mysterious dark knight, and Princess Nell had to reconstruct them, learning the language, which was extremely pithy and made heavy use of parentheses. Along the way, she proved what was a foregone conclusion, namely, that the system for processing this language was essentially a more complex version of the mechanical organ, hence a Turing machine in essence.

Next was a castle divided into many small rooms, with a system for passing messages between rooms through a pneumatic tube. In each room was a group of people who responded to the messages by following certain rules laid out in books, which usually entailed sending more messages to other rooms. After familiarizing herself with some of these rule-books and establishing that the castle was another Turing machine, Princess Nell fixed a problem in the message-delivery system that had been created by the vexatious dark knight, collected another ducal coronet, and moved on to castle number six.

This place was entirely different. It was much bigger. It was much richer. And unlike all of the other castles in the domain of King Coyote, it worked. As she approached the castle, she learned to keep her horse to the edge of the road, for messengers were constantly blowing past her at a full gallop in both directions.

It was a vast open marketplace with thousands of stalls, filled with carts and runners carrying product in all directions. But no vegetables, fish, spices, or fodder were to be seen here; all the product was information written down in books. The books were trundled from place to place on wheelbarrows and carried here and there on great long seedy-looking conveyor belts made of hemp and burlap. Book-carriers bumped into each other, compared notes as to what they were carrying and where they were going, and swapped books for other books. Stacks of books were sold in great, raucous auctions—and paid for not with gold but with other books. Around the edges of the market were stalls where books were exchanged for gold, and beyond that, a few alleys where gold could be exchanged for food.

In the midst of this hubbub, Princess Nell saw a dark knight sitting on a black horse, paging through one of these books. Without further ado, she spurred her horse forward and drew her sword. She slew him in single combat, right there in the middle of the marketplace, and the book-sellers simply backed out of their way and ignored them as Princess Nell and the dark knight hacked and slashed at each other. When the dark knight fell dead and Princess Nell sheathed her sword, the commotion closed in about her again, like the waters of a turbulent river closing over a falling stone.

Nell picked up the book that the dark knight had been reading and found that it contained nothing but gibberish. It was written in some kind of a cipher.

She spent some time reconnoitering, looking for the

center of the place, and found no center. One stall was the same as the next. There was no tower, no throne room, no clear system of authority.

Examining the market stalls in more detail, she saw that each one included a man who did nothing but sit at a table and decipher books, writing them out on long sheets of foolscap and handing them over to other people, who would read through the contents, consult rule-books, and dictate responses to the man with the quill pen, who enciphered them and wrote them out in books that were then tossed out into the marketplace for delivery. The men with the quill pens, she noticed, always wore jeweled keys on chains around their necks; the key was apparently the badge of the cipherers' guild.

This castle proved fiendishly difficult to figure out, and Nell spent a few weeks working on it. Part of the problem was that this was the first castle Princess Nell had visited that was actually functioning as intended; the dark knight had not been able to foul the place up, probably because everything was done in ciphers here, and everything was decentralized. Nell discovered that a smoothly functioning system was much harder to puzzle out than one that was broken.

In the end, Princess Nell had to apprentice herself to a master cipherer and learn everything there was to know about codes and the keys that unlocked them. This done, she was given her own key, as a badge of her office, and found a job in one of the stalls enciphering and deciphering books. As it turned out, the key was more than just a decoration; rolled up inside its shaft was a strip of parchment inscribed with a long number that could be used to decipher a message, if the sender wanted you to decipher it.

From time to time she would go to the edge of the market, exchange a book for some gold, then go buy some food and drink.

On one of these trips, she saw another member of the cipherer's guild, also taking his break, and noticed that the key hanging around his neck looked familiar: it was one of the eleven keys that Nell and her Night Friends had taken from the Faery Kings and Queens! She concealed her excitement and followed this cipherer back to his stall, making a note of where he worked. Over the next few days, going from stall to stall and examining each cipherer, she was able to locate the rest of the eleven keys.

She was able to steal a look at the rule-books that her employers used to respond to the encoded messages. They were written in the same special language used at the previous two castles.

In other words, once Princess Nell had deciphered the messages, her stall functioned like another Turing machine.

It would have been easy enough to conclude that this whole castle was, like the others, a Turing machine. But the Primer had taught Nell to be very careful about making unwarranted assumptions. Just because her stall functioned according to Turing rules did not mean that all of the others did. And even if every stall in this castle was, in fact, a Turing machine, she still could not come to any fixed conclusions. She had seen riders carrying books to and from the castle, which meant that cipherers must be at work elsewhere in this kingdom. She could not verify that all of them were Turing machines.

It did not take long for Nell to attain prosperity here. After a few months (which in the Primer were summarized in as many sentences) her employers announced that they were getting more work than they could handle. They decided to split their operation. They erected a new stall at the edge of the market and gave Nell some of their rule-books.

They also obtained a new key for her. This was done by dispatching a special coded message to the Castle of King Coyote himself, which was three days' ride to the north. Seven days later, Nell's key came back to her in a scarlet box bearing the seal of King Coyote himself.

From time to time, someone would come around to her stall and offer to buy her out. She always turned them down but found it interesting that the keys could be bought and sold in this fashion.

All Nell needed was money, which she quickly accumulated through shrewd dealings in the market. Before long, all eleven of the keys were in her possession, and after liquidating her holdings and turning them into jewels, which she sewed into her clothes, she rode her horse out of the sixth castle and turned north, heading for the seventh: the Castle of King Coyote, and the ultimate goal of her life-long quest.

Nell goes to Madame Ping's Theatre; rumors of the Fists; an important client; assault of the Fists of Righteous Harmony; ruminations on the inner workings of ractives.

Like much that was done with nanotechnology, Feed lines were assembled primarily from a few species of small and uncomplicated atoms in the upper right-hand corner of Mendeleev's grid: carbon, nitrogen, oxygen, silicon, phosphorus, sulfur, and chlorine. The Fists of Righteous Harmony had discovered, to their enduring delight, that objects made of these atoms burned rather nicely once you got them going. The flat, low Yangtze Delta country east of Shanghai was a silk district well stocked with mulberry trees, which when felled, stacked, and burned beneath the Feed lines would eventually ignite them like road flares.

The Nipponese Feed was heavy on the phosphorus and burned with a furious white flame that lit up the night sky in several places as seen from the tall buildings in Pudong. One major line led toward Nanjing, one toward Suzhou, one toward Hangzhou: these distant flares inevitably led to rumors, among the hordes of refugees in Shanghai, that those cities were themselves burning.

The New Atlantan Feed had a higher sulfur content that, when burned, produced a plutonic reek that permeated everything for dozens of miles downwind, making the fires seem much closer than they really were. Shanghai was smelling pretty sulfurous as Nell walked into it across one of the bridges linking downtown Pudong with the much lower and older Bund. The Huang Pu had been too wide to bridge easily until nano had come along, so the four downtown bridges were made of the new materials and seemed impossibly fragile compared with the reinforced-concrete behemoths built to the north and south during the previous century.

A few days ago, working on a script in Madame Ping's offices far above, Nell had gazed out the window at a barge making its way down the river, pulled by a rickety old diesel tug, swathed in dun tarps. A few hundred meters upstream of this very bridge she was now crossing, the tarps had begun squirming and boiling, and a dozen young men in white tunics had jumped out from beneath, scarlet bands tied about their waists, scarlet ribbons around their wrists and foreheads. They had swarmed across the top of the barge hacking at ropes with knives, and the tarps had reluctantly and unevenly fallen away to expose a patchy new coat of red paint and, lined up on the top of the barge like a string of enormous firecrackers, several dozen compressed gas tanks, also painted a festive red for the occasion. Under the circumstances, she did not doubt for a moment that the men were Fists and the gas hydrogen or something else that burned well. But before they had been able to reach the bridge, the tanks had been burst and ignited by something too small and fast for Nell to see from her high post. The barge silently turned into a carbuncle of yellow flame that took up half the width of the Huang Pu, and though the diamond window filtered all of the heat out of its radiance, Nell was able to put her hand on the pane and feel the absorbed warmth, not much hotter than a person's skin. The whole operation had been touchingly hapless, in an age when a hand-size battery could contain as much energy as all those cylinders of gas. It had a quaint twentieth-century feel and made Nell oddly nostalgic for the days when dangerousness was a function of mass and bulk. The passives of that era were so fun to watch, with their big, stupid cars and big, stupid guns and big, stupid people.

Up- and downstream of the bridge, the funeral piers were crowded with refugee families heaving corpses into the Huang Pu; the emaciated bodies, rolled up in white sheets, looked like cigarettes. The Coastal Republic authorities had instituted a pass system on the bridges to prevent rural refugees from swarming across into the relatively spacious streets, plazas, atria, and lobbies of Pudong and gumming up the works for the office crowd. By the time Nell made it across, a couple of hundred refugees had already picked her out as a likely alms source and were waiting with canned demonstrations: women holding up their gaunt babies, or older children who were trained to hang comatose in their arms; men with open wounds, and legless gaffers dauntlessly knuckle-walking through the crowd, butting at people's knees. The taxi-drivers were stronger and more aggressive than the rurals, though, and had a fearsome reputation that created space around them in the crowd, and that was more valuable than an actual vehicle; a vehicle would always get stuck in traffic, but a taxi-driver's hat generated a magic force field that enabled the wearer to walk faster than anyone else.

The taxi-drivers converged on Nell too, and she picked out the biggest one and haggled with him, holding up fingers and essaying a few words in Shanghainese. When the numbers had climbed into the right range for him, he spun around suddenly to face the crowd. The suddenness of the movement drove people back, and the meter-long bamboo stick in his hand didn't hurt either. He stepped forward and Nell hurried after him, ignoring the myriad tuggings at her long skirts, trying not to wonder which of the beggars was a Fist with a concealed knife. If her clothes hadn't been made of untearable, uncuttable nanostuff, she would have been stripped naked within a block.

Madame Ping's was still doing a decent business. Its clientele were willing to put up with some inconvenience to get there. It was only a short distance from the bridgehead, and the Madame had put a few truculent taxi-drivers on retainer as personal escorts. The business was startlingly large given the scarcity of real estate in Shanghai; it occupied most of a five-story reinforced-concrete Mao Dynasty apartment block, having started out with just a couple of flats and expanded room by room as the years went on.

The reception area reminded one of a not-bad hotel lobby, except that it had no restaurant or bar; none of the clients wanted to see or be seen by any other. The desk was staffed by concierges whose job was to get the clients out of view as quickly as possible, and they did it so well that an uninitiated passerby might get the impression that Madame Ping's was some kind of a walk-in kidnapping operation.

One of these functionaries, a tiny woman who seemed oddly prim and asexual considering that she was wearing a black leather miniskirt, briskly took Nell to the top floor, where the large apartments had been built and elaborate scenarios were now realized for Madame Ping's clients.

As the writer, Nell of course never actually entered the same room as the client. The woman in the miniskirt escorted her into a nearby observation room, where a high-res cine feed from the next room covered most of one wall.

If she hadn't known it already, Nell would have seen from the client's uniform that he was a colonel in Her Majesty's Joint Forces. He was wearing a full dress uniform, and the various pins and medals on his coat indicated that he had spent a good deal of his career attached to various Protocol Enforcement units, been wounded in action several times, and displayed exceptional heroism on one occasion. In fact, it was clear that he was a rather important fellow. Reviewing the previous half-hour, Nell saw that, not surprisingly, he had arrived in mufti, carrying the uniform in a leather satchel. Wearing the uniform must be part of the scenario.

At the moment he was seated in a rather typical Victorian parlor, sipping tea from a Royal Albert china cup decorated with a somewhat agonistic briar rose pattern. He looked fidgety; he'd been kept waiting for half an hour, which was also part of the scenario. Madame Ping kept telling her that no one ever complained about having to wait too long for an orgasm; that men could do that to themselves any time they wanted, and that it was the business leading up to it that they would pay for. The biological readouts seemed to confirm Madame Ping's rule: Perspiration and pulse were rather high, and he was about half erect.

Nell heard the sound of a door opening. Switching to a different angle she saw a parlormaid entering the room. Her uniform was not as overtly sexy as most of the ones in Madame Ping's wardrobe department; the client was sophisticated. The woman was Chinese, but she played the role with the mid-Atlantic accent currently in vogue among neo-Victorians: "Mrs. Braithwaite will see you now."

The client stepped into an adjoining drawing room, where two women awaited him: a heavy Anglo in late middle age and a very attractive Eurasian woman, about thirty. Introductions were performed: The old woman was Mrs. Braithwaite, and the younger woman was her daughter. Mrs. was somewhat addled, and Miss was obviously running the show.

This section of the script never changed, and Nell had been over it a hundred times trying to troubleshoot it. The client went through a little speech in which he informed

Mrs. Braithwaite that her son Richard had been killed in action, displaying great heroism in the process, and that he was recommending him for a posthumous Victoria Cross.

Nell had already done the obvious, going back through the *Times* archives to see whether this was a reconstruction of an actual event in the client's life. As far as she could determine, it was more like a composite of many similar events, perhaps with a dollop of fantasy thrown in.

At this point, the old lady got a case of the vapors and had to be helped from the room by the parlormaid and other servants, leaving the client alone with Miss Braithwaite, who was taking the whole thing quite stoically. "Your composure is admirable, Miss Braithwaite," said the client, "but please be assured that no one will blame you for giving vent to your emotions at such a time." When the client spoke this line, there was an audible tremor of excitement in his voice.

"Very well, then," said Miss Braithwaite. She withdrew a small black box from her reticule and pressed a button. The client grunted and arched his back so violently that he fell out of his chair onto the rug, where he lay paralyzed.

"Mites—you have infected my body with some insidious nanosite," he gasped.

"In the tea."

"But that is impossible—most mites highly susceptible to thermal damage—boiling water would destroy them."

"You underestimate the capabilities of CryptNet, Colonel Napier. Our technology is advanced far beyond your knowledge—as you will discover during the next few days!"

"Whatever your plan is—be assured that it will fail!"

"Oh, I have no plan in particular," Miss Braithwaite said. "This is not a CryptNet operation. This is personal. You are responsible for the death of my brother Richard—and I will have you show the proper contrition."

"I assure you that I was as deeply saddened—"

She zapped him again. "I do not want your sadness," she said. "I want you to admit the truth: that you are responsible for his death!"

She pressed another button, which caused Colonel Napier's body to go limp. She and a maid wrestled him into a dumbwaiter and moved him down to a lower floor, where, after descending via the stairway, they tied him to a rack.

This was where the problem came in. By the time they had finished tying him up, he was sound asleep.

"He did it again," said the woman playing the role of Miss Braithwaite, addressing herself to Nell and anyone else who might be monitoring. "Six weeks in a row now."

When Madame Ping had explained this problem to Nell, Nell wondered what the problem was. Let the man sleep, as long as he kept coming and paid his bill. But Madame Ping knew her clients and feared that Colonel Napier was losing interest and might shift his business to some other establishment unless they put some variety into the scenario.

"The fighting has been very bad," the actress said. "He's probably exhausted."

"I don't think it's that," Nell said. She had now opened a private voice channel direct to the woman's eardrum. "I think it is a personal change."

"They never change, sweetheart," said the actress. "Once they get the taste, they have it forever."

"Yes, but different situations may trigger those feelings at different times of life," Nell said. "In the past it has been guilt over the deaths of his soldiers. Now he has made his peace. He has accepted his guilt, and so he accepts the punishment. There is no longer a contest of wills, because he has become submissive."

"So what do we do?"

"We must create a genuine contest of wills. We must force him to do something he really doesn't want to do," Nell said, thinking aloud. What would fit that bill?

"Wake him up," Nell said. "Tell him you were lying when you said this wasn't a CryptNet operation. Tell him you want real information. You want military secrets."

Miss Braithwaite sent the maid out for a bucket of cold water and heaved it over Colonel Napier's body. Then she played the role as Nell had suggested, and did it well; Madame Ping hired people who were good at improvisation, and since most of them never actually had to have sex with clients, she had no trouble finding good ones.

Colonel Napier seemed surprised, not unpleasantly so, at the script change. "If you suppose that I will divulge information that might lead to the deaths of more of my soldiers, you are sadly mistaken," he said. But his voice sounded a little bored and disappointed, and the bio read-outs coming in from the nanosites in his body did not show the full flush of sexual excitement that, presumably, he was paying for. They still were not meeting their client's needs:

On the private channel to Miss Braithwaite, Nell said, "He still doesn't get it. This isn't a fantasy scenario anymore. This is real. Madame Ping's is actually a CryptNet operation. We've been drawing him in for the last several years. Now he belongs to us, and he's going to give us information, and he's going to keep giving it to us, because he's our slave."

Miss Braithwaite acted the scene as suggested, making up more florid dialogue as she went along. Watching the bio readouts, Nell could see that Colonel Napier was just as scared and excited, now, as he had been on his very first visit to Madame Ping's several years ago (they kept records). They were making him feel young again, and fully alive.

"Are you connected with Dr. X?" Colonel Napier said.

"We'll ask the questions," Nell said.

"I shall do the asking. Lotus, give him twenty for that!" said Miss Braithwaite, and the maid went to work on Colonel Napier with a cane.

The rest of the session almost ran itself, which was good for Nell, because she had been startled by Napier's reference to Dr. X and had gone into a reverie, remembering comments that Harv had made about the same person many years ago.

Miss Braithwaite knew her job and understood Nell's strategy instantly: the scenario did not excite the client unless there was a genuine contest of wills, and the only way for them to create that contest was to force Napier to reveal real classified information. Reveal it he did, bit by bit, under the encouragement of Lotus's bamboo and Miss Braithwaite's voice. Most of it had to do with troop movements and other minutiae that he probably thought was terribly interesting. Nell didn't.

"Get more about Dr. X," she said. "Why did he assume a connection between CryptNet and Dr. X?"

After a few more minutes of whacking and verbal domination, Colonel Napier was ready to spill. "Big operation of ours for many years now—Dr. X is working in collusion with a high-level CryptNet figure, the Alchemist. Working on something they mustn't be allowed to have."

"Don't you dare hold back on me," Miss Braithwaite said.

But before she could extract more information about the Alchemist, the building was jolted by a tremendous force that sent thin cracks racing through the old concrete. In the silence that followed, Nell could hear women screaming all over the building, and a crackling, hissing sound as dust and sand sifted out of a fissure in the ceiling. Then her ears began to resolve another sound: men shouting, "Sha! Sha!"

"I suggest that someone has just breached the wall of your building with an explosive charge," Colonel Napier said, perfectly calm. "If you would be so good as to terminate the scenario now and release me, I shall try to make myself useful in whatever is to follow."

Whatever is to follow. The shouting meant simply, "Kill! Kill!" and was the battle cry of the Fists of Righteous Harmony.

Perhaps they wanted Colonel Napier. But it was more likely that they had decided to attack this place for its symbolic value as a den of barbarian decadence.

Miss Braithwaite and Lotus had already gotten Colonel Napier out of his restraints, and he was pulling on his trousers. "That we are not all dead implies that they are not making use of nanotechnological methods," he said professorially. "Hence this attack may safely be assumed to originate from a low-level neighborhood cell. The attackers probably believe the Fist doctrine that they are immune from all weapons. It never hurts, in these situations, to give them a reality check of some sort."

The door to Napier's room flew open, splinters of blond naked wood hissing across the floor. Nell watched, as though watching an old movie, as Colonel Napier drew a ridiculously shiny cavalry saber from its scabbard and ran it through the chest of the attacking Fist. This one fell back into another, creating momentary confusion; Napier took advantage of it, methodically planting his feet in a rather prissy-looking stance, squaring his shoulders, calmly reaching out, as if he were using the saber to poke around in a dark closet, and twitching the point beneath the second Fist's chin, incidentally cutting his throat in the process. A third Fist had gotten into the room by this point, this one bearing a long pole with a knife lashed to the end of it with the gray polymer ribbon peasants used for rope. But as he tried to wheel the weapon around, its butt end got tangled up in the rack to which Napier had lately been tied. Napier stepped forward cautiously, checking his footing as he went, as if he did not want to get any blood on his boots, parried a belated attack, and stabbed the Fist in the thorax three times in quick succession.

Someone kicked at the door to Nell's room.

"Ah," Colonel Napier sighed, when it seemed clear that there were no more attackers in this party, "it is really very singular that I happen to have brought the full dress uniform, as edged weapons are not a part of our usual kit."

Several kicks had failed to open Nell's door, which unlike the ones in the scenario rooms was made of a modern substance and could not possibly be broken in that way. But Nell could hear voices out in the corridor and suspected that contrary to Napier's speculation, they might have nanotech devices of a very primitive sort—small explosives, say, capable of blowing doors open.

She ditched her long dress, which would only get in the way, and got down on knees and elbows to peer through the crack under the door. There were two pairs of feet. She could hear them conversing in low, businesslike tones.

Nell opened the door suddenly with one hand, reaching through with the other to shove a fountain pen into the throat of the Fist standing closest to the door. The other one reached for an old automatic rifle slung over his shoulder. This gave Nell more than enough time to kick him in the knee, which may or may not have done permanent damage but certainly threw him off balance. The Fist kept trying to bring his rifle to bear, as Nell kicked him over and over again. In the end she was able to twist the rifle free from his feeble one-handed grasp, whirl it around, and butt him in the head.

The Fist with the pen in his neck was sitting on the floor watching her calmly. She aimed the rifle his way, and he held up one hand and looked down and away. His wound was bleeding, but not all that much; she had ruined his week but not hit anything big. She reflected that it was probably a healthy thing for him in the long run to be rid of the superstition that he was immune to weapons.

Constable Moore had taught her a thing or two about

rifles. She stepped back into her room, locked the door, and devoted a minute or so to familiarizing herself with its controls, checking the magazine (only half full) and firing a single round (into the door, which stopped it) just to make sure it worked.

She was trying to suppress a flashback to the screwdriver incident. This frightened her until she realized that this time around she was much more in control of the situation. Her conversations with the Constable had not been without effect.

Then she made her way down the corridors and stairwells toward the lobby, slowly gathering a retinue of terrified young women along her way. They passed a few clients, mostly male and mostly European, who had been pulled from their scenario rooms and crudely hacked up by the Fists. Three times she had to fire, surprised each time at how complicated it was. Accustomed to the Primer, Nell had to make allowances when functioning in the real world.

She and her followers found Colonel Napier in the lobby, about three-quarters dressed, carrying on a memorable edged-weapons duel with a couple of Fists who had, perhaps, been left there to keep the path of escape open. Nell considered trying to shoot at the Fists but decided against it, because she did not trust her marksmanship and also because she was mesmerized by the entire scene.

Nell would have been dazzled by Colonel Napier if she had not recently seen him strapped to a rack. Still, there was something about this very contradiction that made him, and by extension all Victorian men, fascinating to her. They lived a life of nearly perfect emotional denial—a form of asceticism as extreme as that of a medieval stylite. Yet they did have emotions, the same as anyone else, and only vented them in carefully selected circumstances.

Napier calmly impaled a Fist who had tripped and fallen, then turned his attention to a new antagonist, a formidable character skilled with a real sword. The duel between Western and Eastern martial arts moved back and forth across the lobby floor, the two combatants staring directly into one another's eyes and trying to intuit the other's thoughts and emotional state. The actual thrusts and parries and ripostes, when they came, were too rapid to be understood. The Fist's style was quite beautiful to watch, involving many slow movements that looked like the stretching of large felines at the zoo. Napier's style was almost perfectly boring: He moved about in a crabbed stance, watched his opponent calmly, and apparently did a lot of deep thinking.

Watching Napier at work, watching the medals and braid swinging and glinting on his jacket, Nell realized that it was precisely their emotional repression that made the Victorians the richest and most powerful people in the world. Their ability to submerge their feelings, far from pathological, was rather a kind of mystical art that gave them nearly magical power over Nature and over the more intuitive tribes. Such was also the strength of the Nipponese.

Before the struggle could be resolved, a smart flechette, horsefly-size, trailing a whip antenna as thick as a hair and as long as a finger, hissed in through a broken window and thunked into the back of the Fist's neck. It did not strike very hard but must have shot some poison into his brain. He sat down quickly on the floor, closed his eyes, and died in that position.

"Not very chivalrous," Colonel Napier said distastefully. "I suppose I have some bureaucrat up on New Chusan to thank for that."

A cautious tour of the building turned up several more Fists who had died in the same fashion. Outside, the same old crowd of refugees, beggars, pedestrians, and cargo-carrying bicyclists streamed on, about as undisturbed as the Yangtze.

Colonel Napier did not return to Madame Ping's the next week, but Madame Ping did not blame Nell for the loss of his custom. To the contrary, she praised Nell for having correctly divined Napier's wishes and for improvising so well. "A fine performance," she said.

Nell had not really thought of her work as a performance, and for some reason Madame Ping's choice of words provoked her in a way that kept her awake late that night, staring into the darkness above her bunk.

Since she had been very small, she had made up stories and recited them to the Primer, which were often digested and incorporated into the Primer's stories. It had come naturally to Nell to do the same work for Madame Ping. But now her boss was calling it a performance, and Nell had to admit that it was, in a way. Her stories were being digested, not by the Primer, but by another human being, becoming a part of that person's mind.

That seemed simple enough, but the notion troubled her for a reason that did not become clear until she had lain half-asleep and fretted over it for several hours.

Colonel Napier did not know her and probably never would. All of the intercourse between him and Nell had been mediated through the actress pretending to be Miss Braithwaite, and through various technological systems.

Nonetheless she had touched him deeply. She had penetrated farther into his soul than any lover. If Colonel Napier had chosen to return the following week and Nell had not been present to make up the story for him, would he have missed her? Nell suspected that he would have. From his point of view, some indefinable essence would have been wanting, and he would have departed unsatisfied.

If this could happen to Colonel Napier in his dealings with Madame Ping's, could it happen to Nell in her dealings with the Primer? She had always felt that there was some essence in the book, something that understood her and even loved her, something that forgave her when she did wrong and appreciated what she did right.

When she'd been very young, she hadn't questioned this at all; it had been part of the book's magic. More recently she had understood it as the workings of a parallel computer of enormous size and power, carefully programmed to understand the human mind and give it what it needed.

Now she wasn't so sure. Princess Nell's recent travels through the lands of King Coyote, and the various castles with their increasingly sophisticated computers that were, in the end, nothing more than Turing machines, had caught her up in a bewildering logical circle. In Castle Turing she had learned that a Turing machine could not really understand a human being. But the Primer was, itself, a Turing machine, or so she suspected; so how could it understand Nell?

Could it be that the Primer was just a conduit, a technological system that mediated between Nell and some human being who really loved her? In the end, she knew, this was basically how all ractives worked. The idea was too alarming to consider at first, and so she circled around it cautiously, poking at it from different directions, like a cavewoman discovering fire for the first time. But as she settled in closer, she found that it warmed her and satisfied her, and by the time her mind wandered into sleep, she had become dependent upon it and would not consider going back into the cold and dark place where she had been traveling for so many years.

Carl Hollywood returns to Shanghai; his forebears
in the territory of the Lone Eagles;
Mrs. Kwan's teahouse.

Heavy rains had come rolling into Shanghai from the West, like a harbinger of the Fists of Righteous Harmony and the thundering herald of the coming Celestial Kingdom. Stepping off the airship from London, Carl Hollywood at once felt himself in a different Shanghai from the one he had left; the old city had always been wild, but in a sophisticated urban way, and now it was wild like a frontier town. He sensed this ambience before he even left the Aerodrome; it leaked in from the streets, like ozone before a thunderstorm. Looking out the windows, he could see a heavy rain rushing down, knocking all the nanotech out of the air and down into the gutters, whence it would eventually stain the Huang Pu and then the Yangtze. Whether it was the wild atmosphere or the prospect of being rained upon, he stopped his porters short of the main exit doors so that he could change hats. The hatboxes were stacked on one of the carts; his bowler went into the smallest and topmost box, which was empty, and then he yanked the largest box out from underneath, popping the stack, and took out a ten-gallon Stetson of breathtaking width and sweep, almost like a head-mounted umbrella. Casting an eye into the street, where a rushing brown stream carried litter, road dust, cholera-ridden sewage, and tons of captive nanotech toward the storm drains, he slipped off his leather shoes and exchanged them for a pair of hand-tooled cowboy boots, made from hides of gaudy reptiles and avians, the pores of which had been corked with mites that would keep his feet dry even if he chose to wade through the gutters.

Thus reconfigured, Carl Hollywood stepped out into the streets of Shanghai. As he came out the doors of the Aerodrome, his duster billowed in the cold wind of the storm and even the beggars stepped away from him. He paused to light a cigar before proceeding and was not molested; even the refugees, who were starving or at least claimed to be, derived more enjoyment from simply looking at him than they would have from the coins in his pocket. He walked the four blocks to his hotel, pursued doggedly by the porters and by a crowd of youngsters entranced by the sight of a real cowboy.

Carl's grandfather was a Lone Eagle who had ridden out from the crowding and squalor of Silicon Valley in the 1990s and homesteaded a patch of abandoned ranch along a violent cold river on the eastern slope of the Wind River Range. From there he had made a comfortable living as a freelance coder and consultant. His wife had left him for the bright lights and social life of California and been startled when he had managed to persuade a judge that he was better equipped to raise their son than she was. Grandfather had raised Carl Hollywood's father mostly in the out-of-doors, hunting and fishing and chopping wood when he wasn't sitting inside studying his calculus. As the years went by, they had gradually been joined by like-minded sorts with similar stories to tell, so that by the time of the Interregnum they had formed a community of several hundred, loosely spread over a few thousand square miles of near-wilderness but, in the electronic sense, as tightly knit as any small village in the Old West. Their technological prowess, prodigious wealth, and numerous large weapons had made them a dangerous group, and the odd pickup-truck-driving desperadoes who attacked an isolated ranch had found themselves surrounded and outgunned with cataclysmic swiftness. Grandfather loved to tell stories of these criminals, how they had tried to excuse their own crimes by pleading that they were economically disadvantaged or infected with the disease of substance abuse, and how the Lone Eagles—many of whom had overcome poverty or addiction themselves—had dispatched them with firing squads and left them posted around the edge of their territory as NO TRESPASSING signs that even the illiterate could read.

The advent of the Common Economic Protocol had settled things down and, in the eyes of the old-timers, begun to soften and ruin the place. There was nothing like getting up at three in the morning and riding the defensive perimeter in subzero cold, with a loaded rifle, to build up one's sense of responsibility and community. Carl Hollywood's clearest and best memories were of going on such rides with his father. But as they squatted on packed snow boiling coffee over a fire, they would listen to the radio and hear stories about the jihad raging across Xinjiang, driving the Han back into the east, and about the first incidents of nanotech terrorism in Eastern Europe. Carl's father didn't have to tell him that their community was rapidly acquiring the character of a historical theme park, and that before long they would have to give up the mounted patrols for more modern defensive systems.

Even after those innovations had been made and the community had mostly joined up with the First Distributed Republic, Carl and his father and grandfather had continued to do things in the old way, hunting elk and heating their houses with wood-burning stoves and sitting behind their computer screens in dark rooms late into the night hand-tooling code in assembly language. It was a purely male household (Carl's mother had died when he was nine years old, in a rafting accident), and Carl had fled the place as soon as he'd found a way, going to San Francisco, then New York, then London, and making himself useful in theatrical productions. But the older he got, the more he understood in how many ways he was rooted in the place where he grew up, and he never felt it more purely than he did striding down a crowded street in a Shanghai thunderstorm, puffing on a thick cigar and watching the rain dribble from the rim of his hat. The most intense and clear sensations of his life had flooded into his young and defenseless mind during his first dawn patrol, knowing the desperadoes were out there somewhere. He kept returning to these memories in later life, trying to recapture the same purity and intensity of sensation, or trying to get his ractors to feel it. Now for the first time in thirty years he felt the same thing, this time on the streets of Shanghai, hot and pulsing on the edge of a

dynastic rebellion, like the arteries of an old man about to
have his first orgasm in years.

He merely touched base at his hotel, where he stuffed
the pockets of his coat with a sheaf of foolscap, a fountain
pen, a silver box loaded with cigars like rounds in an ammo
clip, and some tiny containers of nanosnuff that he could use
to adjust the functioning of his brain and body. He also
hefted a heavy walking-stick, a real wizard's staff loaded
with security aerostats that would shepherd him back to the
hotel in the event of a riot. Then he returned once more to
the streets, shouldering for a mile through the crowd until
he reached a teahouse where he had passed many long
nights during his tenure at the Parnasse. Old Mrs. Kwan
welcomed him warmly, bowing many times and showing
him to his favorite corner table where he could look out on
the intersection of Nanjing Road and a narrow side street
jammed with tiny market stalls. All he could see now were
the backs and buttocks of people in the street, jammed up
against the glass by the pressure of the crowd. He ordered a
big pot of his favorite green tea, the most expensive kind,
picked in April when the leaves were tender and young, and
spread out his sheets of foolscap across the table. This
teahouse was fully integrated into the worldwide media network, and so the pages automatically jacked themselves in.
Under Carl Hollywood's murmured commands they began
to fill themselves with columns of animated text and windows bearing images and cine feeds. He took his first sip of
tea—always the best one—withdrew his big fountain pen
from his pocket, removed the lid, and touched it to the paper. He began to inscribe commands onto the page, in words
and drawings. As he finished the words, they were enacted
before him, and as he drew the lines between the boxes and
circles, links were made and information flowed.

At the bottom of the page he wrote the word MI-
RANDA and drew a circle around it. It was not connected to
anything else in the diagram yet. He hoped that before long
it would be. Carl Hollywood worked on his papers late into
the night, and Mrs. Kwan continued to replenish his teapot
and to bring him little sweets and decorated the edge of his
table with candles as night fell and the teahouse darkened,
for she remembered that he liked to work by candlelight.
The Chinese people outside, separated from him by half an

inch of crosslinked diamond, watched with their noses making white ellipses against the pane, their faces glowing in the
candlelight like ripe peaches hanging in dark lush foliage.

*The Hackworths in transit, and in London; the East
End; a remarkable boatride; Dramatis Personae;
a night at the theatre.*

Smooth, fine-grained arctic clouds undulated slowly like
snow drifts into the distance, a thousand miles looking like
the width of a front yard, lit but not warmed by a low apri-
cot sun that never quite went down. Fiona lay on her stomach on the top bunk, looking out the window, watching her
breath condense on the pane and then evaporate in the
parched air.

"Father?" she said, very softly, to see if he was awake.

He wasn't, but he woke up quickly, as if he'd been in
one of those dreams that just skims beneath the surface of
consciousness, like an airship clipping a few cloud-tops.
"Yes?"

"Who is the Alchemist? Why are you looking for
him?"

"I would rather not explain why I'm looking for him.
Let us say that I have incurred obligations that want settling." Her father seemed more preoccupied with the second
part of the question than she'd expected, and his voice was
steeped in regret.

"Who is he?" she insisted gently.

"Oh. Well, my darling, if I knew that, I'd have found
him."

"Father!"

"What sort of a person is he? I haven't been afforded
many clues, unfortunately. I've tried to draw some deduc-
tions from the sorts of people who are looking for him, and
the sort of person I am."

"Pardon me, Father, but what bearing does your own nature have on that of the Alchemist?"

"More than one knowledgeable sort has arrived at the conclusion that I'm just the right man to find this fellow, even though I know nothing of criminals and espionage and so forth. I'm just a nanotechnological engineer."

"That's not true, Father! You're ever so much more than that. You know so many stories—you told me so many, when you were gone, remember?"

"I suppose so," he allowed, strangely diffident.

"And I read it every night. And though the stories were about faeries and pirates and djinns and such, I could always sense that you were behind them. Like the puppeteer pulling the strings and imbuing them with voices and personalities. So I think you're more than an engineer. It's just that you need a magic book to bring it out."

"Well . . . that's a point I had not considered," her father said, his voice suddenly emotional. She fought the temptation to peer over the edge of the bed and look at his face, which would have embarrassed him. Instead she curled up in her bed and closed her eyes.

"Whatever you may think of me, Fiona—and I must say I am pleasantly surprised that you think of me so favourably—to those who despatched me on this errand, I am an engineer. Without being arrogant, I might add that I have advanced rapidly in that field and attained a position of not inconsiderable responsibility. As this is the only characteristic that distinguishes me from other men, it can be the only reason I was chosen to find the Alchemist. From this I infer that the Alchemist is himself a nanotechnological researcher of some sophistication, and that he is thought to be developing a product that is of interest to more than one of the Powers."

"Are you talking about the Seed, Father?"

He was silent for a few moments. When he spoke again, his voice was high and tight. "The Seed. How did you know about the Seed?"

"You told me about it, Father. You told me it was a dangerous thing, and that Protocol Enforcement mustn't allow it to be created. And besides . . ."

"Besides what?"

She was on the verge of reminding him that her

dreams had been filled with seeds for the last several years, and that every story she had seen in her Primer had been replete with them: seeds that grew up into castles; dragon's teeth that grew up into soldiers; seeds that sprouted into giant beanstalks leading to alternate universes in the clouds; and seeds, given to hospitable, barren couples by itinerant crones, that grew up into plants with bulging pods that contained happy, kicking babies.

But she sensed that if she mentioned this directly, he would slam the steel door in her face—a door that was tantalizingly cracked open at the moment.

"Why do you think that Seeds are so interesting?" she essayed.

"They are interesting inasmuch as a beaker of nitroglycerin is interesting," he said. "They are subversive technology. You are not to speak of Seeds again, Fiona—CryptNet agents could be anywhere, listening to our conversation."

Fiona sighed. When her father spoke freely, she could sense the man who had told her the stories. When certain subjects were broached, he drew down his veil and became just another Victorian gentleman. It was irksome. But she could sense how the same characteristic, in a man who was not her father, could be provocative. It was such an obvious weakness that neither she nor any woman could resist the temptation to exploit it—a mischievous and hence tantalizing notion that was to occupy much of Fiona's thinking for the next few days, as they encountered other members of their tribe in London.

After a simple dinner of beer and pasties in a pub on the fringes of the City, they rode south across the Tower Bridge, pierced a shallow layer of posh development along the right bank of the river, and entered into Southwark. As in other Atlantan districts of London, Feed lines had been worked into the sinews of the place, coursing through utility tunnels, clinging to the clammy undersides of bridges, and sneaking into buildings through small holes bored in the foundations. The tiny old houses and flats of this once impoverished quarter had mostly been refurbished into toeholds for young Atlantans from all around the Anglosphere, poor in equity but rich in expectations, who had come to the great city to incubate their careers. The businesses on the ground floors tended to be pubs, coffeehouses, and music halls. As father and daughter worked their way east, generally paralleling the river, the lustre that was so evident near the approaches to the bridge began to wear thin in places, and the ancient character of the neighborhood began to assert itself, as the bones of the knuckles reveal their shape beneath the stretched skin of a fist. Wide gaps developed between the waterfront developments, allowing them to look across the river into a district whose blanket of evening fog was already stained with the carcinogenic candy-colored hues of big mediatrons.

Fiona Hackworth noticed a glow in the air, which resolved into a constellation when she blinked and focused. A pinprick of green light, an infinitesimal chip of emerald, touched the surface of her eye, expanding into a cloud of light. She blinked twice, and it was gone. Sooner or later it and many others would make their way to the corners of her eyes, giving her a grotesque appearance. She drew a handkerchief from her sleeve and wiped her eyes. The presence of so many lidar-emitting mites prompted her to realize that they had been infiltrating a great expanse of fog for some minutes without really being aware of it; moisture from the river was condensing around the microscopic guardians of the border. Colored light flashed vaguely across the screen of fog before them, silhouetting a stone column planted in the center of the road: wings of a gryphon, horn of a unicorn, crisp and black against a lurid cosmos. A constable stood beside the pediment, symbolically guarding the bar. He nodded to the Hackworths and mumbled something gruff but polite through his chinstrap as father and daughter rode out of New Atlantis and into a gaudy clave full of loutish thetes scrumming and chanting before the entrances of pubs. Fiona caught sight of an old Union Jack, then did a double-take and realized that the limbs of the St. Andrew's Cross had been enhanced with stars, like the Confederate Battle Flag. She gave her chevaline a nudge and pulled up nearly abreast with her father.

Then the city became darker and quieter, though no less crowded, and for a few blocks they saw only dark-haired men with mustaches and women who were nothing more than columns of black fabric. Then Fiona smelled anise and garlic, and they passed into Vietnamese territory for a short time. She would have enjoyed stopping at one of the sidewalk cafés for a bowl of pho, but her father rode on, pursuing the tide that was ebbing down the Thames, and in a few more minutes they had come once again to the bank. It was lined with ancient masonry warehouses—a category of structure now so obsolete as to defy explanation—which had been converted into offices.

A pier rode on the surface of the river, riding up and down on the tide, linked to the rim of the granite embankment by a hinged gangway. A shaggy black vessel was tied up to the pier, but it was completely unlit, visible only by its black shadow against the charcoal-gray water. After the chevalines had planted themselves and the Hackworths had dismounted, they were able to hear low voices coming from below.

John Hackworth withdrew some tickets from his breast pocket and asked them to illuminate themselves; but they were printed on old-fashioned paper that did not contain its own energy source, and so he finally had to use the microtorch dangling from his watch chain. Apparently satisfied that they had arrived at the right place, he offered Fiona his arm and escorted her down the gangway to the pier. A tiny flickering light bobbed toward them and resolved into an Afro-Caribbean man, wearing rimless glasses and carrying an antique hurricane lamp. Fiona watched his face as his enormous eyes, yellowed like antique ivory billiard balls, scanned their tickets. His skin was rich and warm and glowing in the light of the candle, and he smelled faintly of citrus combined with something darker and less ingratiating. When he was finished, he looked up, not at the Hackworths but off into the distance, turned his back, and ambled away. John Hackworth stood there for a few moments, awaiting instructions, then straightened, squared his shoulders, and led Fiona across the pier to the boat.

It was eight or ten meters long. There was no gangway, and persons already on board had to reach out and clutch their arms and pull them in, a breach of formality that happened so quickly that they had no time to become uncomfortable.

The boat was basically a large flat open tub, not much more than a life raft, with some controls in the bow and some sort of modern and hence negligibly small propulsion system built into the stern. As their eyes adjusted to the dim light scattering through the fog, they could see perhaps a dozen other passengers around the edge of the boat, seated so that wakes from passing vessels would not upset them. Seeing wisdom in this, John led Fiona to the only remaining open space, and they sat down between two other groups: a trio of young Nipponese men forcing cigarettes on one another, and a man and woman in bohemian-but-expensive clothes, sipping lager from cans and conversing in Canadian accents.

The man from the pier cast off the painters and vaulted aboard. Another functionary had taken the controls and gently accelerated into the current, cutting the throttle at one point and swinging her about into an oncoming wake. When the boat entered the main channel and came up to speed, it very quickly became chilly, and all the passengers murmured, demanding more warmth from their thermogenic clothing. The Afro-Caribbean man made a circuit lugging a heavy chest stocked with cans of lager and splits of pinot noir. Conversation stopped for several minutes as the passengers, all driven by the same primal impulses, turned their faces into the cool wind and relaxed into the gentle thumping of hull against waves.

The trip took the better part of an hour. After several minutes, conversation resumed, most of the passengers remaining within their little groups. The refreshment chest made a few more circuits. John Hackworth began to realize, from a few subtleties, that one of the Nipponese youths was much more intoxicated than he was letting on and had probably spent a few hours in a dockside pub before reaching the pier. He took a drink from the chest every time it came by, and half an hour into the ride, he rose unsteadily to his feet, leaned over the edge, and threw up. John turned to smirk at his daughter. The boat struck an unseen wave, rolling sideways into the trough. Hackworth clutched first at the railing and then at his daughter's arm.

Fiona screamed. She was staring over John's shoulder at the Nipponese youths. John turned around to see that there were only two of them now; the sick one was gone, and the other two had flung their bellies across the gunwale and stretched out their arms, fingers like white rays shining into the black water. John felt Fiona's arm pull free from his grasp, and as he turned toward her, he just saw her vaulting over the rail.

It was over before he had an opportunity to get really scared. The crew dealt with the matter with a practiced efficiency that suggested to Hackworth that the Nipponese man was really an actor, the entire incident part of the production. The Afro-Caribbean man cursed and shouted for them to hang on, his voice pure and powerful as a Stradivarius cello, a stage voice. He inverted the cooler, dumping out all the beer and wine, then snapped it shut and flung it over the stern as a life preserver. Meanwhile the pilot was swinging the boat round. Several passengers, including Hackworth, had turned on microtorches and focused their beams on Fiona, whose skirts had inflated as she'd jumped in feet-first and now surrounded her like a raft of flowers. With one hand she was clutching the Nipponese man's collar, and with the other, the handle of the ice chest. She did not have the strength or buoyancy to hold the drunken man out of the water, and so both of them were swamped by the estuary's rolling waves.

The man with the dreadlocks hauled Fiona out first and handed her off to her father. The fabricules making up her clothing—countless mites linked elbow-to-elbow in a two-dimensional array—went to work pumping away the water trapped in the interstices. Fiona was wreathed in a sinuous veil of mist that burned with the captured light of the torches. Her thick red hair had been freed from the confines of her hat, which had been torn away by the waves and now fell about her in a cape of fire.

She was looking defiantly at Hackworth, whose adrenal glands had finally jumped into the endocrinological fray. When he saw his daughter in this way, it felt as though someone were inexorably sliding a hundred-pound block of ice up the length of his spine. When the sensation reached his medulla, he staggered and nearly had to sit down. She had somehow flung herself through an unknown and unmarked barrier and become supernatural, a naiad rising from the waves cloaked in fire and steam. In some rational compartment of his mind that had now become irrelevant, Hackworth wondered whether Dramatis Personae (for this was the name of the troupe that was running this show) had got some nanosites into his system, and if so what exactly they were doing to his mind.

Water streamed from Fiona's skirts and ran between the floorboards, and then she was dry, except for her face and hair. She wiped her face on her sleeves, ignoring her father's proffered handkerchief. No words passed between them, and they did not embrace, as if Fiona were conscious now of the impact she was having upon her father and all the others—a faculty that, Hackworth supposed, must be highly acute in sixteen-year-old girls. By now the Nipponese man was just about finished coughing water out of his lungs and gasping piteously for air. As soon as he had the airways up and running, he spoke hoarsely and lengthily. One of his companions translated. "He says that we are not alone—that the water is filled with spirits—that they spoke to him. He followed them beneath the waves. But feeling his spirit about to leave his body, he felt fear and swam to the surface and was saved by the young woman. He says that the spirits are talking to all of us, and we must listen to them!"

This was, needless to say, embarrassing, and so all of the passengers doused their torches and turned their backs on the stricken passenger. But when Hackworth's eyes had adjusted, he took another look at this man and saw that the exposed portions of his flesh had begun to radiate colored light.

He looked at Fiona and saw that a band of white light encircled her head like a tiara, bright enough that it shone red through her hair, with a jewel centered upon her forehead. Hackworth marveled at this sight from a distance, knowing that she wanted to be free of him for now.

Fat lights hung low above the water, describing the envelopes of great ships, sliding past each other as their parallax shifted with the steady progress of the boat. They had come to a place near the mouth of the estuary but not on the usual shipping lanes, where ships lay at anchor awaiting shifts in tides, winds, or markets. One constellation of lights did not move but only grew larger as they drew toward it. Experimenting with shadows and examining the pattern of light cast upon the water from this vessel, Hackworth concluded that the lights were being deliberately shone into their faces so that they could not make any judgments about the nature of the source.

The fog slowly congealed into a wall of rust, so vast and featureless that it might have been ten or a hundred feet distant. The helmsman waited until they were about to ram it, then cut the engines. The raft lost speed instantly and nuzzled the hull of the big ship. Chains, slimy and dripping, descended from the firmament, diverging in Hackworth's view like radiance emanating from some heavy-industrial demigod, clanking harbingers of iron that the crew, heads thrown back ecstatically, throats bared to this kinky revelation, received into their bosoms. They snapped the chains onto metal loops fixed into the floor of the boat. Shackled, the boat rose free of the water and began to ascend the wall of rust, which soared vaguely into the infinite fog. Suddenly there was a railing, an open deck beyond it, pools of light here and there, a few red cigar-coals reciprocating through space. The deck swung under and rose to shove at the hull of the little boat. As they disembarked, they could see similar boats scattered about.

"Dodgy" did not begin to describe the reputation of Dramatis Personae in the New Atlantan parts of London, but that was the adjective they always used anyway, delivered in a near-whisper, with brows raised nearly into the hairline and eyes glancing significantly over the shoulder. It had quickly become clear to Hackworth that a man could get a bad reputation simply for having known that Dramatis Personae existed—at the same time, it was clear that almost everyone had heard about it. Rather than being spattered with any more opprobrium, he had sought the tickets among other tribes.

After all this it did not surprise him in the least to see that most of the attendees were fellow Victorians, and not just young bachelors having a night out, but ostensibly respectable couples, strolling the decks in their top hats and veils.

Fiona vaulted out of the boat before it even touched the deck of the ship and vanished. She had repatterned her dress, ditching the chintzy flowered pattern for basic white, and skipped off into the darkness, her integral tiara glowing like a halo. Hackworth took a slow turn around the deck, watching his fellow-tribesmen trying to solve the following problem: get close enough to another couple to recognize them without getting so close that they can recognize you.

From time to time, couples recognized each other simultaneously and had to say something: the women tittered wickedly, and the men laughed from their bellies and called each other scoundrels, the words glancing off the deckplates and burying themselves in the fog like arrows fired into a bale of cotton.

Some kind of amplified music emanated from compartments below; atonal power chords came up through the deck like seismic disturbances. She was a bulk cargo carrier, now empty and bobbing, surprisingly jittery for something so big.

Hackworth was alone and separate from all humanity, a feeling he had grown up with, like a childhood friend living next door. He had found Gwen by some miracle and lost touch with that old friend for a few years, but now he and solitude were back together, out for a stroll, familiar and comfortable. A makeshift bar amidships had drawn a dozen or so congregants, but Hackworth knew that he could not join in with them. He had been born without the ability to blend and socialize as some are born without hands.

"Standing above it all?" said a voice. "Or standing aside perhaps?"

It was a man in a clown outfit. Hackworth recognized it, vaguely, as an advertising fetish for an old American fast-food chain. But the costume was conspicuously ill-used, as if it were the sole garment of a refugee. It had been patched all over with swatches of chintz, Chinese silk, studded black leather, charcoal-gray pinstripe, and jungle camo. The clown wore integral makeup—his face glowed like an injection-molded plastic toy from the previous century with a light bulb stuck inside the head. It was disturbing to see him talk, like watching one of those animated CAT scans of a man swallowing.

"Are you of it? Or just in it?" the Clown said, and looked at Hackworth expectantly.

As soon as Hackworth had realized, quite some time ago, that this Dramatis Personae thing was going to be some kind of participatory theatre, he had been dreading this moment: his first cue. "Please excuse me," he said in a tense and not altogether steady voice, "this is not my milieu."

"That's for damn fucking sure," said the Clown. "Put these on," he continued, taking something out of his pocket.

He reached out to Hackworth, who was two or three meters away from him—but shockingly, his hand detached itself from his arm and flew through the air, the smutty white glove like a dirty ball of ice tumbling elliptically through the inner planets. It shoved something into Hackworth's breast pocket and then withdrew; but because Hackworth was watching, it described a smooth sudden figure-eight pattern in space before reattaching itself to the stump of the forearm. Hackworth realized that the clown was mechanical. "Put 'em on and be yourself, mister alienated loner steppenwolf bemused distant meta-izing technocrat rationalist fucking shithead." The Clown spun on his heel to leave; his floppy clown shoes were built around some kind of trick heel with a swivel built in, so that when he spun on his heel he really did spin on his heel, performing several complete rotations before stopping with his back turned to Hackworth and storming away. "Revolutionary, ain't it?" he snapped.

The thing in Hackworth's pocket was a pair of dark sunglasses: wraparounds with a glimmering rainbow finish, the sort of thing that, decades ago, would have been worn by a Magnum-slinging rebel cop in a prematurely canceled television series. Hackworth unfolded them and slid the polished ends of the bows cautiously over his temples. As the lenses approached, he could see light coming from them; they were phenomenoscopes. Though in this context, the word *phantascope* might have been more appropriate. The image grew to fill his sight but would not focus until he put them all the way on, so he reluctantly plummeted into the hallucination until it resolved, and just then the bows behind his ears came alive, stretched, and grew around the back of his skull like a rubber band snapping in reverse, joining in the back to form an unbreakable band. "Release," Hackworth said, and then ran through a litany of other standard yuvree commands. The spectacles would not release his head. Finally, a cone of light pierced space from somewhere above and behind him and splashed across a stage. Footlights came up, and a man in a top hat emerged from behind a curtain. "Welcome to your show," he said. "You can remove the glasses at any time by securing a standing ovation from not less than ninety percent of the audience." Then the lights and curtain vanished, and Hackworth was left with what he had seen before, namely, a cybernetically enhanced night-vision rendering of the deck of the ship.

He tried a few more commands. Most phenomenoscopes had a transparent mode, or at least translucent, that allowed the wearer to view what was really there. But these ones were doggedly opaque and would only show him a mediatronic rendering of the scene. The strolling and chatting theatregoers were represented by preposterously oversimplified wire-frames, a display technology unused these eighty years or so, clearly intended to irritate Hackworth. Each figure had a large placard strapped to its chest:

JARED MASON GRIFFIN III, aged 35
(too late to become an interesting
character like you!)
Nephew of an earl-level Equity Lord
(don't you envy him?)
Married to that sunken bitch on his right
They go on these little escapades
to escape their own crippled lives.
(why are you here?)

Hackworth looked down and tried to read the placard on his own chest but couldn't focus on it.

When he walked around the deck, his viewpoint changed correspondingly. There was also a standard interface that enabled him to "fly" around the ship; Hackworth himself remained in one fixed location, of course, but his viewpoint in the spectacles became unlinked to his real coordinates. Whenever he used this mode, the following legend was superimposed on his view in giant flashing red block letters:

JOHN PERCIVAL HACKWORTH'S
GODLIKE PERSPECTIVE

sometimes accompanied by a cartoon of a wizardly sort of fellow sitting atop a mountain peering down into a village of squalid midgets. Because of this annoyance, Hackworth did not use this feature very frequently. But on his initial reconnaissance, he discovered a few items of interest. For one thing, the Nipponese fellow who had got pissed and fallen overboard had encountered a group of several other people who had, by a remarkable coincidence, also fallen out of their boats on the way here, and who upon being rescued had all begun to emit colored light and see visions that they insisted on recounting to anyone in the vicinity. These people convened into a poorly organized chorus, all shouting at once and articulating visions that seemed to be linked in an approximate way—as if they had all just now awakened from the same dream and were all doing an equally bad job describing it. They stuck together despite their differences, drawn together by the same mysterious attractive force that causes streetcorner crackpots to set up their soapboxes right next to each other. Shortly after Hackworth zoomed toward them in his phenomenoscopic view, they began to hallucinate something along the lines of a giant eyeball peering at them from the heavens, the black skin of its eyelids studded with stars.

Hackworth skulked away and focused in on another large gathering: a couple of dozen older people of the trim, fit, and active style, tennis sweaters draped over their shoulders and sensible walking shoes firmly but not too tightly laced to their feet, piling off a small airship that had just moored on the old helicopter pad near the ship's stern. The airship had many windows and was festooned with mediatronic advertisements for aerial tours of London. As the tourists climbed off, they tended to stop in their tracks, so that a severe bottleneck was forever forming. They had to be goaded into the outer darkness by their tour guide, a young actress dressed in a cheesy devil outfit, complete with flashing red horns and a trident.

"Is this Whitechapel?" one of them said to the fog, speaking in an American accent. These people were obviously members of the Heartland tribe, a prosperous phyle closely allied with New Atlantis that had absorbed many responsible, sane, educated, white, Midwestern, middle-class types. Listening in on their furtive conversations, Hackworth divined that these tourists had been brought in from a Holiday Inn in Kensington, under the ruse that they were going to take the Jack the Ripper tour in Whitechapel. As Hackworth listened, the diabolical tour guide explained that their drunken airship pilot had accidentally flown them to a floating theatre, and they were welcome to enjoy the show, which would be starting shortly; a free (to them) performance of *Cats*, the longest-running musical of all time, which most of them had already seen on their first night in London.

Hackworth, still peering through the mocking red letters, did a quick scan belowdecks. There were a dozen cavernous compartments down there. Four of them had been consolidated into a capacious theatre; four more served as the stage and backstage. Hackworth located his daughter there. She was seated on a throne of light, rehearsing some lines. Apparently she'd already been cast in a major role.

"I don't want you to watch me like that," she said, and vanished from Hackworth's display in a burst of light.

The ship's foghorn sounded. The sound continued to echo sporadically from other ships in the area. Hackworth returned to his natural view of the deck just in time to see a blazing figment rushing toward him: the Clown again, who apparently possessed the special power of moving through Hackworth's display like a phantasm. "Going to stay up here all night, guessing the distance to the other ships by timing the echoes? Or may I show you to your seat?"

Hackworth decided that the best thing was not to be ruffled. "Please," he said.

"Well, there it is then," said the Clown, gesturing with one maculated glove toward a plain wooden chair right before them on the deck. Hackworth did not believe it was really there, because he hadn't seen it before now. But the spectacles allowed him no way to tell.

He stepped forward like a man making his way to the toilet in a dark and unfamiliar room, knees bent, hands outstretched, moving his feet gingerly so as not to bark shins or toes on anything. The Clown had drawn to one side and was watching him scornfully. "Is this what you call getting into your role? Think you can get away with scientific rationalism all night? What's going to happen the first time you actually start believing what you see?"

Hackworth found his seat exactly where the display told him it would be, but it wasn't a simple wooden chair; it was foam-covered and it had arms. It was like a seat in a theatre, but when he groped to either side, he did not find any others. So he depressed the seat and fell into it.

"You'll be needing this," the Clown said, and snapped

a tubular object into the palm of Hackworth's hand. Hackworth was just recognizing it as some kind of torch when something loud and violent happened just below him. His feet, which had been resting on the deckplates, were now dangling in air. In fact, all of him was dangling. A trapdoor had flown open beneath him, and he was in free fall. "Enjoy the show," the Clown said, tipping his hat and peering down at him through a rapidly diminishing square hole. "And while you're accelerating toward the center of the earth at nine point eight meters per second squared, riddle me this: We can fake sounds, we can fake images, we can even fake the wind blowing over your face, but how do we fake the sensation of free fall?"

Pseudopods had sprouted from the chair's foam and wrapped around Hackworth's waist and upper thighs. This was fortunate as he had gone into a slow backward spin and soon found himself falling face-first, passing through great amorphous clouds of light: a collection of old chandeliers that Dramatis Personae had scavenged from condemned buildings. The Clown was right: Hackworth was definitely in free fall, a sensation that could not be faked with spectacles. If his eyes and ears were to be believed, he was plunging toward the floor of the big theatre he had reconnoitered earlier. But it was not grooved with neat rows of seats like an ordinary theatre. The seats were present but scattered about randomly. And some of them were moving.

The floor continued to accelerate toward him until he got really scared and started to scream. Then he felt gravity again as some force began to slow him down. The chair spun around so that Hackworth was looking up into the irregular constellation of chandeliers, and the acceleration shot up to several gees. Then back to normal. The chair rotated so that he was on the level once more, and the phenomenoscope went brilliant, blinding white. The earpieces were pumping white noise at him; but as it began to diminish, he realized it was actually the sound of applause.

Hackworth was not able to see anything until he fiddled with the interface and got back to a more schematic view of the theatre. Then he determined that the place was about half full of theatregoers, moving about independently on their chairs, which were somehow motorized, and that several dozen of them were aiming their torches toward him, which accounted for the blinding light. He was on center stage, the main attraction. He wondered if he was supposed to say something. A line was written across his spectacles: *Thanks very much, ladies and gentlemen, for letting me drop in. We have a great show for you tonight. . . .*

Hackworth wondered if he was somehow obligated to read this line. But soon the torches turned away from him, as more audience members began to rain down through the astral plane of the chandeliers. Watching them fall, Hackworth realized that he'd seen something like it before at amusement parks: This was nothing more than bungee-jumping. It's just that the spectacles had declined to show Hackworth his own bungee cord, just to add an extra *frisson* to the whole experience.

The armrest of Hackworth's chair included some controls that enabled him to move it around the floor of the house, which was cone-shaped, sloping sharply in toward the center. A pedestrian would have found difficult footing, but the chair had powerful nanotech motors and compensated for the slope.

It was a round theatre, Globe-style. The conical floor was encompassed by a circular wall, pierced here and there by openings of different sizes. Some appeared to be ventilation shafts, some were the apertures of private boxes or technical control rooms, and by far the largest was a proscenium that occupied a quarter of the circumference, and that was currently closed off by a curtain.

Hackworth noted that the lowest and innermost part of the house floor was not occupied. He motored down the slope and was shocked to realize that he was suddenly up to his waist in painfully chilly water. He threw the chair into reverse, but it did not respond to the controls. "Dead in the water!" cried the Clown triumphantly, sounding as if he were standing right there, though Hackworth couldn't see him. He found a way to release the chair's built-in restraints and struggled up the raked floor, his legs stiff from the cold and reeking of seawater. Evidently the central third of the floor actually plunged beneath the waterline and was open to the sea—another fact that Hackworth's spectacles had not bothered to reveal.

Again, dozens of lights were on him. The audience was laughing, and there was even some sarcastic applause.

Come on in, folks, the water's fine! suggested the spectacles, but once again Hackworth declined to read the line. Apparently these were nothing more than suggestions tossed out by Dramatis Personae's writers, which faded from the display as they lost their currency.

The events of the last few minutes—the phenomenoscopes that couldn't be taken off, the unexpected bungee jump, the plunge into cold seawater—had left Hackworth in a state of shock. He felt a strong need to hole up somewhere and shake off the disorientation. He clambered up toward the perimeter of the house, dodging the occasional moving chair, and tracked by a few spotlight beams from fellow audience members who had taken a particular interest in his personal story. An aperture was above him, glowing with warm light, and passing through it, Hackworth found himself in a cozy little bar with a curving window that afforded an excellent view of the theatre. It was a refuge in more ways than one; he could see normally through the spectacles here, they seemed to be giving him an untampered view of reality. He ordered a pint of stout from the barman and took a seat at the counter along the window. Somewhere around his third or fourth gulp of stout, he realized that he had already submitted to the Clown's imperative. The plunge into the water had taught him that he had no choice but to believe in what the spectacles showed his eyes and ears—even though he knew it to be false—and to accept the consequences. A pint of stout went some distance toward warming up his legs, and toward relaxing his mind. He had come here for a show, and he was getting one, and there was no reason to fight it; Dramatis Personae might have a dodgy reputation, but no one had ever accused them of killing a member of the audience.

The chandeliers dimmed. The torch-wielding audience went into motion like sparks stirred by a gust of wind, some motoring toward the high ground and others preferring the water's edge. As the house lights faded to black, they amused themselves playing their torches back and forth across the walls and the curtain, creating an apocalyptic sky torn by hundreds of comets. A tongue of clammy, algae-colored light shone beneath the water, resolving itself into a long narrow thrust stage as it rose toward the surface, like Atlantis resurgent. The audience noticed it and bounced their spotlights off the surface, catching a few dark motes in the crossfire: the heads of a dozen or so performers, slowly rising out of the water. They began to speak in something like unison, and Hackworth realized that they were the chorus of lunatics he had seen earlier.

"Set me up, Nick," said a woman's voice behind him.

"Tucked 'em in, did you?" said the barkeep.

"Ninnies."

Hackworth turned and saw that it was the young woman in the devil costume who had acted as tour guide for the Heartlanders. She was very petite, dressed in a long black skirt slit all the way to the hipbone, and she had nice hair, very thick and black and glossy. She carried a glass of wheat beer over to the counter, primly swept her devil's tail out of the way in a gesture that Hackworth found hopelessly fetching, and took a seat. Then she let out an explosive sigh and put her head down on her arms for a few moments, her blinking red horns reflecting in the curved window like the taillights of a full-laner. Hackworth laced his fingers together around his pint and smelled her perfume. Down below, the chorus had gotten out of hand and was trying to pull off a rather ambitious Busby Berkeley dance number. They showed an uncanny ability to act in unison—something to do with the 'sites that had burrowed into their brains—but their bodies were stiff, weak, and badly coordinated. What they did, they did with absolute conviction, which made it good anyway.

"Did they buy it?" Hackworth said.

"Pardon me?" said the woman, looking up alertly like a bird, as if she hadn't known Hackworth was here.

"Do those Heartlanders really believe that story about the drunken pilot?"

"Oh. Who cares?" the woman said.

Hackworth laughed, pleased that a member of Dramatis Personae was affording him this confidence.

"It's off the point, isn't it," the woman said in a lower voice, getting a bit philosophical now. She squeezed a wedge of lemon into her wheat beer and took a sip. "Belief isn't a binary state, not here at least. Does anyone believe anything one hundred percent? Do you believe everything you see through those goggles?"

"No," Hackworth said, "the only thing I believe at the

moment is that my legs are wet, this stout is good, and I like your perfume."

She looked a bit surprised, not unpleasantly so, but she wasn't nearly that easy. "So why are you here? Which show did you come to see?"

"What do you mean? I suppose I came to see this one."

"But there is no this one. It's a whole family of shows. Interlaced." She parked her beer and executed Phase 1 of the here-is-the-church maneuver. "Which show you see depends on which feed you're viewing."

"I don't seem to have any control over what I see."

"Ah, then you're a performer."

"So far I have felt like a very inept slapstick performer."

"Inept slapstick? Isn't that a bit redundant?"

It wasn't that funny, but she said it wittily, and Hackworth chuckled politely.

"It sounds as though you've been singled out to be a performer."

"You don't say."

"Now, I don't normally reveal our trade secrets," the woman continued in a lower voice, "but usually when someone is singled out as a performer, it's because they have come here for some purpose other than pure, passive entertainment."

Hackworth stuttered and fumbled for words a bit. "Does that—is that done?"

"Oh, yes!" the woman said. She rose from her stool and moved to the one right next to Hackworth. "Theatre's not just a few people clowning about on a stage, being watched by this herd of oxen. I mean, sometimes it's that. But it can be ever so much more—really it can be any sort of interaction between people and people, or people and information." The woman had become quite passionate now, forgotten herself completely. Hackworth got boundless pleasure just from watching her. When she'd first entered the bar, he'd thought she had a sort of nondescript face, but as she let her guard down and spoke without any self-consciousness, she seemed to become prettier and prettier. "We are tied in to everything here—plugged into the whole universe of information. Really, it's a virtual theatre. Instead of

being hardwired, the stage, sets, cast, and script are all soft—
they can be reconfigured simply by shifting bits about."

"Oh. So the show—or interlaced set of shows—can be
different each night?"

"No, you're still not getting it," she said, becoming
very excited. She reached out and gripped his forearm just
below the elbow and leaned toward him, desperate to make
sure he got this. "It's not that we do a set show, reconfigure,
and a different one next night. The changes are dynamic and
take place in real time. The show reconfigures itself dynami-
cally depending upon what happens *moment to moment*—
and mind you, not just what happens here, but what is
happening in the world at large. It is a *smart play*—an intelligent organism."

"So, if, for example, a battle between the Fists of Righteous Harmony and the Coastal Republic were taking place
in the interior of China at this moment, then shifts in the
battle might in some way—"

"Might change the color of a spotlight or a line of
dialogue—not necessarily in any simple and deterministic
fashion, mind you—"

"I think I understand," Hackworth said. "The internal
variables of the play depend on the total universe of information outside—"

The woman nodded vigorously, quite pleased with
him, her huge black eyes shining.

Hackworth continued, "As, for example, a person's
state of mind at any given moment might depend on the
relative concentrations of innumerable chemical compounds
circulating through his bloodstream."

"Yes," the woman said, "like if you're in a pub being
chatted up by a fetching young gentleman, the words coming out of your mouth are affected by the amount of alcohol
you've put into your system, and, of course, by concentrations of natural hormones—again, not in a simple deterministic way—these things are all inputs."

"I think I'm beginning to get your meaning," Hackworth said.

"Substitute tonight's show for the brain, and the information flowing across the net for molecules flowing through
the bloodstream, and you have it," the woman said.

Hackworth was a bit disappointed that she had chosen

to pull back from the pub metaphor, which he had found more immediately interesting.

The woman continued, "That lack of determinism causes some to dismiss the whole process as wanking. But in fact it's an incredibly powerful tool. Some people understand that."

"I believe I do," Hackworth said, desperately wanting her to believe that he did.

"And so some people come here because they are on a quest of some sort—trying to find a lost lover, let's say, or to understand why something terrible happened in their lives, or why there is cruelty in the world, or why they aren't satisfied with their career. Society has never been good at answering these questions—the sorts of questions you can't just look up in a reference database."

"But the dynamic theatre allows one to interface with the universe of data in a more intuitive way," Hackworth said.

"That is *precisely it*," the woman said. "I'm so pleased that you get this."

"When I was working with information, it frequently occurred to me, in a vague and general way, that such a thing might be desirable," Hackworth said. "But this is beyond my imagination."

"Where did you hear of us?"

"I was referred here by a friend who has been associated with you in the past, in some vague way."

"Oh? May I ask who? Perhaps we have a mutual friend," the woman said, as if that would be a fine thing.

Hackworth felt himself reddening and let out a deep breath. "All right," he said, "I lied. It wasn't really a friend of mine. It was someone I was led to."

"Ah, now we're getting into it," the woman said. "I knew there was something mysterious going on with you."

Hackworth was abashed and did not know what to say. He looked into his beer. The woman was staring at him, and he could feel her eyes on his face like the warmth of a follow spot.

"So you did come here in search of something. Didn't you? Something you couldn't find by looking it up in a database."

"I'm seeking a fellow called the Alchemist," Hackworth said.

Suddenly, things got bright. The side of the woman's
face that was toward the window was brilliantly illuminated, like a probe in space lit on one side by the directional
light of the sun. Hackworth sensed, somehow, that this was
not a new development. Looking out over the audience, he
saw that nearly all of them were aiming their spotlights into
the bar, and that everyone in the place had been watching
and listening to his entire conversation with the woman. The
spectacles had deceived him by adjusting the apparent light
levels. The woman looked different too; her face had reverted to the way it looked when she came in, and Hackworth now understood that her image in his spectacles had
been gradually evolving during their conversation, getting
feedback from whatever part of his brain buzzed when he
saw a beautiful woman.

The curtain parted to reveal a large electric sign de-
scending from the fly space: JOHN HACKWORTH in
QUEST FOR THE ALCHEMIST starring JOHN HACK-
WORTH as HIMSELF.

The Chorus sang:

> He's such a stiff, John Hackworth is
> Can't show emotion to save his life
> With nasty repercussions, viz
> He lost his job and lost his wife.
> So now he's on a goshdarn Quest
> Wandering all o'er the world
> Hunting down that Alchemist
> 'Cept when he stops to pick up girls.
> Maybe he'll clean up his act
> And do the job tonight
> A fabulous adventure packed
> With marvelous sounds and sights
> Let's get it on, oh Hacker John
> Let's get it on, on, on.

Something jerked violently at Hackworth's neck. The
woman had tossed a noose around him while he'd been
staring out the window, and now she was hauling him out
the door of the bar like a recalcitrant dog. As soon as she

cleared the doorway, her cape inflated like a time-lapse explosion, and she shot twelve feet into the air, propelled on jets of air built into her clothing somehow—she payed out the leash so that Hackworth wasn't hanged in the process. Flying above the audience like the cone of fire from a rocket engine, she led the stumbling Hackworth down the sloping floor and to the edge of the water. The thrust stage was linked to the water's edge by a couple of narrow bridges, and Hackworth negotiated one of these, feeling hundreds of lights on his shoulders, seemingly hot enough to ignite his clothing. She led him straight back through the center of the Chorus, beneath the electric sign, through the backstage area, and through a doorway, which clanged shut behind him. Then she vanished.

Hackworth was surrounded on three sides by softly glowing blue walls. He reached out to touch one and received a mild shock for his troubles. Stepping forward, he tripped over something that skittered across the floor: a dry bone, big and heavy, larger than a human femur.

He stepped forward through the only gap available to him and found more walls. He had been deposited into the heart of a labyrinth.

It took him an hour or so to realize that escape through normal means was hopeless. He didn't even try to figure out the labyrinth's floor plan; instead, realizing that it couldn't possibly be larger than the ship, he followed the foolproof expedient of turning right at every corner, which as all clever boys knew must always lead to an exit. But it didn't, and he did not understand why until once, in the corner of his eye, he saw a wall segment shift sideways, closing up an old gap and creating a new one. It was a dynamic labyrinth.

He found a rusty bolt on the floor, picked it up, and threw it at a wall. It did not bounce off but passed through and clattered onto the floor beyond. So the walls did not exist except as figments in his spectacles. The labyrinth was constructed of information. In order to escape, he would have to hack it.

He sat down on the floor. Nick the barman appeared, walking unhindered through walls, bearing a tray with another stout on it, and handed it to him along with a bowl of salty peanuts. As the evening went on, other people passed through his area, dancing or singing or dueling or arguing or making love. None of these had anything to do, particularly, with Hackworth's Quest, and they appeared to have nothing to do with each other. Apparently Hackworth's Quest was (as the devil-woman herself had told him) just one of several concurrent stories being acted out tonight, coexisting in the same space.

So what did any of this have to do with the life of John Hackworth? And how was Fiona mixed up in it?

As Hackworth thought about Fiona, a panel in front of him slid to the side, exposing several yards of corridor. During the next couple of hours he noted the same thing several times: An idea would occur to him, and a wall would move.

In this way he moved in fits and starts through the maze, as his mind moved from one idea to the next. The floor was definitely sloping downward, which would obviously bring him below the waterline at some point; and indeed he had begun to sense a heavy drumming noise coming up through the deckplates, which might have been the pounding of mighty engines except that this ship, as far as he knew, wasn't going anywhere. He smelled seawater before him and saw dim lights shining through its surface, broken by the waves, and knew that in the flooded ballast tanks of this ship lay a network of underwater tunnels, and that in those tunnels were Drummers. For all he knew, the whole show was just a figment being enacted in the mind of the Drummers. Probably not the main event either; it was probably just an epiphenomenon of whatever deep processes the Drummers were running down there in their collective mind.

A wall panel slid aside and gave him a clear path to the water. Hackworth squatted at the water's edge for a few minutes, listening to the drums, then stood up and began to undo his necktie.

He was terribly hot and sweaty, and bright light was in his eyes, and none of these things were consistent with being underwater. He awoke to see a bright blue sky overhead, pawed at his face, and found that the spectacles were gone. Fiona was there in her white dress, watching him with a rueful smile. The floor was pounding Hackworth on the buttocks and evidently had been for some time, as the bony parts of his backside were bruised and raw. He realized that they were on the raft, heading back toward the London docks; that he was naked and that Fiona had covered him with a sheet of plastic to protect his skin from the sun. A few other theatergoers were scattered about, slumped against one another, utterly passive, like refugees, or people who've just had the greatest sex of their lives, or people who are tremendously hung over.

"You were quite a hit," Fiona said. And suddenly Hackworth remembered himself being paraded naked and dripping down the thrust stage, waves of applause rolling over him from the standing audience.

"The Quest is finished," he blurted. "We're going to Shanghai."

"You're going to Shanghai," Fiona said. "I'll see you off at the dock. Then I'll be going back." She cocked her head over the stern.

"Back to the ship?"

"I was a bigger hit than you were," she said. "I've found my calling in life, Father. I've accepted an invitation to join Dramatis Personae."

Carl Hollywood's hack.

Carl Hollywood leaned back against the hard lacquered back of his corner seat for the first time in many hours and rubbed his face with both hands, scratching himself with his own whiskers. He had been sitting in the teahouse for almost twenty-four hours, consumed twelve pots of tea, and twice called in masseuses to unknot his back. The afternoon light coming in the windows behind him flickered as the crowd outside began to break up. They had been treated to a remarkable free media show, watching over his shoulders for hours as the dramaturgical exploits of John Percival Hackworth had played themselves out, in several different camera angles, on floating cine windows on Carl Hollywood's pages. None of them could read English, and so they had been unable to follow the story of Princess Nell's adventures in the land of King Coyote, which had been streaming across the pages at the same time, the storyline fluctuating and curling in upon itself like a cloud of smoke spun and torn by invisible currents.

Now the pages were blank and empty. Carl reached out lazily with one hand and began to stack the sheets on top of each other, just for something to occupy his hands while his mind worked—though it wasn't working, at this point, so much as stumbling blindly through a dark labyrinth à la John Percival Hackworth.

Carl Hollywood had long suspected that, among other things, the network of the Drummers was a giant system for breaking codes. The cryptographic systems that made the media network run securely, and that made it capable of securely transferring money, were based on the use of immense prime numbers as magic keys. The keys could theoretically be broken by throwing enough computing power at the problem. But at any given level of computing power, code-making was always much easier than code-breaking, so as long as the system kept moving to larger and larger prime numbers as computers got faster, the code-makers could stay far ahead of the code-breakers forever.

But the human mind didn't work like a digital computer and was capable of doing some funny things. Carl Hollywood remembered one of the Lone Eagles, an older man who could add huge columns of numbers in his head as quickly as they were called out. That, in and of itself, was merely a duplication of something that a digital computer could do. But this man could also do numerical tricks that could not easily be programmed into a computer.

If many minds were gathered together in the network of the Drummers, perhaps they could somehow see through the storm of encrypted data that roared continuously through media space, cause the seemingly random bits to coalesce into meaning. The men who had come to talk to Miranda, who had persuaded her to enter the world of the Drummers, had implied that this was possible; that through them, Miranda could find Nell.

Superficially, this would be disastrous, because it would destroy the system used for financial transactions. It would be as if, in a world where commerce was based upon the exchange of gold, some person had figured out how to change lead into gold. An Alchemist.

But Carl Hollywood wondered if it really made a difference. The Drummers could only do such things by subsuming themselves into a gestalt society. As the case of Hackworth demonstrated, as soon as a Drummer removed himself from that gestalt, he lost touch with it completely. All communication between the Drummers and normal human society took place unconsciously, through their influence upon the Net, in patterns that appeared subliminally in the ractives that everyone played with in their homes and saw playing across the walls of buildings. The Drummers could break the code, but they couldn't take advantage of it in an obvious way, or perhaps they simply did not want to. They could make gold, but they were no longer interested in having it.

John Hackworth, somehow, was better than anyone else at making the transition between the society of Drummers and the Victorian tribe, and each time he crossed the boundary, he seemed to bring something with him, clinging to his garments like traces of scent. These faint echoes of forbidden data entrained in his wake caused tangled and unpredictable repercussions, on both sides of the boundary, that Hackworth himself might not even be aware of. Carl Hollywood had known little of Hackworth until several hours ago, when, alerted by a friend in Dramatis Personae, he had joined his story in progress on the black decks of the show boat. Now he seemed to know a great deal: that Hackworth was the progenitor of the *Young Lady's Illustrated Primer*, and that he had a deep relationship with the Drummers that went far beyond anything as simpleminded as captivity. He had not just been eating lotuses and getting his rocks off during his years beneath the waves.

Hackworth had brought something back with him this time, when he had emerged naked and streaming with cold seawater from the warren of Drummers in the ballast tanks of the ship. He had emerged with a set of numerical keys that were used to identify certain entities: the Primer, Nell, Miranda, and someone else who went by the name of Dr. X. Before he had fully reentered his conscious state, he had supplied those keys to the Clown, who had been there to haul his gasping and shivering body out of the water. The

Clown was a mechanical device, but Dramatis Personae had been good enough to allow Carl Hollywood to control it— and to improvise much of Hackworth's personal script and storyline—for the duration of the show.

Now Carl had the keys and, for the purposes of the Net, was indistinguishable from Miranda or Nell or Dr. X or even Hackworth himself. They were written out across the surface of a page, long columns of digits grouped in bunches of four. Carl Hollywood told this sheet to fold itself and then tucked it into his breast pocket. He could use them to untangle this whole business, but that would be another night's hack. Snuff and caffeine had done as much as they could. It was time to go back to the hotel, soak in a bath, get some sleep, and prepare for the final act.

From the Primer, Princess Nell's ride to the Castle of King Coyote; description of the castle; an audience with a Wizard; her final triumph over King Coyote; an enchanted army.

Princess Nell rode north into an explosive thunderstorm. The horses were driven nearly mad with terror by the cannonlike explosions of the thunder and the unearthly blue flashes of the lightning, but with a firm hand and a soothing voice in the ear, Nell urged them forward. The cairns of bones strewn along the roadside were evidence that this mountain pass was no place to dawdle, and the poor animals would be no less terrified huddling under a rock. For all she knew, the great King Coyote was capable of controlling even the weather itself and had prepared this reception to try Princess Nell's will.

Finally she crested the pass, and none too soon, as the horses' hooves had begun to slip on a thick layer of ice, and ice had begun thickly to coat the reins and to weigh down the animals' manes and tails. Working her way down the switchbacks, she left the high fury of the storm behind and pushed into masses of rain as dense as any jungle. It was well that she had paused for a few days at the foot of the mountains to review all of Purple's magic books, for on this night ride through the mountains she used every spell Purple had taught her: spells for casting light, for choosing the right fork in the road, for calming animals and warming chilled bodies, for bolstering her own failing courage, for sensing the approach of any monsters foolish enough to venture out in such weather, and for defeating those desperate enough to attack. This night ride was, perhaps, a rash act, but Princess Nell proved equal to the challenge. King Coyote would not expect her to make such a crossing. Tomorrow when the storm on high had cleared, he would send his raven sentinels winging through the pass and down into the plain below to spy on her, as he had for the last several days, and they would return with dismaying news: The Princess had vanished! Even King Coyote's best trackers would not be able to follow her path from yesterday's campsite, so craftily had she covered her real tracks and laid false ones.

Dawn found her in the heart of a great forest. King Coyote's castle was built on a high woodland plateau surrounded by mountains; she estimated she was several hours' ride away. Staying well clear of the high road taken by the messengers from the Cipherers' Market, she made camp under an overhanging rock along a river, sheltered from the chill wet wind and safe from the eyes of the raven sentinels, and lit a tiny fire where she made some tea and porridge.

She napped until the middle of the afternoon, then rose, bathed in the bitter water of the stream, and untied the oilcloth packet she had brought with her. It contained one of the costumes worn by the messengers who galloped to and from the Cipherers' Market. It also contained a few books containing enciphered messages—authentic ones dispatched from various stalls in the market addressed to King Coyote's castle.

As she made her way through the woods toward the high road, she heard massed hoofbeats rolling by and knew that the first contingent of messengers had just come over the pass after waiting for the storm to pass. She waited a few minutes and then followed them. Turning onto the high road out of the dense woods, she reined in her horse and sat for a moment, astonished by her first sight of the Castle of King Coyote.

She had never seen its like in all of her travels through the Land Beyond. Its base was as wide as a mountain, and its walls rose sheer and straight into the clouds. Galactic clouds of lights shone from its myriad windows. It was guarded by mighty stockades, each of them a great castle unto itself, but built not on stony foundations, but upon the very clouds themselves; for King Coyote, in his cleverness, had devised a way to make buildings that floated on the air.

Princess Nell spurred her horse forward, for even in her numbness she sensed that someone might be watching the high road from a window high in one of the castle's glittering oriels. As she galloped toward the castle, she was torn between a sense of her own foolishness in daring to assault such a mighty fortress and admiration for King Coyote's work. Faint clouds of diaphanous black oozed between the towers and stockades, and as Princess Nell drew closer, she saw that they were actually regiments of ravens going through their military drills. They were the closest thing King Coyote had to an army; for as one of the ravens had told her, after he had stolen the eleven keys from around her neck,

> Castles, gardens, gold, and jewels
> Contentment signify, for fools
> Like Princess Nell; but those
> Who cultivate their wit
> Like King Coyote and his crows
> Compile their power bit by bit
> And hide it places no one knows.

King Coyote did not preserve his power by armed might but by cleverness, and sentinels were the only army he needed, information his only weapon.

As she galloped the final miles to the gate, wondering whether her legs and back would hold out, a thin steam of black issued from a narrow portal high in one of the floating stockades, thickened into a transparent ball, and dove toward her like a plunging comet. She could not help flinching from the illusion of mass and momentum, but, a stone's throw above her head the cloud of ravens parted into several contingents that whirled around and struck from several directions, converging on her, passing around her so closely that the wind from their rattling wings blew her hair back, finally reforming into a disciplined group that returned to its stockade without a look back. Apparently she had passed the inspection. When she reached the mighty gate, it was standing open for her, and no one was guarding it. Princess Nell rode into the broad streets of King Coyote's castle.

It was the finest place she had ever seen. Here gold and

crystal were not hidden away in the King's treasury but were used as building materials. Green and growing things were everywhere, for King Coyote was fascinated by the secrets of nature and had sent his agents to the farthest reaches of the world to bring back exotic seeds. The wide boulevards of King Coyote's city were lined with trees whose arching limbs closed over the ashlars to form a rustling vault. The undersides of the leaves were silver and seemed to cast a gentle light, and the branches were filled with violet and magenta bromeliads the size of kettles, making a sweet sharp smell, aswarm with ruby-throated hummingbirds and filled with water where tiny fluorescent frogs and beetles lived.

The Messenger's Route was marked with polished brass plates set among the paving-stones. Princess Nell followed it down the grand boulevard, into a park that encircled the city, and then onto a rising street that spiraled around the central promontory. As the horse took her toward the clouds, her ears popped again and again, and from each curve in the road she enjoyed a sweeping view over the lower city and into the constellation of floating stockades where the raven sentinels soared, coming and going in flights and squadrons, bringing news from every corner of the empire.

She rode by a place where King Coyote was adding on to the castle; but instead of an army of stonemasons and carpenters, the builder was a single man, a portly gray-bearded fellow puffing at a long slender pipe, carrying a leather bag on his belt. Arriving at the center of the building site, he reached into his bag and drew out a great seed the size of an apple and pitched it into the soil. By the time this man had walked back to the spiral road, a tall shaft of gleaming crystal had arisen from the soil and grown far above their heads, gleaming in the sunlight, and branched out like a tree. By the time Princess Nell lost sight of it around the corner, the builder was puffing contentedly and looking at a crystalline vault that nearly covered the lot.

This and many other wonders Princess Nell saw during her long ride up the spiral road. The clouds cleared away, and Nell found that she could see great distances in every direction. King Coyote's domain was in the very heart of the Land Beyond, and his castle was built on a high plateau in the center of his domain, so that from his windows he could see all the way to the shining ocean in every direction. Nell kept a sharp eye on the horizon as she climbed toward the King's inner keep, hoping she might get a glimpse of the faraway island where Harv languished in the Dark

Castle; but there were many islands in the distant sea, and it was hard to tell the Dark Castle's towers from mountain crags.

Finally the road became level and turned inward to pierce another unguarded gate in another high wall, and Princess Nell found herself in a green, flowery court before the King's keep—a high palace that appeared to have been hewn from a single diamond the size of an iceberg. By now the sun was sinking low in the west, and its orange rays ignited the walls of the keep and cast tiny rainbows everywhere like shards from a shattered crystal bowl. A dozen or so messengers stood in a queue before the doors of the keep. They had left their horses in a corner of the yard where a watering-trough and manger were available. Princess Nell did likewise and joined the queue.

"I have never had the honor of carrying a message to King Coyote," Princess Nell said to the messenger preceding her in the queue.

"It is an experience you will never forget," said the messenger, a cocky young man with black hair and a goatee.

"Why must we wait in this queue? In the stalls at the Cipherers' Market, we leave the books on the table and continue on our way."

Several of the messengers turned and looked back at Princess Nell disdainfully. The messenger with the goatee made a visible effort to control his amusement and said, "King Coyote is no small-timer sitting in a stall at the Cipherers' Market! This you will soon see for yourself."

"But doesn't he make his decisions the same way as all the others—by consulting rules in a book?"

At this the other messengers made no effort to control their amusement. The one with the goatee took on a distinctly sneering tone. "What would be the point of having a King in that case?" he said. "He does not take his decisions from any book. King Coyote has built a mighty thinking machine, Wizard 0.2, containing all the wisdom in the world. When we bring a book to this place, his acolytes decipher it and consult with Wizard 0.2. Sometimes it takes hours for Wizard to reach its decision. I would advise you to wait respectfully and quietly in the presence of the great machine!"

"That I will certainly do," said Princess Nell, amused rather than angered by this lowly messenger's impertinence.

The queue moved along steadily, and as darkness fell and the orange rays of the sun died away, Princess Nell became aware of colored lights streaming out from within the keep. The lights seemed to be quite brilliant whenever Wizard 0.2 was cogitating and dropped to a low flicker the rest of the time. Princess Nell tried to make out other details of what was going on inside the keep, but the countless facets broke up the light and bent it into all directions so that she could get only hints and fragments; trying to see into King Coyote's inner sanctum was like trying to remember the details of a forgotten dream.

Finally the messenger with the goatee emerged, gave Princess Nell a final smirk, and reminded her to display proper respect.

"Next," intoned the acolyte in a chanting voice, and Princess Nell entered the keep.

Five acolytes sat in the anteroom, each one at a desk piled high with dusty old books and long reels of paper tape. Nell had brought thirteen books from the Cipherers' Market, and at their direction, she distributed these books among the acolytes for decipherment. The acolytes were neither young nor old but in the middle of their lives, all dressed in white coats decorated, in golden thread, with the crest of King Coyote. Each also had a key around his neck. As Princess Nell waited, they deciphered the contents of the books she had brought and punched the results onto strips of paper tape using little machines built into their tables.

Then, with great ceremony, the thirteen paper tapes were coiled up and placed on a tremendous silver platter carried by a young altar boy. A pair of large doors was swung open, and the acolytes, the altar boy, and Princess Nell formed into a procession of sorts, which marched into the Chamber of the Wizard, a vast vaulted room, and down its long central aisle.

At the far end of the chamber was—nothing. A sort of large empty space surrounded by elaborate machinery and clockwork, with a small altar at the front. It reminded Princess Nell of a stage, empty of curtains and scenery. Standing next to the stage was a high priest, older and wearing a more impressive white robe.

When they reached the head of the aisle, the priest went through a perfunctory ceremony, praising the Wizard's excellent features and asking for its cooperation. As he said these words, lights began to come on and the machinery began to whir. Princess Nell saw that this vault was, in fact, nothing more than an anteroom for a much vaster space within, and that this space was filled with machinery: countless narrow shining rods, scarcely larger than pencil leads, laid in a fine gridwork, sliding back and forth under the impetus of geared power shafts running throughout the place. All of the machinery threw off heat as it ran, and the room was quite warm despite a vigorous draught of cold mountain air being pumped through it by windmill-size fans.

The priest took the first of the thirteen rolls of paper tape from the platter and fed it into a slot on the top of the altar. At this point, Wizard 0.2 really went into action, and Princess Nell saw that all the whirring and humming she'd seen to this point had been nothing more than a low idle. Each of its million push-rods was tiny, but the force needed to move all of them at once was seismic, and she could sense the tremendous strains on the power shafts and gearboxes thundering through the sturdy floor of the keep.

Lights came on around the stage, some of them built into the surface of the stage itself and some hidden in the machinery around it. To Princess Nell's surprise, a seemingly three-dimensional shape of light began to coalesce in the center of the empty stage. It gradually formed itself into a head, which took on additional details as the machinery thundered and hissed away: it was an old bald man with a long white beard, his face deeply furrowed in thought. After a few moments, the beard exploded into a flock of white birds and the head turned into a craggy mountain, the white birds swarming about it, and then the mountain erupted in orange lava that gradually filled up the entire volume of the stage until it was a solid glowing cube of orange light. In this fashion did one image merge into another, most astonishingly, for several minutes, and all the time the machinery was screaming away and making Princess Nell most anxious, and she suspected that if she had not seen less sophisticated machines at work at Castle Turing, she might have turned around and fled.

Finally, though, the images died away, the stage became empty again, and the altar spat out a length of paper tape, which the priest carefully folded up and handed to one of the acolytes. After a brief prayer of thanks, the priest fed the second tape into the altar, and the whole process started up again, this time with different but equally remarkable images.

So it went with one tape after another. When Princess Nell became accustomed to the noise and vibration of the Wizard, she began to enjoy the images, which seemed quite artistic to her— like something a human would come up with, and not machine-like at all.

But the Wizard was undoubtedly a machine. She had not yet had the opportunity to study it in detail, but after her experiences in all of King Coyote's other castles, she suspected that it, too, was just another Turing machine.

Her study of the Cipherers' Market, and particularly of the rule-books used by the cipherers to respond to messages, had taught her that for all its complexity, it too was nothing more than another Turing machine. She had come here to the Castle of King Coyote to see whether the King answered his messages according to Turing-like rules. For if he did, then the entire system—the entire kingdom—the entire Land Beyond—was nothing more than a vast Turing machine. And as she had established when she'd been locked up in the dungeon at Castle Turing, communicating with the mysterious Duke by sending messages on a chain, a Turing machine, no matter how complex, was not human. It had no soul. It could not do what a human did.

The thirteenth tape was fed into the altar, and the machinery began to whine, then to whir, and then to rumble. The images appearing above the stage flourished into wilder and more exotic forms than any they had seen yet, and watching the faces of the priest and the acolytes, Princess Nell could see that even they were surprised; they had never seen anything of the like before. As the minutes wore on, the images became fragmented and bizarre, mere incarnations of mathematical ideas, and finally the stage went entirely dark except for occasional random flashes of color. The Wizard had worked itself up to such a pitch that all of them felt trapped within the bowels of a mighty machine that could tear them to shreds in a moment. The little altar boy finally broke away and fled down the aisle. Within a minute or so, the acolytes, one by one, did the same, backing slowly away from the Wizard until they were about halfway down the aisle and then turning away and running. Finally even the high priest turned and fled. The rumbling of the machinery had now reached such a pitch that it felt as though an epochal earthquake were in progress, and Nell had to steady herself with a hand on the altar. The heat coming from back in the machine was like that from a forge, and Nell could see a dim red light from deep inside as some of the push-rods became hot enough to glow.

Finally it all stopped. The silence was astonishing. Nell realized she had been cringing and stood up straight. The red glow from inside the Wizard began to die away.

White light poured in from all around. Princess Nell could

tell that it was coming in from outside the diamond walls of the keep. A few minutes ago it had been nighttime. Now there was light, but not daylight; it came from all directions and was cool and colorless.

She ran down the aisle and opened the door to the anteroom, but it wasn't there. Nothing was there. The anteroom was gone. The flowery garden beyond it was gone, and the horses, the wall, the spiral road, the City of King Coyote, and the Land Beyond. Instead there was nothing but gentle white light.

She turned around. The Chamber of the Wizard was still there.

At the head of the aisle she could see a man sitting atop the altar, looking at her. He was wearing a crown. Around his neck was a key—the twelfth key to the Dark Castle.

Princess Nell walked down the aisle toward King Coyote. He was a middle-aged man, sandy hair losing its color, gray eyes, and a beard, somewhat darker than his hair and not especially well trimmed. As Princess Nell approached, he seemed to become conscious of the crown around his head. He reached up, lifted it from his head, and tossed it carelessly onto the top of the altar.

"Very funny," he said. "You snuck a zero divide past all of my defenses."

Princess Nell refused to be drawn by his studied informality. She stopped several paces away. "As there is no one here to make introductions, I shall take the liberty of doing so myself. I am Princess Nell, Duchess of Turing," she said, and held out her hand.

King Coyote looked slightly embarrassed. He jumped down from the altar, approached Princess Nell, and kissed her hand. "King Coyote at your service."

"Pleased to make your acquaintance."

"The pleasure is mine. Sorry! I should have known that the Primer would have taught you better manners."

"I am not acquainted with the Primer to which you refer," Princess Nell said. "I am simply a Princess on a quest: to obtain the twelve keys to the Dark Castle. I note you have one of them in your possession."

King Coyote held up his hands, palms facing toward her. "Say no more," he said. "Single combat will not be necessary. You are already the victor." He removed the twelfth key from his neck and held it out to Princess Nell. She took it from him with a little curtsy; but as the chain was sliding through his fingers, he tightened his grip suddenly, so that both of them were joined by the chain. "Now that your quest is over," he said, "can we drop the pretense?"

"I'm sure I don't take your meaning, Your Majesty."

He bore a controlled look of exasperation. "What was your purpose in coming here?"

"To obtain the twelfth key."

"Anything else?"

"To learn about Wizard 0.2."

"Ah."

"To discover whether it was, in fact, a Turing machine."

"Well, you have your answer. Wizard 0.2 is most certainly a Turing machine—the most powerful ever built."

"And the Land Beyond?"

"All grown from seeds. Seeds that I invented."

"And it is also a Turing machine, then? All controlled by Wizard 0.2?"

"No," said King Coyote. "Managed by Wizard. Controlled by me."

"But the messages in the Cipherers' Market control all the events in the Land Beyond, do they not?"

"You are most perceptive, Princess Nell."

"Those messages came to Wizard—just another Turing machine."

"Open the altar," said King Coyote, pointing to a large brass plate with a keyhole in the middle.

Princess Nell used her key to open the lock, and King Coyote flipped back the lid of the altar. Inside were two small machines, one for reading tapes and one for writing them.

"Follow me," said King Coyote, and opened a trapdoor set into the floor behind the altar.

Princess Nell followed him down a spiral staircase into a small room. The connecting rods from the altar came down into this room and terminated at a small console.

"Wizard is not even connected to the altar! It does nothing," Princess Nell said.

"Oh, Wizard does a great deal. It helps me keep track of things, does calculations, and so on. But all of that business up there on the stage is just for show—just to impress the commoners. When a message comes here from the Cipherers' Market, I read it myself, and answer it myself.

"So as you can see, Princess Nell, the Land Beyond is not really a Turing machine at all. It's actually a person—a few people, to be precise. Now it's all yours."

King Coyote led Princess Nell back into the heart of his keep and gave her a tour of the place. The best part was the library. He showed her the books containing the rules for programming Wizard 0.2, and other books explaining how to make atoms build themselves into machines, buildings, and whole worlds.

"You see, Princess Nell, you have conquered this world today, and now that you have conquered it, you'll find it a rather boring place. Now it's your responsibility to make new worlds for other people to explore and conquer." King Coyote waved his hand out the window into the vast, empty white space where once had stood the Land Beyond. "There's plenty of empty space out there."

"What will you do, King Coyote?"

"Call me John, Your Royal Highness. As of today, I no longer have a kingdom."

"John, what will you do?"

"I have a quest of my own."

"What is your quest?"

"To find the Alchemist, whoever he may be."

"And is there . . ."

Nell stopped reading the Primer for a moment. Her eyes had filled up with tears.

"Is there what?" said John's voice from the book.

"Is there another? Another who has been with me during my quest?"

"Yes, there is," John said quietly, after a short pause. "At least I have always sensed that she is here."

"Is she here now?"

"Only if you build a place for her," John said. "Read the books, and they will show you how."

With that, John, the former King Coyote and Emperor of the Land Beyond, vanished in a flash of light, leaving Princess Nell alone in her great dusty library. Princess Nell put her head down on an old leather-bound book and smelled its rich fragrance. One tear of joy ran from each eye. But she mastered the impulse to cry and reached for the book instead.

They were magic books, and they drew Princess Nell into

them so deeply that, for many hours, perhaps even days, she was not aware of her surroundings; which scarcely mattered as nothing remained of the Land Beyond. But at some length, she realized that something was tickling her foot. She reached down absently and scratched it. Moments later the tickling sensation returned. This time she looked down and was astonished to see that the floor of the library was covered with a thick gray-brown carpet, flecked here and there with splotches of white and black.

It was a living, moving carpet. It was, in fact, the Mouse Army. All of the other buildings, places, and creatures Princess Nell had seen in the Land Beyond had been figments produced by Wizard 0.2; but apparently the mice were an exception and existed independently of King Coyote's machinations. When the Land Beyond had disappeared, all of the obstructions and impedimenta that had kept the Mouse Army away from Princess Nell had disappeared with it, and in short order they had been able to fix her whereabouts and to converge upon their long-sought Queen.

"What would you have me do?" Princess Nell said. She had never been a Queen before and did not know the protocol.

A chorus of excited squeaking came from the mice as commands were relayed and issued. The carpet went into violent but highly organized motion as the mice drew themselves up into platoons, companies, battalions, and regiments, each of them commanded by an officer. One mouse clambered up the leg of Princess Nell's table, bowed low to her, and then began to squeak commands from on high. The mice executed a close-order drill, withdrew to the edges of the room, and arrayed themselves in an empty box shape, leaving a large open rectangle in the middle of the floor.

The mouse up on the table, whom Nell had dubbed the Generalissima, issued a lengthy series of orders, running to each of the four edges of the table to address different contingents of the Mouse Army. When the Generalissima was finished, very high piping music could be heard as the mouse pipers played their bagpipes and the drummers beat their drums.

Small groups of mice began to encroach on the empty space, each group moving toward a different spot. Once each group had reached its assigned position, the individual mice arranged themselves in such a way that the group as a whole described a letter. In this way, the following message was written across the floor of the library:

WE ARE ENCHANTED
REQUEST ASSISTANCE
REFER TO BOOKS

"I shall bend all my efforts toward your disenchant-ment," Princess Nell said, and a tremendous, earsplitting scream of gratitude rose from the tiny throats of the Mouse Army.

Finding the required book did not take long. The Mouse Army split itself up into small detachments, each of which wrestled a different book from the shelf, opened it up on the floor, and scampered through it one page at a time, looking for relevant spells. Within the hour, Princess Nell noted that a broad open corridor had developed in the Mouse Army, and that a book was making its way toward her, seeming to float an inch above the floor.

She lifted the book carefully from the backs of the mice who were bearing it and flipped through it until she found a spell for the disenchantment of mice. "Very well then," she said, and began to read the spell; but suddenly, excited squeaking filled the air and all the mice were running away in a panic. The Generalissima climbed up onto the page, jumping up and down in a state of extreme agitation and waving her forelegs back and forth over her head.

"Ah, I understand," Princess Nell said. She picked up the book and walked out of the library, taking care not to step on any of her subjects, and followed them out to the vast empty space beyond.

Once again the Mouse Army put on a dazzling display of close-order drill, drawing itself up across the empty, col-orless plain by platoons, companies, battalions, regiments, and brigades; but this time the parade took up a much larger space, because this time the mice took care to space them-selves as far apart as the length of a human arm. Some of the platoons had to march what was, for them, a distance of many leagues in order to reach the edges of the formation. Princess Nell took advantage of the time to wander about and inspect the ranks, and to rehearse the spell.

Finally the Generalissima approached, bowed deeply, and gave her the thumbs-up, though Princess Nell had to pick the tiny leader up and squint to see this gesture.

She went to the place that had been left for her at the head of the formation, opened up the book, and spoke the magic spell.

There was a violent thunderclap, and a rush of wind that knocked Princess Nell flat on her back. She looked up, dazed, to see that she was surrounded by a vast army of some hundreds of thousands of girls, only a few years younger than she was. A wild cheer rose up, and all of the girls fell to their knees as one and, in a scene of riotous jubilation, proclaimed their fealty to Queen Nell.

Hackworth in China; depredations of the Fists; a meeting with Dr. X; an unusual procession.

*T*hey said that the Chinese had great respect for madmen, and that during the days of the Boxer Rebellion, certain Western missionaries, probably unstable characters to begin with, who had been trapped behind walls of rubble for weeks, scurrying through the sniper fire of the encircling Boxers and Imperial troops and listening to the cries of their flock being burned and tortured in the streets of Beijing, had become deranged and had walked unharmed into the ranks of their besiegers and been given food and treated with deference.

Now John Percival Hackworth, having checked into a suite on the top floor of the Shangri-La in Pudong (or Shong-a-lee-lah as the taxi-drivers sang it), put on a fresh shirt; his best waistcoat, girded with the gold chain, adangle with his chop, snuffboxes, fob, and watchphone; a long coat with a swallowtail for riding; boots, the black leather and brass spurs hand-shined in the lobby of the Shong-a-lee-lah by a coolie who was so servile that he was insolent, and Hackworth suspected him of being a Fist; new kid gloves; and his bowler, de-mossed and otherwise spruced up a bit, but obviously a veteran of many travels in rough territory.

As he crossed the western bank of the Huang Pu, the

usual crowd of starving peasants and professional amputees washed around him like a wave running up a flat beach because, though riding here was dangerous, it was not crazy, and they did not know him for a madman. He kept his gray eyes fixed upon the picket of burning Feed lines that demarcated the shrinking border of the Coastal Republic, and let their hands tug at his coattails, but he took no notice of them. At different times, three very rural young men, identifiable as much by their deep tans as their ignorance of modern security technology, made the mistake of reaching for his watch chain and received warning shocks for their trouble. One of them refused to let go until the smell of burned flesh rose from his palm, and then he peeled his hand away slowly and calmly, staring up at Hackworth to show that he didn't mind a little pain, and said something clearly and loudly that caused a titter to run through the crowd.

The ride down Nanjing Road took him through the heart of Shanghai's shopping district, now an endless gauntlet of tanned beggars squatting on their heels gripping the brightly colored plastic bags that served as their suitcases, carefully passing the butts of cigarettes back and forth. In the shop windows above their heads, animated mannikins strutted and posed in the latest Coastal Republic styles. Hackworth noticed that these were much more conservative than they had been ten years ago, during his last trip down Nanjing Road. The female mannikins weren't wearing slit skirts anymore. Many weren't wearing skirts at all, but silk pants instead, or long robes that were even less revealing. One display was centered upon a patriarchal figure who reclined on a dais, wearing a round cap with a blue button on the top: a mandarin. A young scholar was bowing to him. Around the dais, four groups of mannikins were demonstrating the other four filial relationships.

So it was chic to be Confucian now, or at least it was politic. This was one of the few shop windows that didn't have red Fist posters pasted all over it.

Hackworth rode past marble villas built by Iraqi Jews in previous centuries, past the hotel where Nixon had once stayed, past the high-rise enclaves that Western businessmen had used as the beachheads of the post-Communist development that had led to the squalid affluence of the

Coastal Republic. He rode past nightclubs the size of stadiums; jai-alai pits where stunned refugees gaped at the jostling of the bettors; side streets filled with boutiques, one street for fine goods made from alligators, another for furs, another for leathers; a nanotech district consisting of tiny businesses that did bespoke engineering; fruit and vegetable stands; a cul-de-sac where peddlers sold antiques from little carts, one specializing in cinnabar boxes, another in Maoist kitsch. Each time the density began to wane and he thought he must be reaching the edge of the city, he would come to another edge city of miniature three-story strip malls and it would begin again.

But as the day went on, he truly did approach the limit of the city and kept riding anyway toward the west, and it became evident then that he was a madman and the people in the streets looked at him with awe and got out of his way. Bicycles and pedestrians became less common, replaced by heavier and faster military traffic. Hackworth did not like riding on the shoulder of highways, and so he directed Kidnapper to find a less direct route to Suzhou, one that used smaller roads. This was flat Yangtze Delta territory only inches above the waterline, where canals, for transport, irrigation, and drainage, were more numerous than roads. The canals ramified through the black, stinky ground like blood vessels branching into the tissues of the brain. The plain was interrupted frequently by small tumuli containing the coffins of someone's ancestors, just high enough to stay above the most routine floods. Farther to the west, steep hills rose from the paddies, black with vegetation. The Coastal Republic checkpoints at the intersections of the roads were gray and fuzzy, like house-size clots of bread mold, so dense was the fractal defense grid, and staring through the cloud of macro- and microscopic aerostats, Hackworth could barely make out the hoplites in the center, heat waves rising from the radiators on their backs and stirring the airborne soup. They let him pass through without incident. Hackworth expected to see more checkpoints as he continued toward Fist territory, but the first one was the last; the Coastal Republic did not have the strength for defense in depth and could muster only a one-dimensional picket line.

A mile past the checkpoint, at another small intersection, Hackworth found a pair of very makeshift crucifixes fashioned from freshly cut mulberry trees, green leaves still fluttering from their twigs. Two young white men had been bound to the crucifixes with gray plastic ties, burned in many places and incrementally disemboweled. From the looks of their haircuts and the somber black neckties that had been ironically left around their necks, Hackworth guessed they were Mormons. A long skein of intestine trailed from one of their bellies down into the dirt, where a gaunt pig was tugging on it stubbornly.

He did not see much more death, but he smelled it everywhere in the hot wet air. He thought that he might be seeing a network of nanotech defense barriers until he realized that it was a natural phenomenon: Each waterway supported a linear black nimbus of fat, drowsy flies. From this he knew that if he tugged a bit on this or that rein and guided Kidnapper to the bank of the canal, he would find it filled with ballooning corpses.

Ten minutes after passing the Coastal Republic checkpoint, he rode through the center of a Fist encampment. As he looked neither right nor left, he could not really estimate its size; they had taken over a village of low brick-and-stucco buildings. A long straight smudge running across the earth marked the location of a burned Feed line, and as he crossed it, Hackworth fantasized that it was a meridian engraved on the living globe by an astral cartographer. Most of the Fists were shirtless, wearing indigo trousers, scarlet girdles knotted at the waist, sometimes scarlet ribbons tied round necks, foreheads, or upper arms. The ones who weren't sleeping or smoking were practicing martial arts. Hackworth rode slowly through their midst, and they pretended not to notice him, except for one man who came running out of a house with a knife, shouting "Sha! Sha!" and had to be tackled by three comrades.

As he rode the forty miles to Suzhou, nothing changed about the landscape except that creeks became rivers and ponds became lakes. The Fist encampments became somewhat larger and closer together. When the thick air infrequently roused itself to a breeze, he could smell the clammy metallic reek of stagnant water and knew he was close to the great lake of Tai Wu, or Taifu as the Shanghainese pronounced it. A grayscale dome rose from the paddies some miles away, casting a film of shadow before a cluster of tall buildings, and Hackworth knew it must be Suzhou, now a stronghold of the Celestial Kingdom, veiled in its airborne shield like a courtesan behind a translucent sheen of Suzhou silk.

Nearing the shore of the great lake he found his way onto an important road that ran south toward Hangzhou. He set Kidnapper ambling northward. Suzhou had thrown out tendrils of development along its major roads, and so as he drew closer he saw strip malls and franchises, now destroyed, deserted, or colonized by refugees. Most of these places catered to truck drivers: lots of motels, casinos, teahouses, and fast-food places. But no trucks ran on the highway now, and Hackworth rode down the center of a lane, sweating uncontrollably in his dark clothes and drinking frequently from a refrigerated bottle in Kidnapper's glove compartment.

A McDonald's sign lay toppled across the highway like a giant turnpike; something had burned through the single pillar that thrust it into the air. A couple of young men were standing in front of it smoking cigarettes and, as Hackworth realized, waiting for him. As Hackworth drew closer, they ground out their cigarettes, stepped forward, and bowed. Hackworth tipped his bowler. One of them took Kidnapper's reins, which was a purely ceremonial gesture in the case of a robot horse, and the other invited Hackworth to dismount. Both of the men were wearing heavy but flexible coveralls with cables and tubes running through the fabric: the inner layer of armor suits. They could turn themselves into battle-ready hoplites by slapping on the harder and heavier outer bits, which were presumably stashed somewhere handy. Their scarlet headbands identified them as Fists. Hackworth was one of the few members of the Outer Tribes ever to find himself in the presence of a Fist who was not running toward him with a weapon screaming "Kill! Kill!" and found it interesting to see them in a more indulgent mood. They were dignified, formal, and controlled, like military men, with none of the leering and snickering that were fashionable among Coastal Republic boys of the same age.

Hackworth walked across the parking lot toward the McDonald's, followed at a respectful distance by one of the soldiers. Another soldier opened the door for him, and

Hackworth sighed with delight as cold dry air flowed over his face and began to chase the muggy stuff through the weave of his clothing. The place had been lightly sacked. He could smell a cold, almost clinical greasy smell wafting from behind the counter, where containers of fat had spilled onto the floor and congealed like snow. Much of this had been scooped up by looters; Hackworth could see the parallel tracks of women's fingers. The place was decorated in a *Silk Road* motif, transpicuous mediatronic panels portraying wondrous sights between here and the route's ancient terminus in Cadiz.

Dr. X was seated in the corner booth, his face radiant in the cool, UV-filtered sunlight. He was wearing a mandarin cap with dragons embroidered in gold thread and a magnificent brocade robe. The robe was loose at the neck and had short sleeves so that Hackworth could see the inner garment of a hoplite suit underneath. Dr. X was at war, and had emerged from the safe perimeter of Suzhou, and needed to be prepared for an attack. He was sipping green tea from a jumbo McDonald's cup, made in the local style, great clouds of big green leaves swirling around in a tumbler of hot water. Hackworth doffed his hat and bowed in the Victorian style, which was proper under the circumstances. Dr. X returned the bow, and as his head tilted forward, Hackworth could see the button on the top of his cap. It was red, the color of the highest ranks, but it was made of coral, marking him as second rank. A ruby button would have put him at the very highest level. In Western terms this made Dr. X roughly equivalent to a lesser cabinet minister or three-star general. Hackworth supposed that this was the highest rank of mandarin permitted to converse with barbarians.

Hackworth sat down across the table from Dr. X. A young woman padded out of the kitchen on silk slippers and gave Hackworth his own tumbler full of green tea. Watching her mince away, Hackworth was only mildly shocked to see that her feet were no more than four inches long. There must be better ways to do it now, maybe by regulating the growth of the tarsal bones during adolescence. It probably didn't even hurt.

Realizing this, Hackworth also realized, for the first time, that he had done the right thing ten years ago.

Dr. X was watching him and might as well have been reading his mind. This seemed to put him in a pensive mood. He said nothing for a while, just gazed out the window and occasionally sipped his tea. This was fine with Hackworth, who had had a long ride.

"Have you learned anything from your ten-year sentence?" Dr. X finally said.

"It would seem so. But I have trouble pulling it up," Hackworth said.

This was a bit too idiomatic for Dr. X. By way of explanation, Hackworth flipped out a ten-year-old card bearing Dr. X's dynamic chop. As the old fisherman hauled the dragon out of the water, Dr. X suddenly got it, and grinned appreciatively. This was showing a lot of emotion—assuming it was genuine—but age and war had made him reckless.

"Have you found the Alchemist?" Dr. X said.

"Yes," Hackworth said. "I am the Alchemist."

"When did you know this?"

"Only very recently," Hackworth said. "Then I understood it all in an instant—I pulled it up," he said, pantomiming the act of reeling in a fish. "The Celestial Kingdom was far behind Nippon and Atlantis in nanotech. The Fists could always have burned the barbarians' Feed lines, but this would only have plunged the peasants into poverty and made the people long for foreign goods. The decision was made to leapfrog the barbarian tribes by developing Seed technology. At first you pursued the project in cooperation with second-tier phyles like Israel, Armenia, and Greater Serbia, but they proved unreliable. Again and again your carefully cultivated networks were scattered by Protocol Enforcement.

"But through these failures you made contact for the first time with CryptNet, whom you doubtless view as just another triad—a contemptible band of conspirators. However, CryptNet was tied in with something much deeper and more interesting—the society of the Drummers. With their flaky and shallow Western perspective, CryptNet didn't grasp the full power of the Drummers' collective mind. But you got it right away.

"All you required to initiate the Seed project was the rational, analytical mind of a nanotechnological engineer. I fit the bill perfectly. You dropped me into the society of the Drummers like a seed into fertile soil, and my knowledge spread through them and permeated their collective mind—as their thoughts spread into my own unconscious. They became like an extension of my own brain. For years I laboured on the problem, twenty-four hours a day.

"Then, before I was able to finish the job, I was pulled out by my superiors at Protocol Enforcement. I was close to being finished. But not finished yet."

"Your superiors had uncovered our plan?"

"Either they are completely ignorant, or else they know everything and are pretending ignorance," Hackworth said.

"But surely you have told them everything now," Dr. X said almost inaudibly.

"If I were to answer that question, you would have no reason not to kill me," Hackworth said.

Dr. X nodded, not so much to concede the point as to express sympathy with Hackworth's admirably cynical train of thought—as though Hackworth, after a series of seemingly inconclusive moves, had suddenly flipped over a large territory of stones on a go board.

"There are those on a go who would advocate that course, because of what has happened with the girls," Dr. X said.

Hackworth was so startled to hear this that he became somewhat lightheaded for a moment and too self-conscious to speak. "Have the Primers proved useful?" he finally said, trying not to sound giddy.

Dr. X grinned broadly for a moment. Then the emotion dropped beneath the surface again, like a breaching whale. "They must have been useful to someone," he said. "My opinion is that we made a mistake in saving the girls."

"How can this act of humanity possibly have been a mistake?"

Dr. X considered it. "It would be more correct to say that, although it was virtuous to save them, it was mistaken to believe that they could be raised properly. We lacked the resources to raise them individually, and so we raised them with books. But the only proper way to raise a child is within a family. The Master could have told us as much, had we listened to his words."

"Some of those girls will one day choose to follow in

the ways of the Master," Hackworth said, "and then the wisdom of your decisions will be demonstrated."

This seemed to be a genuinely new thought to Dr. X. His gaze returned to the window. Hackworth sensed that the matter of the girls and the Primers had been concluded.

"I will be open and frank," said Dr. X after some ruminative tea-slurping, "and you will not believe that I am being so, because it is in the heads of those from the Outer Tribes to think that we never speak directly. But perhaps in time you will see the truth of my words.

"The Seed is almost finished. When you left, the building of it slowed down very much—more than we expected. We thought that the Drummers, after ten years, had absorbed your knowledge and could continue the work without you. But there is something in your mind that you have gained through your years of scholarly studies that the Drummers, if they ever had it, have given up and cannot get back unless they come out of the darkness and live their lives in the light again.

"The war against the Coastal Republic reaches a critical moment. We ask you to help us now."

"I must say that it is nearly inconceivable for me to help you at this point," Hackworth said, "unless it would be in the interest of my tribe, which does not strike me as a likely prospect."

"We need you to help us finish building the Seed," Dr. X said doggedly.

Only decades of training in emotional repression kept Hackworth from laughing out loud. "Sir. You are a worldly man and a scholar. Certainly you are aware of the position of Her Majesty's government, and indeed of the Common Economic Protocol itself, on the subject of Seed technologies."

Dr. X raised one hand a few inches from the tabletop, palm down, and pawed once at the air. Hackworth recognized it as the gesture that well-to-do Chinese used to dismiss beggars, or even to call bullshit on people during meetings. "They are wrong," he said. "They do not understand. They think of the Seed from a Western perspective. Your cultures—and that of the Coastal Republic—are poorly organized. There is no respect for order, no reverence for authority. Order must be enforced from above lest anarchy break out. You are afraid to give the Seed to your people because they can use it to make weapons, viruses, drugs of their own design, and destroy order. You enforce order through control of the Feed. But in the Celestial Kingdom, we are disciplined, we revere authority, we have order within our own minds, and hence the family is orderly, the village is orderly, the state is orderly. In our hands the Seed would be harmless."

"Why do you need it?" Hackworth said.

"We must have technology to live," Dr. X said, "but we must have it with our own *ti*."

Hackworth thought for a moment that Dr. X was referring to the beverage. But the Doctor began to trace characters on the tabletop, his hand moving deftly and gracefully, the brocade sleeve rasping across the plastic surface. "*Yong* is the outer manifestation of something. *Ti* is the underlying essence. Technology is a *yong* associated with a particular *ti* that is"—the Doctor stumbled here and, through a noticeable effort, refrained from using pejorative terms like *barbarian* or *gwailo*—"that is Western, and completely alien to us. For centuries, since the time of the Opium Wars, we have struggled to absorb the *yong* of technology without importing the Western *ti*. But it has been impossible. Just as our ancestors could not open our ports to the West without accepting the poison of opium, we could not open our lives to Western technology without taking in the Western ideas, which have been as a plague on our society. The result has been centuries of chaos. We ask you to end that by giving us the Seed."

"I do not understand why the Seed will help you."

"The Seed is technology rooted in the Chinese *ti*. We have lived by the Seed for five thousand years," Dr. X said. He waved his hand toward the window. "These were rice paddies before they were parking lots. Rice was the basis for our society. Peasants planted the seeds and had highest status in the Confucian hierarchy. As the Master said, 'Let the producers be many and the consumers few.' When the Feed came in from Atlantis, from Nippon, we no longer had to plant, because the rice now came from the matter compiler. It was the destruction of our society. When our society was based upon planting, it could truly be said, as the Master did, 'Virtue is the root; wealth is the result.' But under the

Western *ti*, wealth comes not from virtue but from cleverness. So the filial relationships became deranged. Chaos," Dr. X said regretfully, then looked up from his tea and nodded out the window. "Parking lots and chaos."

Hackworth remained silent for a full minute. Images had come into his mind again, not a fleeting hallucination this time, but a full-fledged vision of a China freed from the yoke of the foreign Feed. It was something he'd seen before, perhaps something he'd even helped create. It showed something no *gwailo* would ever get to see: the Celestial Kingdom during the coming Age of the Seed. Peasants tended their fields and paddies, and even in times of drought and flood, the earth brought forth a rich harvest: food, of course, but many unfamiliar plants too, fruits that could be made into medicines, bamboo a thousand times stronger than the natural varieties, trees that produced synthetic rubber and pellets of clean safe fuel. In an orderly procession the suntanned farmers brought their proceeds to great markets in clean cities free of cholera and strife, where all of the young people were respectful and dutiful scholars and all of the elders were honored and cared for. This was a ractive simulation as big as all of China, and Hackworth could have lost himself in it, and perhaps did for he knew not how long. But finally he closed his eyes, blinked it away, sipped some tea to bring his rational mind back into control.

"Your arguments are not without merit," Hackworth said. "Thank you for helping me to see the matter in a different light. I will ponder these questions on my return to Shanghai."

Dr. X escorted him to the parking lot of the McDonald's. The heat felt pleasant at first, like a relaxing bath, though Hackworth knew that soon he would feel as if he were drowning in it. Kidnapper ambled over and folded its legs, allowing Hackworth to mount it easily.

"You have helped us willingly for ten years," Dr. X said. "It is your destiny to make the Seed."

"Nonsense," Hackworth said, "I did not know the nature of the project."

Dr. X smiled. "You knew it perfectly well." He freed one hand from the long sleeves of his robe and shook his finger at Hackworth, like an indulgent teacher pretending to scold a clever but mischievous pupil. "You do these things not to serve your Queen but to serve your own nature, John Hackworth, and I understand your nature. For you cleverness is its own end, and once you have seen a clever way to do a thing, you must do it, as water finding a crack in a dike must pass through it and cover the land on the other side."

"Farewell, Dr. X," Hackworth said. "You will understand that although I hold you in the highest personal esteem, I cannot earnestly wish you good fortune in your current endeavour." He doffed his hat and bowed low to one side, forcing Kidnapper to adjust its stance a bit. Dr. X returned the bow, giving Hackworth another look at that coral button on his cap. Hackworth spurred Kidnapper on to Shanghai.

He followed a more northerly route now, along one of the many radial highways that converged on the metropolis. After he had been riding for some time, he became consciously aware of a sound that had been brushing against the outer fringes of perceptibility for some time: a heavy, distant, and rapid drumbeat, perhaps twice as fast as the beat of his own heart. His first thought, of course, was of the Drummers, and he was tempted to explore one of the nearby canals to see whether their colony had spread its tendrils this far inland. But then he looked northward across the flat land for a couple of miles and saw a long procession making its way down another highway, a dark column of pedestrians marching on Shanghai.

He saw that his path was converging with theirs, so he spurred Kidnapper forward at a hand-gallop, hoping to reach the intersection of the roads before it was clogged by this column of refugees. Kidnapper outdistanced them easily, but to no avail; when he reached the intersection, he found it had been seized by the column's vanguard, which had established a roadblock there and would not let him pass.

The contingent now controlling the intersection consisted entirely of girls, some eleven or twelve years old. There were several dozen of them, and they had apparently taken the objective by force from a smaller group of Fists, who could now be seen lying in the shade of some mulberry trees, hogtied with plastic rope. Probably three-quarters of the girls were on guard duty, mostly armed with sharpened bamboo stakes, though a few guns and blades were in evidence. The remaining quarter were on break, hunkered down in a circle near the intersection, sipping freshly boiled water and concentrating intently on books. Hackworth recognized the books; they were all identical, and they all had marbled jade covers, though all of them had been personalized with stickers, graffiti, and other decorations over the years.

Hackworth realized that several more girls, organized in groups of four, had been following him down the road on bicycles; these outriders passed by him now and rejoined their group.

He had no choice but to wait until the column had passed. The drumbeat grew and grew in volume until the pavement shook with each blow, and the shock absorption gear built into Kidnapper's legs went into play, flinching minutely at each beat. Another vanguard passed through: Hackworth easily calculated its size at two hundred and fifty-six. A battalion was four platoons, each of which was four companies of four troops of four girls each. The vanguard consisted of one such battalion, moving at a very brisk double-time, probably going ahead of the main group to fall upon the next major intersection.

Then, finally, the main column passed through, organized in battalions, each foot hitting the ground in unison with all the others. Each battalion carried a few sedan chairs, which were passed from one four-girl troop to another every few minutes to spread out the work. They were not luxurious palanquins but were improvised from bamboo and plastic rope and upholstered with materials stripped from old plastic cafeteria furniture. Riding in these chairs were girls who did not seem all that different from the others, except that they might have been a year or two older. They did not seem to be officers; they were not giving orders and wore no special insignia. Hackworth did not understand why they were riding in sedan chairs until he got a look at one of them, who had crossed one ankle up on her knee and taken her slipper off. Her foot was defective; it was several inches too short.

But all of the other sedan chair girls were deeply absorbed in their Primers. Hackworth unclipped a small optical device from his watch chain, a nanotech telescope/

microscope that frequently came in handy, and used it to look over one girl's shoulder. She was looking at a diagram of a small nanotechnological device, working her way through a tutorial that Hackworth had written several years ago.

The column went past much faster than Hackworth had feared; they moved down the highway like a piston. Each battalion carried a banner, a very modest thing improvised from a painted bedsheet. Each banner bore the number of the battalion and a crest that Hackworth knew well, as it played an important role in the Primer. In all, he counted two hundred and fifty-six battalions. Sixty-five thousand girls ran past him, hell-bent on Shanghai.

From the Primer, Princess Nell's return to the Dark Castle; the death of Harv; The Books of the Book and of the Seed; Princess Nell's quest to find her mother. Destruction of the Causeway; Nell falls into the hands of Fists; she escapes into a greater peril; deliverance.

Princess Nell could have used all of the powers she had acquired during her great quest to dig Harv's grave or caused the work to be done for her by the Disenchanted Army, but it did not seem fitting, and so instead she found an old rusty shovel hung up in one of the Dark Castle's outbuildings. The ground was dry and stony and veined with the roots of thornbushes, and more than once the shovel struck ancient bones. Princess Nell dug throughout the long day, softening the hard earth with her tears, but did not slacken until the ground was level with her own head. Then she went into the little room in the Dark Castle where Harv had died of a consumption, carefully wrapped his withered body in fine white silk, and bore it out to the grave. She had found lilies growing wild in the overgrown flower-garden by the little fisherman's cottage, so she put a spray of these in the grave with him, along with a little children's storybook that Harv had given her for a present many years ago. Harv could not read, and many nights as they had sat round the fire in the courtyard of the Dark Castle, Nell had read to him from this book, and she supposed that he might like to have it wherever he was going now.

Filling in the grave went quickly; the loose dirt more than filled the hole. Nell left more lilies atop the long low mound of earth that marked Harv's resting place. Then she turned her back and walked into the Dark Castle. The stain-colored granite walls had picked up some salmon highlights from the western sky, and she suspected that she could see a beautiful sunset from the room in the high tower where she had established her library.

It was a long climb up a dank and mildewy staircase that wound up the inside of the Dark Castle's highest tower. In the circular room at the top, which was built with mullioned windows looking out in all directions, Nell had placed all of the books she had gathered during her quest: books given her as presents by Purple, books from the library of King Magpie, the first Faery King that she had vanquished, and more from the palace of the djinn, and Castle Turing, and many other hidden libraries and treasuries that she had discovered or pillaged on her way. And, of course, there was the entire library of King Coyote, which contained so many books that she had not even had time to look at them yet.

There was so much work to be done. Copies of all of these books had to be made for all of the girls in the Disenchanted Army. The Land Beyond had vanished, and Princess Nell wanted to make it anew. She wanted to write down her own story in a great book that young girls could read. And she had one remaining quest that had been pressing on her mind of late, during her long voyage across the empty sea back to the island of the Dark Castle: she wanted to solve the mystery of her own origins. She wanted to find her mother. Even after the destruction of the Land Beyond, she had sensed the presence of another in the world, one who had always been there. King Coyote himself had confirmed it. Long ago, her stepfather, the kindly fisherman, had received her from mermaids; whence had the mermaids gotten her?

She suspected that the answer could not be found without the wisdom contained in her library. She began by causing a catalog to be made, starting with the first books she had gotten on her early adventures with her Night Friends. At the same time she established a Scriptorium in the great hall of the castle, where thousands of girls sat at long tables making exact copies of all of the books.

Most of King Coyote's books had to do with the secrets of atoms and how to put them together to make machines. Naturally, all of them were magic books; the pictures moved, and you could ask them questions and get answers. Some of them were primers and workbooks for novices, and Princess Nell spent a few days studying this art, putting atoms together to make simple machines and then watching them run.

Next came a very large set of matched volumes containing reference materials: One contained designs for thousands of sleeve bearings, another for computers made of rods, still another for energy storage devices, and all of them were ractive so that she could use them to design such things to her own specifications. Then there were more books on the general principles of putting such things together into systems.

Finally, King Coyote's library included some books inscribed in the King's own hand, containing designs for his greatest masterpieces. Of these, the two very finest were the Book of the Book and the Book of the Seed. They were magnificent folio-size volumes, as thick as Princess Nell's hand was broad, bound in rich leather illuminated with hair-thin gilt lines in an elaborate interlace pattern, and closed with heavy brass hasps and locks.

The lock on the Book of the Book yielded to the same key that Princess Nell had taken from King Coyote. She had discovered this very early in her exploration of the library but was unable to comprehend the contents of this volume until she had studied the others and learnt the secrets of these machines. The Book of the Book contained a complete set of plans for a magical book that would tell stories to a young person, tailoring them for the child's needs and interests—even teaching them how to read if need be. It was a fearsomely complicated work, and Princess Nell only skimmed it at first, recognizing that to understand the particulars might take years of study.

The lock on the Book of the Seed would not yield to King Coyote's key or to any other key in Princess Nell's possession, and because this book had been built atom by atom, it was stronger than any mortal substance and could not possibly be broken open. Princess Nell did not know what this book was about; but the cover bore an inlaid illustration of a striped seed, like the apple-sized seed that she had seen used in King Coyote's city to build a crystal pavilion, and this foreshadowed the book's purpose clearly enough.

Nell opened her eyes and propped herself up on one elbow. The Primer fell shut and slid off her belly onto the mattress. She had fallen asleep reading it.

The girls on their bunkbeds lay all around her, breathing quietly and smelling of soap. It made her want to lie back down and sleep too. But for some reason she was up on one elbow. Some instinct had told her she had to be up.

She sat up and drew her knees up to her chest, freeing the hem of her nightgown from between the sheets, then spun around and dropped to the floor soundlessly. Her bare feet took her silently between the rows of bunks and into the little lounge in the corner of the floor where the girls sat together, had tea, brushed their hair, watched old passives. It was empty now, the lights were off, the corner windows exposing a vast panorama: to the northeast, the lights of New Chusan and of the Nipponese and Hindustani concessions standing a few kilometers offshore, and the outlying parts of Pudong. Downtown Pudong was all around, its floating, mediatronic skyscrapers like biblical pillars of fire. To the northwest lay the Huang Pu River, Shanghai, its suburbs, and the ravaged silk and tea districts beyond. No fires burned there now; the Feed lines had been burned all the way to the edge of the city, and the Fists had stopped at the outskirts and hunkered down as they sought a way to penetrate the tattered remains of the security grid.

Nell's eye was drawn toward the water. Downtown Pudong offered the most spectacular urban nightscape ever devised, but she always found herself looking past it, staring instead at the Huang Pu, or the Yangzte to the north, or to the curvature of the Pacific beyond New Chusan.

She'd been having a dream, she realized. She had awakened not because of any external disturbance but because of what had happened in that dream. She had to remember it; but, of course, she couldn't.

Just a few snatches: a woman's face, a beautiful young woman, perhaps wearing a crown, but seen muddily, as through turbulent water. And something that glittered in her hands.

No, dangling beneath her hands. A piece of jewelry on a golden chain.

Could it have been a key? Nell could not bring the image back, but an instinct told her that it was.

Another detail too: a gleaming swath of something that passed in front of her face once, twice, three times. Something yellow, with a repeating pattern woven into it: a crest consisting of a book, a seed, and crossed keys.

Cloth of gold. Long ago the mermaids had brought her to her stepfather, and she had been wrapped in cloth of gold, and from this she had always known that she was a Princess.

The woman in the dream, veiled in swirling water, must have been her mother. The dream was a memory from her lost infancy. And before her mother had given her up to the mermaids, she had given Princess Nell a golden key on a chain.

Nell perched herself on the windowsill, leaned against the pane, opened the Primer, and flipped all the way back to the beginning. It started with the same old story, as ever, but told now in more mature prose. She read the story of how her stepfather had gotten her from the mermaids, and read it again, drawing out more details, asking it questions, calling up detailed illustrations.

There, in one of the illustrations, she saw it: her stepfather's lockbox, a humble plank chest bound in rusted iron straps, with a heavy old-fashioned padlock, stored underneath his bed. It was in this chest that he had stored the cloth of gold—and, perhaps, the key as well.

Paging forward through the book, she came across a long-forgotten story of how, following her stepfather's disappearance, her wicked stepmother had taken the lockbox to a high cliff above the sea and flung it into the waves, destroying any evidence that Princess Nell was of royal blood. She had not known that her stepdaughter was watching her from between the branches of a thicket, where she often concealed herself during her stepmother's rages.

Nell flipped to the last page of the *Young Lady's Illustrated Primer*.

As Princess Nell approached the edge of the cliff, picking her way along carefully through the darkness, taking care not to snag the train of her nightgown on thorny shrubs, she experienced a peculiar feeling that the entire ocean had become dimly luminescent. She had often noticed this phenomenon from the high windows of her library in the tower and reckoned that the waves must be reflecting back the light of the moon and stars. But this was a cloudy night, the sky was like a bowl of carved onyx, allowing no light to pass down from the heavens. The light she saw must emanate from beneath.

Arriving cautiously at the rim of the cliff, she saw that her surmise was true. The ocean—the one constant in all the world—the place from where she had come as an infant, from which the Land Beyond had grown out of King Coyote's seed, and into which it had dissolved—the ocean was alive. Since the departure of King Coyote, Princess Nell had supposed herself entirely alone in the world. But now she saw cities of light beneath the waves and knew that she was alone only by her own choice.

" 'Princess Nell gathered the hem of her nightgown in both hands and raised it over her head, letting the chill wind stream over her body and carry the garment away,' " Nell said. " 'Then, drawing a deep breath and closing her eyes, she bent her legs and sprang forward into space.' "

She was reading about the way the illuminated waves rushed up toward her when suddenly the room filled with light. She looked toward the door, thinking that someone had come in and turned the lights on, but she was alone in the room, and the light was flickering against the wall. She turned her head the other way.

The center span of the Causeway had become a ball of white light hurling its marbled shroud of cold dark matter into the night. The sphere expanded until it seemed to occupy most of the interval between New Chusan and the Pudong shoreline, though by this time the color had deepened from white into reddish-orange, and the explosion had punched a sizable crater into the water, which developed into a circular wave of steam and spray that ran effortlessly across the ocean's surface like the arc of light cast by a pocket torch.

Fragments of the giant Feed line that had once constituted most of the Causeway's mass had been pitched into the sky by the explosion and now tumbled end over end through the night sky, the slowness of their motion bespeaking their size, casting yellow sulfurous light over the city as they burned furiously in the wind-blast created by their own movement. The light limned a pair of tremendous pillars of water vapor rising from the ocean north and south of the Causeway; Nell realized that the Fists must have blown the

Nipponese and Hindustani Feeds at the same moment. So the Fists of Righteous Harmony had nanotechnological explosives now; they'd come a long way since they'd tried to torch the bridge over the Huang Pu with a few cylinders of hydrogen.

The shock wave rapped at the window, startling several of the girls from sleep. Nell heard them murmuring to one another in the bunk room. She wondered if she should go in and warn them that Pudong was cut off now, that the final assault of the Fists had commenced. But though she could not understand what they were saying, she could understand their tone of voice clearly enough: They were not surprised by this, nor unhappy.

They were all Chinese and could become subjects of the Celestial Kingdom simply by donning the conservative garb of that tribe and showing due deference to any mandarins who happened by. No doubt this was exactly what they would do as soon as the Fists came to Pudong. Some of them might suffer deprivation, imprisonment, or rape, but within a year they would all be integrated into the C.K., as if the Coastal Republic had never existed.

But if the news feeds from the interior meant anything, the Fists would kill Nell gradually, with many small cuts and burns, when they grew weary of raping her. In recent days she had often seen the Chinese girls talking in little groups and sneaking glances at her, and the suspicion had grown in her breast that some of them might know of the attack in advance and might make arrangements to turn Nell over to the Fists as a demonstration of their loyalty.

She opened the door a crack and saw two of these girls padding toward the bunk room where Nell usually slept, carrying lengths of red polymer ribbon.

As soon as they had stolen into Nell's bunk room, Nell ran down the corridor and got to the elevators. As she awaited the elevator, she was more scared than she had ever been; the sight of the cruel red ribbons in the small hands of the girls had for some reason struck more terror into her heart than the sight of knives in the hands of Fists.

A shrill commotion arose from the bunk room.

The bell for the elevator sounded.

She heard the bunk room door fly open, and someone running down the hall.

The elevator door opened.

One of the girls came into the lobby, saw her, and shrieked something to the others in a dolphinlike squeal.

Nell got into the elevator, punched the button for the lobby, and held down the DOOR CLOSE button. The girl thought for a moment, then stepped forward to hold the door. Several more girls were running down the hall. Nell kicked the girl in the face, and she spun away in a helix of blood. The elevator door began to close. Just as the two doors were meeting in the center, through the narrowing slit she saw one of the other girls diving toward the wall button. The doors closed. There was a brief pause, and then they slid open again.

Nell was already in the correct stance to defend herself. If she had to beat each of the girls to death individually, she would do it. But none of them rushed the elevator. Instead, the leader stepped forward and aimed something at Nell. There was a little popping noise, a pinprick in Nell's midsection, and within a few seconds she felt her arms becoming impossibly heavy. Her bottom drooped. Her head bowed. Her knees buckled. She could not keep her eyes open; as they closed, she saw the girls coming toward her, smiling with pleasure, holding up the red ribbons. Nell could not move any part of her body, but she remained perfectly conscious as they tied her up with the ribbon. They did it slowly and methodically and perfectly; they did it every day of their lives.

The tortures of the next few hours were of a purely experimental and preliminary nature. They did not last for long and accomplished no permanent damage. These girls had made a living out of binding and torturing people in a way that didn't leave scars, and that was all they really knew. When the leader came up with the idea of shoving a cigarette into Nell's cheek, it was something entirely novel and left the rest of the girls startled and silent for a few minutes. Nell sensed that most of the girls had no stomach for such things and merely wanted to turn her over to the Fists in exchange for citizenship in the Celestial Kingdom.

The Fists themselves began to arrive some twelve hours later. Some of them wore conservative business suits, some wore the uniforms of the building's security force, others looked as if they'd arrived to take a girl out to a disco.

They all had things to do when they arrived. It was obvious that this suite would act as local headquarters of some sort when the rebellion began in earnest. They began to bring up supplies on the freight elevator and seemed to spend a lot of time on the telephone. More arrived every hour, until Madame Ping's suite was playing host to between one and two dozen. Some of them were very tired and dirty and went to sleep in the bunks immediately.

In a way, Nell wished that they would do whatever they were going to do and get it over with fast. But nothing happened for quite some time. When the first Fists arrived, the girls brought them in to see Nell, who had been shoved under a bed and was now lying there in a puddle of her own urine. The leader shone a light on her face briefly and then turned away, completely uninterested. It seemed that once he'd verified that the girls had done their bit for the revolution, Nell ceased to be relevant.

She supposed it was inevitable that, in due time, these men would take those liberties with her that have ever been claimed as angary by irregular fighting men, who have willfully severed themselves from the softening feminine influence of civilized society, with those women who have had the misfortune to become their captives. To make this prospect less attractive, she took the desperate measure of allowing her person to become tainted with the noisome issue of her natural internal processes. But most of the Fists were too busy, and when some of the grungy foot-soldier types arrived, Madame Ping's girls were eager to make themselves useful in this regard. Nell reflected that a bunch of soldiers who found themselves billeted in a bawdy-house would naturally arrive with certain expectations, and that the inmates would be unwise to disappoint them.

Nell had gone into the world to seek her fortune and this was what she had found. She understood more forcibly than ever the wisdom of Miss Matheson's remarks about the hostility of the world and the importance of belonging to a powerful tribe; all of Nell's intellect, her vast knowledge and skills, accumulated over a lifetime of intensive training, meant nothing at all when she was confronted with a handful of organized peasants. She could not really sleep in her current position but drifted in and out of consciousness, visited occasionally by hallucinatory waking dreams. More than once she dreamed that the Constable had come in his hoplite suit to rescue her; and the pain she felt when she returned to full consciousness and realized that her mind had been lying to her, was worse than any tortures others might inflict.

Eventually they got tired of the stink under the bed and dragged her out of there on a smear of half-dried body fluids. It had been at least thirty-six hours since her capture. The leader of the girls, the one who had put out the cigarette on Nell's face, cut the red ribbon away and cut off Nell's filthy nightgown with it. Nell's limbs bounced on the floor. The leader had brought a whip that they sometimes used on clients and beat Nell with it until circulation returned. This spectacle drew quite a crowd of Fist soldiers, who crowded into the bunk room to watch.

The girl drove Nell on hands and knees to a maintenance closet and made her get out a bucket and mop. Then she made Nell clean up the mess under the bed, frequently inspecting the results and beating her, apparently acting out a parody of a rich Westerner bossing around some poor running dog. It became clear after the third or fourth scrubbing of the floor that this was being done as much for the entertainment of the soldiers as for hygienic reasons.

Then it was back to the maintenance closet, where Nell was bound again, this time with lightweight police shackles, and left there on the floor in the dark, naked and filthy. A few minutes later, her possessions—some clothes that the girls didn't like and a book they couldn't read—were thrown in there with her.

When she was sure that the girl with the whip had gone, she spoke to her Primer and told it to make light.

She could see a big matter compiler on the floor in the back of the closet; the girls used it to manufacture larger items when they were needed. This building was apparently hooked up to the Coastal Republic's Pudong Feed, because it hadn't lost Feed services when the Causeway had blown up; and indeed the Fists probably would not have bothered to establish their base here if the place had been cut off.

Once every couple of hours or so, a Fist would come into this closet and order the M.C. to create something, usually a simple bulk substance like rations. On two of these occasions, Nell was outraged in the manner she had long suspected was inevitable. She closed her eyes during the commission of these atrocities, knowing that whatever might be done to the mere vessel of her soul by the likes of these, her soul itself was as serene, as remote from their grasp, as is the full moon from the furious incantations of an aboriginal shaman. She tried to think about the machine that she was designing in her head, with the help of the Primer, about how the gears meshed and the bearings spun, how the rod logic was programmed and where the energy was stored.

On her second night in the closet, after most of the Fists had gone to bed and use of the matter compiler had apparently ceased for the night, she instructed the Primer to load her design into the M.C.'s memory, then crept forward and pressed the START button with her tongue.

Ten minutes later, the machine released its vacuum with a shriek. Nell tongued the door open. A knife and a sword rested on the floor of the M.C. She turned herself around, moving in small, cautious increments and breathing deeply so that she would not whimper from the pain emanating from those parts of her that were most tender and vulnerable and yet had been most viciously depredated by her captors. She reached backward with her shackled hands and gripped the handle of the knife.

Footsteps were approaching down the hallway. Someone must have heard the hiss of the M.C. and thought it was dinner time. But Nell couldn't rush this; she had to be careful.

The door opened. It was one of the ranking Fists, perhaps the rough equivalent of a sergeant. He shone a torch in her face, then chuckled and turned on the overhead light.

Nell's body blocked his view of the M.C., but it was obvious that she was reaching for something. He probably assumed it was only food.

He stepped forward and kicked her casually in the ribs, then grabbed her upper arm and jerked her away from the M.C., causing such pain in her wrists that tears spurted down her face. But she held on to the knife.

The Fist was staring into the M.C. He was startled and would be for several moments. Nell maneuvered the knife so that the blade was touching nothing but the link between the shackles, then hit the ON switch. It worked; the edge of the blade came to life like a nanotech chainsaw and zipped through the link in a moment, like clipping a fingernail. Nell brought it around her body in the same motion and buried it in the base of the Fist's spine.

He fell to the ground without speaking—he wasn't feeling any pain from that wound or from anything below his waist. Before he could assess matters any further, she plunged the knife into the base of his skull.

He was wearing simple peasant stuff: indigo trousers and a tank-top. She put them on. Then she tied her hair up behind her head using strings cut from a mop and devoted a precious minute or two to stretching her arms and legs.

And then it was out into the hallway with her knife in her waistband and her sword in her hands. Going round a corner, she cut a man in half as he emerged from the bathroom; the sword kept going of its own momentum and carved a long gash in the wall. This assault released a prodigious amount of blood, which Nell put behind her as quickly as possible. Another man was on guard in the elevator lobby, and as he came to investigate the sounds, she ran him through several times quickly, taking a page from Napier's book this time.

The elevators were now under some kind of central control and probably subject to surveillance; rather than press the button in the lobby, she cut a hole in the doors, sheathed her sword, and clambered out onto a ladder that ran down the shaft.

She forced herself to descend slowly and carefully, pressing herself flat against the rungs whenever the car went by. By the time she had descended perhaps fifty or sixty floors, the building had come awake; all of the cars were in constant motion, and when they went past her, she could hear men talking excitedly inside them.

Light flooded into the shaft several floors below. The doors had been forced open. A couple of Fists thrust their heads out carefully into the shaft and began looking up and down, shining torches here and there. Several floors below them, more Fists pried another door open; but they had to pull their heads in rapidly as the ascending car nearly decapitated them.

She had imagined that Madame Ping's was playing host to an isolated cell of Fists, but it was now clear that most if not all of the building had been taken over. For that matter, all of Pudong might now be a part of the Celestial Kingdom. Nell was much more profoundly isolated than she had feared.

The skin of her arms glowed yellow-pink in the beam of a torch shone up from below. She did not make the mistake of looking down into the dazzling light and did not have to; the excited voice of the Fist below her told her that she had been discovered. A moment later, the light vanished as the ascending elevator interposed itself between Nell and the Fists who had seen her.

She recalled Harv and his buds elevator-surfing in their old building and reckoned that this would be a good time to take up the practice. As the car rose toward her, she jumped off the ladder, trying to give herself enough upward thrust to match its velocity. She landed hard on the roof, for it was moving far more rapidly than she could jump. The roof knocked her feet out from under her, and she fell backward, slamming her arms out as Dojo had taught her so that she absorbed the impact with her fists and forearms, not her back.

More excited talking from inside the car. The access panel on the roof suddenly flew into the air, driven out of its frame by a well-delivered kick from below. A head popped out of the open hatch; Nell skewered it on her knife. The man tumbled down into the car. There was no point in waiting now; the situation had gone into violent motion, which Nell was obliged to use. She rolled onto her belly and kicked both feet downward into the hatch, spun down into the car, landed badly on the corpse, and staggered to one knee. She had barked the point of her chin on the edge of the hatch as she fell through and bitten her tongue, so she was slightly dazed. A gaunt man in a black leather skullcap was standing directly in front of her, reaching for a gun, and while she was shoving her knife up through the center of his thorax, she bumped into someone behind her. She jumped to her feet and spun around, terrified, readying the knife for another blow, and discovered a much more terrified man in a blue coverall, standing by the elevator's control panel, holding his arms up in front of his face and screaming.

Nell stepped back and lowered the point of the knife. The man was wearing the uniform of a building services worker and had obviously been yanked away from whatever he had been doing and put in charge of the elevator's controls. The man whom Nell had just killed, the one in the black leather skullcap, was some sort of low-level official in the rebellion and could not be expected to demean himself by punching the buttons himself.

"Keep going! Up! Up!" she said, pointing at the ceiling. The last thing she wanted was for him to stop the elevator at Madame Ping's.

The man bowed several times in quick succession and did something with the controls, then turned and smiled ingratiatingly at Nell.

As a Coastal Republic citizen working in services, he knew a few words of English, and Nell knew a few of Chinese. "Down below—Fists?" she said.

"Many Fist."

"Ground floor—Fists?"

"Yes, many Fist ground floor."

"Street—Fists?"

"Fist, army have fight in street."

"Around this building?"

"Fist around this building all over."

Nell looked at the elevator's control panel: four columns of tightly spaced buttons, color-coded according to each floor's function: green for shopping, yellow for residential, red for offices, and blue for utility floors. Most of the blue floors were below ground level, but one of them was fifth from the top.

"Building office?" she said, pointing to it.

"Yes."

"Fists there?"

"No, Fist all down below. But Fist on roof!"

"Go there."

When the elevator reached the fifth floor from the top, Nell had the man freeze it there, then climbed on top and trashed its motors so that it would remain there. She dropped back into the car, trying not to look at the bodies or smell the reek of blood and other body fluids that had gotten all over it, and that were now draining out the open doors and dripping down the shaft. It would not take long for any of this to be discovered.

She had some time, though; all she had to do was

decide how to make use of it. The maintenance closet had a
matter compiler, just like the one Nell had used to make her
weapons, and she knew that she could use it to compile
explosives and booby-trap the lobby. But the Fists had explosives of their own and could just as well blow the top
floors of the building to kingdom come.

For that matter, they were probably down in some
basement control room watching traffic on the building's
Feed network. Use of the M.C. would simply announce her
location; they would shut off the Feed and then come after
her slowly and carefully.

She took a quick tour of the offices, sizing up her resources. Looking out the panoramic windows of the finest
office suite, she saw a new state of affairs in the streets of
Pudong. Many of the skyscrapers had been rooted in lines
from the foreign Feeds and were now dark, though in some
places flames vented from broken windows, casting primitive illumination over the streets a thousand feet below.
These buildings had mostly been evacuated, and so the
streets were crowded with far more people than they could
really handle. The plaza immediately surrounding this particular building had been staked out by a picket line of Fists
and was relatively uncrowded.

She found a windowless room with mediatronic walls
that bore a bewildering collage of images: flowers, details of
European cathedrals and Shinto temples, Chinese landscape
art, magnified images of insects and pollen grains, many-
armed Indian goddesses, planets and moons of the solar
system, abstract patterns from the Islamic world, graphs of
mathematical equations, head shots of models male and female. Other than that, the room was empty except for a
model of the building that stood in the center of the room,
about Nell's height. The model's skin was mediatronic, just
like the skin of the building itself, and it was currently echoing (as she supposed) whatever images were being displayed on the outside of the building: mostly advertising
panels, though some Fists had apparently come in here and
scrawled graffiti across them.

On top of the model rested a stylus—just a black stick
pointed on one end—and a palette, covered with a color
wheel and other controls. Nell picked them up, touched the
tip of the stylus to a green area on the palette's color wheel,

and drew it across the surface of the model. A glowing green line appeared along the track of the stylus, disfiguring an ad panel for an airship line.

Whatever other steps Nell might take in the time she had left, there was one thing she could do quickly and easily here. She was not entirely sure why she did it, but some intuition told her that it might be useful; or perhaps it was an artistic urge to make something that would live longer than she would, even if only by a few minutes. She began by erasing all of the big advertising panels on the upper levels of the skyscraper. Then she sketched out a simple line drawing in primary colors: an escutcheon in blue, and within it, a crest depicting a book drawn in red and white; crossed keys in gold; and a seed in brown. She caused this image to be displayed on all sides of the skyscraper, between the hundredth and two-hundredth floors.

Then she tried to think of a way out of this place. Perhaps there were airships on the roof. There would certainly be Fist guards up there, but perhaps through a combination of stealth and suddenness she could overcome them. She used the emergency stairs to make her way up to the next floor, then the next, and then the next. Two flights above, she could hear Fist guards posted at the roof, talking to each other and playing mah-jongg. Many flights below, she could hear more Fists making their way up the stairs one flight at a time, looking for her.

She was pondering her next move when the guards above her were rudely interrupted by orders squawking from their radios. Several Fists came charging down the stairway, shouting excitedly. Nell, trapped in the stairwell, made herself ready to ambush them as they came toward her, but instead they ran into the top floor and made for the elevator lobby. Within a minute or two, an elevator had arrived and carried them away. Nell waited for a while, listening, and could no longer hear the contingent approaching from below.

She climbed up the last flights of stairs and emerged onto the building's roof, exhilarated as much by the fresh air as by the discovery that it was completely deserted. She walked to the edge of the roof and peered down almost half a mile to the street. In the black windows of a dead skyscraper across the way, she could see the mirror image of Princess Nell's crest.

After a minute or two, she noticed that something akin to a shock wave was making its way down the street far below, moving in slow motion, covering a city block every couple of minutes. Details were difficult to make out at this distance: it was a highly organized group of pedestrians, all wearing the same generally dark clothing, ramming its way through the mob of refugees, forcing the panicked barbarians toward the picket line of the Fists or sideways into the lobbies of the dead buildings.

Nell was transfixed for several minutes by this sight. Then she happened to glance down a different street and saw the same phenomenon there.

She made a quick circuit of the building's roof. All in all, several columns were advancing inexorably on the foundations of the building where Nell stood.

In time, one of these columns broke through the last of the obstructing refugees and reached the edge of the broad open plaza that surrounded the foot of Nell's building, where it faced off against the Fist defenses. The column stopped abruptly at this point and waited for a few minutes, collecting itself and waiting for the other columns to catch up.

Nell had supposed at first that these columns might be Fist reinforcements converging on this building, which was clearly intended to be the headquarters of their final assault on the Coastal Republic. But it soon became evident that these newcomers had arrived for other purposes. After a few minutes of unbearable tension had gone by in nearly perfect silence, the columns suddenly, on the same unheard signal, erupted into the plaza. As they debouched from the narrow streets, they spread out into many-pronged formations, arranging themselves with the precision of a professional drill team, and then charged forward into the suddenly panicked and disorganized Fists, throwing up a tremendous battle-cry. When that sound echoed up two hundred stories to Nell's ears, she felt her hair standing on end, because it was not the deep lusty roar of grown men but the fierce thrill of thousands of young girls, sharp and penetrating as the skirl of massed bagpipes.

It was Nell's tribe, and they had come for their leader. Nell spun on her heel and made for the stairway.

By the time she had reached ground level and burst out, somewhat unwisely, into the building's lobby, the girls had breached the walls of the building in several places and rushed in upon the remaining defenders. They moved in groups of four. One girl (the largest) would rush toward an opponent, holding a pointed bamboo stick aimed at his heart. While his attention was thus fixed, two other girls (the smallest) would converge on him from the sides. Each girl would hug one of his legs and, acting together, they would lift him off the ground. The fourth girl (the fastest) would by this point have circled all the way round and would come in from behind, driving a knife or other weapon into the victim's back. During the half-dozen or so applications of this technique that Nell witnessed, it never failed, and none of the girls ever suffered more than the odd bruise or scrape.

Suddenly she felt a moment of wild panic as she thought they were doing the same to *her*; but after she had been lifted into the air, no attack came from front or back, though many girls rushed in from all sides, each adding her small strength to the paramount goal of hoisting Nell high into the air. Even as the last remnants of the Fists were being hunted down and destroyed in the nooks and corners of the lobby, Nell was being borne on the shoulders of her little sisters out the front doors of the building and into the plaza, where something like a hundred thousand girls—Nell could not count all the regiments and brigades—collapsed to their knees in unison, as though struck down by a divine wind, and presented her their bamboo stakes, pole knives, lead pipes, and nunchuks. The provisional commanders of her divisions stood foremost, as did her provisional ministers of defense, of state, and of research and development, all of them bowing to Nell, not with a Chinese bow or a Victorian one but something they'd come up with that was in between.

Nell should have been tongue-tied and paralyzed with astonishment, but she was not; for the first time in her life she understood why she'd been put on the earth and felt comfortable with her position. One moment, her life had been a meaningless abortion, and the next it all made glorious sense. She began to speak, the words rushing from her mouth as easily as if she had been reading them from the pages of the Primer. She accepted the allegiance of the Mouse Army, complimented them on their great deeds, and swept her arm across the plaza, over the heads of her little sisters, toward the thousands upon thousands of stranded sojourners from New Atlantis, Nippon, Israel, and all of the other Outer Tribes. "Our first duty is to protect these," she said. "Show me the condition of the city and all those in it."

They wanted to carry her, but she jumped to the stones of the plaza and strode away from the building, toward her ranks, which parted to make way for her. The streets of Pudong were filled with hungry and terrified refugees, and through them, in simple peasant clothes streaked with the blood of herself and of others, broken shackles dangling from her wrists, followed by her generals and ministers, walked the barbarian Princess with her book and her sword.

Carl Hollywood takes a stroll to the waterfront.

Carl Hollywood was awakened by a ringing in his ears and a burning in his cheek that turned out to be an inch-long fragment of plate glass driven into his flesh. When he sat up, his bed made clanking and crashing noises, shedding a heavy burden of shattered glass, and a foetid exhalation from the wrecked windows blew over his face. Old hotels had their charms, but disadvantages too—such as windowpanes made out of antique materials.

Fortunately some old Wyoming instinct had caused him to leave his boots next to the bed the night before. He inverted each one and carefully probed it for broken glass before he pulled it on. Only when he had put on all of his clothes and gathered his things together did he go to look out the window.

His hotel was near the Huang Pu waterfront. Looking across the river, he could see that great patches of Pudong had gone black against the indigo sky of predawn. A few buildings, connected to the indigenous Feeds, were still lit up. On this side of the river the situation was not so simple; Shanghai, unlike Pudong, had lived through many wars and was therefore made to be robust: the city was rife with secret power sources, old diesel generators, private Sources and Feeds, water tanks and cisterns. People still raised chickens for food in the shadow of the Hongkong & Shanghai Banking Corporation. Shanghai would weather the onslaught of the Fists much better than Pudong.

But as a white person, Carl Hollywood might not weather it very well at all. It was better to be across the river, in Pudong, with the rest of the Outer Tribes.

From here to the waterfront was about three blocks; but since this was Shanghai, those three blocks were fraught with what in any other city would be three miles' worth of complications. The main problem was going to be Fists; he could already hear the cries of "Sha! Sha!" boiling up from the streets, and shining a pocket torch through the bars of his balcony, he could see many Fists, emboldened by the destruction of the foreign Feeds, running around with their scarlet girdles and headbands exposed to the world.

If he weren't six and a half feet tall and blue-eyed, he'd probably try to disguise himself as Chinese and slink to the waterfront, and it probably wouldn't work. He went through his closet and hauled out his big duster, which swept nearly to his ankles. It was proof against bullets and most nanotech projectiles.

There was a long item of luggage he had thrown up on the closet shelf unopened. Hearing the reports of trouble, he had taken the precaution of bringing these relics with him: an engraved lever-action .44 rifle with low-tech iron sights and, as a last-ditch sort of thing, a Colt revolver. These were unnecessarily glorious weapons, but he had long ago gotten rid of any of his guns that did not have historical or artistic value.

Two gunshots sounded from within the building, very close to him. Moments later, someone knocked at his door. Carl wrapped his duster around him, in case someone decided to fire through the door, and peered out through the peephole. To his surprise, he saw a white-haired Anglo gentleman with a handlebar mustache, gripping a semiautomatic. Carl had met him yesterday in the hotel bar; he was here trying to clear up some kind of business before the fall of Shanghai.

He opened the door. The two men regarded each other briefly. "One might think we had come for an antique weapons convention," the gentleman said through his mustache. "Say, I'm frightfully sorry to have disturbed you, but I thought you might like to know that there are Fists in the hotel." He gestured down the corridor with his gun. Carl poked his head out and discovered a dead bellboy sprawled out in front of an open door, still clutching a long knife.

"As it happens, I was already up," said Carl Hollywood, "and contemplating a bit of a stroll to the waterfront. Care to join me?"

"Delighted. Colonel Spence, Royal Joint Forces, Retired."

"Carl Hollywood."

On their way down the fire stairs, Spence killed two more hotel employees whom he had, on somewhat ambiguous grounds, identified as Fists. Carl was skeptical in both cases until Spence ripped their shirts open to reveal the scarlet girdles beneath. "It's not that they're really Fists, you see," Spence explained jovially. "Just that when the Fists come, this sort of nonsense becomes terribly fashionable."

After exchanging some more self-consciously dry humor about whether they should settle their bills before departure, and how much you were supposed to tip a bellboy who came after you with a carving knife, they agreed it might be safest to exit through the kitchens. Half a dozen dead Fists littered the floor here, their bodies striped with the marks of cookie-cutters. Arriving at the exit they found two fellow guests, both Israelis, staring at them with the fixed gaze that implies the presence of a skull gun. Seconds later, they were joined by two Zulu management consultants carrying long, telescoping poles with nanoblades affixed to the ends, which they used to destroy all of the light fixtures in their path. It took Carl a minute to appreciate their plan: They were all about to step out into a dark alley, and they would need their night vision.

The door began to shudder in its frame and make tremendous booming noises. Carl stepped forward and peered through the peephole; it was a couple of urban homeboy types having at it with a fire axe. He stepped away from the door, shrugging the rifle from his shoulder, levered in a shell, and fired it through the door, aiming away from the youths. The booming stopped abruptly, and they heard the head of the axe ringing like a bell as it fell to the pavement.

One of the Zulus kicked the door open and leapt into the alley, whirling his blade in a vast, fatal arc like the blade of a helicopter, slicing through a garbage can but not hitting any people. When Carl came piling through the door a few seconds later, he saw several young toughs scattering down the alley, dodging among several dozen refugees, loiterers, and street people who pointed helpfully at their receding backsides, making sure it was understood that their only reason for being in this alley at this time was to act as a sort of block watch on behalf of the *gwailo* visitors.

Without talking about it much, they fell into an improvised formation there in the alley, where they had a bit of room to maneuver. The Zulus went in front, whirling their poles over their heads and hollering some kind of traditional war-cry that drove a good many of the Chinese out of their path. One of the Jews went behind the Zulus, using his skull gun to pick off any Fists who charged them. Then came Carl Hollywood, who, with his height and his rifle, seemed to have ended up with the job of long-range reconnaissance and defense. Colonel Spence and the other Israeli brought up the rear, walking backward most of the time.

This got them down the alley without much trouble, but that was the easy part; when they reached the street, they were no longer the only focus of action but mere motes in a sandstorm. Colonel Spence discharged most of a clip into the air; the explosions were nearly inaudible in the chaos, but the gouts of light from the weapon's barrel drew some attention, and people in their immediate vicinity actually got out of their way. Carl saw one of the Zulus do something very ugly with his long weapon and looked away; then he reflected that it was the Zulus' job to break trail and his to concentrate on more distant threats. He turned slowly around as he walked, trying to ignore the threat that was just beyond arm's length and to get a view of the larger scene.

They had walked into a completely disorganized street fight between the Coastal Republic forces and the Fists of Righteous Harmony, which was not made any clearer by the fact that many of the Coastals had defected by tying strips of red cloth round the arms of their uniforms, and that many of the Fists were not wearing any markings at all, and that many others who had no affiliation were taking advantage of the situation to loot stores and were being fought off by private guards; many of the looters were themselves being mugged by organized gangs.

They were on Nanjing Road, a broad thoroughfare leading straight to the Bund and the Huang Pu, lined with four- and five-story buildings so that many windows looked out over them, any one of which might have contained a sniper.

A few of them did contain snipers, Carl realized, but many of these were shooting across the street at each other, and the ones who were firing into the street could have been shooting at anyone. Carl saw one fellow with a laser-sighted rifle emptying clip after clip into the street, and he reckoned that this constituted a clear and present danger; so at a moment when their forward progress had stalled momentarily, while the Zulus were waiting for an especially desperate Coastal/Fist melee to resolve itself ahead of them, Carl planted his feet, swung his rifle up to his shoulder, took aim, and fired. In the dim fire- and torch-light rising up from the street, he could see powder explode from the stone window frame just above the sniper's head. The sniper cringed, then began to sweep the street with his laser, looking for the source of the bullet.

Someone jostled Carl from behind. It was Spence, who had been hit with something and lost the use of his leg. A Fist was in the Colonel's face. Carl rammed the butt of the rifle into the man's chin, sending him backward into the melee with his eyes rolled up into their sockets. Then he levered in another shell, raised the weapon to his shoulder again, and tried to find the window with his sniper friend.

He was still there, tracing a ruby-red line patiently across the boiling surface of the crowd. Carl took in a deep breath, released it slowly, prayed that no one would bump into him, and squeezed the trigger. The rifle butted him hard in the shoulder, and at the same moment he saw the sniper's rifle fall out of the window, spinning end over end, the laser beam sweeping through the smoke and steam like the trace on a radar scope.

The whole thing had probably been a bad idea; if any of the other snipers had seen this, they'd be wanting to get rid of him, whatever their affiliation. Carl levered in another shell and then let the rifle dangle from one hand, pointed down at the street, where it wouldn't be so conspicuous. He got the other hand into Spence's armpit and helped him continue down the street. The ends of Spence's mustache wiggled as he continued with his endless and unflappable line of patter; Carl couldn't hear a word but nodded encouragingly. Not even the most literal-minded neo-Victorian could take that stiff-upper-lip thing seriously; Carl realized now that it was all done with a nod and a wink. It was not Colonel Spence's way of saying that he wasn't scared; it was, rather, a code of sorts, a face-saving way for him to admit that he was terrified half out of his wits, and for Carl to admit likewise.

Several Fists rushed them at once; the Zulus got two, the leading Israeli got one, but another came in and bounced his knife from the Israeli's knife-proof jacket. Carl raised the rifle, clamping the stock between his arm and his body, and fired from the hip. The recoil nearly knocked the weapon out of his hand; the Fist practically did a backflip.

He couldn't believe they had not reached the waterfront yet; they had been doing this for hours. Something prodded him hard in the back, causing him to stumble forward; he looked back over his shoulder and saw a man trying to run him through with a bayonet. Another man ran up and tried to wrench the rifle out of Carl's hand. Carl, too startled to respond for a moment, finally let go of Spence, reached across, and poked him in the eyes. A great explosion sounded in his ear, and he looked over to see that Spence had twisted himself round and shot the attacker who had the bayonet. The Israeli who had been guarding their rear had simply vanished. Carl raised his rifle toward the people who were converging on them from the rear; that and Spence's pistol opened up a gratifying clear space in their wake. But something more powerful and terrifying was driving more people toward them from the side, and as Carl tried to see what it was, he realized that a score of Chinese people were now between him and the Zulus. The looks on their faces were pained and panicky; they were not attacking, they were being attacked.

Suddenly all of the Chinese were gone. Carl and Colonel Spence found themselves commingled with a dozen or so Boers—not just men, but women and children and elders too, a whole laager on the move. All of them surged forward instinctively and reabsorbed the vanguard of Carl's group. They were a block from the waterfront.

The Boer leader, a stout man of about fifty, somehow identified Carl Hollywood as the leader, and they quickly redeployed what forces they had for the final push to the waterfront. The only thing Carl remembered of this conversation was the man saying, "Good. You've got Zulus." The Boers in the vanguard were carrying some sort of automatic weapons firing tiny nanotech high-explosive rounds, which, indiscriminately used, could have turned the crowd into a rampart of chewed meat; but they fired the weapons in disciplined bursts even when the charging Fists penetrated to within a sword's length. From time to time, one of them would raise his head and sweep a row of windows with continuous automatic fire; riflemen would tumble out of the darkness and spin down into the street like rag dolls. The Boers must be wearing some kind of night vision stuff. Colonel Spence suddenly felt very heavy on Carl's arm, and he realized that the Colonel was unconscious, or close to it. Carl slung the rifle over his shoulder, bent down, and picked up Spence in a fireman's carry.

They arrived at the waterfront and established a defensive perimeter. The next question was: Were there any boats? But this part of China was half underwater and seemed to have as many boats as bicycles. Most of them seemed to have found their way downstream to Shanghai during the gradual onslaught of the Fists. So when they arrived at the water's edge, they discovered thousands of people with boats, eager to transact some business. But as the Boer leader rightly pointed out, it would be suicide to split up the group among several tiny, unpowered craft; the Fists were paying high bounties for the heads of barbarians. Much safer to wait for one of the larger vessels out in the channel to make its way to shore, where they could cut a deal with the captain and climb on board as a group.

Several vessels, ranging from motor yachts to fishing trawlers, were already vying to be the first to make that deal, shouldering their way inexorably through the organic chaff of small boats crowded along the shore.

A rhythmic beat had begun to resonate in their lungs. At first it sounded like drumbeats, but as it drew closer it developed into the sound of hundreds or thousands of human voices chanting in unison: *"Sha! Sha! Sha! Sha!"* Nanjing Road began to vomit forth a great crowd of people shoved out onto the Bund like exhaust pushed out by a piston. They cleared out of the way, dispersing up and down the riverfront.

An army of hoplites—professional warriors in battle armor—was marching toward the river, a score abreast, completely filling the width of Nanjing Road. These were not Fists; they were the regular army, the vanguard of the Celestial Kingdom, and Carl Hollywood was appalled to realize that the only thing now standing between them and their three-decade march to the banks of the Huang Pu was Carl Hollywood, his .44, and a handful of lightly armed civilians.

A nice-looking yacht had penetrated to within a few meters of the shore. The remaining Israeli, who was fluent in mandarin, had already commenced negotiations with its captain.

One of the Boers, a wiry grandmother with a white bun on her head and a black bonnet pinned primly over that, conferred briefly with the Boer leader. He nodded once, then caught her face in his hands and kissed her.

She turned her back on the waterfront and began to march toward the head of the advancing column of Celestials. The few Chinese crazy enough to remain along the waterfront, respecting her age and possible madness, parted to make way for her.

The negotiations over the boat appeared to have hit some kind of snag. Carl Hollywood could see individual hoplites vaulting two and three stories into the air, crashing headfirst into the windows of the Cathay Hotel.

The Boer grandmother doggedly made her way forward until she was standing in the middle of the Bund. The leader of the Celestial column stepped toward her, covering her with some kind of projectile weapon built into one arm of his suit and waving her aside with the other. The Boer woman carefully got down on both knees in the middle of the road, clasped her hands together in prayer, and bowed her head.

Then she became a pearl of white light in the mouth of the dragon. In an instant this pearl grew to the size of an airship. Carl Hollywood had the presence of mind to close his eyes and turn his head away, but he didn't have time to throw himself down; the shock wave did that, slamming him full-length into the granite paving-stones of the waterfront promenade and tearing about half of his clothes from his body.

Some time passed before he was really conscious; he felt it must have been half an hour, though debris was still raining down around him, so five seconds was probably more like it. The hull of the white yacht had been caved in on one side and most of its crew flung into the river. But a minute later, a fishing trawler pulled up and took the barbarians on board with only perfunctory negotiations. Carl nearly forgot about Spence and almost left him there; he found that he no longer had the strength to raise the Colonel's body from the ground, so he dragged him on board with the help of a couple of young Boers—identical twins, he realized, maybe thirteen years old. As they headed across the Huang Pu, Carl Hollywood huddled on a piled-up fishing net, limp and weak as though his bones had all been shattered, staring at the hundred-foot crater in the center of the Bund and looking into the rooms of the Cathay Hotel, which had been neatly cross-sectioned by the bomb in the Boer woman's body.

Within fifteen minutes, they were free on the streets of Pudong. Carl Hollywood found his way to the local New Atlantan encampment, reported for duty, and spent a few minutes composing a letter to Colonel Spence's widow; the Colonel had bled to death from a leg wound during the voyage across the river.

Then he spread his pages out on the ground before him and returned to the pursuit that had occupied him in his hotel room for the past few days, namely, the search for Miranda. He had begun this search at the bidding of Lord Finkle-McGraw, pursued it with mounting passion over the last few days as he had begun to understand how much he'd been missing Miranda, and was now pressing the work desperately; for he had realized that in this search might reside

the only hope for the salvation of the tens of thousands of
Outer Tribesmen now encamped upon the dead streets of
the Pudong Economic Zone.

*Final onslaught of the Fists; victory of the Celestial
Kingdom; refugees in the domain
of the Drummers; Miranda.*

The Huang Pu stopped the advance of the Celestial Army
toward the sea, but having crossed the river farther inland, it
continued to move northward up the Pudong Peninsula at a
walking pace, driving before it flocks of starving peasants
much like the ones who had been their harbingers in Shanghai.

The occupants of Pudong—a mixture of barbarians,
Coastal Republic Chinese who feared persecution at the
hands of their Celestial cousins, and Nell's little sisters, a
third of a million strong and constituting a new phyle unto
themselves—were thus caught between the Celestials on the
south, the Huang Pu on the west, the Yangtze on the north,
and the ocean on the east. All the links to the artificial islands offshore had been cut.

The geotects of Imperial Tectonics, in their Classical
and Gothic temples high atop New Chusan, made various
efforts to build a temporary bridge between their island and
Pudong. It was simple enough to throw a truss or floating
bridge across the gap, but the Celestials now had the technology to blow such things up faster than they could be
constructed. On the second day of the siege, they caused the
island to reach toward Pudong with a narrow pseudopod of
smart coral, rooted on the ocean floor. But there were very
simple and clear limits to how fast such things could be
grown, and as the refugees continued to throng the narrow
defiles of downtown Pudong, bearing increasingly dire reports of the Celestials' advance, it became evident to everyone that the land bridge would not be completed in time.

The encampments of the various tribes moved north and east as they were forced out of downtown by the pressure of the refugees and fear of the Celestials, until several miles of shoreline had been claimed and settled by the various groups. The southern end, along the seashore, was anchored by the New Atlantans, who had prepared themselves to fend off any assaults along the beach. The chain of camps extended northward from there, curving along the ocean and then eastward along the banks of the Yangtze to the opposite end, which was anchored by Nippon against any onslaught across the tidal flats. The entire center of the line was guarded against a direct frontal assault by Princess Nell's tribe/army of twelve-year-old girls, who were gradually trading in their pointed sticks for more modern weapons compiled from portable Sources owned by the Nipponese and the New Atlantans.

Carl Hollywood had been assigned to military duty as soon as he reported to the New Atlantan authorities, despite his efforts to convince his superiors that he might be of more use pursuing his own line of research. But then a message came through from the highest levels of Her Majesty's government. The first part of it praised Carl Hollywood for his "heroic" actions in getting the late Colonel Spence out of Shanghai and suggested that a knighthood might be waiting for him if he ever got out of Pudong. The second part of it named him as a special envoy of sorts to Her Royal Highness, Princess Nell.

Reading the message, Carl was momentarily stunned that his Sovereign was according equivalent status to Nell; but upon some reflection he saw that it was simultaneously just and pragmatic. During his time in the streets of Pudong, he had seen enough of the Mouse Army (as they called themselves, for some reason) to know that they did, in fact, constitute a new ethnic group of sorts, and that Nell was their undisputed leader. Victoria's esteem for the new sovereign was well-founded. At the same time, that the Mouse Army was currently helping to protect many New Atlantans from being taken hostage, or worse, by the Celestial Kingdom made such recognition an eminently pragmatic step.

It fell to Carl Hollywood, who had been a member of his adopted tribe only for a few months, to forward Her Majesty's greetings and felicitations to Princess Nell, a girl about whom he had heard much from Miranda but whom he had never met and could hardly fathom. It did not take very deep reflection to see the hand of Lord Alexander Chung-Sik Finkle-McGraw in all this.

Freed from day-to-day responsibilities, he walked north from the New Atlantan camp on the third day of the siege, following the tideline. Every few yards he came to a tribal border and presented a visa that, under the provisions of the Common Economic Protocol, was supposed to afford him free passage. Some of the tribal zones were only a meter or two wide, but their owners jealously guarded their access to the sea, sitting up all night staring out into the surf, waiting for some unspecified form of salvation. Carl Hollywood strolled through encampments of Ashantis, Kurds, Armenians, Navajos, Tibetans, Senderos, Mormons, Jesuits, Lapps, Pathans, Tutsis, the First Distributed Republic and its innumerable offshoots, Heartlanders, Irish, and one or two local CryptNet cells who had now been flushed into the open. He discovered synthetic phyles he had never heard of, but this did not surprise him.

Finally he came to a generous piece of beach frontage guarded by twelve-year-old Chinese girls. At this point he presented his credentials from Her Majesty Queen Victoria II, which were extremely impressive, so much so that many of the girls gathered around to marvel at them. Carl Hollywood was surprised to hear them all speaking perfect English in a rather high Victorian style. They seemed to prefer it when discussing things in the abstract, but when it came to practical matters they reverted to mandarin.

He was ushered through the lines into the Mouse Army's encampment, which was mostly an open-air hospice for ragged, sick and injured discards from other phyles. The ones who weren't flat on their backs, being tended to by Mouse Nurses, were sitting on the sand, hugging their knees, staring out across the water in the direction of New Chusan. The slope of the land was quite gentle here, and a person could wade for a good long stone's throw into the waves.

One person had: a young woman whose long hair fell about her shoulders and trailed in the water around her waist. She stood with her back to the shore, holding a book in her hands, and did not move for a long time.

"What is she doing out there?" Carl Hollywood said to his Mouse Army escort, who had five little stars on her lapels. In Pudong, he had figured out their insignia: Five stars meant that she was in charge of 4^5 people, or 1024. A regimental commander, then.

"She is calling to her mother."

"Her mother?"

"Her mother is beneath the waves," the woman said. "She is a Queen."

"Queen of what?"

"She is the Queen of the Drummers who live beneath the sea."

And then Carl Hollywood knew that Princess Nell was searching for Miranda too. He threw his long coat down on the sand and sloshed out into the Pacific, accompanied by the officer, and remained at a judicious distance, partly to show due respect, and partly because Nell had a sword in her waistband. Her face was inclined over the pages of her book like a focusing lens, and he half expected the pages to curl and smoke under her gaze.

She looked up from the book after some time. The officer spoke to her in a low voice. Carl Hollywood did not know the protocol when one was up to midthigh in the East China Sea, so he stepped forward, bowed as low as he could under the circumstances, and handed Princess Nell the scroll from Queen Victoria II.

She accepted it wordlessly and read it through, then went back to the top and read it again. Then she handed it to her officer, who rolled it up carefully. Princess Nell stared out over the waves for a while, then looked Carl in the eye and said quietly, "I accept your credentials and request that you convey my warm thanks and regard to Her Majesty, along with my apologies that circumstances prevent me from composing a more formal response to her kind letter, which at any other time would naturally be my highest priority."

"I shall do so at the earliest opportunity, Your Majesty," Carl Hollywood said. Hearing these words, Princess Nell looked a bit unsteady and shifted her feet to maintain her balance; though this might have been the undertow. Carl realized that she had never been addressed in this way before; that, until she had been recognized in this fashion by Victoria, she had never fully realized her position.

"The woman you seek is named Miranda," he said.

All thoughts of crowns, queens, and armies seemed to vanish from Nell's mind, and she was just a young lady again, looking for—what? Her mother? Her teacher? Her friend? Carl Hollywood spoke to Nell in a low gentle voice, projecting just enough to be heard over the strumming of the waves. He spoke to her of Miranda, and of the book, and of the old stories about the deeds of Princess Nell, which he had watched from the wings, as it were, by looking in on Miranda's feed many years ago at the Parnasse.

Over the next two days many of the refugees on the shore got away on air or surface ships, but a few of these were destroyed in spectacular fashion before they could get out of range of the Celestial Kingdom's weaponry. Three-quarters of the Mouse Army evacuated itself through the technique of stripping naked and walking into the ocean en masse, linked arm-in-arm into a flexible and unsinkable raft that gradually, slowly, exhaustingly paddled across the sea to New Chusan. Rumors spread rapidly up and down the length of the coast; the tribal borders seemed to accelerate rather than hinder this process as interfaces between languages and cultures spawned new variants of each rumor, tailored to the local fears and prejudices. The most popular rumor was that the Celestials planned to give everyone safe passage and that the attacks were being carried out by intelligent mines that had run out of control or, at worst, by a few fanatical commanders who were defying orders and who would soon be brought to heel. There was a second, stranger rumor that gave some people an incentive to remain on the shore and not entrust themselves to the evacuation ships: A young woman with a book and a sword was creating magical tunnels from out of the deep that would carry them all away to safety. Such ideas were naturally met with skepticism among more rational cultures, but on the morning of the sixth day of the siege, the neap tide carried a peculiar omen up onto the sand: a harvest of translucent eggs the size of beach balls. When their fragile shells were torn open, they were found to contain sculpted backpacks pierced with a fractal pattern of delicate louvers. A stiff hose extended from the top and connected to a facemask. Under the circumstances, it was not difficult to divine the use of these objects. People strapped the packs onto their backs, slipped on the facemasks, and plunged into the water. The backpacks acted like the gills of a fish and provided a steady supply of oxygen.

The gill packs did not carry any tribal identification; they merely washed up onto the beach, by the thousands, with each high tide, cast up organically by the sea. The Atlantans, Nipponese, and others each assumed that they had come from their own tribes. But many perceived a connection between this and the rumors of Princess Nell and the tunnels beneath the waves. Such people migrated toward the center of the Pudong coast, where the tiny, weak, and flaky tribes had all been concentrated. This contraction of the defensive line became inevitable as the number of defenders was shrunk by the evacuation. Borders between tribes became unstable and finally dissolved, and on the fifth day of the siege the barbarians had all become fungible and formed into a huddle on the uttermost point of the Pudong Peninsula, several tens of thousands of persons packed into an area not exceeding a few city blocks. Beyond that were the Chinese refugees, mostly persons strongly identified with the Coastal Republic who knew that they could never blend into the Celestial Kingdom. These did not dare to invade the camp of the refugees, who were still armed with powerful weapons, but by advancing an inch at a time and never retreating, they insensibly shrank the perimeter so that many barbarians found themselves standing knee-deep in the ocean.

The rumor spread that the woman called Princess Nell had a wizard and adviser named Carl, who had appeared out of nowhere one day knowing nearly everything that Princess Nell did, and a few things she didn't. This man, according to rumor, had in his possession a number of magic keys that gave him and the Princess power to speak with the Drummers who lived beneath the waves.

On the seventh day, Princess Nell walked naked into the sea at dawn, vanished beneath waves turned pink by the sunrise, and did not return. Carl followed her a minute later, though unlike the Princess he took the precaution of wearing a gill pack. Then all of the barbarians stepped into the ocean, leaving their filthy clothes strewn across the beach, relinquishing the last foothold of Chinese soil to the Celestial Kingdom. They all walked into the ocean until their heads disappeared. The rearguard was made up of the last part of the Mouse Army, which charged naked into the surf, linked up into a raft, and made its way slowly out to sea, nudging a few sick and wounded along with them in makeshift rafts. By the time the last girl's foot broke contact with the sandy ocean bottom, the end of the land had already been claimed by a man with a scarlet girdle round his waist, who stood on the shore laughing to think that now the Middle Kingdom was at last a whole country once more.

The last foreign devil to depart from the Middle Kingdom was a blond Victorian gentleman with gray eyes, who stood in the waves for some time looking back over Pudong before he turned around and continued his descent. As the sea rose over him, it lifted the bowler from his head, and the hat continued to bob on the tide for some minutes as the Chinese detonated strings of firecrackers on the shore and tiny shreds of the red paper wrappers drifted over the sea like cherry petals.

On one of her forays into the surf, Nell had encountered a man—a Drummer—who had come swimming out of the deep, naked except for a gill pack. This should have astonished her; instead, she had known he was out there before she saw him, and when he came close, she could feel things happening in her mind that were coming in from outside. There was something in her brain that made her connected to the Drummers.

Nell had drawn up some general plans and given them to her engineers for further elaboration, and they had given them to Carl, who had taken them to a functioning portable M.C. in the New Atlantan camp and compiled a little system for examining and manipulating nanotechnological devices.

In the dark, motes of light sparkled in Nell's flesh, like airplane beacons in the night sky. They scraped one of these away with a scalpel and examined it. They found similar devices circulating in her bloodstream. These things, they realized, must have been put into Nell's blood when she was raped. It was clear that the sparkling lights in Nell's flesh

were beacons signaling to others across the gulf that sepa-
rates each of us from our neighbors.

Carl opened one of the things from Nell's blood and
found a rod logic system inside, and a tape drive containing
some few gigabytes of data. The data was divided into dis-
crete chunks, each one of which was separately encrypted.
Carl tried all of the keys that he had obtained from John
Percival Hackworth and found that one of them—Hackworth's key—unlocked some of the chunks. When he examined the decrypted contents, he discovered fragments of
a plan for some kind of nanotechnological device.

They drew blood from several volunteers and found
that one of them had the same little devices in his blood.
When they put two of these devices in close proximity, they
locked onto one another using lidar and embraced, exchanging data and performing some sort of computation that
threw off waste heat.

The devices lived in the blood of the human race like
viruses and passed from one person to the next during sex
or any other exchange of bodily fluids; they were smart
packets of data, just like the ones traversing the media network, and by mating with one another in the blood, they
formed a vast system of communication, parallel to and
probably linked with the dry Net of optical lines and copper
wires. Like the dry Net, the wet Net could be used for doing
computations—for running programs. And it was now clear
that John Percival Hackworth was using it for exactly that,
running some kind of vast distributed program of his own
devising. He was designing something.

"Hackworth is the Alchemist," Nell said, "and he is
using the wet Net to design the Seed."

Half a kilometer offshore, the tunnels began. Some of them
must have been there for many years, for they were rough as
tree trunks, encrusted with barnacles and algae. But it was
clear that in the last few days they had forked and split
organically, like roots questing for moisture; clean new tubes
forced their way out through the encrustation and ran uphill
toward the tide line, splitting again and again until many
orifices presented themselves to the refugees. The shoots terminated in lips that grabbed people and drew them in, like
the tip of an elephant's trunk, accepting the refugees with a

minimum of seawater. The tunnels were lined with media-tronic images urging them forward into the deep; it always seemed as though a warm dry well-lit space awaited them just a bit farther down the line. But the light moved along with the viewer so that they were drawn down the tunnels in a kind of peristalsis. The refugees came to the main tunnel, the old encrusted one, and continued moving on, now packed together in a solid mass, until they were disgorged into a large open cavity far below the surface of the ocean. Here, food and fresh water awaited them and they ate hungrily.

Two people did not eat or drink except from the provisions they had brought with them; these were Nell and Carl.

After they had discovered the nanosites in Nell's flesh that made her a part of the Drummers, Nell had stayed up through the night and designed a counternanosite, one that would seek out and destroy the Drummers' devices. She and Carl had both put these devices into their bloodstreams, so that Nell was now free of the Drummers' influences and both of them would remain so. Nevertheless they did not press their luck by eating of the Drummers' food, and it was well, because after their meal the refugees became drowsy and lay down on the floor and slept, steam rising from their naked flesh, and before long the sparks of light began to come on, like stars coming out as the sun goes down. After two hours the stars had merged together into a continuous surface of flickering light, bright enough to read by, as if a full moon were shining down upon the bodies of slumbering revelers in a meadow. The refugees, now Drummers, all slept and dreamed the same dream, and the abstract lights flickering across the mediatronic lining of the cavern began to coalesce and organize themselves into dark memories from deep within their unconscious mind. Nell began to see things from her own life, experiences long since assimilated into the words of the Primer but here shown once more in a raw and terrifying form. She closed her eyes; but the walls made sounds too, from which she could not escape.

Carl Hollywood was monitoring the signals passing through the walls of the tunnels, avoiding the emotional content of these images by reducing them to binary digits and trying to puzzle out their internal codes and protocols.

"We have to go," Nell said finally, and Carl arose and

followed her through a randomly chosen exit. The tunnel forked and forked again, and Nell chose forks by intuition. Sometimes the tunnels would widen into great caverns full of luminescent Drummers, sleeping or fucking or simply pounding on the walls. The caverns always had many outlets, which forked and forked and converged upon other caverns, the web of tunnels so vast and complicated that it seemed to fill the entire ocean, like neural bodies with their dendrites knitting and ramifying to occupy the whole volume of the skull.

A low drumming sound had been skirting the lower limits of perceptibility ever since they had left the cavern where the refugees slumbered. Nell had first taken it for the beat of submarine currents on the walls of the tunnel, but as it grew stronger, she knew that it was the Drummers talking to each other, convened in some central cavern sending messages out across their network. Realizing this, she felt a sense of urgency verging on panic that they find the central assembly, and for some time they ran through the perfectly bewildering three-dimensional maze, trying to locate the epicenter of the drumming.

Carl Hollywood could not run as quickly as the nimble Nell and eventually lost her at a fork in the tunnels. From there he made his own judgments, and after some time had passed—it was impossible to know how long—his tunnel dovetailed with another that was carrying a stream of Drummers downward toward the floor of the ocean. Carl recognized some of these Drummers as former refugees from the beaches at Pudong.

The sound of the drumming did not build gradually but exploded to a deafening, mind-dissolving roar as Carl emerged into a vast cavern, a conical amphitheatre that must have been a kilometer wide, roofed with a storm of mediatronic images that played across a vast dome. The Drummers, visible by the flickering light of the overhead media storm and by their own internal light, moved up and down the slopes of the cone in a kind of convection pattern. Caught up in an eddy, Carl was transported down toward the center and found that an orgy of fantastic dimensions was underway. The steam of vaporized sweat rose from the center of the pit in a cloud. The bodies pressing against Carl's naked skin were so hot that they almost burned him, as if everyone were running a high fever, and in some logical abstract compartment of his mind that was, somehow, continuing to run along its own reasonable course, he realized why: They were exchanging packets of data with their bodily fluids, the packets were mating in their blood, the rod logic throwing off heat that drove up their core temperature.

The orgy went on for hours, but the pattern of convection gradually slowed down and condensed into a stable arrangement, like a circulating crowd in a theatre that settles into its assigned seats as curtain time approaches. A broad open space had formed at the center of the pit, and the innermost ring of spectators consisted of men, as if these were in some sense the winners of the enormous fornication tournament that was nearing its final round. A lone Drummer circulated around this innermost ring, handing something out; the something turned out to be mediatronic condoms that glowed bright colors when they were stripped onto the men's erect phalluses.

A lone woman entered the ring. The floor at the absolute center of the pit rose up beneath her feet, shoving her into the air as on an altar. The drumming built to an unbearable crescendo and then stopped. Then it began again, a very slow steady beat, and the men in the inner circle began to dance around her.

Carl Hollywood saw that the woman in the center was Miranda.

He saw it all now: that the refugees had been gathered into the realm of the Drummers for the harvest of fresh data running in their bloodstreams, that this data had been infused into the wet Net in the course of the great orgy, and that all of it was now going to be dumped into Miranda, whose body would play host to the climax of some computation that would certainly burn her alive in the process. It was Hackworth's doing; this was the culmination of his effort to design the Seed, and in so doing to dissolve the foundations of New Atlantis and Nippon and all of the societies that had grown up around the concept of a centralized, hierarchical Feed.

A lone figure, remarkable because her skin did not emit any light, was fighting her way in toward the center. She burst into the inner circle, knocking down a dancer who got in her way, and climbed up onto the central altar where

Miranda lay on her back, arms outstretched as if crucified, her skin a galaxy of colored lights.

Nell cradled Miranda's head in her arms, bent down, and kissed her, not a soft brush of the lips but a savage kiss with open mouth, and she bit down hard as she did it, biting through her own lips and Miranda's so that their blood mingled. The light shining from Miranda's body diminished and slowly went out as the nanosites were hunted down and destroyed by the hunter-killers that had crossed into her blood from Nell's. Miranda came awake and arose, her arms draped weakly around Nell's neck.

The drumming had stopped; the Drummers all sat impassively, clearly content to wait—for years if necessary—for a woman who could take Miranda's place. The light from their flesh had diminished, and the overhead mediatron had gone dim and vague. Carl Hollywood, seeing at last a role for himself, stepped into the center, got one arm under Miranda's knees and another beneath her shoulders, and lifted her into the air. Nell turned around and led them up out of the cavern, holding her sword out before her; but none of the Drummers moved to stop them.

They passed up through many tunnels, always taking the uphill fork until they saw sunlight shining down from above through the waves, casting lines of white light on the translucent roof. Nell severed the tunnel behind them, wielding her sword like the sweep of a clock's hand. The warm water rushed in on them. Nell swam up toward the light. Miranda was not swimming strongly, and Carl was torn between a panicky desire to reach the surface and his duty to Miranda. Then he saw shadows descending from above, dozens of naked girls swimming downward, garlands of silver bubbles streaming from their mouths, their almond eyes excited and mischievous. Carl and Miranda were gripped by many gentle hands and borne upward into the light.

New Chusan rose above them, a short swim away, and up on the mountain they could hear the bells of the cathedral ringing.

refresh yourself at penguin.co.uk

Visit penguin.co.uk for exclusive information and interviews with
bestselling authors, fantastic give-aways and the
inside track on all our books, from the Penguin Classics
to the latest bestsellers.

BE FIRST

first chapters, first editions, first novels

EXCLUSIVES

author chats, video interviews, biographies, special
features

EVERYONE'S A WINNER

give-aways, competitions, quizzes, ecards

READERS GROUPS

exciting features to support existing groups and
create new ones

NEWS

author events, bestsellers, awards, what's new

EBOOKS

books that click – download an ePenguin today

BROWSE AND BUY

thousands of books to investigate – search, try
and buy the perfect gift online – or treat yourself!

ABOUT US

job vacancies, advice for writers and company
history

Get Closer To Penguin ... www.penguin.co.uk